More Praise for
JACK HIGGINS

JACK HIGGINS

THREE COMPLETE NOVELS

JACK HIGGINS

THREE COMPLETE NOVELS

THE EAGLE HAS LANDED

THE EAGLE HAS FLOWN

NIGHT OF THE FOX

WINGS BOOKS
New York • *Avenel, New Jersey*

This edition contains the complete and unabridged texts of the original editions. They have been completely reset for this volume.

This omnibus was originally published in separate volumes under the titles:

The Eagle Has Landed, copyright © 1975 by Jack Higgins
The Eagle has Flown, copyright © 1990 by Jack Higgins
Night of the Fox, copyright © 1986 by Jack Higgins

"When That Man Is Dead and Gone" by Irving Berlin: Copyright 1941 by Irving Berlin. Copyright renewed 1968 by Irving Berlin. Reprinted by permission of Irving Berlin Music Corporation and Irving Berlin (England) Music.

This 1994 edition is published by Wings Books,
distributed by Outlet Book Company, Inc., a Random House Company, 40 Engelhard Avenue, Avenel, New Jersey 07001, by arrangement with Simon & Schuster, Inc.

Random House
New York • Toronto • London • Sydney • Auckland

Printed and bound in the United States of America

Library of Congress Cataloging-in-Publication Data
Higgins. Jack. 1929–
    [Novels. Selections]
    Three complete novels / Jack Higgins.
        p.   cm.
    Contents: The eagle has landed—The eagle has flown—Night of the fox.
    ISBN 0-517-10181-5
    1. World War, 1939–1945—Fiction.   2. War stories, English.
I. Title.   II. Title: 3 complete novels.
PR6058.I343A6   1994
823'.914—dc20
                                                              94-2435
                                                                CIP

8 7 6 5 4 3 2 1

CONTENTS

THE
EAGLE HAS
LANDED

For my children Sarah, Ruth, young Sean and little Hannah, who each in their separate ways have suffered and sweated through this one, but most of all for my wife Amy.

Prologue

꩜

AT PRECISELY ONE O'CLOCK ON the morning of Saturday, November 6, 1943, Heinrich Himmler, Reichsführer of the SS and Chief of State Police, received a simple message: *The Eagle has landed.* It meant that a small force of German paratroopers were at that moment safely in England and poised to snatch the British Prime Minister, Winston Churchill, from the Norfolk country house where he was spending a quiet weekend near the sea. This book is an attempt to re-create the events surrounding that astonishing exploit. At least fifty per cent of it is documented historical fact. The reader must decide for himself how much of the rest is a matter of speculation, or fiction ...

1

SOMEONE WAS DIGGING A GRAVE in one corner of the cemetery as I went in through the lychgate. I remember that quite clearly because it seemed to set the scene for nearly everything that followed.

Five or six rooks lifted out of the beech trees at the west end of the church like bundles of black rags, calling angrily to each other as I threaded my way between the tombstones and approached the grave, turning up the collar of my trenchcoat against the driving rain.

Whoever was down there was talking to himself in a low voice. It was impossible to catch what he was saying. I moved to one side of the pile of fresh earth, dodging another spadeful, and peered in. "Nasty morning for it."

He looked up, resting on his spade, an old, old man in a cloth cap and shabby, mud-stained suit, a grain sack draped across his shoulders. His cheeks were sunken and hollow, covered with a gray stubble, and his eyes full of moisture and quite vacant.

I tried again. "The rain," I said.

Some kind of understanding dawned. He glanced up at the sombre sky and scratched his chin. "Worse before it gets better, I'd say."

"It must make it difficult for you," I said. There was at least six inches of water swilling about in the bottom.

He poked at the far side of the grave with his spade and it split wide open, like something rotten bursting, earth showering down. "Could be worse. They put so many in this little boneyard over the years, people aren't planted in earth any more. They're buried in human remains."

He laughed, exposing toothless gums, then bent down, scrabbled in the earth at his feet and held up a finger-bone. "See what I mean?"

The appeal, even for the professional writer, of life in all its infinite variety, definitely has its limits on occasion and I decided it was time to move on. "I have got it right? This is a Catholic church?"

"All Romans here," he said. "Always have been."

"Then maybe you can help me. I'm looking for a grave or perhaps even a monument inside the church. Gascoigne—Charles Gascoigne. A sea captain."

"Never heard of him," he said. "And I've been sexton here forty-one years. When was he buried?"

7

"Around sixteen-eighty-five."

His expression didn't alter. He said calmly, "Ah, well then, before my time, you see. Father Vereker—now he might know something."

"Will he be inside?"

"There or the presbytery. Other side of the trees behind the wall."

At that moment, for some reason or other, the rookery in the beech trees above our heads erupted into life, dozens of rooks wheeling in the rain, filling the air with their clamour. The old man glanced up and hurled the finger-bone into the branches. And then he said a very strange thing.

"Noisy bastards!" he called. "Get back to Leningrad."

I'd been about to turn away, but paused, intrigued. "Leningrad?" I said. "What makes you say that?"

"That's where they come from. Starlings, too. They've been ringed in Leningrad and they turn up here in October. Too cold for them over there in the winter."

"Is that so?" I said.

He had become quite animated now, took half a cigarette from behind his ear and stuck it in his mouth. "Cold enough to freeze the balls off a brass monkey over there in the winter. A lot of Germans died at Leningrad during the war. Not shot or anything. Just froze to death."

By now I was quite fascinated. I said, "Who told you all that?"

"About the birds?" he said, and suddenly he changed completely, his face suffused by a kind of sly cunning. "Why, Werner told me. He knew all about birds."

"And who was Werner?"

"Werner?" He blinked several times, the vacant look appearing on his face again, though whether genuine or simulated it was impossible to tell. "He was a good lad, Werner. A good lad. They shouldn't have done that to him."

He leaned over his spade and started to dig again, dismissing me completely. I stayed there for a moment longer, but it was obvious that he had nothing more to say, so, reluctantly, because it had certainly sounded as if it might be a good story, I turned and worked my way through the tombstones to the main entrance.

I paused inside the porch. There was a notice-board on the wall in some sort of dark wood, the lettering in faded gold paint. *Church of St. Mary and All the Saints, Studley Constable* across the top and, underneath, the times for Mass and Confession. At the bottom it said *Father Philip Vereker, S. J.*

The door was oak and very old, held together by iron bands, studded with bolts. The handle was a bronze lion's head with a large ring in its mouth and the ring had to be turned to one side before the door opened, which it did finally with a slight, eerie creaking.

I had expected darkness and gloom inside, but instead, found what was in effect a medieval cathedral in miniature, flooded with light and astonishingly spacious. The nave arcades were superb, great Norman pillars soaring up to an incredible wooden roof, richly carved with an assortment of figures, human and animal, which were really in quite remarkable condition. A row of round, clerestory windows on either side at roof level were responsible for a great deal of the light which had so surprised me.

There was a beautiful stone font and on the wall beside it, a painted board listed all the priests who had served over the years, starting with a Rafe de Courcey in 1132 and ending with Vereker again, who had taken over in 1943.

Beyond was a small, dark chapel, candles flickering in front of an image of the Virgin Mary that seemed to float there in the half-light. I walked past it and down the centre aisle between the pews. It was very quiet, only the ruby light of the sanctuary lamp, a fifteenth-century Christ high on his cross down by the altar, rain drumming against the high windows.

There was a scrape of a foot on stone behind me and a dry, firm voice said, "Can I help you?"

I turned and found a priest standing in the entrance of the Lady Chapel, a tall, gaunt man in a faded black cassock. He had iron-gray hair cropped close to the skull and the eyes were set deep in their sockets as if he had been recently ill, an impression heightened by the tightness of the skin across the cheekbones. It was a strange face. Soldier or scholar, this man could have been either, but that didn't surprise me, remembering from the notice board that he was a Jesuit. But it was also a face that lived with pain as a constant companion if I was any judge and, as he came forward, I saw that he leaned heavily on a blackthorn stick and dragged his left foot.

"Father Vereker?"

"That's right."

"I was talking to the old man out there, the sexton."

"Ah, yes, Laker Armsby."

"If that's his name. He thought you might be able to help me." I held out my hand. "My name's Higgins, by the way. Jack Higgins. I'm a writer."

He hesitated slightly before shaking hands, but only because he had to switch the blackthorn from his right hand to his left. Even so, there was a definite reserve, or so it seemed to me. "And how can I help you, Mr. Higgins?"

"I'm doing a series of articles for an American magazine," I said. "Historical stuff. I was over at St. Margaret's at Cley, yesterday."

"A beautiful church." He sat down in the nearest pew. "Forgive me, I tire rather easily these days."

"There's a table tomb in the churchyard there," I went on. "Perhaps you know it? 'To James Greeve . . . ' "

He cut in on me instantly. " ' . . . who was assistant to Sir Cloudesley Shovel in burning ye ships in Ye Port of Tripoly in Barbary, January fourteenth, sixteen seventy-six.' " He showed that he could smile. "But that's a famous inscription in these parts."

"According to my researches, when Greeve was Captain of the *Orange Tree* he had a mate called Charles Gascoigne who later became a captain in the navy. He died of an old wound in sixteen-eighty-three and it seems Greeve had him brought up to Cley to be buried."

"I see," he said politely, but without any particular interest. In fact, there was almost a hint of impatience in his voice.

"There's no trace of him in Cley churchyard," I said, "or in the parish records and I've tried the churches at Wiveton, Glandford and Blakeney with the same result."

"And you think he might be here?"

"I was going through my notes again and remembered that he'd been raised a Catholic as a boy and it occurred to me that he might have been buried in the faith. I'm staying at the Blakeney Hotel and I was talking to one of the barmen there who told me there was a Catholic church here at Studley Constable. It's certainly an out-of-the-way little place. Took me a good hour to find it."

"All to no purpose, I'm afraid." He pushed himself up. "I've been here at St. Mary's for twenty-eight years now and I can assure you I've never come across any mention of this Charles Gascoigne."

It had been very much my last chance and I suppose I allowed my disappointment to show, but in any case, I persisted. "Can you be absolutely sure? What about church records for the period? There might be an entry in the burial register."

"The local history of this area happens to be a personal interest of mine," he said with a certain acidity. "There is not a document connected with this church with which I am not completely familiar and I can assure you that nowhere is there any mention of a Charles Gascoigne. And now, if you'll excuse me. My lunch will be ready."

As he moved forward, the blackthorn slipped and he stumbled and almost fell. I grabbed his elbow and managed to stand on his left foot. He didn't even wince.

I said, "I'm sorry, that was damned clumsy of me."

He smiled for the second time. "Nothing to hurt, as it happens." He rapped at the foot with the blackthorn. "A confounded nuisance, but, as they say, I've learned to live with it."

It was the kind of remark which required no comment and he

obviously wasn't seeking one. We went down the aisle together, slowly because of his foot, and I said, "A remarkably beautiful church."

"Yes, we're rather proud of it." He opened the door for me. "I'm sorry I couldn't be of more help."

"That's all right," I said. "Do you mind if I have a look around the churchyard while I'm here?"

"A hard man to convince, I see." But there was no malice in the way he said it. "Why not? We have some very interesting stones. I'd particularly recommend you to the section at the west end. Early eighteenth-century and obviously done by the same local mason who did similar work at Cley."

This time he was the one who held out his hand. As I took it, he said, "You know, I thought your name was familiar. Didn't you write a book on the Ulster troubles last year?"

"That's right," I said. "A nasty business."

"War always is, Mr. Higgins." His face was bleak. "Man at his most cruel. Good-day to you."

He closed the door and I moved into the porch. A strange encounter. I lit a cigarette and stepped into the rain. The sexton had moved on and for the moment I had the churchyard to myself, except for the rooks, of course. *The rooks from Leningrad.* I wondered about that again, then pushed the thought resolutely from my mind. There was work to be done. Not that I had any great hope after talking to Father Vereker, of finding Charles Gascoigne's tomb, but the truth was there just wasn't anywhere else to look.

I worked my way through methodically, starting at the west end, noticing in my progress the headstones he'd mentioned. They were certainly curious. Sculptured and etched with vivid and rather crude ornaments of bones, skulls, winged hourglasses and archangels. Interesting, but entirely the wrong period for Gascoigne.

It took me an hour and twenty minutes to cover the entire area and at the end of that time I knew I was beaten. For one thing, unlike most country churchyards these days, this one was kept in very decent order. Grass cut, bushes trimmed back, very little that was overgrown or partially hidden from view or that sort of thing.

So, no Charles Gascoigne. I was standing by the newly dug grave when I finally admitted defeat. The old sexton had covered it with a tarpaulin against the rain and one end had fallen in. I crouched down to pull it back into position and as I started to rise, noticed a strange thing.

A yard or two away, close in to the wall of the church at the base of the tower, there was a flat tombstone set in a mound of green grass. It was early eighteenth-century, an example of the local mason's work I've already mentioned. It had a superb skull and crossbones at its head and was dedicated to a wool merchant named Jeremiah Fuller, his wife and two children. Crouched down as I was, I became aware that there was another slab beneath it.

The Celt in me rises to the top easily and I was filled with a sudden irrational excitement as if conscious that I stood on the threshold of something. I knelt over the tombstone and tried to get my fingers to it, which proved to be rather difficult. But then, quite suddenly, it started to move.

"Come on, Gascoigne," I said softly. "Let's be having you."

The slab slid to one side, tilting on the slope of the mound and all was revealed. I suppose it was one of the most astonishing moments of my life. It was a simple stone, with a German cross at the head—what most people would describe as an iron cross. The inscription beneath it was in German. It read *Hier ruhen Oberstleutnant Kurt Steiner und 13 Deutsche Fallschirmjäger gefallen am 6 November 1943.*

My German is indifferent at the best of times, mainly from lack of use, but it was good enough for this. Here lies Lieutenant-Colonel Kurt Steiner and 13 German paratroopers, killed in action on the 6th November, 1943.

I crouched there in the rain, checking my translation carefully but no, I was right, and that didn't make any kind of sense. To start with, I happened to know, as I'd once written an article on the subject, that when the German Military Cemetery was opened at Cannock Chase in Staffordshire in 1967, the remains of the four thousand, nine hundred and twenty-five German servicemen who died in Britain during the First and Second World Wars were transferred there.

Killed in Action, the inscription said. No, it was quite absurd. An elaborate hoax on somebody's part. It had to be.

Any further thoughts on the subject were prevented by a sudden outraged cry. "What in the hell do you think you're doing?"

Father Vereker was hobbling towards me through the tombstones, holding a large black umbrella over his head.

I called cheerfully, "I think you'll find this interesting, Father. I've made a rather astonishing find."

As he drew closer, I realized that something was wrong. Something was very wrong indeed, for his face was white with passion and he was shaking with rage. "How dare you move that stone? Sacrilege—that's the only word for it."

"All right," I said. "I'm sorry about that, but look what I've found underneath."

"I don't give a damn what you've found underneath. Put it back at once."

I was beginning to get annoyed myself now. "Don't be silly. Don't you realize what it says here? If you don't read German then allow me to tell you. 'Here lies Lieutenant Colonel Kurt Steiner and thirteen

German paratroopers killed in action sixth November nineteen-forty-three.' Now don't you find that absolutely bloody fascinating?''

''Not particularly.''

''You mean you've seen it before.''

''No, of course not.'' There was something hunted about him now, an edge of desperation to his voice when he added, ''Now will you kindly replace the original stone?''

I didn't believe him, not for a moment. I said, ''Who was he, this Steiner? What was it all about?''

''I've already told you, I haven't the slightest idea,'' he said, looking more hunted still.

And then I remembered something. ''You were here in nineteen-forty-three, weren't you? That's when you took over the parish. It says so on the board inside the church.''

He exploded, came apart at the seams. ''For the last time, will you replace that stone as you found it?''

''No,'' I said. ''I'm afraid I can't do that.''

Strangely enough, he seemed to regain some kind of control of himself at that point. ''Very well,'' he said calmly. ''Then you will oblige me by leaving at once.''

There seemed little point in arguing, considering the state of mind he was in, so I said briefly, ''All right, Father, if that's the way you want it.''

I had reached the path when he called, ''And don't come back. If you do I shall call the local police without the slightest hesitation.''

I went out through the lychgate, got into the Peugeot and drove away. His threats didn't worry me. I was too excited for that, too intrigued. Everything about Studley Constable was intriguing. It was one of those places that seem to turn up in North Norfolk and nowhere else. The kind of village that you find by accident one day and can never find again, so that you begin to question whether it ever existed in the first place.

Not that there was very much of it. The church, the old presbytery in its walled garden, fifteen or sixteen cottages of one kind or another scattered along the stream, the old mill with its massive water wheel, the village inn on the opposite side of the green, the Studley Arms.

I pulled into the side of the road beside the stream, lit a cigarette and gave the whole thing a little quiet thought. Father Vereker was lying. He'd seen that stone before, he knew its significance, of that I was convinced. It was rather ironic when one thought about it. I'd come to Studley Constable by chance in search of Charles Gascoigne. Instead I'd discovered something vastly more intriguing, a genuine mystery. But what was I going to do about it, that was the thing?

The solution presented itself to me almost instantly in the person of Laker Armsby, the sexton, who appeared from a narrow alley between two cottages. He was still splashed with mud, still had that old grain sack over his shoulders. He crossed the road and entered the Studley Arms and I got out of the Peugeot instantly and went after him.

According to the plate over the entrance, the licensee was one George Henry Wilde. I opened the door and found myself in a stone-flagged corridor with panelled walls. A door to the left stood ajar and there was a murmur of voices, a burst of laughter.

Inside, there was no bar, just a large, comfortable room with an open fire on a stone hearth, several highbacked benches, a couple of wooden tables. There were six or seven customers and none of them young. I'd have said that sixty was about the average age—a pattern that's distressingly common in such rural areas these days.

They were countrymen to the backbone, faces weathered by exposure, tweed caps, gumboots. Three played dominoes watched by two more, an old man sat by the fire playing a mouth-organ softly to himself. They all looked up to consider me with the kind of grave interest close-knit groups always have in strangers.

"Good afternoon," I said.

Two or three nodded in a cheerful enough way, though one massively-built character with a black beard flecked with gray didn't look too friendly. Laker Armsby was sitting at a table on his own, rolling a cigarette between his fingers laboriously, a glass of ale in front of him. He put the cigarette in his mouth and I moved to his side and offered him a light. "Hello, there."

He glanced up blankly and then his face cleared. "Oh, it's you again. Did you find Father Vereker then?"

I nodded. "Will you have another drink?"

"I wouldn't say no." He emptied his glass in a couple of swallows. "A pint of brown ale would go down very nicely. Georgy!"

I turned and found a short, stocky man in shirt-sleeves standing behind me, presumably the landlord, George Wilde. He seemed about the same age range as the others and was a reasonable enough looking man except for one unusual feature. At some time in his life he'd been shot in the face at close quarters. I'd seen enough gunshot wounds in my time to be certain of that. In his case the bullet had scoured a furrow in his left cheek, obviously taking bone with it as well. His luck was good.

He smiled pleasantly. "And you, sir?"

I told him I'd have a large vodka and tonic which brought amused looks from the farmers or whatever they were, but that didn't particularly worry me as it happens to be the only alcohol I can drink with any kind of pleasure. Laker Armsby's hand-rolled cigarette hadn't lasted too long so I gave him one of mine which he accepted with alacrity. The drinks came and I pushed his ale across to him.

"How long did you say you'd been sexton up at St. Mary's?"

"Forty-one years."

He drained his pint glass. I said, "Here, have another and tell me about Steiner."

The mouth-organ stopped playing abruptly, all conversation died. Old Laker Armsby stared at me across the top of his glass, that look of sly cunning on his face again. "Steiner?" he said. "Why, Steiner was . . ."

George Wilde cut in, reached for the empty glass and ran a cloth over the table. "Right, sir, time please."

I looked at my watch. It was two-thirty. I said, "You've got it wrong. Another half-hour till closing time."

He picked up my glass of vodka and handed it to me. "This is a free house, sir, and in a quiet little village like this we generally do as we please without anybody getting too upset about it. If I say I'm closing at two-thirty then two-thirty it is." He smiled amiably. "I'd drink up if I were you, sir."

There was tension in the air that you could cut with a knife. They were all sitting looking at me, hard, flat faces, eyes like stones and the giant with the black beard moved across to the end of the table and leaned on it, glaring at me.

"You heard him," he said in a low, dangerous voice. "Now drink up like a good boy and go home, wherever that is."

I didn't argue because the atmosphere was getting worse by the minute. I drank my vodka and tonic, taking a certain amount of time over it, though whether to prove something to them or myself I'm not certain, then I left.

Strange, but I wasn't angry, just fascinated by the whole incredible affair and by now, of course, I was too far in to draw back. I had to have some answers and it occurred to me that there was a rather obvious way of getting them.

I got into the Peugeot, turned over the bridge and drove up out of the village, passing the church and the presbytery, taking the road to Blakeney. A few hundred yards past the church, I turned the Peugeot into a cart track, left it there and walked back, taking a small Pentax camera with me from the glove compartment of the car.

I wasn't afraid. After all, on one famous occasion I'd been escorted from the Europa Hotel in Belfast to the airport by men with guns in their pockets who'd suggested I got the next plane out for the good of my health and didn't return. But I had and on several occasions; had even got a book out of it.

When I went back into the churchyard I found the stone to Steiner and his men exactly as I'd left it. I checked the inscription once again just to make sure I wasn't making a fool of myself, took several photos of it from different angles, then hurried to the church and went inside.

There was a curtain across the base of the tower and I went behind it. Choirboys' scarlet cottas and white surplices hung neatly on a rail, there was an old iron-bound trunk, several bell ropes trailed down through the gloom above and a board on the wall informed the world that on 22 July 1936, a peal of five thousand and fifty-eight changes of Bob Minor was rung at the church. I was interested to note that Laker Armsby was listed as one of the six bell-ringers involved.

Even more interesting was a line of holes cutting across the board which had at some time been filled in with plaster and stained. They continued into the masonry, for all the world like a machine-gun burst, but that was really too outrageous.

What I was after was the burial register and there was no sign of any kind of books or documents there. I went out through the curtain and almost instantly noticed the small door in the wall behind the font. It opened easily enough when I tried the handle and I stepped inside and found myself in what was very obviously the sacristy, a small, oak-panelled room. There was a rack containing a couple of cassocks, several surplices and copes, an oak cupboard and a large, old-fashioned desk.

I tried the cupboard first and struck oil at once. Every kind of ledger possible was in there, stacked neatly on one of the shelves. There were three burial registers and 1943 was in the second one. I leafed through the pages quickly, conscious at once of a feeling of enormous disappointment.

There were two deaths entered during November 1943 and they were both women. I hurriedly worked my way back to the beginning of the year, which didn't take very long, then closed the register and replaced it in the cupboard. So one very obvious avenue was closed to me. If Steiner, whoever he was, had been buried here, then he should have gone into the register. That was an incontrovertible point of English law. So what in the hell did it all mean?

I opened the sacristy door and stepped out, closing it behind me. There were two of them there from the pub. George Wilde and the man with the black beard whom I was disturbed to notice carried a double-barrelled shotgun.

Wilde said gently, "I did advise you to move on, sir, you must admit that. Now why weren't you sensible?"

The man with the black beard said, "What in the hell are we waiting for? Let's get this over with."

He moved with astonishing speed for a man of such size and grabbed hold of the lapels of my trenchcoat. In the same moment the sacristy door opened behind me and Vereker stepped out. God knows where he'd come from, but I was distinctly pleased to see him.

"What on earth's going on here?" he demanded.

Blackbeard said, "You just leave this to us, Father, we'll handle it."

"You'll handle nothing, Arthur Seymour," Vereker said. "Now step back."

Seymour stared at him flatly, still hanging on to me. I could have cut him down to size in several different ways, but there didn't seem a great deal of point.

Vereker said again, "Seymour!" and there was really iron in his voice this time.

Seymour slowly released his grip and Vereker said, "Don't come back again, Mr. Higgins. It should be obvious to you by now that it wouldn't be in your best interests."

"A good point."

I didn't exactly expect a hue and cry, not after Vereker's intervention, but it hardly seemed politic to hang around, so I hurried back to the car at a jog trot. Further consideration of the whole mysterious affair could come later.

I turned into the cart track and found Laker Armsby sitting on the bonnet of the Peugeot rolling a cigarette. He stood up as I approached. "Ah, there you are," he said. "You got away then?"

There was that same look of low cunning on his face again. I took out my cigarettes and offered him one. "Do you want to know something?" I said. "I don't think you're anything like as simple as you look."

He grinned slyly and puffed out smoke in a cloud into the rain. "How much?"

I knew what he meant instantly, but for the moment, played him along. "What do you mean, how much?"

"Is it worth to you. To know about Steiner."

He leaned back against the car looking at me, waiting, so I took out my wallet, extracted a five-pound note and held it up between my fingers. His eyes gleamed and he reached. I pulled back my hand.

"Oh, no. Let's have some answers first."

"All right, mister. What do you want to know?"

"This Kurt Steiner—who was he?"

He grinned, the eyes furtive again, that sly, cunning smile on his lips. "That's easy," he said. "He was the German lad who came here with his men to shoot Mr. Churchill."

I was so astonished that I simply stood there staring at him. He snatched the fiver from my hand, turned and cleared off at a shambling trot.

⚜

Some things in life are so enormous in their impact that they are almost impossible to take in, like a strange voice on the other end of a telephone telling you that someone you greatly loved has just died. Words become meaningless, the mind cuts itself off from reality for a little while, a necessary breathing space until one is ready to cope.

Which is roughly the state I found myself in after Laker Armsby's astonishing assertion. It wasn't just that it was so incredible. If there's one lesson I've learned in life it's that if you say a thing is impossible, it will probably happen next week. The truth is that the implications, if what Armsby had said was true, were so enormous that for the moment, my mind was incapable of handling the idea.

It was there. I was aware of its existence, but didn't consciously think about it. I went back to the Blakeney Hotel, packed my bags, paid my bill and started home, the first stop in a journey which, although I didn't realize it then, was to consume a year of my life. A year of hundreds of files, dozens of interviews, travelling half-way round the world. San Francisco, Singapore, the Argentine, Hamburg, Berlin, Warsaw and even—most ironic of all—the Falls Road in Belfast. Anywhere there seemed to be a clue, however slight, that would lead me to the truth and particularly, because he is somehow central to the whole affair, some knowledge, some understanding of the enigma that was Kurt Steiner.

2

IN A SENSE A MAN called Otto Skorzeny started it all on Sunday 12 September 1943 by bringing off one of the most brilliantly audacious commando coups of the Second World War—thus proving once again to Adolf Hitler's entire satisfaction that he, as usual, had been right and the High Command of the Armed Forces wrong.

Hitler himself had suddenly wanted to know why the German Army did not have commando units like the English ones which had operated so successfully since the beginning of the war. To satisfy him, the High Command decided to form such a unit. Skorzeny, a young SS lieutenant, was kicking his heels in Berlin at the time after being invalided out of his regiment. He was promoted captain and made Chief of German

Special Forces, none of which meant very much, which was exactly what the High Command intended.

Unfortunately for them, Skorzeny proved to be a brilliant soldier, uniquely gifted for the task in hand. And events were soon to give him a chance to prove it.

On 3 September 1943 Italy surrendered, Mussolini was deposed and Marshal Badoglio had him arrested and spirited away. Hitler insisted that his former ally be found and set free. It seemed an impossible task and even the great Erwin Rommel himself commented that he could see no good in the idea and hoped that it wouldn't be put on to his plate.

It wasn't, for Hitler gave it to Skorzeny personally who threw himself into the task with energy and determination and soon discovered that Mussolini was being held in the Sports Hotel on top of the ten-thousand-foot Gran Sasso in the Abruzzi, guarded by two hundred and fifty men.

Skorzeny landed by glider with fifty paratroopers, stormed the hotel and freed Mussolini. He was flown out in a tiny Stork spotter plane to Rome, then transhipped by Dornier to the Wolf's Lair, Hitler's head-quarters for the Eastern Front, which was situated at Rastenburg in a gloomy, damp and heavily-wooded part of East Prussia.

The feat earned Skorzeny a hatful of medals, including the Knight's Cross, and started him on a career that was to embrace countless similar daring exploits and make him a legend in his own time. The High Command, as suspicious of such irregular methods as senior officers the world over, remained unimpressed.

Not so the Führer. He was in his seventh heaven, transported with delight, danced as he had not danced since the fall of Paris and this mood was still with him on the evening of the Wednesday following Mussolini's arrival at Rastenburg, when he held a meeting in the conference hut to discuss events in Italy and the Duce's future role.

The map room was surprisingly pleasant, with pine walls and ceiling. There was a circular table at one end surrounded by eleven rush chairs, flowers in a vase in the centre. At the other end of the room was the long map table. The small group of men who stood beside it discussing the situation on the Italian front included Mussolini himself, Josef Goebbels, Reich Minister of Propaganda and Minister for Total War, Heinrich Himmler, Reichsführer of the SS, Chief of the State Police and of the State Secret Police, amongst other things, and Admiral Wilhelm Canaris, Chief of Military Intelligence, the Abwehr.

When Hitler entered the room they all stiffened to attention. He was in a jovial mood, eyes glittering, a slight fixed smile on his mouth, full of charm as only he could be on occasion. He descended on Mussolini and shook his hand warmly, holding it in both of his. ''You look better tonight, Duce. Decidedly better.''

To everyone else present the Italian dictator looked terrible. Tired and listless, little of his old fire left in him.

He managed a weak smile and the Führer clapped his hands. "Well, gentlemen, and what should our next move be in Italy? What does the future hold? What is your opinion, Herr Reichsführer?"

Himmler removed his silver pince-nez and polished their lenses meticulously as he replied. "Total victory, my Führer. What else? The presence of the Duce here with us now is ample proof of the brilliance with which you saved the situation after that traitor Badoglio signed an armistice."

Hitler nodded, his face serious, and turned to Goebbels. "And you, Josef?"

Goebbels' dark, mad eyes blazed with enthusiasm. "I agree, my Führer. The liberation of the Duce has caused a great sensation at home and abroad. Friend and foe alike are full of admiration. We are able to celebrate a first-class moral victory, thanks to your inspired guidance."

"And no thanks to my generals." Hitler turned to Canaris, who was standing looking down at the map, a slight, ironic smile on his face. "And you, Herr Admiral? You also think this a first-class moral victory?"

There are times when it pays to speak the truth, others when it does not. With Hitler it was always difficult to judge the occasion.

"My Führer, the Italian Battle Fleet now lies at anchor under the guns of the fortress of Malta. We have had to abandon Corsica and Sardinia and news is coming through that our old allies are already making arrangements to fight on the other side."

Hitler had turned deathly pale, his eyes glittered, there was the faint damp of perspiration on his brow, but Canaris continued, "As for the new Italian Socialist Republic as proclaimed by the Duce." Here, he shrugged. "Not a single neutral country so far, not even Spain, has agreed to set up diplomatic relations. I regret to say, my Führer, that in my opinion, they won't."

"Your opinion?" Hitler exploded with fury. "Your opinion? You're as bad as my generals and when I listen to them what happens? Failure everywhere." He moved to Mussolini, who seemed rather alarmed, and placed an arm around his shoulders. "Is the Duce here because of the High Command? No, he's here because I insisted that they set up a commando unit, because my intuition told me it was the right thing to do."

Goebbels looked anxious, Himmler as calm and enigmatic as usual, but Canaris stood his ground. "I implied no criticism of you personally, my Führer."

Hitler had moved to the window and stood looking out, hands tightly clenched behind him. "I have an instinct for these things and I knew how successful this kind of operation could be. A handful of brave men, daring all.'' He swung round to face them. ''Without me there would have been no Gran Sasso because without me there would have been no Skorzeny.'' He said that as if delivering Biblical writ. ''I don't wish to be too hard on you, Herr Admiral, but after all, what have you and your people at the Abwehr accomplished lately? It seems to me that all you can do is produce traitors like Dohnanyi.''

Hans von Dohnanyi, who had worked for the Abwehr, had been arrested for treason against the state in April.

Canaris was paler than ever now, on dangerous ground indeed. He said, ''My Führer, there was no intention on my part . . . ''

Hitler ignored him and turned to Himmler. ''And you, Herr Reichsführer—what do you think?''

''I accept your concept totally, my Führer,'' Himmler told him. ''Totally; but then, I'm also slightly prejudiced. Skorzeny, after all, is an SS officer. On the other hand, I would have thought the Gran Sasso affair to be exactly the kind of business the Brandenburgers were supposed to take care of.''

He was referring to the Brandenburg Division, a unique unit formed early in the war to perform special missions. Its activities were supposedly in the hands of Department Two of the Abwehr, which specialized in sabotage. In spite of Canaris's efforts, this elite force had, for the most part, been frittered away in hit-and-run operations behind the Russian lines which had achieved little.

''Exactly,'' Hitler said. ''What have your precious Brandenburgers done? Nothing worth a moment's discussion.'' He was working himself into a fury again now, and as always at such times, seemed able to draw on his prodigious memory to a remarkable degree.

''When it was originally formed, this Brandenburg unit, it was called the Company for Special Missions, and I remember hearing that von Hippel, its first commander, told them they'd be able to fetch the Devil from hell by the time he'd finished with them. I find that ironic, Herr Admiral, because as far as I can remember, they didn't bring me the Duce. I had to arrange for that myself.''

His voice had risen to a crescendo, the eyes sparked fire, the face was wet with perspiration. ''Nothing!'' he shrieked. ''You have brought me nothing and yet with men like that, with such facilities, you should have been capable of bringing me Churchill out of England.''

There was a moment of complete silence as Hitler glanced from face to face. ''Is that not so?''

Mussolini looked hunted, Goebbels nodded eagerly. It was Himmler who added fuel to the flames by saying quietly, ''Why not, my Führer? After all, anything is possible, no matter how miraculous, as you have shown by bringing the Duce out of Gran Sasso.''

''Quite right.'' Hitler was calm again now. ''A wonderful opportunity to show us what the Abwehr is capable of, Herr Admiral.''

Canaris was stunned. ''My Führer, do I understand you to mean . . . ?''

''After all, an English commando unit attacked Rommel's headquarters in Africa,'' Hitler said, ''and similar groups have raided the French coast on many occasions. Am I to believe that German boys are capable of less?'' He patted Canaris on the shoulder and said affably, ''See to it, Herr Admiral. Get things moving. I'm sure you'll come up with something.'' He turned to Himmler. ''You agree, Herr Reichsführer?''

''Certainly,'' Himmler said without hesitation. ''A feasibility study at the very least—surely the Abwehr can manage that?''

He smiled slightly at Canaris who stood there, thunderstruck. He moistened dry lips and said in a hoarse voice, ''As you command, my Führer.''

Hitler put an arm around his shoulder. ''Good. I knew I could rely on you as always.'' He stretched out his arm as if to pull them all forward and leaned over the map. ''And now, gentlemen—the Italian situation.''

Canaris and Himmler were returning to Berlin by Dornier that night. They left Rastenburg at the same time in separate cars for the nine-mile drive to the airfield. Canaris was fifteen minutes late and when he finally mounted the steps into the Dornier he was not in the best of moods. Himmler was already strapped into his seat and, after a moment's hesitation, Canaris joined him.

''Trouble?'' Himmler asked as the plane bumped forward across the runway and turned into the wind.

''Burst tyre.'' Canaris leaned back. ''Thanks very much, by the way. You were a great help back there.''

''Always happy to be of service,'' Himmler told him.

They were airborne now, the engine note deepening as they climbed. ''My God, but he was really on form tonight,'' Canaris said. ''Get Churchill. Have you ever heard anything so crazy?''

''Since Skorzeny got Mussolini out of Gran Sasso, the world will never be quite the same again. The Führer now believes miracles can actually take place and this will make life increasingly difficult for you and me, Herr Admiral.''

''Mussolini was one thing,'' Canaris said. ''Without in any way detracting from Skorzeny's magnificent achievement, Winston Churchill would be something else again.''

''Oh, I don't know,'' Himmler said. ''I've seen the enemy newsreels as you have. London one day—Manchester or Leeds the next. He walks the streets with that stupid cigar in his mouth talking to the people. I would say that of all the major world leaders, he is probably the least protected.''

"If you believe that, you'll believe anything," Canaris said drily. "Whatever else they are, the English aren't fools. MI five and six employ lots of very well-spoken young men who've been to Oxford or Cambridge and who'd put a bullet through your belly as soon as look at you. Anyway, take the old man himself. Probably carries a pistol in his coat pocket and I bet he's still a crack shot."

An orderly brought them some coffee. Himmler said, "So you don't intend to proceed in this affair?"

"You know what will happen as well as I do," Canaris said. "Today's Wednesday. He'll have forgotten the whole crazy idea by Friday."

Himmler nodded slowly, sipping his coffee. "Yes, I suppose you're right."

Canaris stood up. "Anyway, if you'll excuse me, I think I'll get a little sleep."

He moved to another seat, covered himself with a blanket provided and made himself as comfortable as possible for the three-hour trip that lay ahead.

From the other side of the aisle Himmler watched him, eyes cold, fixed, staring. There was no expression on his face—none at all. He might have been a corpse lying there had it not been for the muscle that twitched constantly in his right cheek.

When Canaris reached the Abwehr offices at 74–76 Tirpitz Ufer in Berlin it was almost dawn. The driver who had picked him up at Tempelhof had brought the Admiral's two favourite dachshunds with him and when Canaris got out of the car, they scampered at his heels as he walked briskly past the sentries.

He went straight up to his office. Unbuttoning his naval greatcoat as he went, he handed it to the orderly who opened the door for him. "Coffee," the Admiral told him. "Lots of coffee." The orderly started to close the door and Canaris called him back. "Do you know if Colonel Radl is in?"

"I believe he slept in his office last night, Herr Admiral."

"Good, tell him I'd like to see him."

The door closed. He was alone and suddenly tired and he slumped down in the chair behind the desk. Canaris's personal style was modest. The office was old-fashioned and relatively bare, with a worn carpet. There was a portrait of Franco on the wall with a dedication. On the desk was a marble paperweight with three bronze monkeys seeing, hearing and speaking no evil.

"That's me," he said softly, tapping them on the head.

He took a deep breath to get a grip on himself: it was the very knife-edge of danger he walked in that insane world. There were things he suspected that even he should not have known. An attempt by two senior officers earlier that year to blow up Hitler's plane in flight from Smolensk to Rastenburg, for instance, and the constant threat of what might happen if von Dohnanyi and his friends cracked and talked.

The orderly appeared with a tray containing coffee pot, two cups and a small pot of real cream, something of a rarity in Berlin at that time. "Leave it," Canaris said. "I'll see to it myself."

The orderly withdrew and as Canaris poured the coffee, there was a knock at the door. The man who entered might have stepped straight off a parade ground, so immaculate was his uniform. A lieutenant-colonel of mountain troops with the ribbon for the Winter War, a silver wound badge and a Knight's Cross at his throat. Even the patch which covered his right eye had a regulation look about it, as did the black leather glove on his left hand.

"Ah, there you are, Max," Canaris said. "Join me for coffee and restore me to sanity. Each time I return from Rastenburg I feel increasingly that I need a keeper, or at least that someone does."

Max Radl was thirty and looked ten or fifteen years older, depending on the day and weather. He had lost his right eye and left hand during the Winter War in 1941 and had worked for Canaris ever since being invalided home. He was at that time Head of Section Three, which was an office of Department Z, the Central Department of the Abwehr and directly under the Admiral's personal control. Section Three was a unit which was supposed to look after particularly difficult assignments and as such, Radl was authorized to poke his nose into any other Abwehr section that he wanted, an activity which made him considerably less than popular amongst his colleagues.

"As bad as that?"

"Worse," Canaris told him. "Mussolini was like a walking automaton, Goebbels hopped as usual from one foot to the other like some ten-year-old schoolboy bursting for a pee."

Radl winced, for it always made him feel decidedly uneasy when the Admiral spoke in that way of such powerful people. Although the offices were checked daily for microphones, one could never really be sure.

Canaris carried on, "Himmler was his usual pleasant corpse-like self and as for the Führer . . . "

Radl cut in hastily. "More coffee, Herr Admiral?"

Canaris sat down again. "All he could talk about was Gran Sasso and what a bloody miracle the whole thing was and why didn't the Abwehr do something as spectacular."

He jumped up, walked to the window and peered out through the curtains into the gray morning. "You know what he suggests we do, Max? Get Churchill for him."

Radl started violently. "Good God, he can't be serious."

"Who knows? One day, yes, another day, no. He didn't actually specify whether he wanted him alive or dead. This business with Mussolini has gone to his head. Now he seems to think anything is possible. Bring the Devil from Hell if necessary, was a phrase he quoted with some feeling."

"And the others—how did they take it?" Radl asked.

"Goebbels was his usual amiable self, the Duce looked hunted. Himmler was the difficult one. Backed the Führer all the way. Said that the least we could do was look into it. A feasibility study, that was the phrase he used."

"I see, sir." Radl hesitated. "You do think the Führer is serious?"

"Of course not." Canaris went over to the army cot in the corner, turned back the blankets, sat down and started to unlace his shoes. "He'll have forgotten it already. I know what he's like when he's in that kind of mood. Comes out with all sorts of rubbish." He got into the cot and covered himself with the blanket. "No, I'd say Himmler's the only worry. He's after my blood. He'll remind him about the whole miserable affair at some future date when it suits him, if only to make it look as if I don't do as I'm told."

"So what do you want me to do?"

"Exactly what Himmler suggested. A feasibility study. A nice, long report that will look as if we've really been trying. For example, Churchill's in Canada at the moment, isn't he? Probably coming back by boat. You can always make it look as if you've seriously considered the possibility of having a U-boat in the right place at the right time. After all, as our Führer assured me personally not six hours ago, miracles do happen, but only under the right divine inspiration. Tell Krogel to wake me in one hour and a half."

He pulled the blanket over his head and Radl turned off the light and went out. He wasn't at all happy as he made his way back to his office and not because of the ridiculous task he'd been given. That sort of thing was commonplace. In fact, he often referred to Section Three as the Department of Absurdities.

No, it was the way Canaris talked which worried him and as he was one of those individuals who liked to be scrupulously honest with himself, Radl was man enough to admit that he wasn't just worried about the Admiral. He was very much thinking of himself and his family.

Technically the Gestapo had no jurisdiction over men in uniform. On the other hand he had seen too many acquaintances simply disappear off the face of the earth to believe that. The infamous Night and Fog Decree, in which various unfortunates were made to vanish into the mists of night in the most literal sense, was supposed to only apply to inhabitants of conquered territories, but as Radl was well aware, there were more than fifty thousand non-Jewish German citizens in concentration camps at that particular point in time. Since 1933, nearly two hundred thousand had died.

When he went into the office, Sergeant Hofer, his assistant, was going through the night mail which had just come in. He was a quiet, dark-haired man of forty-eight, an innkeeper from the Harz Mountains, a superb skier who had lied about his age to join up and had served with Radl in Russia.

Radl sat down behind his desk and gazed morosely at a picture of his wife and three daughters, safe in Bavaria in the mountains. Hofer, who knew the signs, gave him a cigarette and poured him a small brandy from a bottle of Courvoisier kept in the bottom drawer of the desk.

"As bad as that, Herr Oberst?"

"As bad as that, Karl," Radl answered, then he swallowed his brandy and told him the worst.

And there it might have rested had it not been for an extraordinary coincidence. On the morning of the 22nd, exactly one week after his interview with Canaris, Radl was seated at his desk, fighting his way through a mass of paperwork which had accumulated during a three-day visit to Paris.

He was not in a happy mood and when the door opened and Hofer entered, he glanced up with a frown and said impatiently, "For God's sake, Karl, I asked to be left in peace. What is it now?"

"I'm sorry, Herr Oberst. It's just that a report has come to my notice which I thought might interest you."

"Where did it come from?"

"Abwehr One."

Which was the department which handled espionage abroad and Radl was aware of a faint, if reluctant stirring of interest. Hofer stood there waiting, hugging the manilla folder to his chest and Radl put down his pen with a sigh. "All right, tell me about it."

Hofer placed the file in front of him and opened it. "This is the latest report from an agent in England. Code name Starling."

Radl glanced at the front sheet as he reached for a cigarette from the box on the table. "Mrs. Joanna Grey."

"She's situated in the northern part of Norfolk close to the coast, Herr Oberst. A village called Studley Constable."

"But of course," Radl said, suddenly rather more enthusiastic. "Isn't she the woman who got the details of the Oboe installation?" He turned over the first two or three pages briefly and frowned. "There's a hell of a lot of it. How does she manage that?''

''She has an excellent contact at the Spanish Embassy who puts her stuff through in the diplomatic bag. It's as good as the post. We usually take delivery within three days.''

''Remarkable,'' Radl said. ''How often does she report?''

''Once a month. She also has a radio link, but this is seldom used, although she follows normal procedure and keeps her channel open three times a week for one hour in case she's needed. Her link man at this end is Captain Meyer.''

''All right, Karl,'' Radl said. ''Get me some coffee and I'll read it.''

''I've marked the interesting paragraph in red, Herr Oberst. You'll find it on page three. I also put in a large-scale, British ordnance survey map of the area,'' Hofer told him and went out.

The report was very well put together, lucid and full of information of worth. A general description of conditions in the area, the location of two new American B17 squadrons south of the Wash, a B24 squadron near Sheringham. It was all good, useful stuff without being terribly exciting. And then he came to page three and that brief paragraph, underlined in red, and his stomach contracted in a spasm of nervous excitement.

It was simple enough. The British Prime Minister, Winston Churchill, was to inspect a station of RAF Bomber Command near the Wash on the morning of Saturday 6 November. Later on the same day, he was scheduled to visit a factory near King's Lynn and make a brief speech to the workers.

Then came the interesting part. Instead of returning to London he intended to spend the weekend at the home of Sir Henry Willoughby, Studley Grange, which was just five miles outside the village of Studley Constable. It was a purely private visit, the details supposedly secret. Certainly no one in the village was aware of the plan, but Sir Henry, a retired naval commander, had apparently been unable to resist confiding in Joanna Grey, who was, it seemed, a personal friend.

Radl sat staring at the report for a few moments, thinking about it, then he took out the ordnance survey map Hofer had provided and unfolded it. The door opened and Hofer appeared with the coffee. He placed the tray on the table, filled a cup and stood waiting, face impassive.

Radl looked up. ''All right, damn you. Show me where the place is. I expect you know.''

''Certainly, Herr Oberst.'' Hofer placed a finger on the Wash and ran it south along the coast. ''Studley Constable, and here are Blakeney and Cley on the coast, the whole forming a triangle. I have looked at Mrs. Grey's report on the area from before the war. An isolated place—very rural. A lonely coastline of vast beaches and salt marshes.''

Radl sat there staring at the map for a while and then came to a decision. "Get me Hans Meyer. I'd like to have a word with him, only don't even hint what it's about."

"Certainly, Herr Oberst."

Hofer moved to the door. "And Karl," Radl added, "every report she's ever sent. Everything we have on the entire area."

The door closed and suddenly it seemed very quiet in the room. He reached for one of his cigarettes. As usual they were Russian, half-tobacco, half-cardboard tube. An affectation with some people who had served in the East. Radl smoked them because he liked them. They were far too strong and made him cough. That was a matter of indifference to him: the doctors had already warned of a considerably shortened life-span due to his massive injuries.

He went and stood at the window feeling curiously deflated. It was all such a farce really. The Führer, Himmler, Canaris—like shadows behind the white sheet in a Chinese play. Nothing substantial. Nothing real and this silly business—this Churchill thing. While good men were dying on the Eastern Front in the thousands he was playing damned stupid games like this which couldn't possibly come to anything.

He was full of self-disgust, angry with himself for no known reason and then a knock at the door pulled him up short. The man who entered was of medium height and wore a Donegal tweed suit. His gray hair was untidy and the horn-rimmed spectacles made him seem curiously vague.

"Ah, there you are, Meyer. Good of you to come."

Hans Meyer was at that time fifty years of age. During the First World War he had been a U-boat commander, one of the youngest in the German Navy. From 1922 onwards he had been wholly employed in intelligence work and was considerably sharper than he looked.

"Herr Oberst," he said formally.

"Sit down, man, sit down." Radl indicated a chair. "I've been reading the latest report from one of your agents—Starling. Quite fascinating."

"Ah, yes." Meyer took off his spectacles and polished them with a grubby handkerchief. "Joanna Grey. A remarkable woman."

"Tell me about her."

Meyer paused, a slight frown on his face. "What would you like to know, Herr Oberst?"

"Everything!" Radl said.

Meyer hesitated for a moment, obviously on the point of asking why and then thought better of it. He replaced his spectacles and started to talk.

❦

Joanna Grey had been born Joanna Van Oosten in March, 1875, at a small town called Vierskop in the Orange Free State. Her father was a farmer and pastor of the Dutch Reform Church and, at the age of ten, had taken part in the Great Trek, the migration of some ten thousand Boer farmers between 1836 and 1838 from Cape Colony to new lands north of the Orange River to escape British domination.

She had married, at twenty, a farmer named Dirk Jansen. She had one child, a daughter born in 1898, a year before the outbreak of hostilities with the British of the following year that became known as the Boer War.

Her father raised a mounted commando and was killed near Bloem-fontein in May, 1900. From that month the war was virtually over, but the two years which followed proved to be the most tragic of the whole conflict for, like others of his countrymen, Dirk Jansen fought on, a bitter guerrilla war in small groups, relying upon outlying farms for shelter and support.

The British cavalry patrol who called at the Jansen homestead on 11 June 1901 were in search of Dirk Jansen, ironically, and unknown to his wife, already dead of wounds in a mountain camp two months earlier. There was only Joanna, her mother and the child at home. She had refused to answer the corporal's questions and had been taken into the barn for an interrogation that had involved being raped twice.

Her complaint to the local area commander was turned down and, in any case, the British were at that time attempting to combat the guerrillas by burning farms, clearing whole areas and placing the population in what soon became known as concentration camps.

The camps were badly run—more a question of poor administration than of any deliberate ill-will. Disease broke out and in fourteen months over twenty thousand people died, amongst them Joanna Jansen's mother and daughter. Greatest irony of all, she would have died herself had it not been for the careful nursing she had received from an English doctor named Charles Grey who had been brought into her camp in an attempt to improve things after a public outcry in England over the disclosure of conditions.

Her hatred of the British was now pathological in its intensity, burned into her forever. Yet she married Grey when he proposed to her. On the other hand, she was twenty-eight years of age and broken by life. She had lost husband and child, every relative she had in the world, had not a penny to her name.

That Grey loved her there can be no doubt. He was fifteen years older and made few demands, was courteous and kind. Over the years she developed a certain affection for him, mixed with the kind of constant irritation and impatience one feels for an unruly child.

He accepted work with a London Bible Society as a medical mission-ary and for some years held a succession of appointments in Rhodesia and Kenya and finally amongst the Zulu. She could never understand his preoccupation with what to her were kaffirs, but accepted it, just as she accepted the drudgery of the teaching she was expected to do to help his work.

In March, 1925 he died of a stroke and on the conclusion of his affairs, she was left with little more than one hundred and fifty pounds to face life at the age of fifty. Fate had struck her another bitter blow, but she fought on, accepting a post as governess to an English civil servant's family in Cape Town.

During this time she started to interest herself in Boer nationalism, attending meetings held regularly by one of the more extreme organizations engaged in the campaign to take South Africa out of the British Empire. At one of these meetings she met a German civil engineer named Hans Meyer. He was ten years her junior and yet a romance flowered briefly, the first, genuine physical attraction she had felt for anyone since her first marriage.

Meyer was in reality an agent of German Naval Intelligence, in Cape Town to obtain as much information as he could about naval installations in South Africa. By chance, Joanna Grey's employer worked for the Admiralty and she was able, at no particular risk, to take from the safe at his house certain interesting documents which Meyer had copied before she returned them.

She was happy to do it because she felt a genuine passion for him, but there was more to it than that. For the first time in her life she was striking a blow against England. Some sort of return for everything she felt had been done to her.

Meyer had gone back to Germany and continued to write to her and then, in 1929, when for most people the world was cracking into a thousand pieces as Europe nose-dived into a depression, Joanna Grey had the first piece of genuine good fortune of her entire life.

She received a letter from a firm of solicitors in Norwich, informing her that her late husband's aunt had died leaving her a cottage outside the village of Studley Constable in North Norfolk and an income of a little over four thousand pounds a year. There was only one snag. The old lady had had a sentimental regard for the house and it was a strict provision of the will that Joanna Grey would have to take up residence.

To live in England. The very idea made her flesh crawl, but what was the alternative? To continue her present life of genteel slavery, her only prospect a poverty-stricken old age? She obtained a book on Norfolk from the library and read it thoroughly, particularly the section covering the northern coastal area.

The names bewildered her. Stiffkey, Morston, Blakeney, Cley-next-the-Sea, salt marshes, shingle beaches. None of this made any kind of sense for her so she wrote to Hans Meyer with her problem and Meyer wrote back at once, urging her to go and promising to visit her as soon as he could.

It was the best thing she had ever done in her life. The cottage turned out to be a charming five-bedroomed Georgian house set in half an acre of walled garden. Norfolk at that time was still the most rural county in England, had changed comparatively little since the nineteenth century so that in a small village like Studley Constable she was regarded as a wealthy woman, a person of some importance. And another, stranger thing happened. She found the salt marshes and the shingle beaches fascinating, fell in love with the place, was happier than at any other time in her life.

Meyer came to England in the autumn of that year and visited her several times. They went for long walks together. She showed him everything. The endless beaches stretching into infinity, the salt marshes, the dunes of Blakeney Point. He never once referred to the period in Cape Town when she had helped him obtain the information he needed, she never once asked him about his present activities.

They continued to correspond and she visited him in Berlin in 1935. He showed her what National Socialism was doing for Germany. She was intoxicated by everything she saw, the enormous rallies, uniforms everywhere, handsome boys, laughing, happy women and children. She accepted completely that this was the new order. This was how it should be.

And then, one evening as they strolled back along Unter den Linden after an evening at the opera in which she had seen the Führer himself in his box, Meyer had calmly told her that he was now with the Abwehr, had asked her if she would consider working for them as an agent in England.

She had said yes instantly, without needing to think about it, her whole body pulsing with an excitement that she had never known in her life before. So, at sixty, she had become a spy, this upper-class English lady, for so she was considered, with the pleasant face, walking the countryside in sweater and tweed skirt with her black retriever at her heels. A pleasant, white-haired lady who had a wireless transmitter and receiver in a small cubbyhole behind the panelling in her study and a contact in the Spanish Embassy in London who passed anything of a bulky nature out to Madrid in the diplomatic bag from where it was handed on to German Intelligence.

Her results had been consistently good. Her duties as a member of the Women's Voluntary Service took her into many military installations and she had been able to pass out details of most RAF heavy bomber stations in Norfolk and a great deal of additional relevant information. Her greatest coup had been at the beginning of 1943 when the RAF had introduced two new blind bombing devices which were hoped to greatly increase the success of the night bombing offensive against Germany.

The most important of these, Oboe, operated by linking up with two ground stations in England. One was in Dover and known as Mouse, the other was situated in Cromer on the North Norfolk coast and rejoiced in the name of Cat.

It was amazing how much information RAF personnel were willing to give a kindly WVS lady handing out library books and cups of tea, and during half-a-dozen visits to the Oboe installation at Cromer, she was able to put one of her miniature cameras to good use. A single phone call to Señor Lorca, the clerk at the Spanish Embassy who was her contact, a trip by train to London for the day, a meeting in Green Park, was all it took.

Within twenty-four hours the information on Oboe was leaving England in the Spanish diplomatic bag. Within thirty-six, a delighted Hans Meyer was laying it on the desk of Canaris himself in his office at the Tirpitz Ufer.

When Hans Meyer had finished, Radl laid down the pen with which he had been making brief notes. "A fascinating lady," he said. "Quite remarkable. Tell me one thing—how much training has she done?"

"An adequate amount, Herr Oberst," Meyer told him. "She holidayed in the Reich in 1936 and 1937. On each occasion she received instruction in certain obvious matters. Codes, use of radio, general camera work, basic sabotage techniques. Nothing too advanced admittedly, except for her morse code which is excellent. On the other hand, her function was never intended to be a particularly physical one."

"No, I can see that. What about use of weapons?"

"Not much need for that. She was raised on the veld. Could shoot the eye out of a deer at a hundred yards by the time she was ten years old."

Radl nodded, frowning into space and Meyer said tentatively, "Is there something special involved here, Herr Oberst? Perhaps I could be of assistance?"

"Not now," Radl told him, "but I could well need you in the near future. I'll let you know. For the moment, it will be sufficient to pass all files on Joanna Grey to this office and no radio communication until further orders."

Meyer was aghast and quite unable to contain himself. "Please, Herr Oberst, if Joanna is in any kind of danger . . . "

"Not in the slightest," Radl said. "I understand your concern, believe me, but there is really nothing more I can say at this time. A matter of the highest security, Meyer."

Meyer recovered himself enough to apologize. "Of course, Herr

Oberst. Forgive me, but as an old friend of the lady . . . ''

He withdrew. A moment or so after he had gone, Hofer came in from the anteroom carrying several files and a couple of rolled-up maps under his arm. ''The information you wanted, Herr Oberst, and I've also brought two British Admiralty charts which cover the coastal area—numbers one hundred and eight and one hundred and six.''

''I've told Meyer to let you have everything he has on Joanna Grey and I've told him no more radio communication,'' Radl said. ''You take over from now on.''

He reached for one of those eternal Russian cigarettes and Hofer produced a lighter made from a Russian 7.62 mm cartridge case. ''Do we proceed, then, Herr Oberst?''

Radl blew a cloud of smoke and looked up at the ceiling. ''Are you familiar with the works of Jung, Karl?''

''The Herr Oberst knows I sold good beer and wine before the war.''

''Jung speaks of what he calls synchronicity. Events sometimes having a coincidence in time and, because of this, the feeling that some much deeper motivation is involved.''

''Herr Oberst?'' Hofer said politely.

''Take this affair. The Führer, whom heaven protect naturally, has a brainstorm and comes up with the comical and absurd suggestion that we should emulate Skorzeny's exploit at Gran Sasso by getting Churchill, although whether alive or dead has not been specified. And then synchronicity rears its ugly head in a routine Abwehr report. A brief mention that Churchill will be spending a weekend no more than seven or eight miles from the coast at a remote country house in as quiet a part of the country as one could wish. You take my meaning? At any other time that report of Mrs. Grey's would have meant nothing.''

''So we do proceed then, Herr Oberst?''

''It would appear that fate has taken a hand, Karl,'' Radl said. ''How long did you say Mrs. Grey's reports take to come in through the Spanish diplomatic bag?''

''Three days, Herr Oberst, if someone is waiting in Madrid to collect. No more than a week, even if circumstances are difficult.''

''And when is her next radio contact time?''

''This evening, Herr Oberst.''

''Good—send her this message.'' Radl looked up at the ceiling again, thinking hard, trying to compress his thoughts. ''Very interested in your visitor of sixth November. Like to drop some friends in to meet him in the hope that they might persuade him to come back with them. Your early comments looked for by usual route with all relevant information.''

''Is that all, Herr Oberst?''

''I think so.''

⮞

That was Wednesday and it was raining in Berlin, but the following morning when Father Philip Vereker limped out through the lychgate of St. Mary's and All the Saints, Studley Constable, and walked down through the village, the sun was shining and it was that most beautiful of all things, a perfect autumn day.

At that time, Philip Vereker was a tall, gaunt young man of thirty, the gauntness emphasized even more by the black cassock. His face was strained and twisted with pain as he limped along, leaning heavily on his stick. He had only been discharged from a military hospital four months earlier.

The younger son of a Harley Street surgeon, he had been a brilliant scholar who at Cambridge had shown every sign of an outstanding future. Then, to his family's dismay, he had decided to train for the priesthood, had gone to the English College in Rome and joined the Society of Jesus.

He had entered the army as a padre in 1940 and had finally been assigned to the Parachute Regiment and had seen action only once in November, 1942, in Tunisia when he had jumped with units of the First Parachute Brigade with orders to seize the airfield at Oudna, ten miles from Tunis. In the end, they had been compelled to make a fighting retreat over fifty miles of open country, strafed from the air every yard of the way and under constant attack from ground forces.

One hundred and eighty made it to safety. Two hundred and sixty didn't. Vereker was one of the lucky ones, in spite of a bullet which had passed straight through his left ankle, chipping bone. By the time he reached a field hospital, sepsis had set in. His left foot was amputated and he was invalided out.

Vereker found it difficult to look pleasant these days. The pain was constant and would not go away, and yet he did manage a smile as he approached Park Cottage and saw Joanna Grey emerge pushing her bicycle, her retriever at her heels.

"How are you, Philip?" she said. "I haven't seen you for several days."

She wore a tweed skirt, polo-necked sweater underneath a yellow oilskin coat and a silk scarf was tied around her white hair. She really did look very charming with that South African tan of hers that she had never really lost.

"Oh, I'm all right," Vereker said. "Dying by inches of boredom more than anything else. One piece of news since I last saw you. My sister, Pamela. Remember me speaking of her? She's ten years younger than me. A corporal in the WAAF."

"Of course I remember," Mrs. Grey said. "What's happened?"

"She's been posted to a bomber station only fifteen miles from here at Pangbourne, so I'll be able to see something of her. She's coming over this weekend. I'll introduce you."

"I'll look forward to that." Joanna Grey climbed on to her bike.

"Chess tonight?" he asked hopefully.

"Why not? Come around eight and have supper as well. Must go now."

She pedalled away along the side of the stream, the retriever, Patch, loping along behind. Her face was serious now. The radio message of the previous evening had come as an enormous shock to her. In fact, she had decoded it three times to make sure she hadn't made an error.

She had hardly slept, certainly not much before five and had lain there listening to the Lancasters setting out across the sea to Europe and then, a few hours later, returning. The strange thing was that after finally dozing off, she had awakened at seven-thirty full of life and vigour.

It was as if for the first time she had a really important task to handle. This—this was so incredible. To kidnap Churchill—snatch him from under the very noses of those who were supposed to be guarding him.

She laughed out loud. Oh, the damned English wouldn't like that. They wouldn't like that one little bit, with the whole world amazed.

As she coasted down the hill to the main road, a horn sounded behind her and a small saloon car passed and drew into the side of the road. The man behind the wheel had a large white moustache and the florid complexion of one who consumes whisky in large quantities daily. He was wearing the uniform of a lieutenant-colonel in the Home Guard.

"Morning, Joanna," he called jovially.

The meeting could not have been more fortunate. In fact it saved her a visit to Studley Grange later in the day. "Good morning, Henry," she said and dismounted from her bike.

He got out of the car. "We're having a few people on Saturday night. Bridge and so on. Supper afterwards. Nothing very special. Jean thought you might like to join us."

"That's very kind of her. I'd love to," Joanna Grey said. "She must have an awful lot on, getting ready for the big event at the moment."

Sir Henry looked slightly hunted and dropped his voice a little. "I say, you haven't mentioned that to anyone else, have you?"

Joanna Grey managed to look suitably shocked. "Of course not. You did tell me in confidence, remember."

"Shouldn't have mentioned it at all actually, but then I knew I could trust you, Joanna." He slipped an arm about her waist. "Mum's the word on Saturday night, old girl, just for me, eh. Any of that lot get a hint of what's afoot and it will be all over the county."

"I'd do anything for you, you know that," she said calmly.

"Would you, Joanna?" His voice thickened and she was aware of his thigh pushed against her, trembling slightly. He pulled away suddenly. "Well, I'll have to be off. Got an area command meeting in Holt."

"You must be very excited," she said, "at the prospect of having the Prime Minister."

"Indeed I am. Very great honour." Sir Henry beamed. "He's hoping to do a little painting and you know how pretty the views are from the Grange." He opened the door and got back into the car. "Where are you off to, by the way?"

She'd been waiting for exactly that question. "Oh, a little bird-watching, as usual. I may go down to Cley or the marsh. I haven't made up my mind yet. There are some interesting passage migrants about at the moment."

"You damn well watch it." His face was serious. "And remember what I told you."

As local Home Guard commander he had plans covering every aspect of coastal defence in the area, including details of all mined beaches and—more importantly—beaches which were only supposedly mined. On one occasion, full of solicitude for her welfare, he had spent two careful hours going over the maps with her, showing her exactly where not to go on her bird-watching expeditions.

"I know the situation changes all the time," she said. "Perhaps you could come round to the cottage again with those maps of yours and give me another lesson."

His eyes were slightly glazed. "Would you like that?"

"Of course. I'm at home this afternoon, actually."

"After lunch," he said. "I'll be there about two," and he released the handbrake and drove rapidly away.

Joanna Grey got back on her bicycle and started to pedal down the hill towards the main road, Patch running behind. Poor Henry. She was really quite fond of him. Just like a child and so easy to handle.

Half-an-hour later, she turned off the coast road and cycled along the top of a dyke through desolate marshes known locally as Hobs End. It was a strange, alien world of sea creeks and mudflats and great pale barriers of reeds higher than a man's head, inhabited only by the birds, curlew and redshank and brent geese coming south from Siberia to winter on the mud flats.

Half-way along the dyke, a cottage crouched behind a mouldering flint wall, sheltered by a few sparse pine trees. It looked substantial enough with outbuildings and a large barn, but the windows were shuttered and there was a general air of desolation about it. This was the marsh warden's house and there had been no warden since 1940.

She moved on to a high ridge lined with pines. She dismounted from her bicycle and leaned it against a tree. There were sand dunes beyond and then a wide, flat beach stretching with the tide out a quarter of a mile towards the sea. In the distance she could see the Point on the other side of the estuary, curving in like a great bent forefinger, enclosing an area of channels and sandbanks and shoals that, on a rising tide, was probably as lethal as anywhere on the Norfolk coast.

She produced her camera and took a great many pictures from various angles. As she finished, the dog brought her a stick to throw, which he laid carefully down between her feet. She crouched and fondled his ears. "Yes, Patch," she said softly. "I really think this will do very well indeed."

She tossed the stick straight over the line of barbed wire which prevented access to the beach and Patch darted past the post with the notice board that said *Beware of mines*. Thanks to Henry Willoughby, to her certain knowledge there wasn't a mine on the beach.

To her left was a concrete blockhouse and a machine-gun post, a very definite air of decay to both of them, and in the gap between the pine trees, the tank trap had filled with drifting sand. Three years earlier, after the Dunkirk debacle, there would have been soldiers here. Even a year ago, Home Guard, but not now.

In June, 1940, an area up to twenty miles inland from the Wash to the Rye was declared a Defence Area. There were no restrictions on people living there, but outsiders had to have a good reason for visiting. All that had altered considerably and now, three years later, virtually no one bothered to enforce the regulations for the plain truth was that there was no longer any need.

Joanna Grey bent down to fondle the dog's ears again. "You know what it is, Patch? The English just don't expect to be invaded anymore."

3

IT WAS THE FOLLOWING TUESDAY before Joanna Grey's report arrived at the Tirpitz Ufer. Hofer had put a red flag out for it. He took it straight in to Radl who opened it and examined the contents.

There were photos of the marsh at Hobs End and the beach

approaches, their position indicated only by a coded map reference. Radl passed the report itself to Hofer.

"Top priority. Get that deciphered and wait while they do it."

The Abwehr had just started using the new Sonlar coding unit that took care in a matter of minutes of a task that had previously taken hours. The machine had a normal typewriter keyboard. The operator simply copied the coded message, which was automatically deciphered and delivered in a sealed reel. Even the operator did not see the actual message involved.

Hofer was back in the office within twenty minutes and waited in silence while the colonel read the report. Radl looked up with a smile and pushed it across the desk. "Read that, Karl, just you read that. Excellent—really excellent. What a woman."

He lit one of his cigarettes and waited impatiently for Hofer to finish. Finally the sergeant glanced up. "It looks quite promising."

"Promising? Is that the best you can do? Good God, man, it's a definite possibility. A very real possibility."

He was more excited now than he had been for months, which was bad for him, for his heart, so appallingly strained by his massive injuries. The empty eye socket under the black patch throbbed, the aluminum hand inside the glove seemed to come alive, every tendon taut as a bow string. He fought for breath and slumped into his chair.

Hofer had the Courvoisier bottle out of the bottom drawer in an instant, half-filled a glass and held it to the colonel's lips. Radl swallowed most of it down, coughed heavily, then seemed to get control of himself again.

He smiled wryly. "I can't afford to do that too often, eh, Karl? Only two more bottles left. It's like liquid gold these days."

"The Herr Oberst shouldn't excite himself so," Hofer said and added bluntly, "You can't afford to."

Radl swallowed some more of the brandy. "I know, Karl, I know, but don't you see? It was a joke before—something the Führer threw out in an angry mood on a Wednesday, to be forgotten by Friday. A feasibility study, that was Himmler's suggestion and only because he wanted to make things awkward for the Admiral. The Admiral told me to get something down on paper. Anything, just so long as it showed we were doing our job."

He got up and walked to the window. "But now it's different, Karl. It isn't a joke any longer. It could be done."

Hofer stood stolidly on the other side of the desk, showing no emotion. "Yes, Herr Oberst, I think it could."

"And doesn't that prospect move you in any way at all?" Radl shivered. "God, but it frightens me. Bring me those Admiralty charts and the ordnance survey map."

Hofer spread them on the desk and Radl found Hobs End and examined it in conjunction with the photos. "What more could one ask for? A perfect dropping zone for parachutists and that weekend the tide comes in again by dawn and washes away any signs of activity."

"But even quite a small force would have to be conveyed in a transport type of aircraft or a bomber," Hofer pointed out. "Can you imagine a Dornier or a Junkers lasting for long over the Norfolk coast these days, with so many bomber stations protected by regular night fighter patrols?"

"A problem," Radl said, "I agree, but hardly insurmountable. According to the Luftwaffe target chart for the area there is no low-level radar on that particular section of coast, which means an approach under six hundred feet would be undetected. But that kind of detail is immaterial at the moment. It can be handled later. A feasibility study, Karl, that's all we need at this stage. You agree that in theory it would be possible to drop a raiding party on that beach?"

Hofer said, "I accept that as a proposition, but how do we get them out again? By U-boat?"

Radl looked down at the chart for a moment, then shook his head. "No, not really practical. The raiding party would be too large. I know that they could all be crammed on board somehow, but the rendezvous would need to be some distance off-shore and there would be problems getting so many out there. It needs to be something simpler, more direct. An E-boat, perhaps. There's plenty of E-boat activity in that area in the coastal shipping lanes. I don't see any reason why one couldn't slip in between the beach and the Point. It would be on a rising tide and according to the report, there are no mines in that channel, which would simplify things considerably."

"One would need Navy advice on that," Hofer said cautiously. "Mrs. Grey does say in her report that those are dangerous waters."

"Which is exactly what good sailors are for. Is there anything else you're not happy with?"

"Forgive me, Herr Oberst, but it would seem to me that there is a time factor involved which could be quite crucial to the success of the entire operation and frankly, I don't see how it could be reconciled." Hofer pointed to Studley Grange on the ordnance survey map. "Here is the target, approximately eight miles from the dropping zone. Considering the unfamiliar territory and the darkness. I would say it would take the raiding party two hours to reach it and however brief the visit, it would still take as long for the return journey. My estimate would be an action span of six hours. If one accepts that the drop would have to be made around midnight for security reasons, this means that the rendezvous with the E-boat would take place at dawn if not after, which would be completely unacceptable. The E-boat must have at least two hours of darkness to cover her departure."

Radl had been lying back in the chair, face turned up to the ceiling, eyes closed. "Very lucidly put, Karl. You're learning." He sat up. "You're absolutely right, which is why the drop would have to be made the night before."

"Herr Oberst?" Hofer said, astonishment on his face. "I don't understand."

"It's quite simple. Churchill will arrive at Studley Grange during the afternoon or evening of the sixth and spend the night there. Our party drops in on the previous night, November fifth."

Hofer frowned, considering the point. "I can see the advantage, of course, Herr Oberst. The additional time would give them room to manoeuvre in case of any unlooked-for eventuality."

"It would also mean that there would no longer be any problem with the E-boat," Radl said. "They could be picked up as early as ten or eleven o'clock on the Saturday." He smiled and took another cigarette from the box. "So, you agree that this, too, is feasible?"

"There would be a grave problem of concealment on the Saturday itself," Hofer pointed out. "Especially for a sizeable group."

"You're absolutely right." Radl stood up and started to pace up and down the room again. "But it seems to me there's a rather obvious answer. Let me ask you a question as an old forester, Karl? If you wanted to hide a pine tree, what would be the safest place on earth?"

"In a forest of pines, I suppose."

"Exactly. In a remote and isolated area like this a stranger—any stranger—stands out like a sore thumb, especially in wartime. No holiday makers, remember. The British, like good Germans, spend their holidays at home to help the war effort. And yet, Karl, according to Mrs. Grey's report, there are strangers constantly passing through the lanes and the villages every week who are accepted without question." Hofer looked mystified and Radl continued. "Soldiers, Karl, on manoeuvres, playing war-games, hunting each other through the hedgerows." He reached for Joanna Grey's report from the desk and turned the pages. "Here, on page three, for example, she speaks of this place Meltham House eight miles from Studley Constable. During the past year used as a training establishment for commando-type units on four occasions. Twice by British commandos, once by a similar unit composed of Poles and Czechs with English officers and once by American Rangers."

He passed the report across and Hofer looked at it.

"All they need are British uniforms to be able to pass through the countryside with no difficulty. A Polish commando unit would do famously."

"It would certainly take care of the language problem," Hofer said. "But that Polish unit Mrs. Grey mentioned had English officers, not just

English-speaking. If the Herr Oberst will forgive me for saying so, there's a difference.''

"Yes, you're right," Radl told him. "All the difference in the world. If the officer in charge is English or apparently English, then that would make the whole thing so much tighter."

Hofer looked at his watch. "If I might remind the Herr Oberst, the Heads of Section weekly meeting is due to start in the Admiral's office in precisely ten minutes."

"Thank you, Karl." Radl tightened his belt and stood up. "So, it would appear that our feasibility study is virtually complete. We seem to have covered everything."

"Except for what is perhaps the most important item of all, Herr Oberst."

Radl was halfway to the door and now he paused. "All right, Karl, surprise me."

"The leader of such a venture, Herr Oberst. He would have to be a man of extraordinary abilities."

"Another Otto Skorzeny," Radl suggested.

"Exactly," Hofer said. "With, in this case, one thing more. The ability to pass as an Englishman."

Radl smiled beautifully. "Find him for me, Karl. I'll give you forty-eight hours." He opened the door quickly and went out.

As it happened, Radl had to go to Munich unexpectedly the following day and it was not until after lunch on Thursday that he re-appeared in his office at the Tirpitz Ufer. He was extremely tired, having slept very little in Munich the night before. The Lancaster bombers of the RAF had pressed their attentions on that city with more than usual severity.

Hofer produced coffee instantly and poured him a brandy. "Good trip, Herr Oberst?"

"Fair," Radl said. "Actually, the most interesting happening was when we were landing yesterday. Our Junkers was buzzed by an American Mustang fighter. Caused more than a little panic, I can tell you. Then we saw that it had a Swastika on the tailplace. Apparently it was one which had crash-landed and the Luftwaffe had put it into working order and were flight testing."

"Extraordinary, Herr Oberst."

Radl nodded. "It gave me an idea, Karl. That little problem you had about Dorniers or Junkers surviving over the Norfolk coast." And then he noticed a fresh green manilla folder on the desk. "What's this?"

"The assignment you gave me, Herr Oberst. The officer who could pass as an Englishman. Took some digging out, I can tell you, and there's a report of some court martial proceedings which I've indented for. They should be here this afternoon.''

"Court martial?" Radl said. "I don't like the sound of that." He opened the file. "Who on earth is this man?"

"His name is Steiner. Lieutenant-Colonel Kurt Steiner," Hofer said, "and I'll leave you in peace to read about him. It's an interesting story."

It was more than interesting. It was fascinating.

Steiner was the only son of Major-General Karl Steiner, at present area commander in Brittany. He had been born in 1916 when his father was a major of artillery. His mother was American, daughter of a wealthy wool merchant from Boston who had moved to London for business reasons. In the month that her son was born, her only brother had died on the Somme as a captain in a Yorkshire infantry regiment.

The boy had been educated in London, spending five years at St. Paul's during the period his father was military attaché at the German Embassy, and spoke English fluently. After his mother's tragic death in a car crash in 1931, he had returned to Germany with his father, but had continued to visit relatives in Yorkshire until 1938.

For a while, he had studied art in Paris, maintained by his father, the bargain being that if it didn't work out he would enter the Army. That was exactly what had happened. He had a brief period as a second lieutenant in the Artillery and in 1936 had answered the call for volunteers to do parachute training at Stendhal, more to relieve the boredom of military life than anything else.

It had become obvious immediately that he had a talent for that kind of freebooter soldiery. He'd seen ground action in Poland and parachuted into Narvik in the Norwegian campaign. As a full lieutenant he'd crash-landed by glider with the group that took the Albert Canal in 1940 during the big push for Belgium and had been wounded in the arm.

Greece came next—the Corinth Canal, and then a new kind of hell. May, 1941, a captain by then, in the big drop over Crete, severely wounded in savage fighting for Maleme airfield.

Afterwards, the Winter War. Radl was aware of a sudden chill in his bones at the very name. *God, will we ever forget Russia? he asked himself, those of us who were there then?*

As an acting major Steiner had led a special assault group of three hundred volunteers, dropped by night to contact and lead out two divisions cut off during the battle for Leningrad. He had emerged from that affair with a bullet in the right leg which had left him with a slight limp, a Knight's Cross and a reputation for that kind of cutting-out operation.

He had been in charge of two further affairs of a similar nature and had been promoted lieutenant-colonel in time to go to Stalingrad where he had lost half his men, but had been ordered out several weeks before the end when there were still planes running. In January, he and the one hundred and sixty-seven survivors of his original assault group were dropped near Kiev, once again to contact and lead out two infantry divisions which had been cut off. The end product was a fighting retreat for three hundred bloodstained miles and during the last week in April, Kurt Steiner had crossed into German lines with only thirty survivors of his original assault force.

There was an immediate award of the Oak leaves to his Knight's Cross and Steiner and his men had been packed off to Germany by train as soon as possible, passing through Warsaw on the morning of the 1st of May. He had left it with his men that same evening under close arrest by order of Jurgen Stroop, SS Brigadeführer and Major-General of Police.

There had been a court martial the following week. The details were missing, only the verdict was on file. Steiner and his men had been sentenced to serve as a penal unit to work on Operation Swordfish on Alderney in the German-occupied Channel Islands. Radl sat looking at the file for a moment, then closed it and pressed the buzzer for Hofer who came in at once.

"Herr Oberst?"

"What happened in Warsaw?"

"I'm not sure, Herr Oberst. I'm hoping to have the court martial papers available later this afternoon."

"All right," Radl said. "What are they doing in the Channel Islands?"

"As far as I can find out, Operation Swordfish is a kind of suicide unit, Herr Oberst. Their purpose is the destruction of allied shipping in the Channel."

"And how do they achieve that?"

"Apparently they sit on a torpedo with the charge taken out, Herr Oberst and a glass cupola fitted to give the operator some protection. A live torpedo is slung underneath which during an attack, the operator is supposed to release, turning away at the last moment himself."

"Good God Almighty," Radl said in horror. "No wonder they had to make it a penal unit."

He sat there in silence for a while looking down at the file. Hofer coughed and said tentatively, "You think he could be a possibility?"

"I don't see why not," Radl said. "I should imagine that anything would seem like an improvement on what he's doing now. Do you know if the Admiral is in?"

"I'll find out, Herr Oberst."

"If he is, try and get me an appointment this afternoon. Time I showed him how far we've got. Prepare me an outline—nice and brief. One page only and type it yourself. I don't want anyone else getting wind of this thing. Not even in the Department.''

At that precise moment Lieutenant-Colonel Kurt Steiner was up to his waist in the freezing waters of the English Channel, colder than he had ever been in his life before, colder even than in Russia, cold eating into his brain as he crouched behind the glass cupola on his torpedo.

His exact situation was almost two miles to the north-east of Braye Harbour on the island of Alderney, and north of the smaller off-shore island of Burhou, although he was cocooned in a sea-fog of such density that for all he could see, he might as well have been at the end of the world. At least he was not alone. Lifelines of hemp rope disappeared into the fog on either side of him like umbilical cords connecting him with Sergeant Otto Lemke on his left and Lieutenant Ritter Neumann on his right.

Steiner had been amazed to get called out that afternoon. Even more astonishing was the evidence of a radar contact, indicating a ship so close inshore, for the main route up-channel was much further north. As it transpired later, the vessel in question, an eight-thousand-ton Liberty ship *Joseph Johnson* out of Boston for Plymouth with a cargo of high explosives, had sustained damage to her steering in a bad storm near Land's End three days earlier. Her difficulties in this direction and the heavy fog had conspired to put her off course.

North of Burhou, Steiner slowed, jerking on the lifelines to alert his companions. A few moments later, they coasted out of the fog on either side to join him. Ritter Neumann's face was blue with cold in the black cowl of his rubber suit. "We're close, Herr Oberst," he said. "I'm sure I can hear them."

Sergeant Lemke drifted in to join them. The curly black beard, of which he was very proud, was a special dispensation from Steiner in view of the fact that Lemke's chin was badly deformed by a Russian high-velocity bullet. He was very excited, eyes sparkling, and obviously looked upon the whole thing as a great adventure.

"I, too, Herr Oberst."

Steiner raised a hand to silence him and listened. The muted throbbing was quite close now for the *Joseph Johnson* was taking it very steady indeed.

"An easy one, Herr Oberst." Lemke grinned in spite of the fact that his teeth were chattering in the cold. "The best touch we've had yet. She won't even know what's hit her."

"You speak for yourself, Lemke," Ritter Neumann said. "If there's one thing I've learned in my short and unhappy life it's never to expect anything and to be particularly suspicious of that which is apparently served up on a plate.''

As if to prove his words, a sudden flurry of wind tore a hole in the curtain of the fog. Behind them was the gray-green sweep of Alderney, the old Admiralty breakwater poking out like a granite finger for a thousand yards from Braye, the Victorian naval fortification of Fort Albert clearly visible.

No more than a hundred and fifty yards away, the *Joseph Johnson* moved on a north-westerly course for the open Channel at a steady eight or ten knots. It could only be a matter of moments before they were seen. Steiner acted instantly. ''All right, straight in, release torpedoes at fifty yards and out again and no stupid heroics, Lemke. There aren't any medals to be had in the penal regiments, remember. Only coffins.''

He increased power and surged forward, crouching behind the cupola as waves started breaking over his head. He was aware of Ritter Neumann on his right, roughly abreast of him, but Lemke had surged on and was already fifteen or twenty yards in front.

''The silly young bastard,'' Steiner thought. ''What does he think this is, the Charge of the Light Brigade?''

Two of the men at the rail of the *Joseph Johnson* had rifles in their hands and an officer came out of the wheelhouse and stood on the bridge firing a Thompson sub-machine-gun with a drum magazine. The ship was picking up speed now, driving through a light curtain of mist, as the blanket of fog began to settle again. Within another few moments she would have disappeared altogether. The riflemen at the rail were having difficulty in taking aim on a heaving deck at a target so low in the water and their shots were very wide of the mark. The Thompson, not too accurate at the best of times, was doing no better and making a great deal of noise about it.

Lemke reached the fifty-yard line several lengths in front of the others and kept right on going. There wasn't a thing Steiner could do about it. The riflemen started to get the range and a bullet ricocheted from the body of his torpedo in front of the cupola.

He turned and waved to Neumann. ''Now!'' he cried and fired his torpedo.

The one upon which he was seated, released from the weight it had been carrying, sprang forward with new energy and he turned to starboard quickly, following Neumann round in a great sweeping curve intended to take them away from the ship as fast as possible.

Lemke was turning away now also, no more than twenty-five yards from the *Joseph Johnson*, the men at the rail firing at him for all they were worth. Presumably one of them scored a hit, although Steiner could never be sure. The only certain thing was that one moment Lemke was crouched astride his torpedo, surging away from danger. The next, he wasn't there any more.

A second later one of the three torpedoes scored a direct hit close to the stern and the stern hold contained hundreds of tons of high explosive bombs destined for use by Flying Fortresses of bombardment groups of the 1st Air Division of the American 8th Air Force in Britain. As the *Joseph Johnson* was swallowed by the fog, she exploded, the sound re-echoing from the island again and again. Steiner crouched low as the blast swept over, swerving when an enormous piece of twisted metal hurtled into the sea in front of him.

Debris cascaded down. The air was full of it and something struck Neumann a glancing blow on the head. He threw up his hands with a cry and catapulted backwards into the sea, his torpedo running away from him, plunging over the next wave and disappearing.

Although unconscious, blood on his forehead from a nasty gash, he was kept afloat by his inflatable jacket. Steiner coasted in beside him, looped one end of a line under the lieutenant's jacket and kept on going, pushing towards the breakwater and Braye, already fading as the fog rolled in towards the island again.

The tide was ebbing fast. Steiner didn't have one chance in hell of reaching Braye Harbour and he knew it, as he wrestled vainly against a tide that must eventually sweep them far out into the Channel beyond any hope of return.

He suddenly realized that Ritter Neumann was conscious again and staring up at him. "Let me go!" he said faintly. "Cut me loose. You'll make it on your own."

Steiner didn't bother to reply at first, but concentrated on turning the torpedo over towards the right. Burhou was somewhere out there in that impenetrable blanket of fog. There was a chance the ebbing tide might push them in, a slim one perhaps, but better than nothing.

He said calmly, "How long have we been together now, Ritter?"

"You know damn well," Ritter said. "The first time I clapped eyes on you was over Narvik when I was afraid to jump out of the plane."

"I remember now," Steiner said. "I persuaded you otherwise."

"That's one way of putting it," Ritter said. "You threw me out."

His teeth were chattering and he was very cold and Steiner reached down to check the line. "Yes, a snotty eighteen-year-old Berliner, fresh from the University. Always with a volume of poetry in your hip pocket. The professor's son who crawled fifty yards under fire to bring me a medical kit when I was wounded at the Albert Canal."

"I should have let you go," Ritter said. "Look what you got me into. Crete, then a commission I didn't want, Russia and now this. What a bargain." He closed his eyes and added softly, "Sorry, Kurt, but it's no good."

Quite suddenly, they were caught in a great eddy of water that swept them in towards the rocks of L'Equet on the tip of Burhou. There was a ship there, or half one; all that was left of a French coaster that had run on the reef in a storm earlier in the year. What was left of her stern deck sloped into deep water. A wave swept them in, the torpedo high on the swell and Steiner rolled away from it, grabbing for the ship's rail with one hand and hanging on to Neumann's lifeline with the other.

The wave receded, taking the torpedo with it. Steiner got to his feet and went up the sloping deck to what was left of the wheelhouse. He wedged himself in the broken doorway and hauled his companion after him. They crouched in the roofless shell of the wheelhouse and it started to rain softly.

"What happens now?" Neumann asked weakly.

"We sit tight," Steiner said. "Brandt will be out with the recovery boat as soon as this fog clears a little."

"I could do with a cigarette," Neumann said, and then he stiffened suddenly and pointed out through the broken doorway. "Look at that."

Steiner went to the rail. The water was moving fast now as the tide ebbed, twisting and turning amongst the reefs and rocks, carrying with it the refuse of war, a floating carpet of wreckage that was all that was left of the *Joseph Johnson*.

"So, we got her," Neumann said. Then he tried to get up. "There's a man down there, Kurt, in a yellow lifejacket. Look, under the stern."

Steiner slid down the deck into the water and turned under the stern, pushing his way through a mass of planks to the man who floated there, head back, eyes closed. He was very young with blond hair plastered to the skull. Steiner grabbed him by the lifejacket and started to tow him towards the safety of the shattered stern, and he opened his eyes and stared at him. Then he shook his head, trying to speak.

Steiner floated beside him for a moment. "What is it?" he said in English.

"Please," the boy whispered. "Let me go."

His eyes closed again and Steiner swam with him to the stern. Neumann, watching from the wheelhouse, saw Steiner start to drag him up the sloping deck. He paused for a long moment, then slid the boy gently back into the water. A current took him away and out of sight beyond the reef, and Steiner clambered wearily back up the deck again.

"What was it?" Neumann demanded weakly.

"Both legs were gone from the knees down." Steiner sat very carefully and braced his feet against the rail. "What was that poem of Eliot's that you were always quoting at Stalingrad? The one I didn't like?"

"I think we are in rat's alley," Neumann said. "Where the dead men lost their bones."

"Now I understand it," Steiner told him. "Now I see exactly what he meant."

They sat there in silence. It was colder now, the rain increasing in force, clearing the fog rapidly. About twenty minutes later they heard an engine not too far away. Steiner took the small signalling pistol from the pouch on his right leg, charged it with a waterproof cartridge and fired a maroon.

A few moments later, the recovery launch appeared from the fog and slowed, drifting in towards them. Sergeant-Major Brandt was in the prow with a line ready to throw. He was an enormous figure of a man, well over six feet tall and broad in proportion, rather incongruously wearing a yellow oilskin coat with *Royal National Lifeboat Institution* on the back. The rest of the crew were all Steiner's men. Sergeant Sturm at the wheel, Lance-Corporal Briegel and Private Berg acting as deckhands. Brandt jumped for the sloping deck of the wreck and hitched the line about the rail as Steiner and Neumann slid down to join him.

"You made a hit, Herr Oberst. What happened to Lemke?"

"Playing heroes as usual," Steiner told him. "This time he went too far. Careful with Lieutenant Neumann. He's had a bad crack on the head."

"Sergeant Altmann's out in the other boat with Riedel and Meyer. They might see some sign of him. He has the Devil's own luck, that one." Brandt lifted Neumann up over the rail with astonishing strength. "Get him in the cabin."

But Neumann wouldn't have it and slumped down on the deck with his back against the stern rail. Steiner sat beside him and Brandt gave them cigarettes as the motor boat pulled away. Steiner felt tired. More tired than he had been in a very long time. *Five years of war*. Sometimes it seemed as if it was not only all there was, but all there ever had been.

They rounded the end of the Admiralty breakwater and followed the thousand yards or so of its length into Braye. There was a surprising number of ships in the harbour, French coasters mostly, carrying building supplies from the continent for the new fortifications that were being raised all over the island.

The small landing stage had been extended. An E-boat was tied up there and as the motor boat drifted in astern, the sailors on deck raised a cheer and a young, bearded lieutenant in a heavy sweater and salt-stained cap stood smartly to attention and saluted.

"Fine work, Herr Oberst."

Steiner acknowledged the salute as he went over the rail. "Many thanks, Koenig."

He went up the steps to the upper landing stage, Brandt following, supporting Neumann with a strong arm. As they came out on top a large black saloon car, an old Wolseley, turned on to the landing stage and braked to a halt. The driver jumped out and opened the rear door.

The first person to emerge was the man who at that time was acting-commandant of the island, Hans Neuhoff, a full colonel of artillery. Like Steiner, a Winter War veteran, wounded in the chest at Leningrad, he had never recovered his health, his lungs damaged beyond repair, and his face had the permanently resigned look of a man who is dying by inches and knows it. His wife got out of the car after him.

Ilse Neuhoff was at that time twenty-seven years of age, a slim, aristocratic-looking blonde with a wide, generous mouth and good cheek-bones. Most people turned to look at her twice and not only because she was beautiful, but because she usually seemed familiar. She had enjoyed a successful career as a film starlet working for UFA in Berlin. She was one of those odd people that everyone likes and she had been much in demand in Berlin society. She was a friend of Goebbels. The Führer himself had admired her.

She had married Hans Neuhoff out of a genuine liking that went far beyond sexual love, something of which he was no longer capable anyway. She had nursed him back on his feet after Russia, supported him every step of the way, used all her influence to secure him his present post, had even obtained a pass to visit him by influence of Goeb-bels himself. They had an understanding—a warm and mutual under-standing and it was because of this that she was able to go forward to Steiner and kiss him openly on the cheek.

"You had us worried, Kurt."

Neuhoff shook hands, genuinely delighted. "Wonderful work, Kurt. I'll get a signal off to Berlin at once."

"Don't do that, for God's sake," Steiner said in mock alarm. "They might decide to send me back to Russia."

Ilse took his arm. "It wasn't in the cards when I last read Tarot for you, but I'll look again tonight if you like."

There was a hail from the lower landing stage and they moved forward to the edge in time to see the second recovery boat coming in. There was a body on the stern deck covered with a blanket and Sergeant Alt-mann, another of Steiner's men, came out of the wheelhouse. "Herr Oberst?" he called, awaiting orders.

Steiner nodded and Altmann raised the blanket briefly. Neumann had moved to join Steiner and now he said bitterly, "Lemke. Crete, Lenin-grad, Stalingrad—all those years and this is how it ends."

"When your name's on the bullet, that's it," Brandt said.

Steiner turned to look into Ilse Neuhoff's troubled face. "My poor Ilse, better to leave those cards of yours in the box. A few more after-noons like this and it won't be so much a question of *will* the worse come to pass as *when*."

He took her arm, smiling cheerfully and led her towards the car.

ᴥ

Canaris had a meeting with Ribbentrop and Goebbels during the afternoon and it was six o'clock before he could see Radl. There was no sign of Steiner's court martial papers.

At five minutes to six Hofer knocked on the door and entered Radl's office. "Have they come?" Radl demanded eagerly.

"I'm afraid not, Herr Oberst."

"Why not, for God's sake?" Radl said angrily.

"It seems that as the original incident was concerned with a complaint from the SS, the records are at Prinz Albrechtstrasse."

"Have you got the outline that I asked you for?"

"Herr Oberst." Hofer handed him a neatly typed sheet of paper.

Radl examined it quickly. "Excellent, Karl. Really excellent." He smiled and straightened his already immaculate uniform. "You're off duty now, aren't you?"

"I'd prefer to wait until the Herr Oberst returns," Hofer said.

Radl smiled and clapped him on the shoulder. "All right, let's get it over with."

ᴥ

The Admiral was being served with coffee by an orderly when Radl went in. "Ah, there you are, Max," he said cheerfully. "Will you join me?"

"Thank you, Herr Admiral."

The orderly filled another cup, adjusted the blackout curtains and went out. Canaris sighed and eased himself back in the chair, reaching down to fondle the ears of one of his dachshunds. He seemed weary and there was evidence of strain in the eyes and around the mouth.

"You look tired," Radl told him.

"So would you if you'd been closeted with Ribbentrop and Goebbels all afternoon. Those two really get more impossible every time I see them. According to Goebbels we're still winning the war, Max. Was there ever anything more absurd?" Radl didn't really know what to say but was saved by the Admiral carrying straight on. "Anyway, what did you want to see me about?"

Radl placed Hofer's typed outline on the desk and Canaris started to read it. After a while he looked up in obvious bewilderment. "What is it, for God's sake?"

"The feasibility study you asked for, Herr Admiral. The Churchill business. You asked me to get something down on paper."

"Ah, yes." There was understanding on the Admiral's face now and he looked again at the paper. After a while he smiled. "Yes, very good, Max. Quite absurd, of course, but on paper it does have a kind of mad logic to it. Keep it handy in case Himmler reminds the Führer to ask me if we've done anything about it."

"You mean that's all, Herr Admiral?" Radl said. "You don't want me to take it any further?"

Canaris had opened a file and now he looked up in obvious surprise. "My dear Max, I don't think you quite get the point. The more absurd the idea put forward by your superiors in this game, the more rapturously should you receive it, however crazy. Put all your enthusiasm—assumed, of course—into the project. Over a period of time allow the difficulties to show, so that very gradually your masters will make the discovery for themselves that it just isn't on. As nobody likes to be involved in failure if he can avoid it, the whole project will be discreetly dropped." He laughed lightly and tapped the outline with one finger. "Mind you, even the Führer would need to be having a very off-day indeed to see any possibilities in such a mad escapade as this."

Radl found himself saying, "It would work, Herr Admiral. I've even got the right man for the job."

"I'm sure you have, Max, if you've been anything like as thorough as you usually are." He smiled and pushed the outline across the desk. "I can see that you've taken the whole thing too seriously. Perhaps my remarks about Himmler worried you. But there's no need, believe me. I can handle him. You've got enough on paper to satisfy them if the occasion arises. Plenty of other things you can get on with now—really important matters."

He nodded in dismissal and picked up his pen. Radl said stubbornly, "But surely, Herr Admiral, if the Führer wishes it . . . "

Canaris exploded angrily, throwing down his pen. "God in heaven, man, kill Churchill when we have already lost the war? In what way is that supposed to help?"

He had jumped up and leaned across the desk, both hands braced. Radl stood rigidly to attention, staring woodenly into space a foot above the Admiral's head. Canaris flushed, aware that he had gone too far, that there had been treason implicit in his angry words and too late to retract them.

"At ease," he said.

Radl did as he was ordered. "Herr Admiral."

"We've known each other a long time, Max."

"Yes, sir."

"So trust me now. I know what I'm doing."

"Very well, Herr Admiral," Radl said crisply.

He stepped back, clicked his heels, turned and went out. Canaris stayed where he was, hands braced against the desk, suddenly looking haggard and old. "My God," he whispered. "How much longer?"

When he sat down and picked up his coffee, his hand was trembling so much that the cup rattled in the saucer.

When Radl went into the office, Hofer was straightening the papers on his desk. The sergeant turned eagerly and then saw the expression on Radl's face.

"The Admiral didn't like it, Herr Oberst?"

"He said it had a certain mad logic, Karl. Actually, he seemed to find it quite amusing."

"What happens now, Herr Oberst?"

"Nothing, Karl," Radl said wearily and sat down behind his desk. "It's on paper, the feasibility study they wanted and may never ask for again and that's all we were required to do. We get on with something else."

He reached for one of his Russian cigarettes and Hofer gave him a light. "Can I get you anything, Herr Oberst?" he said, his voice sympathetic, but careful.

"No, thank you, Karl. Go home now. I'll see you in the morning."

"Herr Oberst." Hofer clicked his heels and hesitated.

Radl said, "Go on, Karl, there's a good fellow and thank you."

Hofer went out and Radl ran a hand over his face. His empty socket was burning, the invisible hand ached. Sometimes he felt as if they'd wired him up wrongly when they'd put him back together again. Amazing how disappointed he felt. A sense of real, personal loss.

"Perhaps it's as well," he said softly. "I was beginning to take the whole damn thing too seriously."

He sat down, opened Joanna Grey's file and started to read it. After a while he reached for the ordnance survey map and began to unfold it. He stopped suddenly. He'd had enough of this tiny office for one day, enough of the Abwehr. He pulled his briefcase from under the desk, stuffed the files and the map inside and took his leather greatcoat down from behind the door.

It was too early for the RAF and the city seemed unnaturally quiet when he went out of the front entrance. He decided to take advantage of the brief calm and walk home to his small apartment instead of calling for a staff car. In any case his head was splitting and the light rain which was falling was really quite refreshing. He went down the steps, acknowledging the sentry's salute and passed under the shaded street light at the bottom. A car started up somewhere further along the Tirpitz Ufer and pulled in beside him.

It was a black Mercedes saloon, as black as the uniforms of the two

Gestapo men who got out of the front seats and stood waiting. As Radl saw the cuff-title of the one nearest to him, his heart seemed to stop beating. RFSS. Reichsführer der SS. The cuff-title of Himmler's personal staff.

The young man who got out of the rear seat wore a slouch hat and a black leather coat. His smile had the kind of ruthless charm that only the genuinely insincere possess. "Colonel Radl?" he said. "So glad we were able to catch you before you left. The Reichsführer presents his compliments. If you could find it convenient to spare him a little time, he'd appreciate it." He deftly removed the briefcase from Radl's hand. "Let me carry that for you."

Radl moistened dry lips and managed a smile. "But of course," he said and got into the rear of the Mercedes.

The young man joined him, the other got into the front and they moved away. Radl noticed that the one who wasn't driving had an Erma police sub-machine-gun across his knees. He breathed deeply in an effort to control the fear that rose inside him.

"Cigarette, Herr Oberst?"

"Thank you," Radl said. "Where are we going, by the way?"

"Prinz Albrechtstrasse." The young man gave him a light and smiled. "Gestapo Headquarters."

4

WHEN RADL WAS USHERED INTO the office on the first floor at Prinz Albrechtstrasse, he found Himmler seated behind a large desk, a stack of files in front of him. He was wearing full uniform as Reichsführer SS, a devil in black in the shaded light, and when he looked up the face behind the silver pince-nez was cold and impersonal.

The young man in the black leather coat who had brought Radl in gave the Nazi salute and placed the briefcase on the table. "At your orders, Herr Reichsführer."

"Thank you, Rossman," Himmler replied. "Wait outside. I may need you later."

Rossman went out and Radl waited as Himmler moved the files very precisely to one side of the desk, as if clearing the decks for action. He pulled the briefcase forward and looked at it thoughtfully. Strangely enough, Radl had got back some of his nerve, and a certain black humour that had been a saving grace to him on many occasions surfaced now.

"Even the condemned man is entitled to a last cigarette, Herr Reichsführer."

Himmler actually smiled, which was quite something considering that tobacco was one of his pet aversions. "Why not?" He waved a hand. "They told me you were a brave man, Herr Oberst. You earned your Knight's Cross during the Winter War?"

"That's right, Herr Reichsführer." Radl got his cigarette case out, one-handed, and opened it deftly.

"And have worked for Admiral Canaris ever since?"

Radl waited, smoking his cigarette, trying to make it last while Himmler stared down at the briefcase again. The room was really quite pleasant in the shaded light. An open fire burned brightly and above it there was an autographed picture of the Führer in a gilt frame.

Himmler said, "There is not much that happens at the Tirpitz Ufer these days that I don't know about. Does that surprise you? For example, I am aware that on the twenty-second of this month you were shown a routine report from an Abwehr agent in England, a Mrs. Joanna Grey, in which the magic name of Winston Churchill figured."

"Herr Reichsführer, I don't know what to say," Radl told him.

"Even more fascinating, you had all her files transferred from Abwehr One into your custody, and relieved Captain Meyer, who had been this lady's link man for many years, of duty. I understand he's most upset." Himmler placed a hand on the briefcase. "Come, Herr Oberst, we're too old to play games. You know what I'm talking about. Now, what have you got to tell me?"

Max Radl was a realist. He had no choice at all in the matter. He said, "In the briefcase, the Reichsführer will find all that there is to know except for one item."

"The court martial papers of Lieutenant-Colonel Kurt Steiner of the Parachute Regiment?" Himmler picked up the top file from the pile at the side of his desk and handed it over. "A fair exchange. I suggest you read it outside." He opened the briefcase and started to extract the contents. "I'll send for you when I need you."

Radl almost raised his arm, but one last stubborn grain of self-respect turned it into a smart, if conventional salute. He turned on his heel, opened the door and went out into the ante-room.

Rossman sprawled in an easy chair reading a copy of *Signal*, the Wehrmacht magazine. He glanced up in surprise. "Leaving us already?"

"No such luck." Radl dropped the file on to a low coffee table and started to unbuckle his belt. "It seems I've got some reading to do."

Rossman smiled amiably. "I'll see if I can find us some coffee. It looks to me as if you could be with us for quite some time.''

He went out and Radl lit another cigarette, sat down and opened the file.

The date chosen for the final erasing of the Warsaw Ghetto from the face of the earth was the 19th April. Hitler's birthday was on the 20th and Himmler hoped to present him with the good news as a suitable present. Unfortunately when the commander of the operation, SS Oberführer von Sammern-Frankenegg and his men marched in, they were chased out again by the Jewish Combat Organization, under the command of Mordechai Anielewicz.

Himmler immediately replaced him with SS Brigade führer and Major-General of Police, Jurgen Stroop, who, aided by a mixed force of SS and renegade Poles and Ukrainians, applied himself seriously to the task in hand: to leave not one brick standing, not one Jew alive. To be able to report to Himmler personally that *The Warsaw Ghetto is no more*. It took him twenty-eight days to accomplish.

Steiner and his men arrived in Warsaw on the morning of the Thirteenth Day on a hospital train from the Eastern Front bound for Berlin. There was a stopover time of between one to two hours, depending on how long it took to rectify a fault in the engine's cooling system, and orders were broadcast over the loudspeaker that no one was to leave the station. There were military police on the entrances to see that the order was obeyed.

Most of his men stayed inside the coach, but Steiner got out to stretch his legs and Ritter Neumann joined him. Steiner's jump boots were worn through, his leather coat had definitely seen better days and he was wearing a soiled white scarf and sidecap of a type more common amongst NCO's than officers.

The military policeman guarding the main entrance held his rifle across his chest in both hands and said roughly, ''You heard the order, didn't you? Get back in there!''

''It would seem they want to keep us under wraps for some reason, Herr Oberst,'' Neumann said.

The military policeman's jaw dropped and he came to attention hurriedly. ''I ask the Herr Oberst's pardon. I didn't realize.''

There was a quick step behind them and a harsh voice demanded, ''Schultz—what's all this about?''

Steiner and Neumann ignored it and stepped outside. A pall of black smoke hung over the city, there was a crump of artillery in the distance, the rattle of small arms fire. A hand on Steiner's shoulder spun him round and he found himself facing an immaculately uniformed major. Around his neck was suspended on a chain the gleaming brass gorget plate of the military police. Steiner sighed and pulled away the white scarf at his neck exposing not only the collar patches of his rank, but also the Knight's Cross with Oak Leaves for a second award.

"Steiner," he said. "Parachute Regiment."

The major saluted politely, but only because he had to. "I'm sorry, Herr Oberst, but orders are orders."

"What's your name?" Steiner demanded.

There was an edge to the colonel's voice now in spite of the lazy smile, that hinted at the possibility of a little unpleasantness. "Otto Frank, Herr Oberst."

"Good, now that we've established that, would you be kind enough to explain exactly what's going on here? I thought the Polish Army surrendered in 'thirty-nine?"

"They are razing the Warsaw Ghetto to the ground," Frank said.

"Who is?"

"A special task force. SS and various other groups commanded by Brigadeführer Jurgen Stroop. Jewish bandits, Herr Oberst. They've been fighting from house to house, in the cellars, in the sewers, for thirteen days now. So we're burning them out. Best way to exterminate lice."

During convalescent leave after being wounded at Leningrad, Steiner had visited his father in France and had found him considerably changed. The General had had his doubts about the new order for some considerable time. Six months earlier he had visited a concentration camp at Auschwitz in Poland.

"The commander was a swine named Rudolf Hoess, Kurt. Would you believe it, a murderer serving a life sentence and released from gaol in the amnesty of nineteen-twenty-eight. He was killing Jews by the thousand in specially constructed gas chambers, disposing of their bodies in huge ovens. After extracting such minor items as gold teeth and so forth."

The old general had been drunk by then and yet not drunk. "Is this what we're fighting for, Kurt? To protect swine like Hoess? And what will the rest of the world say when the time comes? That we are all guilty? That Germany is guilty because we stood by? Decent and honourable men stood by and did nothing? Well not me, by God. I couldn't live with myself."

Standing there in the entrance to Warsaw Station, the memory of all this welling up inside, Kurt Steiner produced an expression on his face that sent the major back a couple of steps. "That's better," Steiner said, "and if you could make it downwind as well I'd be obliged."

Major Frank's look of astonishment quickly turned to anger as Steiner walked past him, Neumann at his side. "Easy, Herr Oberst. Easy," Neumann said.

On the platform at the other side of the track, a group of SS were herding a line of ragged and filthy human beings against a wall. It was virtually impossible to differentiate between the sexes and as Steiner watched, they all started to take their clothes off.

A military policeman stood on the edge of the platform watching and Steiner said, "What's going on over there?"

"Jews, Herr Oberst," the man replied. "This morning's crop from the Ghetto. They'll be shipped out to Treblinka to finish them off later today. They make them strip like that before a search mainly because of the women. Some of them have been carrying loaded pistols inside their pants."

There was brutal laughter from across the track and someone cried out in pain. Steiner turned to Neumann in disgust and found the lieutenant staring along the platform to the rear of the troop train. A young girl of perhaps fourteen or fifteen, with ragged hair and smoke-blackened face, wearing a cut-down man's overcoat tied with string, crouched under the coach. She had presumably slipped away from the group opposite and her intention was obviously to make a bid for freedom by riding the rods under the hospital train when it pulled out.

In the same moment the military policeman on the edge of the platform saw her and raised the alarm, jumping down on to the track and grabbing for her. She screamed, twisting from his grasp, scrambled up to the platform and ran for the entrance, straight into the arms of Major of Police Frank as he came out of his office.

He had her by the hair and shook her like a rat. "Dirty little Jew bitch. I'll teach you some manners."

Steiner started forward. "No, Herr Oberst!" Neumann said, but he was too late.

Steiner got a firm grip on Frank's collar, pulling him off balance so that he almost fell down, grabbed the girl by the hand and stood her behind him.

Major Frank scrambled to his feet, his face contorted with rage. His hand went to the Walther in the holster at his belt, but Steiner produced a Luger from the pocket of his leather coat and touched him between the eyes. "You do," he said, "and I'll blow your head off. Come to think of it, I'd be doing humanity a favour."

At least a dozen military policemen ran forward, some carrying machine pistols, others rifles and paused in a semi-circle three or four yards away. A tall sergeant aimed his rifle and Steiner got a hand in Frank's tunic and held him close, screwing the barrel of the Luger in hard.

"I wouldn't advise it."

An engine coasted through the station at five or six miles an hour hauling a line of open wagons loaded with coal. Steiner said to the girl without looking at her, "What's your name, child?"

"Brana," she told him. "Brana Lezemnikof."

"Well, Brana," he said, "if you're half the girl I think you are, you'll grab hold of one of those coal trucks and hang on till you're out of here. The best I can do for you." She was gone in a flash and he raised his voice. "Anyone takes a shot at her puts one in the major here as well."

The girl jumped for one of the trucks, secured a grip and pulled herself up between two of them. The train coasted out of the station. There was complete silence.

Frank said, "They'll have her off at the first station, I'll see to it personally."

Steiner pushed him away and pocketed his Luger. Immediately the military policemen closed in and Ritter Neumann called out, "Not today, gentlemen."

Steiner turned and found the lieutenant holding an MP-40 machine pistol. The rest of his men were ranged behind him, all armed to the teeth.

At that point, anything might have happened, had it not been for a sudden disturbance in the main entrance. A group of SS stormed in, rifles at the ready. They took up position in a V formation and a moment later, SS Brigadeführer and Major-General of Police Jurgen Stroop entered, flanked by three or four SS officers of varying ranks, all carrying drawn pistols. He wore a field cap and service uniform and looked surprisingly nondescript.

"What's going on here, Frank?"

"Ask him, Herr Brigadeführer," Frank said, his face twisted with rage. "This man, an officer of the German Army, has just allowed a Jewish terrorist to escape."

Stroop looked Steiner over, noting the rank badges and the Knight's Cross plus the Oak Leaves. "Who are you?" he demanded.

"Kurt Steiner—Parachute Regiment," Steiner told him. "And who might you be?"

Jurgen Stroop was never known to lose his temper. He said calmly, "You can't talk to me like that, Herr Oberst. I'm a Major-General as you very well know."

"So is my father," Steiner told him, "so I'm not particularly impressed. However, as you've raised the matter, are you Brigadeführer Stroop, the man in charge of the slaughter out there?"

"I am in command here, yes."

Steiner wrinkled his nose. "I rather thought you might be. You know what you remind me of?"

"No, Herr Oberst," Stroop said. "Do tell me."

"The kind of thing I occasionally pick up on my shoe in the gutter,"

Steiner said. "Very unpleasant on a hot day."

Jurgen Stroop, still icy calm, held out his hand. Steiner sighed, took the Luger from his pocket and handed it across. He looked over his shoulder to his men. "That's it, boys, stand down." He turned back to Stroop. "They feel a certain loyalty for some reason unknown to me. Is there any chance you could content yourself with me and overlook their part in this thing?"

"Not the slightest," Brigadeführer Jurgen Stroop told him.

"That's what I thought," Steiner said. "I pride myself I can always tell a thoroughgoing bastard when I see one."

Radl sat with the file on his knee for a long time after he'd finished reading the account of the court martial. Steiner had been lucky to escape execution but his father's influence would have helped and after all, he and his men were war heroes. Bad for morale to have to shoot a holder of the Knight's Cross with Oak Leaves. And Operation Swordfish, in the Channel Islands, was just as certain in the long run for all of them. A stroke of genius on somebody's part.

Rossman sprawled in the chair opposite, apparently asleep, the black slouch hat tipped over his eyes, but when the light at the door flashed, he was on his feet. He went straight in without knocking and was back in a moment.

"He wants you."

The Reichsführer was still seated behind the desk. He now had the ordnance survey map spread out in front of him. He looked up. "And what did you make of friend Steiner's little escapade in Warsaw?"

"A remarkable story," Radl said carefully. "An—an unusual man."

"I would say one of the bravest you are ever likely to encounter," Himmler said calmly. "Gifted with high intelligence, courageous, ruthless, a brilliant soldier—and a romantic fool. I can only imagine that to be the American half of him." The Reichsführer shook his head. "The Knight's Cross with Oak Leaves. After that Russian affair the Führer had asked to meet him personally. And what does he do? Throws it all away, career, future, everything, for the sake of a little Jewish bitch he'd never clapped eyes on in his life before."

He looked up at Radl as if waiting for a reply and Radl said lamely, "Extraordinary, Herr Reichsführer."

Himmler nodded and then, as if dismissing the subject completely, rubbed his hands together and leaned over the map. "The Grey woman's reports are really quite brilliant. An outstanding agent." He leaned down, eyes very close to the map. "Will it work?"

"I think so," Radl replied without hesitation.

"And the Admiral? What does the Admiral think?"

Radl's mind raced as he tried to frame a suitable reply. "That's a difficult question to answer."

Himmler sat back, hands folded. For a wild moment Radl felt as if he were back in short trousers and in front of his old village schoolmaster.

"You don't need to tell me, I think I can guess. I admire loyalty, but in this case you would do well to remember that loyalty to Germany, to your Führer, comes first."

"Naturally, Herr Reichsführer," Radl said hastily.

"Unfortunately there are those who would not agree," Himmler went on. "Subversive elements at every level in our society. Even amongst the generals of the High Command itself. Does that surprise you?"

Radl, genuinely astonished, said, "But Herr Reichsführer, I can hardly believe . . . "

"That men who have taken an oath of personal loyalty to the Führer can behave in such a dastardly fashion?" He shook his head almost sadly. "I have every reason to believe that in March of this year, high ranking officers of the Wehrmacht placed a bomb on the Führer's plane, set to explode during its flight from Smolensk to Rastenburg."

"God in heaven," Radl said.

"The bomb failed to explode and was removed by the individuals concerned later. Of course, it makes one realize more strongly than ever that we cannot fail, that ultimate victory must be ours. That the Führer was saved by some divine intervention seems obvious. That doesn't surprise me of course. I have always believed that some higher being is behind nature, don't you agree?"

"Of course, Herr Reichsführer," Radl said.

"Yes, if we refused to recognize that we would be no better than Marxists. I insist that all members of the SS believe in God." He removed his pince-nez for a moment and stroked the bridge of his nose gently with one finger. "So, traitors everywhere. In the Army and in the Navy, too, at the highest level."

He replaced his pince-nez and looked up at Radl. "So you see, Radl," Himmler went on, "I have the very best of reasons for being sure that Admiral Canaris must have vetoed this scheme of yours."

Radl stared at him dumbly. His blood ran cold. Himmler said gently, "It would not be in accordance with his general aim and that aim is not the victory of the German Reich in this war, I assure you."

That the Head of the Abwehr was working against the State? The idea was monstrous. But then Radl remembered the Admiral's acid tongue. The derogatory remarks about high state officials, about the Führer himself on occasion. His reaction earlier that evening. *We have lost the war.* And that from the Head of the Abwehr.

Himmler pressed the buzzer and Rossman came in. "I have an important phone call to make. Show the Herr Oberst around for ten minutes then bring him back." He turned to Radl. "You haven't seen the cellars here, have you?"

"No, Herr Reichsführer."

He might have added that the Gestapo cellars at Prinz Albrechtstrasse were the last places on earth he wanted to see. But he knew that he was going to whether he liked it or not, knew from the slight smile on Rossman's mouth that it was all arranged.

On the ground floor they went along a corridor that led to the rear of the building. There was an iron door guarded by two Gestapo men wearing steel helmets and armed with machine pistols. "Are you expecting a war or something?" Radl enquired.

Rossman grinned. "Let's say it impresses the customers."

The door was unlocked and he led the way down. The passage at the bottom was brilliantly lit, brickwork painted white, doors opening to right and left. It was extraordinarily quiet.

"Might as well start in here," Rossman said and opened the nearest door and switched on the light.

It was a conventional enough looking cellar painted white except for the opposite wall which had been faced with concrete in a surprisingly crude way, for the surface was uneven and badly marked. There was a beam across the ceiling near that wall, chains hanging down with coil spring stirrups on the end.

"Something they're supposed to have a lot of success with lately." Rossman took out a packet of cigarettes and offered Radl one. "I think it's a dead loss myself. I can't see much point in driving a man insane when you want him to talk."

"What happens?"

"The suspect is suspended in those stirrups, then they simply turn the electricity on. They throw buckets of water on that concrete wall to improve the electrical flow or something. Extraordinary what it does to people. If you look close you'll see what I mean."

When Radl approached the wall he saw that what he had taken to be a crudely finished surface was in fact a patina of hand prints in raw concrete where victims had clawed in agony.

"The Inquisition would have been proud of you."

"Don't be bitter, Herr Oberst, it doesn't pay, not down here. I've seen generals on their knees down here and begging." Rossman smiled genially. "Still, that's neither here nor there." He walked to the door. "Now what can I show you next?"

"Nothing, thank you," Radl said. "You've made your point, wasn't that the object of the exercise? You can take me back now."

"As you say, Herr Oberst." Rossman shrugged and turned out the light.

When Radl went back into the office, he found Himmler busily writing in a file. He looked up and said calmly, "Terrible the things that have to be done. It personally sickens me to my stomach. I can't abide violence of any sort. It is the curse of greatness, Herr Oberst, that it must step over dead bodies to create new life."

"Herr Reichsführer," Radl said. "What do you want of me?"

Himmler actually smiled, however slightly, contriving to look even more sinister. "Why, it's really very simple. This Churchill business. I want it seen through."

"But the Admiral doesn't."

"You have considerable autonomy, is it not so? Run your own office? Travel extensively? Munich, Paris, Antwerp within the past fortnight?" Himmler shrugged. "I see no reason why you shouldn't be able to manage without the Admiral realizing what's going on. Most of what needs to be done could be handled in conjunction with other business."

"But why, Herr Reichsführer, why is it so important that it be done this way?"

"Because, in the first place, I think the Admiral totally wrong in this affair. This scheme of yours could work if everything falls right for it, just like Skorzeny at Gran Sasso. If it succeeds, if Churchill is either killed or kidnapped—and personally, I'd sooner see him dead—then we have a world sensation. An incredible feat of arms."

"Which if the Admiral had had his way would never have taken place," Radl said. "I see now. Another nail in his coffin?"

"Would you deny that he would have earned it in such circumstances?"

"What can I say?"

"Should such men be allowed to get away with it? Is that what you want, Radl, as a loyal German officer?"

"But the Herr Reichsführer must see what an impossible position this puts me in," Radl said. "My relations with the Admiral have always been excellent." It occurred to him, too late, that that was hardly the point to make under the circumstances and he added hurriedly, "Naturally my personal loyalty is beyond question, but what kind of authority would I have to carry such a project through?"

Himmler took a heavy manilla envelope from his desk drawer. He opened it and produced a letter which he handed to Radl without a word. It was headed by the German Eagle with the Iron Cross in gold.

FROM THE LEADER AND CHANCELLOR OF THE STATE

MOST SECRET

Colonel Radl is acting under my direct and personal orders in a matter of the utmost importance to the Reich. He is answerable only to me. All personnel, military and civil, without distinction of rank, will assist him in any way he sees fit.

ADOLF HITLER

Radl was stunned. It was the most incredible document he had ever held in his hand. With such a key, a man could open any door in the land, be denied nothing. His flesh crawled and a strange thrill ran through him.

"As you can see, anyone who wishes to query that document would have to be prepared to take it up with the Führer himself." Himmler rubbed his hands together briskly. "So, it is settled. You are prepared to accept this duty your Führer places on you?"

There was really nothing to be said except the obvious thing. "Of course, Herr Reichsführer."

"Good." Himmler was obviously pleased. "To business then. You are right to think of Steiner. The very man for the job. I suggest that you go and see him without delay."

"It occurs to me," Radl said carefully, "that in view of his recent history he may not be interested in such an assignment."

"He will have no choice in the matter," Himmler said. "Four days ago his father was arrested on suspicion of treason against the state."

"General Steiner?" Radl said in astonishment.

"Yes, the old fool seems to have got himself involved with entirely the wrong sort of people. He's being brought to Berlin at the moment."

"To—to Prinz Albrechtstrasse?"

"But of course. You might point out to Steiner that not only would it be in his own best interests to serve the Reich in any way he can at the moment. Such evidence of loyalty might well affect the outcome of his father's case." Radl was genuinely horrified, but Himmler carried straight on. "Now, a few facts. I would like you to elaborate on this question of disguise that you mention in your outline. That interests me."

Radl was aware of a feeling of total unreality. No one was safe—no one. He had known of people, whole families, who had disappeared after the Gestapo called. He thought of Trudi, his wife, his three cherished daughters and the same fierce courage that had brought him through the Winter War flowed through him again. For them, he thought, I've got to survive for them. Anything it takes—anything.

He started to speak, amazed at the calmness in his own voice. "The British have many commando regiments as the Reichsführer is aware, but perhaps one of the most successful has been the unit formed by a British officer named Stirling to operate behind our lines in Africa. The Special Air Service."

"Ah, yes, the man they called the Phantom Major. The one Rommel thought so highly of."

"He was captured in January of this year, Herr Reichsführer. I believe he is in Colditz now, but the work he started has not only continued, but expanded. According to our present information there are due to return to Britain soon, probably to prepare for an invasion of Europe, the First and Second SAS Regiments and the Third and Fourth French Parachute Battalions. They even have a Polish Independent Parachute Squadron."

"And the point you are trying to make?"

"Little is known of such units by the more conventional branches of the army. It is accepted that their purposes are secret, therefore less likely that they would be challenged by anyone."

"You would pass off our men as Polish members of this unit?"

"Exactly, Herr Reichsführer."

"And uniforms?"

"Most of these people are now wearing camouflage smock and trousers in action, rather similar to SS pattern. They also wear the English parachutists' red beret with a special badge. A winged dagger with the inscription *Who dares—wins.*"

"How dramatic," Himmler said drily.

"The Abwehr has ample supplies of such clothing from those taken prisoner during SAS operations in the Greek Islands, Yugoslavia and Albania."

"And equipment?"

"No problem. The British Special Operations Executive still do not appreciate the extent to which we have penetrated the Dutch resistance movement."

"Terrorist movement," Himmler corrected him. "But carry on."

"Almost nightly they drop further supplies of arms, sabotage equipment, radios for field use, even money. They still don't realize that all the radio messages they receive are from the Abwehr."

"My God," Himmler said, "and still we continue to lose the war." He got up, walked to the fire and warmed his hands. "This whole question of wearing enemy uniform is a matter of great delicacy and it is forbidden under the Geneva Convention. There is only one penalty. The firing squad."

"True, Herr Reichsführer."

"In this case it seems to me a compromise would be in order. The

raiding party will wear normal uniform underneath these British camouflage outfits. That way they will be fighting as German soldiers, not
gangsters. Just before the actual attack, they could remove these dis-
guises. You agree?''

Radl personally thought it probably the worst idea he'd ever heard of,
but realized the futility of argument. ''As you say, Herr Reichsführer.''

''Good. Everything else seems to me simply a question of organization. The Luftwaffe and the Navy for transportation. No trouble there.
The Führer's Directive will open all doors for you. Is there anything you
wish to raise with me?''

''As regards Churchill himself,'' Radl said. ''Is he to be taken alive?''

''If possible,'' Himmler said. ''Dead if there is no other way.''

''I understand.''

''Good, then I may safely leave the matter in your hands. Rossman
will give you a special phone number on the way out. I wish to be kept
in daily touch with your progress.'' He replaced the reports and the map
in the briefcase and pushed it across.

''As you say, Herr Reichsführer.''

Radl folded the precious letter, put it back in the manilla envelope
which he slipped inside his tunic. He picked up the briefcase and his
leather greatcoat and moved to the door.

Himmler, who had started writing again, said, ''Colonel Radl.''

Radl turned. ''Herr Reichsführer?''

''Your oath as a German soldier, to your Führer and the State. You
remember it?''

''Of course, Herr Reichsführer.''

Himmler looked up, the face cold, enigmatic. ''Repeat it now.''

''I swear by God this holy Oath. I will render unconditional obedience
to the Führer of the German Reich and People, Adolf Hitler, the Supreme
Commander of the Armed Forces and will be ready, as a brave soldier,
to stake my life at any time to this oath.''

His eye socket was on fire again, his dead hand ached. ''Excellent,
Colonel Radl. And remember one thing. Failure is a sign of weakness.''

Himmler lowered his head and continued to write. Radl got the door
open as fast as he could and stumbled outside.

He changed his mind about going home to his apartment. Instead he got
Rossman to drop him at the Tirpitz Ufer, went up to his office and
bedded down on the small camp bed that he kept for such emergencies.
Not that he slept much. Every time he closed his eyes he saw the silver
pince-nez, the cold eyes, the calm, dry voice making its monstrous state-
ments.

One thing was certain, or so he told himself at five o'clock when he finally surrendered and reached for the bottle of Courvoisier. He had to see this thing through, not for himself, but for Trudi and the children. Gestapo surveillance was bad enough for most people. "But me," he said as he put the light out again. "I have to have Himmler himself on my tail."

After that he slept and was awakened by Hofer at eight o'clock with coffee and hot rolls. Radl got up and walked across to the window, eating one of the rolls. It was a gray morning and raining heavily.

"Was it a bad raid, Karl?"

"Not too bad. I hear eight Lancasters were shot down."

"If you look in the inside breast pocket of my tunic you'll find an envelope," Radl said. "I want you to read the letter inside."

He waited, peering out into the rain and turned after a moment or so. Hofer was staring down at the letter, obviously shaken. "But what does this mean, Herr Oberst?"

"The Churchill affair, Karl. It proceeds. The Führer wishes it so. I had that from Himmler himself last night."

"And the Admiral, Herr Oberst?"

"Is to know nothing."

Hofer stared at him in honest bewilderment, the letter in one hand. Radl took it from him and held it up. "We are little men, you and I, caught in a very large web and we must tread warily. This directive is all we need. Orders from the Führer himself. Do you follow me?"

"I think so."

"And trust me?"

Hofer sprang to attention. "I have never doubted you, Herr Oberst. Never."

Radl was aware of a surge of affection. "Good, then we proceed as I have indicated and under conditions of the strictest secrecy."

"As you say, Herr Oberst."

"Good, Karl, then bring me everything. Everything we have, and we'll go over it again."

He moved to the window, opened it and took a deep breath. There was the acrid tang of smoke on the air from last night's fires. Parts of the city that he could see were a desolate ruin. Strange how excited he felt.

"She needs a man, Karl."

"Herr Oberst?" Hofer said.

They were leaning over the desk, the reports and charts spread before them. "Mrs. Grey," Radl explained. "She needs a man."

"Ah, I see now, Herr Oberst," Hofer said. "Someone with broad shoulders. A blunt instrument?"

"No." Radl frowned and took one of his Russian cigarettes from the box on the table. "Brains as well—that is essential."

Hofer lit the cigarette for him. "A difficult combination."

"It always is. Who does Section One have working for them in England at the moment, who might be able to help? Someone thoroughly reliable?"

"There are perhaps seven or eight agents who may be so considered. People like Snow White, for example. He's been working in the offices at the Naval Department in Portsmouth for two years. We receive regular and valuable information on North Atlantic convoys from him."

Radl shook his head impatiently. "No, no one like that. Such work is too important to be jeopardized in any way. Surely to God there are others?"

"At least fifty." Hofer shrugged. "Unfortunately the BIA section of M15 has had a remarkably successful run during the past eighteen months."

Radl got up and went to the window. He stood there tapping one foot impatiently. He was not angry—worried more than anything else. Joanna Grey was sixty-eight years of age and no matter how dedicated, no matter how reliable, she needed a man. As Hofer had put it, a blunt instrument. Without him the whole enterprise could founder.

His left hand was hurting, the hand which was no longer there, a sure sign of stress, and his head was splitting. *Failure is a sign of weakness, Colonel.* Himmler had said that, the dark eyes cold. Radl shivered uncontrollably, fear almost moving his bowels as he remembered the cellars at Prinz Albrechtstrasse.

Hofer said diffidently, "Of course, there is always the Irish Section."

"What did you say?"

"The Irish Section, sir. The Irish Republican Army."

"Completely useless," Radl said. "The whole IRA connection was aborted long ago, you know that, after that fiasco with Goertz and the other agents. A total failure, the entire enterprise."

"Not quite, Herr Oberst."

Hofer opened one of the filing cabinets, leafed through it quickly and produced a manilla folder which he laid on the desk. Radl sat down with a frown and opened it.

"But, of course . . . and he's still here? At the university?"

"So I understand. He also does a little translation work when needed."

"And what does he call himself now?"

"Devlin. Liam Devlin."

"Get him!"

"Now, Herr Oberst?"

"You heard me. I want him here within the hour. I don't care if you have to turn Berlin upside down. I don't care if you have to call in the Gestapo."

Hofer clicked his heels and went out quickly. Radl lit another cigarette with trembling fingers and started to go through the file.

He had not been far wrong in his earlier remarks, for every German attempt to make terms with the IRA since the beginning of the war had come to nothing and the whole business was probably the biggest tale of woe in Abwehr files.

None of the German agents sent to Ireland had achieved anything worth having. Only one had remained at large for any length of time, Captain Goertz, who had been parachuted from a Heinkel over Meath in May, 1940, and who had succeeded in remaining at large for nineteen wasted months.

Goertz found the IRA exasperatingly amateur and unwilling to take any kind of advice. As he was to comment years later, they knew how to die for Ireland, but not how to fight for her and German hopes of regular attacks on British military installations in Ulster faded away.

Radl was familiar with all this. What really interested him was the man who called himself Liam Devlin. Devlin had actually parachuted into Ireland for the Abwehr, had not only survived, but had eventually made his way back to Germany, a unique achievement.

Liam Devlin had been born in Lismore in County Down in the North of Ireland in July, 1908, the son of a small tenant farmer who had been executed in 1921 during the Anglo-Irish War for serving with an IRA flying column. The boy's mother had gone to keep house for her brother, a Catholic priest in the Falls Road area of Belfast and he had arranged for him to attend a Jesuit boarding school in the South. From there Devlin had moved to Trinity College, Dublin, where he had taken an excellent degree in English Literature.

He'd had a little poetry published, was interested in a career in journalism, would probably have made a successful writer if it had not been for one single incident which had altered the course of his entire life. In 1931 while visiting his home in Belfast during a period of serious sectarian rioting, he had witnessed an Orange mob sack his uncle's church. The old priest had been so badly beaten that he lost an eye. From that moment Devlin had given himself completely to the Republican cause.

In a bank raid in Derry in 1932 to gather funds for the movement, he was wounded in a gun battle with the police and sentenced to ten years imprisonment. He had escaped from the Crumlin Road gaol in 1934 and while on the run, led the defence of Catholic areas in Belfast during the rioting of 1935.

Later that year he had been sent to New York to execute an informer who had been put on a boat to America by the police for his own good after selling information which had led to the arrest and hanging of a young IRA volunteer named Michael Reilly. Devlin had accomplished this mission with an efficiency that could only enhance a reputation that was already becoming legendary. Later that year he repeated the performance. Once in London and again in America, although this time the venue was Boston.

In 1936 he had taken himself to Spain, serving in the Lincoln Washington Brigade. He had been wounded and captured by Italian troops who, instead of shooting him, had kept him intact, hoping to effect an exchange for one of their own officers. Although this had never come to anything, it meant that he survived the war, being eventually sentenced to life imprisonment by the Franco government.

He had been freed at the instigation of the Abwehr in the autumn of 1940 and brought to Berlin, where it was hoped he might prove of some use to German Intelligence. It was at this stage that things had gone sadly wrong, for according to the record, Devlin, while having little sympathy with the Communist cause, was very definitely anti-fascist, a fact which he had made abundantly clear during his interrogation. A bad risk, then considered fit only for minor translation duties and English tutoring at the University of Berlin.

But the position had changed drastically. The Abwehr had made several attempts to get Goertz out of Ireland. All had failed. In desperation, the Irish Section had called in Devlin and asked him to parachute into Ireland with forged travel documents, contact Goertz and get him out via a Portuguese ship or some similar neutral vessel. He was dropped over County Meath on the 18 October 1941 but some weeks later, before he could contact Goertz, the German was arrested by the Irish Special Branch.

Devlin had spent several harrowing months on the run, betrayed at every turn, for so many IRA supporters had been interned in the Curragh by the Irish Government that there were few reliable contacts left. Surrounded by police in a farmhouse in Kerry in June, 1942, he wounded two of them and was himself rendered unconscious when a bullet creased his forehead. He had escaped from a hospital bed, made his way to Dun Laoghaire and had managed to get passage on a Brazilian boat bound for Lisbon. From there he had passed through Spain via the usual channels until he once more stood in the offices at the Tirpitz Ufer.

From then on, Ireland was a dead end as far as the Abwehr was concerned and Liam Devlin was sent back to kick his heels in translation duties and occasionally, so farcical can life be, to take tutorials again in English literature at the University of Berlin.

It was just before noon when Hofer came back into the office. "I've got him, Herr Oberst."

Radl looked up and put down his pen. "Devlin?" He stood up and walked to the window, straightening his tunic, trying to work out what he was going to say. This had to go right, had to work. Yet Devlin would require careful handling. He was, after all, a neutral. The door clicked open and he turned.

Liam Devlin was smaller than he had imagined. No more than five feet five or six. He had dark, wavy hair, pale face, eyes of the most vivid blue that Radl had ever seen and a slight, ironic smile that seemed to permanently lift the corner of his mouth. The look of a man who had found life a bad joke and had decided that the only thing to do was laugh about it. He was wearing a black, belted trenchcoat and the ugly puckered scar of the bullet wound that he had picked up on his last trip to Ireland showed clearly on the left side of his forehead.

"Mr. Devlin," Radl went round the desk and held out his hand. "My name is Radl—Max Radl. It's good of you to come."

"That's nice," Devlin said in excellent German. "The impression I got was that I didn't have much choice in the matter." He moved forward, unbuttoning his coat. "So this is Section Three where it all happens?"

"Please, Mr. Devlin." Radl brought a chair forward and offered him a cigarette.

Devlin leaned forward for a light. He coughed, choking as the harsh cigarette smoke pulled at the back of his throat. "Mother Mary, Colonel, I knew things were bad, but not that bad. What's in them or shouldn't I ask?"

"Russian," Radl said. "I picked up the taste for them during the Winter War."

"Don't tell me," Devlin said. "They were the only thing that kept you from falling asleep in the snow."

Radl smiled, warming to the man. "Very likely." He produced the bottle of Courvoisier and two glasses. "Cognac?"

"Now you're being too nice." Devlin accepted the glass, swallowed, closing his eyes for a moment. "It isn't Irish, but it'll do to be going on with. When do we get to the nasty bit? The last time I was at Tirpitz Ufer they asked me to jump out of a Dornier at five thousand feet over Meath in the dark and I've a terrible fear of heights."

"All right, Mr. Devlin," Radl said. "We do have work for you if you're interested."

"I've got work."

"At the university? Come now, for a man like you that must be rather like being a thoroughbred racing horse that finds itself pulling a milk cart."

Devlin threw back his head and laughed out loud. "Ah, Colonel, you've found my weak spot instantly. Vanity, vanity. Stroke me any more and I'll purr like my Uncle Sean's old tomcat. Are you trying to lead up, in the nicest way possible, to the fact that you want me to go back to Ireland? Because if you are you can forget it. I wouldn't stand a chance, not for any length of time the way things are now, and I've no intention of sitting on my arse in the Curragh for five years. I've had enough of prisons to last me quite some time."

"Ireland is still a neutral country, Mr. de Valera has made it quite clear that she will not take sides."

"Yes, I know," Devlin said, "which is why a hundred thousand Irishmen are serving in the British forces. And another thing—every time an RAF plane crashlands in Ireland, the crew are passed over the border in a matter of days. How many German pilots have they sent you back lately?" Devlin grinned. "Mind you, with all that lovely butter and cream and the colleens, they probably think they're better off where they are."

"No, Mr. Devlin, we don't want you to go back to Ireland," Radl said. "Not the way you mean."

"Then what in the hell do you want?"

"Let me ask you something first. You are still a supporter of the IRA."

"Soldier of," Devlin corrected him. "We have a saying back home, Colonel. Once in, never out."

"So, your total aim is victory against England?"

"If you mean a united Ireland, free and standing on her own two feet, then I'll cheer for that: I'll believe it when it happens, mind you, but not before."

Radl was mystified. "Then why fight?"

"God save us, but don't you ask the questions?" Devlin shrugged. "It's better than fist-fighting outside Murphy's Select Bar on Saturday nights. Or maybe it's just that I like playing the game."

"And which game would that be?"

"You mean to tell me you're in this line of work and you don't know?"

For some reason Radl felt strangely uncomfortable so he said hurriedly, "Then the activities of your compatriots in London, for instance, don't commend themselves to you?"

"Hanging round Bayswater making Paxo in their landlady's saucepans?" Devlin said. "Not my idea of fun."

"Paxo?" Radl was bewildered.

"A joke. Paxo is a well-known package gravy, so that's what the boys call the explosive they mix. Potassium chlorate, sulphuric acid and a few other assorted goodies."

"A volatile brew."

"Especially when it goes up in your face."

"This bombing campaign your people started with the ultimatum they sent to the British Prime Minister in January, 1939 . . . "

Devlin laughed. "And Hitler and Mussolini and anyone else they thought might be interested including Uncle Tom Cobley."

"Uncle Tom Cobley?"

"Another joke," Devlin said. "A weakness of mine, never having been able to take anything too seriously."

"Why, Mr. Devlin? That interests me."

"Come now, Colonel," Devlin said. "The world was a bad joke dreamed up by the Almighty on an off-day. I've always felt myself that he probably had a hangover that morning. But what was your point about the bombing campaign?"

"Did you approve of it?"

"No. I don't like soft target hits. Women, kids, passers-by. If you're going to fight, if you believe in your cause and it is a just one, then stand up on your two hind legs and fight like a man."

His face was white and very intense, the bullet scar in his head glowing like a brand. He relaxed just as suddenly and laughed. "There you go, bringing out the best in me. Too early in the morning to be serious."

"So, a moralist," Radl said. "The English would not agree with you. They bomb the heart out of the Reich every night."

"You'll have me in tears if you keep that up. I was in Spain fighting for the Republicans remember. What in the hell do you think those German Stukas were doing flying for Franco? Ever heard of Barcelona or Guernica?"

"Strange, Mr. Devlin, you obviously resent us and I had presumed it was the English you hated."

"The English?" Devlin laughed. "Sure and they're just like your mother-in-law. Something you put up with. No, I don't *hate* the English—it's the bloody British Empire I hate."

"So, you wish to see Ireland free?"

"Yes." Devlin helped himself to another of the Russian cigarettes.

"Then would you accept that from your point of view the best way of achieving that aim would be for Germany to win this war?"

"And pigs might fly one of these days," Devlin told him, "but I doubt it."

"Then why stay here in Berlin?"

"I didn't realize that I had any choice?"

"But you do, Mr. Devlin," Colonel Radl said quietly. "You can go to England for me."

Devlin stared at him in amazement, for once in his life stopped dead in his tracks. "God save us, the man's mad."

"No, Mr. Devlin, quite sane I assure you." Radl pushed the Courvoisier bottle across the desk and placed the manilla file next to it. "Have another drink and read that file then we'll talk again."

He got up and walked out.

When at the end of a good half-hour there was no sign of Devlin, Radl steeled himself to open the door and go back in. Devlin was sitting with his feet on the desk, Joanna Grey's reports in one hand, a glass of Courvoisier in the other. The bottle looked considerably depleted.

He glanced up. "So there you are? I was beginning to wonder what had happened to you."

"Well, what do you think," Radl demanded.

"It reminds me of a story I heard when I was a boy," Devlin said. "Something that happened during the war with the English back in nineteen-twenty-one. May, I think. It concerned a man called Emmet Dalton. He that was a General in the Free State Army later. Did you ever hear tell of him?"

"No, I'm afraid not," said Radl with ill-concealed impatience.

"What we Irish would call a lovely man. Served as a major in the British Army right through the war, awarded the Military Cross for bravery, then he joined the IRA."

"Forgive me, Mr. Devlin, but is any of this relevant?"

Devlin didn't seem to have heard him. "There was a man in Mountjoy prison in Dublin called McEoin, another lovely man, but in spite of that he only had the gallows before him." He helped himself to more Courvoisier. "Emmet Dalton had other ideas. He stole a British armoured car, put on his old major's uniform, dressed a few of the boys as *Tommis*, bluffed his way into the prison and right into the governor's office. Would you believe that?"

By now Radl was interested in spite of himself. "And did they save this McEoin?"

"By bad luck, it was the one morning his application to see the governor was refused."

"And these men—what happened to them?"

"Oh, there was a little shooting, but they got clean away. Bloody cheek, though." He grinned and held up Joanna Grey's report. "Just like this."

"You think it would work?" Radl demanded eagerly. "You think it possible?"

"It's impudent enough." Devlin threw the report down. "And I thought the Irish were supposed to be the crazy ones. To tumble the great Winston Churchill out of his bed in the middle of the night and away with him.'' He laughed out loud. ''Now that would be something to see. Something that would stand the whole world on its ear in amazement.''

''And you'd like that?''

''A great ploy, surely.'' Devlin smiled hugely and was still smiling when he added, ''Of course, there is the point that it wouldn't have the slightest effect on the course of the war. The English will simply promote Attlee to fill the vacancy, the Lancasters will still come over by night and the Flying Fortresses by day.''

''In other words it is your considered opinion that we'll still lose the war?'' Radl said.

''Fifty marks on that any time you like.'' Devlin grinned. ''On the other hand, I'd hate to miss this little jaunt, if you're really serious, that is?''

''You mean you're willing to go?'' Radl was by now thoroughly bewildered. ''But I don't understand. Why?''

''I know, I'm a fool,'' Devlin said. ''Look what I'm giving up. A nice safe job at the University of Berlin with the RAF bombing by night, the Yanks by day, food getting shorter, the Eastern Front crumbling.''

Radl raised both hands, laughing. ''All right, no more questions, the Irish are quite obviously mad. I was told it, now I accept it.''

''The best thing for you and, of course, we mustn't forget the twenty thousand pounds you're going to deposit to a numbered account in a Geneva bank of my choosing.''

Radl was aware of a feeling of acute disappointment. ''So, Mr. Devlin, you also have your price like the rest of us?''

''The movement I serve has always been notoriously low on funds.'' Devlin grinned. ''I've seen revolutions started on less than twenty thousand pounds, Colonel.''

''Very well,'' Radl said. ''I will arrange it. You will receive confirmation of the deposit before you leave.''

''Fine,'' Devlin said. ''So what's the score then?''

''Today is the first October. That gives us exactly five weeks.''

''And what would my part be?''

''Mrs. Grey is a first-rate agent, but she is sixty-eight years of age. She needs a man.''

''Someone to do the running around? Handle the rough stuff?''

''Exactly.''

''And how do you get me there and don't tell me you haven't been thinking about it?''

Radl smiled. ''I must admit I've given the matter considerable thought. See how this strikes you. You're an Irish citizen who has served with the British Army. Badly wounded and given a medical discharge. That scar on your forehead will help there.''

''And how does this fit in with Mrs. Grey?''

''An old family friend who has found you some sort of employment in Norfolk. We'll have to put it to her and see what she comes up with. We'll fill the story out, supply you with every possible document from an Irish passport to your army discharge papers. What do you think?''

''It sounds passable enough,'' Devlin said. ''But how do I get there?''

''We'll parachute you into Southern Ireland. As close to the Ulster border as possible. I understand it to be extremely easy to walk across the border without passing through a customs post.''

''No trouble there,'' Devlin said. ''Then what?''

''The night boat from Belfast to Heysham, train to Norfolk, everything straight and above board.''

Devlin pulled the ordnance survey map forward and looked down at it. ''All right, I'll buy that. When do I go?''

''A week, ten days at the most. For the moment, you will obviously observe total security. You must also resign your post at the University and vacate your present apartment. Drop completely out of sight. Hofer will arrange other accommodation for you.''

''Then what?''

''I'm going to see the man who will probably command the assault group. Tomorrow or the next day depending on how soon I can arrange flights to the Channel Islands. You might as well come too. You're going to have a lot in common. You agree?''

''And why shouldn't I, Colonel? Won't the same bad old roads all lead to hell in the end?'' He poured what was left of the Courvoisier into his glass.

5

ALDERNEY IS THE MOST NORTHERLY of the Channel Islands and the closest to the French coast. As the German Army rolled inexorably westward in the summer of 1940 the islanders had voted to evacuate. When the first Luftwaffe plane landed on the tiny grass strip on top of the cliffs on 2 July 1940, the place was deserted, the narrow cobbled streets of St. Anne eerily quiet.

By the autumn of 1942 there was a garrison of perhaps three thousand, mixed Army, Navy and Luftwaffe personnel and several Todt camps employing slave labour from the continent to work on the massive concrete gun emplacements of the new fortifications. There was also a concentration camp staffed by members of the SS and Gestapo, the only such establishment ever to exist on British soil.

Just after noon on Sunday Radl and Devlin flew in from Jersey in a Stork spotter plane. It was only a half-hour run and as the Stork was unarmed the pilot did the entire trip at sea level only climbing up to seven hundred feet at the last moment.

As the Stork swept in over the enormous breakwater Alderney was spread out for them like a map. Braye Bay, the harbour, St. Anne, the island itself, perhaps three miles long and a mile and a half wide, vividly green, great cliffs on one side, the land sliding down into a series of sandy bays and coves on the other.

The Stork turned into the wind and dropped down on to one of the grass runways of the airfield on top of the cliffs. It was one of the smallest Radl had ever seen, hardly deserving of the name. A tiny control tower, a scattering of prefabricated buildings and no hangars.

There was a black Wolseley car parked beside the control tower and as Radl and Devlin went towards it, the driver, a sergeant of Artillery, got out and opened the rear door. He saluted. "Colonel Radl? The commandant asks you to accept his compliments. I'm to take you straight to the Feldkommandantur."

"Very well," Radl said.

They got in and were driven away, soon turning into a country lane. It was a fine day, warm and sunny, more like late spring than early autumn.

"It seems a pleasant enough place," Radl commented.

"For some." Devlin nodded over towards the left where hundreds of Todt workers could be seen in the distance labouring on what looked like some enormous concrete fortification.

The houses in St. Anne were a mixture of French Provincial and English Georgian, streets cobbled, gardens high-walled against the constant winds. There were plenty of signs of war—concrete pillboxes, barbed wire, machine-gun posts, bomb damage in the harbour far below—but it was the Englishness of it all that fascinated Radl. The incongruity of seeing two SS men in a field car parked in Connaught Square and of a Luftwaffe private giving another a light for his cigarette under a sign that said "Royal Mail."

Feldkommandantur 515, the German civilian administration for the Channel Islands, had its local headquarters in the old Lloyds Bank premises in Victoria Street and as the car drew up outside, Neuhoff himself appeared in the entrance.

He came forward, hand outstretched. "Colonel Radl? Hans Neuhoff, temporarily in command here. Good to see you."

Radl said, "This gentleman is a colleague of mine."

He made no other attempt to introduce Devlin and a certain alarm showed in Neuhoff's eyes instantly, for Devlin, in civilian clothes and a black leather military greatcoat Radl had procured for him, was an obvious curiosity. The logical explanation would seem to be that he was Gestapo. During the trip from Berlin to Brittany and then on to Guernsey, the Irishman had seen the same wary look on other faces and had derived a certain malicious satisfaction from it.

"Herr Oberst," he said, making no attempt to shake hands.

Neuhoff, more put out than ever, said hurriedly, "This way, gentlemen, please."

Inside, three clerks worked at the mahogany counter. Behind them on the wall was a new Ministry of Propaganda poster showing an eagle, with a swastika in its talons, rearing proudly above the legend *Am ende steht der Sieg*! At the end stands victory.

"My God," Devlin said softly, "some people will believe anything."

A military policeman guarded the door of what had presumably been the manager's office. Neuhoff led the way in. It was sparsely furnished, a workroom more than anything else. He brought two chairs forward. Radl took one, but Devlin lit a cigarette and went and stood at the window.

Neuhoff glanced at him uncertainly and tried to smile. "Can I offer you gentlemen a drink? Schnapps or a Cognac perhaps?"

"Frankly I'd like to get straight down to business," Radl told him.

"But, of course, Herr Oberst."

Radl unbuttoned his tunic, took the manilla envelope from his inside pocket and produced the letter. "Please read that."

Neuhoff picked it up, frowning slightly and ran his eyes over it. "The Führer himself commands." He looked up at Radl in amazement. "But I don't understand. What is it that you wish of me?"

"Your complete co-operation, Colonel Neuhoff," Radl said. "And no questions. You have a penal unit here, I believe? Operation Swordfish."

There was a new kind of wariness in Neuhoff's eyes, Devlin noticed it instantly, and the colonel seemed to stiffen. "Yes, Herr Oberst, that is so. Under the command of Colonel Steiner of the Parachute Regiment."

"So I understand," Radl said. "Colonel Steiner, a Lieutenant Neumann and twenty-nine paratroopers."

Neuhoff corrected him. "Colonel Steiner, Ritter Neumann and fourteen paratroopers."

Radl stared at him in surprise. "What are you saying? Where are the others?"

"Dead, Herr Oberst," Neuhoff said simply. "You know about Operation Swordfish? You know what they do, these men? They sit astride torpedoes and . . . "

"I'm aware of that." Radl stood up, reached for the Führer Directive and replaced it in its envelope. "Are there any operations planned for today?"

"That depends on whether there is a radar contact."

"No more," Radl said. "It stops now, from this moment." He held up the envelope. "My first order under this directive."

Neuhoff actually smiled. "I am delighted to comply with such an order."

"I see," Radl said. "Colonel Steiner is a friend?"

"My privilege," Neuhoff said simply. "If you knew the man, you'd know what I mean. There is also the point of view that someone of his extraordinary gifts is of more use to the Reich alive than dead."

"Which is exactly why I am here," Radl said. "Now, where can I find him?"

"Just before you get to the harbour there's an inn. Steiner and his men use it as their headquarters. I'll take you down there."

"No need," Radl said. "I'd like to see him alone. Is it far?"

"A quarter of a mile."

"Good, then we'll walk."

Neuhoff stood up. "Have you any idea how long you will be staying?"

"I have arranged for the Stork to pick us up first thing in the morning," Radl said. "It is essential that we're at the airfield in Jersey no later than eleven. Our plane for Brittany leaves then."

"I'll arrange accommodation for you and your—your friend." Neuhoff glanced at Devlin. "Also, if you would care to dine with me tonight? My wife would be delighted and perhaps Colonel Steiner could join us."

"An excellent idea," Radl said. "I'll look forward to it."

As they walked down Victoria Street past the shuttered shops and empty houses Devlin said, "What's got into you? You were laying it on a bit strong, weren't you? Are we feeling our oats today?"

Radl laughed, looking slightly shamefaced. "Whenever I take that damned letter out I feel strange. A feeling of—of power comes over me. Like the centurion in the Bible, who says do this and they do it, go there and they go."

As they turned into Braye Road a fieldcar drove past them, the artillery sergeant who had brought them in from the airfield at the wheel.

"Colonel Neuhoff sending a warning of our coming," Radl

commented. "I wondered whether he would."

"I think he thought I was Gestapo," Devlin said. "He was afraid."

"Perhaps," Radl said. "And you, Herr Devlin? Are you ever afraid?"

"Not that I can remember." Devlin laughed, without mirth. "I'll tell you something I've never told another living soul. Even at the moment of maximum danger and, God knows, I've known enough of those in my time, even when I'm staring Death right between the eyes, I get the strangest feeling. It's as if I want to reach out and take his hand. Now isn't that the funniest thing you ever heard of?"

Ritter Neumann, wearing a black rubber wet suit, was sitting astride a torpedo moored to the number one recovery boat tinkering with its engine, when the fieldcar roared along the jetty and braked to a halt. As Neumann looked up, shading his eyes against the sun, Sergeant-Major Brandt appeared.

"What's your hurry?" Neumann called. "Is the war over?"

"Trouble, Herr Leutnant," Brandt said. "There's some staff officer flown in from Jersey. A Colonel Radl. He's come for the Colonel. We've just had a tip-off from Victoria Street."

"Staff officer?" Neumann said and he pulled himself over the rail of the recovery boat and took the towel that Private Riedel handed him. "Where's he from?"

"Berlin!" Brandt said grimly. "And he has someone with him who looks like a civilian, but isn't."

"Gestapo?"

"So it would appear. They're on their way down now—walking."

Neumann pulled on his jump boots and scrambled up the ladder to the jetty. "Do the lads know?"

Brandt nodded, a savage look on his face, "And don't like it. If they find he's come to put the screws in the Colonel they're quite likely to push him and his pal off the end of the jetty with sixty pounds of chain apiece around their ankles."

"Right," said Neumann. "Back to the pub as fast as you can and hold them. I'll take the fieldcar and get the Colonel. He went for a walk along the breakwater with Frau Neuhoff."

Steiner and Ilse Neuhoff were at the very end of the breakwater. She was sitting above on the rampart, those long legs dangling into space, the wind off the sea ruffling the blonde hair, tugging at her skirt. She was laughing down at Steiner. He turned as the fieldcar braked to a halt.

Neumann scrambled out and Steiner took one look at his face and smiled sardonically. "Bad news, Ritter, and on such a lovely day."

"There's some staff officer in from Berlin looking for you, a Colonel

Radl,'' Neumann said grimly. ''They say he has a Gestapo man with him.''

Steiner wasn't put out in the slightest. ''That certainly adds a little interest to the day.''

He put up his hands to catch Ilse as she jumped down, and held her close for a moment. Her face was full of alarm. ''For God's sake, Kurt, can't you ever take anything seriously?''

''He's probably only here for a head count. We should all be dead by now. They must be very put out at Prinz Albrechtstrasse.''

The old inn stood at the side of the road on the approach to the harbour backing on to the sands of Braye Bay. It was strangely quiet as Radl and the Irishman approached.

''As nice a looking pub as I've seen,'' Devlin said. ''Would you think it possible they might still have a drink on the premises?''

Radl tried the front door. It opened and they found themselves in a dark passageway. A door clicked open behind them. ''In here, Herr Oberst,'' a soft, cultured voice said.

Sergeant Hans Altmann leaned against the outside door as if to bar their exit. Radl saw the Winter War ribbon, the Iron Cross, First and Second Class, a silver wound badge which meant at least three wounds, the Air Force Ground Combat badge and, most coveted honour of all amongst paratroopers, the *Kreta* cuff-title, proud mark of those who had spearheaded the invasion of Crete in May, 1941.

''Your name?'' Radl said crisply.

Altmann didn't reply, but simply pushed with his foot so that the door marked ''Saloon Bar'' swung open and Radl, sensing something, but uncertain what, stuck out his chin and advanced into the room.

The room was only fair-sized. There was a bar counter to the left, empty shelves behind it, a number of framed photographs of old wrecks on the walls, a piano in one corner. There were a dozen or so paratroopers scattered around the room, all remarkably unfriendly. Radl, looking them over coolly, was impressed. He'd never before seen a group of men with so many decorations between them. There wasn't a man there who didn't have the Iron Cross, First Class and such minor items as wound badges and tank destruction badges were ten a penny.

He stood in the centre of the room, his briefcase under his arm, his hands in his pockets, coat collar still turned up. ''I'd like to point out,'' he said mildly, ''that men have been shot before now for this kind of behaviour.''

There was a shout of laughter. Sergeant Sturm, who was behind the bar cleaning a Luger said, ''That really is very good, Herr Oberst. Do you want to hear something funny? When we went operational here ten weeks ago, there were thirty-one of us, including the Colonel. Fifteen now, in spite of a lot of lucky breaks. What can you and this Gestapo shit offer that's worse than that?''

"Don't go including me in this thing," Devlin said. "I'm neutral."

Sturm, who had worked the Hamburg barges since the age of twelve and was inclined to be a trifle direct in his speech, went on, "Listen to this because I'm only going to say it once. The Colonel isn't going anywhere. Not with you. Not with anyone." He shook his head. "You know that's a very pretty hat, Herr Oberst, but you've been polishing a chair with your backside for so long up there in Berlin that you've forgotten how real soldiers feel. You've come to the wrong place if you're hoping for a chorus from the *Horst Wessel*."

"Excellent," Radl said. "However, your completely incorrect reading of the present situation argues a lack of wit which I, for one, find deplorable in someone of your rank."

He dumped his briefcase on the counter, opened the buttons of his coat with his good hand and shrugged it off. Sturm's jaw dropped as he saw the Knight's Cross, the Winter War ribbon. Radl moved straight into the attack.

"Attention!" he barked. "On your feet, all of you." There was an instant burst of activity and in the same moment the door swung open and Brandt rushed in. "And you, Sergeant-Major," Radl snarled.

There was pin-drop silence as every man stood rigidly to attention and Devlin, thoroughly enjoying this new turn events had taken, pulled himself up on to the bar and lit a cigarette.

Radl said, "You think you are German soldiers, a natural error in view of the uniforms you wear, but you are mistaken." He moved from one man to another, pausing as if committing each face to memory. "Shall I tell you what you are?"

Which he did in simple and direct terms that made Sturm look like a beginner. When he paused for breath after two or three minutes, there was a polite cough from the open doorway and he turned to find Steiner there, Ilse Neuhoff behind him.

"I couldn't have put it better myself, Colonel Radl. I can only hope that you are willing to put down anything which has happened here to misguided enthusiasm and let it go at that. Their feet won't touch the ground when I get through with them, I promise you." He held out his hand and smiled with considerable charm. "Kurt Steiner."

Radl was always to remember that first meeting. Steiner possessed that strange quality to be found in the airborne troops of every country. A kind of arrogant self-sufficiency bred of the hazards of the calling. He was wearing a blue-gray flying blouse with the yellow collar patches bearing the wreath and two stylized wings of his rank, jump trousers and

the kind of sidecap known as a *Schiff*, an affectation of many of the old-
timers. The rest, for a man who had every conceivable decoration in the
book, was extraordinarily simple. The *Kreta* cuff-title, the ribbon for the
Winter War and the silver and gold eagle of the paratroopers' qualification badge. The Knight's Cross with Oak Leaves was concealed by a
silk scarf tied loosely about his neck.

"To be honest, Colonel Steiner, I've rather enjoyed putting these
rogues of yours in their place."

Ilse Neuhoff chuckled. "An excellent performance, Herr Oberst, if I
may say so."

Steiner made the necessary introductions and Radl kissed her hand.
"A great pleasure, Frau Neuhoff." He frowned. "Have we by any
chance met before?"

"Undoubtedly," Steiner said and pulled forward Ritter Neumann who
had been lurking in the background in his rubber wet suit. "And this,
Herr Oberst, is not as you may imagine, a captive Atlantic seal, but
Oberleutnant Ritter Neumann."

"Lieutenant." Radl glanced at Ritter Neumann briefly, remembering
the citation for the Knight's Cross that had been quashed because of the
court martial, wondering whether he knew.

"And this gentleman?" Steiner turned to Devlin who jumped down
from the counter and came forward.

"Actually everyone round here seems to think I'm your friendly
neighbourhood Gestapo man," Devlin said. "I'm not sure I find that too
flattering." He held out his hand. "Devlin, Colonel. Liam Devlin."

"Herr Devlin is a colleague of mine," Radl explained quickly.

"And you?" Steiner said politely.

"From Abwehr Headquarters. And now, if it is convenient, I would
like to talk to you privately on a matter of grave urgency."

Steiner frowned and again, there was that pin-drop silence in the room.
He turned to Ilse. "Ritter will see you home."

"No, I'd rather wait until your business with Colonel Radl is over."

She was desperately worried, it showed in her eyes. Steiner said gently, "I shouldn't imagine I'll be very long. Look after her, Ritter." He
turned to Radl. "This way, Herr Oberst."

Radl nodded to Devlin and they went after him.

"All right, stand down," Ritter Neumann said. "You damned fools."

There was a general easing of tension. Altmann sat at the piano and
launched into a popular song which assured everyone that everything
would get better by and by. "Frau Neuhoff," he called. "What about a
song?"

Ilse sat on one of the old bar stools. "I'm not in the mood," she said.
"You want to know something, boys? I'm sick of this damned war. All
I want is a decent cigarette and a drink, but that would be too much like
a miracle, I suppose."

"Oh, I don't know, Frau Neuhoff." Brandt vaulted clean over the bar and turned to face her. "For you, anything is possible. Cigarettes, for example, London gin."

His hands went beneath the counter and came up clutching a carton of Gold Flake and a bottle of Beefeater.

"Now will you sing for us, Frau Neuhoff," Hans Altmann called.

Devlin and Radl leaned on the parapet looking down into the water, clear and deep in the pale sunshine. Steiner sat on a bollard at the end of the jetty working his way through the contents of Radl's briefcase. Across the bay, Fort Albert loomed on the headland and below, the cliffs were splashed with birdlime, seabirds wheeling in great clouds, gulls, shags, razorbills and oystercatchers.

Steiner called, "Colonel Radl."

Radl moved towards him and Devlin followed, stopping two or three yards away to lean on the wall. Radl said, "You have finished?"

"Oh, yes." Steiner put the various papers back into the briefcase. "You're serious, I presume?"

"Of course."

Steiner reached forward and tapped a forefinger on Radl's Winter War ribbon. "Then all I can say is that some of that Russian cold must have got into your brain, my friend."

Radl took the manilla envelope from his inside pocket and produced the Führer Directive. "I think you had better have a look at that."

Steiner read it, with no evidence of emotion, and shrugged as he handed it back. "So what?"

"But Colonel Steiner," Radl said. "You are a German soldier. We swore the same oath. This is a direct order from the Führer himself."

"You seem to have forgotten one highly important thing," Steiner told him. "I'm in a penal unit, under suspended sentence of death, officially disgraced. In fact, I only retain my rank because of the peculiar circumstances of the job in hand." He produced a crumpled packet of French cigarettes from his hip pocket and put one in his mouth. "Anyway, I don't like Adolf. He has a loud voice and bad breath."

Radl ignored this remark. "We must fight. We have no other choice."

"To the last man?"

"What else can we do?"

"We can't win."

Radl's good hand was clenched into a fist, he was filled with nervous excitement. "But we can force them to change their views. See that some sort of settlement is better than this continual slaughter."

"And knocking off Churchill would help?" Steiner said with obvious scepticism.

"It would show them we still have teeth. Look at the furore when Skorzeny lifted Mussolini off the Gran Sasso. A sensation all over the world."

Steiner said, "As I heard it, General Student and a few paratroopers had a hand in that as well."

"For God's sake," Radl said impatiently. "Imagine how it would look. German troops dropping into England for one thing, but with such a target. Of course, perhaps you don't think it could be done."

"I don't see why not," Steiner said calmly. "If those papers I've just looked at are accurate and if you've done your homework correctly, the whole thing could go like a Swiss watch. We could really catch the *Tommis* with their pants down. In and out again before they know what's hit them, but that isn't the point."

"What is?" demanded Radl, completely exasperated. "Is thumbing your nose at the Führer more important because of your court martial? Because you're here? Steiner, you and your men are dead men if you stay here. Thirty-one of you eight weeks ago. How many left—fifteen? You owe it to your men, to yourself, to take this last chance to live."

"Or die in England instead."

Radl shrugged. "Straight in, straight out, that's the way it could go. Just like a Swiss watch, you said that yourself."

"And the terrible thing about those is that if anything goes wrong with even the tiniest part, the whole damn thing stops working," Devlin put in.

Steiner said, "Well put, Mr. Devlin. Tell me something. Why are you going?"

"Simple," Devlin said. "Because it's there. I'm the last of the great adventurers."

"Excellent," Steiner laughed delightedly. "Now that, I can accept. To play the game. The greatest game of all. But it doesn't help, you see," he went on. "Colonel Radl here tells me that I owe it to my men to do the thing because it is a way out from certain death here. Now, to be perfectly frank with you, I don't think I owe anything to anybody."

"Not even your father?" Radl said.

There was a silence, only the sea washing over the rocks below. Steiner's face turned pale, the skin stretched tight on the cheekbones, eyes dark. "All right, tell me."

"The Gestapo have him at Prinz Albrechtstrasse. Suspicion of treason."

And Steiner, remembering the week he had spent at his father's headquarters in France in 'forty-two, remembering what the old man had said, knew instantly that it was true.

"Ah, I see now," he said softly. "If I'm a good boy and do as I'm told, it would help his case." Suddenly his face changed and he looked about as dangerous as any man could and when he reached for Radl, it was in a kind of slow motion. "You bastard. All of you, bastards."

He had Radl by the throat. Devlin moved in fast and found that it took all his considerable strength to pull him off. "Not him, you fool. He's under the boot as much as you. You want to shoot somebody, shoot Himmler. He's the man you want."

Radl fought to get his breath and leaned against the parapet, looking very ill. "I'm sorry." Steiner put a hand on his shoulder in genuine concern. "I should have known."

Radl raised his dead hand. "See this, Steiner, and the eye? And other damage that you can't see. Two years if I'm lucky, that's what they tell me. Not for me. For my wife and daughters because I wake up at night sweating at the thought of what might happen to them. That's why I'm here."

Steiner nodded slowly. "Yes, of course, I understand. We're all up the same dark alley looking for a way out." He took a deep breath. "All right, we'll go back. I'll put it to the lads."

"Not the target," Radl said. "Not at this stage."

"The destination then. They're entitled to know that. As for the rest— I'll only discuss it with Neumann for the moment."

He started to walk away and Radl said, "Steiner, I must be honest with you." Steiner turned to face him. "In spite of everything I've said, I also think it's worth a try, this thing. All right, as Devlin says, getting Churchill, alive or dead, isn't going to win us the war, but perhaps it will give them a shake. Make them think again about a negotiated peace."

Steiner said, "My dear Radl, if you believe that you'll believe anything. I'll tell you what this affair, even if it's successful, will buy you from the British. Damn all!"

He turned and walked away along the jetty.

The saloon bar was full of smoke. Hans Altmann was playing the piano and the rest of the men were crowded round Ilse, who was sitting at the bar, a glass of gin in one hand, recounting a slightly unsavoury story current in high society and relevant only to Reichsmarschall Hermann Goering's love life, such as it was. There was a burst of laughter as Steiner entered the room followed by Radl and Devlin. Steiner surveyed the scene in astonishment, particularly the array of bottles on the bar counter.

"What the hell's going on here?"

The men eased away from the bar. Ritter Neumann, who was standing behind it with Brandt, said, "Altmann found a trap door under that old rush mat behind the bar this morning, sir, and a cellar below that we didn't know about. Two parcels of cigarettes not even unwrapped. Five thousand in each." He waved a hand along the counter. "Gordon's gin, Beefeater, White Horse Scotch Whisky, Haig and Haig." He picked up a bottle and spelled out the English with difficulty. "Bushmills Irish Whiskey. Pot distilled."

Liam Devlin gave a howl of delight and grabbed it from him. "I'll shoot the first man that touches a drop," he declared. "I swear it. It's all for me."

There was a general laugh and Steiner calmed them with a raised hand. "Steady down, there's something to discuss. Business." He turned to Ilse Neuhoff. "Sorry, my love, but this is top security."

She was enough of a soldier's wife not to argue. "I'll wait outside. But I refuse to let that gin out of my sight." She exited, the bottle of Beefeater in one hand, her glass in the other.

There was silence, now, in the saloon bar, everyone suddenly sober, waiting to hear what he had to say. "It's simple," Steiner told them. "There's a chance to get out of here. A special mission."

"Doing what, Herr Oberst?" Sergeant Altmann asked.

"Your old trade. What you were trained to do."

There was an instant reaction, a buzz of excitement. Someone whispered, "Does that mean we'll be jumping again?"

"That's exactly what I mean," Steiner said. "But it's volunteers only. A personal decision for every man here."

"Russia, Herr Oberst?" Brandt asked.

Steiner shook his head. "Somewhere no German soldier has ever fought." The faces were full of curiosity, tight, expectant as he looked from one to the other. "How many of you speak English?" he asked softly.

There was a stunned silence and Ritter Neumann so far forgot himself as to say in a hoarse voice, "For God's sake, Kurt, you've got to be joking."

Steiner shook his head. "I've never been more serious. What I tell you now is top secret, naturally. To be brief, in approximately five weeks we'd be expected to do a night drop over a very isolated part of the English coast across the North Sea from Holland. If everything went according to plan we'd be taken off again the following night."

"And if not?" Neumann said.

"You'd be dead, naturally, so it wouldn't matter." He looked around the room. "Anything else?"

"Can we be told the purpose of the mission, Herr Oberst?" Altmann asked.

"The same sort of thing Skorzeny and those lads of the Paratroop School Battalion pulled at Gran Sasso. That's all I can say."

"Well, it's enough for me." Brandt glared around the room. "If we go, we might die, if we stay here we die for certain. If you go—we go."

"I agree," Ritter Neumann echoed and snapped to attention.

Every man in the room followed suit. Steiner stood there for a long moment, staring into some dark, secret place in his own mind and then he nodded. "So be it. Did I hear someone mention White Horse Whisky?"

The group broke for the bar and Altmann sat down and started to play *We march against England* on the piano. Someone threw his cap at him and Sturm called, "You can stick that load of old crap. Let's have something worth listening to."

The door opened and Ilse Neuhoff appeared. "Can I come in now?"

There was a roar from the whole group. In a moment she was lifted up on to the bar. "A song!" they chorused.

"All right," she said, laughing. "What do you want?"

Steiner got in before everyone, his voice sharp and quick. *"Alles ist verrückt."*

There was a sudden silence. She looked down at him, face pale. "You're sure?"

"Highly appropriate," he said. "Believe me."

Hans Altmann moved into the opening chords, giving it everything he had and Ilse paraded slowly up and down the bar, her hands on her hips, as she sang that strange melancholy song known to every man who had ever served in the Winter War.

What are we doing here? What is it all about? Alles ist verriükt. Everything's crazy. Everything's gone to hell.

There were tears in her eyes now. She spread her arms wide as if she would embrace them all and suddenly everyone was singing, slow and deep, looking up at her, Steiner, Ritter, all of them—even Radl.

Devlin looked from one face to the other in bewilderment then turned, pulled open the door and lurched outside. "Am I crazy or are they?" he whispered.

It was dark on the terrace because of the blackout, but Radl and Steiner went out there to smoke a cigar after dinner, more for privacy than anything else. Through the thick curtains that covered the French windows they could hear Liam Devlin's voice, Ilse Neuhoff and her husband laughing gaily.

"A man of considerable charm," Steiner said.

Radl nodded. "He has other qualities also. Many more like him and the British would have thankfully got out of Ireland years ago. You had a mutually profitable meeting after I left you this afternoon, I trust?"

"I think that you could say that we understand each other," Steiner said, "and we examined the map together very closely. It will be of great assistance to have him as an advance party, believe me."

"Anything else I should know?"

"Yes, young Werner Briegel's actually been to that area."

"Briegel?" Radl said. "Who's he?"

"Lance-corporal. Twenty-one. Three years service. Comes from a place called Barth on the Baltic. He says some of that coastline is rather similar to Norfolk. Enormous lonely beaches, sand dunes and lots of birds."

"Birds?" Radl said.

Steiner smiled through the darkness. "I should explain that birds are the passion of young Werner's life. Once, near Leningrad, we were saved from a partisan ambush because they disturbed a huge flock of starlings. Werner and I were temporarily caught in the open, under fire and flat on our faces in the mud. He filled in the time by giving me chapter and verse on how the starlings were probably migrating to England for the winter."

"Fascinating," Radl said ironically.

"Oh, you may laugh, but it passed a nasty thirty minutes rather quickly for us. That's what took him and his father to North Norfolk in nineteen-thirty-seven, by the way. The birds. Apparently the whole coast is famous for them."

"Ah, well," Radl said. "Each one to his own taste. What about this question of who speaks English? Did you get that sorted out?"

"Lieutenant Neumann, Sergeant Altmann and young Briegel all speak good English, but with accents, naturally. No hope of passing for natives. Of the rest, Brandt and Klugl both speak the broken variety. Enough to get by. Brandt, by the way, was a deck hand on cargo boats as a youngster. Hamburg to Hull."

Radl nodded. "It could be worse. Tell me, has Neuhoff questioned you at all?"

"No, but he's obviously very curious. And poor Ilse is beside herself with worry. I'll have to make sure she doesn't try to take the whole thing up with Ribbentrop in a misguided attempt to save me from she knows not what."

"Good," Radl said. "You sit tight then and wait. You'll have movement orders within a week to ten days, depending on how quickly I can find a suitable base in Holland. Devlin, as you know, will probably go over in about a week. I think we'd better go in now."

Steiner put a hand on his arm. "And my father?"

Radl said, "I would be dishonest if I led you to believe I have any influence in the matter. Himmler is personally responsible. All that I can do—and I will certainly do this—is make it plain to him how co-operative you are being."

"And do you honestly think that will be enough?"

"Do you?" Radl said.

Steiner's laugh had no mirth in it at all. "He has no conception of honour."

It seemed a curiously old-fashioned remark, and Radl was intrigued. "And you?" he said. "You have?"

"Perhaps not. Perhaps it's too fancy a word for what I mean. Simple things like giving your word and keeping it, standing by friends whatever comes. Does the sum of these things total honour?"

"I don't know, my friend," Radl said. "All I can confirm with any certainty is the undoubted fact that you are too good for the Reichs-führer's world, believe me." He put an arm around Steiner's shoulders. "And now, we'd really better go in."

Ilse, Colonel Neuhoff and Devlin were seated at a small round table by the fire and she was busy laying out a Celtic Circle from the Tarot pack in her left hand.

"Go on, amaze me," Devlin was saying.

"You mean you are not a believer, Mr. Devlin?" she asked him.

"A decent Catholic lad like me? Proud product of the best the Jesuits could afford, Frau Neuhoff?" He grinned. "Now what do you think?"

"That you are an intensely superstitious man, Mr. Devlin." His smile slipped a little. "You see," she went on, "I am what is known as a sensitive. The cards are not important. They are a tool only."

"Go on then."

"Very well, your future on one card, Mr. Devlin. The seventh I come to."

She counted them out quickly and turned the seventh card over. It was a skeleton carrying a scythe and the card was upside down.

"Isn't he the cheerful one?" Devlin remarked, trying to sound unconcerned and failing.

"Yes, Death," she said, "but reversed it doesn't mean what you imagine." She stared down at the card for a full half-minute and then said very quickly, "You will live long, Mr. Devlin. Soon for you begins a lengthy period of inertia, of stagnation even and then, in the closing years of your life, revolution, perhaps assassination." She looked up calmly. "Does that satisfy you?"

"The long life bit does," Devlin said cheerfully. "I'll take my chance on the rest."

"May I join in, Frau Neuhoff," Radl said.

"If you like."

She counted out the cards. This time the seventh was the Star reversed. She looked at it for another long moment. "Your health is not good, Herr Oberst."

"That's true," Radl said.

She looked up and said simply, "I think you know what is here?"

"Thank you, I believe I do," he said, smiling calmly.

There was a slightly uncomfortable atmosphere then, as if a sudden chill had fallen and Steiner said, "All right, Ilse, what about me?"

She reached for the cards as if to gather them up. "No, not now, Kurt, I think we've had enough for one night."

"Nonsense," he said. "I insist." He picked up the cards. "There, I hand you the pack with my left hand, isn't that right?"

Very hesitantly she took it, looked at him in mute appeal, then started to count. She turned the seventh card over quickly, long enough to glance at it herself and put it back on top of the pack. "Lucky in cards as well, it seems, Kurt. You drew Strength. Considerable good fortune, a triumph in adversity, sudden success." She smiled brightly. "And now, if you gentlemen will excuse me, I'll see to the coffee," and she walked out of the room.

Steiner reached down and turned the card over. It was The Hanged Man. He sighed heavily. "Women," he said, "can be very silly at times. Is it not so, gentlemen?"

There was fog in the morning. Neuhoff had Radl wakened just after dawn and broke the bad news to him over coffee.

"A regular problem here, I'm afraid," he said. "But there it is and the general forecast is lousy. Not a hope of anything getting off the ground here before evening. Can you wait that long?"

Radl shook his head. "I have to be in Paris by this evening and to do that it's essential that I catch the transport leaving Jersey at eleven to make the necessary connection in Brittany. What else can you offer?"

"I could arrange passage by E-boat if you insist," Neuhoff told him. "Something of an experience, I warn you, and rather hazardous. We've more trouble with the Royal Navy than we do with the RAF in this area. But it would be essential to leave without delay if you are to make St. Helier in time."

"Excellent," Radl said. "Please make all necessary arrangements at once and I'll rouse Devlin."

Neuhoff drove them down to the harbour himself in his staff car shortly after seven, Devlin huddled in the rear seat showing every symptom of a king-size hangover. The E-boat waited at the lower jetty. When they went down the steps they found Steiner in sea boots and reefer jacket, leaning on the rail talking to a young bearded naval lieutenant in heavy sweater and salt-stained cap.

He turned to greet them. "A nice morning for it. I've just been making sure Koenig realizes he's carrying precious cargo."

The lieutenant saluted. "Herr Oberst."

Devlin, the picture of misery, stood with his hands pushed deep into his pockets. "Not too well this morning, Mr. Devlin?" Steiner enquired.

Devlin moaned. "Wine is a mocker; strong drink is raging."

Steiner said, "You won't be wanting this then?" He held up a bottle. "Brandt found another Bushmills."

Devlin relieved him of it instantly. "I wouldn't dream of allowing it to do to anyone else what it's done to me." He shook hands. "Let's hope that when you're coming down I'll be looking up," and he clambered over the rail and sat in the stern.

Radl shook hands with Neuhoff, then turned to Steiner. "You'll hear from me soon. As for the other matter, I'll do everything I can."

Steiner said nothing. Did not even attempt to shake hands and Radl hesitated, then scrambled over the rail. Koenig issued orders crisply, leaning out of an open window in the wheelhouse. The lines were cast off and the E-boat slipped away into the mist of the harbour.

They rounded the end of the breakwater and picked up speed. Radl looked about him with interest. The crew were a rough-looking lot, half of them bearded, and all attired in either Guernseys or thick fishermen's sweaters, denim pants and sea boots. In fact, there was little of the Navy about them at all and the craft itself, festooned with strange aerials, was like no E-boat he had ever seen before now that he examined it thoroughly.

When he went on to the bridge he found Koenig leaning over the chart table, a large black-bearded seaman at the wheel who wore a faded reefer jacket that carried a chief petty officer's rank badges. A cigar jutted from between his teeth, something else which, it occurred to Radl, did not seem very naval.

Koenig saluted decently enough. "Ah, there you are, Herr Oberst. Everything all right?"

"I hope so." Radl leaned over the chart table. "How far is it?"

"About fifty miles."

"Will you get us there on time?"

Koenig glanced at his watch. "I estimate we'll arrive at St. Helier just before ten, Herr Oberst, as long as the Royal Navy doesn't get in the way."

Radl looked out of the window. "Your crew, Lieutenant, do they always dress like fishermen? I understood the E-boats to be the pride of the Navy."

Koenig smiled. "But this isn't an E-boat, Herr Oberst. Only classed as one."

"Then what in the hell is it?" Radl demanded in bewilderment.

"Actually we're not too sure, are we, Muller?" The petty officer grinned and Koenig said, "A motor gun boat, as you can see, Herr Oberst, constructed in Britain for the Turks and commandeered by the Royal Navy."

"What's the story?"

"Ran aground on a sandbank on an ebb tide near Morlaix in Brittany. Her captain couldn't scuttle her, so he fired a demolition charge before abandoning her."

"And?"

"It didn't go off and before he could get back on board to rectify the error an E-boat turned up and grabbed him and his crew."

"Poor devil," Radl said. "I almost feel sorry for him."

"But the best is yet to come, Herr Oberst," Koenig told him. "As the captain's last message was that he was abandoning his ship and blowing her up, the British Admiralty naturally assumed that he had succeeded."

"Which leaves you free to make the run between the islands in what is to all intents and purposes a Royal Navy boat? I see now."

"Exactly. You were looking at the jack staff earlier and were no doubt puzzled to find that it is the White Ensign of the Royal Navy we keep ready to unfurl."

"And it's saved you on occasion?"

"Many times. We hoist the White Ensign, make a courtesy signal and move on. No trouble at all."

Radl was aware of that cold finger of excitement moving inside him again. "Tell me about the boat," he said. "How fast is she?"

"Top speed was originally twenty-five knots, but the Navy yard at Brest did enough work on her to bring that to thirty. Still not up to an E-boat, of course, but not bad. A hundred and seventeen feet long and as for armaments, a six-pounder, a two-pounder, two twin point five machine-guns, twin twenty millimetre antiaircraft cannon."

"Fine," Radl cut him off. "A gun boat indeed. What about range?"

"A thousand miles at twenty-one knots. Of course, with the silencers on, she burns up much more fuel."

"And what about that lot?" Radl pointed out to the aerials which festooned her.

"Navigational some of them. The rest are S-phone aerials. It's a micro-wave wireless set for two-way voice communication between a moving ship and an agent on land. Far better than anything we've got. Obviously used by agents to talk them in before a landing. I'm sick of singing its praises at Naval Headquarters in Jersey. Nobody takes the slightest interest. No wonder we're . . . ''

He stopped himself just in time. Radl glanced at him and said calmly, "At what range does this remarkable gadget function?''

"Up to fifteen miles on a good day; for reliability I'd only claim half that distance, but at that range it's as good as a telephone call.''

Radl stood there for a long moment, thinking about it all and then he nodded abruptly. "Thank you, Koenig,'' he said and went out.

He found Devlin in Koenig's cabin, flat on his back, eyes closed, hands folded over the bottle of Bushmills. Radl frowned, annoyance and even a certain alarm stirring inside him and then saw that the seal on the bottle was unbroken.

"It's all right, Colonel dear,'' Devlin said without apparently opening his eyes. "The Devil hasn't got me by the big toe yet.''

"Did you bring my briefcase with you?''

Devlin squirmed to pull it from underneath him. "Guarding it with my life.''

"Good.'' Radl moved back to the door. "They've got a wireless in the wheelhouse that I'd like you to look at before we land.''

"Wireless?'' Devlin grunted.

"Oh, never mind,'' Radl said. "I'll explain later.''

When he went back to the bridge Koenig was seated at the chart table in a swivel chair drinking coffee from a tin mug. Muller still had the wheel.

Koenig got up, obviously surprised, and Radl said, "The officer commanding naval forces in Jersey—what's his name?''

"Kapitän zur See Hans Olbricht.''

"I see—can you get us to St. Helier half an hour earlier than your estimated time of arrival?''

Koenig glanced dubiously at Muller. "I'm not sure, Herr Oberst. We could try. Is it essential?''

"Absolutely. I must have time to see Olbricht to arrange your transfer.''

Koenig looked at him in astonishment. "Transfer, Herr Oberst? To which command?''

"My command.'' Radl took the manilla envelope from his pocket and produced the Führer Directive. "Read that.''

He turned away impatiently and lit a cigarette. When he turned again, Koenig's eyes were wide. "My God!'' he whispered.

"I hardly think He enters into the matter.'' Radl took the letter from him and replaced it in the envelope. He nodded at Muller. "This big ox is to be trusted?''

"To the death, Herr Oberst.''

"Good,'' Radl said. "For a day or two you'll stay in Jersey until orders are finalized, then I want you to make your way along the coast to Boulogne where you will await my instructions. Any problems in getting there?''

Koenig shook his head. ''None that I can see. An easy enough trip for a boat like this staying inshore.'' He hesitated. ''And afterwards, Herr Oberst?''

''Oh, somewhere on the North Dutch coast near Den Helder. I haven't found a suitable place yet. Do you know it?''

It was Muller who cleared his throat and said, ''Begging the Herr Oberst's pardon, but I know that coast like the back of my hand. I used to be first mate on a Dutch salvage tug out of Rotterdam.''

''Excellent. Excellent.''

He left them, then went and stood in the prow beside the six-pounder smoking a cigarette. ''It marches,'' he said softly. ''It marches,'' and his stomach was hollow with excitement.

6

JUST BEFORE NOON ON WEDNESDAY 6 October Joanna Grey took possession of a large envelope deposited inside a copy of *The Times* left on a certain bench in Green Park by her usual contact at the Spanish Embassy.

Once in possession of the package she went straight back to Kings Cross station and caught the first express north, changing at Peterborough to a local train for King's Lynn where she had left her car, taking advantage of the surplus she had managed to accumulate from the petrol allocation given to her for WVS duties.

When she turned into the yard at the back of Park Cottage it was almost six o'clock and she was dog tired. She let herself in through the kitchen where she was greeted enthusiastically by Patch. He trailed at her heels when she went into the sitting-room and poured herself a large Scotch—of which, thanks to Sir Henry Willoughby, she had a plentiful supply. Then she climbed the stairs to the small study next to her bedroom.

The panelling was Jacobean and the invisible door in the corner was none of her doing, but part of the original, a common device of the period and designed to resemble a section of panelling. She took a key from a chain around her neck and unlocked the door. A short wooden stairway gave access to a cubby-hole loft under the roof. Here she had a radio receiver and transmitter. She sat down at an old deal table, opened a drawer in it, pushing a loaded Luger to one side and rummaged for a pencil, then took out her code books and got to work.

When she sat back an hour later her face was pinched with excitement. "My God!" she said to herself in Afrikaans. "They meant it—they actually meant it."

Then she took a deep breath, pulled herself together and went back downstairs. Patch was waiting patiently at the door and followed at her heels all the way to the sitting-room where she picked up the telephone and dialled the number of Studley Grange. Sir Henry Willoughby himself answered.

She said, "Henry—it's Joanna Grey."

His voice warmed immediately. "Hello there, my dear. I hope you're not ringing to say you won't be coming over for bridge or something. You hadn't forgotten? Eight-thirty?"

She had, but that didn't matter. She said, "Of course not, Henry. It's just that I've got a little favour to ask and I wanted to speak to you privately about it."

His voice deepened. "Fire away, old girl. Anything I can do."

"Well, I've heard from some Irish friends of my late husband and they've asked me to try and do something for their nephew. In fact, they're sending him over. He'll be arriving in the next few days."

"Do what exactly?"

"His name is Devlin—Liam Devlin, and the thing is, Henry, the poor man was very badly wounded serving with the British Army in France. He received a medical discharge and he's been convalescing for almost a year. He's quite fit now though and ready for work, but it needs to be the outdoor variety."

"And you thought I might be able to fix him up?" said Sir Henry jovially. "No difficulty there, old girl. You know what it's like getting any kind of workers for the estate these days."

"He wouldn't be able to do much at first," she said. "Actually I was wondering about the marsh warden's job at Hobs End. That's been vacant since young Tom King went off to the Army two years ago, hasn't it, and there's the house standing empty? It would be good to have somebody in. It's getting very run down."

"I'll tell you what, Joanna, I think you might have something there. We'll go into the whole thing in depth. No sense in discussing it over bridge with other people there. Are you free tomorrow afternoon?"

"Of course," she said. "You know, it's so good of you to help in this way, Henry. I always seem to be bothering you with my problems these days.''

"Nonsense," he told her sternly. "That's what I'm here for. Woman needs a man to smooth over the rough spots for her." His voice was shaking slightly.

"I'd better go now," she said. "I'll see you soon."

"Goodbye, my dear."

She put down the receiver and patted Patch on the head and he trailed along at her heels when she went back upstairs. She sat at the transmitter and made the briefest of signals on the frequency of the Dutch beacon for onward transmission to Berlin. An acknowledgement that her instructions had been safely received and a given code word that meant that the business of Devlin's employment had been taken care of.

In Berlin it was raining, black, cold rain drifting across the city pushed by a wind so bitter that it must have come all the way from the Urals. In the ante-room outside Himmler's office at Prinz Albrechtstrasse, Max Radl and Devlin sat facing each other, as they had been sitting for more than an hour now.

"What in the hell goes on?" Devlin said. "Does he want to see us or doesn't he?"

"Why don't you knock and ask?" Radl suggested.

Just then the outer door opened and Rossman came in, beating rain from his slouch hat, his coat dripping water. He smiled brightly. "Still here, you two?"

Devlin said to Radl, "He's got the great wit to him, that one, isn't it a fact?"

Rossman knocked at the door and went in. He didn't bother closing it. "I've got him, Herr Reichsführer."

"Good," they heard Himmler say. "Now I'll see Radl and this Irish fellow."

"What in the hell is this?" Devlin muttered. "A command performance?"

"Watch your tongue," Radl said, "and let me do the talking."

He led the way into the room, Devlin at his heels, and Rossman closed the door behind them. Everything was exactly the same as on that first night. The room in half-darkness, the open fire flickering, Himmler seated behind the desk.

The Reichsführer said, "You've done well, Radl. I'm more than pleased with the way things are progressing. And this is Herr Devlin?"

"As ever was," Devlin said cheerfully. "Just a poor, old Irish peasant, straight out of the bog, that's me, your honour."

Himmler frowned in puzzlement. "What on earth is the man talking about?" he demanded of Radl.

"The Irish, Herr Reichsführer, are not as other people," Radl said weakly.

"It's the rain," Devlin told him.

Himmler stared at him in astonishment, then turned to Radl. "You are certain he is the man for this?"

"Perfectly."

"And when does he go?"

"On Sunday."

"And your other arrangements? They are proceeding satisfactorily?"

"So far. My trip to Alderney I combined with Abwehr business in Paris and I have perfectly legal reasons for visiting Amsterdam next week. The Admiral knows nothing. He has been preoccupied with other matters."

"Good." Himmler sat staring into space, obviously thinking about something.

"Was there anything else, Herr Reichsführer?" Radl asked as Devlin stirred impatiently.

"Yes, I brought you here for two reasons tonight. In the first place I wanted to see Herr Devlin for myself. But secondly, there is the question of the composition of Steiner's assault group."

"Maybe I should leave," Devlin suggested.

"Nonsense," Himmler said brusquely. "I would be obliged if you would simply sit in the corner and listen. Or are the Irish incapable of such a feat?"

"Oh, it's been known," Devlin said. "But not often."

He went and sat by the fire, took out a cigarette and lit it. Himmler glared at him, seemed about to speak and obviously thought better of it. He turned back to Radl.

"You were saying, Herr Reichsführer?"

"Yes, there seems to me one weakness in the composition of Steiner's group. Four or five of the men speak English to some degree, but only Steiner can pass as a native. This isn't good enough. In my opinion he needs the backing of someone of similar ability."

"But people with that sort of ability are rather thin on the ground."

"I think I have a solution for you," Himmler said. "There is a man called Amery—John Amery. Son of a famous English politician. He ran guns for Franco. Hates the Bolsheviks. He's been working for us for some time now."

"Is he of any use?"

"I doubt it, but he came up with the idea of founding what he called the British Legion of St. George. The idea was to recruit Englishmen from the prisoner of war camps, mainly to fight in the Eastern Front."

"Did he get any takers?"

"A few—not many and mostly rogues. Amery has nothing to do with it now. For a while the Wehrmacht was responsible for the unit, but now the SS has taken over."

"These volunteers—are there many?"

"Fifty or sixty as I last heard. They now rejoice in the name British Free Corps." Himmler opened a file in front of him and took out a record card. "Such people do have their uses on occasion. This man, for instance, Harvey Preston. When captured in Belgium he was wearing the uniform of a captain in the Coldstream Guards, and having what I am informed are the voice and mannerisms of the English aristocrat, no one doubted him for some time."

"And he was not what he seemed?"

"Judge for yourself."

Radl examined the card. Harvey Preston had been born in Harrogate, Yorkshire in 1916, the son of a railway porter. He had left home at fourteen to work as a prop boy with a touring variety company. At eighteen he was acting in repertory in Southport. In 1937 he was sentenced to two years imprisonment at Winchester Assizes on four charges of fraud.

Discharged in January, 1939, he was arrested a month later and sentenced to a further nine months on a charge of impersonating an RAF officer and obtaining money by false pretenses. The judge had suspended the sentence on condition that Preston joined the forces. He had gone to France as an orderly room clerk with an RASC transport company and, when captured, held the rank of acting corporal.

His prison camp record was bad or good according to which side you were on, for he had informed on no fewer than five separate escape attempts. On the last occasion this had become known to his comrades and if he had not volunteered to serve in the Free Corps, he would in any case have had to be moved for reasons of his own safety.

Radl walked across to Devlin and handed him the card, then turned to Himmler. "And you want Steiner to take this . . . this . . . "

"Rogue," Himmler said, "who is quite expendable, but who simulates the English aristocrat quite well? He really does have presence, Radl. The sort of man to whom policemen touch their helmets the moment he opens his mouth. I've always understood that the English working classes know an officer and a gentleman when they see one, and Preston should do very well."

"But Steiner and his men, Herr Reichsführer, are soldiers—real soldiers. You know their record. Can you see such a man fitting in? Taking orders?"

"He will do as he is told," Himmler said. "That goes without question. We'll have him in, shall we?"

He pressed the buzzer and a moment later, Rossman appeared in the doorway. "I'll see Preston now." Rossman went out, leaving the door open, and a moment later Preston entered the room, closed the door behind him and gave the Nazi Party salute.

He was at that time twenty-seven years of age, a tall, handsome man in a beautifully-tailored uniform of field gray. It was the uniform particularly which fascinated Radl. He had the death's head badge of the SS in his peaked cap and collar patches depicting the three leopards. Under the eagle on his left sleeve was a Union Jack shield and a black and silver cuff-title carried the legend in Gothic lettering, *Britisches Freikorps*.

"Very pretty," Devlin said, but so softly that only Radl heard.

Himmler made the introductions. "Untersturmführer Preston—Colonel Radl of the Abwehr and Herr Devlin. You will be familiar with the role each of these gentlemen plays in the affair at hand from the documents I gave you to study earlier today."

Preston half-turned to Radl, inclined his head and clicked his heels. Very formal, very military, just like someone playing a Prussian officer in a play.

"So," Himmler said. "You have had ample opportunity to consider this matter. You understand what is required of you?"

Preston said carefully, "Do I take it that Colonel Radl is looking for volunteers for this mission?" His German was good, although the accent could have been improved on.

Himmler removed his pince-nez, stroked the bridge of his nose gently with a forefinger and replaced them with great care. It was a gesture somehow infinitely sinister. His voice, when he spoke, was like dry leaves brushed by the wind. "What exactly are you trying to say, Untersturmführer?"

"It's just that I find myself in rather a difficulty here. As the Reichsführer knows, members of the British Free Corps were given a guarantee that at no time would they have to wage war or take part in any armed act against Britain or the Crown or indeed to support any act detrimental to the interests of the British people."

Radl said, "Perhaps this gentleman would be happier serving on the Eastern Front, Herr Reichsführer? Army Group South, under Field Marshal von Manstein. Plenty of hot spots there for those who crave real action."

Preston, realizing that he had made a very bad mistake, hastily tried to make amends. "I can assure you, Herr Reichsführer, that . . . "

Himmler didn't give him a chance. "You talk of volunteering, where I see only an act of sacred duty. An opportunity to serve the Führer and the Reich."

Preston snapped to attention. It was an excellent performance and

Devlin, for one, was thoroughly enjoying himself. "Of course, Herr Reichsführer It is my total aim."

"I am right, am I not, in assuming that you have taken an oath to this effect? A holy oath?"

"Yes, Herr Reichsführer."

"Then nothing more need be said. You will from this moment consider yourself to be under the orders of Colonel Radl here."

"As you say, Herr Reichsführer."

"Colonel Radl, I'd like to have a word with you in private." Himmler glanced at Devlin. "Herr Devlin, if you would be kind enough to wait in the ante-room with Untersturmführer Preston."

Preston gave him a crisp Heil Hitler, turned on heel with a precision that would not have disgraced the Grenadier Guards, and went out. Devlin followed, closing the door behind them.

There was no sign of Rossman and Preston kicked the side of one of the armchairs viciously and threw his cap down on the table. He was white with anger and when he produced ·a silver case and extracted a cigarette, his hand trembled slightly.

Devlin strolled across and helped himself to a cigarette before Preston could close the case. He grinned. "By God, the old bugger's got you by the balls."

He had spoken in English and Preston, glaring at him, replied in the same language. "What in the hell do you mean?"

"Come on, son," Devlin said. "I've heard of your little lot. Legion of St. George; British Free Corps. How was it they bought you? Unlimited booze and as many women as you can handle, if you're not too choosy, that is. Now it's all got to be paid for."

At an inch above six feet, Preston was able to look down with some contempt at the Irishman. His left nostril curled. "My God, the people one has to deal with—straight out of the bogs, too, from the smell. Now go away and try playing nasty little Irishman elsewhere, there's a good chap, or I might have to chastise you."

Devlin, in thc act of putting a match to his cigarette, kicked Preston with some precision under the right kneecap.

In the office Radl had just come to the end of a progress report. "Excellent," Himmler said, "and the Irishman leaves on Sunday?"

"By Dornier from a Luftwaffe base outside Brest—Laville. A northwesterly course from there will take them to Ireland without the necessity of passing over English soil. At twenty-five thousand feet for most of the way they should have no trouble."

"And the Irish Air Force?"

"What air force, Herr Reichsführer?"

"I see." Himmler closed the file. "So, things seem to be really moving at last. I'm very pleased with you, Radl. Continue to keep me informed."

He picked up his pen in a dismissive gesture and Radl said, "There is one other matter."

Himmler looked up. "And what is that?"

"Major-General Steiner."

Himmler laid down his pen. "What about him?"

Radl didn't know how to put it, but he had to make the point somehow. He owed it to Steiner. In fact, considering the circumstances, the intensity with which he wanted to keep that promise surprised him. "It was the Reichsführer himself who suggested I make it clear to Colonel Steiner that his conduct in this affair could have a significant effect on his father's case."

"That is so," Himmler said calmly. "But what is the problem?"

"I promised Colonel Steiner, Herr Reichsführer," Radl said lamely. "Gave him an assurance that . . . that . . . "

"Which you had no authority to offer," Himmler said. "However, under the circumstances, you may give Steiner that assurance in my name." He picked up his pen again. "You may go now and tell Preston to remain. I want another word with him. I'll have him report to you tomorrow."

When Radl went out into the ante-room, Devlin was standing at the window peering through a chink in the curtains and Preston was sitting in one of the armchairs. "Raining cats and dogs out there," he said cheerfully. "Still, it might keep the RAF at home for a change. Are we going?"

Radl nodded and said to Preston, "You stay. He wants you. And don't come to Abwehr Headquarters tomorrow. I'll get in touch with you."

Preston was on his feet, very military again, arm raised. "Very well, Herr Oberst. Heil Hitler!"

Radl and Devlin moved to the door and as they went out, the Irishman raised a thumb and grinned amiably. "Up the Republic, me old son!"

Preston dropped his arm and swore viciously. Devlin closed the door and followed Radl down the stairs. "Where in the hell did they find him? Himmler must have lost his wits entirely."

"God knows," Radl said as they paused beside the SS guards in the main entrance to turn up their collars against the heavy rain. "There is some merit in the idea of another officer who is obviously English, but this Preston." He shook his head. "A badly flawed man. Second-rate actor, petty criminal. A man who has spent most of his life living some sort of private fantasy."

"And we're stuck with him," Devlin said. "I wonder what Steiner will make of it?"

They ran through the rain as Radl's staff car approached and settled themselves in the back. "Steiner will cope," Radl said. "Men like Steiner always do. But now to business. We fly to Paris tomorrow afternoon."

"Then what?"

"I've important business in Holland. As I told you, the entire operation will be based on Landsvoort, which is the right kind of end-of-the-world spot. During the operational period I shall be there myself, so, my friend, if you make a transmission, you'll know who is on the other end. As I was saying, I'll leave you in Paris when I fly to Amsterdam. You, in your turn, will be ferried down to the airfield at Laville near Brest. You take off at ten o'clock on Sunday night."

"Will you be there?" Devlin asked.

"I'll try, but it may not be possible."

They arrived at Tirpitz Ufer a moment later and hurried through the rain to the entrance just as Hofer, in cap and heavy greatcoat, was emerging. He saluted and Radl said, "Going off duty, Karl? Anything for me?"

"Yes, Herr Oberst, a signal from Mrs. Grey."

Radl was filled with excitement. "What is it, man, what does she say?"

"Message received and understood, Herr Oberst and the question of Herr Devlin's employment has been taken care of."

Radl turned triumphantly to Devlin, rain dripping from the peak of his mountain cap. "And what do you have to say to that, my friend?"

"Up the Republic," Devlin said morosely. "Right up! Is that patriotic enough for you? If so, could I go in now and have a drink?"

When the office door clicked open Preston was sitting in the corner reading an English-language edition of *Signal*. He glanced up and finding Himmler there watching him, jumped to his feet. "Your pardon, Herr Reichsführer."

"For what?" Himmler said. "Come with me. I want to show you something."

Puzzled and also faintly alarmed, Preston followed him downstairs and along the ground floor corridor to the iron door guarded by two Gestapo men. One of them got the door open, they sprang to attention, Himmler nodded and started down the steps.

The white-painted corridor seemed quiet enough and then Preston became aware of a dull, rhythmic slapping, strangely remote, as if it came from a great distance. Himmler paused outside a cell door and opened a metal gate. There was a small window of armoured glass.

A gray-haired man of sixty or so in a tattered shirt and military breeches was sprawled across a bench while a couple of heavily muscled SS men beat him systematically across the back and buttocks with rubber truncheons. Rossman stood watching, smoking a cigarette, his shirt sleeves rolled up.

"I detest this sort of mindless violence," Himmler said. "Don't you, Herr Untersturmführer?"

Preston's mouth had gone dry and his stomach heaved. "Yes, Herr Reichsführer. Terrible."

"If only these fools would listen. A nasty business, but how else can one deal with treason against the State? The Reich and the Führer demand an absolute and unquestioning loyalty and those who give less than this must accept the consequences. You understand me?"

Which Preston did—perfectly. And when the Reichsführer turned and went back up the stairs he stumbled after him, a handkerchief in his mouth in an attempt to stop himself from being sick.

In the darkness of his cell below, Major-General of Artillery Karl Steiner crawled into a corner and crouched there, arms folded as if to stop himself from falling apart. "Not one word," he said softly through swollen lips. "Not one word—I swear it."

⚔

At precisely 02.20 hours on the morning of Saturday 9 October Captain Peter Gericke of Night Fighter Group 7, operating out of Grandjeim on the Dutch coast, made his thirty-eighth confirmed kill. He was flying a Junkers 88 in heavy cloud, one of those apparently clumsy, black, twin-engined planes festooned with strange radar aerials, that had proved so devastating in their attacks on RAF bombing groups engaged on night raids over Europe.

Not that Gericke had had any luck earlier that night. A blocked fuel pipe in the port engine had kept him grounded for thirty minutes while the rest of the Staffel had taken off to pounce upon a large force of British bombers returning home across the Dutch coast after a raid on Hanover.

By the time Gericke reached the area most of his comrades had turned for home. And yet there were always stragglers, so he remained on patrol for a while longer.

Gericke was twenty-three years of age. A handsome, rather saturnine young man whose dark eyes seemed full of impatience, as if life itself were too slow for him. Just now he was whistling softly between his teeth the first movement of the Pastoral Symphony.

Behind him, Haupt, the radar operator, huddled over the Lichtenstein set gave an excited gasp. "I've got one."

In the same moment base took over smoothly and the familiar voice of Major Hans Berger, ground controller of NJG7, crackled over Gericke's headphones. "Wanderer Four, this is Black Knight. I have a Kurier for you. Are you receiving?"

"Loud and clear," Gericke told him.

"Steer nought-eight-seven degrees. Target range ten kilometres."

The Junkers burst out of cloud cover only seconds later and Bohmler, the observer, touched Gericke's arm. Gericke saw his prey instantly, a Lancaster bomber limping home in bright moonlight, a feathered plume of smoke drifting from the port outer motor.

"Black Knight, this is Wanderer Four," Gericke said. "I have visual sighting and require no further assistance."

He slipped back into the clouds, descended five hundred feet then banked steeply to port, emerging a couple of miles to the rear and below the crippled Lancaster. It was a sitting target, drifting above them like a gray ghost, that plume of smoke trailing gently.

During the second half of 1943, many German night fighters began operating with a secret weapon that was known as *Schraege Musik*, a pair of twenty millimetre cannon mounted in the fuselage and arranged to fire upwards at an angle of between ten and twenty degrees. This weapon enabled night fighters to attack from below, from which position the bomber presented an enormous target and was virtually blind. As tracer rounds were not used, scores of bombers were brought down without their crews even knowing what hit them.

So it was now. For a split second, Gericke was on target, then as he turned away to port, the Lancaster banked steeply and plunged towards the sea three thousand feet below. There was one parachute, then another. A moment later, the plane itself exploded in a brilliant ball of orange fire. Fuselage dropped down towards the sea, one of the parachutes ignited and flared briefly.

"Dear God in heaven!" Bohmler said in horror.

"What God?" Gericke demanded savagely. "Now send base a fix on that poor sod down there so someone can pick him up and let's go home."

When Gericke and his two crewmen reported to the Intelligence Room in the Operations building it was empty except for Major Adler, the senior Intelligence officer, a jovial fifty-year-old with the slightly frozen face of someone who had been badly burned. He had actually flown during the First War in von Richthofen's Staffel and wore the Blue Max at his throat.

"Ah, there you are, Peter," he said. "Better late than never. Your kill's been confirmed by radio from an E-boat in the area."

"What about the man who got clear?" Gericke demanded. "Have they found him?"

"Not yet, but they're searching. There's an air-sea rescue launch in the area, too."

He pushed a sandalwood box across his desk. It contained very long, pencil-slim Dutch cheroots. Gericke took one.

Adler said, "You seem concerned, Peter. I had never imagined you a humanitarian."

"I'm not," Gericke told him bluntly as he put a match to his cheroot, "but tomorrow night that could be me. I like to think those air-sea rescue bastards are on their toes."

As he turned away, Adler said, "Prager wants to see you."

Lieutenant-Colonel Otto Prager was Gruppenkommandeur of Grandjeim, responsible for three Staffeln including Gericke's. He was a strict disciplinarian and an ardent National Socialist, neither of which qualities Gericke found particularly pleasing. He atoned for these minor irritations by being a first-rate pilot in his own right, totally dedicated to the welfare of the aircrew in his Gruppe.

"What does he want?"

Adler shrugged. "I couldn't say, but when he telephoned, he made it plain it was to be at the earliest possible moment."

"I know," Bohmler said, "Goering's been on the phone. Invited you to Karinhall for the weekend and about time."

It was a well-known fact that when a Luftwaffe pilot was awarded the Knight's Cross, the Reichsmarschall, as an old flyer himself, liked to hand it over in person.

"That'll be the day," Gericke said grudgingly. The fact was that men with fewer kills to their credit than he had received the coveted award. It was a distinctly sore point.

"Never mind, Peter," Adler called as they went out. "Your day will come."

"If I live that long," Gericke said to Bohmler as they paused on the steps of the main entrance to the Operations building. "What about a drink?"

"No, thanks," Bohmler said. "A hot bath and eight hours sleep are my total requirements. I don't approve of it at this time in the morning, you know that, even if we are living backwards way round."

Haupt was already yawning and Gericke said morosely, "Bloody Lutheran. All right, sod both of you."

As he started to walk away, Bohmler called, "Don't forget Prager wants to see you."

"Later," Gericke said. "I'll see him later."

"He's really asking for it," Haupt remarked as they watched him go. "What's got into him lately?"

"Like the rest of us, he lands and takes off too often," Bohmler said.

Gericke walked towards the officers' mess wearily, his flying boots drubbing on the tarmac. He felt unaccountably depressed, stale, somehow at the final end of things. It was strange how he couldn't get that *Tommi*, the sole survivor of the Lancaster, out of his mind. What he needed was a drink. A cup of coffee, very hot, and a large Schnapps or perhaps a Steinhager?

He walked into the ante-room and the first person he saw was Colonel Prager sitting in an easy chair in the far corner with another officer, their heads together as they talked in subdued tones. Gericke hesitated, debating whether to turn tail, for the Gruppenkommandeur was particularly strict on the question of flying clothes being worn in the mess. Prager looked up and saw him.

"There you are, Peter. Come and join us."

He snapped his finger for the mess waiter who hovered nearby and ordered coffee as Gericke approached. He didn't approve of alcohol where pilots were concerned. "Good morning, Herr Oberst," Gericke said brightly, intrigued by the other officer, a lieutenant-colonel of Mountain Troops with a black patch over one eye and a Knight's Cross to go with it.

"Congratulations," Prager said. "I hear you've got another confirmed kill."

"That's right, a Lancaster. One man got clear, I saw his chute open. They're looking for him now."

"Colonel Radl," Prager said.

Radl held out his good hand and Gericke shook it briefly. "Herr Oberst."

Prager was more subdued than he had ever known him. In fact, he was very obviously labouring under some kind of strain, easing himself in the chair as if in acute physical discomfort as the mess waiter brought a tray with a fresh pot of coffee and three cups.

"Leave it, man, leave it!" Prager ordered curtly.

There was a slight strained silence after the waiter had departed. Then the Gruppenkommandeur said abruptly, "The Herr Oberst here is from the Abwehr. With fresh orders for you."

"Fresh orders, Herr Oberst?"

Prager got to his feet. "Colonel Radl can tell you more than I can, but obviously you're being given an extraordinary opportunity to serve the Reich." Gericke stood up and Prager hesitated, then stuck out his hand. "You've done well here, Peter. I'm proud of you. As for the other business—I've recommended you three times now so it's right out of my hands."

"I know, Herr Oberst," Gericke said warmly, "and I'm grateful."

Prager walked away and Gericke sat down. Radl said, "This Lancaster makes thirty-eight confirmed kills, is it not so?''

''You seem remarkably well informed, Herr Oberst,'' Gericke said. ''Will you join me in a drink?''

''Why not? A cognac, I think.''

Gericke called to the waiter and gave the order.

''Thirty-eight confirmed kills and no Knight's Cross,'' Radl commented. ''Isn't that unusual?''

Gericke stirred uncomfortably. ''The way it goes sometimes.''

''I know,'' Radl said. ''There is also the fact to be taken into consideration that during the summer of nineteen-forty, when you were flying ME one-o-nines out of a base near Calais, you told Reichsmarschall Goering who was inspecting your Staffel, that in your opinion, the Spitfire was a better aircraft.'' He smiled gently. ''People of his eminence don't forget junior officers who make remarks like that.''

Gericke said, ''With all due respect, might I point out to the Herr Oberst that in my line of work I can only rely on today because tomorrow I might very possibly be dead, so some idea of what all this is about would be appreciated.''

''It's simple enough,'' Radl said. ''I need a pilot for a rather special operation.''

''*You* need?''

''All right, the Reich,'' Radl told him. ''Does that please you any better?''

''Not particularly.'' Gericke held up his empty Schnapps glass to the waiter and signalled for another. ''As it happens, I'm perfectly happy where I am.''

''A man who consumes Schnapps in such an amount at four o'clock in the morning? I doubt that. In any case, you've no choice in the matter.''

''Is that so?'' Gericke said angrily.

''You are perfectly at liberty to confirm this with the Gruppenkommandeur,'' Radl said.

The waiter brought him the second glass of Schnapps, Gericke poured it down in one quick swallow and made a face. ''God, how I hate that stuff.''

''Then why drink it?'' Radl asked.

''I don't know. Maybe I've been out there in the dark too much or flying too long.'' He smiled sardonically. ''Or perhaps I just need a change, Herr Oberst.''

''I think I may say without any exaggeration that I can certainly offer you that.''

''Fine.'' Gericke swallowed the rest of his coffee. ''What's the next move?''

''I have an appointment in Amsterdam at nine o'clock. Our destination after that is about twenty miles north of the city, on the way to Den Helder.'' He glanced at his watch. ''We'll need to leave here no later than seven-thirty.''

''That gives me time for breakfast and a bath,'' Gericke said. ''I can catch a little sleep in the car if that's all right with you.''

As he got up, the door opened and an orderly came in. He saluted and passed the young captain a signal flimsy. Gericke read it and smiled. ''Something important?'' Radl asked.

''The *Tommi* who parachuted out of that Lancaster I shot down earlier. They've picked him up. A pilot officer navigator.''

''His luck is good,'' Radl commented.

''A good omen,'' Gericke said. ''Let's hope mine is.''

Landsvoort was a desolate little place about twenty miles north of Amsterdam between Schagen and the sea. Gericke slept soundly for the entire journey, only coming awake when Radl shook his arm.

There was an old farmhouse and barn, two hangars roofed with rusting corrugated iron and a single runway of crumbling concrete, grass growing between the cracks. The wire perimeter fence was nothing very special and the steel and wire swing gate, which looked new, was guarded by a sergeant with the distinctive gorget plate of the military police hanging around his neck. He was armed with a Schmeisser machine pistol and held a rather savage-looking Alsatian on the end of a steel chain.

He checked their papers impassively while the dog growled deep in its throat, full of menace. Radl drove on through the gate and pulled up in front of the hangars. ''Well, this is it.''

The landscape was incredibly flat, stretching out towards the distant sand dunes and the North Sea beyond. As Gericke opened the door and got out, rain drifted in off the sea in a fine spray and there was the tang of salt to it. He walked across to the edge of the crumbling runway and kicked with his foot until a piece of concrete broke away.

''It was built by a shipping magnate in Rotterdam for his own use ten or twelve years ago,'' Radl said as he got out of the car to join him. ''What do you think?''

''All we need now are the Wright brothers.'' Gericke looked out towards the sea, shivered and thrust his hands deep into the pockets of his leather coat. ''What a dump—the last place on God's list, I should imagine.''

''Therefore exactly right for our purposes,'' Radl pointed out. ''Now, let's get down to business.''

He led the way across to the first hangar which was guarded by another military policeman complete with Alsatian. Radl nodded and the man pulled back one of the sliding doors.

It was damp and rather cold inside, rain drifting in through a hole in the roof. The twin-engined aircraft which stood there looked lonely and rather forlorn, and very definitely far from home. Gericke prided himself that he had long since got past being surprised at anything in this life, but not that morning.

The aircraft was a Douglas DC3, the famous Dakota, probably one of the most successful general transport planes ever built, as much a workhorse for the Allied Forces during the war as was the Junkers 52 to the German Army. The interesting thing about this one was that it carried Luftwaffe insignia on the wings and a Swastika on the tail.

Peter Gericke loved aeroplanes as some men love horses, with a deep and unswerving passion. He reached up and touched a wing gently and his voice was soft when he said, ''You old beauty.''

''You know this aircraft?'' Radl said.

''Better than any woman.''

''Six months with the Landros Air Freight Company in Brazil from June to November, nineteen-thirty-eight. Nine hundred and thirty flying hours. Quite something for a nineteen-year-old. That must have been hard flying.''

''So that's why I was chosen?''

''All on your records.''

''Where did you get her?''

''RAF Transport Command, dropping supplies to the Dutch Resistance four months ago. One of your night fighter friends got her. Superficial engine damage only. Something to do with the fuel pump, I understand. The observer was too badly wounded to jump so the pilot managed to bring her down in a ploughed field. Unfortunately for him he was next door to an SS barracks. By the time he got his friend out, it was too late to blow her up.''

The door was open and Gericke pulled himself inside. In the cockpit, he sat behind the controls and for a moment he was back in Brazil, green jungle below, the Amazon twisting through it like a great, silver snake from Manaus down to the sea.

Radl took the other seat. He produced a silver case and offered Gericke one of his Russian cigarettes. ''You could fly this thing, then?''

''Where to?''

''Not very far. Across the North Sea to Norfolk. Straight in, straight out.''

''To do what?''

''Drop sixteen paratroopers.''

In his astonishment, Gericke inhaled too deeply and almost choked, the harsh Russian tobacco catching at the back of his throat.

He laughed wildly. "Operation Sealion at last. Don't you think it's a trifle late in the war for the invasion of England?"

"This particular section of the coast has no low level radar cover," Radl said calmly. "No difficulty at all if you go in below six hundred feet. Naturally I'll have the plane cleaned up and the RAF rondels replaced on the wings. If anyone does see you, they see an RAF aircraft presumably going about its lawful business."

"But why?" said Gericke. "What in the hell are they going to do when they get there?"

"None of your affair," Radl said firmly. "You are just a bus driver, my friend."

He got up and went out and Gericke followed him. "Now look here, I think you could do better than that."

Radl walked to the Mercedes without replying. He stood looking out across the airfield to the sea. "Too tough for you?"

"Don't be stupid," Gericke told him angrily. "I just like to know what I'm getting into, that's all."

Radl opened his coat and unbuttoned his tunic. From the inside pocket he took out the stiff manilla envelope that housed the precious letter and handed it to Gericke. "Read that," he said crisply.

When Gericke looked up, his face was suddenly bleak. "That important? No wonder Prager was so disturbed."

"Exactly."

"All right, how long have I got?"

"Approximately four weeks."

"I'll need Bohmler, my observer, to fly with me. He's the best bloody navigator I've ever come across."

"Anything you need. Just ask. Top secret, the whole thing, of course. I can get you a week's leave if you like. After that, you stay here, at the farm under strict security."

"Can I test flight?"

"If you must, but only at night and preferably only once. I'll have a team of the finest aircraft mechanics the Luftwaffe can supply. Anything you need. You'll be in charge of that side. I don't want engines failing for some absurd mechanical reason when you're four hundred feet above a Norfolk marsh. We'll go back to Amsterdam now."

At precisely two forty-five on the following morning, Seumas O'Broin, a sheep farmer of Conroy in County Monaghan, was endeavouring to find his way home across a stretch of open moorland. And was making a bad job of it.

Which was understandable enough for when one is seventy-six, friends have a tendency to disappear with monotonous regularity and Seumas O'Broin was on his way home from a funeral wake for one who had just departed—a wake which had lasted for seventeen hours.

He had not only, as the Irish so delightfully put it, drink taken. He had consumed quantities so vast that he was not certain whether he was in this world or the next; so that when what he took to be a large, white bird sailed out of the darkness over his head without a sound and plunged into the field beyond the next wall, he felt no fear at all, only a mild curiosity.

Devlin made an excellent landing, the supply bag dangling twenty feet below from a line clipped to his belt, hitting the ground first, warning him to be ready. He followed a split second later, rolling in springy Irish turf, scrambling to his feet instantly and unfastening his harness.

The clouds parted at that moment, exposing a quarter-moon which gave him exactly the right amount of light to do what had to be done. He opened the supply bag, took out a small trenching shovel, his dark raincoat, a tweed cap, a pair of shoes and a large, leather Gladstone bag.

There was a thorn hedge nearby, a ditch beside it and he quickly scraped a hole in the bottom with the shovel. Then he unzipped his flying overalls. Underneath he was wearing a tweed suit and he transferred the Walther which he had carried in his belt to his right-hand pocket. He pulled on his shoes and then put the overalls, the parachute and the flying boots into the bag and dropped it into the hole, raking the soil back into place quickly. He scraped a mass of dry leaves and twigs over everything, just to finish things off and tossed the spade into a nearby copse.

He pulled on his raincoat, picked up the Gladstone bag and turned to find Seumas O'Broin leaning on the wall watching him. Devlin moved fast, his hand on the butt of the Walther. But then the aroma of good Irish whiskey, the slurred speech told him all he needed to know.

"What are ye, man or divil?" the old farmer demanded, each word slow and distinct. "Of this world or the next?"

"God save us, old man, but from the smell of you, if one of us lit a match right now we'd be in hell together soon enough. As for your question, I'm a little of both. A simple Irish boy, trying a new way of coming home after years in foreign parts."

"Is that a fact?" O'Broin said.

"Aren't I telling you?"

The old man laughed delightedly. *"Cead mile failte sa bhaile romhat,"* he said in Irish. "A hundred thousand welcomes home to you."

Devlin grinned. *"Go raibh maith agat,"* he said. "Thanks." He picked up the Gladstone bag, vaulted over the wall and set off across the meadow briskly, whistling softly between his teeth. It was good to be home, however brief the visit.

The Ulster border, then, as now, was wide open to anyone who knew the area. Two and a half hours of brisk walking by country lanes and field paths and he was in the county of Armagh and standing on British soil. A lift in a milk truck had him in Armagh itself by six o'clock. Half-an-hour later, he was climbing into a third-class compartment on the early morning train to Belfast.

7

ON WEDNESDAY IT RAINED all day and in the afternoon mist drifted in off the North Sea across the marshes at Cley and Hobs End and Blakeney.

In spite of the weather, Joanna Grey went into the garden after lunch. She was working in the vegetable patch beside the orchard, lifting potatoes, when the garden gate creaked. Patch gave a sudden whine and was off like a flash. When she turned, a smallish, pale-faced man with good shoulders, wearing a black, belted trenchcoat and tweed cap was standing at the end of the path. He carried a Gladstone bag in his left hand and had the most startling blue eyes she had ever seen.

"Mrs. Grey?" he enquired in a soft, Irish voice. "Mrs. Joanna Grey?"

"That's right." Her stomach knotted with excitement. For a brief moment she could hardly breathe.

He smiled. "I shall light a candle of understanding in the heart which shall not be put out."

"*Magna est veritas et praevalet.*"

"Great is Truth and mighty above all things," Liam Devlin smiled. "I could do with a cup of tea, Mrs. Grey. It's been one hell of a trip."

Devlin had been unable to secure a ticket for the night crossing from Belfast to Heysham on Monday and the situation was no better on the Glasgow route. But the advice of a friendly booking clerk had sent him up to Larne where he'd had better luck, obtaining a passage on the Tuesday morning boat on the short run to Stranraer in Scotland.

The exigencies of wartime travel by train had left him with a seemingly interminable journey from Stranraer to Carlisle, changing for Leeds. And in that city, a lengthy wait into the small hours of Wednesday morning before making a suitable connection for Peterborough where he had made the final change to a local train for Kings Lynn.

Much of this passed through his mind again when Joanna Grey turned from the stove where she was making tea and said, "Well, how was it?"

"Not too bad," he said. "Surprising in some ways."

"How do you mean?"

"Oh, the people, the general state of things. It wasn't quite as I expected."

He thought particularly of the station restaurant at Leeds, crowded all night with travellers of every description, all hopefully waiting for a train to somewhere, the poster on the wall which had said with particular irony in his case: *It is more than ever vital to ask yourself: Is my journey really necessary?* He remembered the rough good humour, the general high spirits and contrasted it less than favourably with his last visit to the central railway station in Berlin.

"They seem to be pretty sure they're going to win the war," he said as she brought the tea tray to the table.

"A fool's paradise," she told him calmly. "They never learn. They've never had the organization, you see, the discipline that the Führer has given to Germany."

Remembering the bomb-scarred Chancellery as he had last seen it, the considerable portions of Berlin that were simply heaps of rubble after the Allied bombing offensive, Devlin felt almost constrained to point out that things had changed rather a lot since the good old days. On the other hand, he got the distinct impression that such a remark would not be well received.

So, he drank his tea and watched her as she walked to a corner cupboard, opened it and took down a bottle of Scotch, marvelling that this pleasant-faced, white-haired woman in the neat, tweed skirt and Wellington boots could be what she was.

She poured a generous measure into two glasses and raised one in a kind of salute. "To the English Enterprise," she said, her eyes shining.

Devlin could have told her that the Spanish Armada had been so described, but remembering what had happened to that ill-fated venture decided, once again, to keep his mouth shut.

"To the English Enterprise," he said solemnly.

"Good." She put down her glass. "Now let me see all your papers. I must make sure you have everything."

He produced his passport, army discharge papers, a testimonial purporting to be from his old commanding officer, a similar letter from his parish priest and various documents relating to his medical condition.

"Excellent," she said. "These are really very good. What happens now is this. I've fixed you up with a job working for the local squire, Sir Henry Willoughby. He wants to see you as soon as you arrive so we'll get that over with today. Tomorrow morning I'll run you into Fakenham, that's a market town about ten miles from here."

"And what do I do there?"

"Report to the local police station. They'll give you an alien's registration form which all Irish citizens have to fill in and you'll also have to provide a passport photo, but we can get that with no trouble. Then you'll need insurance cards, an identity card, ration book, clothing coupons."

She numbered them off on the fingers of one hand and Devlin grinned. "Heh, hold on now. It sounds like one hell of a lot of trouble to me. Three weeks on Saturday, that's all, and I'll be away from here so fast they'll think I've never been."

"All these things are essential," she said. "Everyone has them, so you must. It only needs one petty clerk in Pakenham or Kings Lynn to notice that you haven't applied for something and put an enquiry in hand and then where would you be?"

Devlin said cheerfully, "All right, you're the boss. Now what about this job?"

"Warden of the marshes at Hobs End. It couldn't be more isolated. There's a cottage to go with it. Not much, but it will do."

"And what will be expected of me?"

"Gamekeeping duties in the main and there's a system of dyke gates that needs regular checking. They haven't had a warden for two years since the last one went off to the war. And you'll be expected to keep the vermin in check. The foxes play havoc with the wildfowl."

"What do I do? Throw stones at them?"

"No, Sir Henry will supply you with a shotgun."

"That's nice of him. What about transport?"

"I've done the best I can. I've managed to persuade Sir Henry to allocate you one of the estate motorbikes. As an agricultural worker it's legitimate enough. Buses have almost ceased to exist, so most people are allowed a small monthly ration to help them get into town occasionally for essential purposes."

A horn sounded outside. She went into the sitting-room and was back in an instant. "It's Sir Henry. Leave the talking to me. Just act properly servile and speak only when you're spoken to. He'll like that. I'll bring him in here."

She went out and Devlin waited. He heard the front door open and her feigned surprise. Sir Henry said, "Just on my way to another command meeting in Holt, Joanna. Wondered if there was anything I could get you?"

She replied much more quietly so that Devlin couldn't hear what she said. Sir Henry dropped his voice in return, there was a further murmur of conversation and then they came into the kitchen.

Sir Henry was in uniform as a lieutenant-colonel in the Home Guard, medal ribbons for the First World War and India making a splash of colour above his left breast pocket. He glanced piercingly at Devlin, one hand behind his back, the other brushing the wide sweep of his moustache.

"So you're Devlin?"

Devlin lurched to his feet and stood there twisting and untwisting his tweed cap in his two hands. "I'd like to thank you, sir," he said, thickening the Irish accent noticeably. "Mrs. Grey's told me how much you've done for me. It's more than kind."

"Nonsense, man," Sir Henry said brusquely although it was observable that he stretched to his full height and placed his feet a little further apart. "You did your best for the old country, didn't you? Caught a packet in France, I understand?"

Devlin nodded eagerly and Sir Henry leaned forward and examined the furrow on the left side of the forehead made by an Irish Special Branch detective's bullet. "By heavens," he said softly. "You're damn lucky to be here if you ask me."

"I thought I'd settle him in for you," Joanna Grey said. "If that's all right, Henry? Only you're so busy, I know."

"I say, would you, old girl?" He glanced at his watch. "I'm due in Holt in half an hour."

"No more to be said. I'll take him along to the cottage, show him around the marsh generally and so on."

"Come to think of it you probably know more about what goes on at Hobs End than I do." He forgot himself for a moment and slipped an arm about her waist, then withdrew it hastily and said to Devlin, "Don't forget to present yourself to the police in Fakenham without delay. You know all about that?"

"Yes, sir."

"Anything you want to ask me?"

"The gun, sir," Devlin said. "I understand you want me to do a little shooting."

"Ah, yes. No trouble there. Call at the Grange tomorrow afternoon and I'll see you fixed up. You can pick the bike up tomorrow afternoon, too. Mrs. Grey's told you about that, has she? Only three gallons of petrol a month, mind you, but you'll have to make out the best way you can. We've all got to make sacrifices." He brushed his moustache again. "A single Lancaster, Devlin, uses two thousand gallons of petrol to reach the Ruhr. Did you know that?"

"No, sir."

"There you are, then. We've all got to be prepared to do our best."
Joanna Grey took his arm. "Henry, you're going to be late."

"Yes, of course, my dear." He nodded to the Irishman. "All right,
Devlin, I'll see you tomorrow afternoon."

Devlin actually touched his forelock and waited until they'd gone out
of the front door before moving into the sitting-room. He watched Sir
Henry drive away and was lighting a cigarette when Joanna Grey returned.

"Tell me something," he said. "Are he and Churchill supposed to be
friends?"

"As I understand it, they've never met. Studley Grange is famous for
its Elizabethan gardens. The Prime Minister fancied the idea of a quiet
weekend and a little painting before returning to London."

"With Sir Henry falling over himself to oblige? Oh, yes, I can see
that."

She shook her head. "I thought you were going to say begorrah any
minute. You're a wicked man, Mr. Devlin."

"Liam," he said. "Call me Liam. It'll sound better, especially if I
still call you Mrs. Grey. He fancies you, then, and at his age?"

"Autumn romance is not completely unheard of."

"More like winter, I should have thought. On the other hand it must
be damn useful."

"More than that—essential," she said. "Anyway, bring your bag and
I'll get the car and take you along to Hobs End."

The rain pushed in on the wind from the sea was cold and the marsh
was shrouded in mist. When Joanna Grey braked to a halt in the yard
of the old marsh warden's cottage, Devlin got out and looked about him
thoughtfully. It was a strange, mysterious sort of place, the kind that
made the hair lift on the back of his head. Sea creeks and mudflats, the
great, pale reeds merging with the mist and somewhere out there, the
occasional cry of a bird, the invisible beat of wings.

"I see what you mean about being isolated."

She took a key from under a flat stone by the front door and opened
it, leading the way into the flagged passageway. There was rising damp
and the whitewash was flaking from the wall. On the left a door opened
into a large kitchen-cum-living room. Again, the floor was stone flags,
but there was a huge open-hearth fireplace and rush mats. At the other
end of the room was an iron cooking stove and a chipped, white pot
sink with a single tap. A large pine table flanked by two benches and an
old wing-back chair by the fire were the only furniture.

"I've news for you," Devlin said. "I was raised in a cottage exactly like this in County Down in the North of Ireland. All it needs is a bloody good fire to dry the place out.''

"And it has one great advantage—seclusion," she said. "You probably won't see a soul the whole time you're here.''

Devlin opened the Gladstone bag and took out some personal belongings, clothing and three or four books. Then he ran a finger through the lining to find a hidden catch, and removed a false bottom. In the cavity he revealed was a Walther P38, a Sten gun, the silenced version, in three parts, and a land agent's S-phone receiver and transmitter which was no more than pocket size. There was a thousand pounds in pound notes and another thousand in fivers. There was also something in a white cloth which he didn't bother to unwrap.

"Operating money," he said.

"To obtain the vehicles?"

"That's right. I've been given the address of the right sort of people.''

"Where from?"

"The kind of thing they have on file at Abwehr Headquarters.''

"Where is it?"

"Birmingham. I thought I'd take a run over there this weekend. What do I need to know?''

She sat on the edge of the table and watched as he screwed the barrel unit of the Sten into the main body and slotted the shoulder stock in place. "It's a fair way," she said. "Say three hundred miles the round trip."

"Obviously my three gallons of petrol isn't going to get me very far. What can I do about that?''

"There's plenty of black market petrol available, at three times the normal price, if you know the right garages. The commercial variety is dyed to make it easy for the police to detect wrongful use, but you can get rid of the dye by straining the petrol through an ordinary civilian gas mask filter.''

Devlin rammed a magazine into the Sten, checked it, then took the whole thing to pieces again and replaced it in the bottom of the bag.

"A wonderful thing, technology," he observed. "That thing can be fired at close quarters and the only sound you can hear is the bolt clicking. It's English, by the way. Another of the items SOE fondly imagine it's been dropping in to the Dutch underground.'' He took out a cigarette and put it into his mouth. "What else should I know when I make this trip? What are the risks?''

"Very few," she said. "The lights on the machine will have the regulation blackout fittings so there's no problem there. The roads, particularly in country areas, are virtually traffic free. And white lines have been painted down the centre of most of them. That helps.''

"What about the police or the security forces?''

She gazed at him blankly. "Oh, there's nothing to worry about there. The military would only stop you if you tried to enter a restricted area. Technically this still is a Defence Area, but nobody bothers with the regulations these days. As for the police, they're entitled to stop you and ask for your identity card or they might stop a vehicle on the main road as part of a spot check in the campaign against misuse of petrol."

She almost sounded indignant and, remembering what he had left, Devlin had to fight an irresistible compulsion to open her eyes a little. Instead he said, "Is that all?"

"I think so. There's a twenty-mile-an-hour speed limit in built-up areas and of course you won't find signposts anywhere, but they started putting place names up again in many places earlier this summer."

"So, the odds are that I shouldn't have any trouble?"

"No one's stopped me. Nobody bothers now." She shrugged. "There's no problem. At the local WVS aid centre we have all sorts of official forms from the old Defence Area days. There was one that allowed you to visit relatives in hospital. I'll make one out referring to some brother in hospital in Birmingham. That and those medical discharge papers from the Army should be enough to satisfy anyone. Everybody has a soft spot for a hero these days."

Devlin grinned. "You know something, Mrs. Grey? I think we're going to get on famously." He went and rummaged in the cupboard under the sink and returned with a rusty hammer and a nail. "The very thing."

"For what?" she demanded.

He stepped inside the hearth and drove the nail partially home at the back of the smoke-blackened beam which supported the chimney breast. Then he hung the Walther up there by its trigger guard. "What I call my ace-in-the-hole. I like to have one around, just in case. Now, show me round the rest of the place."

There was an assortment of outbuildings, mostly in decay, and a barn in quite reasonable condition. There was another standing behind it on the very edge of the marsh, a decrepit building of considerable age, the stonework green with mildew. Devlin got one half of the large door open with difficulty. Inside it was cold and damp and obviously hadn't been used for anything for years.

"This will do just fine," he said. "Even if old Sir Willoughby comes poking his nose in I shouldn't think he'd go this far."

"He's a busy man," she said. "County affairs, magistrate, running the local Home Guard. He still takes that very seriously. Doesn't really have much time for anything else."

"But you," he said. "The randy old bastard still has enough time left for you."

She smiled. "Yes, I'm afraid that's only too true." She took his arm.

"Now, I'll show you the dropping zone."

They walked up through the marsh along the dyke road. It was raining quite hard now and the wind carried with it the damp, wet smell of rotting vegetation. Some Brent geese flew in out of the mist in formation like a bombing squadron going in for the kill and vanished into the gray curtain.

They reached the pine trees, the pill boxes, the sand-filled tank trap, the warning *Beware of Mines* so familiar to Devlin from the photographs he had seen. Joanna Grey tossed a stone out over the sands and Patch bounded through the wire to retrieve it.

"You're sure?" Devlin said.

"Absolutely."

He grinned crookedly. "I'm Catholic, remember that if it goes wrong."

"They all are here. I'll see you're put down properly."

He stepped over the coils of wire, paused on the edge of the sand, then walked forward. He paused again, then started to run, leaving wet footprints for the tide had not long ebbed. He turned, ran back and once again negotiated the wire.

He was immensely cheerful and put an arm around her shoulders. "You were right—from the beginning. It's going to work, this thing. You'll see." He looked out to sea across the creeks and the sandbanks, through the mist towards the Point. "Beautiful. The thought of leaving all this must break your heart."

"Leave?" She looked up at him blankly. "What do you mean?"

"But you can't stay," he said. "Not afterwards. Surely you must see that?"

She looked out to the Point as if for the last time. Strange, but it had never occurred to her that she would have to leave. She shivered as the wind drove rain in hard off the sea.

At twenty to eight that evening Max Radl, in his office at the Tirpitz Ufer, decided he'd had enough for the day. He'd not felt well since his return to Brittany and the doctor he'd gone to see had been horrified at his condition.

"If you carry on like this, Herr Oberst, you will kill yourself," he had declared firmly. "I think I can promise you that."

Radl had paid his fee and taken the pills—three different kinds—which with any kind of luck might keep him going. As long as he could stay out of the hands of the Army medics he had a chance, but one more physical check-up with that lot and he was finished. They'd have him into a civilian suit before he knew where he was.

He opened a drawer, took out one of the pill bottles and popped two into his mouth. They were supposed to be pain killers, but just to make sure, he half-filled a tumbler with Courvoisier to wash them down. There was a knock on the door and Hofer entered. His normally composed face was full of emotion and his eyes were bright.

"What is it, Karl, what's happened?" Radl demanded.

Hoffer pushed a signal flimsy across the desk. "It's just in, Herr Oberst. From Starling—Mrs. Grey. He's arrived safely. He's with her now."

Radl looked down at the flimsy in a kind of awe. "My God, Devlin," he whispered. "You brought it off. It worked."

A sense of physical release surged through him. He reached inside his bottom drawer and found another glass. "Karl, this very definitely calls for a drink."

He stood up, full of a fierce joy, aware that he had not felt like this in years, not since that incredible euphoria when racing for the French coast at the head of his men in the summer of 1940.

He raised his glass and said to Hofer, "I give you a toast, Karl. To Liam Devlin and 'Up the Republic.' "

As a staff officer in the Lincoln Washington Brigade in Spain, Devlin had found a motorcycle the most useful way of keeping contact between the scattered units of his command in difficult mountain country. Very different from Norfolk, but there was that same sense of freedom, of being off the leash, as he rode from Studley Grange through quiet country lanes towards the village.

He'd obtained a driving licence in Holt that morning along with his other documents, without the slightest difficulty. Wherever he'd gone, from the police station to the local labour exchange, his cover story of being an ex-infantryman, discharged because of wounds, had worked like a charm. The various officials had really put themselves out to push things through for him. It was true what they said. In wartime, everyone loved a soldier, and a wounded hero even more so.

The motorcycle was pre-war, of course, and had seen better days. A 350 cc BSA, but when he took a chance and opened the throttle wide on the first straight, the needle swung up to sixty with no trouble at all. He throttled back quickly once he'd established that the power was there if needed. No sense in asking for trouble. There was no village policeman in Studley Constable. Joanna Grey had warned him that one occasionally appeared from Holt on a motorcycle.

He came down the steep hill into the village itself past the old mill with the waterwheel which didn't seem to be turning and slowed for a young girl in a pony and trap carrying three milk churns. She wore a blue beret and a very old, First-World-War trenchcoat at least two sizes too big for her. She had high cheekbones, large eyes, a mouth that was too wide and three of her fingers poked through holes in the woollen gloves she wore.

"Good day to you, *a colleen*," he said cheerfully as he waited for her to cross his path to the bridge. "God save the good work."

Her eyes widened in a kind of astonishment, her mouth opened slightly. She seemed bereft of speech and clicked her tongue, urging the pony over the bridge and into a trot as they started up the hill past the church.

"A lovely, ugly little peasant," he quoted softly, "who turned my head not once, but twice." He grinned. "Oh, no, Liam, me old love. Not that. Not now."

He swung the motorcycle in towards the Studley Arms and became aware of a man standing in the window glaring at him. An enormous individual of thirty or so with a tangled black beard. He was wearing a tweed cap and an old reefer coat.

And what in the hell have I done to you, son? Devlin asked himself. The man's gaze travelled to the girl and the trap just breasting the hill beside the church and moved back again. It was enough. Devlin pushed the BSA up on to its stand, unstrapped the shotgun in its canvas bag which was hanging about his neck, tucked it under his arm and went inside.

There was no bar, just a large comfortable room with a low-beamed ceiling, several high-backed benches, a couple of wooden tables. A wood fire burned brightly on an open hearth.

There were only three people in the room. The man sitting beside the fire playing a mouth organ, the one with the black beard at the window and a short, stocky man in shirt sleeves who looked to be in his late twenties.

"God bless all here," Devlin announced, playing the bog Irishman to the hilt.

He put the gun in its canvas bag on the table and the man in the shirt sleeves smiled and stuck out his hand. "I'm George Wilde the publican here and you'll be Sir Henry's new warden down on the marshes. We've heard all about you."

"What, already?" Devlin said.

"You know how it is in the country."

"Or does he?" the big man at the window said harshly.

"Oh, I'm a farm boy from way back myself," Devlin said.

Wilde looked troubled, but attempted the obvious introduction. "Arthur Seymour and the old goat by the fire is Laker Armsby."

As Devlin discovered later, Laker was in his late forties, but looked older. He was incredibly shabby, his tweed cap torn, his coat tied with string and his trousers and shoes were caked with mud.

"Would you gentlemen join me in a drink?" Devlin suggested.

"I wouldn't say no to that," Laker Armsby told him. "A pint of brown ale would suit me fine."

Seymour drained his flagon and banged it down on the table. "I buys my own." He picked up the shotgun and hefted it in one hand. "The Squire's really looking after you, isn't he? This and the bike. Now I wonder why you should rate that, an incomer like you, when there's those amongst us who've worked the estate for years and still must be content with less."

"Sure and I can only put it down to my good looks," Devlin told him.

Madness sparked in Seymour's eyes, the Devil looked out, hot and wild. He had Devlin by the front of the coat and pulled him close. "Don't make fun of me, little man. Don't ever do that or I'll step on you as I'd step on a slug."

Wilde grabbed his arm. "Now come on, Arthur," but Seymour pushed him away.

"You walk soft round here, you keep your place and we might get on. Understand me?"

Devlin smiled anxiously. "Sure and if I've given offence, I'm sorry."

"That's better." Seymour released his grip and patted his face. "That's much better. Only in future, remember one thing. When I come in, you leave."

He went out, the door banged behind him and Laker Armsby cackled wildly, "He's a bad bastard is Arthur."

George Wilde vanished into the back room and returned with a bottle of Scotch and some glasses. "This stuff's hard to come by at the moment, but I reckon you've earned one on me, Mr. Devlin."

"Liam," Devlin said. "Call me Liam." He accepted the glass of whisky. "Is he always like that?"

"Ever since I've known him."

"There was a girl outside in a pony and trap as I came in. Does he have some special interest there?"

"Fancies his chances." Laker Armsby chuckled. "Only she won't have any of it."

"That's Molly Prior," Wilde said. "She and her mother have a farm a couple of miles this side of Hobs End. Been running it between them since last year when her father died. Laker gives them a few hours when he isn't busy at the church."

"Seymour does a bit for them as well. Some of the heavy stuff."

"And thinks he owns the place, I suppose? Why isn't he in the Army?"

"That's another sore point. They turned him down because of a perforated eardrum."

"Which he took as an insult to his great manhood, I suppose?" Devlin said.

Wilde said awkwardly, as if he felt some explanation was necessary, "I picked up a packet myself with the Royal Artillery at Narvik in April, nineteen-forty. Lost my right knee-cap, so it was a short war for me. You got yours in France I understand?"

"That's right," Devlin said calmly. "Near Arras. Came out through Dunkirk on a stretcher and never knew a thing about it."

"And over a year in hospitals Mrs. Grey tells me?"

Devlin nodded. "A grand woman. I'm very grateful to her. Her husband knew my people back home years ago. If it wasn't for her I wouldn't have this job."

"A lady," Wilde said. "A real lady. There's nobody better liked round here."

Laker Armsby said, "Now me, I copped my first packet on the Somme in nineteen-sixteen. With the Welsh Guards, I was."

"Oh, no." Devlin took a shilling from his pocket, slapped it down on the table and winked at Wilde. "Give him a pint, but I'm off. Got work to do."

When he reached the coast road, Devlin took the first dyke path that he came to at the northerly end of Hobs End marsh and drove out towards the fringe of pine trees. It was a crisp, autumnal sort of day, cold but bracing, white clouds chasing each other across a blue sky. He opened the throttle and roared along the narrow dyke path. A hell of a risk, for one wrong move and he'd be into the marsh. Stupid really, but that was the kind of mood he was in, and the sense of freedom was exhilarating.

He throttled back, braking to turn into another path, working his way along the network of dykes towards the coast, when a horse and rider suddenly appeared from the reeds thirty or forty yards to his right and scrambled up on top of the dyke. It was the girl he'd last seen in the village in the pony and trap, Molly Prior. As he slowed, she leaned low over the horse's neck and urged it into a gallop, racing him on a parallel course.

Devlin responded instantly, opening the throttle and surging forward in a burst of speed, kicking dirt out in a great spray into the marsh behind him. The girl had an advantage, in that the dyke she was on ran straight to the pine trees, whereas Devlin had to work his way through a maze, turning from one path into another and he lost ground.

She was close to the trees now and as he skidded out of one path broadside on and finally found a clear run, she plunged her mount into the water and mud of the marsh, urging it through the reeds in a final short cut. The horse responded well and a few moments later, bounded free and disappeared into the pines.

Devlin left the dyke path at speed, shot up the side of the first sand dune, travelled some little distance through the air and alighted in soft white sand, going down on one knee in a long slide.

Molly Prior was sitting at the foot of a pine tree gazing out to sea, her chin on her knees. She was dressed exactly as she had been when Devlin had last seen her except that she had taken off the beret, exposing short-cropped, tawny hair. The horse grazed on a tuft of grass that pushed up through the sand.

Devlin got the bike up on its stand and threw himself down beside her. "A fine day, thanks be to God."

She turned and said calmly, "What kept you?"

Devlin had taken off his cap to wipe sweat from his forehead and he looked up at her in astonishment. "What kept me, is it? Why, you little . . ."

And then she smiled. More than that, threw back her head and laughed and Devlin laughed too. "By God, and I'll know you till the crack of Doomsday, that's for sure."

"And what's that supposed to mean?" She spoke with the strong and distinctive Norfolk accent that was still so new to him.

"Oh, a saying they have where I come from." He found a packet of cigarettes and put one in his mouth. "Do you use these things?"

"No."

"Good for you, they'd stunt your growth and you with your green years still ahead of you."

"I'm seventeen, I'll have you know," she told him. "Eighteen in February."

Devlin put a match to his cigarette and lay back pillowing his head on his hands, the peak of his cap over his eyes. "February what?"

"The twenty-second."

"Ah, a little fish, is it? Pisces. We should do well together, me being a Scorpio. You should never marry a Virgo, by the way. No chance of them and Pisces hitting it off at all. Take Arthur, now. I've a terrible hunch he's a Virgo. I'd watch it there if I were you."

"Arthur?" she said. "You mean Arthur Seymour? Are you crazy?"

"No, but I think he is," Devlin replied and carried on. "Pure, clean, virtuous and not very hot, which is a terrible pity from where I'm lying."

She had turned round to look down at him and the old coat gaped open. Her breasts were full and firm, barely contained by the cotton blouse she was wearing.

"Oh, girl dear, you'll have a terrible problem with your weight in a year or two if you don't watch your food.''

Her eyes flashed, she glanced down and instinctively pulled her coat together. ''You bastard,'' she said, somehow drawing the word out. And then she saw his lips quiver and leaned down to peer under the peak of the cap. ''Why, you're laughing at me!'' She pulled off his cap and threw it away.

''And what else would I do with you, Molly Prior?'' He put out a hand defensively. ''No, don't answer that.''

She sat back against the tree, her hands in her pockets. ''How did you know my name?''

''George Wilde told me at the pub.''

''Oh, I see now. And Arthur—was he there?''

''You could say that. I get the impression he looks upon you as his personal property.''

''Then he can go to hell,'' she said, suddenly fierce. ''I belong to no man.''

He looked up at her from where he lay, the cigarette hanging from the corner of his mouth, and smiled. ''Your nose turns up, has anyone ever told you that? And when you're angry, your mouth goes down at the corners.''

He had gone too far, touched some source of secret inner hurt. She flushed and said bitterly, ''Oh, I'm ugly enough, Mr. Devlin. I've sat all night long at dances in Holt without being asked, too often not to know my place. You wouldn't throw me out on a wet Saturday night, I know. But that's men for you. Anything's better than nothing.''

She started to get up, Devlin had her by the ankle and dragged her down, pinning her with one strong arm as she struggled. ''You know my name? How's that?''

''Don't let it go to your head. Everybody knows about you. Everything there is to know.''

''I've news for you.'' he said pushing himself up on one elbow and leaning over her. ''You don't know the first thing about me because if you did, you'd know I prefer fine autumn afternoons under the pine trees to wet Saturday nights. On the other hand, the sand has a terrible way of getting where it shouldn't.'' She went very still. He kissed her briefly on the mouth and rolled away. ''Now get the hell out of it before I let my mad passion run away with me.''

She grabbed her beret, jumped to her feet and reached for the horse's bridle. When she turned to glance at him her face was serious, but after she'd scrambled into the saddle and pulled her mount round to look at him again, she was smiling. ''They told me all Irishmen were mad. Now I believe them. I'll be at Mass Sunday evening. Will you?''

''Do I look as though I will?''

The horse was stamping, turning in half-circles, but she held it well.

"Yes," she said seriously, "I think you do," and she gave the horse its head and galloped away.

"Oh, you idiot, Liam," Devlin said softly as he pushed his motorcycle off its stand and shoved it alongside the sand dune, through the trees and on to the path. "Won't you ever learn?"

He drove back along the main dyke top, sedately this time, and ran the motorcycle into the barn. He found the key where he'd left it under the stone by the door and let himself in. He put the shotgun in the hallstand, went into the kitchen, unbuttoning his raincoat, and paused. There was a pitcher of milk on the table, a dozen brown eggs in a white bowl.

"Mother Mary," he said softly. "Would you look at that now?"

He touched the bowl gently with one finger, but when he finally turned to take off his coat, his face was bleak.

8

IN BIRMINGHAM A COLD WIND drifted across the city, hurling rain against the plate glass window of Ben Garvald's flat above the garage in Saltley. In the silk dressing gown and with a scarf at the throat, the dark, curly hair carefully combed, he made an imposing figure; the broken nose added a sort of rugged grandeur. A closer inspection was not so flattering, the fruits of dissipation showing clearly on the fleshy arrogant face.

But this morning he faced something more—a considerable annoyance with the world at large. At eleven-thirty on the previous night, one of his business ventures, a small illegal gaming club in a house in an apparently respectable street in Aston had been turned over by the City of Birmingham Police. Not that Garvald was in any personal danger of being arrested himself. That was what the front man was paid for, and he would be taken care of. Much more serious was the three and a half thousand pounds on the gaming tables which had been confiscated by the police.

The kitchen door swung open and a young girl of seventeen or eighteen came in. She wore a pink lace dressing gown, her peroxide-blonde hair was tousled and her face was blotched, the eyes swollen from weeping. "Can I get you anything else, Mr. Garvald?" she said in a low voice.

"Get me anything?" he said. "That's good. That's bloody rich, that is, seeing as how you haven't bleeding well *given* me anything yet."

He spoke without turning round. His interest had been caught by a man on a motorcycle who had just ridden into the yard below and parked beside one of the trucks.

The girl who had found herself quite unable to cope with some of Garvald's more bizarre demands of the previous night said tearfully, "I'm sorry, Mr. Garvald."

The man below had walked across the yard and disappeared now. Garvald turned and said to the girl, "Go on, get your clothes on and piss off." She was frightened to death, shaking with fear and staring at him, mesmerized. A delicious feeling of power, almost sexual in its intensity, flooded through him. He grabbed her hair and twisted it cruelly. "And learn to do as you're told. Understand?"

As the girl fled, the outer door opened and Reuben Garvald, Ben's younger brother, entered. He was small and sickly-looking, one shoulder slightly higher than the other, but the black eyes in the pale face were constantly on the move, missing nothing.

His eyes followed the girl disapprovingly as she disappeared into the bedroom. "I wish you wouldn't, Ben. A dirty little cow like that. You might catch something."

"That's what they invented penicillin for," Garvald said. "Anyway, what do you want?"

"There's a bloke to see you. Just came in on a motorcycle."

"So I noticed. What's he want?"

"Wouldn't say. Cheeky little Mick with too much off." Reuben held out half a five pound note. "Told me to give you that. Said you could have the other half if you'd see him."

Garvald laughed, quite spontaneously, and plucked the torn banknote from his brother's hand. "I like it. Yes, I very definitely go for that." He took it to the window and examined it. "It looks Kosher, too." He turned, grinning. "I wonder if he's got any more, Reuben? Let's see."

Reuben went out and Garvald crossed to a sideboard in high good humour and poured himself a glass of Scotch. Maybe the morning was not going to turn out to be such a dead loss after all. It might even prove to be quite entertaining. He settled himself in an easy chair by the window.

The door opened and Reuben ushered Devlin into the room. He was wet through, his raincoat saturated, and he took off his tweed cap and squeezed it over a Chinese porcelain bowl filled with bulbs. "Would you look at that now?"

"All right," Garvald said. "I know all you bleedin' Micks are cracked. You needn't rub it in. What's the name?''

''Murphy, Mr. Garvald,'' Devlin told him. ''As in spuds.''

''And I believe that, too,'' Garvald said. ''Take that coat off, for Christ's sake. You'll ruin the bloody carpet. Genuine Axminster. Costs a fortune to get hold of that these days.''

Devlin removed his dripping trenchcoat and handed it to Reuben, who looked mad but took it anyway and draped it over a chair by the window.

''All right, sweetheart,'' Garvald said. ''My time's limited so let's get to it.''

Devlin rubbed his hands dry on his jacket and took out a packet of cigarettes. ''They tell me you're in the transport business,'' he said. ''Amongst other things.''

''Who tells you?''

''I heard it around.''

''So?''

''I need a truck. Bedford three-tonner. Army type.''

''Is that all?'' Garvald was still smiling, but his eyes were watchful.

''No, I also want a jeep, a compressor plus spray equipment and a couple of gallons of khaki-green paint. And I want both trucks to have service registration.''

Garvald laughed out loud. ''What are you going to do, start the Second Front on your own or something?''

Devlin took a large envelope from his inside breast pocket and held it out. ''There's five hundred quid on account in there, just so you know I'm not wasting your time.''

Garvald nodded to his brother who took the envelope, opened it and checked the contents. ''He's right, Ben. In brand new fivers, too.''

He pushed the money across. Garvald weighed it in his hand then dropped it on the coffee table in front of him. He leaned back. ''All right, let's talk. Who are you working for?''

''Me,'' Devlin said.

Garvald didn't believe him for a moment and showed it, but he didn't argue the point. ''You must have something good lined up to be going to all this trouble. Maybe you could do with a little help.''

''I've told you what I need, Mr. Garvald,'' Devlin said. ''One Bedford three-ton truck, a jeep, a compressor, and a couple of gallons of khaki-green paint. Now if you don't think you can help, I can always try elsewhere.''

Reuben said angrily, ''Who the hell do you think you are? Walking in here's one thing. Walking out again isn't always so easy.''

Devlin's face was very pale and when he turned to look at Reuben, the blue eyes seemed to be fixed on some distant point, cold and remote. ''Is that a fact, now?''

He reached for the bundle of fivers, his left hand in his pocket on the butt of the Walther. Garvald slammed a hand down across them hard. "It'll cost you," he said softly. "A nice, round figure. Let's say two thousand quid."

He held Devlin's gaze in a kind of challenge, there was a lengthy pause and then Devlin smiled. "I bet you had a mean left hand in your prime."

"I still do, boy." Garvald clenched his fist. "The best in the business."

"All right," Devlin said. "Throw in fifty gallons of petrol in Army jerrycans and you're on."

Garvald held out his hand. "Done. We'll have a drink on it. What's your pleasure?"

"Irish if you've got it. Bushmills for preference."

"I got everything, boy. Anything and everything." He snapped his fingers. "Reuben, how about some of that Bushmills for our friend here?" Reuben hesitated, his face set and angry, and Garvald said in a low, dangerous voice, "The Bushmills, Reuben."

His brother went over to the sideboard and opened the cupboard, disclosing dozens of bottles underneath. "You do all right for yourself," Devlin observed.

"The only way." Garvald took a cigar from a box on the coffee table. "You want to take delivery in Birmingham or someplace else?"

"Somewhere near Peterborough on the A1 would do," Devlin said.

Reuben handed him a glass. "You're bloody choosy, aren't you?"

Garvald cut in. "No, that's all right. You know Norman Cross? That's on the A1 about five miles out of Peterborough. There's a garage called Fogarty's a couple of miles down the road. It's closed at the moment."

"I'll find it," Devlin said.

"When do you want to take delivery?"

"Thursday the twenty-eighth and Friday the twenty-ninth. I'll take the truck and the compressor and the jerrycans the first night, the jeep on the second."

Garvald frowned slightly. "You mean you're handling the whole thing yourself?"

"That's right."

"Okay—what kind of time were you thinking of?"

"After dark. Say about nine to nine-thirty."

"And the cash?"

"You keep that five hundred on account. Seven-fifty when I take delivery of the truck, the same for the jeep and I want delivery licences for each of them."

"That's easy enough," Garvald said. "But they'll need filling in with purpose and destination."

"I'll see to that myself when I get them."

Garvald nodded slowly, thinking about it. "That looks all right to me. Okay, you're on. What about another snort?"

"No, thanks," Devlin said. "I've places to go."

He pulled on the wet trenchcoat and buttoned it quickly. Garvald got up and went to the sideboard and came back with the freshly opened bottle of Bushmills. "Have that on me, just to show there's no ill will."

"The last thought in my mind," Devlin told him. "But thanks anyway. A little something in return." He produced the other half of the five pound note from his breast pocket. "Yours, I believe."

Garvald took it and grinned. "You've got the cheek of the Devil, you know that, Murphy?"

"It's been said before."

"All right, we'll see you at Norman Cross on the twenty-eighth. Show him out, Reuben. Mind your manners."

Reuben moved to the door sullenly and opened it and went out. Devlin followed him, but turned as Garvald sat down again. "One more thing, Mr. Garvald."

"What's that?"

"I keep my word."

"That's nice to know."

"See that you do."

He wasn't smiling now, the face bleak for the moment longer than he held Garvald's gaze before turning and going out.

Garvald stood up, walked to the sideboard and poured himself another Scotch, then he went to the window and looked down into the yard. Devlin pulled his motorcycle off the stand and kicked the engine into life. The door opened and Reuben entered the room.

He was thoroughly aroused now. "What's got into you, Ben? I don't understand. You let a little Mick, so fresh out of the bogs he's still got mud on his boots, walk all over you. You took more from him than I've seen you take from anyone."

Garvald watched Devlin turn into the main road and ride away through the heavy rain. "He's on to something, Reuben, boy," he said softly. "Something nice and juicy."

"But why the Army vehicles?"

"Lots of possibilities there. Could be almost anything. Look at that case in Shropshire the other week. Some bloke dressed as a soldier drives an Army lorry into a big NAAFI depot and out again with thirty thousand quid's worth of Scotch on board. Imagine what that lot would be worth on the black market."

"And you think he could be on to something like that?"

"He's got to be," Garvald said, "and whatever it is, I'm in, whether he likes it or not." He shook his head in a kind of bewilderment. "Do you know, he threatened me, Reuben—me! We can't have that, now can we?"

Although it was only mid-afternoon, the light was beginning to go as Koenig took the E-boat in towards the low-lying coastline. Beyond, thunderclouds towered into the sky, black and swollen and edged with pink.

Muller who was bending over the chart table said, "A bad storm soon, Herr Leutnant."

Koenig peered out of the window. "Another fifteen minutes before it breaks. We'll be well up by then."

Thunder rumbled ominously, the sky darkened and the crew, waiting on deck for the first glimpse of their destination, were strangely quiet.

Koenig said, "I don't blame them. What a bloody place after St. Helier."

Beyond the line of sand dunes the land was flat and bare, swept clean by the constant wind. In the distance he could see the farmhouse and the hangars at the airstrip, black against a pale horizon. The wind brushed across the water and Koenig reduced speed as they approached the inlet. "You take her in, Erich."

Muller took the wheel. Koenig pulled on an old pilot coat and went out on deck and stood at the rail smoking a cigarette. He felt strangely depressed. The voyage had been bad enough, but in a sense his problems were only beginning. The people he was to work with, for example. That was of crucial importance. In the past he'd had certain unfortunate experiences in similar situations.

The sky seemed to split wide open and rain began to fall in torrents. As they coasted in towards the concrete pier, a field car appeared on the track between the dunes. Muller cut the engines and leaned out of the window shouting orders. As the crew bustled to get a line ashore, the field car drove on to the pier and braked to a halt. Steiner and Ritter Neumann got out and walked to the edge.

"Hello, Koenig, so you made it?" Steiner called cheerfully. "Welcome to Landsvoort."

Koenig, halfway up the ladder, was so astonished that he missed his footing and almost fell into the water. "You, Herr Oberst, but . . . " And then as the implication struck home, he started to laugh. "And here was I worrying like hell about who I was going to have to work with."

He scrambled up the ladder and grabbed Steiner's hand.

It was half past four when Devlin rode down through the village past the Studley Arms. As he went over the bridge he could hear the organ playing and lights showed very dimly at the windows of the church for it was not yet dark. Joanna Grey had told him that evening Mass was held in the afternoon to avoid the blackout. As he went up the hill he remembered Molly Prior's remark. Smiling, he pulled up outside the church. She was there, he knew, because the pony stood patiently in the shafts of the trap, its nose in a feed bag. There were two parked cars, a flat-backed truck and several bicycles parked there also.

When Devlin opened the door, Father Vereker was on his way down the aisle with three young boys in scarlet cassocks and white cottas, one of them carrying a bucket of holy water, Vereker sprinkling the heads of the congregation as he passed, washing them clean. *"Asperges me,"* he intoned as Devlin slipped down the right-hand aisle and found a pew.

There were no more than seventeen or eighteen people in the congregation. Sir Henry and a woman who was presumably his wife and a young, dark-haired girl in her early twenties in the uniform of the Women's Auxiliary Air Force who sat with them and who was obviously Pamela Vereker. George Wilde was there with his wife. Laker Armsby sat with them, scrubbed clean in stiff white collar and an ancient, black suit.

Molly Prior was across the aisle with her mother, a pleasant, middle-aged woman with a kind face. Molly wore a straw hat decorated with some kind of fake flowers, the brim tilted over her eyes, and a flowered cotton dress with a tightly buttoned bodice and a rather short skirt. Her coat was folded neatly over the pew.

I bet she's been wearing that dress for at least three years now, he told himself. She turned suddenly and saw him. She didn't smile, simply looked at him for a second or so, then glanced away.

Vereker in his faded rose cope was up at the altar, hands together as he commenced Mass. "I confess to Almighty God, and to you, my brothers and sisters, that I have sinned through my own fault."

He struck his breast and Devlin, aware that Molly Prior's eyes had swivelled sideways under the brim of the straw hat to watch him, joined in out of devilment, asking Blessed Mary ever Virgin, all the Angels and Saints and the rest of the congregation to pray for him to the Lord our God.

When she went down on her knees on the hassock, she seemed to descend in slow motion, lifting her skirt perhaps six inches too high. He had to choke back his laughter at the demureness of it. But he sobered soon enough when he became aware of Arthur Seymour's mad eyes glaring from the shadows beside a pillar on the far aisle.

When the service was over, Devlin made sure he was first out. He was astride the motorcycle and ready for off when he heard her call, "Mr. Devlin, just a minute." He turned as she hurried towards him, an umbrella over her head, her mother a few yards behind her. "Don't be in such a rush to be off," Molly said. "Are you ashamed or something?"

"Damn glad I came," Devlin told her.

Whether she blushed or not, it was impossible to say for the light was bad. In any case, her mother arrived at that moment. "This is my mum," Molly said. "And this is Mr. Devlin."

"I know all about you," Mrs. Prior said. "Anything we can do, you just ask now. Difficult for a man on his own."

"We thought you might like to come back and have tea with us," Molly told him.

Beyond them, he saw Arthur Seymour standing by the lychgate, glowering. Devlin said, "It's very nice of you, but to be honest, I'm in no fit state."

Mrs. Prior reached out to touch him. "Lord bless us, boy, but you're soaking. Get you home and into a hot bath on the instant. You'll catch your death."

"She's right," Molly told him fiercely. "You get off and mind you do as she says."

Devlin kicked the starter. "God protect me from this monstrous regiment of women," he said and rode away.

He was hungry, but too tired to do anything much about it, so he took a glass and the bottle of Bushmills Garvald had given him and one of his books and sat in the old wing-back chair and roasted his feet and read by the light of the fire. It was perhaps an hour later that a cold wind touched the back of his neck briefly. He had not heard the latch, but she was there, he knew that.

"What kept you?" he said without turning round.

"Very clever. I'd have thought you could have done better than that after I've walked a mile and a quarter over wet fields in the dark to bring you your supper."

She moved round to the fire. She was wearing her old raincoat, Wellington boots and a headscarf and carried a basket in one hand. "A meat and potato pie, but then I suppose you've eaten?"

He groaned aloud. "Don't go on. Just get it in the oven as quick as you can."

She put the basket down and pulled off her boots and unfastened the raincoat. Underneath she was wearing the flowered dress. She pulled off the scarf, shaking her hair. "That's better. What are you reading?"

He handed her the book. "Poetry," he said, "by a blind Irishman called Raftery who lived a long time ago.''

She peered at the page in the firelight. ''But I can't understand it,'' she said. ''It's in a foreign language.''

''Irish,'' he said. ''The language of kings.'' He took the book from her and read:

Anois, teacht an Earraigh, beidh an la dul chun sineadh,
is tar eis feile Bride, ardochaidh me mo sheol . . .
. . . Now, in the springtime, the day's getting longer,
On the feastday of Bridget, up my sail will go,
Since my journey's decided, my step will get stronger,
Till once more I stand in the plains of Mayo . . .

''That's beautiful,'' she said. ''Really beautiful.'' She dropped down on the rush mat beside him, leaning against the chair, her left hand touching his arm. ''Is that where you come from, this place Mayo?''

''No,'' he said, keeping his voice steady with some difficulty. ''From rather farther north, but Raftery had the right idea.''

''Liam,'' she said. ''Is that Irish, too?''

''Yes, m'am.''

''What does it mean?''

''William.''

She frowned. ''No, I think I prefer Liam. I mean, William's so ordinary.''

Devlin hung on to the book in his left hand and caught hold of her hair at the back with his right. ''Jesus, Joseph and Mary aid me.''

''And what's that supposed to mean?'' she asked, all innocence.

''It means, girl dear, that if you don't get that pie out of the oven and on to the plate this instant, I won't be responsible.''

She laughed suddenly, deep in the throat, leaning over for a moment, her head on his knee. ''Oh, I do like you,'' she said. ''Do you know that? From the first moment I saw you, Mr. Devlin, sir, sitting astride that bike outside the pub, I liked you.''

He groaned, closing his eyes, and she got to her feet, eased the skirt over her hips and got his pie from the oven.

When he walked her home over the fields it had stopped raining and the clouds had blown away, leaving a sky glowing with stars. The wind was cold and beat amongst the trees over their heads as they followed the field path, showering them with twigs. Devlin had the shotgun over his shoulder and she hung on to his left arm.

They hadn't talked much after the meal. She'd made him read more poetry to her, leaning against him, one knee raised. It had been infinitely worse than he could have imagined. Not in his scheme of things at all. He had three weeks, that was all, and a great deal to do in that time and no room for distraction.

They reached the farmyard wall and paused beside the gate.

"I was wondering. Wednesday afternoon if you've nothing on, I could do with some help in the barn. Some of the machinery needs moving for winter storage. It's a bit heavy for Mum and me. You could have your dinner with us."

It would have been churlish to refuse. "Why not?" he said.

She reached a hand up behind his neck, pulling his face down and kissed him with a fierce, passionate, inexperienced urgency that was incredibly moving. She was wearing some sort of lavender perfume, infinitely sweet, probably all she could afford. He was to remember it for the rest of his life.

She leaned against him and he said into her ear gently, "You're seventeen and I'm a very old thirty-five. Have you thought about that?"

She looked up at him, eyes blind. "Oh, you're lovely," she said. "So lovely."

A silly, banal phrase, laughable in other circumstances, but not now. Never now. He kissed her again, very lightly on the mouth. "Go in!"

She went without any attempt at protest, wakening only the chickens as she crossed the farmyard. Somewhere on the other side of the house, a dog barked hollowly, a door banged, Devlin turned and started back.

It began to rain again as he skirted the last meadow above the main road. He crossed to the dyke path opposite with the old wooden sign, *Hobs End Farm*, which no one had ever thought worth taking down. Devlin trudged along, head bowed against the rain. Suddenly there was a rustling in the reeds to his right and a figure bounded into his path.

In spite of the rain, the cloud cover was only sparse and in the light of the quarter moon he saw that Arthur Seymour crouched in front of him. "I told you," he said. "I warned you, but you wouldn't take no notice. Now you'll have to learn the hard way."

Devlin had the shotgun off his shoulder in a second. It wasn't loaded, but no matter. He thumbed the hammer back with a very definite double click and rammed the barrel under Seymour's chin.

"Now you be careful," he said. "Because I've licence to shoot vermin here from the squire himself and you're on the squire's property."

Seymour jumped back. "I'll get you, see if I don't. And that dirty little bitch. I'll pay you both out."

He turned and ran into the night. Devlin shouldered his gun and moved on towards the cottage, head down as the rain increased in force. Seymour was mad—no, not quite—just not responsible. He wasn't worried about his threats in the slightest, but then he thought of Molly and his stomach went hollow.

"My God," he said softly. "If he harms her, I'll kill the bastard. I'll kill him."

9

THE STEN MACHINE CARBINE WAS probably the greatest mass produced weapon of the Second World War and the standby of most British infantrymen. Shoddy and crude it may have looked, but it could stand up to more ill-treatment than any other weapon of its type. It came to pieces in seconds and would fit into a handbag or the pockets of an overcoat— a fact which made it invaluable to the various European resistance groups to whom it was parachuted by the British. Drop it in the mud, stamp on it and it would still kill as effectively as the most expensive Thompson gun.

The MK IIS version was specially developed for use by commando units, fitted with a silencer which absorbed the noise of the bullet explosions to an amazing degree. The only sound when it fired was the clicking of the bolt and that could seldom be heard beyond a range of twenty yards.

The one which Staff Sergeant Willi Scheid held in his hands on the improvised firing range amongst the sand dunes at Landsvoort on the morning of Wednesday 20 October, was a mint specimen. There was a row of targets at the far end, lifesize replicas of charging *Tommis*. He emptied the magazine into the first five, working from left to right. It was an eerie experience to see the bullets shredding the target and to hear only the clicking of the bolt. Steiner and the rest of his small assault force, standing in a semi-circle behind him, were suitably impressed.

"Excellent!" Steiner held out his hand and Scheid passed the Sten to him. "Really excellent!" Steiner examined it and handed it to Neumann.

Neumann cursed suddenly. "Dammit, the barrel's hot."

"That is so, Herr Oberleutnant," Scheid said. "You must be careful to hold only the canvas insulating cover. The silencer tubes heat rapidly when the weapon is fired on full automatic."

Scheid was from the Ordnance Depot at Hamburg, a small, rather insignificant man in steel spectacles and the shabbiest uniform Steiner had ever seen. He moved across to a ground-sheet on which various weapons were displayed. "The Sten gun, in both the silenced and normal versions, will be the machine pistol you will use. As regards a light machine-gun, the Bren. Not as good a general purpose weapon as our own MG-forty-two, but an excellent section weapon. It fires in either single shots or bursts of four or five rounds so it's very economical and highly accurate."

"What about rifles?" Steiner asked.

Before Scheid could reply, Neumann tapped Steiner on the shoulder and the Colonel turned in time to see the Stork come in low from the direction of the Ijsselmeer and turn for its first circuit over the airstrip.

Steiner said, "I'll take over for a moment, Sergeant." He turned to the men. "From now on what Staff Sergeant Scheid says goes. You've got a couple of weeks, and by the time he's finished with you I'll expect you to be able to take these things apart and put them together again with your eyes closed." He glanced at Brandt. "Any assistance he wants, you see that he gets it, understand?"

Brandt sprang to attention. "Herr Oberst."

"Good." Steiner's glance seemed to take in each man as an individual. "Most of the time Oberleutnant Neumann and myself will be in there with you. And don't worry. You'll know what it's all about soon enough, I promise you."

Brandt brought the entire group to attention. Steiner saluted, then turned and hurried across to the field car which was parked nearby, followed by Neumann. He got into the passenger seat, Neumann climbed behind the wheel and drove away. As they approached the main entrance to the airstrip the military policeman on duty opened the gate and saluted awkwardly, hanging on to his snarling guard dog with the other hand.

"One of these days that brute is going to get loose," Neumann said, "and frankly, I don't think it knows which side it's on."

The Stork dropped in for an excellent landing and four or five Luftwaffe personnel raced out to meet it in a small truck. Neumann followed in the field car and pulled up a few yards away from the Stork. Steiner lit a cigarette as they waited for Radl to disembark.

Neumann said, "He's got someone with him."

Steiner looked up with a frown as Max Radl came towards him, a cheerful smile on his face. "Kurt, how goes it?" he called, hand outstretched.

But Steiner was more interested in his companion, the tall, elegant young man with the deathshead of the SS in his cap. "Who's your friend, Max?" he asked softly.

Radl's smile was awkward as he made the necessary introduction.

"Colonel Kurt Steiner—Untersturmführer Harvey Preston of the British Free Corps."

Steiner had had the old living room of the farmhouse converted into the nerve centre for the entire operation. There were a couple of army cots at one end of the room for himself and Neumann and two large tables placed down the centre were covered with maps and photos of the Hobs End and Studley Constable general area. There was also a beautifully made three-dimensional mock-up as yet only half completed. Radl leaned over it with interest, a glass of brandy in one hand. Ritter Neumann stood on the other side of the table and Steiner paced up and down by the window, smoking furiously.

Radl said, "This model is really superb. Who's working on it?"

"Private Klugl," Neumann told him. "He was an artist, I think, before the war."

Steiner turned impatiently. "Let's stick to the matter in hand, Max. Do you seriously expect me to take that—that object out there?"

"It's the Reichsführer's idea, not mine," Radl said mildly. "In matters like this, my dear Kurt, I take orders, I don't give them."

"But he must be mad."

Radl nodded and went to the sideboard to help himself to more cognac. "I believe that has been suggested before."

"All right," Steiner said. "Let's look at it from the purely practical angle. If this thing is to succeed it's going to need a highly disciplined body of men who can move as one, think as one, act as one and that's exactly what we've got. Those lads of mine have been to hell and back. Crete, Leningrad, Stalingrad and a few places in between and I was with them every step of the way. Max, there are times when I don't even have to give a spoken order."

"I accept that completely."

"Then how on earth do you expect them to function with an outsider at this stage, especially one like Preston?" He picked up the file Radl had given him and shook it. "A petty criminal, a poseur who's acted since the day he was born, even to himself." He threw the file down in disgust. "He doesn't even know what real soldiering is."

"What's more to the point at the moment, or so it seems to me," Ritter Neumann put in, "he's never jumped out of an aeroplane in his life."

Radl took out one of his Russian cigarettes and Neumann lit it for him. "I wonder, Kurt, whether you're letting your emotions run away with you in this matter."

"All right," Steiner said. "So my American half hates his lousy guts because he's a traitor and a turncoat and my German half isn't too keen on him either." He shook his head in exasperation. "Look, Max, have you any idea what jump training is like?" He turned to Neumann. "Tell him, Ritter."

"Six jumps go into the paratroopers qualification badge and after that, never less than six a year if he wants to keep it," Neumann said. "And that applies to everyone from private to general officer. Jump pay is sixty-five to one hundred and twenty Reichsmarks per month, according to rank."

"So?" Radl said.

"To earn it you train on the ground for two months, make your first jump alone from six hundred feet. After that, five jumps in groups and in varying light conditions, including darkness, bringing the altitude down all the time and then the grand finale. Nine plane-loads dropping together in battle conditions at under four hundred feet."

"Very impressive," Radl said. "On the other hand, Preston has to jump only once, admittedly at night, but to a large and very lonely beach. A perfect dropping zone as you have admitted yourselves. I would have thought it not beyond the bounds of possibility to train him sufficiently for that single occasion."

Neumann turned in despair to Steiner. "What more can I say?"

"Nothing," Radl said, "because he goes. He goes because the Reichsführer thinks it a good idea."

"For God's sake," Steiner said. "It's impossible, Max, can't you see that?"

"I'm returning to Berlin in the morning," Radl replied. "Come with me and tell him yourself if that's how you feel. Or would you rather not?"

Steiner's face was pale. "Damn you to hell, Max, you know I can't and you know why." For a moment he seemed to have difficulty in speaking. "My father—he's all right? You've seen him?"

"No," Radl said. "But the Reichsführer instructed me to tell you that you have his personal assurance in this matter."

"And what in the hell is that supposed to mean?" Steiner took a deep breath and smiled ironically. "I know one thing. If we can take Churchill, who I might as well tell you now is a man I've always personally admired, and not just because we both had an American mother, then we can drop in on Gestapo Headquarters in Prinz Albrechtstrasse and grab that little shit any time we want. Come to think of it, that's quite an idea." He grinned at Neumann. "What do you think, Ritter?"

"Then you'll take him?" Radl said eagerly. "Preston, I mean?"

"Oh, I'll take him all right," Steiner said, "only by the time I've finished, he'll wish he'd never been born." He turned to Neumann. "All right, Ritter. Bring him in and I'll give him some idea of what hell is going to be like.''

When Harvey Preston was in repertory he'd once played a gallant young British officer in the trenches of the First World War in that great play *Journey's End*. A brave, war-weary young veteran, old beyond his years, able to meet death with a wry smile on his face and a glass raised, at least symbolically, in his right hand. When the roof of the dug-out finally collapsed and the curtain fell, you simply picked yourself up and went back to the dressing room to wash the blood off.

But not now. This was actually happening, terrifying in its implication and quite suddenly he was sick with fear. It was not that he had lost any faith in Germany's ability to win the war. He believed in that totally. It was simply that he preferred to be alive to see the glorious day for himself.

It was cold in the garden and he paced nervously up and down, smoking a cigarette and waiting impatiently for some sign of life from the farmhouse. His nerves were jagged. Steiner appeared at the kitchen door. ''Preston!'' he called in English. ''Get in here.''

He turned without another word. When Preston went into the living room, he found Steiner, Radl and Ritter Neumann grouped around the map table.

''Herr Oberst,'' he began.

''Shut up!'' Steiner told him coldly. He nodded to Radl. ''Give him his orders.''

Radl said formally, ''Untersturmführer Harvey Preston of the British Free Corps, from this moment you are to consider yourself under the total and absolute command of Lieutenant-Colonel Steiner of the Parachute Regiment. This by direct order of Reichsführer Heinrich Himmler himself. You understand?''

As far as Preston was concerned Radl might as well have worn a black cap for his words were like a death sentence. There was sweat on his forehead as he turned to Steiner and stammered, ''But Herr Oberst, I've never made a parachute jump.''

''The least of your deficiencies,'' Steiner told him grimly. ''But we'll take care of all of them, believe me.''

''Herr Oberst, I must protest,'' Preston began and Steiner cut in on him like an axe falling.

''Shut your mouth and get your feet together. In future you speak when you're spoken to and not before.'' He walked round behind Preston who was by now standing rigidly to attention. ''All you are at the moment is excess baggage. You're not even a soldier, just a pretty uniform.

We'll have to see if we can change that, won't we?'' There was silence and he repeated the question quite softly into Preston's left ear. "Won't we?''

He managed to convey an infinite menace, and Preston said hurriedly, "Yes, Herr Oberst.''

"Good. So now we understand each other.'' Steiner walked round to the front of him again. "Point number one—at the moment the only people at Landsvoort who know the purpose for which this whole affair had been put together are the four of us present in this room. If anyone else finds out before I'm ready to tell them because of a careless word from you, I'll shoot you myself. Understand?''

"Yes, Herr Oberst.''

"As regards rank, you cease to hold any for the time being. Lieutenant Neumann will see that you're provided with parachutists' overalls and a jump smock. You'll therefore be indistinguishable from the rest of your comrades with whom you will be training. Naturally there will be certain additional work necessary in your case, but we'll come to that later. Any questions?''

Preston's eyes burned, he could hardly breathe so great was his rage. Radl said gently, "Of course, Herr Untersturmführer, you could always return to Berlin with me if dissatisfied and take up the matter personally with the Reichsführer.''

In a choked whisper, Preston said, "No questions.''

"Good.'' Steiner turned to Ritter Neumann. "Get him kitted out, then hand him over to Brandt. I'll speak to you about his training schedule later.'' He nodded to Preston. "All right, you're dismissed.''

Preston didn't give the Nazi party salute because it suddenly occurred to him that it would very possibly not be appreciated. Instead he saluted, turned and stumbled out. Ritter Neumann grinned and went after him.

As the door closed, Steiner said, "After that I really do need a drink,'' and he moved across to the sideboard and poured a cognac.

"Will it work out, Kurt?'' Radl asked.

"Who knows?'' Steiner smiled wolfishly. "With luck he might break a leg in training.'' He swallowed some of his brandy. "Anyway, to more important matters. How's Devlin doing at the moment? Any more news?''

In her small bedroom in the old farmhouse above the marsh at Hobs End, Molly Prior was trying to make herself presentable for Devlin, due to arrive for his dinner as promised at any moment. She undressed quickly and stood in front of the mirror in the old mahogany wardrobe for a moment in pants and bra and examined herself critically. The underwear was neat and clean, but showed signs of numerous repairs. Well, that was all right and the same for everybody. There were never enough clothing coupons to go round. It was what was underneath that mattered and that wasn't too bad. Nice, firm breasts, round hips, good thighs.

She placed a hand on her belly and thought of Devlin touching her like that and her stomach churned. She opened the top drawer of the dresser, took out her only pair of pre-war silk stockings, each one darned many times, and rolled them on carefully. Then she got the cotton dress that she had worn on Saturday from the wardrobe.

As she pulled it over her head, there was the sound of a car horn. She peered out of the window in time to see an old Morris drive into the farmyard. Father Vereker was at the wheel. Molly cursed softly, eased the dress over her head, splitting a seam under one arm, and pulled on her Sunday shoes with the two-inch heels.

As she went downstairs she ran a comb through her hair, wincing as it snagged on the tangles. Vereker was in the kitchen with her mother and he turned and greeted her with what for him was a surprisingly warm smile.

"Hello, Molly, how are you?"

"Hard pressed and hard worked, Father." She tied an apron about her waist and said to her mother, "That meat and tatie pie. Ready is it? He'll be here any minute."

"Ah, you're expecting company." Vereker stood up, leaning on his stick. "I'm in the way. A bad time."

"Not at all, Father," Mrs. Prior said. "Only Mr. Devlin, the new warden at Hobs End. He's having his dinner here, then giving us an afternoon's work. Was there anything special?"

Vereker turned to look at Molly, speculatively, noting the dress, the shoes and there was a frown on his face as if he disapproved of what he saw. Molly flared angrily. She put her left hand on her hip and faced him belligerently.

"Was it me you wanted, Father?" she asked, her voice dangerously calm.

"No, it was Arthur I wanted a word with. Arthur Seymour. He helps you up here Tuesdays and Wednesdays, doesn't he?"

He was lying, she knew that instantly. "Arthur Seymour doesn't work here anymore, Father. I'd have thought you'd have known that. Or didn't he tell you I sacked him?"

Vereker was very pale. He would not admit it, yet he was not prepared to lie to her face. Instead he said, "Why was that, Molly?"

"Because I didn't want him round here anymore."

He turned to Mrs. Prior inquiringly. She looked uncomfortable, but shrugged. "He's not fit company for man nor beast."

He made a bad mistake then and said to Molly, "The feeling in the village is that he's been hard done to. That you should have a better reason than preference for an outsider. Hard on a man who's bided his time and helped where he could, Molly.''

''Man,'' she said. ''Is that what he is, Father? I never realized. You could tell 'em he was always sticking his hand up my skirt and trying to feel me.'' Vereker's face was very white now, but she carried on remorselessly. ''Of course, people in the village might think that all right, him having acted no different round females since he was twelve years old and no one ever did a thing about it. And you don't seem to be shaping no better.''

''Molly!'' her mother cried, aghast.

''I see,'' Molly said. ''One mustn't offend a priest by telling him the truth, is that what you're trying to say?'' There was contempt on her face when she looked at Vereker. ''Don't tell me you don't know what he's like, Father. He never misses Mass Sundays so you must confess him often enough.''

She turned from the furious anger in his eyes as there was a knock at the door, smoothing her dress over her hips as she hurried to answer. But when she opened the door it wasn't Devlin, but Laker Armsby who stood there rolling a cigarette beside the tractor with which he'd just towed in a trailer loaded with turnips.

He grinned. ''Where you want this lot then, Molly?''

''Damn you, Laker, you choose your times, don't you? In the barn. Here, I'd better show you myself or you're bound to get it wrong.''

She started across the yard, picking her way through the mud in her good shoes and Laker trailed after her. ''Dressed up like a dog's dinner today. Now I wonder why that should be, Molly?''

''You mind your business, Laker Armsby,'' she told him, ''and get this door open.''

Laker tipped the holding bar and started to open one of the great barn doors. Arthur Seymour was standing on the other side, his cap pulled low over the mad eyes, the massive shoulders straining the seams of the old reefer coat.

''Now then, Arthur,'' Laker said warily.

Seymour shoved him to one side and grabbed Molly by the right wrist, pulling her towards him. ''You get in here, you bitch. I want words with you.''

Laker pawed at his arm ineffectually. ''Now look here, Arthur,'' he said. ''No way to behave.''

Seymour slapped him back-handed, bringing blood from his nose in a sudden gush. ''Get out of it!'' he said and shoved Laker backwards into the mud.

Molly kicked out furiously. ''You let me go!''

''Oh, no,'' he said. He pushed the door closed behind him and shot the bolt. "Never again, Molly." He grabbed for her hair with his left hand. "Now you be a good girl and I won't hurt you. Not so long as you give me what you've been giving that Irish bastard."

His fingers were groping for the hem of her skirt.

"You stink," she said. "You know that? Like an old sow that's had a good wallow."

She leaned down and bit his wrist savagely. He cried out in pain, releasing his grip, but clutched at her with his other hand as she turned, dress tearing, and ran for the ladder to the loft.

Devlin, on his way across the fields from Hobs End, reached the crest of the meadow above the farm in time to see Molly and Laker Armsby crossing the farmyard to the barn. A moment later Laker was propelled from the barn to fall flat on his back in the mud and the great door slammed. Devlin tossed his cigarette to one side and went down the hill on the run.

By the time he was vaulting the fence into the farmyard, Father Vereker and Mrs. Prior were at the barn. The priest hammered on the door with his stick. "Arthur?" he shouted. "Open the door—stop this foolishness."

The only reply was a scream from Molly. "What's going on?" Devlin demanded.

"It's Seymour," Laker told him, holding a bloody handkerchief to his nose. "Got Molly in there, he has, and he's bolted the door."

Devlin tried a shoulder and realized at once that he was wasting his time. He glanced about him desperately as Molly cried out again and his eyes lit on the tractor where Laker had left it, engine ticking over. Devlin was across the yard in a moment, scrambled up into the high seat behind the wheel and rammed the stick into gear, accelerating so savagely that the tractor shot forward, trailer swaying, turnips scattering across the yard like cannon balls. Vereker, Mrs. Prior and Laker got out of the way just in time as the tractor collided with the doors, bursting them inwards and rolling irresistibly forward.

Devlin braked to a halt. Molly was up in the loft, Seymour down below trying to re-position the ladder which she had obviously thrown down. Devlin switched off the engine and Seymour turned and looked at him, a strange, dazed look in his eyes.

"Now then, you bastard," Devlin said.

Vereker limped in. "No, Devlin, leave this to me!" he called and turned to Seymour. "Arthur, this won't do, will it?"

Seymour paid not the slightest heed to either of them. It was as if they didn't exist and he turned and started to climb the ladder. Devlin jumped down from the tractor and kicked the ladder from under him. Seymour fell heavily to the ground. He lay there for a moment or so, shaking his head. Then his eyes cleared.

As Seymour got to his feet, Father Vereker lurched forward. "Now, Arthur, I've told you . . . ''

It was as far as he got for Seymour hurled him so violently to one side that he fell down. "I'll kill you, Devlin!''

He gave a cry of rage and rushed in, great hands outstretched to destroy. Devlin dodged to one side and the weight of Seymour's progress carried him into the tractor. Devlin gave him a left and right to the kidneys and danced away as Seymour cried out in agony.

He came in with a roar and Devlin feinted with his right and smashed his left fist into the ugly mouth, splitting the lips so that blood spurted. He followed up with a right under the ribs that sounded like an axle going into wood.

He ducked in under Seymour's next wild punch and hit him under the ribs again. "Footwork, timing and hitting, that is the secret. The Holy Trinity, we used to call them, Father. Learn those and ye shall inherit the earth as surely as the meek. Always helped out by a little dirty work now and then, of course.''

He kicked Seymour under the right kneecap and as the big man doubled over in agony, put a knee into the descending face, lifting him back through the door into the mud of the yard. Seymour got to his feet slowly and stood there like a dazed bull in the centre of the plaza, blood on his face.

Devlin danced in. "You don't know when to lie down, do you, Arthur, but that's hardly surprising with a brain the size of a pea.''

He advanced his right foot, slipped in the mud and went down on one knee. Seymour delivered a stunning blow to his forehead that put him flat on his back. Molly screamed and rushed in, hands clawing at Seymour's face. He threw her away from him and raised a foot to crush Devlin. But the Irishman got a hand to it and twisted, sending him staggering into the barn entrance again.

When he turned, Devlin was reaching for him, no longer smiling, the white killing face on him now. "All right, Arthur. Let's get it over with. I'm hungry.''

Seymour tried to rush him again and Devlin circled, driving him across the yard, giving him neither quarter nor peace, evading his great swinging punches with ease, driving his knuckles into the face again and again until it was a mask of blood.

There was an old zinc water trough near the back door and Devlin pushed him towards it relentlessly. "And now you will listen to me, you bastard!'' he said. "Touch that girl again, harm her in any way and I'll take the shears to you myself. Do you understand me?'' He punched under the ribs again and Seymour groaned, his hands coming down. "And in future, if you are in a room and I enter, you get up and walk out. Do you understand that too?"

His right connected twice with the unprotected jaw and Seymour fell across the trough and rolled on to his back.

Devlin dropped to his knees and pushed his face into the rain water in the trough. He surfaced for air to find Molly crouched beside him, and Father Vereker bending over Seymour. "My God, Devlin, you might have killed him," the priest said.

"Not that one," Devlin said. "Unfortunately."

As if anxious to prove him right, Seymour groaned and tried to sit up. At the same moment Mrs. Prior came out of the house with a double-barrelled shotgun in her hands. "You get him out of here," she told Vereker. "And tell him from me, when his brains are unscrambled, that if he comes back here bothering my girl again, I'll shoot him like a dog and answer for it."

Laker Armsby dipped an old enamel bucket into the trough and emptied it over Seymour. "There you go, Arthur," he said cheerfully. "First bath you've had since Michaelmas, I dare say."

Seymour groaned and grabbed for the trough to pull himself up. Father Vereker said, "Help me, Laker," and they took him between them across to the Morris.

Quite suddenly, the earth moved for Devlin, like the sea turning over. He closed his eyes. He was aware of Molly's cry of alarm, her strong, young shoulder under his arm and then her mother was on the other side of him and they were walking him towards the house between them.

He surfaced to find himself in the kitchen chair by the fire, his face against Molly's breasts, while she held a damp cloth to his forehead. "You can let me go now, I'm fine," he told her.

She looked down at him, face anxious. "God, but I thought he'd split your skull with that one punch."

"A weakness of mine," Devlin told her, aware of her concern and momentarily serious. "After periods of intense stress I sometimes keel over, go out like a light. Some psychological thing."

"What's that?" she demanded, puzzled.

"Never mind," he said. "Just let me put my head back where I can see your right nipple."

She put a hand to her torn bodice and flushed. "You devil."

"You see," he said. "Not much difference between Arthur and me when it comes right down to it."

She tapped a finger very gently between his eyes. "I never heard such rubbish from a grown man in all my life."

Her mother bustled into the kitchen fastening a clean apron about her waist. "By God, boy, but you must have a powerful hunger on you after that little bout. Are you ready for your meat and potato pie now, then?''

Devlin looked up at Molly and smiled. ''Thank you kindly, ma'am. As a matter of fact, I think I could say with some truth that I'm ready for anything.''

The girl choked back laughter, shook a clenched fist under his nose and went to help her mother.

It was late evening when Devlin returned to Hobs End. It was very still and quiet on the marsh as if rain threatened and the sky was dark and thunder rumbled uneasily on the far horizon. He took the long way round to check the dyke gates that controlled the flow into the network of waterways and when he finally turned into the yard, Joanna Grey's car was parked by the door. She was wearing a WVS uniform and leaning on the wall looking out to sea, the retriever sitting beside her patiently. She turned to look at him as he joined her. There was a sizeable bruise on his forehead where Seymour's fist had landed.

''Nasty,'' she said. ''Do you try to commit suicide often?''

He grinned. ''You should see the other fella.''

''I have.'' She shook her head. ''It's got to stop, Liam.''

He lit a cigarette, match flaring in cupped hands. ''What has?''

''Molly Prior. You're not here for that. You've got a job to do.''

''Come off it,'' he said. ''I haven't a thing to lay hand to before my meeting with Garvald on the twenty-eighth.''

''Don't be silly. People in places like this are the same the world over, you know that. Distrust the stranger and look after your own. They don't like what you did to Arthur Seymour.''

''And I didn't like what he tried to do to Molly.'' Devlin half-laughed in a kind of astonishment. ''God save us, woman, if only half the things Laker Armsby told me about Seymour this afternoon are true, they should have locked him up years ago and thrown away the key. Sexual assaults of one kind or another too numerous to mention and he's crippled at least two men in his time.''

''They never use the police in places like this. They handle it themselves.'' She shook her head impatiently. ''But this isn't getting us anywhere. We can't afford to alienate people so do the sensible thing. Leave Molly alone.''

''Is that an order, ma'am?''

''Don't be an idiot. I'm appealing to your good sense, that's all.''

She walked to the car, put the dog in the back and got behind the wheel. ''Any news from the Sir Henry front?'' Devlin asked as she switched on the engine.

She smiled. ''I'm keeping him warm, don't worry. I'll be on the radio to Radl again on Friday night. I'll let you know what comes up.''

She drove away and Devlin unlocked the door and let himself in. Inside he hesitated for a long moment and then shot the bolt and went into the living room. He pulled the curtain, lit a small fire and sat in front of it, a glass of Garvald's Bushmills in his hand.

It was a shame—one hell of a shame, but perhaps Joanna Grey was right. It would be silly to go looking for trouble. He thought of Molly for one brief moment, then resolutely selected a copy of *The Midnight Court* in Irish from his small stock of books and forced himself to concentrate.

It started to rain, brushing the window pane. It was about seven-thirty when the handle of the front door rattled vainly. After a while, there was a tap at the window on the other side of the curtain and she called his name softly. He kept on reading, straining to follow the words in the failing light of the small fire and after a while, she went away.

He swore softly, black rage in his heart and threw the book at the wall, resisting with every fibre of his being the impulse to run to the door, unlock it and go after her. He poured himself another large whiskey and stood at the window, feeling suddenly lonelier than he had ever felt in his life before, as rain hurtled in across the marsh in a sudden fury.

And at Landsvoort there was a gale blowing in off the sea, with the kind of bitter drenching rain that cut to the bone like a surgeon's knife. Harvey Preston, on guard duty at the garden gate of the old farmhouse, huddled against the wall, cursing Steiner, cursing Radl, cursing Himmler and whatever else had combined to reduce him to this, the lowest and most miserable level of his entire life.

10

During the Second World War, the German paratrooper differed from his British counterpart in one highly important aspect—the type of parachute used.

The German version, unlike that issued to Luftwaffe pilots and aircrew, did not have straps, known as lift webs, fastening the shroud lines to the harness. Instead, the shroud lines connected directly to the pack itself. It made the whole process of jumping entirely different and because of that, on Sunday morning at Landsvoort, Steiner arranged for a demonstration of the standard British parachute in the old barn at the back of the farmhouse.

The men stood in front of him in a semi-circle, Harvey Preston in the centre, dressed, like the others, in jump boots and overalls. Steiner faced them, Ritter Neumann and Brandt on either side of him.

Steiner said, "The whole point of this operation, as I've already explained, is that we pass ourselves off as a Polish unit of the Special Air Service. Because of this, not only will all your equipment be British— you'll jump using the standard parachute used by British airborne forces." He turned to Ritter Neumann. "All yours."

Brandt picked up a parachute pack and held it aloft. Neumann said, "X Type parachute as used by British Airborne forces. Weighs around twenty-eight pounds and as the Herr Oberst says, very different from ours."

Brandt pulled the ripcord, the pack opened, disgorging the khaki chute. Neumann said, "Note the way the shroud lines are fastened to the harness by shoulder straps, just like the Luftwaffe."

"The point being," Steiner put in, "that you can manipulate the chute, change direction, have the kind of control over your own destiny that you just don't get with the one you're used to."

"Another thing," Ritter said. "With our parachute the centre of gravity is high which means you get snagged up in the shroud lines unless you exit in a partially facedown position, as you all know. With the X type, you can go out in the standing posture and that's what we're going to practise now."

He nodded to Brandt, who said, "All right, let's have you all down here."

There was a loft perhaps fifteen feet high at the far end of the barn. A rope had been looped over a beam above it, an X type parachute harness fastened to one end. "A trifle primitive," Brandt announced jovially, "but good enough. You jump off the loft and there'll be half a dozen of us on the other end to make sure you don't hit the dirt too hard. Who's first?"

Steiner said, "I'd better claim that honour, mainly because I've things to do elsewhere."

Ritter helped him into the harness, then Brandt and four others got on the other end of the rope and hauled him up to the loft. He paused on the edge for a moment or so, Ritter signalled and Steiner swung out into space. The other end of the rope went up, taking three of the men with it, but Brandt and Sergeant Sturm hung on, cursing. Steiner hit the dirt, rolled over in a perfect fall and sprang to his feet.

"All right," he told Ritter. "Usual stick formation. I've time to see everyone do it once. Then I must go."

He moved to the rear of the group and lit a cigarette as Neumann buckled himself into the harness. From the back of the barn it looked reasonably hair-raising as the Oberleutnant was hoisted up to the loft, but there was a roar of laughter when Ritter made a mess of his landing and ended up flat on his back.

"See?" Private Klugl said to Werner Briegel. "That's what riding those damn torpedoes does for you. The Herr Leutnant's forgotten everything he ever knew."

Brandt went next and Steiner observed Preston closely. The Englishman was very pale, sweat on his face——obviously terrified. The group worked through with varying success, the men on the end of the rope in one unfortunate lapse mistaking the signal and leaving go at the wrong moment so that Private Hagl descended the full fifteen feet under his own power with all the grace of a sack of potatoes. But he picked himself up, none the worse for his experience.

Finally, it was Preston's turn. The good humour faded abruptly.

Steiner nodded to Brandt. "Up with him."

The five men on the end of the rope hauled with a will and Preston shot up, banging against the loft on the way, finishing just below the roof. They lowered him till he stood on the edge, gazing down at them wildly.

"All right, English," Brandt called. "Remember what I told you. Jump when I signal."

He turned to instruct the men on the rope, and there was a cry of alarm from Briegel as Preston simply fell forward into space. Ritter Neumann jumped for the rope. Preston came to rest three feet above the ground, swinging like a pendulum, arms hanging at his side, head down.

Brandt put a hand under the chin and looked into the Englishman's face. "He's fainted."

"So it would appear," Steiner said.

"What do we do with him, Herr Oberst?" Ritter Neumann demanded.

"Bring him round," Steiner said calmly. "Then put him up again. As many times as it takes until he can do it satisfactorily—or breaks a leg." He saluted. "Carry on, please," turned and went out.

There were at least a dozen men in the tap room of the Studley Arms when Devlin went in. Laker Armsby in his usual place by the fire with his mouth organ, the rest seated around the two large tables playing dominoes. Arthur Seymour was staring out of the window, a pint in his hand.

"God save all here!" Devlin announced cheerfully. There was complete silence, every face in the room turned towards him except for Seymour's. "God save you kindly, was the answer to that one," Devlin said. "Ah, well."

There was a step behind him and he turned to find George Wilde emerging from the back room, wiping his hands on a butcher's apron. His face was grave and steady, no emotion there at all. "I was just closing, Mr. Devlin," he said politely.

"Time for a jar, surely."

"I'm afraid not. You'll have to leave, sir."

The room was very quiet. Devlin put his hands in his pockets and hunched his shoulders, head down. And when he looked up, Wilde took an involuntary step back, for the Irishman's face had turned very pale, the skin stretched tight over the cheekbones, blue eyes glittering.

"There is one man here who will leave," Devlin said quietly, "and it is not me."

Seymour turned from the window. One eye was still completely closed, his lips scabbed and swollen. His entire face seemed lopsided and was covered with purple and green bruises. He stared at Devlin dully, then put down his half-finished pint of ale and shuffled out.

Devlin turned back to Wilde. "I'll have that drink, now, Mr. Wilde. A drop of Scotch, Irish being something you'll never have heard of here at the edge of your own little world, and don't try to tell me you don't have a bottle or two under the counter for favoured customers."

Wilde opened his mouth as if to speak and obviously thought better of it. He went into the back and returned with a bottle of White Horse and a small glass. He poured out a single measure and placed the glass on the shelf next to Devlin's head.

Devlin produced a handful of change. "One shilling and sixpence," he said cheerfully, counting it out on the nearest table. "The going price for a nip. I'm taking it for granted, of course, that such a fine, upstanding pillar of the church as yourself wouldn't be dealing in black market booze."

Wilde made no reply. The whole room waited. Devlin picked up the glass, held it to the light, then emptied it in a golden stream to the floor. He put the glass down carefully on the table. "Lovely," he said. "I enjoyed that."

Laker Armsby broke into a wild cackle of laughter, Devlin grinned. "Thank you, Laker, my old son. I love you too," he said and walked out.

⚓

It was raining hard at Landsvoort as Steiner drove across the airstrip in his field car. He braked to a halt outside the first hangar and ran for its shelter. The starboard engine of the Dakota was laid bare and Peter Gericke, in a pair of old overalls, grease up to his elbows, worked with a Luftwaffe sergeant and three mechanics.

"Peter?" Steiner called. "Have you got a moment? I'd like a progress report."

"Oh, things are going well enough."

"No problems with the engines?"

"None at all. They're nine-hundred horsepower Wright Cyclones. Really first class and as far as I can judge, they've done very little time. We're only stripping as a precaution."

"Do you usually work on your own engines?"

"Whenever I'm allowed." Gericke smiled. "When I flew these things in South America you had to service your own engines, because there was nobody else who could."

"No problems?"

"Not as far as I can see. She's scheduled to have her new paint job some time next week. No rush on that and Bohmler's fitting a Lichtenstein set so we'll have good radar coverage. A milk run. An hour across the North Sea, an hour back. Nothing to it."

"In an aircraft whose maximum speed is half that of most RAF or Luftwaffe fighters."

Gericke shrugged. "It's all in how you fly them, not in how fast they go."

"You want a test flight, don't you?"

"That's right."

"I've been thinking," Steiner said. "It might be a good idea to combine it with a practice drop. Preferably one night when the tide is well out. We could use the beach north of the sand pier. It will give the lads a chance to try out these British parachutes."

"What altitude are you thinking of?"

"Probably four hundred feet. I want them down fast and from that height fifteen seconds is all it takes."

"Rather them than me. I've only had to hit the silk three times in my career and it was a lot higher than that." The wind howled across the airstrip, driving rain before it, and he shivered. "What a bloody awful place."

"It serves its purpose."

"And what's that?"

Steiner grinned. "You ask me that at least five times a day. Don't you ever give up?"

"I'd like to know what it's all about, that's all."

"Maybe you will, one day, that's up to Radl, but for the moment we're here because we're here."

"And Preston?" Gericke said. "I wonder what his reason is? What makes a man do what he's done."

"All sorts of things," Steiner said. "In his case, he's got a pretty uniform, officer status. He's somebody for the first time in his life, that means a lot when you've been nothing. As regards the rest—well, he's here as the result of a direct order from Himmler himself."

"What about you?" Gericke asked. "The greater good of the Third Reich? A life for the Führer?"

Steiner smiled. "God knows. War is only a matter of perspective. After all, if it had been my father who was American and my mother German, I'd have been on the other side. As for the Parachute Regiment—I joined that because it seemed like a good idea at the time. After a while, of course, it grows on you."

"I do it because I'd rather fly anything than nothing," Gericke said, "and I suppose it's much the same for most of those RAF lads on the other side of the North Sea. But you . . . " He shook his head. "I don't really see it. Is it a game to you, then, just that and nothing more?"

Steiner said wearily, "I used to know, now I'm not so sure. My father was a soldier of the old school. Prussian blue. Plenty of blood and iron, but honour, too."

"And this task they've given you to do," Gericke said, "this—this English business, whatever it is. You have no doubts?"

"None at all. A perfectly proper military venture, believe me. Churchill himself couldn't fault it, in principle, at least." Gericke tried to smile and failed and Steiner put a hand on his shoulder. "I know, there are days when I could weep myself—for all of us," and he turned and walked away through the rain.

In the Reichsführer's private office, Radl stood in front of the great man's desk while Himmler read through his report. "Excellent, Herr Oberst," he said finally. "Really quite excellent." He laid the report down. "Everything would appear to be progressing more than satisfactorily. You have heard from the Irishman?"

"No, only from Mrs. Grey, that is the arrangement. Devlin has an excellent radio-telephone set. Something which we picked up from the British SOE, which will keep him in touch with the E-boat on its way in. That is the part of the operation he will handle as regards communication."

"The Admiral has not become suspicious in any way? Has picked up no hint of what is happening? You're sure of that?"

"Perfectly, Herr Reichsführer. My visits to France and Holland, I've been able to handle in conjunction with Abwehr business in Paris and Antwerp or Rotterdam. As the Reichsführer is aware, I have always had considerable latitude from the Admiral as regards running my own section."

"And when do you go to Landsvoort again?"

"Next weekend. By a fortunate turn of events, the Admiral goes to Italy on the first or second of November. This means I can afford to stay at Landsvoort myself during the final crucial days and indeed, for the period of the operation itself."

"No coincidence, the Admiral's visit to Italy, I can assure you." Himmler smiled thinly. "I suggested it to the Führer at exactly the right moment. Within five minutes he'd quite decided he'd thought of it himself." He picked up his pen. "So, it progresses, Radl. Two weeks from today and it will all be over. Keep me informed."

He bent over his work and Radl licked dry lips and yet it had to be said. "Herr Reichsführer."

Himmler sighed heavily. "I'm really very busy, Radl. What is it now?"

"General Steiner, Herr Reichsführer. He is—he is well?"

"Of course," Himmler said calmly. "Why do you ask?"

"Colonel Steiner," Radl explained, his stomach churning. "He is naturally extremely anxious . . . "

"There is no need to be," Himmler said gravely. "I gave you my personal assurance, is that not so?"

"Of course." Radl backed to the door. "Thank you again," and he turned and got out as fast as he could.

Himmler shook his head, sighed in a kind of exasperation and returned to his writing.

When Devlin went into the church, Mass was almost over. He slipped down the right-hand aisle and eased into a pew. Molly was on her knees beside her mother dressed exactly as she had been on the previous Sunday. Her dress showed no evidence of the rough treatment it had received from Arthur Seymour. He was present also, in the same position he usually occupied, and he saw Devlin instantly. He showed no emotion at all, but simply got to his feet and slipped down the aisle in the shadows and went out.

Devlin waited, watching Molly at prayer, all innocence kneeling there in the candlelight. After a while, she opened her eyes and turned very slowly as if physically aware of his presence. Her eyes widened, she looked at him for a long moment, then turned away again.

Devlin left just before the end of the service and went out quickly. By the time the first of the congregation exited, he was already at his motorcycle. It was raining slightly and he turned up the collar of his trenchcoat and sat astride the bike and waited. When Molly finally came down the path with her mother she ignored him completely. They got into the trap, her mother took the reins and they drove away.

"Ah, well, now," Devlin told himself softly. "And who would blame her?"

He kicked the engine into life, heard his name called and found Joanna Grey bearing down on him. She said in a low voice, "I had Philip Vereker at me for two hours this afternoon. He wanted to complain to Sir Henry about you."

"I don't blame him."

She said, "Can't you ever be serious for more than five minutes at any one time?"

"Too much of a strain," he said and she was prevented from continuing the conversation by the arrival of the Willoughbys.

Sir Henry was in uniform. "Now then, Devlin, how's it working out?"

"Fine, sir," Devlin rolled out the Irish. "I can't thank you enough for this wonderful opportunity to make good."

He was aware of Joanna Grey standing back, tightlipped, but Sir Henry liked it well enough. "Good show, Devlin. Getting excellent reports on you. Excellent. Keep up the good work."

He turned to speak to Joanna Grey and Devlin, seizing his opportunity, rode away.

It was raining very heavily by the time he reached the cottage, so he put the motorcycle in the first barn, changed into waders and an oilskin coat, got his shotgun and started out into the marsh. The dyke gates needed checking in such heavy rain and trudging round in such conditions was a nice negative sort of occupation to take his mind off things.

It didn't work. He couldn't get Molly Prior out of his thoughts. The image recurred constantly of her dropping to her knees in prayer the previous Sunday in a kind of slow motion, the skirt sliding up her thighs. Would not go away.

"Holy Mary and all the Saints," he said softly. "If this is what love is really like, Liam my boy, you've taken one hell of a long time finding out about it."

As he came back along the main dyke towards the cottage he smelt woodsmoke heavy on the damp air. There was a light at the window in the evening gloom, the tiniest chink where the blackout curtains had failed to come together. When he opened the door he could smell cooking. He put the shotgun in the corner, hung the oilskin up to dry and went into the living room.

She was on one knee at the fire, putting on another log. She turned to look over her shoulder gravely. ''You'll be wet through.''

''Half an hour in front of that fire and a couple of whiskies inside me and I'll be fine.''

She went to the cupboard, got the bottle of Bushmills and a glass. ''Don't pour it on the floor,'' she said. ''Try drinking it this time.''

''So you know about that?''

''Not much you don't hear in a place like this. Irish stew on the go. That all right?''

''Fine.''

''Half an hour, I'd say.'' She crossed to the sink and reached for a glass dish. ''What went wrong, Liam? Why did you keep out of the way?''

He sat down in the old wing-back chair, legs wide to the fire, steam rising from his trousers. ''I thought it best at first.''

''Why?''

''I had my reasons.''

''And what went wrong today?''

''Sunday, bloody Sunday. You know how it is.''

''Damn your eyes.'' She crossed the room, drying her hands on her apron and looked down at the steam rising from Devlin's trousers. ''You'll catch your death if you don't change those. Rheumatism at least.''

''Not worth it,'' he said. ''I'll go to bed soon. I'm tired.''

She reached out hesitantly and touched his hair. He seized her hand and kissed it. ''I love you, you know that?''

It was as if a lamp had been switched on inside her. She glowed, seemed to expand and take on an entirely new dimension. ''Well, thank God for that. At least it means I can go to bed now with a clear conscience.''

''I'm bad for you, girl dear, there's nothing in it. No future, I warn you. There should be a notice above that bedroom door. Abandon hope all ye who enter here.''

''We'll see about that,'' she said. ''I'll get your stew,'' and she moved across to the stove.

Later, lying in the old brass bed, an arm about her, watching the shadow patterns on the ceiling from the fire, he felt more content, more at peace with himself than he had for years.

There was a radio on a small table at her side of the bed. She switched it on, then turned her stomach against his thigh and sighed, eyes closed. ''Oh, that was lovely. Can we do it again some time?''

''Would you give a fella time to catch his breath?''

She smiled and ran a hand across his belly. "The poor old man. Just listen to him."

A record was playing on the radio.

> When that man is dead and gone . . .
> Some fine day the news will flash,
> Satan with a small moustache
> Is asleep beneath the lawn.

"I'll be glad when that happens," she said drowsily.

"What?" he asked.

"Satan with a small moustache asleep beneath the lawn. Hitler. I mean, it'll all be over then, won't it?" She snuggled closer. "What's going to happen to us, Liam? When the war's over?"

"God knows."

He lay there staring at the fire. After a while her breathing steadied and she was asleep. *After the war was over.* Which war? He'd been on the barricades one way or another for twelve years now. How could he tell her that? It was a nice little farm, too, and they needed a man. God, the pity of it. He held her close and the wind moaned about the old house, rattling the windows.

And in Berlin, at Prinz Albrechtstrasse, Himmler still sat at his desk, methodically working his way through dozens of reports and sheets of statistics, mainly those relating to the extermination squads who, in the occupied lands of Eastern Europe and Russia, liquidated Jews, gypsies, the mentally and physically handicapped and any others who did not fit into the Reichsführer's plan for a Greater Europe.

There was a polite knock at the door and Karl Rossman entered. Himmler looked up. "How did you get on?"

"I'm sorry, Herr Reichsführer, he won't budge and we really have tried just about everything. I'm beginning to think he might be innocent after all."

"Not possible." Himmler produced a sheet of paper. "I received this document earlier this evening. A signed confession from an artillery sergeant who was his batman for two years and who during that time engaged in work prejudicial to State Security on Major-General Karl Steiner's direct order."

"So what now, Herr Reichsführer?"

"I'd still prefer a signed confession from General Steiner himself. It makes everything that much tighter." Himmler frowned slightly. "Let's try a little more psychology. Clean him up, get an SS doctor to him, plenty of food. You know the drill. The whole thing has been a shocking mistake on somebody's part. Sorry you have still to detain him, but one or two points still remain to be cleared up.''

''And then?''

''When he's had say ten days of that, go to work on him again. Right out of the blue. No warning. The shock might do it.''

''I'll do as you suggest, Herr Reichsführer,'' Rossman said.

11

AT FOUR O'CLOCK ON THE afternoon of Thursday, the twenty-eighth October, Joanna Grey drove into the yard of the cottage at Hobs End and found Devlin in the barn working on the motorcycle.

''I've been trying to get hold of you all week,'' she said. ''Where have you been?''

''Around,'' he told her cheerfully, wiping grease from his hands on an old rag. ''Out and about. I told you there was nothing for me to do till my meeting with Garvald so I've been having a look at the countryside.''

''So I've heard,'' she said grimly. ''Riding around on that motorcycle with Molly Prior on the pillion. You were seen in Holt at a dance on Tuesday night.''

''A very worthy cause,'' he said. ''Wings for Victory. Actually your friend Vereker turned up and made an impassioned speech about how God would help us crush the bloody Hun. I found that ironic in view of the fact that everywhere I went in Germany I used to see signs saying *God with us*.''

''I told you to leave her alone.''

''I tried that, it didn't work. Anyway, what did you want? I'm busy. I'm having a certain amount of magneto trouble and I want this thing to be in perfect working order for my run to Peterborough tonight.''

''Troops have moved into Meltham House,'' she said. ''They arrived on Tuesday night.''

He frowned. ''Meltham House—isn't that the place where Special Force outfits train?''

"That's right. It's about eight miles up the coast road from Studley Constable."

"Who are they?"

"American Rangers."

"I see. Should it make any difference, their being here?"

"Not really. They usually stay up at that end, the units who use the facilities. There's a heavily wooded area, a salt marsh and a good beach. It's a factor to be considered, that's all."

Devlin nodded. "Fair enough. Let Radl know about it in your next broadcast and there's your duty done. And now, I must get on."

She turned to go to the car and hesitated. "I don't like the sound of this man Garvald."

"Neither do I, but don't worry, my love. If he's going to turn nasty, it won't be tonight. It will be tomorrow."

She got to the car and drove away and he returned to his work on the motorcycle. Twenty minutes later Molly rode up out of the marsh, a basket hanging from her saddle. She slipped to the ground and tied the horse to a hitching ring in the wall above the trough. "I've brought you a shepherd's pie."

"Yours or your mother's?" She threw a stick at him and he ducked. "It'll have to wait. I've got to go out tonight. Put it in the oven for me and I'll heat it up when I get in."

"Can I go with you?"

"Not a chance. Too far. And besides, it's business." He slapped her behind. "A cup of tea is what I crave, woman of the house, or maybe two, so off with you and put the kettle on."

He reached for her again, she dodged him, grabbed her basket and ran for the cottage. Devlin let her go. She went into the living room and put the basket on the table. The Gladstone bag was at the other end and as she turned to go to the stove, she caught it with her left arm, knocking it to the floor. It fell open disgorging packets of banknotes and the Sten gun parts.

She knelt there, stunned for the moment, suddenly icy cold, as if aware by some kind of precognition that nothing ever would be the same again.

There was a step in the doorway and Devlin said quietly, "Would you put them back, now, like a good girl?"

She looked up, white-faced, but her voice was fierce. "What is it? What does it mean?"

"Nothing," he said, "for little girls."

"But all this money."

She held up a packet of fivers. Devlin took the bag from her, stuffed the money and the weapons back inside and replaced the bottom. Then he opened the cupboard under the window, took out a large envelope and tossed it to her.

"Size ten. Was I right?"

She opened the envelope, peered inside and there was an immediate look of awe on her face. "Silk stockings. Real silk and two pairs. Where on earth did you get these?"

"Oh, a man I met in a pub in Fakenham. You can get anything you want if you know where to look."

"The black market," she said. "That's what you're mixed up in, isn't it?"

There was a certain amount of relief in her eyes and he grinned. "The right color for me. Now would you kindly get the tea on and hurry? I want to be away by six and I've still got work to do on the bike."

She hesitated, clutching the stockings and moved close. "Liam, it's all right, isn't it?"

"And why wouldn't it be?" He kissed her briefly, turned and went out, cursing his own stupidity.

And yet as he walked towards the barn, he knew in his heart that there was more to it than that. For the first time he had been brought face to face with what he was doing to this girl. Within little more than a week, her entire world was going to be turned upside down. That was absolutely inevitable and nothing he could do about it except leave her, as he must, to bear the hurt of it alone.

Suddenly, he felt physically sick and kicked out at a packing case savagely. "Oh, you bastard," he said. "You dirty bastard, Liam."

Reuben Garvald opened the judas in the main gate of the workshop of Fogarty's garage and peered outside. Rain swept across the cracked concrete of the forecourt where the two rusting petrol pumps stood forlornly. He closed the judas hurriedly and stepped back inside.

The workshop had once been a barn and was surprisingly spacious. A flight of wooden steps led up to a loft, but in spite of a wrecked saloon car in one corner, there was still plenty of room for the three-ton Bedford truck and the van in which Garvald and his brother had travelled from Birmingham. Ben Garvald himself walked up and down impatiently, occasionally beating his arms together. In spite of the heavy overcoat and scarf he wore, he was bitterly cold.

"Christ what a dump," he said. "Isn't there any sign of that little Irish sod?"

"It's only a quarter to nine, Ben," Reuben told him.

"I don't care what bleeding time it is." Garvald turned on a large, hefty young man in a sheepskin flying jacket who leaned against the truck reading a newspaper. "You get me some heat in here tomorrow night, Sammy boy, or I'll have your balls. Understand?"

Sammy, who had long dark sideburns and a cold, rather dangerous-looking face, seemed completely unperturbed. "Okay, Mr. Garvald. I'll see to it."

"You'd better, sweetheart, or I'll send you back to the Army." Garvald patted his face. "And you wouldn't like that, would you?"

He took out a packet of Gold Flake, selected one and Sammy gave him a light with a fixed smile. "You're a card. Mr. Garvald. A real card."

Reuben called urgently from the door. "He's just turned on to the forecourt."

Garvald tugged at Sammy's arm. "Get the door open and let's have the bastard in."

Devlin entered in a flurry of rain and wind. He wore oilskin leggings with his trenchcoat, and an old leather flying helmet and goggles which he'd bought in a second-hand shop in Fakenham. His face was filthy and when he switched off and pushed up his goggles, there were great white circles round his eyes.

"A dirty night for it, Mr. Garvald," he said as he shoved the BSA on its stand.

"It always is, son," Garvald replied cheerfully. "Nice to see you." He shook hands warmly. "Reuben you know and this is Sammy Jackson, one of my lads. He drove the Bedford over for you."

There was an implication that Jackson had somehow done him a great personal favour and Devlin responded in kind, putting on the Irish as usual. "Sure and I appreciate that. It was damn good of you," he said, wringing Sammy's hand.

Jackson looked him over contemptuously but managed a smile and Garvald said, "All right then, I've got business elsewhere and I don't expect you want to hang around. Here's your truck. What do you think?"

The Bedford had definitely seen better days, the paintwork badly fading and chipped, but the tyres weren't too bad and the canvas tilt was almost new. Devlin heaved himself over the tailboard and noted the Army jerrycans, the compressor and the drum of paint he'd asked for.

"It's all there, just like you said." Garvald offered him a cigarette. "Check the petrol if you want."

"No need, I'll take your word for it."

Garvald wouldn't have tried any nonsense with the petrol, he was sure of that. After all, he wanted him to return on the following evening. He went round to the front and lifted the bonnet. The engine seemed sound enough.

"Try it," Garvald invited.

He switched on and tapped the accelerator, and the engine broke into a healthy enough roar as he had expected. Garvald would be much too interested in finding out exactly what he was up to to spoil things by trying to push second-class goods at this stage.

Devlin jumped down and looked at the truck again, noting the military registration. "All right?" Garvald asked.

"I suppose so." Devlin nodded slowly. "From the state of it, it looks as if it's been having a hard time in Tobruk or somewhere."

"Very probably, old son." Garvald kicked a wheel. "But these things are built to take it."

"Have you got the delivery licence I asked for?"

"Sure thing." Garvald snapped a finger. "Let's have that form, Reuben."

Reuben produced it from his wallet and said sullenly, "When do we see the colour of his money?"

"Don't be like that, Reuben. Mr. Murphy here is as sound as a bell."

"No, he's right enough, a fair exchange." Devlin took a fat manilla envelope from his breast pocket and passed it to Reuben. "You'll find seven hundred and fifty in there in fivers, as agreed."

He pocketed the form Reuben had given him after glancing at it briefly and Ben Garvald said, "Aren't you going to fill that thing in?"

Devlin tapped his nose and tried to assume an expression of low cunning. "And let you see where I'm going? Not bloody likely, Mr. Garvald."

Garvald laughed delightedly. He put an arm about Devlin's shoulder. The Irishman said, "If someone could give me a hand to put my bike in the back, I'll be off."

Garvald nodded to Jackson who dropped the tailboard of the Bedford and found an old plank. He and Devlin ran the BSA up and laid it on its side. Devlin clipped the tailboard in place and turned to Garvald. "That's it then, Mr. Garvald, same time tomorrow."

"Pleasure to do business with you, old son," Garvald told him, wringing his hand again. "Get the door open, Sammy."

Devlin climbed behind the wheel and started the engine. He leaned out of the window. "One thing, Mr. Garvald. I'm not likely to find the military police on my tail, now am I?"

"Would I do that to you, son?" Garvald beamed. "I ask you." He banged the side of the truck with the flat of his hand. "See you tomorrow night. Repeat performance. Same time, same place and I'll bring you another bottle of Bushmills."

Devlin drove out into the night and Sammy Jackson and Reuben got the doors closed. Garvald's smile disappeared. "It's up to Freddy now."

"What if he loses him?" Reuben asked.

"Then there's tomorrow night, isn't there." Garvald patted him on the face. "Where's that half of brandy you brought?"

"Lose him?" Jackson said. "That little squirt?" He laughed harshly. "Christ, he couldn't even find the way to the men's room unless you showed him."

Devlin, a quarter of a mile down the road, was aware of the dim lights behind him indicating the vehicle which had pulled out of a lay-by a minute or so earlier as he passed, exactly as he expected.

An old ruined windmill loomed out of the night on his left and a flat stretch of cleared ground in front of it. He switched off all his lights suddenly, swung the wheel and drove into the cleared area blind, and braked. The other vehicle carried straight on, increasing its speed and Devlin jumped to the ground, went to the back of the Bedford and removed the bulb from the rear light. Then he got back behind the wheel, turned the truck in a circle on to the road and only switched on his lights when he was driving back towards Norman Cross.

A quarter of a mile this side of Fogarty's he turned right into a side road, the B660, driving through Holme, stopping fifteen minutes later outside Doddington to replace the bulb. When he returned to the cab, he got out the delivery licence form and filled it in in the light of a torch. There was the official stamp of a Service Corps unit near Birmingham at the bottom and the signature of the commanding officer, a Major Thrush. Garvald had thought of everything. Well, not quite everything. Devlin grinned and filled in his destination as the RAF radar station at Sheringham ten miles further along the coast road from Hobs End.

He got back behind the wheel and drove away again. Swaffham first, then Fakenham. He'd worked it all out very carefully on the map and he sat back and took it steadily because the blackout visors on his headlamps didn't give him a great deal of light to work by. Not that it mattered. He'd all the time in the world. He lit a cigarette and wondered how Garvald was getting on.

It was just after midnight when he turned into the yard outside the cottage at Hobs End. The journey had proved to be completely uneventful and in spite of the fact that he had boldly used the main roads for most of the way, he had passed no more than a handful of vehicles during the entire trip. He coasted round to the old barn on the very edge of the marsh, jumped out into the heavy rain and unlocked the padlock. He got the doors open and drove inside.

There were only a couple of round loft windows and it had been easy enough to black those out. He primed two Tilley lamps, pumped them until he had plenty of light, went outside to check that nothing showed, then he went back in and got his coat off.

Within half an hour, he had the truck unloaded, running the BSA out on an old plank and sliding the compressor to the ground the same way.

The jerrycans, he stacked in a corner, covering them with an old tarpaulin. Then he washed down the truck. When he was satisfied that it was as clean as he was going to get it he brought newspapers and tape which he had laid by earlier and proceeded to mask the windows. He did this very methodically, concentrating all the time and when he was finished went across to the cottage and had some of Molly's shepherd pie and a glass of milk.

It was still raining very hard when he ran back to the barn, hissing angrily into the waters of the marsh, filling the night with sound. Conditions were really quite perfect. He filled the compressor, primed the pump and turned its motor over, then he put the spraying equipment together and mixed some paint. He started on the tailboard first, taking his time, but it really worked very well indeed and within five minutes he had covered it with a glistening new coat of khaki green.

"God save us," he said to himself softly. "It's a good thing I haven't a criminal turn of mind for I could be making a living at this sort of thing and that's a fact."

He moved round to the left and started on the side panels.

After lunch on Friday, he was touching up the numbers on the truck with white paint when he heard a car drive up. He wiped his hands and let himself out of the barn quickly, but when he went round the corner of the cottage it was only Joanna Grey. She was trying the front door, a trim and surprisingly youthful figure in the green WVS uniform.

"You always look your best in that outfit," he said. "I bet it has old Sir Henry crawling up the wall."

She smiled. "You're on form, anyway. Things must have gone well."

"See for yourself?"

He opened the barn door and led her in. The Bedford, in its fresh coat of khaki green paint, really looked very well indeed. "As my information has it, Special Force vehicles don't usually carry divisional flashes or insignia. Is that so?"

"That's true," she said. "The stuff I've seen operating out of Meltham House in the past have never advertised who they are." She was obviously very impressed. "This is really good, Liam. Did you have any trouble?"

"He had someone try to follow me, but I soon shook him off. The big confrontation should be tonight."

"Can you handle it?"

"This can." He picked up a cloth bundle lying on the packing case beside his brushes and tins of paint, unwrapped it and took out a Mauser with a rather strange bulbous barrel. "Ever seen one of these before?"

"I can't say I have." She weighed it in her left hand with professional interest and took aim.

"Some of the SS security people use them," he said, "but there just aren't enough to go round. Only really efficient silenced handgun I've ever come across."

She said dubiously, "You'll be on your own."

"I've been on my own before." He wrapped the Mauser in the cloth again and went to the door with her. "If everything goes according to plan I should be back with the jeep around midnight. I'll check with you first thing in the morning."

"I don't think I can wait that long."

Her face was tense and anxious. She put out her hand impulsively and he held it tight for a moment. "Don't worry. It'll work. I have the sight, or so my old grannie used to say. I know about these things."

"You rogue," she said and leaned forward and kissed him on the cheek in genuine affection. "I sometimes wonder how you've survived so long."

"That's easy," he said. "Because I've never particularly cared whether I do or not."

"You say that as if you mean it?"

"Tomorrow." He smiled gently. "I'll be round first thing. You'll see."

He watched her drive away, then kicked the door of the barn shut behind him and stuck a cigarette in his mouth. "You can come out now," he called.

There was a moment's delay and then Molly emerged from the rushes on the far side of the yard. Too far to have heard anything which was why he had let it go. He padlocked the door, then walked towards her. He stopped a yard away, hands pushed into his pockets. "Molly, my own sweet girl," he said gently. "I love you dearly, but any more games like this and I'll give you the thrashing of your young life."

She flung her arms about his neck. "Is that a promise?"

"You're entirely shameless."

She looked up at him, hanging on. "Can I come over tonight?"

"You can't," he said, "because I won't be here," and he added a half-truth. "I'm going to Peterborough on private business and I won't be back until the small hours." He tapped the end of her nose with a finger. "And that's between us. No advertising."

"More silk stockings?" she said, "or is it Scotch whisky this time."

"Five quid a bottle the Yanks will pay, so they tell me."

"I wish you wouldn't." Her face was troubled. "Why can't you be nice and normal like everyone else?"

"Would you have me in my grave so early?" He turned her round. "Go and put the kettle on the stove and if you're a good girl, I'll let you make my dinner—or something.''

She smiled briefly over her shoulder, looking suddenly quite enchanting, then ran across to the cottage. Devlin put the cigarette back into his mouth, but didn't bother to light it. Thunder rumbled far out on the horizon, heralding more rain. *Another wet ride*. He sighed and went after her across the yard.

In the workshop at Fogarty's garage it was even colder than it had been on the previous night, in spite of Sammy Jackson's attempts to warm things up by punching holes in an old oil drum and lighting a coke fire. The fumes it gave off were quite something.

Ben Garvald, standing beside it, a half-bottle of brandy in one hand, a plastic cup in the other, retreated hastily. ''What in the hell are you trying to do, poison me?''

Jackson, who was sitting on a packing case on the opposite side of the fire nursing a sawn-off, double-barrelled shotgun across his knees, put it down and stood up. ''Sorry, Mr. Garvald. It's the coke—that's the trouble. Too bloody wet.''

Reuben, at the judas, called suddenly, ''Here, I think he's coming.''

''Get that thing out of the way,'' Garvald said quickly, ''and remember you don't make your move till I tell you.'' He poured some more brandy into the plastic cup and grinned. ''I want to enjoy this, Sammy boy. See that I do.''

Sammy put the shotgun under a piece of sacking beside him on the packing case and hurriedly lit a cigarette. They waited as the sound of the approaching engine grew louder, then moved past and died away into the night.

''For Christ's sake,'' Garvald said in disgust. ''It wasn't him. What time is it?''

Reuben checked his watch. ''Just on nine. He should be here any moment.''

If they had but known it Devlin was, in fact, already there, standing in the rain at the broken rear window which had been roughly boarded up with planks. His vision, through a crack, was limited, but at least covered Garvald and Jackson beside the fire. And he'd certainly heard every word spoken during the past five minutes.

Garvald said, ''Here, you might as well do something useful while we're waiting, Sammy. Top up the jeep's tank with a couple of those jerrycans so you're ready for the run back to Brum.''

Devlin withdrew, worked his way through the yard, negotiating with caution the wrecks of several cars, regained the main road and ran back along the verge to the lay-by, a quarter of a mile away where he had left the BSA.

He unbuttoned the front flap of his trenchcoat, took out the Mauser and checked it in the light of the headlamp. Satisfied, he pushed it back inside, but left the flap unbuttoned, then he got back in the saddle. He wasn't afraid, not in the slightest. A little excited, true, but only enough to put an edge to him. He kicked the starter and turned into the road.

Inside the workshop, Jackson had just finished filling the jeep's tank when Reuben turned from the judas again excitedly. "It's him. Definitely this time. He's just turned on to the forecourt."

"Okay, get the doors open and let's have him in," Garvald said.

The wind was so strong it caused a massive draught when Devlin entered that had the coke crackling like dried wood. Devlin switched off and shoved the bike up on its stand. His face was in an even worse state than it had been in the night before, plastered with mud. But when he pushed up his goggles he was smiling cheerfully.

"Hello there, Mr. Garvald."

"Here we are again." Garvald passed him the half of brandy. "You look as if you could do with a nip."

"Did you remember my Bushmills?"

"Course I did. Get those two bottles of Irish out of the van for Mr. Murphy, Reuben."

Devlin took a quick pull at the brandy bottle while Reuben went to the van and returned with the two bottles of Bushmills. His brother took them from him. "There you are, boy, just like I promised." He went across to the jeep and put the bottles down on the passenger seat. "Everything went off all right last night, then?"

"No problems at all," Devlin said.

He approached the jeep. Like the Bedford, its coachwork was badly in need of a fresh coat of paint, but otherwise it was fine. It had a strip canvas roof with open sides and a mounting point for a machine gun. The registration, in contrast to the rest of the vehicle, had been freshly painted and when Devlin looked closely he could see traces of another underneath.

"There's a thing now, Mr. Garvald," he said. "Would some Yank airbase be missing one of these?"

"Now, look here, you," Reuben put in angrily.

Devlin cut him off. "Come to think of it, Mr. Garvald, there was a moment last night when I thought someone was trying to follow me. Nerves, I suppose. Nothing came of it."

He turned back to the jeep and had another quick pull at the bottle. Garvald's anger, contained with considerable difficulty, overflowed now. "You know what you need?"

"And what would that be?" Devlin enquired softly. He turned, still holding the half of brandy, clutching one lapel of his trenchcoat with his right hand.

"A lesson in manners, sweetheart," Garvald said. "You need putting in place and I'm just the man to do it." He shook his head. "You should have stayed back home in the bogs."

He started to unbutton his overcoat and Devlin said, "Is that a fact now? Well, before you start, I'd just like to ask Sammy boy, here, if that shotgun he's got under the sacking is cocked or not, because if it isn't, he's in big trouble."

In that single, frozen moment of time, Ben Garvald suddenly knew beyond any shadow of a doubt that he'd just made the worst mistake of his life. "Take him, Sammy!" he cried.

Jackson was way ahead of him, had already grabbed for the shotgun under the sacking—already too late. As he frantically thumbed back the hammers, Devlin's hand was inside his trenchcoat and out again. The silenced Mauser coughed once, the bullet smashed into Jackson's left arm, turning him in a circle. The second shot shattered his spine, driving him headfirst into the wrecked car in the corner. In death his finger tightened convulsively on the triggers of the shotgun, discharging both barrels into the ground.

The Garvald brothers backed away slowly, inching towards the door. Reuben was shaking with fear, Garvald watchful, waiting for any kind of chance to seize on.

Devlin said, "That's far enough."

In spite of his size, the old flying helmet and goggles, the soaking-wet coat, he seemed a figure of infinite menace as he faced them from the other side of the fire, the Mauser with the bulbous silencer in his hand.

Garvald said, "All right, I made a mistake."

"Worse than that, you broke your word," Devlin said. "And where I come from, we have an excellent specific for people who let us down."

"For God's sake, Murphy . . . "

He didn't get any further because there was a dull thud as Devlin fired again. The bullet splintered Garvald's right kneecap. He went back against the door with a stifled cry and fell to the ground. He rolled over, clutching at his knee with both hands, blood pumping between his fingers.

Reuben crouched, hands raised in futile protection, head down. He spent two or three of the worst moments of his life in that position and when he finally had the courage to look up, discovered Devlin positioning an old plank at the side of the jeep. As Reuben watched, the Irishman ran the BSA up and into the rear.

He came forward and opened one half of the garage doors. Then he snapped his fingers at Reuben. "The delivery licence."

Reuben produced it from his wallet with shaking fingers and handed it over. Devlin checked it briefly, then took out an envelope which he dropped at Garvald's feet. "Seven hundred and fifty quid, just to keep the books straight. I told you, I'm a man of my word. You should try it some time." He got into the jeep, pressed the starter and drove out into the night.

"The door," Garvald said to his brother through clenched teeth. "Get the bloody door closed or you'll have every copper for miles turning up to see what the light is."

Reuben did as he was told, then turned to survey the scene. The air was full of hazy blue smoke and the stench of cordite.

Reuben shuddered. "Who was that bastard, Ben?"

"I don't know and I don't really care." Garvald pulled free the white silk scarf he wore around his neck. "Use this to bandage this bloody knee."

Reuben looked at the wound in fascinated horror. The 7.63 mm cartridge had gone in one side and out of the other, and the kneecap had fragmented, splinters of white bone protruding through flesh and blood.

"Christ, it's bad, Ben. You need a hospital."

"Like hell I do. You carry me into any casualty department in this country with a gunshot wound and they'll shout for the coppers so fast you'll think you're standing still." There was sweat on his face. "Go on, bandage it for Christ's sake."

Reuben started to wind the scarf round the shattered knee. He was almost in tears. "What about Sammy, Ben?"

"Leave him where he is. Just cover him with one of the tarpaulins for the moment. You can get some of the boys over here tomorrow to get rid of him." He cursed as Reuben tightened the scarf. "Hurry up, and let's get out of here."

"Where to, Ben?"

"We'll go straight to Birmingham. You can take me to that nursing home in Aston. The one that Indian doctor runs. What's his name?"

"You mean Das?" Reuben shook his head. "He's in the abortion racket, Ben. No good to you."

"He's a doctor, isn't he?" Ben said. "Now give me a hand up and let's get out of here."

Devlin drove into the yard at Hobs End half an hour after midnight. It was a dreadful night with gale-force winds, torrential rain and when he had unlocked the doors of the barn and driven inside, he had all on to get them closed again.

He lit the Tilley lamps and manoeuvred the BSA out of the back of the jeep. He was tired and bitterly cold, but not tired enough to sleep. He lit a cigarette and walked up and down, strangely restless.

It was quiet in the barn, only the rain drumming against the roof, the quiet hissing of the Tilley lamps. The door opened in a flurry of wind and Molly entered, closing it behind her. She wore her old trenchcoat, Wellington boots and a headscarf and was soaked to the skin so that she shook with cold, but it didn't seem to matter. She walked to the jeep, a puzzled frown on her face.

She gazed at Devlin dumbly. "Liam?" she said.

"You promised," he told her. "No more prying. It's useful to know how you keep your word."

"I'm sorry, but I was so frightened, and then all this." She gestured at the vehicles. "What does it mean?"

"None of your business," he told her brutally. "As far as I'm concerned you can clear off right now. If you want to report me to the police—well, you must do as you see fit."

She stood staring at him, eyes very wide, mouth working. "Go on!" he said. "If that's what you want. Get out of it!"

She ran into his arms, bursting into tears. "Oh, no, Liam, don't send me away. No more questions, I promise and from now on I'll mind my own business, only don't send me away."

It was the lowest point in his life and the self-contempt he felt as he held her in his arms was almost physical in its intensity. But it had worked. She would cause him no more trouble, of that he was certain.

He kissed her on the forehead. "You're freezing. Get on over to the house with you and build up the fire. I'll be with you in a few minutes."

She gazed up at him searchingly, then turned and went out. Devlin sighed and went over to the jeep and picked up one of the bottles of Bushmills. He eased out the cork and took a long swallow.

"Here's to you, Liam, old son," he said with infinite sadness.

In the tiny operating theatre in the nursing home at Aston, Ben Garvald lay back on the padded table, eyes closed. Reuben stood beside him while Das, a tall, cadaverous Indian in an immaculate white coat, cut away the trouser leg with surgical scissors.

"Is it bad?" Reuben asked him, his voice shaking.

"Yes, very bad," Das replied calmly. "He needs a first-rate surgeon, if he is not to be crippled. There is also the question of sepsis."

"Listen, you bleeding wog bastard," Ben Garvald said, eyes opening. "It says physician and surgeon on that fancy brass plate of yours by the door, doesn't it?"

"True, Mr. Garvald," Das told him calmly. "I have degrees of the

Universities of Bombay and London, but that is not the point. You need specialist assistance in this instance.''

Garvald pushed himself up on one elbow. He was in considerable pain and sweat was pouring down his face. ''You listen to me and listen good. A girl died in here three months ago. What the law would call an illegal operation. I know about that and a lot more. Enough to put you away for seven years at least, so if you don't want the coppers in here, get moving on this leg.''

Das seemed quite unperturbed. ''Very well, Mr. Garvald, on your own head be it. I'll have to give you an anaesthetic. You understand this?''

''Give me anything you bleeding well like, only get on with it.''

Garvald closed his eyes. Das opened a cupboard, took out a gauze face mask and a bottle of chloroform. He said to Reuben, ''You'll have to help. Add chloroform to the pad as I tell you, drop by drop. Can you manage it?''

Reuben nodded, too full to speak.

12

It was still raining on the following morning when Devlin rode over to Joanna Grey. He parked his bike by the garage and went to the back door. She opened it instantly and drew him inside. She was still in her dressing gown and her face was strained and anxious.

''Thank God, Liam.'' She took his face between her two hands and shook him. ''I hardly slept a wink. I've been up since five o'clock drinking whisky and tea alternately. A hell of a mixture at this time in the morning.'' She kissed him warmly. ''You rogue, it's good to see you.''

The retriever swung its hindquarters frantically from side-to-side, anxious to be included. Joanna Grey busied herself at the stove and Devlin stood in front of the fire.

''How was it?'' she asked.

''All right.''

He was deliberately noncommittal, for it seemed likely she might not be too happy about the way he had handled things.

She turned, surprise on her face. ''They didn't try anything?''

"Oh, yes," he said. "But I persuaded them otherwise."

"Any shooting?"

"No need," he said calmly. "One look at that Mauser of mine was enough. They're not used to guns, the English criminal fraternity. Razors are more their style."

She carried the tea things on a tray across to the table. "God, the English. Sometimes I despair of them."

"I'll drink to that in spite of the hour. Where's the whisky?"

She went and got the bottle and a couple of glasses. "This is disgraceful at this time of day, but I'll join you. What do we do now?"

"Wait," he said. "I've got the jeep to fix up, but that's all. You'll need to squeeze old Sir Henry dry right up to the last moment, but other than that, all we can do is bite our nails for the next six days."

"Oh, I don't know," she said. "We can always wish ourselves luck." She raised her glass. "God bless you, Liam, and long life."

"And you, my love."

She raised her glass and drank. Suddenly something moved inside Devlin like a knife in his bowels. In that moment he knew, beyond any shadow of a doubt, that the whole bloody thing was going to go about as wrong as it could do.

Pamela Vereker had a thirty-six-hour pass that weekend, coming off duty at seven A.M., and her brother had driven over to Pangbourne to pick her up. Once at the presbytery, she couldn't wait to get out of uniform and into a pair of jodhpurs and a sweater.

In spite of this symbolic turning away, however temporarily, from the dreadful facts of daily life on a heavy bomber station, she still felt edgy and extremely tired. After lunch she cycled six miles along the coast road to Meltham Vale Farm where the tenant, a parishioner of Vereker's, had a three-year-old stallion badly in need of exercise.

Once over the dunes behind the farm, she gave the stallion his head and galloped along the winding track through the tangled gorse, climbing towards the wooded ridge above. It was completely exhilarating, with the rain beating in her face, and for a while she was back in another, safer place, the world of her childhood that had ended at four forty-five on the morning of 1 September 1939 when General Gerd von Runstedt's Army Group South had invaded Poland.

She entered the trees, following the old forestry commission track and the stallion slowed as it approached the crest of the hill. There was a pine tree across the track a yard or two further on, a windfall. It was no more than three feet high and the stallion took it in its stride. As it landed on the other side, a figure stood up in the undergrowth on the right. The stallion swerved. Pamela Vereker lost her stirrups and was tossed to one side. A rhododendron bush broke her fall, but for a moment she was winded and lay there fighting for breath, aware of voices all around.

"You stupid bastard, Krukowski," someone said. "What were you trying to do, kill her?"

The voices were American. She opened her eyes and found a ring of soldiers in combat jackets and steel helmets surrounding her, faces daubed with camouflage cream, all heavily armed. Kneeling beside her was a large rugged Negro with a master sergeant's stripes on his arm. "You all right, miss?" he asked anxiously.

She frowned and shook her head, and suddenly felt rather better. "Who are you?"

He touched his helmet in a kind of half-salute. "Name's Garvey. Master Sergeant. Twenty-first Specialist Raiding Force. We're based at Meltham House for a couple of weeks for field training."

A jeep arrived at that moment, skidding to a halt in the mud. The driver was an officer, she could tell that, although not sure of his rank, having had little to do with American forces during her service career. He wore a forage cap and normal uniform and was certainly not dressed for manoeuvres.

"What in the hell is going on here?" he demanded.

"Lady got thrown from her horse, Major," Garvey replied. "Krukowski jumped out of the bushes at the wrong moment."

Major, she thought, surprised at his youth. She scrambled to her feet. "I'm all right, really I am."

She swayed and the major took her arm. "I don't think so. Do you live far, ma'am?"

"Studley Constable. My brother is parish priest there."

He guided her firmly towards the jeep. "I think you'd better come with me. We've got a medical officer down at Meltham House. I'd like him to make sure you're still in one piece."

The flash on his shoulder said *Rangers* and she remembered having read somewhere that they were the equivalent of the British Commandos. "Meltham House?"

"I'm sorry, I should introduce myself. Major Harry Kane, attached to the Twenty-first Specialist Raiding Force under the command of Colonel Robert E. Shafto. We're here for field training."

"Oh, yes," she said. "My brother was telling me that Meltham was being used for some such purpose these days." She closed her eyes. "Sorry, I feel a little faint."

"You just relax. I'll have you there in no time."

It was a nice voice. Most definitely. For some absurd reason it made her feel quite breathless. She lay back and did exactly as she was told.

The five acres of garden at Meltham House were surrounded by a typical Norfolk flint wall, some eight feet in height. It had been spiked with barbed wire at the top for extra security. Meltham itself was of modest size, a small manor house dating from the early part of the seventeenth century. Like the wall, a great deal of split flint had been used, the construction of the building, particularly the design of the gable ends, showed the Dutch influence typical of the period.

Harry Kane and Pamela strolled through the shrubbery towards the house. He had spent a good hour showing her over the estate and she had enjoyed every minute of it. "How many of you are there?"

"At the present time, about ninety. Most of the men are under canvas, of course, in the camp area I pointed out on the other side of the spinney."

"Why wouldn't you take me down there. Secret training or something?"

"Good God, no." He chuckled. "You're entirely too good-looking, it's as simple as that."

A young soldier hurried down the steps of the terrace and came towards them. He saluted smartly. "Colonel's back, sir. Master Sergeant Garvey is with him now."

"Very well, Appleby."

The boy returned Kane's salute, turned and doubled away.

"I thought Americans were supposed to take things terribly easy," Pamela said.

Kane grinned. "You don't know Shafto. I think they must have coined the term martinet especially for him."

As they went up the steps to the terrace, an officer came out through the French windows. He stood facing them, slapping a riding crop against his knee, full of a restless animal vitality. Pamela did not need to be told who he was. Kane saluted. "Colonel Shafto, allow me to present Miss Vereker."

Robert Shafto was at that time forty-four years of age, a handsome, arrogant-looking man; a flamboyant figure in polished top boots and riding breeches. He wore a forage cap slanted to his left eye and the two rows of medal ribbons above his left pocket made a bright splash of colour. Perhaps the most extraordinary thing about him was the pearl handled Colt .45 he carried in an open holster on his left hip.

He touched his riding crop to his brow and said gravely, "I was distressed to hear of your accident, Miss Vereker. If there is anything I can do to make up for the clumsiness of my men . . . "

"That's most kind of you," she said. "However, Major Kane here has very kindly offered to run me back to Studley Constable, if you can spare him, that is. My brother is priest there."

"The least we can do."

She wanted to see Kane again and there seemed to be only one sure way she could accomplish that. She said, "We're having a little party at the presbytery tomorrow night. Nothing very special. Just a few friends for drinks and sandwiches. I was wondering whether you and Major Kane would care to join us." Shafto hesitated. It seemed obvious that he was going to make some excuse and she carried on hurriedly, "Sir Henry Willoughby will be there, the local squire. Have you met yet?"

Shafto's eyes lit up. "No, I haven't had that pleasure."

"Miss Vereker's brother was a padre with the First Parachute Brigade," Kane said. "Dropped with them at Oudna in Tunisia last year. You remember that one, Colonel?"

"I certainly do," Shafto said. "That was one hell of an affair. Your brother must be quite a man to have survived that, young lady."

"He was awarded the Military Cross," she said. "I'm very proud of him."

"And so you should be. I'll be happy to attend your little soirée tomorrow night and have the pleasure of meeting him. You make the necessary arrangements, Harry." He saluted again with the riding crop. "And now you must excuse me. I have work to do."

"Were you impressed?" Kane asked her as they drove back along the coast road in his jeep.

"I'm not sure," she said. "He's rather a flamboyant figure, you must admit."

"The understatement of this or any other year," he said. "Shafto is what is known in the trade as a fighting soldier. The kind of guy who used to lead his men over the top of some trench in Flanders in the old days armed with a swagger stick. Like that French general said at Balaclava, magnificent, but it isn't war."

"In other words he doesn't use his head?"

"Well, he does have one hell of a fault from the Army's point of view. He can't take orders—from anybody. Fighting Bobby Shafto, the pride of the infantry. Got himself out of Bataan back in April last year when the Japs overran the place. Only trouble was, he left an infantry regiment behind. That didn't sit too well at the Pentagon. Nobody wanted him so they shipped him over to London to work on the staff at Combined Operations."

"Which he didn't like?"

"Naturally. Used it as a stepping stone to further glory. He discovered the British had their Small Scale Raiding Force slipping over the Channel by night playing Boy Scouts and decided the American Army should have the same. Unfortunately some imbecile at Combined Operations thought it was a good idea.''

''Don't you?'' she said.

He seemed to evade the question. ''During the past nine months, men from the Twenty-first have raided across the Channel on no fewer than fourteen separate occasions.''

''But that's incredible.''

''Which includes,'' he carried on, ''the destruction of an empty light-house in Normandy and several landings on uninhabited French islands.''

''You don't think much of him, it seems?''

''The great American public certainly does. Three months ago some war reporter, in London and short of a story, heard how Shafto had captured the crew of a lightship off the Belgian coast. There were six of them and as they happened to be German soldiers, it looked pretty good, especially the photos of the landing craft coming into Dover in the gray dawn, Shafto and his boys, one helmet strap dangling, the prisoners looking suitably cowed. Straight off Stage Ten at MGM.'' He shook his head. ''How the folks back home bought that one. Shafto's Raiders. *Life, Collier's, Saturday Evening Post.* You name it, he was in there some-place. The people's hero. Two DSCs, Silver Star with Oak Leaf clusters. Everything but the Congressional Medal of Honor and he'll have that before he's through, even if he has to kill the lot of us doing it.''

She said stiffly, ''Why did you join this unit, Major Kane?''

''Stuck behind a desk,'' he said. ''That about sums it up. Guess I'd have done just about anything to get out—and did.''

''So you weren't on any of the raids you mention?''

''No, ma'am.''

''Then I suggest you think twice in future before dismissing so lightly the action of a brave man, especially from the vantage point of a desk.''

He pulled into the side of the road and braked to a halt. He turned to her, smiling cheerfully. ''Heh, I like that. Mind if I write it down to use in that great novel we journalists are always going to write?''

''Damn you, Harry Kane.''

She raised a hand as if to strike him, and he pulled out a pack of Camels and shook one out. ''Have a cigarette instead. Soothes the nerves.''

She took it and the light which followed and inhaled deeply, staring out over the salt marsh towards the sea. ''Sorry, I suppose I am reacting too strongly, but this war has become very personal for me.''

''Your brother?''

''Not only that. My job. When I was on duty yesterday afternoon, I got a fighter pilot on the RT. Badly shot up in a dogfight over the North Sea. His Hurricane was on fire and he was trapped in the cockpit. He screamed all the way down.''

"It started out by being a nice day," Kane said. "Suddenly it isn't."

He reached for the steering wheel and she put her hand on his impulsively. "I'm sorry—really I am."

"That's okay."

Her expression changed to one of puzzlement and she raised his hand. "What's wrong with your fingers? Several of them are crooked. Your nails . . . Good God, Harry, what happened to your nails?"

"Oh, that?" he said. "Somebody pulled them out for me."

She stared at him in horror. "Was it—was it the Germans, Harry?" she whispered.

"No." He switched on the engine. "As a matter of fact they were French, but working for the other side, of course. It's one of life's more distressing discoveries, or so I've found, that it very definitely takes all sorts to make a world."

He smiled crookedly and drove away.

On the evening of the same day in his private room in the nursing home at Aston, Ben Garvald took a decided turn for the worse. He lost consciousness at six o'clock. His condition was not discovered for another hour. It was eight before Doctor Das arrived in answer to the nurse's urgent phone call, ten past when Reuben walked in and discovered the situation.

He had been back to Fogarty's on Ben's instructions, with a hearse and a coffin obtained from the funeral firm which was another of the Garvald brothers' many business ventures. The unfortunate Jackson had just been disposed of at a local private crematorium in which they also had an interest, not the first time, by any means, that they had got rid of an inconvenient corpse in this way.

Ben's face was bathed in sweat and he groaned, moving from side to side. There was a faint unpleasant odour like rotten meat. Reuben caught a glimpse of the knee as Das lifted the dressing. He turned away, fear rising into his mouth like bile.

"Ben?" he said.

Garvald opened his eyes. For a moment he didn't seem to recognize his brother and then he smiled. "You get it done, Reuben boy? Did you get rid of him?"

"Ashes to ashes, Ben."

Garvald closed his eyes and Reuben turned to Das. "How bad is it?"

"Very bad. There is a chance of gangrene here. I warned him."

"Oh, my God," Reuben said. "I knew he should have gone to hospital."

Ben Garvald's eyes opened and he glared feverishly. He reached for his brother's wrist. "No hospital, you hear me? What do you want to do? Give those bleeding coppers the opening they've been looking for for years?"

He fell back, eyes closed again. Das said, "There is one chance. There is a drug called penicillin. You have heard of it?"

"Sure I have. They say it'll cure anything. Fetches a fortune on the black market."

"Yes, it has quite miraculous results in cases like this. Can you get hold of some? Now—tonight?"

"If it's in Birmingham, you'll have it within an hour." Reuben walked to the door and turned. "But if he dies, then you go with him, son. That's a promise."

He went out and the door swung behind him.

At the same moment in Landsvoort the Dakota lifted off the runway and turned out to sea. Gericke didn't waste any time. Simply took her straight up to a thousand feet, banked to starboard and dropped down towards the coast. Inside, Steiner and his men made ready. They were all dressed in full British paratroop gear, all weapons and equipment stowed in suspension bags in the British manner. "All right," Steiner called.

They all stood and clipped their static lines to the anchor line cable, each man checking the comrade in front of him, Steiner seeing to Harvey Preston who was last in line. The Englishman was trembling, Steiner could feel it as he tightened his straps for him.

"Fifteen seconds," he said, "so you haven't got long—understand? And get this straight, all of you. If you're going to break a leg, do it here. Not in Norfolk."

There was a general laugh and he walked to the front of the line where Ritter Neumann checked his straps. Steiner slid back the door as the red light blinked above his head and there was the sudden roaring of the wind.

In the cockpit, Gericke throttled back and went in low. The tide was out, the wide, wet lonely beaches pale in the moonlight, stretching into infinity. Bohmler, beside him, was concentrating on the altimeter. "Now!" Gericke cried and Bohmler was ready for him.

The green light flared above Steiner's head, he slapped Ritter on the shoulder. The young Oberleutnant went out followed by the entire stick, very fast, ending with Brandt. As for Preston, he stood there, mouth gaping, staring out into the night.

"Go on!" Steiner cried and grabbed for his shoulder.

Preston pulled away, holding on to a steel strut to support himself. He shook his head, mouth working. ''Can't!'' he finally managed to say. ''Can't do it!''

Steiner struck him across the face back-handed, grabbed him by the right arm and slung him towards the open door. Preston hung there, bracing himself with both hands. Steiner put a foot in his rear and shoved him out into space. Then he clipped on to the anchor line and went after him.

When you jump at four hundred feet there isn't really time to be frightened. Preston was aware of himself somersaulting, the sudden jerk, the slap of the 'chute catching air and then he was swinging beneath the dark khaki umbrella.

It was fantastic. The moon pale on the horizon, the flat wet sands, the creamy line of the surf. He could see the E-boat by the sand pier quite clearly, men watching and further along the beach a line of collapsed parachutes as the others gathered them in. He glanced up and caught a glimpse of Steiner above him and to the left and then seemed to be going in very fast.

The supply bag, swinging twenty feet below at the end of a line clipped to his waist, hit the sand with a solid thump warning him to get ready. He went in hard, too hard, or so it seemed, rolled and miraculously found himself on his feet, the parachute billowing up like some pale flower in the moonlight.

He moved in quickly to deflate it as he had been taught and suddenly paused there on his hands and knees, a sense of overwhelming joy, of personal power sweeping through him of a kind he had never known in his life before.

''I did it!'' he cried aloud. ''I showed the bastards. I did it! I did it! I did it!''

In the bed at the nursing home in Aston Ben Garvald lay very still. Reuben stood at the end and waited as Doctor Das probed for a heartbeat with his stethoscope.

''How is he?'' Reuben demanded.

''Still alive, but only just.''

Reuben made his decision and acted on it. He grabbed Das by the shoulder and shoved him at the door. ''You get an ambulance round here quick as you like. I'm having him in hospital.''

''But that will mean the police, Mr. Garvald,'' Das pointed out.

''Do you think I care?'' Reuben said hoarsely. ''I want him alive, understand? He's my brother. Now get moving!''

He opened the door and pushed Das out. When he turned back to the bed there were tears in his eyes. "I promise you one thing, Ben," he said brokenly. "I'll have that little Irish bastard for this if it's the last thing I do."

13

⚬⚬

AT FORTY-FIVE, JACK ROGAN HAD been a policeman for nearly a quarter of a century—a long time to work a three-shift system and be disliked by the neighbors. But that was the policeman's lot, and only to be expected, as he frequently pointed out to his wife.

It was nine-thirty on Tuesday 2 November when he entered his office at Scotland Yard. By rights, he shouldn't have been there at all. Having spent a lengthy night at Muswell Hill interrogating members of an Irish club, he was entitled to a few hours in bed, but there was a little paperwork to clear up first.

He'd just settled down at his desk when there was a knock at the door and his assistant, Detective Inspector Fergus Grant, entered. Grant was the younger son of a retired Indian Army colonel. Winchester and Hendon Police College. One of the new breed who were supposed to revolutionize the Force. In spite of this, he and Rogan got on well together.

Rogan put up a hand defensively. "Fergus, all I want to do is sign a few letters, have a cup of tea and go home to bed. Last night was hell."

"I know, sir," Grant said. "It's just that we've had a rather unusual report in from the City of Birmingham Police. I thought it might interest you."

"You mean me in particular or the Irish Section?"

"Both."

"All right." Rogan pushed back his chair and started to fill his pipe from a worn, leather pouch. "I'm not in the mood for reading so tell me about it."

"Ever hear of a man called Garvald, sir?"

Rogan paused. "You mean Ben Garvald? He's been bad news for years. Biggest villain in the Midlands."

"He died early this morning. Gangrene as the result of a gunshot wound. The hospital got their hands on him too late."

Rogan struck a match. "There are people I know who might say that was the best bit of news they'd heard in years but how does it affect us?"

"He was shot in the right kneecap, by an Irishman."

Rogan stared at him. "That *is* interesting. The statutory IRA punishment when someone tries to cross you." He cursed as the match in his left hand burned down to his fingers and dropped it. "What was his name, this Irishman?"

"Murphy, sir."

"It would be. Is there more?"

"You could say that," Grant told him. "Garvald had a brother who's so cut up about his death that he's singing like a bird. He wants friend Murphy nailing to the door."

Rogan nodded. "We'll have to see if we can oblige him. What was it all about?"

Grant told him in some detail and by the time he had finished, Rogan was frowning. "An Army truck, a jeep, khaki-green paint? What would he want with that little lot?"

"Maybe they're going to try a raid on some army camp, sir, to get arms."

Rogan got up and walked to the window. "No, I can't buy that, not without firm evidence. They're just not active enough at the moment. Not capable of that kind of ploy, you know that." He came back to the desk. "We've broken the back of the IRA here in England and in Ireland, de Valera's put most of them in internment at the Curragh." He shook his head. "It wouldn't make sense that kind of operation at this stage. What did Garvald's brother make of it?"

"He seemed to think Murphy was organizing a raid on a NAAFI depot or something like that. You know the sort of thing? Drive in dressed as soldiers in an army truck."

"And drive out again with fifty thousand quid's worth of Scotch and cigarettes. It's been done before," Rogan said.

"So Murphy's just another thief on the take, sir? Is that your hunch?"

"I'd accept that if it wasn't for the bullet in the kneecap. That's pure IRA. No, my left ear's twitching about this one, Fergus. I think we could be on to something."

"All right, sir, what's the next move?"

Rogan walked over to the window thinking about it. Outside it was typical autumn weather, fog drifting across the rooftops from the Thames, rain dripping from the sycamore trees.

He turned. "I know one thing. I'm not having Birmingham cock this up for us. You handle it personally. Book a car from the pool and get up there today. Take the files with you, photos, the lot. Every known IRA man not under wrappers. Maybe Garvald can pick him out for us."

"And if not, sir?"

"Then we start asking questions at this end. All the usual channels. Special Branch in Dublin will help all they can. They hate the IRA worse than ever since they shot Detective Sergeant O'Brien last year. You always feel worse when it's one of your own."

"Right, sir," Grant said. "I'll get moving."

It was eight that evening when General Karl Steiner finished the meal which had been served to him in his room on the second floor at Prinz Albrechtstrasse. A chicken leg, potatoes fried in oil, just as he liked them, a tossed salad and a half-bottle of Riesling, served ice-cold. Quite incredible. And real coffee to follow.

Things had certainly changed since the final terrible night when he had collapsed after the electrical treatment. The following morning he had awakened to find himself lying between clean sheets in a comfortable bed. No sign of that bastard Rossman and his Gestapo bully boys. Just an Obersturmbannführer named Zeidler, a thoroughly decent type, even if he was SS. A gentleman.

He had been full of apologies. A dreadful mistake had been made. False information had been laid with malicious intent. The Reichsführer himself had ordered the fullest possible enquiry. Those responsible would undoubtedly be apprehended and punished. In the meantime, he regretted the fact that the Herr General still had to be kept under lock and key, but this would only be for a matter of a few days. He was sure he understood the situation.

Which Steiner did perfectly. All they had ever had against him was innuendo, nothing concrete. And he hadn't said a word in spite of everything Rossman had done, so the whole thing was going to look like one God-Almighty foul-up on someone's part. They were hanging on to him now to make sure he looked good for when they released him. Already, the bruises had almost faded. Except for the rings around his eyes he looked fine. They'd even given him a new uniform.

The coffee was really quite excellent. He started to pour another cup and the key rattled in the lock and the door opened behind him. There was an uncanny silence. The hair seemed to lift on the back of his head.

He turned slowly and found Karl Rossman standing in the doorway. He was wearing his slouch hat, the leather coat over his shoulders and a cigarette dangled from the corner of his mouth. Two Gestapo men in full uniform stood on either side of him.

"Hello, there, Herr General," Rossman said. "Did you think we'd forgotten you?"

Something seemed to break inside Steiner. The whole thing became dreadfully clear. "You bastard!" he said and threw the cup of coffee at Rossman's head.

"Very naughty," Rossman said. "You shouldn't have done that."

One of the Gestapo men moved in quickly. He rammed the end of his baton into Steiner's groin, who dropped to his knees with a scream of agony. A further blow to the side of the head put him down completely.

"The cellars," Rossman said simply, and went out.

The two Gestapo men got an ankle apiece and followed, dragging the General behind them facedown, keeping in step with a military precision that didn't even falter when they reached the stairs.

Max Radl knocked at the door of the Reichsführer's office and went in. Himmler was standing in front of the fire, drinking coffee. He put down his cup and crossed to the desk. "I had hoped that you would have been on your way by now."

"I leave on the overnight flight for Paris," Radl told him. "As the Herr Reichsführer is aware, Admiral Canaris only flew to Italy this morning."

"Unfortunate," Himmler said. "However, it should still leave you plenty of time." He removed his pince-nez and polished them as meticulously as usual. "I've read the report you gave Rossman this morning. What about these American Rangers who have appeared in the area? Show me."

He unfolded the ordnance survey map in front of him and Radl put a finger on Meltham House. "As you can see, Herr Reichsführer, Meltham House is eight miles to the north along the coast from Studley Constable. Twelve or thirteen from Hobs End. Mrs. Grey anticipates no trouble whatsoever in that direction in her latest radio message."

Himmler nodded. "Your Irishman seems to have earned his wages. The rest is up to Steiner."

"I don't think he'll let us down."

"Yes, I was forgetting," Himmler said dryly. "He has, after all, a personal stake in this."

Radl said, "May I be permitted to enquire after Major-General Steiner's health?"

"I last saw him yesterday evening," Himmler replied with perfect truth, "although I must confess he did not see me. At that time he was working his way through a meal consisting of roast potatoes, mixed vegetables and a rather large rump steak." He sighed. "If only these meat eaters realized the effect on the system of such a diet. Do you eat meat, Herr Oberst?"

"I'm afraid so."

"And smoke sixty or seventy of those vile Russian cigarettes a day and drink. What is your brandy consumption now?" He shook his head as he shuffled his papers into a neat pile in front of him. "Ah, well, in your case I don't suppose it really matters.''

Is there anything the swine doesn't know? Radl thought. "No, Herr Reichsführer.''

"What time do they leave on Friday?''

"Just before midnight. A one-hour flight, weather permitting.''

Himmler looked up instantly, eyes cold. "Colonel Radl, let me make one thing perfectly plain. Steiner and his men go in as arranged, weather or no weather. This is not something that can be postponed until another night. This is a once in a lifetime opportunity. There will be a line kept open to these headquarters at all times. From Friday morning you will communicate with me each hour on the hour and continue so doing until the operation is successfully concluded.''

"I will, Herr Reichsführer.''

Radl turned for the door and Himmler said, "One more thing. I have not kept the Führer informed of our progress in this affair for many reasons. These are hard times, Radl, the destiny of Germany rests on his shoulders. I would like this to be, how can I put it, a surprise for him?''

For a moment, Radl thought he must be going out of his mind. Then realized that Himmler was serious. "It is essential that we don't disappoint him,'' Himmler went on. "We are all in Steiner's hands now. Please impress that on him.''

"I will, Herr Reichsführer.'' Radl choked back an insane desire to laugh.

Himmler flipped up his right arm in a rather negligent party salute. "Heil Hitler!''

Radl, in what he afterwards swore to his wife was the bravest action of his entire life, gave him a punctilious military salute, turned to the door and got out as fast as he could.

When he went into his office at the Tirpitz Ufer, Hofer was packing an overnight bag for him. Radl got out the Courvoisier and poured himself a large one. "Is the Herr Oberst all right?'' Hofer enquired anxiously.

"You know what our esteemed Reichsführer has just let slip, Karl? He hasn't told the Führer about how far along the road we are with this thing. He wants to surprise him. Now isn't that sweet?''

"Herr Oberst, for God's sake.''

Radl raised his glass. "To our comrades, Karl, the three hundred and ten of the regiment who died in the Winter War, I'm not sure what for. If you find out, let me know.'' Hofer stared at him and Radl smiled. "All right, Karl, I'll be good. Did you check the time of my Paris flight?''

"Ten-thirty from Tempelhof. I've ordered a car for nine-fifteen. You have plenty of time.''

"And the onward flight to Amsterdam?"

"Some time tomorrow morning. Probably about eleven, but they couldn't be sure."

"That's cutting it fine. All I need is a little dirty weather and I won't get to Landsvoort till Thursday. What's the met report?"

"Not good. A cold front coming in from Russia."

"There always is," Radl told him bleakly. He opened the desk drawer and took out a sealed envelope. "That's for my wife. See that she gets it. Sorry you can't come with me, but you must hold the fort here, you understand that?"

Hofer looked down at the letter and there was fear in his eyes. "Surely the Herr Oberst doesn't think . . . "

"My dear, good Karl," Radl told him. "I think nothing. I simply prepare for any unpleasant eventuality. If this thing goes wrong then it seems to me that those connected with it might not be considered—how shall I put it?—persona grata at court. In any such eventuality your own line should be to deny all knowledge of the affair. Anything I've done, I've done alone."

"Herr Oberst, please," Hofer said hoarsely. There were tears in his eyes.

Radl took out another glass, filled it and handed it to him. "Come now, a toast. What shall we drink to?"

"God knows, Herr Oberst."

"Then I shall tell you. To life, Karl, and love and friendship and hope." He smiled wryly. "You know, it's just occurred to me that the Reichsführer very probably doesn't know the first thing about any one of those items. Ah, well . . . "

He threw back his head and emptied his glass at a single swallow.

Like most senior officers at Scotland Yard, Jack Rogan had a small camp bed in his office for use on those occasions when air raids made traveling home a problem. When he came back from the Assistant Commissioner, Special Branch's, weekly coordinating meeting with section heads on Wednesday morning just before noon, he found Grant asleep on it, eyes closed.

Rogan stuck his head out of the door and told the duty constable to make some tea. Then he gave Grant a friendly kick and went and stood at the window filling his pipe. The fog was worse than ever. A real London particular, as Dickens had once aptly phrased it.

Grant got up, adjusting his tie. His suit was crumpled and he needed a shave. "Hell of a journey back. The fog was really quite something."

"Did you get anywhere?"

Grant opened his briefcase, took out a file and produced a card which he laid on Rogan's desk. A photo of Liam Devlin was clipped to it. Strangely enough he looked older. There were several different names typed underneath. "That's Murphy, sir."

Rogan whistled softly. "Him? Are you sure?"

"Reuben Garvald is."

"But this doesn't make sense," Rogan said. "Last I heard, he was in trouble in Spain, fighting for the wrong side. Serving a life sentence on some penal farm."

"Evidently not, sir."

Rogan jumped up and walked to the window. He stood there, hands in pockets, for a moment. "You know, he's one of the few top-liners in the movement I've never met. Always the mystery man. All those bloody aliases for one thing."

"Went to Trinity College according to his file, which is unusual for a Catholic," Grant said. "Good degree in English Literature. There's irony, considering he's in the IRA."

"That's the bloody Irish for you." Rogan turned, prodding a finger into his skull. "Puddled from birth. Round the twist. I mean his uncle's a priest, he has a university degree and what is he? The most cold-blooded executioner the movement's had since Collins and his Murder Squad."

"All right, sir," Grant said. "How do we handle it?"

"First of all get in touch with the Special Branch in Dublin. See what they've got."

"And next?"

"If he's here legally he must have registered with his local police, wherever that is. Alien's registration form plus photograph."

"Which are then passed on to the headquarters of the force concerned."

"Exactly." Rogan kicked the desk. "I've been arguing for two years now that we should have them on a central file, but with nearly three-quarters of a million micks working over here nobody wants to know."

"That means circulating copies of this photo to all city and county forces and asking for someone to go through every registration on file." Grant picked up the card. "It'll take time."

"What else can we do, stick it in the paper and say: *Has anybody seen this man?* I want to know what he's up to, Fergus, I want to catch him at it, not frighten him off."

"Of course, sir."

"Just get on with it. Top Priority. Give it a National Security Red File rating. That will make the buggers jump to it."

Grant went out and Rogan picked up Devlin's file, leaned back in the chair and started to read it.

In Paris, all aircraft were grounded and the fog was so thick that when Radl walked out of the entrance of the departure lounge at Orly he couldn't see his hand in front of his face. He went back inside and spoke to the Duty Officer. "What do you think?"

"I'm sorry, Herr Oberst, but on the basis of the latest met report, nothing before morning. To be honest with you, there could be further delays even then. They seem to think this fog could last for some days." He smiled amiably. "It keeps the *Tommis* at home, anyway."

Radl made his decision and reached for his bag. "Absolutely essential that I'm in Rotterdam no later than tomorrow afternoon. Where's the motor pool?"

Ten minutes later he was holding the Führer Directive under the nose of a middle-aged transport captain and twenty minutes after that was being driven out of the main gate of Orly Airport in a large, black Citroën saloon.

At the same moment in the sitting room of Joanna Grey's cottage at Studley Constable, Sir Henry Willoughby was playing bezique with Father Vereker and Joanna Grey. He had had more to drink than was perhaps good for him and was in high good humor.

"Let me see now, I had a Royal Marriage—forty points and now a sequence in trumps."

"How many is that?" Vereker demanded.

"Two hundred and fifty," Joanna Grey said. "Two-ninety with his Royal Marriage."

"Just a minute," Vereker said. "He's got a ten above the Queen."

"But I explained that earlier," Joanna told him. "In bezique, the ten *does* come before the Queen."

Philip Vereker shook his head in disgust. "It's no good. I'll never understand this damned game."

Sir Henry laughed delightedly. "A gentleman's game, my boy. The aristocrat of card games." He jumped up, knocking his chair over and righted it. "Mind if I help myself, Joanna?"

"Of course not, my dear," she said brightly.

"You seem pleased with yourself tonight," Vereker remarked.

Sir Henry, warming his backside in front of the fire, grinned. "I am, Philip, I am and good cause to be." It all came flowing out of him in a sudden burst. "Don't see why I shouldn't tell you. You'll know soon enough now."

God, the old fool. Joanna Grey's alarm was genuine as she said hastily, "Henry, do you think you should?"

"Why not?" he said. "If I can't trust you and Philip, who can I trust." He turned to Vereker. "Fact is, the Prime Minister is coming to stay the weekend on Saturday."

"Good heavens. I'd heard he was speaking at King's Lynn, of course." Vereker was astounded. "To be honest, sir, I didn't realize you knew Mr. Churchill."

"I don't," Sir Henry said. "Thing is he fancied a quiet weekend and a little painting before going back to town. Naturally he'd heard about the gardens at Studley, I mean who hasn't? Laid down in the Armada year. When Downing Street got in touch to ask if he could stay, I was only too delighted."

"Naturally," Vereker said.

"Now you must keep it to yourselves, I'm afraid," Sir Henry said. "Villagers can't know till he's gone. They're most insistent about that. Security, you know. Can't be too careful."

He was very drunk now, slurring his words. Vereker said, "I suppose he'll be quite heavily guarded."

"Not at all," Sir Henry said. "Wants as little fuss as possible. He'll only have three or four people with him. I've arranged for a platoon of my Home Guard chaps to guard the perimeter of the Grange while he's there. Even they don't know what it's all about. Think it's an exercise."

"Is that so?" Joanna said.

"Yes, I'm to go up to King's Lynn on Saturday to meet him. We'll come back by car." He belched and put down his glass. "I say, would you excuse me? Don't feel too good."

"Of course," Joanna Grey said.

He walked to the door, turned and put a finger to his nose. "Mum's the word now."

After he'd gone, Vereker said, "That is a turn-up for the book."

"He's really very naughty," Joanna said. "He isn't supposed to say a word and yet he told me in exactly similar circumstances when he'd had too much to drink. Naturally I felt bound to keep quiet about it."

"Of course," he said. "You were absolutely right." He stood up, groping for his stick. "I'd better run him home. He's not fit to drive."

"Nonsense." She took his arm and steered him to the door. "That would mean you having to walk up to the presbytery to get your own car out. There's no need. I'll take him."

She helped him into his coat. "If you're sure, then?"

"Of course." She kissed his cheek. "I'm looking forward to seeing Pamela on Saturday."

He limped away into the night. She stood at the door listening as the sound of his progress faded. It was so still and quiet, almost as quiet as the veldt when she was a young girl. Strange, but she hadn't thought of that for years.

She went back inside and closed the door. Sir Henry appeared from the downstairs cloakroom and weaved an unsteady path to his chair by the fire. "Must go, old girl."

"Nonsense," she said. "Always time for another one." She poured two fingers of Scotch into his glass and sat on one arm of the chair, gently stroking his neck. "You know, Henry, I'd love to meet the Prime Minister. I think I'd like that more than anything else in the world."

"Would you, old girl?" He gazed up at her foolishly.

She smiled and gently brushed her lips along his forehead. "Well, almost anything."

It was very quiet in the cellars at Prinz Albrechtstrasse as Himmler went down the stairs. Rossman was waiting at the bottom. His sleeves were rolled up to the elbows and he was very pale.

"Well?" Himmler demanded.

"He's dead, I'm afraid, Herr Reichsführer."

Himmler was not pleased and showed it. "That seems singularly careless of you, Rossman. I told you to take care."

"With all due respect, Herr Reichsführer, it was his heart which gave out. Dr. Prager will confirm this. I sent for him at once. He's still in there."

He opened the nearest door. Rossman's two Gestapo assistants stood at one side, still wearing rubber gloves and aprons. A small, brisk-looking man in a tweed suit was leaning over the body on the iron cot in the corner, probing the naked chest with a stethoscope.

He turned as Himmler entered and gave the party salute. "Herr Reichsführer."

Himmler stood looking down at Steiner for a while. The General was stripped to the waist and his feet were bare. His eyes were partly open, fixed, staring into eternity.

"Well?" Himmler demanded.

"His heart, Herr Reichsführer. No doubt about it."

Himmler removed his pince-nez and gently rubbed between his eyes. He'd had a headache all afternoon and it simply would not go away. "Very well, Rossman," he said. "He was guilty of treason against the State, of plotting against the life of the Führer himself. As you know, the Führer has decreed a statutory punishment for this offense and Major-General Steiner cannot evade this, even in death."

"Of course, Herr Reichsführer."

"See that the sentence is carried out. I won't stay myself, I am summoned to Rastenburg but take photographs and dispose of the body in the usual way.''

They all clicked their heels in the party salute and left.

⋙

''He was arrested where?'' Rogan said in astonishment. It was just before five and already dark enough for the blackout curtains to be drawn.

''At a farmhouse near Caragh Lake in Kerry in June last year, after a gunfight in which he shot two policemen and was wounded himself. He escaped from the local hospital the following day and dropped out of sight.''

''Dear God and they call themselves policemen,'' Rogan said in despair.

''The thing is, Special Branch, Dublin, weren't involved in any of this, sir. They only identified him later by the prints on the revolver. The arrest was made by a patrol from the local *Garda* barracks checking for an illicit still. One other point, sir. Dublin say they checked with the Spanish Foreign Office, our friend supposedly being in gaol over there. They were reluctant to come across, you know how difficult they can be about this kind of thing. They finally admitted that he'd escaped from a penal farm in Granada in the autumn of 1940. Their information was that he'd made it to Lisbon and taken passage to the States.''

''And now he's back,'' Rogan said. ''But what for, that's the thing. Have you heard from any of the provincial forces yet?''

''Seven, sir—all negative, I'm afraid.''

''All right. There's nothing more we can do at the moment except hope. The moment you have anything, contact me instantly. Day or night, no matter where I am.''

''Very well, sir.''

14

⋙

IT WAS PRECISELY ELEVEN-FIFTEEN ON Friday morning at Meltham Grange when Harry Kane, who was supervising a squad's progress over the assault course, received an urgent summons to report to Shafto at once. When he reached his commanding officer's outer office he found things in something of a turmoil. The clerks looked frightened and Master-Sergeant Garvey paced up and down, smoking a cigarette nervously.

"What's happened?" Kane demanded.

"God knows, Major. All I know is he blew his stack about fifteen minutes ago after receiving an urgent despatch from Headquarters. Kicked young Jones clean out of the office. And I mean kicked."

Kane knocked at the door and went in. Shafto was standing at the window, his riding crop in one hand, a glass in the other. He turned angrily and then his expression changed. "Oh, it's you, Harry."

"What is it, sir?"

"It's simple. Those bastards up at Combined Operations who've been trying to get me out of the way have finally managed it. When we finish here next weekend, I hand over command to Sam Williams."

"And you, sir?"

"I'm to go back Stateside. Chief Instructor in Fieldcraft at Fort Benning."

He kicked a wastepaper bin clean across the room and Kane said, "Isn't there anything you can do about it, sir?"

Shafto turned on him like a madman. "Do about it?" He picked up the order and pushed it into Kane's face. "See the signature on that? Eisenhower himself." He crumpled it into a ball and threw it away. "And you know something, Kane? He's never been in action. Not once in his entire career."

At Hobs End Devlin was lying in bed writing in his personal notebook. It was raining hard and outside, mist draped itself over the marsh in a damp, clinging shroud. The door was pushed open and Molly came in. She was wearing Devlin's trenchcoat and carried a tray which she put down on the table beside the bed.

"There you are, O lord and master. Tea and toast, two boiled eggs, four and a half minutes as you suggested, and cheese sandwiches."

Devlin stopped writing and looked at the tray appreciatively. "Keep up this standard and I might be tempted to take you on permanently."

She took off the trenchcoat. Underneath she was only wearing pants and a bra and she picked up her sweater from the end of the bed and pulled it over her head. "I'll have to get moving. I told Mum I'd be in for my dinner."

He poured himself a cup of tea and she picked up the notebook. "What's this?" She opened it. "Poetry?"

He grinned. "A matter of opinion in some quarters."

"Yours?" she said and there was genuine wonder on her face. She opened it at the place where he had been writing that morning. "There

is no certain knowledge of my passing, where I have walked in wood-
land after dark.'' She looked up. ''Why, that's beautiful, Liam.''

''I know,'' he said. ''Like you keep telling me, I'm a lovely boy.''

''I know one thing, I could eat you up.'' She flung herself on top of
him and kissed him fiercely. ''You know what today is? The fifth of
November only we can't have no bonfire because of rotten old Adolf.''

''What a shame,'' he jeered.

''Never you mind.'' She wriggled into a comfortable position, her legs
straddling him. ''I'll come round tonight and cook you supper and we'll
have a nice little bonfire all our own.''

''No you won't,'' he said. ''Because I shan't be here.''

Her face clouded. ''Business?''

He kissed her lightly. ''Now you know what you promised.''

''All right,'' she said. ''I'll be good. I'll see you in the morning.''

''No, I probably won't get back till tomorrow afternoon. Far better to
leave it that I'll call for you—all right?''

She nodded reluctantly. ''If you say so.''

''I do.''

He kissed her and there was the sound of a horn outside. Molly darted
to the window and came back in a hurry grabbing for her denim trousers.
''My God, it's Mrs. Grey.''

''That's what's called being caught with your pants down,'' Devlin
told her, laughing.

He pulled on a sweater. Molly reached for her coat. ''I'm off. I'll see
you tomorrow, beautiful. Can I take this? I'd like to read the others.''

She held up his notebook of poetry. ''God, but you must like punishment,'' he said.

She kissed him hard and he followed her out, opening the back door
for her, standing watching her run through the reeds to the dyke, knowing
that this could well be the end. ''Ah, well,'' he said softly. ''The best
thing for her.''

He turned and went to open the door in answer to Joanna Grey's
repeated knocking. She surveyed him grimly as he tucked his shirt into
his trousers. ''I caught a glimpse of Molly on the dyke path a second
ago.'' She walked past him. ''You really should be ashamed of yourself.''

''I know,'' he said as he followed her into the sitting room. ''I'm a
terrible bad lot. Well, the big day. I'd say that warrants a little nip. Will
you join me?''

''Quarter of an inch in the bottom of the glass and no more,'' she
said sternly.

He brought the Bushmills and two glasses and poured a couple of
drinks. ''Up the Republic!'' he told her, ''Both the Irish and South
African varieties. Now, what's the news?''

"I switched to the new wavelength last night as ordered, transmitting directly to Landsvoort. Radl himself is there now."

"And it's still on?" Devlin said. "In spite of the weather?"

Her eyes were shining. "Come hell or high water, Steiner and his men will be here at approximately one o'clock."

Steiner was addressing the assault group in his quarters. The only person present other than those actually making the drop was Max Radl. Even Gericke had been excluded. They all stood around the map table. There was an atmosphere of nervous excitement as Steiner turned from the window where he had been talking to Radl in a low voice and faced them. He indicated Gerhard Klugl's model, the photos, the maps.

"All right. You all know where you're going. Every stick, every stone of it, which has been the object of the exercise for the past few weeks. What you don't know is what we're supposed to do when we get there."

He paused, glancing at each face in turn, tense, expectant. Even Preston, who, after all, had known for some time, seemed caught by the drama of the occasion.

So Steiner told them.

Peter Gericke could hear the roar from as far away as the hangar.

"Now what's happening, for God's sake?" Bohmler said.

"Don't ask me," Gericke replied sourly. "Nobody tells me anything around here." The bitterness suddenly overflowed. "If we're good enough to risk our necks flying the sods in, you'd think we might at least be told what it's all about."

"If it's as important as that," Bohmler said, "I'm not sure I want to know. I'm going to check the Lichtenstein set."

He climbed into the plane and Gericke lit a cigarette and moved a little further away, looking the Dakota over again. Sergeant Witt had done a lovely job on the RAF rondels. He turned and saw the field car moving across the airstrip towards him, Ritter Neumann at the wheel, Steiner beside him, Radl in the rear. It braked to a halt a yard or two away. No one got out.

Steiner said, "You don't look too pleased with life, Peter."

"Why should I?" Gericke said. "A whole month I've spent in this dump, worked all the hours God sends on that plane in there and for what?" His gesture took in the mist, the rain, the entire sky. "In this kind of shit I'll never even get off the ground."

"Oh, we have every confidence that a man of your very special calibre will be able to accomplish that."

They started to get out of the field wagon and Ritter particularly was having the greatest difficulty in holding back his laughter. "Look, what's going on here?" Gericke said truculently. "What's it all about?"

"Why, it's really quite simple, you poor, miserable, hard-done-to son of a bitch," Radl said. "I have the honor to inform you that you have just been awarded the Knight's Cross."

Gericke stared at him, open-mouthed and Steiner said gently, "So, you see, my dear Peter, you get your weekend at Karinhall after all."

❧

Koenig leaned over the chart table with Steiner and Radl and Chief Petty Officer Muller stood at a respectful distance, but missing nothing.

The young lieutenant said, "Four months ago a British armed trawler was torpedoed off the Hebrides by a U-boat under the command of Horst Wengel, an old friend of mine. There were only fifteen in the crew so he took them all prisoner. Unfortunately for them, they hadn't managed to get rid of their documents, which included some interesting charts of the British coastal minefields."

"That was a break for somebody," Steiner said.

"For all of us, Herr Oberst, as these latest charts from Wilhelmshaven prove. See, here, east of the Wash where the minefield runs parallel to the coast to protect the inshore shipping lane? There is a route through quite clearly marked. The British Navy made it for their own purposes, but units of the Eighth E-boat Flotilla out of Rotterdam have used it with perfect safety for some time now. In fact, as long as navigation is accurate enough, one may proceed at speed."

"There would seem to be an argument for saying that the minefield itself in such circumstances will afford you considerable protection," Radl said.

"Exactly, Herr Oberst."

"And what about the estuary approach behind the Point to Hobs End?"

"Difficult certainly, but Muller and I have studied the Admiralty Charts until we know them by heart. Every sounding, every sandbank. We will be going in on a rising tide, remember, if we are to make the pick-up at ten."

"You estimate eight hours for the passage which would mean your leaving here at what—one o'clock?"

"If we are to have a margin at the other end in which to operate. Of course, this is a unique craft as you know. She could do the trip in seven hours if it comes to that. I'm just playing safe.''

"Very sensible," Radl said, "because Colonel Steiner and I have decided to modify your orders. I want you off the Point and ready to go in for the pick-up at *any* time between nine and ten. You'll get your final run-in orders from Devlin on the S-phone. Be guided by him.''

"Very well, Herr Oberst.''

"You shouldn't be in any particular danger under cover of darkness," Steiner said and smiled. "After all, this is a British ship.''

Koenig grinned, opened a cupboard under the chart table and took out a British Navy White Ensign. "And we'll be flying this, remember.''

Radl nodded. "Radio silence from the moment you leave. Under no circumstances must you break it until you hear from Devlin. You know the code sign, of course.''

"Naturally, Herr Oberst.''

Koenig was being polite and Radl clapped him on the shoulder. "Yes, I know, to you I am a nervous, old man. I'll see you tomorrow before you leave. You'd better say goodbye to Colonel Steiner now.''

Steiner shook hands with both of them. "I don't quite know what to say except be on time for God's sake.''

Koenig gave him a perfect naval salute. "I'll see you on that beach, Herr Oberst. I promise you.''

Steiner smiled wryly. "I damn well hope so.'' He turned and followed Radl outside.

As they walked along the sand pier towards the field car Radl said, "Well, is it going to work, Kurt?''

At that moment Werner Briegel and Gerhard Klugl came over the sand dunes. They were wearing ponchos and Briegel's Zeiss fieldglasses were slung around his neck.

"Let's seek their opinion," Steiner suggested and called out in English, "Private Kunicki! Private Moczar! Over here, please!'' Briegel and Klugl doubled across without hesitation. Steiner looked them over calmly and continued in English, "Who am I?''

"Lieutenant-Colonel Howard Carter, in command of the Polish Independent Parachute Squadron, Special Air Service Regiment," Briegel replied promptly in good English.

Radl turned to Steiner with a smile. "I'm impressed.''

Steiner said, "What are you doing here?''

"Sergeant-Major Brandt," Briegel began and hastily corrected himself. "Sergeant-Major Kruczek told us to relax.'' He hesitated then added in German, "We're looking for shorelarks, Herr Oberst.''

"Shorelarks?" Steiner said.

"Yes, they're quite easy to distinguish. A most striking black and yellow pattern on face and throat.''

Steiner exploded into laughter. "You see, my dear Max? Shorelarks. How can we possibly fail?"

⚜

But the elements seemed determined to make sure that they did. As darkness fell, fog still blanketed most of Western Europe. At Landsvoort, Gericke inspected the airstrip constantly from six o'clock onwards, but in spite of the heavy rain the fog was as thick as ever.

"There's no wind, you see," he informed Steiner and Radl at eight o'clock. "That's what we need now to clear this damn stuff away. Lots of wind."

⚜

Across the North Sea in Norfolk things were no better. In the secret cubbyhole in the loft of her cottage, Joanna Grey sat by the radio receiver in her headphones and filled in the time reading a book Vereker had lent her in which Winston Churchill described how he had escaped from a prison camp during the Boer War. It was really quite enthralling and she was conscious of a rather reluctant admiration.

Devlin, at Hobs End, had been out to check on the weather as frequently as Gericke, but nothing changed and the fog seemed as impenetrable as ever. At ten o'clock he went along the dyke to the beach for the fourth time that night, but conditions didn't seem to have altered.

He flashed his torch into the gloom then shook his head and said softly to himself, "A good night for dirty work, that's about all you can say for it."

⚜

It seemed obvious that the whole thing was a washout and it was hard to escape that conclusion at Landsvoort, too. "Are you trying to say you can't take off?" Radl demanded when the young Hauptmann came back inside the hangar from another inspection.

"No problem there," Gericke told him. "I can take off blind. Not particularly hazardous in country as flat as this. The difficulty's going to be at the other end. I can't just drop those men and hope for the best. We could be a mile out to sea. I need to see the target, however briefly."

Bohmler opened the judas in one of the big hangar doors and peered in. "Herr Hauptmann."

Gericke moved to join him. "What is it?"

"See for yourself."

Gericke stepped through, Bohmler had switched on the outside light and in spite of its dimness, Gericke could see the fog swirling in strange patterns. Something touched his cheek coldly. "Wind!" he said. "My God, we've got wind."

There was a sudden gap torn in the curtain and he could see the farmhouse for a moment. Dimly, but it was there. "Do we go?" Bohmler demanded.

"Yes," Gericke said. "But it's got to be now," and he turned and plunged back through the judas to tell Steiner and Radl.

Twenty minutes later, at exactly eleven o'clock, Joanna Grey straightened abruptly as her earphones started to buzz. She dropped her book, reached for a pencil and wrote on the pad in front of her. It was a very brief message, decoded in seconds. She sat staring at it, momentarily spellbound, then she made an acknowledgement.

She went downstairs quickly and took her sheepskin coat from behind the door. The retriever sniffed at her heels. "No, Patch, not this time," she said.

She had to drive carefully because of the fog and it was twenty minutes later before she turned into the yard at Hobs End. Devlin was getting his gear together on the kitchen table when he heard the car. He reached for the Mauser quickly and went out into the passageway.

"It's me, Liam," she called.

He opened the door and she slipped in. "What's all this?"

"I've just received a message from Landsvoort, timed eleven o'clock exactly," she said. "The eagle has flown."

He stared at her, astonished. "They must be crazy. It's like pea soup up there on the beach."

"It seemed a little clearer to me as I turned along the dyke."

He went out quickly and opened the front door. He was back in a moment, face pale with excitement. "There's a wind coming in off the sea, not much, but it could get stronger."

"Don't you think it will last?" she said.

"God knows." The silenced Sten gun was assembled on the table and he handed it to her. "You know how to work these?"

"Of course."

He picked up a bulging rucksack and slung it over his shoulders. "Right then, let's you and me get to it. We've got work to do. If your timing's right, they'll be over that beach in forty minutes." As they moved into the passage, he laughed harshly. "By God, but they mean business, I'll say that for them."

He opened the door and they plunged out into the fog.

"I'd close my eyes if I were you," Gericke told Bohmler cheerfully, above the rumbling of the engines warming up as he made his final check before take-off. "This one's going to be pretty hair-raising."

The flares to mark the take-off run had been lit, but only the first few could be seen. Visibility was still no more than forty or fifty yards. The door behind them opened and Steiner poked his head into the cockpit.

"Everything strapped down back there?" Gericke asked him.

"Everything and everybody. We're ready when you are."

"Good, I don't want to be an alarmist, but I should point out that anything could happen and very probably will."

He increased his engine revs and Steiner grinned, shouting to make himself heard above the roaring. "We have every faith in you."

He closed the door and retired. Gericke boosted power instantly and let the Dakota go. To plunge headlong into that gray wall was probably the most terrifying thing he had ever done in his life. He needed a run of several hundred yards, a speed of around eighty miles an hour for lift-off.

"My God," he thought. "Is this it? Is this finally it?"

The vibrations as he gave her more power seemed unbearable. Up came the tail as he pushed the column forward. Just a touch. She yawed to starboard in a slight crosswind and he applied a little rudder correction.

The roar of the engines seemed to fill the night. At eighty, he eased back slightly, but held on. And then, as that feeling flowed through him, that strange sixth sense, the product of several thousand hours of flying that told you when things were just right, he hauled back on the column.

"Now!" he cried.

Bohmler, who had been waiting tensely, his hand on the undercarriage lever, responded frantically, winding up the wheels. Suddenly they were flying. Gericke kept her going, straight into that gray wall, refusing to sacrifice power for height, hanging on till the last possible moment, before pulling the column right back. At five hundred feet they burst out of the fog, he stamped on the right rudder and turned out to sea.

Outside the hangar, Max Radl sat in the passenger seat of the field car staring up into the fog, a kind of awe on his face. "Great God in heaven!" he whispered. "He did it!"

He sat there for a moment longer, listening as the sound of the engines faded into the night, then nodded to Witt behind the wheel. "Back to the farmhouse as quickly as you like, Sergeant. I've got things to do."

In the Dakota there was no easing of tension. There had been none in the first place. They talked amongst themselves in low tones with all the calm of veterans who had done this sort of thing so many times that it was second nature. As nobody had been allowed to have German cigarettes on his person, Ritter Neumann and Steiner moved amongst them handing them out singly.

Altmann said, "He's a flyer, that Hauptmann, I'll say that for him. A real ace to take off in that fog."

Steiner turned to Preston sitting at the end of the stick. "A cigarette, Lieutenant?" he said in English.

"Thanks very much, sir, I think I will." Preston replied in a beautifully clipped voice that suggested he was playing the Coldstream Guards Captain again.

"How do you feel?" Steiner asked in a low voice.

"In excellent spirits, sir," Preston told him calmly. "Can't wait to get stuck in."

Steiner gave up and retreated to the cockpit where he found Bohmler passing Gericke coffee from a thermos flask. They were flying at two thousand feet. Through occasional gaps in the clouds, stars could be seen and a pale sickle moon. Below, fog covered the sea like smoke in a valley, a spectacular sight.

"How are we doing?" Steiner asked.

"Fine. Another thirty minutes. Not much of a wind though. I'd say about five knots."

Steiner nodded down into the cauldron below. "What do you think? Will it be clear enough when you go down?"

"Who knows?" Gericke grinned. "Maybe I'll end up on that beach with you."

At that moment Bohmler, huddled over the Lichtenstein set, gave an excited gasp. "I've got something, Peter."

They entered a short stretch of cloud. Steiner said, "What's it likely to be?"

"Probably a night fighter, as he's on his own." Gericke said. "Better pray it isn't one of ours. He'll blow us out of the sky."

They emerged from the clouds into clear air and Bohmler tapped Gericke's arm. "Coming in like a bat out of hell on the starboard quarter."

Steiner turned his head and after a few moments could plainly see a twin-engined aircraft levelling out to starboard.

"Mosquito," Gericke said and added calmly, "Let's hope he knows a friend when he sees one."

The Mosquito held course with them for only a few more moments, then wagged its wingtips and swung away to starboard at great speed, disappearing into heavy cloud.

"See," Gericke smiled up at Steiner. "All you have to do is live right. Better get back to your lads and make sure they're ready to go. If everything works, we should pick up Devlin on the S-phone twenty miles out. I'll call you when we do. Now get the hell out of here. Bohmler's got some fancy navigating to do."

Steiner returned to the main cabin and sat down beside Ritter

Neumann. "Not long now." He passed him a cigarette.

"Thanks very much," Steiner said. "Just what I needed."

It was cold on the beach and the tide was about two-thirds of the way in. Devlin walked up and down restlessly to keep warm, holding the receiver in his right hand, the channel open. It was almost ten to twelve and Joanna Grey, who had been sheltering from the light rain in the trees, came towards him.

"They must be close now."

As if in direct answer, the S-phone crackled and Peter Gericke said with astonishing clarity, "This is Eagle, are you receiving me, Wanderer?"

Joanna Grey grabbed Devlin's arm. He shook her off and spoke into the S-phone. "Loud and clear."

"Please report conditions over nest."

"Visibility poor," Devlin said. "One hundred to one hundred and fifty yards, wind freshening."

"Thank you, Wanderer. Estimated time of arrival, six minutes."

Devlin shoved the S-phone into Joanna Grey's hand. "Hang on to that while I lay out the markers."

Inside his rucksack he had a dozen cycle lamps. He hurried along the beach, putting them down at intervals of fifteen yards in a line following the direction of the wind, switching each one on. Then he turned and went back in a parallel line at a distance of twenty yards.

When he rejoined Joanna Grey he was slightly breathless. He took out a large and powerful spotlight and ran a hand over his forehead to wipe sweat from his eyes.

"Oh, this damn fog," she said. "They'll never see us. I know they won't."

It was the first time he'd seen her crack in any way and he put a hand on her arm. "Be still, girl."

Faintly, in the distance, there was the rumble of engines.

The Dakota was down to a thousand feet and descending through intermittent fog. Gericke said over his shoulder, "One pass, that's all I'll get, so make it good."

"We will," Steiner told him.

"Luck, Herr Oberst. I've got a bottle of Dom Perignon back there at Landsvoort on ice, remember. We'll drink it together, Sunday morning."

Steiner clapped him on the shoulder and went out. He nodded to Ritter who gave the order. Everyone stood and clipped his static line to the anchor cable. Brandt slid back the exit door and as fog and cold air billowed in, Steiner moved down the line checking each man personally.

Gericke went in very low, so low that Bohmler could see the white of waves breaking in the gloom. Ahead was only fog and more darkness. "Come on!" Bohmler whispered, hammering his clenched fist on his knee. "Come on, damn you!"

As if some unseen power had decided to take a hand, a sudden gust of wind tore a hole in the gray curtain and revealed Devlin's parallel lines of cycle lamps, clear in the night, a little to starboard.

Gericke nodded. Bohmler pressed the switch and the red light in the cabin flashed above Steiner's head. "Ready!" he cried.

Gericke banked to starboard, throttled back until his airspeed indicator stood at a hundred and made his pass along the beach at three hundred and fifty feet. The green light flashed, Ritter Neumann jumped into darkness, Brandt followed, the rest of the men tumbled after them. Steiner could feel the wind on his face, smell the salt tang of the sea and waited for Preston to falter. The Englishman stepped into space without a second's hesitation. It was a good omen. Steiner clipped on to the anchor line and went after him.

Bohmler, peering out through the open door of the cockpit, tapped Gericke on the arm. "All gone, Peter. I'll go and close the door."

Gericke nodded and swung out towards the sea again. It was no more than five minutes later that the S-phone receiver crackled and Devlin said clearly, "All fledglings safe and secure in the nest."

Gericke reached for the mike. "Thank you, Wanderer. Good luck."

He said to Bohmler, "Pass that on to Landsvoort at once. Radl must have been walking on hot bricks for the past hour."

In his office at Prinz Albrechtstrasse, Himmler worked alone in the light of the desk lamp. The fire was low, the room rather cold, but he seemed oblivious of both those facts and wrote on steadily. There was a discreet knock at the door and Rossman entered.

Himmler looked up. "What is it?"

"We've just heard from Radl at Landsvoort, Herr Reichsführer. The Eagle has landed."

Himmler's face showed no emotion whatsoever. "Thank you, Rossman," he said. "Keep me informed."

"Yes, Herr Reichsführer."

Rossman withdrew and Himmler returned to his work, the only sound in the room the steady scratching of his pen.

Devlin, Steiner and Joanna Grey stood together at the table examining a large-scale map of the area. "See here, behind St. Mary's," Devlin was saying, "Old Woman's Meadow. It belongs to the church and the barn with it which is empty at the moment."

"You move in there tomorrow," Joanna Grey said. "See Father Vereker and tell him you're on exercises and wish to spend the night in the barn."

"And you're certain he'll agree?" Steiner said.

Joanna Grey nodded. "No question of it. That sort of thing happens all the time. Soldiers appear either on exercises or forced marches, disappear again. No one ever really knows who they are. Nine months ago we had a Czechoslovakian unit through here and even their officers could only speak a few words of English."

"Another thing, Vereker was a paratrooper padre in Tunisia," Devlin added, "so he'll be leaning over backwards to assist when he sees those red berets."

"There's an even stronger point in our favour where Vereker's concerned," Joanna Grey said. "He knows the Prime Minister is spending the weekend at Studley Grange which is going to work on our behalf very nicely. Sir Henry let it slip the other night at my house when he'd been drinking a little bit too much. Of course Vereker was sworn to secrecy. Can't even tell his own sister until after the great man's gone."

"And how will this help us?" Steiner asked.

"It's simple," Devlin said. "You tell Vereker you're here for the weekend on some exercise or other and ordinarily he would accept that at face value. But this time, remember, he knows that Churchill is visiting the area incognito, so what interpretation does he put on the presence of a crack outfit like the SAS?"

"Of course," Steiner said. "Special security."

"Exactly." Joanna Grey nodded. "Another point in our favour. Sir Henry is giving a small dinner party for the Prime Minister tomorrow night." She smiled and corrected herself. "Sorry, I mean tonight. Seventhirty for eight and I'm invited. I'll go only to make my excuses. Say that I've had a call to turn out on night duty for the WVS emergency service. It's happened before, so Sir Henry and Lady Willoughby will accept it completely. It means, of course, that if we make contact in the vicinity of the Grange, I'll be able to give you a very exact description of the immediate situation there."

"Excellent," Steiner said. "The whole thing seems more plausible by the minute."

Joanna Grey said, "I must go."

Devlin brought her coat and Steiner took it from him and held it open for her courteously. "Is there no danger for you in driving round the countryside alone at this hour of the morning?"

"Good heavens no." She smiled. "I'm a member of the WVS motor pool. That's why I'm allowed the privilege of running a car at all, but it means that I'm required to provide an emergency service in the village and surrounding area. I often have to turn out in the early hours to take people to hospital. My neighbours are perfectly used to it."

The door opened and Ritter Neumann entered. He was wearing a camouflaged jump jacket and trousers and there was an SAS winged dagger badge in his red beret.

"Everything all right out there?" Steiner asked.

Ritter nodded. "Everyone bedded down snugly for the night. Only one grumble. No cigarettes."

"Of course. I knew there was something I'd forgotten. I left them in the car." Joanna Grey hurried out.

She was back in a few moments and put two cartons of Players on the table, five hundred in each in packets of twenty.

"Holy Mother," Devlin said in awe. "Did you ever see the like? They're like gold, those things. Where did they come from?"

"WVS stores. You see, now I've added theft to my accomplishments." She smiled. "And now, gentlemen, I must leave you. We'll meet again, by accident, of course, tomorrow when you are in the village."

Steiner and Ritter Neumann saluted and Devlin took her out to her car. When he returned, the two Germans had opened one of the cartons and were smoking by the fire.

"I'll have a couple of packets of these myself," Devlin said.

Steiner gave him a light. "Mrs. Grey is a remarkable woman. Who did you leave in charge out there, Ritter? Preston or Brandt?"

"I know who thinks he is."

There was a light tap on the door and Preston entered. The camouflaged jump jacket, the holstered revolver at his waist, the red beret slanted at just the right angle towards the left eye, made him seem more handsome than ever.

"Oh, yes," Devlin said. "I like it. Very dashing. And how are you, me old son? Happy to be treading your native soil again, I dare say?"

The expression on Preston's face suggested that Devlin reminded him of something that needed scraping off his shoe. "I didn't find you particularly entertaining in Berlin, Devlin. Even less so now. I'd be pleased if you would transfer your attentions elsewhere."

"God save us," Devlin said, amazed. "Who in the hell does the lad think he's playing now?"

Preston said to Steiner, "Any further orders, sir?"

Steiner picked up the two cartons of cigarettes and handed them to him. "I'd be obliged if you'd give these out to the men," he said gravely.

"They'll love you for that," Devlin put in.

Preston ignored him, put the cartons under his left arm and saluted smartly. "Very well, sir."

In the Dakota, the atmosphere was positively euphoric. The return trip had passed completely without incident. They were thirty miles out from the Dutch coast and Bohmler opened the thermos and passed Gericke another cup of coffee. "Home and dry," he said.

Gericke nodded cheerfully. Then the smile vanished abruptly. Over his headphones he heard a familiar voice. Hans Berger, the controller at his old unit, NJG7.

Bohmler touched his shoulder. "That's Berger, isn't it?"

"Who else?" Gericke said. "You've listened to him often enough."

"Steer o-eight-three degrees." Berger's voice crackled through the static.

"Sounds as if he's leading a night fighter in for the kill," Bohmler said. "On our heading."

"Target five kilometres."

Suddenly Berger's voice seemed like the hammer on the last nail in a coffin, crisp, clear, final. Gericke's stomach knotted in a cramp that was almost sexual in its intensity. And he was not afraid. It was as if after years of looking for Death, he was now gazing upon his face with a kind of yearning.

Bohmler grabbed his arm convulsively. "It's us, Peter!" he screamed. "We're the target!"

The Dakota rocked violently from side to side as cannon shell punched through the floor of the cockpit, tearing the instrument panel apart, shattering the windscreen. Shrapnel ripped into Gericke's right thigh and a heavy blow shattered his left arm. Another part of his brain told him exactly what was happening. *Schraege Musik*, delivered from below by one of his own comrades—only this time he was on the receiving end.

He wrestled with the control column, heaving it back with all his strength as the Dakota started to go down. Bohmler was struggling to rise to his feet, blood on his face.

"Get out!" Gericke shouted above the roaring of the wind through the shattered windscreen. "I can't hold her for long."

Bohmler was on his feet now and trying to speak. Gericke lashed out wildly with his left arm, catching him across the face. The pain was excruciating and he screamed again, "Get out! That's an order."

Bohmler turned and moved back along the Dakota to the exit. The plane was in a hell of a state, great holes ripped in the body, pieces of fuselage rattling in the turbulence. He could smell smoke and burning oil. Panic gave him new strength, as he wrestled with the release handles on the hatch.

"Dear God, don't let me burn," he thought. "Anything but that." Then the hatch eased back and he poised for a moment and tumbled into the night.

The Dakota corkscrewed and the port wing lifted. Bohmler somersaulted, his head caught the tailplane a violent blow even as his right hand fastened convulsively on the metal ring. He pulled his ripcord in the very moment of dying. The parachute opened like a strange, pale flower and carried him gently down into darkness.

The Dakota flew on, descending now, the port engine on fire, flames spreading along the wing, reaching for the main body of the plane. Gericke sat at the controls, still fighting to hold her, unaware that his left arm was broken in two places.

There was blood in his eyes. He laughed weakly as he strained to peer through the smoke. *What a way to go.* No visit to Karinhall now, no Knight's Cross. His father would be disappointed about that. Though they'd simply award the damn thing posthumously.

Suddenly, the smoke cleared and he could see the sea through intermittent fog. The Dutch coast couldn't be far away. There were ships down there, at least two. A line of tracer arched up towards him. Some bloody E-boat showing it had teeth. It was really very funny.

He tried to move in his seat and found that his left foot was trapped by a piece of twisted fuselage. Not that it mattered, for by now he was too far down to jump. He was only three hundred feet above the sea, aware of the E-boat to starboard racing him like a grayhound, firing with everything it had got, cannon shells ripping into the Dakota.

"Bastards!" Gericke shouted. "Stupid bastards!" He laughed weakly again and said softly, as if Bohmler was still there on his left. "Who in the hell am I supposed to be fighting, anyway?"

Quite suddenly, the smoke was torn away in a violent crosswind and he saw the sea no more than a hundred feet below and coming up to meet him fast.

At that moment he became a great pilot for the only time in his life when it really mattered. Every instinct for survival surged up to give him new strength. He pulled on the column and in spite of the agony in his left arm throttled back and dropped what was left of his flaps.

The Dakota almost stalled, the tail started to fall. He gave a final burst of power to straighten her up as she dropped into the waves and pulled hard on the column again. She bounced three times, skimming the water like a gigantic surfboard and came to a halt, the burning engine hissing angrily as a wave slopped across it.

Gericke sat there for a moment. Everything wrong, nothing by the book and yet he had done it and against every conceivable odds. There was water around his ankles. He tried to get up, but his left foot was securely held. He pulled the fire axe on his right from its holding clip and smashed at the crumpled fuselage, and his foot, breaking the ankle in the process. By then he was beyond reason.

It came as no surprise to find himself standing, the foot free. He got the hatch open—no trouble at all, and fell out into the water, bumping against the wing clumsily, pulling at the quick release ring on his life-jacket. It inflated satisfactorily and he kicked out at the wing, pushing himself away as the Dakota started to go under.

When the E-boat arrived behind him he didn't even bother to turn, but floated there watching the Dakota slide under the surface.

"You did all right, old girl. All right," he said.

A rope splashed into the water beside him and someone called in English with a heavy German accent, "Catch hold, *Tommi*, and we'll haul you in. You're safe now."

Gericke turned and looked up at the young German naval lieutenant and half a dozen sailors who leaned over the rail above him.

"Safe, is it?" he demanded in German. "You stupid bastards—I'm on your side."

15

ᴡᴡ

IT WAS JUST AFTER TEN on Saturday morning when Molly rode down through the fields towards Hobs End. The heavy rain of the previous night had slackened into a light drizzle, but the marsh itself was still blanketed in fog.

She'd risen early and worked hard all morning, had fed the livestock and seen to the milking herself, for Laker Armsby had a grave to dig. Her decision to ride down to the marsh had been a sudden impulse for, in spite of the fact that she had promised Devlin to wait until he called for her, she was terrified that something might happen to him. Conviction of those involved in black market activities usually meant a heavy prison sentence.

She took the horse down into the marsh and came to the cottage from the rear through the reed barrier, letting the animal choose its own way.

The muddy water came up to its belly and some slopped inside her Wellington boots. She paid no heed and leaned over the horse's neck, peering through the fog. She was sure she could smell woodsmoke. Then the barn and the cottage gradually materialized from the fog, and there *was* smoke ascending from the chimney.

She hesitated, momentarily undecided. Liam was at home, obviously back earlier than he had intended, but if she went in now he would think she had been snooping again. She dug her heels into her horse's flanks and started to turn it away.

In the barn the men were getting their equipment ready for the move out. Brandt and Sergeant Altmann were supervising the mounting of a Browning M2 heavy machine-gun on the jeep. Preston stood watching, hands clasped behind his back, giving the impression of being somehow in charge of the whole thing.

Werner Briegel and Klugl had partially opened one of the rear shutters and Werner surveyed what he could of the marsh through his Zeiss fieldglasses. There were birds in the *suaeda* bushes, the reedy dykes. Enough to content even him. Grebes and moorhens, curlew, widgeon, brent geese.

"There's a good one," he said to Klugl. "A green sandpiper. Passage migrant, usually in the autumn, but they've been known to winter here." He continued his trajectory and Molly jumped into view. "Christ, we're being watched."

In a moment Brandt and Preston were at his side. Preston said, "I'll get her," and he turned and ran for the door.

Brandt grabbed at him, too late, and Preston was across the yard and into the reeds in a matter of moments. Molly turned, reining in. Her first thought that it was Devlin. Preston grabbed for the reins and she looked down at him in astonishment.

"All right, let's have you."

He reached for her and she tried to back her mount away. "Here, you leave me be. I haven't done anything."

He grabbed her right wrist and pulled her out of the saddle, catching her as she fell. "We'll see about that, shall we?"

She started to struggle and he tightened his grip. He slung her over his shoulder and carried her kicking and shouting through the reeds to the barn.

Devlin had been up to the beach at first light to make certain that the tide had covered all traces of the previous night's activities. He had gone up again with Steiner after breakfast to show him as much of the general pick-up area of the estuary and the Point as could be seen in the fog.

They were on their way back, only thirty yards from the cottage when Preston emerged from the marsh with the girl on his shoulder.

"What is it?" Steiner demanded.

"It's Molly Prior, the girl I told you about."

He started to run, entering the yard as Preston reached the entrance. "Put her down, damn you!" Devlin shouted.

Preston turned. "I don't take orders from you."

But Steiner, hard on Devlin's heel into the yard, took a hand. "Lieutenant Preston," he called in a voice like iron. "You will release the lady now."

Preston hesitated, then set Molly down reluctantly. She promptly slapped his face. "And you keep your hands to yourself, you bugger," she stormed at him.

There was immediate laughter from inside the barn and she turned to see through the open door, a line of grinning faces, the truck beyond, the jeep with the Browning machine gun mounted.

Devlin arrived and shoved Preston out of the way. "Are you all right, Molly?"

"Liam," she said in bewilderment. "What is it? What's going on?"

But it was Steiner who handled it, smooth as silk. "Lieutenant Preston," he said coldly. "You will apologize to this young lady at once." Preston hesitated and Steiner really laid it on. "At once, Lieutenant!"

Preston got his feet together. "Humble apologies, ma'am. My mistake." he said with some irony, turned and went inside the barn.

Steiner saluted gravely. "I can't tell you how sorry I am about this whole unfortunate incident."

"This is Colonel Carter, Molly," Devlin explained.

"Of the Polish Independent Parachute Squadron," Steiner said. "We're here in this area for tactical field training and I'm afraid Lieutenant Preston gets rather carried away when it comes to a question of security."

She was more bewildered than ever now. "But, Liam," she began.

Devlin took her by the arm. "Come on now, let's catch that horse and get you back into the saddle." He pushed her towards the edge of the marsh where her mount nibbled peacefully at the tussocks of grass. "Now look what you've done," he scolded her. "Didn't I tell you to wait for me to call this afternoon? When will you learn to stop sticking your nose into things that don't concern you?"

"But I don't understand," she said. "Paratroopers—here, and that truck and the jeep you painted?"

He gripped her arm fiercely. "Security, Molly, for God's sake. Didn't you get the drift of what the Colonel was saying? Sure and why do you think that lieutenant reacted like he did? They've a very special reason for being here. You'll find out when they've gone, but for the moment it's top secret and you mustn't mention seeing them here to a living soul. As you love me, promise me that.''

She stared up at him and there was a kind of understanding in her eyes. ''I see the way of it now,'' she said. ''All these things you've been doing, the trips at night and so on. I thought it was something to do with the black market and you let me think it. But I was wrong. You're still in the army, that's it, isn't it?''

''Yes,'' he said with some truth. ''I'm afraid I am.''

Her eyes were shining. ''Oh, Liam, can you ever forgive me thinking you some cheap spiv peddling silk stockings and whisky round the pubs?''

Devlin took a very deep breath, but managed a smile. ''I'll think about it. Now go home like a good girl and wait until I call, no matter how long.''

''I will, Liam. I will.''

She kissed him, one hand behind his neck and swung up into the saddle. Devlin said, ''Mind now, not a word.''

''You can rely on me.'' She kicked her heels into the horse's belly and moved away through the reeds.

Devlin went back across the yard walking very fast. Ritter had joined Steiner from the cottage and the Colonel said, ''Is it all right?''

Devlin brushed past him and plunged into the barn. The men were talking together in small groups and Preston was in the act of lighting a cigarette, the match flaring in his cupped hands. He looked up with a slight, mocking smile. ''And we all know what you've been getting up to during the past few weeks. Was it nice, Devlin?''

Devlin got in one beautiful right hand that landed high on Preston's cheekbone and sent the Englishman sprawling over someone's out-stretched foot. Then Steiner had him by the arm.

''I'll kill the bastard!'' Devlin said.

Steiner got in front of him, both hands on the Irishman's shoulders, and Devlin was astonished at the strength. ''Go up to the cottage,'' he said calmly. ''I'll handle it.''

Devlin glared at him, that bone-white killing face on him again, and then the eyes dulled a little. He turned and went out, breaking into a run across the yard. Preston got to his feet, a hand to his face. There was total silence.

Steiner said, ''There is a man who will kill you if he can, Preston. Be warned. Step out of line once more and if he doesn't, I'll shoot you myself.'' He nodded to Ritter, ''Take command!''

When he went into the cottage, Devlin was at the Bushmills. The Irishman turned with a shaky grin. ''God, but I would have killed him. I must be going to pieces.''

''What about the girl?''

"No worries there. She's convinced I'm still in the army and up to my neck in official secrets." The self-disgust was plain on his face. "Her lovely boy, that's what she called me, I'm that all right." He started to pour another whiskey, hesitated then corked the bottle firmly. "All right," he said to Steiner. "What now?"

"We'll move up to the village around noon and go through the motions. My own feeling is that you should keep completely out of the way for the time being. We can meet up again this evening, after dark, when we're closer to making the assault."

"All right," Devlin said. "Joanna Grey is certain to contact you at the village somehow during the afternoon. Tell her I'll be at her place by six-thirty. The E-boat should be available any time between nine and ten. I'll bring the S-phone with me so that you can contact Koenig direct from the scene of operations and fix a pick-up time to fit the circumstances."

"Fine," Steiner said and appeared to hesitate. "There's one thing."

"What's that?"

"My orders regarding Churchill. They're quite explicit. They'd like to have him alive, but if that isn't possible . . . "

"You've got to put a bullet in him. So what's the problem?"

"I wasn't sure whether there might be one for you?"

"Not in the slightest," Devlin said. "This time everyone's a soldier, and takes a soldier's chances. That includes old Churchill."

In London, Rogan was clearing his desk, thoughts of lunch in his mind, when the door opened with no preliminary knock and Grant entered. His face was tense with excitement. "Just in over the teleprinter, sir." He slapped the message down in front of Rogan. "We've got him."

"Norfolk Constabulary, Norwich," Rogan said.

"That's where his registration particulars ended up, but he's some distance from there, right up on the North Norfolk coast near Studley Constable and Blakeney. Very isolated sort of place."

"Do you know the area?" Rogan asked as he read the message.

"Two holidays in Sheringham when I was a nipper, sir."

"So, he's calling himself Devlin and he's working as a marsh warden for Sir Henry Willoughby, the local squire. He's certainly due for a shock. How far is this place?"

"I'd say about a couple of hundred miles." Grant shook his head. "What in the hell could he be up to?"

"We'll find that out soon enough." Rogan looked up from the report.

"What's the next move, sir? Shall I get the Norfolk Constabulary to pick him up?"

"Are you mad?" Rogan said in amazement. "You know what these country police are like? Turnip heads. No, we'll handle this one ourselves, Fergus. You and me. It's a while since I've had a weekend in the country. It'll make a nice change."

"You've got an appointment at the Attorney General's office after lunch," Grant reminded him. "Evidence for the Halloran case."

"I'll be out of there by three o'clock. Three-thirty at the latest. You get a car from the pool and be ready and waiting and we can get straight off."

"Should I clear it with the Assistant Commissioner, sir?"

Rogan flared in irritation. "For Christ's sake, Fergus, what's wrong with you? He's in Portsmouth, isn't he? Now get moving."

Unable to explain his strange reluctance to himself, Grant made an effort. "Very well, sir."

He had a hand on the door when Rogan added, "And Fergus."

"Yes, sir?"

"Call in at the armoury and draw a couple of Browning Hi-Powers. This character shoots first and asks what you wanted afterwards."

Grant swallowed hard. "I'll see to that, sir," he said, his voice shaking slightly and went out.

Rogan pushed back his chair and went to the window. He flexed the fingers of both hands, full of tension. "Right, you bastard," he said softly. "Let's see if you're as good as they say you are."

It was just before noon when Philip Vereker opened the door at the end of the presbytery hall under the back stairs and went down to the cellar. His foot was giving him hell and he had hardly slept at all during the night. That was his own fault. The doctor had offered a plentiful supply of morphine tablets, but Vereker had a morbid fear of becoming addicted.

So he suffered. At least Pamela was coming for the weekend. She'd telephoned early that morning, not only to confirm it, but to tell him that Harry Kane had offered to pick her up from Pangbourne. At least it saved Vereker a gallon of petrol, and that was something. And he liked Kane. Had done instinctively, which was rare for him. It was nice to see Pamela taking an interest in someone at last.

A large torch hung from a nail at the bottom of the cellar steps. Vereker took it down, then opened an ancient, black, oak cupboard opposite, stepped inside and closed the door. He switched on the torch, felt for a hidden catch and the back of the cupboard swung open to reveal a long, dark tunnel with Norfolk flint walls that glistened with moisture.

It was one of the finest remaining examples of such a structure in the country, a priest's tunnel linking the presbytery with the church, a relic of the days of Roman Catholic persecution under Elizabeth Tudor. The secret of it was handed on from one incumbent to the next. From Vereker's point of view it was simply a very great convenience.

At the end of the tunnel, he mounted a flight of stone steps and paused in surprise, listening carefully. Yes, there could be no mistake. Someone was playing the organ, and very well indeed. He went up the rest of the stairs, opened the door at the top (which was in fact a section of the oak-panelled wall in the sacristy), closed it behind him, opened the other door and moved into the church.

When Vereker went up the aisle he saw to his astonishment that a paratrooper sergeant in camouflaged jump jacket was sitting at the organ, his red beret on the seat beside him. He was playing a Bach choral prelude, one highly appropriate to the season, for it was usually sung to the old Advent hymn *Gottes Sohn ist kommen.*

Hans Altmann was thoroughly enjoying himself. A superb instrument, a lovely church. Then he glanced up and in the organist's mirror saw Vereker at the bottom of the chapel steps. He stopped playing abruptly and turned.

"I'm sorry, Father, but I just couldn't help myself." He spread his hands. "One doesn't often get the chance in my—my present occupation." His English was excellent but with a definite accent.

Vereker said, "Who are you?"

"Sergeant Emil Janowski, Father."

"Polish?"

"That's right." Altmann nodded. "Came in here looking for you with my C.O. You were not here, of course, so he told me to wait on while he tried the presbytery."

Vereker said, "You play very well indeed. Bach needs to be played well, a fact I constantly remember with bitterness each time I take that seat."

"Ah, you play yourself?" Altmann said.

"Yes," Vereker said. "I'm very fond of the piece you were playing."

Altmann said, "A favourite of mine." He started to play, singing at the same time, *"Gott, durch deine Güte, wolst uns arme Leute . . ."*

"But that's a Trinity Sunday hymn," Vereker said.

"Not in Thuringia, Father." At that moment the great oak door creaked open and Steiner entered.

He moved down the aisle, a leather swagger stick in one hand, his beret in the other. His boots rang on the flagstones and as he came towards them, the shafts of light, slanting down through the gloom from the clerestory windows above, touched with fire his pale, fair hair.

"Father Vereker?"

"That's right."

"Howard Carter, in command Independent Polish Parachute Squadron of the Special Air Service Regiment.'' He turned to Altmann. ''You been behaving yoursel, Janowski?''

''As the Colonel knows, the organ is my principal weakness.''

Steiner grinned. ''Go on, cut along and wait outside with the others.'' Altmann departed and Steiner looked up into the nave. ''This is really quite beautiful.''

Vereker looked him over curiously, noting the crown and pip of a lieutenant-colonel on the epaulettes of the jump jacket. ''Yes, we're rather proud of it. SAS. Aren't you and your chaps rather a long way from your usual haunts? I thought the Greek Islands and Yugoslavia were your stamping ground?''

''Yes, well so did I until a month or so ago and then the powers-that-be in their wisdom decided to bring us home for special training, although perhaps home isn't exactly the right word to use, my lads all being Polish.''

''Like Janowski?''

''Not at all. He speaks really very good English. Most of the others manage *Hello* or *Will you come out with me tonight* and that's it. They don't seem to think they need any more.'' Steiner smiled. ''Paratroopers can be a pretty arrogant lot, Father. Always the trouble with elite units.''

''I know,'' Vereker said. ''I was one myself. Padre to the First Parachute Brigade.''

''Were you, by God?'' Steiner said. ''You served in Tunisia then?''

''Yes, at Oudna, which was where I got this.'' Vereker tapped his stick against his aluminum foot. ''And now I'm here.''

Steiner reached for his hand and shook it. ''It's a pleasure to meet you. Never expected anything like this.''

Vereker managed one of his rare smiles. ''What can I do for you?''

''Put us up for the night, if you will. You've a barn in the field next door that's had similar use before, I believe.''

''You're on exercise?''

Steiner smiled lightly. ''Yes, you could call it that. I've only got a handful of men with me here. The rest are scattered all over North Norfolk. At a given time tomorrow everyone's supposed to race like hell for a certain map reference, just to see how fast we can come together.''

''So you'll only be here this afternoon and tonight?''

''That's it. We'll try not to be a nuisance, of course. I'll probably give the lads a few tactical exercises round the village and so on, just to keep them occupied. You don't think anyone will mind?''

It worked, exactly as Devlin had predicted. Philip Vereker smiled. ''Studley Constable has been used for military manoeuvres of one kind or another many times before, Colonel. We'll all be only too happy to help in any way we can.''

❧

When Altmann came out of the church he went down the road to where the Bedford stood beside the five-barred gate at the entrance to the track which gave access to the barn in Old Woman's Meadow. The jeep waited beside the lychgate, Klugl at the wheel, Werner Briegel behind the Browning M2.

Werner had his Zeiss fieldglasses trained on the rookery in the beech trees. "Very interesting," he said to Klugl. "I think I'll take a closer look. Are you coming?"

He'd spoken in German as there was no one around and Klugl answered in the same language. "Do you think we should?"

"What harm?" Werner said.

He got out, went in through the lychgate and Klugl followed him reluctantly. Laker Armsby was digging a grave up at the west end of the church. They threaded their way between the tombstones and Laker, seeing them coming, stopped work and took a half-smoked cigarette from behind his ear.

"Hello, there," Werner said.

Laker squinted up at them. "Foreigners, eh? Thought you was British boys in them uniforms."

"Poles," Werner told him, "so you'll have to excuse my friend. He doesn't speak English." Laker fiddled ostentatiously with the dog-end and the young German took the hint and produced a packet of Players. "Have one of these."

"Don't mind if I do." Laker's eyes sparkled.

"Take another."

Laker needed no second bidding. He put one cigarette behind his ear and lit the other. "What's your name, then?"

"Werner." There was a nasty pause as he realized his mistake and added, "Kunicki."

"Oh, aye," Laker said. "Always thought Werner was a German name. I took a prisoner once in France in nineteen-fifteen. He was called Werner. Werner Schmidt."

"My mother was German," Werner explained.

"Not your fault, that," Laker replied. "We can't choose who brings us into this world."

"The rookery," Werner said. "Can I ask you how long it has been here?"

Laker looked at him in puzzlement, then stared up at the trees. "Since I were a lad, that is a fact. Are you interested in birds or something?"

"Certainly," Werner told him. "The most fascinating of living creatures. Unlike man, they seldom fight with each other, they know no boundaries, the whole world is their home."

Laker looked at him as if he was mad and laughed. "Go on. Who'd want to get worked up over a few tatty old rooks?"

"But are they, my friend?" Werner said. "Rooks are an abundant and widespread resident of Norfolk, true, but many arrive during the late autumn and winter from as far afield as Russia."

"Get away," Laker told him.

"No, it's true. Many rooks in this area before the war were found to have been ringed around Leningrad, for example."

"You mean some of these old ragbags sitting above my head could have come from there?" Laker demanded.

"Most certainly."

"Well, I never did."

"So, my friend, in future you must treat them with the respect they deserve as much-travelled ladies and gentlemen, these rooks from Leningrad," Werner told him.

There was a shout, "Kunicki—Moczar," and they turned and found Steiner and the priest standing outside the church porch. "We're leaving," Steiner called and Werner and Klugl doubled back through the cemetery to the jeep.

Steiner and Father Vereker started to walk down the path together. A horn sounded and another jeep came up the hill from the direction of the village and pulled in at the opposite side of the road. Pamela Vereker got out in WAAF uniform. Werner and Klugl eyed her appreciatively and then they stiffened as Harry Kane came round from the other side. He was wearing a side cap, combat jacket and jump boots.

As Steiner and Vereker reached the gate, Pamela joined them and reached up to kiss her brother on the cheek. "Sorry I'm late, but Harry wanted to see a little more of Norfolk than he's been able to manage so far."

"And you took him the long way round?" Vereker said affectionately.

"At least I got her here, Father," Kane said.

"I'd like you both to meet Colonel Carter of the Polish Independent Parachute Squadron," Vereker said. "He and his men are on exercise in this district. They'll be using the barn in Old Woman's Meadow. My sister Pamela, Colonel, and Major Harry Kane."

"Twenty-first Specialist Raiding Force." Kane shook hands. "We're up the road at Meltham House. I noticed your boys on the way up, Colonel. You guys have sure got it made with those crazy red berets. I bet the girls go wild."

"It's been known to happen," Steiner said.

"Polish, eh? We've one or two Polish guys in our outfit. Krukowski for instance. He's from Chicago. Born and raised there and yet his Polish is as good as his English. Funny people. Maybe we can have some sort of get together."

"I'm afraid not," Steiner said. "I'm under special orders. Exercises this afternoon and this evening, move on to join up with other units under my command tomorrow. You know how it is.''

"I certainly do,'' Kane said. "Being in exactly the same position myself.'' He glanced at his watch. "In fact, if I'm not back at Meltham House within twenty minutes the Colonel will have me shot.''

Steiner said pleasantly, "Nice to have met you anyway. Miss Vereker. Father.'' He got into the jeep and nodded to Klugl, who released the brake and moved away.

"Try to remember it's the left-hand side of the road you drive on here, Klugl,'' Steiner said calmly.

The walls of the barn were three feet thick in places. Tradition had it that during the Middle Ages it had been part of a manor house. It was certainly adequate enough for their purposes. There was the usual smell of old hay and mice. A broken wagon stood in one corner and a large loft with round, glassless windows let in light.

They left the Bedford outside with a man on guard, but took the jeep inside. Steiner stood in it and addressed them all.

"So far, so good. From now on we've got to make the whole thing look as natural as possible. First, get the field stoves out and cook a meal.'' He looked at his watch. "That should take us somewhere up towards three o'clock. Afterwards, some field training. That's what we're here for and that's what people will expect to see. Basic infantry tactics across the fields, by the stream, amongst the houses. Another thing—be careful at all times about speaking German. Keep your voices low. Use hand signals wherever possible during the field exercises. The only spoken orders to be in English, naturally. The field telephones are for emergency only and I mean emergency. Oberleutnant Neumann will give section leaders the necessary call signs.''

Brandt said, "What's the drill if people try to speak to us?''

"Pretend you don't understand, even if you've got good English. I'd rather you did that than get involved.''

Steiner turned to Ritter. "I'll leave the field training organization to you. Make sure each group has at least one person who speaks good English. You should be able to manage that.'' He turned back to the men. "Remember it will be dark by six to six-thirty. We have only to look busy until then.''

He jumped down and went outside. He walked down the track and leaned on the gate. Joanna Grey was toiling up the hill on her bicycle, a large bunch of flowers in the basket which hung from her handlebars, Patch running along behind.

"Good afternoon, ma'am.'' Steiner saluted.

She dismounted and came forward, pushing the machine. "How's everything progressing?''

"Fine."

She held out her hand as if introducing herself formally. At a distance it must have looked very natural. "And Philip Vereker?"

"Couldn't be more helpful. Devlin was right. I think he's decided we're here to keep an eye on the great man."

"What happens now?"

"You'll see us playing soldiers round the village. Devlin said he'll be up to see you at six-thirty."

"Good." She held out her hand again. "I'll see you later."

Steiner saluted, turned and went back to the barn and Joanna remounted and continued up the hill to the church. Vereker was standing in the porch waiting for her and she leaned her cycle against the wall and went towards him with the flowers.

"They're nice," he said. "Where on earth did you get them?"

"Oh, a friend in Holt. Iris. Raised under glass, of course. Dreadfully unpatriotic. I suppose she should have put the time in on potatoes or cabbages."

"Nonsense, man does not live by bread alone." Strange how pompous he could sound. "Did you see Sir Henry before he left?"

"Yes, he called in on his way. Full uniform, too. He really looked very splendid."

"And he'll be back with the great man himself before nightfall," Vereker said. "A brief line in some biography of him one of these days. *Spent the night at Studley Grange.* The villagers don't know a thing about it and yet a little piece of history is being made here."

"Yes, I suppose you're right if you look at it that way." She smiled beautifully. "Now, shall we arrange these flowers on the altar?"

He opened the door for her and they went inside.

16

IN LONDON, AS BIG BEN struck three, Rogan came out of the Royal Courts of Justice and hurried along the pavement to where Fergus Grant waited at the wheel of a Humber saloon. In spite of the heavy rain the Chief Inspector was in high good humour as he opened the door.

"Everything go off all right, sir?" Fergus asked him.

Rogan smiled smugly. "If friend Halloran draws less than ten years I'm a monkey's uncle. Did you get them?"

"Glove compartment, sir."

Rogan opened it and found a Browning Hi-Power automatic. He checked the clip, rammed it back into the butt. Strange how good it felt in his hand. How right. He hefted it for a moment, then slipped it into his inside breast pocket.

"All right, Fergus, now for friend Devlin."

At the same moment Molly was approaching St. Mary and All the Saints on horseback by way of the field paths. Because of the light drizzle she wore her old trenchcoat and a scarf around her hair and carried a rucksack on her back covered with a piece of sacking.

She tethered her horse under the trees at the back of the presbytery and went through the back gate into the graveyard. As she went round to the porch, a shouted command drifted up the hill and she paused and looked down towards the village. The paratroops were advancing in skirmishing order towards the old mill by the stream, their red berets very clear against the green of the meadow. She could see Father Vereker, George Wilde's boy, Graham, and little Susan Turner standing on the footbridge above the weir watching. There was another shouted command and the paratroopers flung themselves down.

When she went inside the church she found Pamela Vereker on her knees at the altar polishing the brass rails. "Hello, Molly," she said. "Come to help?"

"Well, it is my mum's weekend for the altar," Molly said, slipping her arms out of the rucksack, "only she has a bad cold and thought she'd spend the day in bed."

Another shouted order echoed faintly from the village. "Are they still at it out there?" Pamela asked. "Wouldn't you think there was enough war to get on with and still they have to play their stupid games. Is my brother down there?"

"He was when I came in."

A shadow crossed Pamela Vereker's face. "I wonder about that sometimes. Wonder if he somehow resents being out of it all now." She shook her head. "Men are strange creatures."

There were no obvious signs of life in the village except for smoke here and there from a chimney. For most people it was a working day. Ritter

Neumann had split the assault group into three sections of five, all linked to each other by field telephone. He and Harvey Preston were deployed amongst the cottages with one section each. Preston was rather enjoying himself. He crouched by the wall at the side of the Studley Arms, revolver in hand and gave his section a hand signal to move forward. George Wilde leaned on the wall watching and his wife, Betty, appeared in the doorway, wiping her hands on her apron.

"Wish you was back in action then?"

Wilde shrugged. "Maybe."

"Men," she said in disgust. "I'll never understand you."

The group in the meadow consisted of Brandt, Sergeant Sturm, Corporal Becker and Privates Jansen and Hagl. They were deployed opposite the old mill. It had not been in use for thirty years or more and there were holes in the roof where slates were missing.

Usually the massive waterwheel stood still, but during the night the rushing water of the stream, flooded by many days of heavy rain, had exerted such pressure that the locking bar, already eaten away by rust, had snapped. Now the wheel was moving round again with an unearthly creaking and groaning, churning the water into foam.

Steiner, who had been sitting in the jeep examining the wheel with interest, turned to watch Brandt correcting young Jansen's technique in the prone firing position. Higher up the stream above the weir, Father Vereker and the two children also watched. George Wilde's son, Graham, was eleven and considerably excited by the activities of the paratroops.

"What are they doing now, Father?" he asked Vereker.

"Well, Graham, it's a question of having the elbows in the right position," Vereker said. "Otherwise he won't be able to get a steady aim. See, now he's demonstrating the leopard crawl."

Susan Turner was bored with the entire proceedings and, hardly surprising in a five-year-old girl, was more interested in the wooden doll her grandfather had made for her the evening before. She was a pretty, fair-haired child, an evacuee from Birmingham. Her grandparents, Ted and Agnes Turner, ran the village Post Office and general store and small telephone exchange. She'd been with them for a year now.

She crossed to the other side of the footbridge, ducked under the rail and squatted at the edge. The floodwaters rushed past not more than two feet below, brown and foam-flecked. She dangled the doll by one of its movable arms just above the surface, chuckling as water splashed across its feet. She leaned still lower, clutching the rail above her head, dipping the doll's legs right into the water now. The rail snapped and with a scream she went head first into the water.

Vereker and the boy turned in time to see her disappear. Before the priest could move she was swept under the bridge. Graham, more by instinct than courage, jumped in after her. At that point the water was usually no more than a couple of feet deep. During the summer he had fished there for tadpoles. But now all was changed. He grabbed the tail of Susan's coat and hung on tight. His feet were scrabbling for the bottom, but there was no bottom, and he cried out in fear as the current swept them towards the weir above the bridge.

Vereker, frozen with horror, had not uttered a sound, but Graham's cry alerted Steiner and his men instantly. As they all turned to see what the trouble was the two children went over the edge of the weir and slid down the concrete apron into the mill pool.

Sergeant Sturm was on his feet and running for the edge of the pool, tearing off his equipment. He had no time to unzip his jump jacket. The children, with Graham still hanging on to Susan, were being carried relentlessly by the current into the path of the water wheel.

Sturm plunged in without hesitation and struck out towards them. He grabbed Graham by the arm. Brandt plunged waist deep into the water behind him. As Sturm pulled Graham in, the boy's head dipped momentarily under the water. He panicked, kicking and struggling, releasing his grip on the girl. Sturm swung him round in an arc so that Brandt could catch hold of him, then plunged on after Susan.

She had been saved by the enormous force of the current, which had kept her on the surface. She was screaming as Sturm's hand fastened on her coat. He pulled her into his arms and tried to stand. But he went right under and when he surfaced again, he felt himself being drawn inexorably into the path of the water wheel.

He was aware of a cry above the roaring, turned and saw that his comrades on the bank had the boy, that Brandt was back in the water again and pushing towards him. Karl Sturm summoned up everything he had, every ounce of strength and hurled the child bodily through the air to the safety of Brandt's arms. A moment later and the current took him in a giant hand and swept him in. The wheel thundered down and he went under.

George Wilde had gone into the pub to get a bucket of water to swill the front step. He came out again in time to see the children go over the weir. He dropped the bucket, called out to his wife and ran across the road to the bridge. Harvey Preston and his section, who had also witnessed the mishap, followed.

Except for being soaked to the skin, Graham Wilde seemed none the worse for his experience. The same held true for Susan, though she was crying hysterically. Brandt thrust the child into George Wilde's arms and ran along the bank to join Steiner and the others, searching beyond the water wheel for Sturm. Suddenly he floated to the surface in calm water. Brandt plunged in and reached for him.

Except for a slight bruise on the forehead there wasn't a mark on him, but his eyes were closed, his lips slightly parted. Brandt waded out of the water holding him in his arms, and everyone seemed to arrive at once. Vereker, then Harvey Preston and his men and finally, Mrs. Wilde, who took Susan from her husband.

"Is he all right?" Vereker demanded.

Brandt ripped the front of the jump jacket open and got a hand inside the blouse, feeling for the heart. He touched the small bruise on the forehead and the skin was immediately suffused with blood, the flesh and bone soft as jelly. In spite of this Brandt remained sufficiently in control to remember where he was.

He looked up at Steiner and said in fair English, "I'm sorry, sir, but his skull is crushed."

For a moment, the only sound was the mill wheel's eerie creaking. It was Graham Wilde who broke the silence, saying loudly, "Look at his uniform, Dad. Is that what the Poles wear?"

Brandt, in his haste, had committed an irretrievable blunder. Beneath the open jump jacket was revealed Karl Sturm's *Fliegerbluse*, with the Luftwaffe eagle badge on the right breast. The blouse had been pierced to take the red, white and black ribbon of the Iron Cross 2nd Class. On the left breast was the Iron Cross 1st Class, the ribbon for the Winter War, the paratrooper's qualification badge, the silver wound badge. Under the jump jacket, full uniform, as Himmler himself had insisted.

"Oh, my God," Vereker whispered.

The Germans closed round in a circle. Steiner said in German to Brandt, "Put Sturm in the jeep." He snapped his fingers at Jansen who was carrying one of the field telephones. "Let me have that. Eagle One to Eagle Two," he called. "Come in please."

Ritter Neumann and his section were at work out of sight on the far side of the cottages. He replied almost instantly. "Eagle Two, I hear you."

"The Eagle is blown," Steiner said. "Meet me at the bridge now."

He passed the phone back to Jansen. Betty Wilde said in bewilderment, "What is it, George? I don't understand?"

"They're Germans," Wilde said. "I've seen uniforms like that before, when I was in Norway."

"Yes," Steiner said. "Some of us were there."

"But what do you want?" Wilde said. "It doesn't make sense. There's nothing for you here."

"You poor stupid bastard," Preston jeered. "Don't you know who's staying at Studley Grange tonight? Mr. Lord-God-Almighty-Winston-bloody-Churchill himself.''

Wilde stared at him in astonishment and then he actually laughed. ''You must be bloody cracked. I never heard such nonsense in all my life. Isn't that so, Father?''

''I'm afraid he's right.'' Vereker got the words out slowly and with enormous difficulty. ''Very well, Colonel. Do you mind telling me what happens now? To start with, these children must be chilled to the bone.''

Steiner turned to Betty Wilde. ''Mrs. Wilde, you may take your son and the little girl home now. When the boy has changed, take Susan in to her grandparents. They run the Post Office and general store, is this not so?''

She glanced wildly at her husband, still bemused by the whole thing. ''Yes, that's right.''

Steiner said to Preston, ''There are only six telephones in the general village area. All calls come through a switchboard at the Post Office and are connected by either Mr. Turner or his wife.''

''Shall we rip it out?'' Preston suggested.

''No, that might attract unnecessary attention. Someone might send a repair man. When the child is suitably changed, send her and her grandmother up to the church. Keep Turner himself on the switchboard. If there are any incoming calls, he's to say that whoever they want isn't in or something like that. It should do for the moment. Now get to it and try not to be melodramatic about it.''

Preston turned to Betty Wilde. Susan had stopped crying and he held out his hands and said with a dazzling smile, ''Come on, beautiful, I'll give you a piggyback.'' The child responded instinctively with a de-lighted smile. ''This way, Mrs. Wilde, if you'd be so kind.''

Betty Wilde, after a desperate glance at her husband, went after him, holding her son by the hand. The rest of Preston's section, Dinter, Meyer, Riedel and Berg followed a yard or two behind.

Wilde said hoarsely, ''If anything happens to my wife . . . ''

Steiner ignored him. He said to Brandt, ''Take Father Vereker and Mr. Wilde up to the church and hold them there. Becker and Jansen can go with you. Hagl, you come with me.''

Ritter Neumann and his section had arrived at the bridge. Preston had just reached them and was obviously telling the Oberleutnant what had happened.

Philip Vereker said, ''Colonel, I've a good mind to call your bluff. If I walk off now you can't afford to shoot me out of hand. You'll arouse the whole village.''

Steiner turned to face him. ''There are sixteen houses or cottages in Studley Constable, Father. Forty-seven people in all and most of the men aren't even here. They are working on any one of a dozen farms within a radius of five miles from here. Apart from that . . . " He turned to Brandt. "Give him a demonstration."

Brandt took Corporal Becker's Mk IIS Sten from him, turned and fired from the hip, spraying the surface of the mill pool. Fountains of water spurted high in the air, but the only sound was the metallic chattering as the bolt reciprocated.

"Remarkable, you must admit," Steiner said. "And a British invention. But there's an even surer way, Father. Brandt puts a knife under your ribs in just the right way to kill you instantly and without a sound. He knows how, believe me. He's done it many times. Then we walk you to the jeep between us, set you up in the passenger seat and drive off with you. Is that ruthless enough for you?"

"It will do to be going on with, I fancy," Vereker said.

"Excellent." Steiner nodded to Brandt. "Get going, I'll be up in a few minutes."

He turned and hurried towards the bridge, walking very fast so that Hagl had to trot to keep up with him. Ritter came to meet them. "Not so good. What happens now?"

"We take over the village. You know what Preston's orders are?"

"Yes, he told me. What do you want us to do?"

"Send a man up for the truck, then start at one end of the village and work your way through house by house. I don't care how you do it, but I want everybody out and up in that church within fifteen to twenty minutes."

"And afterwards?"

"A road block at each end of the village. We'll make it look nice and official, but anyone who comes in stays."

"Shall I tell Mrs. Grey?"

"No, leave her for the time being. She needs to stay free to use the radio. I don't want anyone to know she's on our side until it's absolutely necessary. I'll see her myself later." He grinned. "A tight one, Ritter."

"We've known them before, Herr Oberst."

"Good." Steiner saluted formally. "Get to it then." He turned and started up the hill to the church.

In the living room of the Post Office and General Stores Agnes Turner wept as she changed her granddaughter's clothes. Betty Wilde sat beside her, hanging on tightly to Graham. Privates Dinter and Berg stood on either side of the door waiting for them.

"I'm that feared, Betty," Mrs. Turner said. "I've read such terrible things about them. Murdering and killing. What are they going to do to us?"

In the tiny room behind the Post Office counter that held the switch-board, Ted Turner said in some agitation, "What's wrong with my mis-sus?"

"Nothing." Harvey Preston said. "And there isn't likely to be as long as you do exactly as you're told. If you try shouting a message into the phone when someone rings through. Any tricks at all." He took the revolver from his webbing holster. "I won't shoot you—I'll shoot your wife and that's a promise."

"You swine," the old man said. "Call yourself an Englishman?"

"A better one than you, old man." Harvey struck him across the face with the back of his hand. "Remember that."

He sat back in the corner, lit a cigarette and picked up a magazine.

Molly and Pamela Vereker had finished at the altar and used up what remained of the reeds and marsh grasses Molly had brought to create a display by the font. Pamela said, "I know what it needs. Ivy leaves. I'll get some."

She opened the door, went out through the porch and plucked two or three handfuls of leaves from the vine which climbed the tower at that spot. As she was about to go into the church again, there was a squeal of brakes and she turned to see the jeep draw up. She watched them get out, her brother and Wilde, and at first concluded that the paratroopers had merely given them a lift. Then it occurred to her that the huge sergeant-major was covering her brother and Wilde with the rifle he held braced against his hip. She would have laughed at the absurdity of it had it not been for Becker and Jansen who followed the others through the lychgate carrying Sturm's body.

Pamela retreated through the partly opened door, bumping into Molly. "What is it?" Molly demanded.

Pamela hushed her. "I don't know, but something's wrong—very wrong."

Half-way along the path, George Wilde attempted to make a break for it, but Brandt, who had been expecting such a move, deftly tripped him. He leaned over Wilde, prodding him under the chin with the muzzle of the M1. "All right, *Tommi*, you're a brave man. I salute you. But try anything like that again and I blow your head off."

Wilde, helped by Vereker, scrambled to his feet and the party moved on towards the porch. Inside, Molly looked at Pamela in consternation. "What's it mean?"

Pamela hushed her again. "Quick, in here," she said and opened the sacristy door. They slipped inside, she closed it and slid home the bolt. A moment later they heard voices clearly.

Vereker said, "All right, now what?"

"You wait for the Colonel," Brandt told him. "On the other hand, I don't see why you shouldn't fill in the time by doing what's right for poor old Sturm. As it happens, he was a Lutheran, but I don't suppose it matters. Catholic or Protestant, German or English. It's all the same to the worms."

"Bring him to the Lady Chapel," Vereker said.

The footsteps died away and Molly and Pamela crouched against the door, looked at each other. "Did he say German?" Molly said. "That's crazy."

Footsteps echoed hollowly on the flags of the porch and the outer door creaked open. Pamela put a finger to her lips and they waited.

Steiner paused by the font and looked around him, tapping his swagger stick against his thigh. He hadn't bothered to remove his beret this time. "Father Vereker," he called. "Down here, please." He moved to the sacristy door and tried the handle. On the other side the two girls eased back in alarm. As Vereker limped down the aisle, Steiner said, "This seems to be locked. Why? What's in there?"

The door had never been locked to Vereker's knowledge because the key had been lost for years. That could only mean that someone had bolted it from the inside. Then he remembered that he had left Pamela working on the altar when he had gone to watch the paratroopers. The conclusion was obvious.

He said clearly, "It is the sacristy, Herr Oberst. Church registers, my vestments, things like that. I'm afraid the key is over at the presbytery. Sorry for such inefficiency. I suppose you order things better in Germany?"

"You mean we Germans have a passion for order, Father?" Steiner said. "True. I, on the other hand, had an American mother although I went to school in London. In fact, lived there for many years. Now, what does that mixture signify?"

"That it is highly unlikely that your name is Carter."

"Steiner, actually. Kurt Steiner."

"What of, the SS?"

"It seems to have a rather morbid fascination for you people. Do you imagine all German soldiers serve in Himmler's private army?"

"No, perhaps it is just that they behave as if they do."

"Like Sergeant Sturm, I suppose." Vereker could find nothing to say to that. Steiner added, "For the record, we are not SS. We are Fallschirmjäger. The best in the business, with all due respect to your Red Devils."

Vereker said, "So, you intend to assassinate Mr. Churchill at Studley Grange tonight?"

"Only if we have to," Steiner said. "I'd much prefer to keep him in one piece."

"And now the planning's gone slightly awry? The best laid schemes and so on . . . ''

"Because one of my men sacrificed himself to save the lives of two children of this village, or perhaps you don't wish to know about that? Why should that be, I wonder? Because it destroys this pitiful delusion that all German soldiers are savages whose sole occupation is murder and rape? Or is it something deeper? Do you hate all of us because it was a German bullet that crippled you?"

"Go to hell!" Vereker said.

"The Pope, Father, would not be at all pleased with such a sentiment. To answer your original question. Yes, the plan has gone a little awry, but improvisation is the essence of our kind of soldiering. As a paratrooper yourself, you must know that."

"For heaven's sake, man, you've had it," Vereker said. "No element of surprise."

"There still will be," Steiner told him calmly. "If we hold the entire village incommunicado, so to speak, for the required period."

Vereker was, for the moment, rendered speechless by the audacity of this suggestion. "But that is impossible."

"Not at all. My men are at this very moment rounding up everyone at present in Studley Constable. They'll be up here within the next fifteen or twenty minutes. We control the telephone system, the roads, so that anyone entering will be immediately apprehended."

"But you'll never get away with it."

"Sir Henry Willoughby left the Grange at eleven this morning to travel to King's Lynn where he was to have lunch with the Prime Minister. They were due to leave in two cars with an escort of four Royal Military Police motorcyclists at three-thirty." Steiner looked at his watch. "Which, give or take a minute or two, is right now. The Prime Minister has expressed a particular desire to pass through Walsingham, by the way, but forgive me, I must be boring you with all this."

"You seem to be very well informed?"

"Oh, I am. So, you see, all we have to do is to hang on until this evening as arranged, and the prize will still be ours. Your people, by the way, have nothing to fear as long as they do as they are told."

"You won't get away with it," Vereker said stubbornly.

"Oh, I don't know. It's been done before. Otto Skorzeny got Mussolini out of an apparently impossible situation. Quite a feat of arms as Mr. Churchill himself conceded in a speech at Westminster."

"Or what's left of it after your damned bombs," Vereker said.

"Berlin isn't looking too good either these days," Steiner pointed out, "and if your friend Wilde is interested, tell him that the five-year-old daughter and the wife of the man who died to save his son, were killed by RAF bombs four months ago.'' Steiner held out his hand. ''I'll have the keys of your car. It might come in useful.''

''I haven't got them with me,'' Vereker began.

''Don't waste my time, Father. I'll have my lads strip you if I have to.''

Vereker reluctantly produced his keys and Steiner slipped them into his pocket. ''Right, I have things to do.'' He raised his voice. ''Brandt, hold the fort here. I'll send Preston to relieve you, then report to me in the village.''

He went out, and Private Jansen came and stood against the door with his M1. Vereker walked up the aisle slowly, past Brandt and Wilde who was sitting in one of the pews, shoulders hunched. Sturm was lying in front of the altar in the Lady Chapel. The priest stood looking down at him for a moment, then knelt, folded his hands and in a firm, confident voice, began to recite the prayers for the dying.

''So now we know,'' Pamela Vereker said as the door banged behind Steiner.

''What are we going to do?'' Molly said dully.

''Get out of here, that's the first thing.''

''But how?''

Pamela moved to the other side of the room, found the concealed catch and a section of the panelling swung back to reveal the entrance to the priest's tunnel. She picked up the torch her brother had left on the table. Molly was gaping in amazement. ''Come on,'' Pamela said impatiently. ''We must get moving.''

Once inside, she closed the door and led the way quickly along the tunnel. They exited through the oak cupboard in the presbytery cellar and went up the stairs to the hall. Pamela put the torch on the table beside the telephone and when she turned, saw that Molly was crying bitterly.

''Molly, what is it?'' she said, taking the girl's hands in hers.

''Liam Devlin,'' Molly said. ''He's one of them. Must be. They were at his place, you see. I saw them.''

''When was this?''

''Earlier today. He let me think he was still in the army. Some kind of secret job.'' Molly pulled her hands free and clenched them into fists. ''He used me. All the time he was using me. God help me, but I hope they hang him.''

''Molly, I'm sorry,'' Pamela said. ''Truly I am. If what you say is true then he'll be taken care of. But we've got to get out of here.'' She looked down at the telephone. "No use trying to get through to the police or somebody on that, not if they control the village exchange. And I haven't got the keys of my brother's car."

"Mrs. Grey has a car," Molly said.

"Of course." Pamela's eyes glinted with excitement. "Now if I could only get down to her house."

"Then what would you do? There isn't a phone for miles."

"I'd go straight to Meltham House," Pamela said. "There are American Rangers there. A crack outfit. They'd show Steiner and his bunch a thing or two. How did you get here?"

"Horseback. He's tied up in the woods behind the presbytery."

"All right, leave him. We'll take the field path back of Hawks Wood and see if we can get to Mrs. Grey's without being seen."

Molly didn't argue. Pamela tugged her sleeve, they darted across the road into the shelter of Hawks Wood.

The path was centuries old and cut deep into the earth, giving complete concealment. Pamela led the way, running very fast, not stopping until they came out into the trees on the opposite side of the stream from Joanna Grey's cottage. There was a narrow footbridge and the road seemed deserted.

Pamela said, "All right, let's go. Straight across."

Molly grabbed her arm. "Not me, I've changed my mind."

"But why?"

"You try this way. I'll go back for my horse and try another. Two bites of the apple."

Pamela nodded. "That makes sense. All right then, Molly." She kissed her on the cheek impulsively. "Only watch it! They mean business, this lot."

Molly gave her a little push and Pamela darted across the road and disappeared round the corner of the garden wall. Molly turned and started to run back up the track through Hawks Wood. *Oh, Devlin, you bastard, she thought, I hope they crucify you.*

By the time she reached the top, the tears, slow, sad and incredibly painful were oozing from her eyes. She didn't even bother to see if the road was clear, but simply dashed across and followed the line of the garden wall round to the wood at the back. Her horse was waiting patiently where she'd tethered him, cropping the grass. She untied him quickly, scrambled into the saddle and galloped away.

When Pamela went into the yard at the rear of the cottage the Morris saloon was standing outside the garage. When she opened the car door the keys were in the ignition. She started to get behind the wheel and an indignant voice called, "Pamela, what on earth are you doing?"

Joanna Grey was standing at the back door. Pamela ran towards her. "I'm sorry, Mrs. Grey, but something absolutely terrible has happened. This Colonel Carter and his men who are exercising in the village. They're not SAS at all. His name is Steiner and they're German paratroopers here to kidnap the Prime Minister."

Joanna Grey drew her into the kitchen and closed the door. Patch fawned about her knees. "Now calm down," Joanna said. "This really is a most incredible story. The Prime Minister isn't even here."

She turned to her coat hanging behind the door and fumbled in the pocket. "Yes, but he will be this evening," Pamela said. "Sir Henry is bringing him back from King's Lynn."

Joanna turned, a Walther automatic in her hand. "You have been busy, haven't you?" She reached behind and got the cellar door open. "Down you go."

Pamela was thunderstruck. "Mrs. Grey, I don't understand."

"And I don't have time to explain. Let's just say we're on different sides in this affair and leave it at that. Now get down those stairs. I won't hesitate to shoot if I have to."

Pamela went down, Patch scampering in front of her, and Joanna Grey followed. She switched on a light at the bottom and opened a door opposite. Inside was a dark windowless storeroom filled with junk. "In you go."

Patch, circling his mistress, managed to get between her feet. She stumbled against the wall. Pamela gave her a violent push through the doorway. As she fell back, Joanna Grey fired at point-blank range. Pamela was aware of the explosion that half-blinded her, the sudden touch of a white-hot poker against the side of her head, but she managed to slam the door in Joanna Grey's face and ram home the bolt.

The shock of a gunshot wound is so great that it numbs the entire central nervous system for a while. There was a desperate air of unreality to everything as Pamela stumbled upstairs to the kitchen. She leaned on a chest of drawers to stop herself from falling, and looked in the mirror above it. A narrow strip of flesh had been gouged out of the left side of her forehead and bone showed through. There was surprisingly little blood and, when she touched it gently with a fingertip, no pain. *That would come later*.

"I must get to Harry," she said aloud. "I must get to Harry."

Then, like something in a dream, she found herself behind the wheel of the Morris driving out of the yard, as if in slow motion.

As he walked down the road Steiner saw her go and made the natural assumption that Joanna Grey was at the wheel. He swore softly, turned and went back to the bridge where he had left the jeep with Werner

Briegel manning the machine-gun and Klugl at the wheel. As he arrived, the Bedford came back down the hill from the church, Ritter Neumann standing on the running-board and hanging on to the door. He jumped down.

"Twenty-seven people up at the church now, Herr Oberst, including the two children. Five men, nineteen women."

"Ten children at harvest camp," Steiner said. "Devlin estimated a present population of forty-seven. If we allow for Turner in the exchange, and Mrs. Grey, that leaves eight people who are certain to turn up at some time. Mostly men, I would imagine. Did you find Vereker's sister?"

"No sign of her at the presbytery and when I asked him where she was, he told me to go to hell. Some of the women were more forthcoming. It seems she goes riding on Saturday afternoons when she's at home."

"You'll have to keep an eye out for her as well, then," Steiner said. "Have you seen Mrs. Grey?"

"I'm afraid not." Steiner explained what had happened. "I made a bad mistake there. I should have allowed you to go and see her when you suggested it. I can only hope she returns soon."

"Perhaps she's gone to see Devlin?"

"That's a point. Worth checking on. We'll have to let him know what's happening anyway." He slapped the swagger stick against his palm.

There was a crash of breaking glass and a chair came through the window of Turner's shop. Steiner and Ritter Neumann drew their Brownings and ran across the road.

For most of the day Arthur Seymour had been felling the trees of a small plantation on a farm to the east of Studley Constable. He sold the logs to his own benefit in and around the village. Mrs. Turner had given him an order only that morning. When he was finished at the plantation, he filled a couple of sacks, put them on his handcart and went down to the village across the field tracks, coming into the yard at the back of the Turners' shop from the rear.

He kicked open the kitchen door without knocking and walked in, a sack of logs on his shoulder—and came face-to-face with Dinter and Berg who were sitting on the edge of the table drinking coffee. If anything, they were more surprised than Seymour.

"Here, what's going on?" he demanded.

Dinter, who had his Sten slung across his chest, moved it on target and Berg picked up his M1. At the same moment Harvey Preston appeared in the door. He stood there, hands on hips, looking Seymour over.

"My God," he said. "The original walking ape."

Something stirred in Seymour's dark mad eyes. "You watch your mouth, soldier boy."

"It can talk as well," Preston said. "Wonders will never cease. All right, put him with the others."

He turned to go back into the exchange and Seymour tossed the sack of logs at Dinter and Berg and jumped on him, one arm clamping around Preston's throat, a knee in his back. He snarled like an animal. Berg got to his feet and slammed the butt of his M1 into Seymour's kidneys. The big man cried out in pain, released his hold on Preston and launched himself at Berg with such force that they went through the open door behind into the shop, a display cabinet collapsing beneath them.

Berg lost his rifle but managed to get to his feet and back away. Seymour advanced on him, sweeping the counter clear of the pyramids of tinned goods and packages, growling deep in his throat. Berg picked up the chair Mrs. Turner habitually sat on behind the counter. Seymour knocked it aside in mid-flight and it went out through the shop window. Berg drew his bayonet and Seymour crouched.

Preston took a hand then, moving in from behind, Berg's M1 in his hands. He raised it high and drove the butt into the back of Seymour's skull. Seymour cried out and swung round. "You bloody great ape," Preston cried. "We'll have to teach you your manners, won't we?"

He smashed the butt into Seymour's stomach and as the big man started to fold, hit him again in the side of the neck. Seymour fell back, grabbed for support and only succeeded in bringing a shelf and its contents down on top of him as he slid to the floor.

Steiner and Ritter Neumann burst in through the shop doorway at that moment, guns ready. The place was a shambles, cans of various descriptions, sugar, flour, scattered everywhere. Harvey Preston handed Berg his rifle. Dinter appeared in the doorway, swaying slightly, a streak of blood on his forehead.

"Find some rope," Preston said, "and tie him up or next time you might not be so lucky."

Old Mr. Turner was hovering in the door of the exchange. There were tears in his eyes as he surveyed the shambles. "And who's going to pay for that lot."

"Try sending the bill to Winston Churchill, you never know your luck," Preston said brutally. "I'll have a word with him for you if you like. Press your case."

The old man slumped down in a chair in the small exchange, the picture of misery and Steiner said, "All right, Preston, I won't need you down here any more. Get on up to the church and take that specimen behind the counter with you. Relieve Brandt. Tell him to report to Oberleutnant Neumann."

"What about the switchboard?"

"I'll send Altmann in. He speaks good English. Dinter and Berg can keep an eye on things until then."

Seymour was stirring, pushing himself up on his knees and making the discovery that his hands were lashed behind his back. "Comfortable are we?" Preston kicked him in the backside and hauled him to his feet. "Come on, ape, start putting one foot in front of the other."

At the church, the villagers sat in pews as instructed and awaited their fate, talking to each other in low voices. Most of the women were plainly terrified. Vereker moved amongst them, bringing what comfort he could. Corporal Becker stood guard near the chapel steps, a Sten gun in his hands, Private Jansen at the door. Neither spoke English.

After Brandt had departed, Harvey Preston found a length of rope in the bell room at the bottom of the tower, lashed Seymour's ankles together, then turned him over and dragged him on his face to the Lady Chapel where he dumped him beside Sturm. There was blood on Seymour's cheek where the skin had rubbed away and there were gasps of horror, particularly from the women.

Preston ignored them and kicked Seymour in the ribs. "I'll cool you down before I'm through, I promise you."

Vereker limped forward and grabbed him by the shoulder, turning him round. "Leave that man alone."

"Man?" Preston laughed in his face. "That isn't a man, it's a thing." Vereker reached down to touch Seymour and Preston knocked him away and drew his revolver. "You just won't do as you're told, will you?"

One of the women choked back a scream. There was a terrible silence as Preston thumbed back the hammer. A moment in time. Vereker crossed himself and Preston laughed again and lowered the revolver. "A lot of good that will do you."

"What kind of man are you?" Vereker demanded. "What moves you to act like this?"

"What kind of man?" Preston said. "That's simple. A special breed. The finest fighting men that ever walked the face of the earth. The Waffen SS in which I have the honour to hold the rank of Untersturmführer."

He walked up the aisle, turned at the chancel steps, unzipped his jump jacket and took it off, revealing the tunic underneath, the collar patches with the three leopards, the eagle on his left arm, the Union Jack shield beneath and the black and silver cuff-title.

It was Laker Armsby sitting beside George Wilde who said, "Here, he's got a Union Jack on his sleeve."

Vereker moved forward, a frown on his face and Preston held out his arm. "Yes, he's right. Now read the cuff-title."

"Britisches Freikorps," Vereker said aloud and glanced up sharply. "British Free Corps?"

"Yes, you damned fool. Don't you realize? Don't any of you realize? I'm English, like you, only I'm on the right side. The only side."

Susan Turner started to cry. George Wilde came out of his pew, walked up the aisle slowly and deliberately and stood looking up at Preston. "The Jerries must be damned hard up, because the only place they could have found you was under a stone."

Preston shot him at point-blank range. As Wilde fell back across the steps below the roodscreen, blood on his face, there was pandemonium. Women were screaming hysterically. Preston fired another shot into the air. "Stay where you are!"

There was the kind of frozen silence produced by complete panic. Vereker got down on one knee awkwardly and examined Wilde as he groaned and moved his head from side to side. Betty Wilde ran up the aisle, followed by her son, and dropped to her knees beside her husband.

"He'll be all right, Betty, his luck is good," Vereker told her. "See, the bullet has just gouged his cheek."

At that moment the door at the other end of the church crashed open and Ritter Neumann rushed in, his Browning in his hand. He ran up the centre aisle and paused. "What's going on here?"

"Ask your colleague from the SS," Vereker suggested.

Ritter glanced at Preston, then dropped to one knee and examined Wilde. "Don't you touch him, you—you bloody German swine," Betty said.

Ritter took a field dressing from one of his breast pockets and gave it to her. "Bandage him with that. He'll be fine." He stood up and said to Vereker, "We are Fallschirmjäger, Father, and proud of our name. This gentleman, on the other hand . . . " He turned in an almost casual gesture and struck Preston a heavy blow across the face with the Browning. The Englishman cried out and crumpled to the floor.

The door opened again and Joanna Grey ran in. "Herr Oberleutnant," she called in German. "Where's Colonel Steiner? I must speak with him."

Her face was streaked with dirt and her hands were filthy. Neumann went down the aisle to meet her. "He isn't here. He's gone to see Devlin. Why?"

Vereker said, "Joanna?" There was a question in his voice, but more than that, a kind of dread as if he was afraid to know for certain what he feared.

She ignored him and said to Ritter, "I don't know what's been going on here, but about forty-five minutes ago, Pamela Vereker turned up at the cottage and she knew everything. Wanted my car to go to Meltham House to get the Rangers."

"What happened?"

"I tried to stop her and ended up locked in the cellar. I only managed to break out five minutes ago. What are we going to do?"

Vereker put a hand on her arm and pulled her round to face him. "Are you saying you're one of them?"

"Yes," she said impatiently. "Now will you leave me alone? I've work to do." She turned back to Ritter.

"But why?" Vereker said. "I don't understand. You're British . . ."

She rounded on him then. "British?" she shouted. "Boer, damn you! Boer! How could I be British? You insult me with that name."

There was a genuine horror on virtually every face there. The agony in Philip Vereker's eyes was plain for all to see. "Oh, my God," he whispered.

Ritter took her by the arm. "Back to your house fast. Contact Landsvoort on the radio. Let Radl know the position. Keep the channel open."

She nodded and hurried out. Ritter stood there, for the first time in his military career totally at a loss. *What in the hell are we going to do?* he thought. But there was no answer. Couldn't be without Steiner.

He said to Corporal Becker, "You and Jansen stay here," and he hurried outside.

There was silence in the church. Vereker walked up the aisle, feeling inexpressibly weary. He mounted the chancel steps and turned to face them. "At times like these there is little left, but prayer," he said. "And it frequently helps. If you would all please kneel."

He crossed himself, folded his hands and began to pray aloud in a firm and remarkably steady voice.

17

ᨠᨠ

HARRY KANE WAS SUPERVISING A course in field tactics in the wood behind Meltham Farm when he received Shafto's urgent summons to report to the house and bring the training squad with him. Kane left the Sergeant, a Texan named Hustler from Fort Worth, to follow with the men and went on ahead.

As he arrived, Sections which had been training on various parts of the estate were all coming in together. He could hear the revving of engines from the motor pool in the stabling block at the rear. Several jeeps turned into the gravel drive in front of the house and drew up line abreast.

The crews started to check their machine-guns and equipment. An officer jumped out of the lead vehicle, a captain named Mallory.

"What gives, for Christ's sake?" Kane demanded.

"I haven't the slightest idea," Mallory said. "I get the orders, I follow them through. He wants you in a hurry, I know that." He grinned. "Maybe it's the Second Front."

Kane went up the steps on the run. The outer office was a scene of frenzied activity. Master Sergeant Garvey paced up and down outside Shafto's door, nervously smoking a cigarette. His face brightened as Kane entered.

"What in the hell is going on?" Kane demanded. "Have we orders to move out or something?"

"Don't ask me, Major. All I know is that lady friend of yours arrived in one hell of a state about fifteen minutes ago and nothing's been the same since."

Kane opened the door and went in. Shafto, in breeches and riding boots, was standing at the desk with his back to him. When he swung round Kane saw that he was loading the pearl-handled Colt. The change in him was extraordinary. He seemed to crackle with electricity, his eyes sparkled as if he was in a high fever, his face was pale with excitement.

"Fast action, Major, that's what I like."

He reached for belt and holster and Kane said, "What is it, sir? Where's Miss Vereker?"

"In my bedroom. Under sedation and badly shocked."

"But what happened?"

"She took a bullet in the side of the head." Shafto buckled his belt quickly, easing the holster low down on his right hip. "And the finger on the trigger was that friend of her brother's, Mrs. Grey. Ask her yourself. I can only spare you three minutes."

Kane opened the bedroom door. Shafto followed him in. The curtains had been partially drawn and Pamela was in bed, the blankets up to her chin. She looked pale and very ill and there was a bandage around her head, a little blood soaking through.

As Kane approached, her eyes opened and she stared up at him fixedly. "Harry?"

"It's all right." He sat on the edge of the bed.

"No, listen to me." She pushed herself up and tugged at his sleeve and when she spoke, her voice was remote, far-away. "Mr. Churchill leaves King's Lynn at three-thirty for Studley Grange with Sir Henry

Willoughby. They'll be coming by way of Walsingham. You must stop him.''

"Why must I?" Kane said gently.

"Because Colonel Steiner and his men will get him if you don't. They're waiting at the village now. They're holding everyone prisoner at the church.''

"Steiner?"

"The man you know as Colonel Carter. And his men, Harry. They aren't Poles. They're German paratroops.''

"But Pamela," Kane said. "I met Carter. He's as English as you are.''

"No, his mother was American and he went to school in London. Don't you see? That explains it.'' There was a kind of exasperation in her voice now. "I overheard them talking in the church, Steiner and my brother. I was hiding with Molly Prior. After we got away, we split up and I went to Joanna's, only she's one of them. She shot me and I—I locked her in the cellar.'' She frowned, trying hard. "Then I took her car and came here.''

There was a sudden release that was almost physical in its intensity. It was as if she had been holding herself together by willpower alone and now it didn't matter. She lay back against the pillow and closed her eyes. Kane said, "But how did you get away from the church, Pamela?''

She opened her eyes and stared at him, dazed, uncomprehending. "The church? Oh, the—the usual way.'' Her voice was the merest whisper. "And then I went to Joanna's and she shot me.'' She closed her eyes again. "I'm so tired, Harry.''

Kane stood up and Shafto led the way back into the other room. He adjusted his sidecap in the mirror. "Well, what do you think? That Grey woman for a start. She must be the great original bitch of all time.''

"Who have we notified? The War Office and GOC East Anglia for a start and . . . ''

Shafto cut right in. "Have you any idea how long I'd be on the phone while those chair-bound bastards at Staff try to decide whether I've got it right or not?'' He slammed a fist down on the table. "No, by Godfrey. I'm going to nail these Krauts myself, here and now and I've got the men to do it. Action this day!'' He laughed harshly. "Churchill's personal motto. I'd say that's rather appropriate.''

Kane saw it all then. To Shafto it must have seemed like a dispensation from the gods themselves. Not only the salvaging of his career, but the making of it. The man who had saved Churchill. A feat of arms that would take its place in the history books. Let the Pentagon try to keep that general's star from him after this and there would be rioting in the streets.

"Look, sir," Kane said stubbornly. "If what Pamela said is true, this might be just about the hottest potato of all time. If I might respectfully suggest, the British War Office won't take too kindly . . . ''

Shafto's fist slammed down on the desk again. "What's got into you? Maybe those Gestapo boys did a better job than they knew?" He turned to the window restlessly, then swung back as quickly, smiling like a contrite schoolboy. "Sorry, Harry, that was uncalled for. You're right, of course."

"Okay, sir, what do we do?"

Shafto looked at his watch. "Four-fifteen. That means the Prime Minister must be getting close. We know the road he's coming on. I think it might be a good idea if you took a jeep and headed him off. From what the girl said you should be able to catch him this side of Walsingham."

"I agree, sir. At least we can offer him one hundred and ten per cent security here."

"Exactly." Shafto sat down behind the desk and picked up the telephone. "Now get moving and take Garvey with you."

"Colonel."

As Kane opened the door he heard Shafto say, "Get me the General Officer commanding East Anglia District and I want him personally— no one else."

When the door closed Shafto removed his left index finger from the telephone rest. The operator's voice crackled in his ear. "Did you want something, Colonel?"

"Yes, get Captain Mallory in here on the double."

Mallory was with him in about forty-five seconds. "You wanted me, Colonel?"

"That's right, plus a detail of forty men ready to move out five minutes from now. Eight jeeps should do it. Cram 'em in."

"Very well, sir." Mallory hesitated, breaking one of his strictest rules. "Is it permitted to ask what the Colonel intends?"

"Well, let's put it this way," Shafto said, "You'll be a major by nightfall—or dead."

Mallory went out, his heart pumping and Shafto went to the cupboard in the corner and took out a bottle of Bourbon and half-filled a glass. Rain beat against the window and he stood there, drinking his Bourbon, taking his time. Within twenty-four hours he would probably have the best-known name in America. His day had come, he knew that with absolute conviction.

When he went outside three minutes later the jeeps were drawn up in line, the crews on board. Mallory was standing in front talking to the unit's youngest officer, a second lieutenant named Chalmers. They sprang to attention and Shafto paused at the top of the steps.

"You're wondering what all this is about. I'll tell you. There's a village named Studley Constable about eight miles from here. You'll find it marked plainly enough on your maps. Most of you will have heard that Winston Churchill was visiting an RAF station near King's Lynn today. What you don't know is that he's spending tonight at Studley Grange. This is where it gets interesting. There are sixteen men from the Polish Independent Parachute Squadron of the SAS training in Studley Constable. You can't miss them in those pretty red berets and camouflage uniforms." Somebody laughed and Shafto paused until there was complete silence again. "I've got news for you. Those guys are Krauts. German paratroops here to get Churchill and we're going to nail them to the wall." The silence was total and he nodded slowly. "One thing I can promise you boys. Handle this right and by tomorrow, your names will ring from California to Maine. Now get ready to move out."

There was an instant burst of activity as engines roared into life. Shafto went down the steps and said to Mallory, "Make sure they go over those maps on the way. No time for any fancy briefing when we get there." Mallory hurried away and Shafto turned to Chalmers. "Hold the fort, boy, until Major Kane gets back." He slapped him on the shoulder. "Don't look too disappointed. He'll have Mr. Churchill with him. You see he gets the hospitality of the house." He jumped into the lead jeep and nodded to the driver. "Okay, son, let's move out."

They roared down the drive, the sentries on the massive front gate got it open fast and the convoy turned into the road. A couple of hundred yards farther on, Shafto waved them to a halt and told his driver to pull in close to the nearest telephone pole. He turned to Sergeant Hustler in the rear seat. "Give me that Thompson gun."

Hustler handed it over. Shafto cocked it, took aim and sprayed the top of the pole, reducing the crossbars to matchwood. The telephone lines parted, springing wildly through the air.

Shafto handed the Thompson back to Hustler. "I guess that takes care of any unauthorized phone calls for a while." He slapped the side of the vehicle. "Okay, let's go, let's go, let's go!"

Garvey handled the jeep like a man possessed, roaring along the narrow country lanes at the kind of speed which assumed that nothing was coming the other way. Even then, they almost missed their target, for as they drove along the final stretch to join the Walsingham road, the small convoy flashed past at the end of the lane. Two military policemen on motorcycles leading the way, two Humber saloon cars, two more policemen bringing up the rear.

"It's him!" Kane cried.

The jeep skidded into the main road, Garvey rammed his foot down hard. It was only a matter of moments before they caught up with the convoy. As they roared up behind, the two military policemen at the rear glanced over their shoulders. One waved them back.

Kane said, "Sergeant, pull out and overtake and if you can't stop them any other way you have my permission to ram that front car."

Dexter Garvey grinned. "Major, I'm going to tell you something. If this goes wrong we'll end up in that Leavenworth stockade so fast you won't know which day it is."

He swerved out to the right past the motorcyclists and pulled alongside the rear Humber. Kane couldn't see much of the man in the back seat because the side curtains were pulled forward just sufficiently to ensure privacy. The driver, who was in dark blue chauffeur's uniform, glanced sideways in alarm and the man in the gray suit in the front passenger seat drew a revolver.

"Try the next one," Kane ordered and Garvey pulled alongside the front saloon, blaring his horn.

There were four men in there, two in army uniform, both colonels, one with the red tabs of a staff officer. The other turned in alarm and Kane found himself looking at Sir Henry Willoughby. There was instant recognition and Kane shouted to Garvey, "Okay, pull out in front. I think they'll stop now."

Garvey accelerated, overtaking the military policemen at the head of the small convoy. A horn blared three times behind them, obviously some pre-arranged signal. When Kane looked over his shoulder they were pulling-in at the side of the road. Garvey braked and Kane jumped out and ran back.

The military policemen had a Sten gun apiece trained on him before he was anywhere close and the man in the gray suit, presumably the Prime Minister's personal detective, was already out of the rear car, revolver in hand.

The staff colonel with the red tabs got out of the first car, Sir Henry in Home Guard uniform at his heels. "Major Kane," Sir Henry said in bewilderment. "What on earth are you doing here?"

The staff colonel said curtly, "My name is Corcoran, Chief Intelligence Officer to the GOC, East Anglia District. Will you kindly explain yourself, sir?"

"The Prime Minister mustn't go to Studley Grange," Kane told him. "The village has been taken over by German paratroops and . . ."

"Good God," Sir Henry interrupted. "I've never heard such nonsense . . ."

Corcoran waved him to silence. "Can you substantiate this statement, Major?"

"Dear God Almighty," Kane shouted. "They're here to get Churchill like Skorzeny dropped in for Mussolini, don't you understand? What in the hell does it take to convince you guys? Won't anybody listen?"

A voice from behind, a voice that was entirely familiar to him said, "I will, young man. Tell your story to me."

Harry Kane turned slowly, leaned down at the rear window and was finally face-to-face with the great man himself.

When Steiner tried the door of the cottage at Hobs End it was locked. He went round to the barn, but there was no sign of the Irishman there either. Briegel shouted, "Herr Oberst, he's coming."

Devlin was riding the BSA across the network of narrow dyke paths. He turned into the yard, shoved the bike up on its stand and pushed up his goggles. "A bit public, Colonel."

Steiner took him by the arm and led him across to the wall where, in a few brief sentences, he filled him in on the situation. "Well," he said when he was finished. "What do you think?"

"Are you sure your mother wasn't Irish?"

"*Her* mother was."

Devlin nodded. "I might have known. Still, who knows? We might get away with it." He smiled. "I know one thing. My fingernails will be down to the quick by nine tonight."

Steiner jumped into the jeep and nodded to Klugl. "I'll keep in touch."

From the wood on the hill on the other side of the road Molly stood beside her horse and watched Devlin take out his key and unlock the front door. She had intended to confront him, filled with the desperate hope that even now she might be mistaken, but the sight of Steiner and his two men in the jeep was the ultimate truth of things.

A half mile outside Studley Constable Shafto waved the column to a halt and gave his orders. "No time for any nonsense now. We've got to hit them and hit them hard before they know what's happening. Captain Mallory, you take three jeeps and fifteen men, cross the fields to the east of the village using those farm tracks marked on the map. Circle round till you come out on the Studley Grange road north of the watermill. Sergeant Hustler, the moment we reach the edge of the village, you dismount and take a dozen men on foot and make your way up this sunken track through Hawks Wood to the church. The remaining men stay with me. We'll plug the road by the Grey woman's house."

"So we've got them completely bottled up, Colonel," Mallory said.

"Bottled up hell. When everyone's in position and I give the signal on field telephone, we go in and finish this thing fast."

There was silence. It was Sergeant Hustler who finally broke it. "Begging the Colonel's pardon, but wouldn't some sort of reconnaissance be in order?" He tried to smile. "I mean, from what we hear, these Kraut paratroopers ain't exactly Chesterfields."

"Hustler," Shafto said coldly. "You ever query an order of mine again and I'll have you down to private so fast you won't know your own first name." A muscle twitched in his right cheek as his glance took in the assembled NCOs one by one. "Hasn't anybody got any guts here?"

"Of course, sir," Mallory answered. "We're right behind you, Colonel."

"Well you'd better be," Shafto said. "Because I'm going in there now on my own with a white flag."

"You mean you're going to invite them to surrender, sir?"

"Surrender, my backside, Captain. While I do some talking, the rest of you will be getting into position and you've got exactly ten minutes from the moment I enter that dump so let's get to it."

Devlin was hungry. He heated a little soup, fried an egg and made a sandwich of it with two thick slices of bread, Molly's own baking. He was eating it in the chair by the fire when a cold draught on his left cheek told him that the door had opened. When he looked up, she was standing there.

"So there you are?" he said cheerfully. "I was having a bit before coming looking for you." He held up the sandwich. "Did you know these things were invented by a belted earl, no less?"

"You bastard!" she said. "You dirty swine! You used me."

She flung herself on him, hands clawing at his face. He grabbed her wrists and fought to control her. "What is it?" he demanded. Yet in his heart, he knew.

"I know all about it. Carter isn't his name—it's Steiner and he and his men are bloody Germans come for Mr. Churchill. And what's your name? Not Devlin, I'll be bound."

He pushed her away from him, went and got the Bushmills and a glass. "No, Molly, it isn't." He shook his head. "You weren't meant to be any part of this, my love. You just happened."

"You bloody traitor!"

He said in a kind of exasperation, "Molly, I'm Irish, that means I'm as different from you as a German is from a Frenchman. I'm a foreigner.

We're not the same just because we both speak English with different accents. When will you learn, you people?''

There was uncertainty in her eyes now, but still she persisted. "Traitor!''

His face was bleak then, the eyes very blue, the chin tilted. "No traitor, Molly. I am a soldier of the Irish Republican Army. I serve a cause as dear to me as yours.''

She needed to hurt him then, to wound and had the weapon to do it. "Well, much good may it do you and your friend Steiner. He's finished or soon will be. You next.''

"What are you talking about?''

"Pamela Vereker was with me up at the church when he and his men took her brother and George Wilde up there. We overheard enough to send her flying off to Meltham to get those Yankee Rangers.''

He grabbed her by the arms. "How long ago?''

"You go to hell!''

"Tell me, damn you!'' he shook her roughly.

"I'd say they must be there by now. If the wind was in the right direction you could probably hear the shooting, so there isn't a bloody thing you can do about it except run while you have the chance.''

He released her and said wryly, "Sure and it would be the sensible thing to do, but I was never one for that.''

He pulled on his cap and goggles, his trenchcoat, and belted it around his waist. He crossed to the fireplace and felt under a pile of old newspapers behind the log basket. There were two hand grenades there which Ritter Neumann had given him. He primed them and placed them carefully inside the front flap of his trenchcoat. He put the Mauser into his right pocket and lengthened the sling on his Sten, suspending it around his neck almost to waist level so that he could fire it one-handed if necessary.

Molly said, "What are you going to do?''

"Into the valley of death, Molly, my love, rode the six hundred and all that sort of good old British rubbish.'' He poured himself a glass of Bushmills and saw the look of amazement on her face. "Did you think I'd run for the hills and leave Steiner in the lurch?'' He shook his head. "God, girl, and I thought you knew something about me.''

"You can't go up there.'' There was panic in her voice now. "Liam, you won't stand a chance.'' She caught hold of him by the arm.

"Oh, but I must, my pet.'' He kissed her on the mouth and pushed her firmly to one side. He turned at the door. "For what it's worth, I wrote you a letter. Not much, I'm afraid, but if you're interested, it's on the mantelpiece.''

The door banged, she stood there rigid, frozen. Somewhere in another world the engine roared into life and moved away.

She found the letter and opened it feverishly. It said: *Molly, my own true love. As a great man once said, I have suffered a sea-change and nothing can ever be the same again. I came to Norfolk to do a job, not to fall in love for the first and last time in my life with an ugly little peasant girl that should have known better. By now you'll know the worst of me, but try not to think it. To leave you is punishment enough. Let it end there. As they say in Ireland, we knew the two days. Liam.*

The words blurred, there were tears in her eyes. She stuffed the letter into her pocket and stumbled outside. Her horse was at the hitching ring. She untied him quickly, scrambled up on his back and urged him into a gallop, beating her clenched fist against his neck. At the end of the dyke she took him straight across the road, jumped the hedge and galloped for the village, taking the shortest route across the fields.

Otto Brandt sat on the parapet of the bridge and lit a cigarette as if he didn't have a care in the world. "So what do we do, run for it?"

"Where to?" Ritter looked at his watch. "Twenty to five. It should be dark by six-thirty at the latest. If we can hang on until then, we could fade away in twos and threes and make for Hobs End across country. Maybe some of us could catch that boat."

"The Colonel could have other ideas," Sergeant Altmann said.

Brandt nodded. "Exactly, only he isn't here, so for the moment it seems to me we'd better get ready to do a little fighting."

"Which raises an important point," Ritter said. "We fight only as German soldiers. That was made clear from the beginning. It seems to me that the time has come to drop the pretence."

He took off his red beret and jump jacket, revealing his *Fliegerbluse*. From his hip pocket he produced a Luftwaffe sidecap or *Schiff* and adjusted it to the correct angle.

"All right," he said to Brandt and Altmann. "The same for everybody, so you'd better get moving."

Joanna Grey had witnessed the entire scene from her bedroom window and the sight of Ritter's uniform brought a chill to her heart. She watched Altmann go in to the Post Office. A moment later Mr. Turner emerged. He crossed the bridge and started up the hill to the church.

Ritter was in an extraordinary dilemma. Ordinarily in such circumstances he would have ordered an immediate withdrawal, but as he had said to Brandt, where to? Including himself, he had twelve men to guard the prisoners and hold the village. An impossible situation. *But so was the Albert Canal and Eban Emael*, that's what Steiner would have said. It occurred to him and not for the first time, how much he had come to depend on Steiner over the years.

He tried to raise him again on the field telephone. "Come in Eagle One," he said in English. "This is Eagle Two."

There was no reply. He handed the phone back to Private Hagl who lay in the shelter of the bridge wall, the barrel of his Bren protruding through a drainage hole giving him a fair field of fire. A supply of magazines was neatly stacked beside him. He, too, had divested himself of the red beret and jump jacket and wore *Schiff* and *Fliegerbluse* while still retaining his camouflaged trousers.

"No luck, Herr Oberleutnant?" he said and then stiffened. "I think that's a jeep I hear now."

"Yes, but from the wrong direction entirely," Ritter told him grimly.

He vaulted over the wall beside Hagl, turned and saw a jeep come round the corner by Joanna Grey's cottage. A white handkerchief fluttered at the end of the radio aerial. There was one occupant only, the man at the wheel. Ritter stepped from behind the wall and waited, hands on hips.

Shafto hadn't bothered swopping to a tin hat and still wore his sidecap. He took a cigar from one of his shirt pockets, and put it between his teeth purely for effect. He took his time over lighting it, then got out of the jeep and came forward. He stopped a yard or two away from Ritter and stood, legs apart, looking him over.

Ritter noted the collar tabs and saluted formally. "Colonel."

Shafto returned the salute. His glance took in the two Iron Crosses, the Winter War ribbon, the wound badge in silver, the combat badge for distinguished service in ground battles, the paratroopers qualification badge, and knew that in this fresh-faced young man he was looking on a hardened veteran.

"So, no more pretence, Herr Oberleutnant? Where's Steiner? Tell him Colonel Robert E. Shafto, in command Twenty-first Specialist Raiding Force, would like to speak with him."

"I am in charge here, Herr Oberst. You must deal with me."

Shafto's eyes took in the barrel of the Bren poking through the drainage hole in the bridge parapet, swivelled to the Post Office, the first floor of the Studley Arms where two bedroom windows stood open. Ritter said politely, "Is there anything else, Colonel, or have you seen enough?"

"What happened to Steiner? Has he run out on you or something?" Ritter made no reply and Shafto went on, "Okay, son, I know how many men you have under your command and if I have to bring my boys in here you won't last ten minutes. Why not be practical and throw in the towel?"

"So sorry," Ritter said. "But the fact is I left in such a hurry that I forgot to put one in my overnight bag."

Shafto tapped ash from his cigar. "Ten minutes, that's all I'll give you, then we come in."

"And I'll give you two, Colonel," Ritter said. "To get to hell out of here before my men open fire."

There was the metallic click of weapons being cocked. Shafto looked up at the windows and said grimly, "Okay, sonny, you asked for it."

He dropped the cigar, stamped it very deliberately into the ground, walked back to the jeep and got behind the wheel. As he drove away he reached for the mike on the field radio. "This is Sugar One. Twenty seconds and counting. Nineteen, eighteen, seventeen . . . "

He was passing Joanna Grey's cottage at twelve, disappeared round the bend in the road on ten.

She watched him go from the bedroom window, turned and went into the study. She opened the secret door to the cubbyhole loft, closed it behind her and locked it. She went upstairs, sat down at the radio, took the Luger from the drawer and laid it down on the table where she could reach it quickly. Strange, but now that it had come to this she wasn't in the least afraid. She reached for a bottle of Scotch and as she poured a large one, firing started outside.

The lead jeep in Shafto's section roared round the corner into the straight. There were four men inside and the two in the rear were standing up working a Browning machine-gun. As they passed the garden of the cottage next to Joanna Grey's, Dinter and Berg stood up together, Dinter supporting the barrel of a Bren gun across his shoulder while Berg did the firing. He loosed one long continuous burst that knocked the two men at the Browning off their feet. The jeep bounced over the verge and rolled over, coming to rest upside down in the stream.

The next jeep in line swerved away wildly, the driver taking it round in a circle over the grass bank that almost had it into the stream with the other. Berg swung the barrel of the Bren, continuing to fire in short bursts, driving one of the jeep's machine gun crew over the side of the vehicle and smashing its windscreen before it scrambled round the corner to safety.

In the rubble of Stalingrad, Dinter and Berg had learned that the essence of success in such situations was to make your hit, then get out fast. They exited immediately through a wrought-iron gate in the wall and worked their way back to the Post Office, using the cover of the back garden hedges at the rear of the cottages.

Shafto, who had witnessed the entire debacle from a rise in the woods further down the road, ground his teeth with rage. It had suddenly become all too obvious that Ritter had let him see exactly what he had wanted him to see. "Why, that little bastard was setting me up," he said softly.

The jeep which had just been shot-up pulled in at the side of the road in front of number three. Its driver had a bad cut on the face. A sergeant named Thomas was putting a field dressing on it. Shafto shouted down, "For Christ's sake, Sergeant, what are you playing at? There's a machine-gun behind the wall of the garden of the second cottage along. Go forward with three men on foot now and take care of it."

Krukowski, who waited behind him with the field telephone, winced. *Five minutes ago we were thirteen. Now it's nine. What in the hell does he think he's playing at?*

There was heavy firing from the other side of the village. Shafto raised his field glasses, but could see little except for a piece of the road curving beyond the bridge and the roof of the mill standing up beyond the end houses. He snapped a finger and Krukowski passed him the phone. "Mallory, do you read me?"

Mallory answered instantly. "Affirmative, Colonel."

"What in the hell goes on up there? I expected you with bells on by now."

"They've got a strong point set up in the mill on the first floor. Commands one hell of a field of fire. They knocked out the lead jeep. It's blocking the road now. I've already lost four men."

"Then lose some more," Shafto yelled into the phone. "Get in there, Mallory. Burn them out. Whatever it takes."

The firing was very heavy now as Shafto tried the other section. "You there, Hustler?"

"Colonel, this is Hustler." His voice sounded rather faint.

"I expected to see you up on the hill at that church by now."

"It's been tough going, Colonel. We started across the fields like you said and got tangled up in a bog. Just approaching the south end of Hawks Wood now."

"Well, get the lead out, for Christ's sake!"

He handed the phone back to Krukowski. "Christ Jesus!" he said bitterly. "You can't rely on anybody: when it comes right down to it, anything I need doing right, I've got to see to myself."

He slid down the bank into the ditch as Sergeant Thomas and the three men he'd taken with him returned. "Nothing to report, Colonel."

"What do you mean, nothing to report?"

"No one there, sir, just these." Thomas held out a handful of .303 cartridge cases.

Shafto struck his hand violently, spilling them to the ground. "Okay, I want both jeeps out in front, two men to each Browning. I want that bridge plastered. I want you to lay down such a field of fire that even a blade of grass won't be able to stand up."

"But Colonel," Thomas began.

"And you take four men and work your way on foot back of the cottages. Hit that Post Office by the bridge from the rear. Krukowski stays with me." He slammed his hand hard down on the bonnet of the jeep. "Now move it!"

Otto Brandt had Corporal Walther, Meyer and Riedel with him in the mill. From a defence point of view it was perfect: the ancient stone walls were about three feet thick and downstairs the oak doors were bolted and barred. The windows of the first floor commanded an excellent field of fire and Brandt had a Bren gun set up there.

Down below a jeep burned steadily, blocking the road. One man was still inside, two more sprawled in the ditch. Brandt had disposed of the jeep personally, making no sign at first, letting Mallory and his men come roaring in, only lobbing down a couple of grenades from the loft door at the last moment. The effect had been catastrophic. From behind the hedges further up the road the Americans poured in a considerable amount of fire to little effect because of those massive stone walls.

"I don't know who's in charge down there, but he doesn't know his business," Walther observed as he reloaded his M1.

"Well, what would you have done?" Brandt asked him, squinting along the barrel of the Bren as he loosed off a quick burst.

"There's the stream, isn't there? No windows on that side. They should be moving in from the rear . . . "

Brandt held up his hand. "Everyone stop firing."

"Why?" Walther demanded.

"Because they have, or hadn't you noticed?"

There was a deathly silence and Brandt said softly, "I'm not sure I really believe this, but get ready."

A moment later, with a rousing battlecry, Mallory and eight or nine men emerged from shelter and ran for the next ditch, firing from the hip. In spite of the fact that they were getting covering fire from the Brownings of the two remaining jeeps on the other side of the hedge, it was an incredible act of folly.

"My God!" Brandt said. "Where do they think they are? The Somme?"

He put a long, almost leisurely burst into Mallory and killed him instantly. Three more went down as the Germans all fired at once. One of them picked himself up and staggered back to the safety of the first hedge as the survivors retreated.

In the quiet which followed, Brandt reached for a cigarette. "I make that seven. Eight if you count the one who dragged himself back."

"Crazy," Walther said. "Suicide. I mean, why are they in such a hurry? All they have to do is wait."

~

Kane and Colonel Corcoran sat in a jeep two hundred yards down the road from the main gate at Meltham House and looked up at the shattered telephone pole. "Good God!" Corcoran said. "It's really quite incredible. What on earth was he thinking of?"

Kane could have told him, but refrained. He said, "I don't know, Colonel. Maybe some notion he had about security. He sure was anxious to get to grips with those paratroopers."

A jeep turned out of the main gate and moved towards them. Garvey was at the wheel and when he braked, his face was serious. "We just got a message in the radio room."

"From Shafto?"

Garvey shook his head. "Krukowski, of all people. He asked for you, Major, personally. It's a mess down there. He says they walked right into it. Dead men all over the place."

"And Shafto?"

"Krukowski was pretty hysterical. Kept saying the Colonel was acting like a crazy man. Some of it didn't make much sense."

Dear God, Kane thought, *he's gone riding straight in, guidons fluttering in the breeze*. He said to Corcoran, "I think I should get down there, Colonel."

"So do I," Corcoran said. "Naturally, you'll leave adequate protection for the Prime Minister."

Kane turned to Garvey. "What have we got left in the motor pool?"

"A White Scout car and three jeeps."

"All right, we'll take them plus a detail of twenty men. Ready to move out in five minutes if you please, Sergeant."

Garvey swung the jeep in a tight circle and drove away fast. "That leaves twenty-five for you, sir," Kane told Corcoran. "Will that be all right?"

"Twenty-six with me," Corcoran said. "Perfectly adequate, especially as I shall naturally assume command. Time someone licked you colonials into shape."

"I know, sir," Harry Kane said as he switched on the engine. "Nothing but a mass of complexes since Bunker Hill." He let in the clutch and drove away.

18

THE VILLAGE WAS STILL A good mile and a half away when Steiner first became aware of the persistent electronic buzz from the Grauman field phone. Someone was on channel, but too far away to be heard. "Put your foot down," he told Klugl. "Something's wrong."

When they were a mile away, the rattle of small arms fire in the distance confirmed his worst fears. He cocked his Sten gun and looked up at Werner. "Be ready to use that thing. You might have to."

Klugl had the jeep pushed right up to its limit, his foot flat on the boards. "Come on, damn you! Come on!" Steiner cried.

The Grauman had ceased the buzz and as they drew closer to the village, he tried to make voice contact. "This is Eagle One. Come in, Eagle Two."

There was no reply. He tried again, but with no better success. Klugl said, "Maybe they're too busy, Herr Oberst."

A moment later they topped the rise at Garrowby Heath three hundred yards west of the church at the top of the hill and the whole panorama was spread below. Steiner raised his field glasses, took in the mill and Mallory's detail in the field beyond. He moved on, noting the Rangers behind the hedges at the rear of the Post Office and the Studley Arms and Ritter, young Hagl beside him, pinned down behind the bridge by the heavy concentration of machine-gun fire from the Brownings of Shafto's two remaining jeeps. One of them had been sited alongside Joanna Grey's garden wall from where the gun crew were able to fire over the top and yet remain in good cover. The other employed the same technique against the wall of the next cottage.

Steiner tried the Grauman again. "This is Eagle One. Do you read me?"

On the first floor of the mill, his voice crackled in the ear of Riedel, who had just switched on during a lull in the fighting. "It's the Colonel," he cried to Brandt and said into the phone, "This is Eagle Three, in the water mill. Where are you?"

249

"On the hill above the church," Steiner said. "What is your situation?"

Several bullets passed through the glassless windows and ricocheted from the wall. "Give it to me!" Brandt called from his position flat on the floor behind the Bren.

"He's on the hill," Riedel said. "Trust Steiner to turn up to pull us out of the shit." He crawled along to the loft door above the waterwheel and kicked it open.

"Come back here," Brandt called.

Riedel crouched to peer outside. He laughed excitedly and raised the Grauman to his mouth. "I can see you, Herr Oberst, we're . . . "

There was a heavy burst of automatic fire from outside, blood and brains sprayed across the wall as the back of Riedel's skull disintegrated and he went headfirst out of the loft, still clutching the field phone.

Brandt flung himself across the room and peered over the edge. Riedel had fallen on top of the waterwheel. It kept on turning, carrying him with it, down into the churning waters. When it came round again, he was gone.

On the hill, Werner tapped Steiner on the shoulder. "Below, Herr Oberst, in the wood on the right. Soldiers."

Steiner swung his field glasses. With the height advantage the hill gave him it was just possible to see down into one section of the sunken track through Hawks Wood about half-way along. Sergeant Hustler and his men were passing through.

Steiner made his decision and acted on it. "It seems we're Fallschirmjäger again, boys."

He tossed his red beret away, unbuckled his webbing belt and the Browning in its holster and took off his jump jacket. Underneath he was wearing his *Fliegerbluse*, the Knight's Cross with Oak Leaves at his throat. He took a *Schiff* from his pocket and jammed it down on his head. Klugl and Werner followed his example.

Steiner said, "Right, boys, the grand tour. Straight down that track through the wood, across the footbridge for a few words with those jeeps. I think you can make it, Klugl, if you go fast enough, then on to Oberleutnant Neumann." He looked up at Werner. "And don't stop firing. Not for anything."

The jeep was doing fifty as they went down the final stretch towards the church. Corporal Becker was outside the porch. He crouched in alarm,

Steiner waved, then Klugl swung the wheel and turned the jeep into the Hawks Wood track.

They bounced over a slight rise, hurtled round a bend between the steep walls and there was Hustler with his men, no more than twenty yards away, strung out on either side of the track. Werner started to fire at point-blank range, had no more than a few seconds in which to take aim because by then, the jeep was into them. Men were jumping for their lives, trying to scramble up the steep banks. The offside front wheel bounced over a body and then they were through, leaving Sergeant Horace Hustler and seven of his men dead or dying behind them.

The jeep emerged from the end of the track like a thunderbolt. Klugl kept right on going as ordered, straight across the four-foot-wide footbridge over the stream, snapping the rustic pole handrails like matchsticks, and shot up the bank to the road, all four wheels clear of the ground as they bounced over the rise.

The two men comprising the machine-gun crew of the jeep sheltering behind Joanna Grey's garden wall swung their Browning frantically, already too late as Werner raked the wall with a sustained burst that knocked them both off their feet.

But the fact of their dying gave the crew of the second jeep, positioned at the side of the next garden wall, the two or three precious seconds to react—the seconds that meant the difference between life and death. They had their Browning round and were already firing as Klugl swung the wheel and drove back towards the bridge.

It was the Rangers' turn now. Werner got in a quick burst as they flashed past that caught one of the machine-gun crew, but the other kept on firing his Browning, bullets hammering into the Germans' jeep, shattering the windscreen. Klugl gave a sudden sharp cry and fell forward across the steering wheel, the jeep swerved wildly and smashed into the parapet at the end of the bridge. It seemed to hang there for a moment, then tipped over on to its side very slowly.

Klugl lay huddled in the shelter of the jeep and Werner crouched over him, blood on his face where flying glass had cut him. He looked up at Steiner. "He's dead, Herr Oberst," he said and his eyes were wild.

He reached for a Sten gun and started to stand. Steiner dragged him down. "Pull yourself together, boy. He's dead, you're alive."

Werner nodded dully. "Yes, Herr Oberst."

"Now get this Browning set up and keep them busy down there."

As Steiner turned, Ritter Neumann crawled out from behind the parapet carrying a Bren gun. "You certainly created hell back there."

"They had a section moving up through the wood to the church," Steiner said. "We didn't do them any good either. What about Hagl?"

"Done for, I'm afraid." Neumann nodded to where Hagl's boots protruded from behind the parapet.

Werner had the Browning set up at the side of the jeep now and started to fire in short bursts. Steiner said, "All right, Herr Oberleutnant, and what exactly did you have in mind?"

"It should be dark in an hour," Ritter said. "I thought if we could hold on till then and slip away in twos and threes. We could lie low in the marsh at Hobs End under cover of darkness. Still make the boat if Koenig arrives as arranged. After all, we'll never get near the old man now." He hesitated and added rather awkwardly, "It gives us some sort of chance."

"The only one," Steiner said. "But not here. I think it's time we regrouped again. Where is everybody?"

Ritter gave him a quick run-down on the general situation and when he was finished, Steiner nodded. "I managed to raise them in the mill on the way in. Got Riedel on the Grauman plus a lot of machine-gun fire. You get Altmann and his boys and I'll see if I can get through to Brandt."

Werner gave Ritter covering fire as the Oberleutnant darted across the road and Steiner tried to raise Brandt on the Grauman. He had no success at all and as Neumann emerged from the door of the Post Office with Altmann, Dinter and Berg, there was an outbreak of heavy firing up at the mill.

They all crouched behind the parapet and Steiner said, "I can't raise Brandt. God knows what's happening. I want the rest of you to make a run for it to the church. You've good cover for most of the way if you keep to the hedge. You're in charge, Ritter."

"What about you?"

"I'll keep them occupied with the Browning for a while then I'll follow on."

"But Herr Oberst," Ritter began.

Steiner cut him off short. "No buts about it. Today's my day for playing hero. Now get to hell out of it, all of you and that's an order."

Ritter hesitated, but only fractionally. He nodded to Altmann then slipped past the jeep and ran across the bridge, crouching behind the parapet. Steiner got down to the Browning and started to fire.

At the other end of the bridge there was a stretch of open ground, no more than twenty-five feet before the safety of the hedge. Ritter, crouching on one knee, said, "Taking it one by one is no good because after he's seen the first, that joker on the machine-gun will be ready and waiting for whoever comes next. When I give the word, we all go together."

A moment later he was out of cover and dashing across the road, vaulting the stile and dropping into the safety of the hedge, Altmann right on his heels and followed by the others. The Ranger on the Browning at the other end of the village was a corporal named Bleeker, a Cape Cod fisherman in happier times. Just now, he was nearly out of his mind with pain, a piece of glass having buried itself just beneath his right eye. More than anything else in the world he hated Shafto for bringing him into this, but right now any target would do. He saw the Germans crossing the road and swung the Browning, too late. In his rage and frustration he raked the hedge anyway.

On the other side Berg tripped and fell and Dinter turned to help him. "Give me your hand, you daft bastard," he said. "Two left feet as usual."

Berg stood up to die with him as bullets shredded the hedge, hammering into them, driving them both back across the meadow in a last frenzied dance. Werner turned with a cry and Altmann grabbed him by the shoulder and pushed him after Ritter.

From the loft entrance above the waterwheel, Brandt and Meyer saw what had happened in the meadow. "So now we know," Meyer said. "From the looks of things I'd say we've taken up permanent residence here."

Brandt watched Ritter, Altmann and Briegel toil up the long run of the hedge and scramble over the wall into the churchyard. "They made it," he said. "Wonders will never cease."

He moved across to Meyer, who was propped against a box in the middle of the floor. He'd been shot in the stomach. His blouse was open and there was an obscene hole with swollen purple lips just below his navel. "Look at that," he said, sweat on his face. "At least I'm not losing any blood. My mother always did say I had the luck of the Devil."

"So I've observed." Brandt put a cigarette in Meyer's mouth, but before he could light it, heavy firing started again from outside.

Shafto crouched in the shelter of the wall in Joanna Grey's front garden, stunned by the enormity of the news one of the survivors of Hustler's section had just brought him. The catastrophe seemed complete. In a little over half-an-hour he had lost at least twenty-two men dead or wounded. More than half his command. The consequences now were too appalling to contemplate.

Krukowski, crouching behind him with the field telephone, said, "What are you going to do, Colonel?"

"What do you mean, what am *I* going to do?" Shafto demanded. "It's always me when it comes right down to it. Leave things to other people, people with no conception of discipline or duty, and see what happens."

He slumped against the wall and looked up. At that exact moment

Joanna Grey peered from behind the bedroom curtain. She drew back instantly, too late. Shafto growled deep in his throat. "My God, Krukowski, that Goddamned, double-dealing bitch is still in the house."

He pointed up at the window as he scrambled to his feet. Krukowski said, "I can't see anyone, sir."

"You soon will, boy!" Shafto cried, drawing his pearl-handled Colt. "Come on!" and he ran up the path to the front door.

Joanna Grey locked the secret door and went up the stairs quickly to the cubbyhole loft. She sat down at the radio and started to transmit on the Landsvoort channel. She could hear noise downstairs. Doors were flung open and furniture knocked over as Shafto ransacked the house. He was very close now, stamping about in the study. She heard his cry of rage quite clearly as he went out on the stairs.

"She's got to be in here someplace."

A voice echoed up the stairs. "Heh, Colonel, there was this dog locked up in the cellar. He's on his way up to you now like a bat out of hell."

Joanna Grey reached for the Luger and cocked it, continuing to transmit without faltering. On the landing, Shafto stood to one side as Patch scurried past him. He followed the retriever into the study and found him scratching at the panelling in the corner.

Shafto examined it quickly and found the tiny keyhole almost at once. "She's here, Krukowski!" There was a savage, almost insane joy in his voice. "I've got her!"

He fired three shots point blank in the general area of the keyhole. The wood splintered as the lock disintegrated and the door swung open of its own accord, just as Krukowski entered the room, his M1 ready.

"Take it easy, sir."

"Like hell I will." Shafto started up the stairs, the Colt held out in front of him as Patch flashed past. "Come down out of there, you bitch!"

As his head rose above floor level, Joanna Grey shot him between the eyes. He tumbled back down into the study. Krukowski poked the barrel of his M1 round the corner and loosed off an eight-round clip so fast that it sounded like one continuous burst. The dog howled, there was the sound of a body falling, and then silence.

Devlin arrived outside the church as Ritter, Altmann and Werner Briegel ran through the tombstones towards the porch. They veered towards him as Devlin braked to a halt at the lychgate. "It's a mess," Ritter said. "And the Colonel's still down there by the bridge."

Devlin looked down to the village where Steiner continued to fire the Browning from behind the damaged jeep and Ritter grabbed his arm and pointed. "My God, look what's coming!"

Devlin turned and saw, on the other side of the bend in the road beyond Joanna Grey's cottage, a White Scout Car and three jeeps. He revved his motor and grinned. "Sure and if I don't go now I might think better of it and that would never do."

He went straight down the hill and skidded broadside on into the entrance to Old Woman's meadow, leaving the track within a few yards and taking the direct route straight across the field to the footbridge above the weir. He seemed to take off again and again as the machine bounced over the tussocky grass and Ritter watched from the lychgate, marvelling that he remained in the saddle.

The Oberleutnant ducked suddenly as a bullet chipped the woodwork beside his head. He dropped into the shelter of the wall with Werner and Altmann and started to return the fire as the survivors of Hustler's section, finally re-grouped, reached the fringe of the wood opposite the church.

Devlin shot across the footbridge and followed the track through the wood on the other side. There were men up there by the road, he was sure of it. He pulled one of the grenades from inside his coat and yanked the pin with his teeth. And then he was through the trees and there was a jeep on the grass verge, men turning in alarm.

He simply dropped the grenade behind him. He took out the other. There were more Rangers behind the hedge on his left and he tossed the second grenade over towards them as the first exploded. He kept right on going, down the road past the mill and round the corner, skidding to a halt behind the bridge where Steiner still crouched with the machine-gun.

Steiner didn't say a word. He simply stood up, holding the Browning in both hands and emptied it in a long burst of such savagery that it sent Corporal Bleeker diving for cover behind the garden wall. In the same moment, Steiner tossed the Browning to one side and swung a leg over the pillion. Devlin gunned the motor, swerved across the bridge and went straight up the hill as the White Scout Car nosed round the corner of Joanna Grey's cottage. Harry Kane stood up to watch them go.

"And what in the hell was *that*?" Garvey demanded.

Corporal Bleeker fell out of his jeep and stumbled towards them, blood on his face. "Is there a medic there, sir? I think maybe I lost my right eye. I can't see a thing."

Someone jumped down to hold him and Kane surveyed the shambles of the village. "The crazy, stupid bastard," he whispered.

Krukowski came out of the front gate and saluted. "Where's the Colonel?" Kane asked.

"Dead, sir, upstairs in the house. The lady in there—she shot him."

Kane got down in a hurry. "Where is she?"

"I—I killed her, Major," Krukowski said, and there were tears in his eyes.

Kane couldn't think of a single damn thing to say. He patted Krukowski on the shoulder and went up the path to the cottage.

At the top of the hill, Ritter and his two comrades were still firing from behind the wall at the Rangers in the wood when Devlin and Steiner arrived on the scene. The Irishman changed gear, got his foot down and let the bike drift, turning at just the right moment for a clear run through the lychgate and up the path to the porch. Ritter, Altmann and Werner retreated steadily using the tombstones for cover and finally made the safety of the porch without further casualties.

Corporal Becker had the door open, they all passed inside and he slammed it shut and bolted it. The firing resumed outside with renewed intensity. The villagers huddled together, tense and anxious. Philip Vereker limped down the aisle to confront Devlin, his face white with anger. "Another damned traitor!"

Devlin grinned. "Ah, well," he said. "It's nice to be back amongst friends."

In the mill everything was quiet. "I don't like it," Walther commented.

"You never do," Brandt said and frowned. "What's that?"

There was the sound of a vehicle approaching. Brandt tried to peer out of the loft entrance over the road and immediately came under fire. He drew back. "How's Meyer?"

"I think he's dead."

Brandt reached for a cigarette as the noise of the approaching vehicle drew close. "Just think," he said. "The Albert Canal, Crete, Stalingrad and where does the end of the road turn out to be? Studley Constable." He put a light to his cigarette.

The White Scout Car was doing at least forty when Garvey swung the wheel and smashed it straight through the mill doors. Kane stood in the back behind a Browning anti-aircraft machine-gun and was already firing up through the wood floor above, the enormous .50 calibre rounds smashing their way through with ease, ripping the planking to pieces.

He was aware of the cries of agony, but kept on firing, working the gun from side to side, only stopping when there were great gaping holes in the floor.

A bloodstained hand showed at one of them. It was very quiet. Garvey took a Thompson gun from one of the men, jumped down and went up the flight of wooden steps in the corner. He came down again almost instantly.

"That's it, Major."

Harry Kane's face was pale, but he was completely in command of himself. "All right," he said. "Now for the church."

Molly arrived on Garrowby Heath in time to see a jeep drive up the hill, a white handkerchief fluttering from its radio aerial. It pulled up at the lychgate and Kane and Dexter Garvey got out. As they went up the path through the churchyard Kane said softly, "Use your eyes, Sergeant. Make sure you'd know this place again if you saw it."

"Affirmative, Major."

The church door opened and Steiner moved out of the porch and Devlin leaned against the wall behind him smoking a cigarette. Harry Kane saluted formally. "We've met before, Colonel."

Before Steiner could reply, Philip Vereker pushed past Becker at the door and limped forward. "Kane, where's Pamela? Is she all right?"

"She's fine, Father," Kane told him. "I left her back at Meltham House."

Vereker turned to Steiner, face pinched and very white. There was a glitter of triumph in his eyes. "She fixed you beautifully, didn't she, Steiner? Without her you might actually have got away with it."

Steiner said calmly, "Strange how the perspective changes with the point of view. I thought we failed because a man called Karl Sturm sacrificed himself to save two children's lives." He didn't wait for an answer, but turned to Kane. "What can I do for you?"

"Surely that's obvious. Surrender. There's no point in further useless bloodshed. The men you left down in the mill are all dead. So is Mrs. Grey."

Vereker caught him by the arm. "Mrs. Grey is dead? How?"

"She killed Colonel Shafto when he tried to arrest her, died herself in the exchange of gunfire which followed." Vereker turned away, a look of utter desolation on his face and Kane said to Steiner, "You are quite alone now. The Prime Minister is safe at Meltham House under as heavy a guard as he's likely to see in his lifetime. It's all over."

Steiner thought of Brandt and Walther and Meyer, Gerhard Klugl, Dinter and Berg and nodded, his face very pale. "Honourable terms?"

"No terms!" Vereker shouted it aloud like a cry to heaven. "These men came here in British uniform, must I remind you of that, Major?"

"But did not fight in them," Steiner cut in. "We fought only as German soldiers, in German uniforms. As Fallschirmjäger. The other was a legitimate *ruse de guerre*."

"And a direct contravention of the Geneva Convention," Vereker answered. "Which not only expressly forbids the wearing of an enemy's uniform in time of war, but also prescribes the death penalty for offenders."

Steiner saw the look on Kane's face and smiled gently. "Don't worry, Major, not your fault. The rules of the game and all that." He turned to Vereker. "Well now, Father, your God is a God of Wrath indeed. You would dance on my grave, it seems."

"Damn you, Steiner!" Vereker lurched forward, raising his stick to strike, stumbled over the long skirts of his cassock and fell, striking his head on the edge of a tombstone.

Garvey dropped to one knee beside him and made a quick examination. "Out for the count." He looked up. "Somebody should check him out, though. We've got a good medic down in the village."

"Take him by all means," Steiner said. "Take all of them."

Garvey glanced at Kane, then picked Vereker up and carried him to the jeep. Kane said, "You'll let the villagers go?"

"The obvious thing to do since a further outbreak of hostilities seems imminent." Steiner looked faintly amused. "Why, did you think we'd hold the entire village hostage or come out fighting, driving the women in front of us? The brutal Hun? Sorry I can't oblige." He turned. "Send them out, Becker, all of them."

The door swung open with a crash and the villagers started to pour through, led by Laker Armsby. Most of the women were crying hysterically as they rushed past. Betty Wilde came last with Graham and Ritter Neumann supported her husband, who looked dazed and ill. Garvey hurried back up the path and got an arm round him and Betty Wilde reached for Graham's hand and turned to Ritter.

"He'll be all right, Mrs. Wilde," the young Oberleutnant said. "I'm sorry about what happened in there, believe me."

"That's all right," she said. "It wasn't your fault. Would you do something for me? Would you tell me your name?"

"Neumann," he said. "Ritter Neumann."

"Thank you," she said simply. "I'm sorry I said the things I did." She turned to Steiner. "And I want to thank you and your men for Graham."

"He's a brave boy," Steiner said. "He didn't even hesitate. He jumped straight in. That takes courage and courage is something that never goes out of fashion."

The boy stared up at him. "Why are you a German?" he demanded. "Why aren't you on our side?"

Steiner laughed out loud. "Go on, get him out of here," he said to Betty Wilde. "Before he completely corrupts me."

She took the boy by the hand and hurried away. Beyond the wall the women streamed down the hill. At that moment the White Scout Car emerged from the Hawks Wood track and stopped, its anti-aircraft gun and heavy machine-gun traversing on to the porch.

Steiner nodded wryly. "So, Major, the final act. Let battle commence then." He saluted and went back into the porch where Devlin had been standing throughout the entire conversation without saying a word.

"I don't think I've ever heard you silent for so long before," Steiner said.

Devlin grinned. "To tell you the truth I couldn't think of a single damned thing to say except *Help*. Can I go in now and pray?"

From her vantage point on the heath Molly watched Devlin disappear inside the porch with Steiner and her heart sank like a stone. *Oh, God, she thought, I must do something.* She got to her feet and at the same moment, a dozen Rangers headed by the big black sergeant cut across the road from the wood well up from the church where they couldn't be seen. They ran back along the wall and entered the presbytery garden through the wicket gate.

But they didn't go into the house. They slipped over the wall into the cemetery, approaching the church from the tower end and worked their way round to the porch. The big sergeant had a coil of rope over his shoulder and as she watched, he jumped for the porch guttering and pulled himself over, then scrambled fifteen feet up the ivy vine to the lower leads. Once there, he uncoiled the rope and tossed the end down and the other Rangers began to follow.

Seized by a sudden new determination, Molly swung into the saddle and urged her horse across the heath, turning down to the woods at the rear of the presbytery.

It was very cold inside the church, a place of shadows, only the flickering candles, the ruby light of the sanctuary lamp. There were eight of them left now including Devlin. Steiner and Ritter, Werner Briegel, Altmann, Jansen, Corporal Becker and Preston. There was also, unknown to any of them, Arthur Seymour who, overlooked in the stampede to get out, still lay beside Sturm in the darkness of the Lady Chapel, his hands and feet bound. He had managed to push himself into a sitting position against the wall and was working on his wrists, his strange mad eyes fixed on Preston.

Steiner tried the tower door and the sacristy, both of which appeared to be locked and looked behind the curtain at the foot of the tower where ropes soared through holes in the wooden floor thirty feet up to bells which hadn't rung since 1939.

He turned and walked up the aisle to face them. "Well, all I can offer you is another fight."

Preston said, "It's a ludicrous situation. How can we fight? They've got the men, the equipment. We couldn't hold this place for ten minutes once they really start."

"It's quite simple," Steiner said. "We don't have any other choice. As you heard, under the terms of the Geneva Convention we have put ourselves gravely at risk by wearing British uniforms."

"We fought as German soldiers," Preston insisted. "In German uniforms. You said that yourself."

"A neat point," Steiner said. "I'd hate to stake my life on it, even with a good lawyer. If it's to be a bullet, rather now than from a firing squad later."

"I don't know what you're getting so worked up about anyway, Preston," Ritter said. "It's the Tower of London for you without a doubt. The English, I'm afraid, have never held traitors in particularly high regard. They'll hang you so high the crows won't be able to get at you."

Preston sank down in a pew, head in hands.

The organ rumbled into life and Hans Altmann, sitting high above the choir stalls, called, "A choral prelude of Johann Sebastian Bach, particularly appropriate to our situation as it is entitled *For the Dying*."

His voice echoed up into the nave as the music swelled. *Ach wie nichtig, ach wie fluchtig. O how cheating, O how fleeting are our days departing . . .*

One of the clerestory windows high up in the nave smashed. A burst of automatic fire knocked Altmann off the seat into the choir stalls. Werner turned, crouching, firing his Sten. A Ranger pitched headlong through the window and landed between two pews. In the same moment, several more clerestory windows crashed in and heavy fire was poured down into the church. Werner was hit in the head as he ran along the south aisle and fell on his face without a cry. Someone was using a Thompson gun up there now, spraying it back and forth.

Steiner crawled to Werner, turned him over, then moved on, dodging up the chancel steps to check on Altmann. He returned by way of the south aisle, keeping down behind the pews as intermittent firing continued.

Devlin crawled to meet him. "What's the situation up there?"

"Altmann and Briegel both gone."

"It's a bloodbath," the Irishman said. "We don't stand a chance. Ritter's been hit in the legs and Jansen's dead."

Steiner crawled back with him to the rear of the church and found Ritter on his back behind the pews binding a field dressing round one thigh. Preston and Corporal Becker crouched beside him.

"Are you all right, Ritter?" Steiner asked.

"They'll run out of wound badges, Herr Oberst." Ritter grinned, but was obviously in great pain.

They were still firing from above and Steiner nodded towards the sacristy door, barely visible now in the shadows and said to Becker, "See if you can shoot your way in through that door. We can't last long out here, that's for certain."

Becker nodded and slipped through the shadows behind the font, keeping low. There was that strange metallic clicking of the bolt reciprocating as he fired the silenced Sten, he stamped against the sacristy door, it swung open.

All firing stopped and Garvey called from high above. "You had enough yet, Colonel? This is like shooting fish in a barrel and I'd rather not, but we'll carry you out on a plank if we have to."

Preston cracked then, jumped to his feet and ran out into the open by the font. "Yes, I'll come! I've had enough!"

"Bastard!" Becker cried and he ran out of the shadows by the sacristy door and rammed the butt of his rifle against the side of Preston's skull. The Thompson gun rattled, a short burst only, but it caught Becker full in the back, driving him headlong through the curtains at the base of the tower. He grabbed at the ropes in dying as if trying to hang on to life itself and somewhere overhead, a bell tolled sonorously for the first time in years.

There was silence again and Garvey called, "Five minutes, Colonel."

"We'd better get moving," Steiner said to Devlin in a low voice. "We'll do better inside that sacristy than out here."

"How long for?" Devlin asked.

There was a slight eerie creaking and straining his eyes, Devlin saw that someone was standing in the entrance to the sacristy where the broken door swung crazily. A familiar voice whispered, "Liam?"

"My God," he said to Steiner. "It's Molly. Where in the hell did she spring from?" He crawled across the floor to join her and was back in a moment. "Come on!" he said, getting a hand under Ritter's left arm. "The little darling's got a way out for us. Now let's have this one on his feet and get moving while those lads up on the leads are still waiting."

They slipped through the shadows, Ritter between them, and moved into the sacristy. Molly waited by the secret panel. Once they were inside, she closed it and led the way down the stairs and along the tunnel.

It was very quiet when they came out into the hall at the presbytery. "Now what?" Devlin said. "We'll not get far with Ritter like this."

"Father Vereker's car is in the yard at the back," Molly said.

And Steiner, remembering, put a hand in his pocket. "And I've got his keys."

"Don't be silly," Ritter told him. "The moment you start the motor you'll have Rangers swarming all over you."

"There's a gate at the back," Molly said. "A track over the fields beside the hedge. We can push that little Morris Eight of his between us for a couple of hundred yards. Nothing to it."

They were at the bottom of the first meadow and a hundred and fifty yards away, when shooting began again at the church. Only then did Steiner start the engine and drive away, following Molly's directions, sticking to farm tracks across the fields, all the way down to the coast road.

After the tiny click of the panel door in the sacristy closing, there was a stirring in the Lady Chapel and Arthur Seymour stood up, hands free. He padded down the north aisle without a sound, holding in his left hand the coil of rope with which Preston had bound his feet.

It was totally dark now, the only light the candles at the altar and the sanctuary lamp. He leaned down to satisfy himself that Preston was still breathing, picked him up and slung him over one massive shoulder. Then he turned and walked straight up the centre aisle towards the altar.

On the leads, Garvey was beginning to worry. It was so dark down there that you couldn't see a damn thing. He snapped his fingers for the field telephone and spoke to Kane who was at the gate with the White Scout Car. "Silent as the grave in here, Major. I don't like it."

"Try a burst. See what happens," Kane told him.

Garvey pushed the barrel of his Thompson through the clerestory window and fired. There was no response and then the man on his right grabbed his arm. "Down there, Sergeant, near the pulpit. Isn't someone moving?"

Garvey took a chance and flashed his torch. The young private on his right gave a cry of horror. Garvey ran the torch quickly along the south aisle, then said into the field phone, "I don't know what's happening, Major, but you'd better get in there."

A moment later, a burst from a Thompson gun shattered the lock on the main door, it crashed back and Harry Kane and a dozen Rangers moved in fast, ready for action. But there was no Steiner and no Devlin. Only Arthur Seymour kneeling in the front pew in the guttering candle-light, staring up into the hideously swollen face of Harvey Preston hanging by his neck from the center pole of the rood screen.

19

THE PRIME MINISTER HAD TAKEN the library overlooking the rear terrace at Meltham House for his personal use. When Harry Kane came out at seven-thirty Corcoran was waiting. "How was he?"

"Very interested," Kane said. "Wanted chapter and verse on the whole battle. He seems fascinated by Steiner."

"Aren't we all. What I'd like to know is where the damn man is now and that Irish scoundrel."

"Nowhere near the cottage he's been living in, that's for sure. I had a report over the radio from Garvey just before I went in. It seems that when they went to check out this cottage of Devlin's, they found two inspectors from Special Branch waiting for him."

"Good God," Corcoran said. "How on earth did they get on to him?"

"Some police investigation or other. Anyway, he's highly unlikely to turn up there now. Garvey is staying in the area and setting up a couple of road blocks on the coast road, but we can't do much more till we get more men."

"They're coming in, my boy, believe me," Corcoran said. "Since your chaps got the telephones working again, I've had several lengthy discussions with London. Another couple of hours should see the whole of North Norfolk sealed up tight. By morning most of this area will be, to all intents and purposes, under martial law. And it will certainly stay that way until Steiner is caught."

Kane nodded. "There's no question that he could get anywhere near the Prime Minister. I've got men on his door, on the terrace outside and at least two dozen prowling out there in the garden, with blackened faces and Thompson guns. I've given it to them straight. They shoot first. Accidents we can argue about afterwards."

The door opened and a young corporal entered, a couple of typewritten sheets in his hand. "I've got the final lists if you'd like to see them, Major."

He went out and Kane looked at the first sheet. "They've had Father Vereker and some of the villagers look at the German bodies."

"How is he?" Corcoran asked.

"Concussed, but otherwise he seems okay. From what they say everyone is accounted for except for Steiner, his second in command, Neumann, and the Irishman, of course. The other fourteen are all dead."

"But how in the hell did they get away, that's what I'd like to know?"

"Well, they blasted their way into the sacristy to get out of the line of fire from Garvey and his men up on the leads. My theory is that when Pamela and the Prior girl got out through this priest's tunnel, they were in such a hurry they didn't close the secret door properly."

Corcoran said, "I understand the young Prior girl was rather sweet on this scoundrel Devlin. You don't think she could be involved in any way?"

"I wouldn't have thought so. According to Pamela the kid was really bitter about the whole thing."

"I suppose so," Corcoran said. "Anyway, what about casualties on your side?"

Kane glanced at the second list. "Including Shafto and Captain Mallory, twenty-one dead, eight wounded." He shook his head. "Out of forty. There's going to be one God Almighty rumpus when this gets out."

"*If* it gets out."

"What do you mean?"

"London is already making it clear they want a very low profile on this one. They don't want to alarm the people for one thing. I ask you, German Fallschirmjäger dropping into Norfolk to seize the Prime Minister. And coming too damn close for comfort. And what about this British Free Corps? Englishmen in the SS. Can you imagine how *that* would look in the papers?" He shuddered. "I'd have hung the damn man myself."

"I see what you mean."

"And look at it from the Pentagon's point of view. A crack American unit, the elite of the elite, takes on a handful of German paratroops and sustains a seventy per cent casualty rate."

"I don't know," Kane shook his head. "It's expecting a hell of a lot of people to keep quiet."

"There's a war on, Kane," Corcoran said. "And in wartime, people can be made to do as they are told, it's as simple as that."

The door opened, the young corporal looked in. "London on the phone again, Colonel."

Corcoran went out in a hurry, and Kane followed. He lit a cigarette which he held in the palm of his hand when he went out of the front door and down the steps past the sentries. It was raining hard and very dark, but he could smell fog on the air as he walked across the front terrace. Maybe Corcoran was right? It could happen that way. A world at war was crazy enough for anything to be believable.

He went down the steps and in a moment had an arm about his throat, a knee in his back. A knife gleamed dully. Someone said, "Identify yourself."

"Major Kane."

A torch flicked on and off. "Sorry, sir. Corporal Bleeker."

"You should be in bed, Bleeker. How's that eye?"

"Five stitches in it, Major, but it's going to be fine. I'll move on now, sir, with your permission."

He faded away and Kane stared into the darkness. "I will never," he said softly, "to the end of my days even begin to understand my fellow human beings."

In the North Sea area generally, as the weather report had it, the winds were three to four with rain squalls and some sea fog persisting till morning. The E-boat had made good time and by eight o'clock they were through the minefields and into the main coastal shipping lane.

Muller was at the wheel and Koenig looked up from the chart table where he had been laying off their final course with great care. "Ten miles due east of Blakeney Point, Erich."

Muller nodded, straining his eyes into the murk ahead. "This fog isn't helping."

"Oh, I don't know," Koenig said. "You might be glad of it before we're through."

The door banged open and Teusen, the leading telegraphist, entered. He held out a signal flimsy. "Message from Landsvoort, Herr Leutnant."

He held out the flimsy, Koenig took it from him and read it in the light of the chart table. He looked down at it for a long moment, then crumbled it into a ball in his right hand.

"What is it?" Muller asked.

"The Eagle is blown. The rest is just words."

There was a short pause. Rain pattered against the window. Muller said, "And our orders?"

"To proceed as I see fit." Koenig shook his head. "Just think of it. Colonel Steiner, Ritter Neumann—all those fine men."

For the first time since childhood he felt like crying. He opened the door and stared out into the darkness, rain beating against his face. Muller said carefully, "Of course, it's always possible some of them might make it. Just one or two. You know how these things go?"

Koenig slammed the door. "You mean you'd still be willing to go in there?'' Muller didn't bother to reply and Koenig turned to Teusen. "You, too?''

Teusen said, "We've been together a long time, Herr Leutnant. I've never asked where we were going before.''

Koenig was filled with wild elation. He slapped him on the back. "All right, then send this signal.''

Radl's condition had deteriorated steadily during the late afternoon and evening, but he had refused to remain in bed in spite of Witt's pleadings. Since Joanna Grey's final message he had insisted on staying in the radio room, lying back in an old armchair Witt had brought in while the operator tried to raise Koenig. The pain in his chest was not only worse, but had spread to his left arm. He was no fool. He knew what that meant. Not that it mattered. Not that anything mattered now.

At five minutes to eight, the operator turned, a smile of triumph on his face. "I've got them, Herr Oberst. Message received and understood.''

"Thank God,'' Radl said and fumbled to open his cigarette case, but suddenly his fingers seemed too stiff and Witt had to do it for him.

"Only one left, Herr Oberst,'' he said as he took out the distinctive Russian cigarette and put it in Radl's mouth.

The operator was writing feverishly on his pad. He tore off the sheet and turned. "Reply, Herr Oberst.''

Radl felt strangely dizzy and his vision wasn't good. He said, "Read it, Witt.''

"Will still visit nest. Some fledglings may need assistance. Good luck.'' Witt looked bewildered. "Why does he add that, Herr Oberst?''

"Because he is a very perceptive young man who suspects I'm going to need it as much as he does.'' He shook his head slowly. "Where do we get them from, these boys? To dare so much, sacrifice everything and for what?''

Witt looked troubled. "Herr Oberst, please.''

Radl smiled. "Like this last of my Russian cigarettes, my friend, all good things come to an end sooner or later.'' He turned to the radio operator and braced himself to do what should have been done at least two hours earlier. "Now you can get me Berlin.''

There was a decaying farm cottage on the eastern boundary of Prior Farm, at the back of the wood on the opposite side of the main road above Hobs End. It provided some sort of shelter for the Morris.

It was seven-fifteen when Devlin and Steiner left Molly to look after Ritter and went down through the trees to make a cautious reconnaissance. They were just in time to see Garvey and his men go up the dyke road to the cottage. They retreated through the trees and crouched in the lee of a wall to consider the situation.

"Not so good," Devlin said.

"You don't need to go to the cottage. You can cut through the marsh on foot and still reach that beach in time," Steiner pointed out.

"For what?" Devlin sighed. "I've a terrible confession to make, Colonel. I went off in such a Devil of a hurry that I left the S-phone at the bottom of a carrier-bag filled with spuds that's hanging behind the kitchen door."

Steiner laughed softly. "My friend you are truly yourself alone. God must have broken the mold after turning you out."

"I know," Devlin said. "A hell of a thing to live with, but staying with the present situation, I can't call Koenig without it."

"You don't think he'll come in without a signal?"

"That was the arrangement. Any time between nine and ten as ordered. Another thing. Whatever happened to Joanna Grey, it's likely she got some sort of message off to Landsvoort. If Radl has passed it on to Koenig, he and his boys could be already on their way back."

"No," Steiner said. "I don't think so. Koenig will come. Even if he fails to get your signal, he will come in to that beach."

"Why should he?"

"Because he told me he would," Steiner said simply. "So you see, you could manage without the S-phone. Even if the Rangers search the area, they won't bother with the beach because the signs say it is mined. If you get there in good time you can walk along the estuary for at least a quarter of a mile with the tide as it is."

"With Ritter in his state of health?"

"All he needs is a stick and a shoulder to lean on. Once in Russia he walked eighty miles in three days through snow with a bullet in his right foot. When a man knows he'll die if he stays where he is, it concentrates his mind wonderfully on moving somewhere else. You'll save a considerable amount of time. Meet Koenig on his way in."

"You're not going with us." It was a statement of fact, not a question.

"I think you know where I must go, my friend."

Devlin sighed. "I was always the great believer in letting a man go to hell his own way, but I'm willing to make an exception in your case. You won't even get close. They'll have more guards round him than there are flies on a jam jar on a hot summer day."

"In spite of that I must try."

"Why, because you think it might help your father's case back home? That's an illusion. Face up to it. Nothing you do can help him if that old sod at Prinz Albrechtstrasse decides otherwise.''

"Yes, you're very probably right. I think I've always known that.''

"Then why?''

"Because I find it impossible to do anything else.''

"I don't understand.''

"I think you do. This game you play. Trumpets on the wind, the tricolour fluttering bravely in the gray morning. Up the Republic. Remember Easter nineteen-sixteen. But tell me this, my friend. In the end, do you control the game, or does the game possess you? Can you stop, if you want, or must it always be the same? Trenchcoats and Thompson guns, my life for Ireland until the day you lie in the gutter with a bullet in your back?''

Devlin said hoarsely, "God knows, I don't.''

"But I do, my friend. And now, I think, we should rejoin the others. You will naturally say nothing about my personal plans. Ritter could prove difficult.''

"All right,'' Devlin said reluctantly.

They moved back through the night to the ruined cottage where they found Molly rebandaging one of Ritter's thighs. "How are you doing?'' Steiner asked him.

"Fine,'' Ritter answered, but when Steiner put a hand on his forehead it was damp with sweat.

Molly joined Devlin in the angle of the two walls where he sheltered from the rain, smoking a cigarette. "He's not good,'' she said. "Needs a doctor if you ask me.''

"You might as well send for an undertaker,'' Devlin said. "But never mind him. It's you I'm worried about now. You could be in serious trouble from this night's work.''

She was curiously indifferent. "Nobody saw me get you out of the church, nobody can prove I did. As far as they're concerned I've been sitting on the heath in the rain crying my heart out at finding the truth about my lover.''

"For God's sake, Molly.''

"Poor, silly little bitch, they'll say. Got her fingers burned and serves her right for trusting a stranger.''

He said awkwardly, "I haven't thanked you.''

"It doesn't matter. I didn't do it for you. I did it for me.'' She was a simple girl in many ways and content to be so and yet now, more than at any other time in her life, she wanted to be able to express herself with complete certainty. "I love you. That doesn't mean I like what you are or what you've done or even understand it. That's something different. The love is a separate issue. It's in a compartment of its own. That's why I got you out of that church tonight. Not because it was right or wrong, but because I couldn't have lived with myself if I'd stood by and let you die." She pulled herself free. "I'd better check on how the lieutenant is getting on."

She walked over to the car and Devlin swallowed hard. Wasn't it the strange thing? The bravest speech he'd ever heard in his life, a girl to cheer from the rooftops, and here he felt more like crying at the tragic waste of it all.

⚓

At twenty past eight, Devlin and Steiner went down through the trees again. The cottage out there in the marsh was in darkness but on the main road, there were subdued voices, the dim shape of a vehicle. "Let's move a little closer," Steiner whispered.

They got to the boundary wall between the wood and the road and peered over. It was raining hard now. There were two jeeps, one on either side of the road and several Rangers were sheltering under the trees. A match flared in Garvey's cupped hands, lighting his face for a brief moment.

Steiner and Devlin retreated. "The big negro," Steiner said. "The Master Sergeant who was with Kane, waiting to see if you show up."

"Why not at the cottage?"

"He probably has men out there, too. This way he covers the road as well."

"It doesn't matter," Devlin said. "We can cross the road further down. Make it to the beach on foot as you said."

"Easier if you had a diversion."

"Such as?"

"Me in a stolen car passing through that road block. I could do with your trenchcoat, by the way, if you'd consider a permanent loan."

Devlin couldn't see his face in the darkness and suddenly didn't want to. "Damn you, Steiner, go to hell your own way," he said wearily. He unslung his Sten gun, took off the trenchcoat and handed it over. "You'll find a silenced Mauser in the right-hand pocket and two extra magazines."

"Thank you." Steiner took off his *Schiff* and pushed it inside his *Fliegerbluse*. He pulled on the trenchcoat and belted it. "So, the final end of things. We'll say goodbye here, I think."

"Tell me one thing," Devlin said. "Has it been worth it? Any of it?"

"Oh, no." Steiner laughed lightly. "No more philosophy, please." He held out his hand. "May you find what you are searching for, my friend."

"I already have and lost it in the finding," Devlin told him.

"Then from now on, nothing really matters," Steiner said. "A dangerous situation. You will have to take care,'' and he turned and went back to the ruined cottage.

They got Ritter out of the car and pushed it to where the track started to slope to a five-barred gate, the road on the other side. Steiner ran down and opened it, pulling a six-foot length of rail off the fence which he gave to Ritter when he got back.

"How's that?" he asked.

"Fine," Ritter said bravely. "Do we go now?"

"You, not me. There are Rangers down there on the road. I thought I might arrange a small diversion while you get across. I'll catch up with you later."

Ritter grabbed his arm and there was panic in his voice. "No, Kurt, I can't let you do this."

Steiner said, "Oberleutnant Neumann, you are undoubtedly the finest soldier I've ever known. From Narvik to Stalingrad, you've never shirked your duty or disobeyed an order of mine and I haven't the slightest intention of letting you start now."

Ritter tried to straighten up, bracing himself against the rail. "As the Herr Oberst wishes," he said formally.

"Good," Steiner said. "Go now, please, Mr. Devlin, and good luck."

He opened the car door and Ritter called softly, "Herr Oberst."

"Yes?"

"A privilege to serve with you, sir."

"Thank you, Herr Oberleutnant."

Steiner got into the Morris, released the brake and the car started to roll down the track.

⌇

Devlin and Molly went through the trees, Ritter between them and paused at the side of the low wall. Devlin whispered, "Time for you to go, girl."

"I'll see you to the beach, Liam," she said firmly.

He had no chance to argue because the car engine started forty yards up the road and the Morris's slotted headlights were turned on. One of the Rangers took a red lamp from under his cape and waved it. Devlin had expected the German to drive straight on, but to his astonishment, he slowed. Steiner was taking a coldly calculated risk, something designed to draw every last man there. There was only one way he could do that. He waited for Garvey's approach, his left hand on the wheel, his right holding the Mauser.

Garvey said as he approached, "Sorry, but you'll have to identify yourself."

He switched on the torch in his left hand, picking Steiner's face out of the darkness. The Mauser coughed once as Steiner fired, apparently at point-blank range, but a good two inches to one side, the wheels skidded as he stamped on the accelerator and was away.

"That was Steiner himself, Goddammit!" Garvey cried. "Get after him!"

There was a mad scramble as everyone jumped to get on board, Garvey's jeep was away first, the other hard behind. The sound dwindled into the night.

Devlin said, "Right, let's get out of it then," and he and Molly helped Ritter over the wall and started across the road.

Built in 1933, the Morris was still on the road only because of the wartime shortage of new cars. Her engine was virtually worn out and although she suited Vereker's requirements adequately enough, they were not those of Steiner that night. With his foot flat on the boards, the needle hovered on forty and obstinately refused to move beyond that point.

He had minutes only, not even that, for as he debated the merits of stopping suddenly and taking to the woods on foot, Garvey, in the lead jeep, started to fire its Browning. Steiner ducked over the wheel, bullets hammered through the body, the windscreen dissolved in a snowstorm of flying glass.

The Morris swerved to the right, smashed through some wooden railings and lumbered down a slope of young firs. The braking effect of these was such that the speed was not very great. Steiner got the car door open and tumbled out. He was on his feet in a moment, moving away through the trees into the darkness as the Morris went into the flooded waters of the marsh below and started to sink.

The jeep skidded to a halt on the road above. Garvey was first out, going down the bank fast, the torch ready in his hand. As he reached the bank, the muddy waters of the marsh closed over the roof of the Morris.

He took off his helmet and started to unbuckle his belt and Krukowski, sliding down after him, grabbed him by the arm. "Don't even think it. That isn't just water down there. The mud in some of these places is deep enough to swallow a man whole."

Garvey nodded slowly. "Yes, I suppose you're right." He played his torch on the surface of the muddy pool where bubbles broke through, then turned and went back up the slope to radio in.

Kane and Corcoran were having supper in the ornate front drawing room, when the corporal from the radio room rushed in with the signal. Kane looked at it briefly then slid it across the polished surface of the table.

"My God, and he was pointing in this direction, you realize that?" Corcoran frowned in distaste. "What a way for such a man to go."

Kane nodded. He should have been pleased and felt curiously depressed. He said to the corporal, "Tell Garvey to stay where he is, then get the motor pool to send some sort of recovery vehicle out to him. I want Colonel Steiner's body out of there."

The corporal went out and Corcoran said, "What about the other one and the Irishman?"

"I don't think we need worry. They'll turn up, but not here." Kane sighed. "No, in the end it was Steiner on his own, I think. The sort of man who never knows when to give up."

Corcoran went to the sideboard and poured two large whiskies. He handed one to Kane. "I won't say cheers because I think I know how you feel. A strange sense of personal loss."

"Exactly."

"I've been at this game for too long, I think." Corcoran shivered and downed his whisky. "Will you tell the Prime Minister or shall I?"

"Your privilege, I fancy, sir." Kane managed a smile. "I'd better let the men know."

When he went out of the front door it was pouring with rain and he stood at the top of the steps in the porch and shouted, "Corporal Bleeker?"

Bleeker ran out of the darkness within a few moments and came up the steps. His combat jacket was soaked, his helmet shiny with rain and the dark camouflage cream on his face had streaked.

Kane said, "Garvey and his boys got Steiner back along the coast road. Spread the word."

Bleeker said, "That's it then. Do we stand down, sir?"

"No, but you can phase the guard system now. Work it so you get some time off in turns for a hot meal and so on."

Bleeker started down the steps and vanished into the darkness. The Major stayed there for quite some time, staring out into the rain and then finally turned and went back inside.

The cottage at Hobs End was in total darkness as Devlin, Molly and Ritter Neumann approached. They paused by the wall and Devlin whispered, "It looks quiet enough to me."

"Not worth the risk," Ritter whispered.

But Devlin, thinking of the S-phone, said stubbornly, "And bloody daft we'd be and no one in the place. You two keep moving along the dyke. I'll catch you up.''

He slipped away before either of them could protest, and went across the yard cautiously and listened at the window. All was quiet, only the rain falling, not a chink of light anywhere. The front door opened to his touch with a slight creak and he moved into the hall, the Sten gun ready.

The living room door stood ajar, a few embers from the dying fire glowing redly on the hearth. He stepped inside and knew instantly that he had made a very bad mistake. The door slammed behind him, the muzzle of a Browning was rammed into the side of his neck and the Sten plucked from his hand.

"Hold it right there," Jack Rogan said. "All right, Fergus, let's have a little light on the situation."

A match flared as Fergus Grant touched the wick of the oil lamp and replaced the glass chimney. Rogan put his knee into Devlin's back and sent him staggering across the room. "Let's have a look at you."

Devlin half-turned, a foot on the hearth. He put a hand on the mantelpiece. "I haven't had the honour."

"Chief Inspector Rogan, Inspector Grant, Special Branch."

"The Irish Section, is it?"

"That's right, son, and don't ask for my warrant card or I'll belt you." Rogan sat on the edge of the table, holding his Browning against his thigh. "You know, you've been a very naughty boy from what I hear."

"Do you tell me?" Devlin said, leaning a little further into the hearth, knowing that even if he got to the Walther his chances were of the slimmest. Whatever Rogan might be doing, Grant was taking no chances and had him covered.

"Yes, you really give me a pain, you people," Rogan said. "Why can't you stay back there in the bogs where you belong?"

"It's a thought," Devlin said.

Rogan took a pair of handcuffs out of his coat pocket. "Get over here."

A stone crashed through the window on the other side of the blackout curtain and both policemen turned in alarm. Devlin's hand reached for the Walther hanging on the nail at the back of the beam that supported the chimney breast. He shot Rogan in the head, knocking him back off the table, but Grant was already turning. He got off one wild shot that caught the Irishman in the right shoulder and Devlin fell back in the easy chair, still firing, shattering the young inspector's left arm, putting another bullet into the shoulder on the same side.

Grant fell back against the wall and slid down to the floor. He seemed in deep shock and gazed across the room uncomprehendingly at Rogan lying on the other side of the table. Devlin picked up the Browning and stuffed it in his waistband, then went to the door, took down the carrier bag and emptied the potatoes on the floor. The small canvas bag at the bottom contained the S-phone and a few other odds and ends and he slung it over his shoulder.

"Why don't you kill me as well?" Fergus Grant said weakly.

"You're nicer than he was," Devlin said. "I'd find a better class of work, son, if I was you."

He went out quickly. When he opened the front door, Molly was standing against the wall. "Thank God!" she said, but he put a hand to her mouth and hurried her away. They reached the wall where Ritter waited. Molly said, "What happened?"

"I killed a man, wounded another, that's what happened," Devlin told her. "Two Special Branch detectives."

"I helped you do that?"

"Yes," he said. "Will you go now, Molly, while you still can?"

She turned from him suddenly and started to run back along the dyke. Devlin hesitated and then, unable to contain himself, went after her. He caught her within a few yards and pulled her into his arms. Her hands went to his neck, she kissed him with a passion that was all-consuming. He pushed her away. "Go now, girl, and God go with you."

She turned without a word and ran into the night and Devlin went back to Ritter Neumann. "A very remarkable young woman," the Oberleutnant said.

"Yes, you could say that," Devlin told him, "And you'd be making the understatement of the age." He got the S-phone out of the bag and switched on to channel. "Eagle to Wanderer. Eagle to Wanderer. Come in please."

On the bridge of the E-boat where the S-phone receiver had been situated, his voice sounded as clearly as if he was just outside the door. Koenig reached for the mike quickly, his heart beating. "Eagle, this is Wanderer. What is your situation?"

"Two fledglings still in the nest," Devlin said. "Can you come immediately?"

"We're on our way," Koenig told him. "Over and out." He put the mike back on its hook and turned to Muller. "Right, Erich, switch to silences and break out the White Ensign. We're going in."

As Devlin and Neumann reached the trees, the Irishman glanced back and saw car headlights turn out of the main road and move along the dyke path. Ritter said, "Who do you think it is?"

"God knows," Devlin told him.

Garvey, waiting a couple of miles along the road for the recovery vehicle, had decided to send the other jeep back to check on the two Special Branch men.

Devlin got a hand under Ritter's arm. "Come on, son, we'd better get out of this." He cursed suddenly at the searing pain in his shoulder now that the shock was beginning to wear off.

"Are you all right?" Ritter asked.

"Bleeding like Mrs. O'Grady's pig. I stopped one in the shoulder back there, but never mind that now. Nothing like a sea voyage to cure what ails you."

They went past the warning notice, picked their way gingerly through the barbed wire and started across the beach. Ritter was gasping with pain at every step. He leaned heavily on the rail Steiner had given him, yet he never faltered. The sands stretched wide and flat before them, fog rolling in on the wind, and then they were walking on water, only an inch or two at first, rather more in the depressions.

They paused to take stock and Devlin looked back and saw lights moving in the trees. "Christ almighty," he said. "Don't they ever give up?"

They stumbled on towards the estuary across the sands and as the tide flowed in, the water grew deeper. At first knee-deep and then it was up to their thighs. They were well out in the estuary now and Ritter groaned suddenly and fell to one knee, dropping his rail. "It's no good, Devlin. I've had it. I've never known such pain."

Devlin crouched beside him and raised the S-phone to his mouth again. "Wanderer, this is Eagle. We are waiting for you in the estuary a quarter of a mile off-shore. Signalling now."

From the canvas bag he took out a luminous signal ball, another gift from the Abwehr by courtesy of SOE, and held it up in the palm of his right hand. He glanced round towards the shore, but the fog had rolled in now, blanketing everything back there.

Twenty minutes later, the water was up to his chest. He had never been so cold in his life before. He stood on the sandbank, legs apart, his left arm supporting Ritter, his right hand holding the luminous signalling ball high, the tide flowing around them.

"It's no good," Ritter whispered. "I can't feel a thing. I'm finished. I can't take any more."

"As Mrs. O'Flynn said to the Bishop," Devlin said. "Come on, boy, don't give in now. What would Steiner say?"

"Steiner?" Ritter coughed, choking a little as salt water slopped over his chin and into his mouth. "He'd have swum across."

Devlin forced a laugh. "That's the way, son, keep smiling." He started to sing at the top of his voice, "And down the glen rode Sarsfield's men all in their jackets green."

A wave passed right over his head and they went under. Oh, Christ, he thought, this is it, but when it had rolled on, still managed to find his feet, his right hand holding the signalling ball high, although by now, the water was up to his chin.

It was Teusen who caught sight of the light to port and ran to the bridge instantly. Three minutes later, the E-boat slid out of the darkness and someone shone a torch down on the two men. A net was thrown over, four seamen clambered down and willing hands reached for Ritter Neumann.

"Watch him," Devlin urged. "He's in a bad way."

When he went over the rail himself a couple of moments later and collapsed, it was Koenig who knelt beside him with a blanket. "Mr. Devlin, drink some of this." He passed him a bottle.

"Cead mile Failte," Devlin said.

Koenig leaned close. "I'm sorry, I don't understand."

"And how would you? It's Irish, the language of kings. I simply said, a hundred thousand welcomes."

Koenig smiled through the darkness. "I am glad to see you, Mr. Devlin. A miracle."

"The only one you're likely to get this night."

"You are certain?"

"As the coffin lid closing."

Koenig stood up. "Then we will go now. Please excuse me."

A moment later, the E-boat swung round and surged forward. Devlin got the cork out of the bottle and sniffed at the contents. Rum. Not one of his favourites, but he swallowed deep and huddled against the stern rail looking back towards the land.

In her bedroom at the farm, Molly sat up suddenly, then moved across the room and drew the curtains. She threw the windows open and leaned out into the rain, a tremendous feeling of elation, of release filling her and at that very moment, the E-boat moved from behind the Point and turned out towards the open sea.

In his office at Prinz Albrechtstrasse, Himmler worked at his eternal files in the light of the desk lamp. There was a knock at the door and Rossman entered.

"Well?" Himmler said.

"I'm sorry to disturb you, Herr Reichsführer, but we've had a signal from Landsvoort. The Eagle is blown."

Himmler showed no emotion whatsoever. He laid down his pen carefully and held out his hand. "Let me see." Rossman gave him the signal and Himmler read it through. After a while, he looked up. "I have an errand for you."

"Herr Reichsführer."

"Take two of your most trusted men. Fly to Landsvoort at once and arrest Colonel Radl. I will see that you have all necessary authorization before you leave."

"Of course, Herr Reichsführer. And the charge?"

"Treason against the state. That should do for a start. Report to me as soon as you get back." Himmler picked up his pen and started to write again and Rossman withdrew.

Just before nine o'clock Corporal George Watson of the Military Police ran his motorcycle into the side of the road a couple of miles south from Meltham House and pushed it up on its stand. Having ridden from Norwich with almost torrential rain the whole way, he was soaked to the skin, in spite of his long dispatch rider's coat—bitterly cold and very hungry. He was also lost.

He opened his map case in the light of his headlamp and leaned down to check it. A slight movement to his right made him look up. A man in a trenchcoat was standing there. "Hello," he said. "Lost, are you?"

"I'm trying to find Meltham House," Watson told him. "All the way from Norwich in this bloody rain. These country districts all look the same with the damned signposts missing."

"Here, let me show you," Steiner said.

Watson leaned down to examine the map again in the light from the headlamp, the Mauser rose and fell across the back of his neck. He lay in a puddle of water and Steiner pulled his dispatch case over his head and examined the contents quickly. There was only one letter, heavily sealed and marked *Urgent*. It was addressed to Colonel William Corcoran, Meltham House.

Steiner got hold of Watson under the armpits and dragged him into the shadows. When he re-appeared a few moments later, he was wearing the dispatch rider's long raincoat, helmet and goggles and leather gauntlets. He pulled the sling of the dispatch case over his head, pushed the motorcycle off its stand, kicked the engine into life and rode away.

At the side of the road they had a spotlight set up and as the Scammel recovery truck's winch started to revolve, the Morris came up out of the marsh on to the bank. Garvey stayed up on the road, waiting.

The corporal in charge had the door open. He peered inside and looked up. "There's nothing here."

"What in the hell are you talking about?" Garvey demanded and he moved down through the trees quickly.

He looked inside the Morris, but the corporal was right. Lots of stinking mud, a certain amount of water, but no Steiner. "Oh, my God," Garvey said as the full implication hit him and he turned, scrambled up the bank, and grabbed for the mike on his jeep's radio.

Steiner turned in at the gate of Meltham House, which was closed, and halted. The Ranger on the other side shone a torch on him and called, "Sergeant of the Guard."

Sergeant Thomas came out of the lodge and approached the gate. Steiner sat there, anonymous in helmet and goggles. "What is it?" Thomas demanded.

Steiner opened his dispatch case, took out the letter and held it close to the bars. "Dispatch from Norwich for Colonel Corcoran."

Thomas nodded, the Ranger next to him unbolted the gate. "Straight up to the front of the house. One of the sentries will take you in."

Steiner rode up the drive and turned away from the front door, following a branch that finally brought him to the motor pool at the rear of the building. He stopped beside a parked truck, switched off and pushed the motorcycle up on its stand, then turned and followed the path round towards the garden. When he'd gone a few yards, he stepped into the shelter of the rhododendrons.

He removed the crash helmet, the raincoat and gauntlets, took his *Schiff* from inside his *Fliegerbluse* and put it on. He adjusted the Knight's Cross at his throat and moved off, the Mauser ready.

He paused on the edge of a sunken garden below the terrace to get his bearings. The blackout wasn't too good, chinks of light showing at several windows. He took a step forward and someone said, "That you, Bleeker?"

Steiner grunted. A dim shape moved forward. The Mauser coughed in his right hand, there was a startled gasp as the Ranger slumped to the ground. In the same moment, a curtain was pulled back and light fell across the terrace above.

When Steiner looked up, he saw the Prime Minister standing at the balustrade smoking a cigar.

When Corcoran came out of the Prime Minister's room he found Kane waiting. "How is he?" Kane asked.

"Fine. Just gone out on the terrace for a last cigar and then he's going to bed."

They moved into the hall. "He probably wouldn't sleep too well if he heard my news, so I'll keep it till morning,'' Kane told him. ''They hauled that Morris out of the marsh and no Steiner.''

Corcoran said, ''Are you suggesting he got away? How do you know he isn't still down there? He might have been thrown out or something.''

''It's possible,'' Kane said. ''But I'm doubling the guard anyway.''

The front door opened and Sergeant Thomas came in. He unbuttoned his coat to shake the rain from it. ''You wanted me, Major?''

''Yes,'' Kane said. ''When they got the car out, Steiner was missing. We're taking no chances and doubling the guard. Nothing to report from the gate?''

''Not a damn thing since the recovery Scammel went out. Only that military policeman from Norwich with the dispatch for Colonel Corcoran.''

Corcoran stared at him, frowning. ''That's the first I've heard of it. When was this?''

''Maybe ten minutes ago, sir.''

''Oh, my God!'' Kane said. ''He's here! The bastard's here!'' And he turned, tugging at the Colt automatic in the holster at his waist and ran for the library door.

Steiner went up the steps to the terrace slowly. The scent of the good Havana cigar perfumed the night. As he put his foot on the top step it crunched in gravel. The Prime Minister turned sharply and looked at him.

He removed the cigar from his mouth, that implacable face showing no kind of reaction, and said, ''Oberstleutnant Kurt Steiner of the Fallschirmjäger, I presume?''

''Mr. Churchill.'' Steiner hesitated. ''I regret this, but I must do my duty, sir.''

''Then what are you waiting for?'' the Prime Minister said calmly.

Steiner raised the Mauser, the curtains at the French windows billowed and Harry Kane stumbled through, firing wildly. His first bullet hit Steiner in the right shoulder spinning him round, the second caught him in the heart, killing him instantly, pushing him back over the balustrade.

Corcoran arrived on the terrace a moment later, revolver in hand, and below in the sunken garden, Rangers appeared from the darkness on the run, to pause and stand in a semi-circle. Steiner lay in the pool of light from the open window, the Knight's Cross at his throat, the Mauser still gripped firmly in his right hand.

''Strange,'' the Prime Minister said. ''With his finger on the trigger, he hesitated. I wonder why?''

"Perhaps that was his American half speaking, sir?" Harry Kane said.

The Prime Minister had the final word. "Whatever else may be said, he was a fine soldier and a brave man. See to him, Major." He turned and went back inside.

20

❧

IT WAS ALMOST A YEAR to the day since I had made that astonishing discovery in the churchyard at St. Mary and All the Saints when I returned to Studley Constable, this time by direct invitation of Father Philip Vereker. I was admitted by a young priest with an Irish accent.

Vereker was sitting in a wing-back chair in front of a huge fire in the study, a rug about his knees, a dying man if ever I've seen one. The skin seemed to have shrunk on his face, exposing every bone and the eyes were full of pain. "It was good of you to come."

"I'm sorry to see you so ill," I said.

"I have a cancer of the stomach. Nothing to be done. The Bishop has been very good in allowing me to end it here, arranging for Father Damian to assist with parish duties, but that isn't why I sent for you. I hear you've had a busy year."

"I don't understand," I said. "When I was here before you wouldn't say a word. Drove me out, in fact."

"It's really very simple. For years I've only known half the story myself. I suddenly discover that I have an insatiable curiosity to know the rest before it is too late."

So I told him because there didn't really seem any reason why I shouldn't. By the time I had finished, the shadows were falling across the grass outside and the room was half in darkness.

"Remarkable," he said. "How on earth did you find it all out?"

"Not from any official source, believe me. Just from talking to people, those who are still alive and who were willing to talk. The biggest stroke of luck was in being privileged to read a very comprehensive diary kept by the man responsible for the organization of the whole thing, Colonel Max Radl. His widow is still alive in Bavaria. What I'd like to know now is what happened here afterwards."

"There was a complete security clampdown. Every single villager involved was interviewed by the intelligence and security people. The Official Secrets Act invoked. Not that it was really necessary. These are a peculiar people. Drawing together in adversity, hostile to strangers, as you have seen. They looked upon it as their business and no one else's."

"And there was Seymour."

"Exactly. Did you know that he was killed last February?"

"No."

"Driving back from Holt one night drunk. He ran his van off the coast road into the marsh and was drowned."

"What happened to him after the other business?"

"He was quietly certified. Spent eighteen years in an institution before he managed to obtain his release when the mental health laws were relaxed."

"But how could people stand having him around?"

"He was related by blood to at least half the families in the district. George Wilde's wife, Betty, was his sister."

"Good God," I said. "I didn't realize."

"In a sense, the silence of the years was also a kind of protection for Seymour."

"There is another possibility," I said. "That the terrible thing he did that night was seen as a reflection on all of them. Something to hide rather than reveal."

"That, too."

"And the tombstone?"

"The military engineers who were sent here to clean up the village, repair damage and so on, placed all the bodies in a mass grave in the churchyard. Unmarked, of course, and we were told it was to remain so."

"But you thought differently?"

"Not just me. All of us. Wartime propaganda was a pernicious thing then, however necessary. Every war picture we saw at the cinema, every book we read, every newspaper, portrayed the average German soldier as a ruthless and savage barbarian, but these men were not like that. Graham Wilde is alive today, Susan Turner married with three children because one of Steiner's men gave his life to save them. And at the church, remember, he let the people go."

"So, a secret monument was decided on?"

"That's right. It was easy enough to arrange. Old Ted Turner was a retired monumental mason. It was laid, dedicated by me at a private service, then concealed from the casual observer as you know. The man Preston is down there, too, but was not included on the monument."

"And you all agreed with this?"

He managed one of his rare, wintry smiles. "As some kind of personal penance if you like. Dancing on his grave was the term Steiner used and he was right. I hated him that day. Could have killed him myself.''

"Why?'' I said. ''Because it was a German bullet that crippled you?''

"So I pretended until the day I got down on my knees and asked God to help me face the truth.''

"Joanna Grey?'' I said gently.

His face was completely in shadow. I found it impossible to see his expression. ''I am more used to hearing confessions than making them, but yes, you are right. I worshipped Joanna Grey. Oh, not in any silly superficial sexy way. To me she was the most wonderful woman I'd ever known. I can't even begin to describe the shock I experienced on discovering her true role.''

"So in a sense, you blamed Steiner?''

"I think that was the psychology of it.'' He sighed. ''So long ago. How old were you in nineteen-forty-three? Twelve, thirteen? Can you remember what it was like?''

"Not really—not in the way you mean.''

"People were tired because the war seemed to have gone on for ever. Can you possibly imagine the terrible blow to national morale if the story of Steiner and his men and what took place here, had got out? That German paratroopers could land in England and come within an ace of snatching the Prime Minister himself?''

"Could come as close as the pull of a finger on the trigger to blowing his head off.''

He nodded. ''Do you still intend to publish?''

"I don't see why not.''

"It didn't happen, you know. No stone anymore and who is to say it ever existed? And have you found one single official document to substantiate any of it?''

"Not really,'' I said cheerfully. ''But I've spoken to a lot of people and together they've told me what adds up to a pretty convincing story.''

"It could have been.'' He smiled faintly. ''If you hadn't missed out on one very important point.''

"And what would that be?''

"Look up any one of two dozen history books on the last war and check what Winston Churchill was doing during the weekend in question. But perhaps that was too simple, too obvious.''

"All right,'' I said. ''You tell me.''

"Getting ready to leave in HMS *Renown* for the Teheran conference. Called at Algiers on the way, where he invested Generals Eisenhower and Alexander with special versions of the North Africa ribbon and arrived at Malta, as I remember, on the seventeenth November.''

It was suddenly very quiet. I said, ''Who was he?''

"His name was George Howard Foster, known in the profession as the Great Foster.''

"The profession?"

"The stage, Mr. Higgins. Foster was a music hall act, an impressionist. The war was his salvation."

"How was that?"

"He not only did a more than passable imitation of the Prime Minister. He even looked like him. After Dunkirk, he started doing a special act, a kind of grand finale to the show. *I have nothing to offer but blood sweat and tears. We will fight them on the beaches.* The audiences loved it."

"And Intelligence pulled him in?"

"On special occasions. If you intend to send the Prime Minister to sea at the height of the U-boat peril, it's useful to have him publicly appearing elsewhere." He smiled. "He gave the performance of his life that night. They all believed it was him, of course. Only Corcoran knew the truth."

"All right," I said. "Where's Foster now?"

"Killed, along with a hundred and eight other people when a flying bomb hit a little theatre in Islington in February, nineteen-forty-four. So you see, it's all been for nothing. It never happened. Much better for all concerned."

He went into a bout of coughing that racked his entire body. The door opened and the nun entered. She leaned over him and whispered. He said, "I'm sorry, it's been a long afternoon. I think I should rest. Thank you for coming and filling in the gaps."

He started to cough again so I left as quickly as I could and was ushered politely to the door by young Father Damian. On the step I gave him my card. "If he gets worse." I hesitated. "You know what I mean? I'd appreciate hearing from you."

I lit a cigarette and leaned on the flint wall of the churchyard beside the lychgate. I would check the facts, of course, but Vereker was telling the truth, I knew that beyond any shadow of a doubt and did it really change anything? I looked towards the porch where Steiner had stood that evening so long ago in confrontation with Harry Kane, thought of him on the terrace at Meltham House, the final, and for him, fatal hesitation. *And even if he had pulled that trigger it would still all have been for nothing.*

There's irony for you, as Devlin would have said. I could almost hear his laughter. Ah, well, in the final analysis there was nothing I could find to say that would be any improvement on the words of a man who had played his own part so well on that fatal night.

Whatever else may be said, he was a fine soldier and a brave man. Let it end there. I turned and walked away through the rain.

THE
EAGLE HAS
FLOWN

For my mother
Henrietta Higgins Bell

Prologue

AT ONE O'CLOCK ON THE morning of Saturday, November 6, 1943, Heinrich Himmler, Reichsführer of the SS and Chief of State Police, received a simple message: *The Eagle has landed.* A small force of German paratroopers under the command of Oberstleutnant Kurt Steiner, aided by IRA gunman Liam Devlin, were at that moment safely in England and poised to snatch the British Prime Minister, Winston Churchill, from the Norfolk country house where he was spending a quiet weekend near the sea. By the end of the day—thanks to a bloody confrontation in the village of Studley Constable between American Rangers and the Germans—the mission was a failure, Liam Devlin apparently the only survivor. As for Kurt Steiner . . .

LONDON
BELFAST
1975

1

THERE WAS AN ANGEL OF Death on top of an ornate mausoleum in one corner, arms extended. I remember that well because someone was practicing the organ and light drifted across the churchyard in colored bands through stained-glass windows. The church wasn't particularly old, built on a high tide of Victorian prosperity like the tall houses surrounding it. St. Martin's Square. A good address once. Now just a shabby backwater in Belsize Park, but a nice, quiet area where a woman alone might walk down to the corner shop at midnight in safety and people minded their own business.

The flat at number thirteen was on the ground floor. My agent had borrowed it for me from a cousin who had gone to New York for six months. It was old-fashioned and comfortable and suited me fine. I was on the downhill slope of a new novel and needed to visit the reading room at the British Museum most days.

But that November evening, the evening it all started, it was raining heavily, and just after six I passed through the iron gates and followed the path through the forest of Gothic monuments and gravestones. In spite of my umbrella, the shoulders of my trench coat were soaked, not that it bothered me. I've always liked the rain, the city at night, wet streets stretching into winter darkness, a peculiar feeling of freedom that it contains. And things had gone well that day with the work; the end was very definitely in sight.

The Angel of Death was closer now shadowed in the half-light from the church, the two marble attendants on guard at the mausoleum's bronze doors, everything as usual, except that tonight I could have sworn there was a third figure and that it moved out of the darkness toward me.

For a moment I knew genuine fear, and then, as it came into the light, I saw a young woman, quite small and wearing a black beret and soaked raincoat. She had a briefcase in one hand. The face was pale, the eyes dark and somehow anxious.

"Mr. Higgins? You are Jack Higgins, aren't you?"

She was American, that much was obvious. I took a deep breath to steady my nerves. "That's right. What can I do for you?"

"I must talk to you, Mr. Higgins. Is there somewhere we could go?"

I hesitated, reluctant for all sorts of obvious reasons to take this any further, and yet there was something quite out of the ordinary about her. Something not to be resisted.

I said, "My flat's just over the square there."

"I know," she said. I still hesitated, and she added, "You won't regret it, believe me. I've information of vital importance to you."

"About what?" I asked.

"What really happened afterward at Studley Constable. Oh, lots of things you don't know."

Which was enough. I took her arm and said, "Right, let's get in out of this damn rain before you catch your death, and you can tell me what the hell this is all about."

The house interior had changed very little, certainly not in my flat, where the tenant had stayed with a late Victorian decor, lots of mahogany furniture, red velvet curtains at the bow window and a sort of Chinese wallpaper in gold and green, heavily patterned with birds. Except for the central heating radiators, the only other concession to modern living was the kind of gas fire which made it seem as if logs burned brightly in a stainless steel basket.

"That's nice," she said and turned to face me, even smaller than I had thought. She held out her right hand awkwardly, still clutching the briefcase in the other. "Cohen," she said. "Ruth Cohen."

I said, "Let's have that coat. I'll put it in front of one of the radiators."

"Thank you." She fumbled at her belt awkwardly with one hand, and I laughed and took the briefcase from her.

"Here, let me." As I put it down on the table, I saw that her initials were etched on the flap in black. The only difference was that it said Ph.D. at the end of it.

"Ph.D.?" I said.

She smiled slightly as she struggled out of the coat. "Harvard, modern history."

"That's interesting," I said. "I'll make some tea, or would you prefer coffee?"

She smiled again. "Six months post doc at London University, Mr. Higgins. I'd very definitely prefer your tea."

I went through to the kitchen and put on the kettle and made a tray ready. I lit a cigarette as I waited and turned to find her leaning on the doorway, arms folded.

"Your thesis," I said. "For your doctorate. What was the subject?"

"Certain aspects of the Third Reich in the Second World War."

"Interesting. Cohen—are you Jewish?" I turned to make the tea.

"My father was a German Jew. He survived Auschwitz and made it to the U.S., but died the year after I was born.''

I could think of no more than the usual inadequate response. ''I'm sorry.''

She stared at me blankly for a moment, then turned and went back to the sitting room. I followed with the tray, placed it on a small coffee table by the fire, and we sat opposite each other in wingback chairs.

''Which explains your interest in the Third Reich,'' I said as I poured the tea.

She frowned and took the cup of tea I handed her. ''I'm just a historian. No ax to grind. My particular obsession is with the Abwehr, German Military Intelligence. Why they were so good and why they were so bad at the same time.''

''Admiral Wilhelm Canaris and his merry men?'' I shrugged. ''I'd say his heart was never in it, but as the SS hanged him at Flossenburg concentration camp in April forty-five, we'll never know.''

''Which brings me to you,'' she said. ''And your book *The Eagle Has Landed*.''

''A novel, Dr. Cohen.'' I said. ''Pure speculation.''

''At least fifty percent of which is documented historical fact; you claim that yourself at the beginning of the book.''

She leaned forward, hands clenched on her knees, a kind of fierceness there. I said softly, ''All right, so what exactly are you getting at?''

''Remember how you found out about the affair in the first place?'' she said. ''The thing that started you off?''

''Of course,'' I said. ''The tombstone to Steiner and his men that the villagers of Studley Constable had hidden under another tombstone in the churchyard.''

''Remember what it said?''

''*Hier ruhen Oberstleutnant Kurt Steiner und thirteen Deutsche Fallschirmjäger gefallen am six November nineteen forty-three.*''

''Exactly,'' she said. '' 'Here lies Lieutenant Colonel Kurt Steiner and thirteen German paratroopers killed in action on six November nineteen forty-three.' ''

''So what's your point?''

''Thirteen plus one makes fourteen, only there aren't fourteen bodies in that grave. There are only thirteen.''

I stared at her incredulously. ''How in the hell do you make that out?''

''Because Kurt Steiner didn't die that night on the terrace at Meltham House, Mr. Higgins.'' She reached for the briefcase, had it open in a second and produced a brown manila folder. ''And I have the proof right here.''

Which very definitely called for Bushmills whiskey. I poured one and said, ''All right, do I get to see it?''

''Of course, that's why I'm here, but first let me explain. Any study of Abwehr intelligence affairs during the Second World War constantly refers to the work of SOE, the Special Operations Executive set up by British intelligence in 1940 on Churchill's instructions to coordinate resistance and the underground movement in Europe.''

"Set Europe ablaze, that's what the old man ordered,'' I said.

"I was fascinated to discover that a number of Americans worked for SOE before America came into the war. I thought there might be a book in it. I arranged to come over here to do the research, and a name that came up again and again was Munro—Brigadier Dougal Munro. Before the war he was an archeologist at Oxford. At SOE he was head of Section D. What was commonly known as the dirty-tricks department.''

"I had heard of him,'' I said.

"I did most of my research at the Public Records Office. As you know, few files dealing with intelligence matters are immediately available. Some are on a twenty-five-year hold, some fifty—''

"And exceptionally sensitive material, a hundred years,'' I said.

"That's what I have here.'' She held up the folder. "A hundred-year hold file concerning Dougal Munro, Kurt Steiner, Liam Devlin and others. Quite a story, believe me.''

She passed it across, and I held it on my knees without opening it. "How on earth did you come by this?''

"I checked out some files concerning Munro yesterday. There was a young clerk on duty on his own. Got careless, I guess. I found the file sandwiched in between two others, sealed, of course. You have to do your research on the premises at the Records Office, but since it wasn't on the booking-out form, I slipped it into my briefcase.''

"A criminal offense under the Defence of the Realm Act,'' I told her.

"I know. I opened the seals as carefully as I could and read the file. It's only a thirty-page resumé of certain events—certain astonishing events.''

"And then?''

"I photocopied it.''

"The wonders of modern technology allow them to tell when that's been done.''

"I know. Anyway, I resealed the file and took it back this morning.''

"And how did you manage to return it?'' I asked.

"Checked out the same file yesterday. Took the Munro file back to the desk and told the duty clerk there'd been an error.''

"Did he believe you?''

"I suppose so. I mean, why wouldn't he?''

"The same clerk?''

"No—an older man.''

I sat there thinking about it, feeling decidedly uneasy. Finally I said, "Why don't you make us some fresh tea while I have a go at this?''

"All right."

She took the tray and went out. I hesitated, then opened the file and started to read.

I wasn't even aware that she was there, so gripped was I by the events recorded in that file. When I was finished, I closed it and looked up. She was back in the other chair watching me, a curiously intent look on her face.

I said, "I can understand the hundred-year hold. The powers that be wouldn't want this to come out, not even now."

"That's what I thought."

"Can I hang on to it for a while?"

She hesitated, then nodded. "Till tomorrow if you like. I'm going back to the States on the evening flight. Pan Am."

"A sudden decision?"

She went and got her raincoat. "That's right. I've decided I'd rather be back in my own country."

"Worried?" I asked.

"I'm probably being hypersensitive, but sure. I'll pick the file up tomorrow afternoon. Say three o'clock on my way to Heathrow?"

"Fine." I put the file down on top of my coffee table.

The clock on the mantelpiece chimed the half-hour, seven-thirty, as I walked her to the door. I opened it and we stood for a moment, rain driving down hard.

"Of course there is someone who could confirm the truth of that file," she said. "Liam Devlin. You said in your book he was still around, operating with the Provisional IRA in Ireland."

"Last I heard," I said. "Sixty-seven he'll be now, but lively with it."

"Well, then." She smiled again. "I'll see you tomorrow afternoon."

She went down the steps and walked away through the rain, vanishing in the early evening mist at the end of the street.

I sat by the fire and read the file twice, then I went back into the kitchen, made myself some more tea and a chicken sandwich and sat at the table eating the sandwich and thinking about things.

Extraordinary how events coming right out of the blue can change everything. It had happened to me once before, the discovery of that hidden memorial to Steiner and his men in the churchyard at Studley Constable. I'd been researching an article for a historical magazine. Instead, I'd found something unlooked-for that had changed the course of my entire life. Produced a book which had gone around the world from New York to Moscow, made me rich. Now this—Ruth Cohen and her stolen file, and I was filled with the same strange, tingling excitement.

I needed to come down. Get things in perspective. So I went to have a shower, took my time over it, shaved and dressed again. It was only eight-thirty, and it didn't seem likely that I'd go to bed early, if I went at all.

I didn't have any more whiskey. I needed to think, so I made even more tea and settled on the chair by the fire, lit a cigarette and started to work my way through the file again.

The doorbell rang, shaking me from my reverie. I glanced at the clock. It was just before nine. The bell rang again insistently, and I replaced the file in the folder, put it on the coffee table and went out into the hall. It occurred to me that it might be Ruth Cohen again, but I couldn't have been more wrong, for when I opened the door I found a young police constable standing there, his navy-blue mac wet with rain.

"Mr. Higgins?" He looked at a piece of paper in his left hand. "Mr. Jack Higgins?"

Strange the certainty of bad news so that we don't even need to be told. "Yes," I said.

He stepped into the hall. "Sorry to trouble you, sir, but I'm making an inquiry relevant to a Miss Ruth Cohen. Would you be a friend of hers, sir?"

"Not exactly," I said. "Is there a problem?"

"I'm afraid the young lady's dead, sir. Hit-and-run accident at the back of the British Museum an hour ago."

"My God!" I whispered.

"The thing is, sir, we found your name and address on a card in her handbag."

It was so difficult to take in. She'd stood there at the door where he was, such a short time before. He was no more than twenty-one or -two. Still young enough to feel concern and he put a hand on my arm.

"Are you all right, sir?"

I said, "Rather shocked, that's all." I took a deep breath. "What is it you want of me?"

"It seems the young lady was at London University. We've checked the student accommodation she was using. No one there, with it being the weekend. It's a question of official identification. For the coroner's office."

"And you'd like me to do it?"

"If you wouldn't mind, sir. It's not far. She's at Kensington Mortuary."

I took another deep breath to steady myself. "All right. Just let me get my raincoat."

The mortuary was a depressing-looking building in a side street, more like a warehouse than anything else. When we went into the foyer, there was a uniformed porter on duty at the desk and a small dark man in his early fifties standing at the window looking out at the rain, a cigarette dangling from the corner of his mouth. He wore a trilby hat and trench coat.

He turned to meet me, hands in pockets. "Mr. Higgins, is it?"

"Yes," I said.

He didn't take his hands out of his pockets and coughed, ash falling from the tip of his cigarette onto his coat. "Detective Chief Superintendent Fox. An unfortunate business, sir."

"Yes," I said.

"This young lady, Ruth Cohen, was she a friend of yours?"

"No," I said. "I only met her for the first time earlier this evening."

"Your name and address were in her handbag." Before I could reply, he carried on. "Anyway, best to get it over with. If you'd come this way."

The room they took me into was walled with white tiles and bright fluorescent lighting. There was a line of operating tables. The body was on the end one covered with a white rubber sheet. Ruth Cohen looked very calm, eyes closed, but her head was enclosed in a plastic hood and blood seeped through.

"Would you formally identify the deceased as Ruth Cohen, sir?" the constable asked.

I nodded. "Yes, that's her." And he replaced the sheet.

When I turned, Fox was sitting on the end of the table in the corner lighting another cigarette. "As I said, we found your name in her handbag."

It was then, as if something had gone click in my head, that I came back to reality. Hit and run—a serious offense, but when had it merited the attention of a detective chief superintendent, and wasn't there something about Fox with his saturnine face and dark watchful eyes? This was no ordinary policeman. I smelled Special Branch.

It always pays to stick as closely to the truth as possible, I found that out a long time ago. I said, "She told me she was over from Boston, working at London University, researching a book."

"About what, sir?"

Which confirmed my suspicions instantly. "Something to do with the Second World War, Superintendent, which happens to be an area I've written about myself."

"I see. She was looking for help, advice, that sort of thing?"

Which was when I lied totally. "Not at all. Hardly needed it. A Ph.D., I believe. The fact is, Superintendent, I wrote a rather successful book set during the Second World War. She simply wanted to meet me. As I understood it, she was flying back to the States tomorrow.''

The contents of her handbag and briefcase were on the table beside him, the Pan Am ticket conspicuous. He picked it up. "So it would appear.''

"Can I go now?''

"Of course. The constable will run you home.''

We went out into the foyer and paused at the door. He coughed as he lit another cigarette. "Damn rain. I suppose the driver of that car skidded. An accident really, but then he shouldn't have driven away. We can't have that, can we?''

"Goodnight, Superintendent,'' I told him and went down the steps to the police car.

I'd left the light on in the hall. When I went in, I went into the kitchen without taking my coat off, put the kettle on and then went into the living room. I poured a Bushmills and turned toward the fire. It was then that I saw that the folder I'd left on the coffee table was gone. For a wild moment I thought I'd made a mistake, had put it elsewhere, but that was nonsense of course.

I put the glass of whiskey down and lit a cigarette, thinking about it. The mysterious Fox—I was more certain than ever that he was Special Branch now—that wretched young woman lying there in the mortuary, and I remembered my unease when she'd told me how she had returned that file at the Records Office. I thought of her walking along the pavement and crossing that street in the rain at the back of the British Museum, and then the car. A wet night and a skidding car, as Fox had said. It could have been an accident, but I knew that was hardly likely, not with the file missing. Which raised the problem of my own continued existence.

Time to move on for a while, but where? And then I remembered what she had said. There was one person still left who could confirm the story in that file. I packed an overnight bag and went and checked the street through a chink in the curtain. Cars parked everywhere, so it was impossible to see if I was being watched.

I left by the kitchen door at the rear of the house walked cautiously up the back alley and quickly worked my way through a maze of quiet back streets thinking about it. It had to be a security matter, of course. Some anonymous little department at D15 that took care of people who got out of line, but would that necessarily mean they'd have a go at me? After all, the girl was dead, the file back in the Records Office, the only copy recovered. What could I say that could be proved or in any way be believed? On the other hand, I had to prove it to my own satisfaction, and I hailed a cab on the next corner.

The Green Man, in Kilburn, an area of London popular with the Irish, featured an impressive painting of an Irish tinker over the door which indicated the kind of custom the place enjoyed. The bar was full. I could see that through the saloon window, and I went around to the yard at the rear. The curtains were drawn, and Sean Riley sat at a crowded desk doing his accounts. He was a small man with cropped white hair, active for his age, which I knew was seventy-two. He owned The Green Man, but more importantly was an organizer for Sinn Fein, the political wing of the IRA, in London. I knocked at the window, he got up and moved to peer out. He turned and moved away. A moment later the door opened.

"Mr. Higgins. What brings you here?"

"I won't come in, Sean. I'm on my way to Heathrow."

"Is that a fact. A holiday in the sun, is it?"

"Not exactly. Belfast. I'll probably miss the last shuttle, but I'll be on the breakfast plane. Get word to Liam Devlin. Tell him I'll be staying at the Europa Hotel and I must see him."

"Jesus, Mr. Higgins, and how would I be knowing such a desperate fella as that?"

Through the door I could hear the music from the bar. They were singing "Guns of the IRA." "Don't argue, Sean, just do it," I said. "It's important."

I knew he would, of course, and turned away without another word. A couple of minutes later I hailed a cab and was on my way to Heathrow

⌬

The Europa Hotel in Belfast was legendary among newspaper men from all over the world. It had survived numerous bombing attacks by the IRA and stood in Great Victoria Street next to the railway station. I stayed in my room on the eighth floor for most of the day, just waiting. Things seemed quiet enough, but it was an uneasy calm, and in the late afternoon there was a crump of a bomb; and when I looked out of the window, I saw a black pall of smoke in the distance.

Just after six, with darkness falling, I decided to go down to the bar for a drink, was pulling on my jacket when the phone rang. A voice said, "Mr. Higgins? Reception here, sir. Your taxi's waiting."

It was a black cab, the London variety, and the driver was a middle-aged woman, a pleasant-faced lady who looked like your favorite aunt. I pulled back the glass panel between us and gave her the ritual Belfast greeting: "Goodnight to you."

"And you."

"Not often I see a lady cab driver, not in London anyway."

"A terrible place that. What would you expect? You sit quiet now like a good gentleman and enjoy the trip."

She closed the panel with one hand. The journey took no more than ten minutes. We passed along the Falls Road, a Catholic area I remembered well from boyhood, and turned into a warren of mean side streets, finally stopping outside a church. She opened the glass panel.

"The first confessional box on the right as you go in."

"If you say so."

I got out and she drove away instantly. The board said *Church of the Holy Name*, and it was in surprisingly good condition, the times of Mass and Confession listed in gold paint. I opened the door at the top of the steps and went in. It was not too large and dimly lit, candles flickering down at the altar, the Virgin in a chapel to one side. Instinctively, I dipped my fingers in the holy water and crossed myself, remembering the Catholic aunt in South Armagh who'd raised me for a while as a child and had anguished over my black little Protestant soul.

The confessional boxes stood to one side. No one waited, which was hardly surprising, for according to the board outside I was an hour early. I went in the first on the right and closed the door. I sat there in the darkness for a moment and then the grille slid open.

"Yes?" a voice asked softly.

I answered automatically. "Bless me, Father, for I have sinned."

"You certainly have, my old son." The light was switched on in the other box, and Liam Devlin smiled through at me.

He looked remarkably well. In fact, rather better than he'd seemed the last time I'd seen him. Sixty-seven, but as I'd said to Ruth Cohen, lively with it. A small man with enormous vitality, hair as black as ever, and vivid blue eyes. There was the scar of an old bullet wound on the left side of his forehead, and a slight ironic smile was permanently in place. He wore a priest's cassock and clerical collar and seemed perfectly at home in the sacristy at the back of the church to which he'd taken me.

"You're looking well, son. All that success and money." He grinned. "We'll drink to it. There's a bottle here surely."

He opened a cupboard and found a bottle of Bushmills and two glasses. "And what would the usual occupant think of all this?" I asked.

"Father Murphy?" He splashed whiskey into the glasses. "Heart of corn, that one. Out doing good, as usual."

"He looks the other way, then?"

"Something like that." He raised his glass. "To you, my old son."

"And you, Liam." I toasted him back. "You never cease to amaze me. On the British army's most wanted list for the last five years and you still have the nerve to sit here in the middle of Belfast.''

''Ah, well, a man has to have some fun.'' He took a cigarette from a silver case and offered me one. ''Anyway, to what do I owe the pleasure of this visit?''

''Does the name Dougal Munro mean anything to you?''

His eyes widened in astonishment. ''What in the hell have you come up with now? I haven't heard that old bastard's name mentioned in years.''

''Or Schellenberg?''

''Walter Schellenberg? There was a man for you. General at thirty. Schellenberg—Munro? What is this?''

''And Kurt Steiner,'' I said, ''who, according to everyone, including you, died trying to shoot the fake Churchill on the terrace at Meltham House.''

Devlin swallowed some of his whiskey and smiled amiably. ''I was always the terrible liar. Now, tell me what this is all about.''

So I told him about Ruth Cohen, the file and its contents, everything, and he listened intently without interrupting.

When I was finished, he said, ''Convenient, the girl's death, you were right about that.''

''Which doesn't look very good for me.''

There was an explosion not too far away and, as he went to open the door to the rear yard, the rattle of small-arms fire.

''It sounds like a lively night,'' I said.

''Oh, it will be. Safer off the streets at the moment.''

He closed the door and turned to face me. I said, ''The facts in that file. Were they true?''

''A good story.''

''In outline.''

''Which means you'd like to hear the rest?''

''I need to hear it.''

''Why not.'' He smiled, sat down at a table in the corner and reached for the Bushmills. ''Sure and it'll keep me out of mischief for a while. Now, where would you like me to begin?''

BERLIN

LISBON

LONDON

1943

2

BRIGADIER DOUGAL MUNRO'S FLAT IN Haston Place was only ten minutes' walk from the London headquarters of SOE in Baker Street. As head of Section D, he needed to be on call twenty-four hours a day, and besides the normal phone he had a secure line routed directly to his office. It was this particular phone he answered on that late November evening as he sat by the fire working on some files.

"Carter here, Brigadier. Just back from Norfolk."

"Good," Munro told him. "Call in on your way home and tell me about it."

He put the phone down and went and got himself a malt whisky, a squat, powerful-looking man with white hair who wore steel-rimmed spectacles. Strictly a non-professional, his rank of brigadier was simply for purposes of authority in certain quarters; and at sixty-five, an age when most men faced retirement, even at Oxford, the war had been the saving of him, that was the blunt truth. He was thinking about that when the doorbell rang and he admitted Captain Jack Carter.

"You look frozen, Jack. Help yourself to a drink."

Jack Carter leaned his walking stick against a chair and shrugged off his greatcoat. He was in the uniform of a captain in the Green Howards, the ribbon of the Military Cross on his battledress. His false leg was a legacy of Dunkirk, and he limped noticeably as he went to the drinks cupboard and poured a whisky.

"So, what's the situation at Studley Constable?" Munro asked.

"Back to normal, sir. All the German paratroopers buried in a common grave in the churchyard."

"No marker of course?"

"Not at the moment, but they're a funny lot those villagers. They actually seem to think quite highly of Steiner."

"Yes, well, one of his sergeants was killed saving the lives of two village children who fell into the millrace remember. In fact, that single action was the one thing that blew their cover, caused the failure of the entire operation."

"And he did let the villagers go before the worst of the fighting started," Carter said.

"Exactly. Have you got the file on him?"

Carter got his briefcase and extracted a couple of sheets stapled together. Munro examined them. "Oberstleutnant Kurt Steiner, age twenty-seven. Remarkable record. Crete, North Africa, Stalingrad. Knight's Cross with Oak Leaves."

"I'm always intrigued by his mother, sir. Boston socialite. What they call 'Boston Brahmin.' ''

"All very fine, Jack, but don't forget his father was a German general and a damn good one. Now, what about Steiner? How is he?"

"There seems no reason to doubt a complete recovery. There's an RAF hospital for bomber crews with burn problems just outside Norwich. Rather small. Used to be a nursing home. We have Steiner there under secure guard. The cover story is that he's a downed Luftwaffe pilot. Rather convenient that German paratroopers and Luftwaffe aircrews wear roughly the same uniform."

"And his wounds?"

"He was damn lucky there, sir. One round hit him in the right shoulder, at the rear. The second was a heart shot, but it turned on the breastbone. The surgeon doesn't think it will take long, especially as he's in remarkable physical shape."

Munro went and got another small whisky. "Let's go over what we know, Jack. The whole business, the plot to kidnap Churchill, the planning. Everything was done without Admiral Canaris's knowledge?"

"Apparently so, sir, all Himmler's doing. He pressured Max Radl at Abwehr headquarters to plan it all behind the admiral's back. At least that's what our sources in Berlin tell us."

"He knows all about it now, though?" Munro said. "The admiral, I mean."

"Apparently, sir, and not best pleased, not that there's anything he can do about it. Can't exactly go running to the Führer."

"And neither can Himmler," Munro said. "Not when the whole project was mounted without the Führer's knowledge."

"Of course Himmler did give Max Radl a letter of authorization signed by Hitler himself," Carter said.

"*Purporting* to be signed by Hitler, Jack. I bet that was the first thing to go into the fire. No, Himmler won't want to advertise this one."

"And we don't want it on the front of the *Daily Express*, sir. German paratroopers trying to grab the Prime Minister, battling it out with American Rangers in an English country village."

"Yes, it wouldn't exactly help the war effort." Munro looked at the file again. "This IRA chap, Devlin. Quite a character. You say that your information is that he was wounded?"

"That's right, sir. He was in hospital in Holland and simply took off one night. We understand he's in Lisbon."

"Probably hoping to make it to the States in some way. Are we keeping an eye on him? Who's SOE's man in Lisbon?''

"Major Arthur Frear, sir. Military attache at the Embassy. He's been notified,'' Carter told him.

"Good.'' Munro nodded.

"So what do we do about Steiner, sir?''

Munro frowned, thinking about it. "The moment he's fit enough, bring him to London. Do we still house German prisoners of war in the Tower?''

"Only occasionally, sir, transients passing through the small hospital. Not like the early days of the war when most of the captured U-boat people were housed there.''

"And Hess.''

"A special case, sir.''

"All right. We'll have Steiner at the Tower. He can stay in the hospital till we decide on a safe house. Anything else?''

"One development, sir. Steiner's father was involved, as you know, in a series of army plots aimed at assassinating Hitler. The punishment is statutory. Hanging by piano wire, and by the Führer's orders the whole thing is recorded on film.''

"How unpleasant,'' Munro said.

"The thing is, sir, we've received a copy of the film of General Steiner's death. One of our Berlin sources got it out via Sweden. I don't know if you'll want to see it. It's not very nice.''

Munro was angry, got up and paced the room. He paused suddenly, a slight smile on his mouth. "Tell me, Jack, is that little toad Vargas still at the Spanish Embassy?''

"José Vargas, sir, trade attaché. We haven't used him in a while.''

"But German intelligence are convinced he's on their side?''

"The only side Vargas is on is the one with the biggest bankbook, sir. Works through his cousin at the Spanish Embassy in Berlin.''

"Excellent.'' Munro was smiling now. "Tell him to pass the word to Berlin that we have Kurt Steiner. Tell him to say in the Tower of London. Sounds very dramatic. Most important, he makes sure that *both* Canaris and Himmler get the information. That should get them stirred up.''

"What on earth are you playing at, sir?'' Carter asked.

"War, Jack, war. Now have another drink, then get yourself off home to bed. You're going to have a full day tomorrow.''

Near Paderborn in Westphalia in the small town of Wewelsburg was the castle of that name which Heinrich Himmler had taken over from the local council in 1934. His original intention had been to convert it into a school for Reich SS leaders, but by the time the architects and builders had finished and many millions of marks had been spent, he had created a Gothic monstrosity worthy of stage six at MGM, a vast film set of the kind Hollywood was fond of when historical pictures were the vogue. The castle had three wings, towers, a moat, and in the southern wing the Reichsführer had his own apartments and his special pride, the enormous dining hall where selected members of the SS would meet in a kind of court of honor. The whole thing had been influenced by Himmler's obsession with King Arthur and the Knights of the Round Table, with a liberal dose of occultism thrown in.

Ten miles away on that December evening, Walter Schellenberg lit a cigarette in the back of the Mercedes which was speeding him toward the castle. He'd received the order to meet the Reichsführer in Berlin that afternoon. The reason had not been specified. He certainly didn't take it as any evidence of preferment.

He'd been to Wewelsburg on several occasions, had even inspected the castle's plans at SD headquarters, so he knew it well. He also knew that the only men to sit around that table with the Reichsführer were cranks like Himmler himself who believed all the dark-age twaddle about Saxon superiority, or timeservers who had their own chairs with names inscribed on a silver plate. The fact that King Arthur had been Romano-British engaged in a struggle against Saxon invaders made the whole thing even more nonsensical, but Schellenberg had long since ceased to be amused by the excesses of the Third Reich.

In deference to the demands of Wewelsburg, he wore the black dress uniform of the SS, the Iron Cross First Class pinned to the left side of his tunic.

"What a world we live in," he said softly as the car took the road up to the castle, snow falling gently. "I sometimes really do wonder who is running the lunatic asylum."

He smiled as he sat back, looking suddenly quite charming, although the dueling scar on one cheek hinted at a more ruthless side to his nature. It was a relic of student days at the University of Bonn. In spite of a gift for languages, he'd started in the Faculty of Medicine, had then switched to law. But times in Germany in 1933 were hard, even for well-qualified young men just out of university.

The SS were recruiting gifted young scholars for their upper echelons. Like many others, Schellenberg had seen it as employment, not as a political ideal, and his rise had been astonishing. Because of his language ability, Reinhard Heydrich himself had pulled him into the Sicherheitsdienst, the SS security service known as the SD. His main responsibility had always been intelligence work abroad, often a conflict with the Abwehr, although his personal relationship with Canaris was excellent. A series of brilliant intelligence coups had pushed him up the ladder rapidly. By the age of thirty, he was an SS Brigadeführer and Major General of Police.

The really astonishing thing was that Walter Schellenberg didn't consider himself a Nazi, looked on the Third Reich as a sorry charade, its main protagonists actors of a very low order indeed. There were Jews who owed their survival to him, intended victims of the concentration camps rerouted to Sweden and safety. A dangerous game, a sop to his conscience, he told himself, and he had his enemies. He had survived for one reason only. Himmler needed his brains and his considerable talents, and that was enough.

There was only a powdering of snow in the moat, no water. As the Mercedes crossed the bridge to the gate, he leaned back and said softly, "Too late to get off the roundabout now, Walter, far too late."

Himmler received him in his private sitting room in the south wing. Schellenberg was escorted there by an SS sergeant in dress uniform and found Himmler's personal aide, a Sturmbannführer named Rossman, sitting at a table outside the door, also in dress uniform.

"Major." Schellenberg nodded.

Rossman dismissed the sergeant. "A pleasure to see you, General. He's waiting. The mood isn't good, by the way."

"I'll remember that."

Rossman opened the door and Schellenberg entered a large room with a vaulted ceiling and flagged floor. There were tapestries on the walls and lots of dark oak furniture. A log fire burned on a great stone hearth. The Reichsführer sat at an oak table working his way through a mound of papers. He was not in uniform, unusual for him, wore a tweed suit, white shirt and black tie. The silver pince-nez gave him the air of a rather unpleasant schoolmaster.

Unlike Heydrich. who had always addressed Schellenberg by his Christian name, Himmler was invariably formal. "General Schellenberg." He looked up. "You got here."

There was an implied rebuke, and Schellenberg said, "I left Berlin the moment I received your message, Reichsführer. In what way can I serve you?"

"Operation Eagle, the Churchill affair. I didn't employ you on that business because you had other duties. However, you by now will be familiar with most of the details."

"Of course, Reichsführer."

Himmler abruptly changed the subject. "Schellenberg, I am increasingly concerned at the treasonable activities of many members of the High Command. As you know, some wretched young major was blown up in his car outside the entrance to the Führer's headquarters at Rastenburg last week. Obviously another attempt on our Führer's life."

"I'm afraid so, Reichsführer."

Himmler stood up and put a hand on Schellenberg's shoulder. "You and I, General, are bound by a common brotherhood, the SS. We are sworn to protect the Führer and yet are constantly threatened by this conspiracy of generals."

"There is no direct proof, Reichsführer," Schellenberg said, which was not strictly true.

Himmler said, "General von Stülpnagel, Von Falkenhausen, Stieff, Wagner and others, even your good friend Admiral Wilhelm Canaris, Schellenberg. Would that surprise you?"

Schellenberg tried to stay calm, envisaging the distinct possibility that *he* might be named next. "What can I say, Reichsführer?"

"And Rommel, General, the Desert Fox himself. The people's hero."

"My God!" Schellenberg gasped, mainly because it seemed the right thing to do.

"Proof." Himmler snorted. "I'll have my proof before I'm done. They have a date with the hangman, all of them. But to other things." He returned to the table and sat. "Have you ever had any dealings with an agent named Vargas?" He examined a paper in front of him. "José Vargas."

"I know of him. An Abwehr contact. A commercial attaché at the Spanish Embassy in London. As far as I know, he has only been used occasionally."

"He has a cousin who is also a commercial attaché at the Spanish Embassy here in Berlin. One Juan Rivera." Himmler glanced up. "Am I right?"

"So I understand, Reichsführer. Vargas would use the Spanish diplomatic bag from London. Most messages would reach his cousin here in Berlin within thirty-six hours. Highly illegal, of course."

"And thank God for it," Himmler said. "This Operation Eagle affair. You say you are familiar with the details?"

"I am, Reichsführer," Schellenberg said smoothly.

"There is a problem here, General. Although the idea was suggested by the Führer, it was, how shall I put it, more a flight of fancy than anything else? One couldn't rely on Canaris to do anything about it. I'm afraid that total victory for the Third Reich is low on his list of priorities. That is why I personally put the plan into operation aided by Colonel Radl of the Abwehr, who's had a heart attack, I understand, and is not expected to live."

Schellenberg said cautiously, "So the Führer knows nothing of the affair?"

"My dear Schellenberg, he carries the responsibility for the war, its every aspect, on his own shoulders. It is our duty to lighten that load as much as possible."

"Of course, Reichsführer."

"Operation Eagle, however brilliantly conceived, ended in failure, and who would wish to take failure into the Führer's office and place it on his desk?" Before Schellenberg could reply, he carried on. "Which brings me to this report which has reached me from Vargas in London via his cousin here in Berlin, the man Rivera."

He handed across a signal flimsy and Schellenberg glanced at it. "Incredible!" he said. "Kurt Steiner alive."

"And in the Tower of London." Himmler took the signal back.

"They won't keep him there for very long," Schellenberg said. "It may sound dramatic, but the Tower isn't really suitable to house high-security prisoners longterm. They'll move him to some safe house just as they did with Hess."

"Have you any other opinion in the matter?"

"Only that the British will keep quiet about the fact that he's in their hands."

"Why do you say that?"

"Operation Eagle almost succeeded."

"But Churchill wasn't Churchill," Himmler reminded him. "Our intelligence people discovered that."

"Of course, Reichsführer, but German paratroopers did land on English soil and fought a bloody battle. If the story was publicized, the effect on the British people at this stage of the war would be appalling. The very fact that it's SOE and their Brigadier Munro who are handling the matter is further proof."

"You know the man?"

"Know of him only, Reichsführer. A highly capable intelligence officer."

Himmler said, "My sources indicate that Rivera has also passed this news on to Canaris. How do you think he will react?"

"I've no idea, Reichsführer."

"You can see him when you get back to Berlin. Find out. My opinion is that he will do nothing. He certainly won't go running to the Führer." Himmler examined another sheet in front of him. "I'll never understand men like Steiner. A war hero. Knight's Cross with Oak Leaves, a brilliant soldier, and yet he ruined his career, failure, everything, for the sake of some little Jewish bitch he tried to help in Warsaw. It was only Operation Eagle that saved him and his men from the penal unit they were serving in." He put the sheet down. "The Irishman, of course, is a different matter."

"Devlin, Reichsführer?"

"Yes, a thoroughly obnoxious man. You know what the Irish are like, Schellenberg. Everything a joke."

"I must say that from all reports he seems to know his business."

"I agree, but then he was only in it for the money. Someone was singularly careless to allow him to walk out of that hospital in Holland.''

"I agree, Reichsführer.''

"My reports indicate that he's in Lisbon now,'' Himmler said. He pushed another sheet across. "You'll find the details there. He's trying to get to America, but no money. According to that, he's been working as a barman.''

Schellenberg examined the signal quickly, then said, "What would you like me to do on this matter, Reichsführer?''

"You'll return to Berlin tonight, fly to Lisbon tomorrow. Persuade this rogue Devlin to return with you. I shouldn't think that would prove too difficult. Radl gave him twenty thousand pounds for taking part in Operation Eagle. It was paid into a numbered account in Geneva.'' Himmler smiled thinly. "He'll do anything for money. He's that sort. Offer him the same—more if you have to. I'll authorize payments up to thirty thousand pounds.''

"But for what, Reichsführer?''

"Why, to arrange Steiner's escape, of course. I should have thought that's obvious. The man is a hero of the Reich, a true hero. We can't leave him in British hands.''

Remembering how General Steiner had met his end in the Gestapo cellars at Prinz Albrechtstrasse, it seemed likely to Schellenberg that Himmler might have other reasons. He said calmly, "I take your point, Reichsführer.''

"You know the confidence I repose in you, General,'' Himmler said. "And you've never let me down. I leave the whole matter in your capable hands.'' He passed an envelope across. "You'll find a letter of authorization in there that should take care of all contingencies.''

Schellenberg didn't open it. Instead he said, "You said you wanted me to go to Lisbon tomorrow, Reichsführer. May I remind you it's Christmas Eve?''

"What on earth has that got to do with anything?'' Himmler seemed genuinely surprised. "Speed is of the essence here, Schellenberg, and reminding you of your oath as a member of the SS, I will now tell you why. In approximately four weeks, the Führer will fly to Cherbourg in Normandy. January twenty-first. I shall accompany him. From there we proceed down the coast to a place called Château de Belle-Île. Such strange names the French employ.''

"May I ask the purpose of the visit?''

"The Führer intends to meet with Field Marshal Rommel personally, to confirm his appointment as Commander of Army Group B. This will give him direct responsibility for the Atlantic Wall defenses. The meeting will be concerned with the strategy necessary if our enemies decide to invade next year. The Führer has given to me the honor of organizing the conference and, of course, responsibility for his safety. It will be purely an SS matter. As I've said, Rommel will be there, probably Canaris. The Führer particularly asked for him.''

He started to sort his papers into a neat pile, putting some of them into a briefcase. Schellenberg said, ''But the urgency on the Steiner affair, Reichsführer, I don't understand.''

''I intend to introduce him to the Führer at that meeting, General. A great coup for the SS, his escape and near victory. His presence, of course, will make things rather difficult for Canaris, which will be all to the good.'' He closed the briefcase and his eyes narrowed. ''That is all you need to know.''

Schellenberg, who felt that he was only hanging on to his sanity by his fingernails, said, ''But, Reichsführer, what if Devlin doesn't wish to be persuaded?''

''Then you must take appropriate action. To that end, I have selected a Gestapo man I wish to accompany you to Lisbon as your bodyguard.'' He rang a bell on the desk and Rossman entered. ''Ah, Rossman. Ill see Sturmbannführer Berger now.''

Schellenberg waited, desperate for a cigarette, but aware also of how totally Himmler disapproved of smoking, and then the door opened and Rossman appeared with another man. Something of a surprise, this one. A young man, only twenty-five or -six, with blond hair that was almost white. Good-looking once, but one side of his face had been badly burned. Schellenberg could see where the skin graft stretched tightly.

He held out his hand. ''General Schellenberg. Horst Berger. A pleasure to work with you.''

He smiled, looking with that marred face like the devil himself and Schellenberg said, ''Major.'' He turned to Himmler. ''May I get started, Reichsführer?''

''Of course. Berger will join you in the courtyard. Send Rossman in.'' Schellenberg got the door open and Himmler added, ''One more thing. Canaris is to know nothing. Not Devlin, not our intentions regarding Steiner and for the moment no mention of Chateau de Belle-Île. You understand the importance of this?''

''Of course, Reichsführer.''

Schellenberg told Rossman to go in and walked along the corridor. On the next floor, he found a toilet, slipped in and lit a cigarette, then took the envelope Himmler had given him from his pocket and opened it.

From the Leader and Chancellor of the State
General Schellenberg acts upon my direct and personal orders in a matter of the utmost importance to the Reich. He is answerable only to me. All personnel, military and civil, without distinction of rank, will assist him in any way he sees fit.

ADOLF HITLER

Schellenberg shivered and put it back in the envelope. The signature certainly looked right, he'd seen it often enough, but then it would be easy for Himmler to get the Führer's signature on something, just one document among many. So, Himmler was giving him the same powers as he had given Max Radl for Operation Eagle. But why? Why was it so important to get Steiner back and in the time scale indicated?

There had to be more to the whole business than Himmler was telling him, that much was obvious. He lit another cigarette and left, losing his way at the end of the corridor. He hesitated, uncertain, then realized that the archway at the end led onto the balcony above the great hall. He was about to turn and go the other way when he heard voices. Intrigued, he moved forward onto the balcony and peered down cautiously. Himmler was standing at the head of the great table flanked by Rossman and Berger. The Reichsführer was speaking.

"There are those, Berger, who are more concerned with people than ideas. They become sentimental too easily. I do not think you are one of them."

"No, Reichsführer," Berger said.

"Unfortunately, General Schellenberg is. That's why I'm sending you with him to Lisbon. The man Devlin comes whether he likes it or not. I look to you to see to it."

"Is the Reichsführer doubting General Schellenberg's loyalty?" Rossman asked.

"He has been of great service to the Reich," Himmler said. "Probably the most gifted officer to serve under my command, but I've always doubted his loyalty to the Party. But there is no problem here, Rossman. He is too useful for me to discard at the present time. We must put all our energies into the preparation for Belle-Île while Schellenberg busies himself with the Steiner affair." He turned to Berger. "You'd better be off."

"Reichsführer." Berger clicked his heels and turned away. When he was halfway across the hall, Himmler called, "Show me what you can do, Sturmbannführer."

Berger had the flap of his holster open, turned with incredible speed, arm extended. There was a fresco of knights on the far wall done in medieval style in plaster. He fired three times very fast and three heads disintegrated. The shots echoed through the hall as he replaced his weapon.

"Excellent," Himmler said.

Schellenberg was already on his way. He was good himself, maybe as good as Berger, but that wasn't the point. In the hall he retrieved his greatcoat and cap and was sitting in the rear of the Mercedes when Berger joined him five minutes later.

"Sorry if I've kept you waiting, General," he said as he got in.

"No problem," Schellenberg said and nodded to the driver, who drove away. "Smoke if you like."

"No vices, I'm afraid," Berger said.

"Really? Now that is interesting." Schellenberg turned up the collar of his greatcoat and leaned back in the corner pulling the peak of his cap over his eyes. "A long way to Berlin. I don't know about you, but I'm going to get some sleep."

He did just that. Berger watched him for a while, and then he also pulled up the collar of his greatcoat and turned into the corner.

Schellenberg's office at Prinz Albrechtstrasse had a military camp bed in one corner, for he often spent the night there. He was in the small bathroom adjacent to it shaving when his secretary, Ilse Huber, entered. She was forty-one at that time, already a war widow, a sensual, attractive woman in white blouse and black skirt. She had once been Heydrich's secretary, and Schellenberg, to whom she was devoted, had inherited her.

"He's here," she said.

"Rivera?" Schellenberg wiped soap from his face. "And Canaris?"

"The Herr Admiral will be riding in the Tiergarten at ten o'clock as usual. Will you join him?"

Schellenberg frequently did, but when he went to the window and saw the powdering of snow in the streets he laughed. "Not this morning, thank you, but I must see him."

Dedicated as she was to Schellenberg's welfare, she had an instinct about things. She went and poured coffee from the pot on the tray she had put on his desk. "Trouble, General?"

"In a way, my love." He drank some of the coffee and smiled that ruthless, dangerous smile of his that made the heart turn over in her. "But don't worry. Nothing I can't handle. I'll fill you in on the details before I leave. I'm going to need your help with this one. Where's Berger, by the way?"

"Downstairs in the canteen, last I saw of him."

"All right. I'll see Rivera now."

She paused at the door and turned. "He frightens me that one. Berger, I mean."

Schellenberg went and put an arm around her. "I told you not to worry. After all, when has the great Schellenberg ever failed to manage?"

His self-mockery, as always, made her laugh. He gave her a squeeze, and she was out of the door smiling. Schellenberg buttoned his tunic and sat down. A moment later the door opened and Rivera came in.

He wore a dark brown suit, an overcoat over one arm, a small man, sallow skin, black hair carefully parted. Just now he looked decidedly anxious.

"You know who I am?" Schellenberg asked him.

"Of course, General. An honor to meet you."

Schellenberg held up a piece of paper which was actually some stationery from the hotel he'd stayed at in Vienna the previous week. "This message you received from your cousin Vargas at the London Embassy concerning the whereabouts of a certain Colonel Steiner. Have you discussed it with anyone?"

Rivera seemed genuinely shocked. "Not a living soul, General. Before God I swear this." He spread his hands dramatically. "On my mother's life."

"Oh, I don't think we need to bring her into it. She's quite comfortable in that little villa you bought her in San Carlos." Rivera looked startled, and Schellenberg said, "You see, there is nothing about you I don't know. There is no place you could go where I couldn't reach you. Do you understand me?"

"Perfectly, General." Rivera was sweating.

"You belong to the SD now and Reichsführer Himmler, but it is me you answer to and no one else, so to start with: This message from your cousin in London. Why did you also send it to Admiral Canaris?"

"My cousin's orders, General. In these matters there is always the question of payment and in this case . . . " He shrugged.

"He thought you might get paid twice?" Schellenberg nodded. It made sense, and yet he had learned never to take anything for granted in this game. "Tell me about your cousin."

"What can I say that the general doesn't know? José's parents died in the influenza epidemic just after the First World War. My parents raised him. We were like brothers. Went to the University of Madrid together. Fought in the same regiment in the Civil War. He's one year older than me, thirty-three."

"He isn't married, you are," Schellenberg said. "Does he have a girlfriend in London?"

Rivera spread his hands. "As it happens, José's tastes do not run to women, General."

"I see." Schellenberg brooded about it for a moment. He had nothing against homosexuals, but such people were susceptible to blackmail, and that was a weakness for anyone engaged in intelligence work. A point against Vargas, then.

"You know London?"

Rivera nodded. "I served at the Embassy there with José in nineteen thirty-nine for one year. I left my wife in Madrid."

"I know London also," Schellenberg said. "Tell me about his life. Does he live at the Embassy?"

"Officially he does, General, but for the purposes of his private life he has a small apartment, a 'flat' as the English call it. He took a seven-year lease on the place while I was there, so he must still have it."

"Where would that be?"

"Stanley Mews, quite close to Westminster Abbey."

"And convenient for the Houses of Parliament. A good address. I'm impressed."

"José always did like the best."

"Which must be paid for." Schellenberg got up and went to the window. It was snowing lightly. He said, "Is he reliable, this cousin of yours? Any question of him ever having had any dealings with our British friends?"

Rivera looked shocked again. "General Schellenberg, I assure you. José, like me, is a good Fascist. We fought together with General Franco in the Civil War. We—"

"All right, I was just making the point. Now listen to me carefully. We may well decide to attempt to rescue Colonel Steiner."

"From the Tower of London, señor?" Rivera's eyes bulged.

"In my opinion, they'll move him to some sort of safe house. May well have done so already. You will send a message to your cousin today asking for all possible information."

"Of course, General."

"Get on with it then." As Rivera reached the door, Schellenberg added, "I need hardly say that if one word of this leaks out you will end up in the river Spree, my friend, and your cousin in the Thames. I have an extraordinarily long arm."

"General, I beg of you." Rivera started to protest again.

"Spare me all that stuff about what a good Fascist you are. Just think about how generous I'm going to be. A much sounder basis for our relationship."

Rivera departed and Schellenberg phoned down for his car, pulled on his overcoat and went out.

Admiral Wilhelm Canaris was fifty-six, a U-boat captain of distinction in the First World War. He had headed the Abwehr since 1935 and despite being a loyal German had always been unhappy with National Socialism. Although he was opposed to any plan to assassinate Hitler, he had been involved with the German Resistance movement for some years, treading a dangerous path that was eventually to lead to his downfall and death.

That morning, as he galloped along the path between the trees in the Tiergarten, his horse's hooves kicked up the powdered snow, filling him with a fierce joy. The two dachshunds which accompanied him everywhere followed with surprising speed. He saw Schellenberg standing beside his Mercedes, waved and turned toward him.

"Good morning, Walter. You should be with me."

"Not this morning," Schellenberg told him. "I'm off on my travels again."

Canaris dismounted, and Schellenberg's driver held the horse's reins. Canaris offered Schellenberg a cigarette, and they went and leaned on a parapet overlooking the lake.

"Anywhere interesting?" Canaris asked.

"No, just routine," Schellenberg said.

"Come on, Walter, out with it. There's something on your mind."

"All right. The Operation Eagle affair."

"Nothing to do with me," Canaris told him. "The Führer came up with the idea. What nonsense! Kill Churchill when we've already lost the war."

"I wish you wouldn't say that sort of thing out loud," Schellenberg said gently.

Canaris ignored him. "I was ordered to prepare a feasibility study. I knew the Führer would forget it within a matter of days and he did, only Himmler didn't. Wanted to make life disagreeable for me as usual. Went behind my back, suborned Max Radl, one of my most trusted aides. And the whole thing turned out to be the shambles I knew it would."

"Of course Steiner almost pulled it off," Schellenberg said.

"Pulled what off? Come off it, Walter, I'm not denying Steiner's audacity and bravery, but the man they were after wasn't even Churchill. Would have been quite something if they'd brought him back. The look on Himmler's face would have been a joy to see."

"And now we hear that Steiner didn't die," Schellenberg said. "That they have him in the Tower of London."

"Ah, so Rivera has passed on his dear cousin's message to the Reichsführer also." Canaris smiled cynically. "Doubling up their reward as usual."

"What do you think the British will do?"

"With Steiner? Lock him up tight until the end of the war like Hess, only they'll keep quiet about it. Wouldn't look too good, just as it wouldn't look too good to the Führer if the facts came to his attention."

"Do you think they're likely to?" Schellenberg asked.

Canaris laughed out loud. "You mean from me? So that's what all this is about? No, Walter, I'm in enough trouble these days without looking for more. You can tell the Reichsführer that I'll keep quiet if he will."

They started to walk back to the Mercedes. Schellenberg said, "I suppose he's to be trusted, this Vargas. We can believe him?"

Canaris took the point seriously. "I'm the first to admit our operations in England have gone badly. The British secret service came up with a stroke of some genius when they stopped having our operatives shot when they caught them and simply turned them into double agents.''

"And Vargas?"

"One can never be sure, but I don't think so. His position at the Spanish Embassy, the fact that he has only worked occasionally and as a free-lance. No contacts with any other agents in England, you see." They had reached the car. He smiled. "Anything else?"

Schellenberg couldn't help saying it, he liked the man so much. "As you well know, there was another attempt on the Führer's life at Rastenburg. As it happened, the bombs the young officer involved was carrying went off prematurely."

"Very careless of him. What's your point, Walter?"

"Take care, for God's sake. These are dangerous times."

"Walter, I have never condoned the idea of assassinating the Führer." The admiral climbed back into the saddle and gathered his reins. "However desirable that possibility may seem to some people. And shall I tell you why, Walter?"

"I'm sure you're going to."

"Stalingrad, thanks to the Führer's stupidity, lost us more than three hundred thousand dead. Ninety-one thousand taken prisoner, including twenty-four generals. The greatest defeat we've ever known. One balls-up after another, thanks to the Führer." He laughed harshly. "Don't you realize the truth of it, my friend? His continued existence actually shortens the war for us."

He put his spurs to his horse, the dachshunds yapping at his heels, and galloped into the trees.

Back at the office, Schellenberg changed into a light gray flannel suit in the bathroom, speaking through the other door to Ilse Huber as he dressed, filling her in on the whole business.

"What do you think?" he asked as he emerged. "Like a fairy tale by the Brothers Grimm?"

"More like a horror story," she said as she held his black leather coat for him.

"We'll refuel in Madrid and carry straight on. Should be in Lisbon by late afternoon."

He pulled on the coat, adjusted a slouch hat and picked up the overnight bag she had prepared. "I expect news from Rivera within two days at the outside. Give him thirty-six hours, then apply pressure." He kissed her on the cheek. "Take care, Ilse. See you soon." And he was gone.

The plane was a Ju-52 with its famous three engines and corrugated metal skin. As it lifted from the Luftwaffe fighter base outside Berlin, Schellenberg undid his seat belt and reached for his briefcase.

Berger, on the other side of the aisle, smiled. "The Herr Admiral was well, General?"

Now that isn't very clever, Schellenberg thought. You weren't supposed to know I was seeing him.

He smiled back. "He seemed his usual self."

He opened his briefcase, started to read Devlin's background report and examined a photo of him. After a while he stopped and looked out of the window, remembering what Canaris had said about Hitler.

His continued existence actually shortens the war for us.

Strange how that thought went around and around in his brain and wouldn't go away.

3

BARON OSWALD VON HOYNINGEN-HEUNE, the minister to the German Legation in Lisbon, was a friend and an aristocrat of the old school who was also no Nazi. He was delighted to see Schellenberg and showed it.

"My dear Walter. Good to see you. How's Berlin at the moment?"

"Colder than this," Schellenberg told him as they moved out through French windows and sat at a table on the pleasant terrace. The garden was a sight to see, winter flowers everywhere. A houseboy in white jacket brought coffee on a tray, and Schellenberg sighed. "Yes, I can understand you hanging on here instead of coming back to Berlin. The best place to be these days, Lisbon."

"I know," the baron told him. "The constant worry all my staff have is of being transferred." He poured the coffee. "A strange time to arrive, Walter, Christmas Eve."

"You know Uncle Heini when he gets the bit between his teeth," Schellenberg told him, using the nickname common in the SS behind Himmler's back.

"It must be important," the baron said. "Especially if he sends you."

"There's a man we want, an Irishman—Liam Devlin." Schellenberg took Devlin's photo from his wallet and passed it across. "He worked for Abwehr for a while. The IRA connection. Walked out of a hospital in Holland the other week. Our information is that he's here, working as a waiter at a club in Alfama."

"The old quarter." The baron nodded. "If he's Irish, this man, I hardly need point out that makes him officially a neutral. A situation of some delicacy."

"No rough stuff needed," Schellenberg said. "I hope we can persuade him to come back peaceably. I have a job to offer him that could be rather lucrative."

"Fine," the baron said. "Just remember that our Portuguese friends really do value their neutrality. Even more so now that victory seems to be slipping away from us. However, Captain Eggar, my police attaché here, should be able to assist you." He picked up his phone and spoke to an aide. As he put it down he said, "I caught a glimpse of your companion."

"Sturmbannführer Horst Berger—Gestapo," Schellenberg said.

"Doesn't look your sort."

"A Christmas present from the Reichsführer. I didn't have much choice."

"Like that, is it?"

There was a knock at the door and a man in his forties slipped in. He had a heavy mustache and wore a brown gabardine suit that didn't fit too well. A professional policeman. Schellenberg recognized the type.

"Ah, there you are, Eggar. You know General Schellenberg, don't you?"

"Of course. A great pleasure to see you again. We met during the course of the Windsor affair in nineteen forty."

"Yes, well we prefer to forget all about that these days." Schellenberg passed Devlin's photo across. "Have you seen this man?"

Eggar examined it. "No, General."

"He's Irish, ex-IRA, if you ever can be ex-IRA, age thirty-five. He worked for Abwehr for a while. We want him back. Our latest information is that he's been working as a waiter at a bar called Flamingo."

"I know the place."

"Good. You'll find my aide, Major Berger of the Gestapo, outside. Bring him in." Eggar went out and returned with Berger, and Schellenberg made the introductions. "Baron von Hoyningen-Heune, minister to the Legation, and Captain Eggar, police attaché. Sturmbannführer Berger." Berger, in his dark suit with that ravaged face of his, was a chilling presence as he nodded formally and clicked his heels. "Captain Eggar knows this Flamingo place. I want you to go there with him and check if Devlin still works there. If he does, you will not, I repeat *not*, contact him in any way. simply report to me." Berger showed no emotion and turned to the door. As he opened it, Schellenberg called, "During the nineteen thirties Liam Devlin was one of the most notorious gunmen in the IRA. You gentlemen would do well to remember that fact."

The remark, as Berger immediately knew, was aimed at him. He smiled faintly. "We will, General." He turned and went out, followed by Eggar.

"A bad one that. You're welcome to him. Still . . ." The baron checked his watch. "Just after five, Walter. How about a glass of champagne?"

Major Arthur Frear was fifty-four and looked older with his crumpled suit and white hair. He'd have been retired by now on a modest pension leading a life of genteel poverty in Brighton or Torquay. Instead, thanks to Adolf Hitler, he was employed as military attaché at the British Embassy in Lisbon, where he unofficially represented SOE.

The Lights of Lisbon at the southern edge of the Alfama district was one of his favorite places. How convenient that Devlin was playing piano there, although there was no sign of him at the moment. Devlin, in fact, was watching him through a bead curtain at the rear. He wore a linen suit in off-white, dark hair falling across his forehead, the vivid blue eyes full of amusement as they surveyed Frear. The first Frear knew of his presence was when Devlin slid onto the stool next to him and ordered a beer.

"Mr. Frear, isn't it?" He nodded to the barman. "Miguel here tells me you're in the Port business."

"That's right," Frear said jovially. "Been exporting it to England for years, my firm."

"Never been my taste," Devlin told him. "Now if it was Irish whiskey you were talking about."

"Can't help you there, I'm afraid." Frear laughed again. "I say, old man, do you realize you're wearing a Guards Brigade tie?"

"Is that a fact? Fancy you knowing that." Devlin smiled amiably. "And me buying it from a stall in the flea market only last week."

He slid off the stool, and Frear said, "Aren't you going to give us a tune?"

"Oh, that comes later." Devlin moved to the door and grinned. "Major," he added, and was gone.

The Flamingo was a shabby little bar and restaurant. Berger was forced to leave things to Eggar, who spoke the language fluently. At first they drew a blank. Yes, Devlin had worked there for a while, but he'd left three days ago. And then a woman who had come in to sell flowers to the customers. overheard their conversation and intervened. The Irishman was working another establishment she called at, the Lights of Lisbon, only he was employed not as a waiter but as a pianist in the bar. Eggar tipped her and they moved outside.

"Do you know the place?" Berger said.

"Oh, yes, quite well. Also in the old quarter. I should warn you, the customers tend to the rougher side. Rather common round here."

"The scum of this life never give me a problem," Berger said. "Now show me the way."

The high walls of the Castelo de São Jorge lifted above them as they worked their way through a maze of narrow alleys, and then, as they came into a small square in front of a church, Devlin emerged from an alley and crossed the cobbles before them toward a café.

"My God, it's him," Eggar muttered. "Exactly like his photo."

"Of course it is, you fool," Berger said. "Is this the Lights of Lisbon?"

"No, Major, another café. One of the most notorious in Alfama. Gypsies, bullfighters, criminals."

"A good job we're armed then. When we go in, have your pistol in your right pocket and your hand on it."

"But General Schellenberg gave us express instructions to—"

"Don't argue. I've no intention of losing this man now. Do as I say and follow me." And Berger led the way toward the café where they could hear guitar music.

Inside, the place was light and airy in spite of the fact that dusk was falling. The bar top was marble, bottles ranged against an old-fashioned mirror behind it. The walls were whitewashed and covered with bullfighting posters. The bartender, squat and ugly with one white eye, wore an apron and soiled shirt and sat at a high stool reading a newspaper. Four other men played poker at a table, swarthy, fierce-looking gypsies. A younger man leaned against the wall and fingered a guitar.

The rest of the place was empty except for Devlin, who sat at a table against the far wall reading a small book, a glass of beer at his hand. The door creaked open and Berger stepped in, Eggar at his back. The guitarist stopped playing, and all conversation died as Berger stood just inside the door, death come to visit them. Berger moved past the men who were playing cards. Eggar went closer as well, standing to the left.

Devlin glanced up, smiling amiably. and picked up the glass of beer in his left hand. "Liam Devlin?" Berger asked.

"And who might you be?"

"I am Sturmbannführer Horst Berger of the Gestapo."

"Jesus and why didn't they send the devil? I'm on reasonable terms there."

"You're smaller than I thought you'd be," Berger told him. "I'm not impressed."

Devlin smiled again. "I get that all the time, son."

"I must ask you to come with us."

"And me only halfway through my book. *The Midnight Court*, and in Irish. Would you believe I found it on a stall in the flea market only last week?"

"Now!" Berger said.

Devlin drank some more beer. "You remind me of a medieval fresco I saw on a church in Donegal once. People running in terror from a man in a hood. Everyone he touched got the Black Death, you see."

"Eggar!" Berger commanded.

Devlin fired through the tabletop, chipping the wall beside the door. Eggar tried to get the pistol out of his pocket. The Walther Devlin had been holding on his knee appeared above the table now and he tried again, shooting Eggar through the right hand. The police attaché cried out, falling against the wall, and one of the gypsies grabbed for his gun as he dropped it.

Berger's hand went inside his jacket, reaching for the Mauser he carried in a shoulder holster there. Devlin tossed the beer in his face and upended the table against him, the edge catching the German's shins so that he staggered forward. Devlin rammed the muzzle of the Walther into his neck and reached inside Berger's coat, removing the Mauser, which he tossed onto the bar.

"Present for you, Barbosa." The barman grinned and picked the Mauser up. The gypsies were on their feet, two of them with knives in their hands. "Lucky for you you picked on the sort of place where they don't call the peelers," Devlin said. "A real bad lot, these fellas. Even the man in the hood doesn't count for much with them. Barbosa there used to meet him most afternoons in the bullrings in Spain. That's where he got the horn in the eye."

The look on Berger's face was enough. Devlin slipped his book into his pocket, stepped around him, holding the Walther against his leg, and reached for Eggar's hand. "A couple of knuckles gone. You're going to need a doctor." He slipped the Walther into his pocket and turned to go.

Berger's iron control snapped. He ran at him, hands outstretched. Devlin swayed, his right foot flicking forward, catching Berger under the left kneecap. As the German doubled over, he raised a knee in his face, sending him back against the bar. Berger pulled himself up, hanging on to the marble top, and the gypsies started to laugh.

Devlin shook his head, "Jesus, son, but I'd say you should find a different class of work, the both of you." And he turned and went out.

When Schellenberg went into the small medical room, Eggar was sitting at the desk while the Legation's doctor taped his right hand.

"How is he?" Schellenberg asked.

"He'll live." The doctor finished and cut off the end of the tape neatly. "He may well find it rather stiffer in future. Some knuckle damage."

"Can I have a moment?" The doctor nodded and went out and Schellenberg lit a cigarette and sat on the edge of the desk. "I presume you found Devlin?"

"Hasn't the Herr General been told?" Eggar asked.

"I haven't spoken to Berger yet. All I heard was that you'd come back in a taxi the worse for wear. Now tell me exactly what happened."

Which Eggar did, for as the pain increased, so did his anger. "He wouldn't listen, Herr General. Had to do it his way."

Schellenberg put a hand on his shoulder. "Not your fault, Eggar. I'm afraid Major Berger sees himself as his own man. Time he was taught a lesson."

"Oh, Devlin took care of that," Eggar said. "When I last saw it, the major's face didn't look too good."

"Really?" Schellenberg smiled. "I didn't think it could look worse."

Berger stood stripped to the waist in front of the washbasin in the small bedroom he had been allocated and examined his face in the mirror. A bruise had already appeared around his left eye and his nose was swollen. Schellenberg came in, closed the door and leaned against it.

"So, you disobeyed my orders."

Berger said, "I acted for the best. I didn't want to lose him."

"And he was better than you are. I warned you about that."

There was rage on Berger's face in the mirror as he touched his cheek. "That little Irish swine. I'll fix him next time."

"No you won't, because from now on I'll handle things myself," Schellenberg said. "Unless, of course, you'd prefer me to report to the Reichsführer that we lost this man because of your stupidity."

Berger swung around. "General Schellenberg, I protest."

"Get your feet together when you speak to me, Sturmbannführer," Schellenberg snapped. Berger did as he was told, the iron discipline of the SS taking control. "You took an oath on joining the SS. You vowed total obedience to your Führer and to those appointed to lead you. Is this not so?"

"*Jawohl, Brigadeführer.*"

"Excellent," Schellenberg told him. "You're remembering. Don't forget again. The consequences could be disastrous." He moved to the door, opened it and shook his head. "You look awful, Major. Try and do something about your face before going down to dinner."

He went out and Berger turned back to the mirror. "Bastard!" he said softly.

ᵥᵥᵥ

Liam Devlin sat at the piano in the Lights of Lisbon, a cigarette dangling from the corner of his mouth, a glass of wine on one side. It was ten o'clock, only two hours till Christmas Day, and the café was crowded and cheerful. He was playing a number called "Moonlight on the Highway," a particular favorite, very slow, quite haunting. He noticed Schellenberg the moment he entered, not because he recognized him, only the kind of man he was. He watched him go to the bar and get a glass of wine, then looked away, aware that he was approaching.

Schellenberg said, " 'Moonlight on the Highway.' I like that. One of Al Bowlly's greatest numbers," he added, mentioning the name of the man who had been England's most popular crooner until his death.

"Killed in the London Blitz, did you know that?" Devlin asked. "Would never go down to the cellars like everyone else when the air-raid siren went. They found him dead in bed from the bomb blast."

"Unfortunate," Schellenberg said.

"I suppose it depends on which side you're on."

Devlin moved into "A Foggy Day in London Town" and Schellenberg said, "You are a man of many talents Mr. Devlin."

"A passable barroom piano, that's all," Devlin told him. "Fruits of a misspent youth." He reached for his wine, continuing to play one-handed. "And who might you be, old son?"

"My name is Schellenberg—Walter Schellenberg. You may have heard of me."

"I certainly have." Devlin grinned. "I lived long enough in Berlin for that. General now, is it, and the SD at that? Are you something to do with the two idiots who had a try at me earlier this evening?"

"I regret that, Mr. Devlin. The man you shot is the police attaché at the Legation. The other, Major Berger, is Gestapo. He's with me only because the Reichsführer ordered it."

"Jesus, are we into old Himmler again? Last time I saw him he didn't exactly approve of me."

"Well he needs you now."

"For what?"

"To go to England for us, Mr. Devlin. To London, to be more precise."

"No, thanks. I've worked for German intelligence twice in this war. The first time in Ireland, where I nearly got my head blown off." He tapped the bullet scar on the side of his forehead.

"And the second time, in Norfolk, you took a bullet in the right shoulder and only got away by the skin of your teeth, leaving Kurt Steiner behind."

"Ah, so you know about that?"

"Operation Eagle? Oh, yes."

"A good man, the colonel. He wasn't much of a Nazi—"

"Did you hear what happened to him?"

"Sure, they brought Max Radl into the hospital I was in in Holland after his heart attack. He got some sort of report from intelligence sources in England that Steiner was killed at a place called Meltham House trying to get at Churchill."

"Two things wrong about that," Schellenberg told him. "Two things Radl didn't know. It wasn't Churchill that weekend. He was on his way to the Tehran conference. It was his double. Some music-hall actor."

"Jesus, Joseph and Mary!" Devlin stopped playing.

"And more importantly, Kurt Steiner didn't die. He's alive and well and at present in the Tower of London, which is why I want you to go to England for me. You see I've been entrusted with the task of getting him safely back to the Reich, and I've little more than three weeks to do it in."

Frear had entered the café a couple of minutes earlier and had recognized Schellenberg instantly. He retreated to a side booth where he summoned a waiter, ordered a beer, and watched as the two men went out into the garden at the rear. They sat at a table and looked down at the lights of the shipping in the Tagus River.

"General, you've lost the war," Devlin said. "Why do you keep trying?"

"Oh, we all have to do the best we can until the damn thing is over. As I keep saying, it's difficult to jump off the merry-go-round once it's in motion. A game we play."

"Like the old sod with the white hair in the end booth watching us now," Devlin observed.

Schellenberg looked around casually. "And who might he be?"

"Pretends to be in the Port business. Name of Frear. My friends tell me he's military attaché at the Brit Embassy here."

"Indeed." Schellenberg carried on calmly. "Are you interested?"

"Now why would I be?"

"Money. You received twenty thousand pounds for your work on

Operation Eagle paid into a Geneva account.''

"And me stuck here without two pennies to scratch myself with.''

"Twenty-five thousand pounds, Mr. Devlin. Paid anywhere you wish.''

Devlin lit another cigarette and leaned back. "What do you want him for? Why go to all the trouble?''

"A matter of security is involved.''

Devlin laughed harshly. "Come off it, General. You want me to go jumping out of Dorniers again at five thousand feet in the dark like that last time over Ireland, and you try to hand me that kind of bollocks.''

"All right.'' Schellenberg put up a hand defensively. "There's a meeting in France on the twenty-first of January. The Führer, Rommel, Canaris and Himmler. The Führer doesn't know about Operation Eagle. The Reichsführer would like to produce Steiner at that meeting. Introduce him.''

"And why would he want to do that?''

"Steiner's mission ended in failure, but he led German soldiers in battle on English soil. A hero of the Reich.''

"And all that old balls?''

"Added to which the Reichsführer and Admiral Canaris do not always see eye to eye. To produce Steiner.'' He shrugged. "The fact that his escape had been organized by the SS—''

"Would make Canaris look bad.'' Devlin shook his head. "What a crew. I don't much care for any of them or that old crow Himmler's motives, but Kurt Steiner's another thing. A great man, that one. But the bloody Tower of London!''

He shook his head again, and Schellenberg said, "They won't keep him there. My guess is they'll move him to one of their London safe houses.''

"And how can you find that out?''

"We have an agent in London working out of the Spanish Embassy.''

"Can you be sure he's not a double?''

"Pretty sure in this case.'' Devlin sat there frowning, and Schellenberg said, "Thirty thousand pounds.'' He smiled. "I'm good at my job, Mr. Devlin. I'll prepare a plan for you that will work.''

Devlin nodded. "I'll think about it.'' He stood up.

"But time is of the essence. I need to get back to Berlin.''

"And I need time to think, and it's Christmas. I've promised to go up country to a bull ranch a friend of mine called Barbosa runs. Used to be a great torero in Spain, where they like sharp horns. I'll be back in three days.''

"But, Mr. Devlin,'' Schellenberg tried again.

"If you want me, you'll have to wait.'' Devlin clapped him on the shoulder. "Come on now, Walter, Christmas in Lisbon. Lights, music, pretty girls. At this present moment they've got a blackout in Berlin, and I bet it's snowing. Which would you rather have?''

Schellenberg started to laugh helplessly, and behind them Frear got up and went out.

Urgent business had kept Dougal Munro at his office at SOE headquarters on the morning of Christmas Day. He was about to leave when Jack Carter limped in. It was just after noon.

Munro said, "I hope it's urgent, Jack. I'm due for Christmas lunch with friends at the Garrick."

"I thought you'd want to know about this, sir." Carter held up a signal flimsy. "From Major Frear, our man in Lisbon. Friend Devlin."

Munro asked, "What about him?"

"Guess who he was locked in conversation with last night at a Lisbon club. Walter Schellenberg."

Munro sat down at his desk. "Now what in the hell is the good Walter playing at?"

"God knows, sir."

"The devil, more like. Signal Frear most immediate. Tell him to watch what Schellenberg gets up to. If he and Devlin leave Portugal together, I want to know at once."

"I'll get right onto it, sir," Carter told him and hurried out.

It had tried to snow over Christmas, but in London on the evening of the twenty-seventh it was raining when Jack Carter turned into a small mews near Portman Square not far from SOE headquarters; which was why he had chosen it when he'd received a phone call from Vargas. The café was called Mary's Pantry, blacked-out, but when he went in, the place was bright with Christmas decorations and holly. It was early evening and there were only three or four customers.

Vargas sat in the corner drinking coffee and reading a newspaper. He wore a heavy blue overcoat and there was a hat on the table. He had olive skin and hollow cheeks and a pencil mustache, his hair brilliantined and parted in the center.

Carter said, "This had better be good."

"Would I bother you if it were not, señor?" Vargas asked. "I've heard from my cousin in Berlin."

"And?"

"They want more information about Steiner. They're interested in mounting a rescue operation."

"Are you certain?"

"That was the message. They want all possible information as to his whereabouts. They seem to think you will move him from the Tower."

"Who's they? The Abwehr?"

"No. General Schellenberg of the SD is in charge. At least that is who my cousin is working for."

Carter nodded, fiercely excited, and got up. "I want you to phone me at the usual number at eleven, old chum, and don't fail." He leaned forward. "This is the big one, Vargas. You'll make a lot of cash if you're smart."

He turned and went out and hurried along Baker Street as fast as his game leg would allow.

In Lisbon at that precise moment Walter Schellenberg was climbing the steep cobbled alley in Alfama toward the Lights of Lisbon. He could hear the music even before he got there. When he went inside, the place was deserted except for the barman and Devlin at the piano.

The Irishman stopped to light a cigarette and smiled. "Did you enjoy your Christmas, General?"

"It could have been worse. And you?"

"The bulls were running well. I got trampled. Too much drink taken."

"A dangerous game."

"Not really. They tip the ends of the horns in Portugal. Nobody dies."

"It hardly seems worth the candle," Schellenberg said.

"And isn't that the fact? Wine, grapes, bulls and lots and lots of sun, that's what I had for Christmas, General." He started to play "Moonlight on the Highway." "And me thinking of old Al Bowlly in the Blitz, London, fog in the streets. Now isn't that the strange thing?"

Schellenberg felt the excitement rise inside him. "You'll go?"

"On one condition. I can change my mind at the last minute if I think the thing isn't watertight."

"My hand on it."

Devlin got up and they walked out to the terrace. Schellenberg said, "We'll fly out to Berlin in the morning."

"You will, General, not me."

"But, Mr. Devlin."

"You have to think of everything in this game, you know that. Look down there."

Over the wall they could see that Frear had come in and was talking to one of the waiters as he wiped down the outside tables. "He's been keeping an eye on me, old Frear. He's seen me talking to the great Walter Schellenberg. I should think that would figure in one of his reports to London."

"So what do you suggest?"

"You fly back to Berlin and get on with the preparations. There'll be plenty to do. Arrange the right papers for me at the Legation, traveling money and so on, and I'll come the low-risk way by rail. Lisbon to Madrid, then the Paris Express. Fix it up for me to fly from there if it suits, or I could carry on by train."

"It would take you two days at least."

"As I say, you'll have things to do. Don't tell me the work won't be piling up."

Schellenberg nodded. "You're right. So, let's have a drink on it. To our English enterprise."

"Holy Mother of God, not that, General. Someone used that phrase to me last time. They didn't realize that's how the Spanish Armada was described, and look what happened to that lot."

"Then to ourselves, Mr. Devlin," Schellenberg said. "I will drink to you and you will drink to me." And they went back inside.

Munro sat at his desk in the Haston Place flat and listened intently as Carter gave him the gist of his conversation with Vargas.

He nodded. "Two pieces of the jigsaw puzzle, Jack. Schellenberg's interested in rescuing Steiner, and where is Schellenberg right now? In Lisbon hobnobbing with Liam Devlin. Now, what conclusion does that lead you to?"

"That he wants to recruit Devlin to the cause, sir."

"Of course. The perfect man." Munro nodded. "This could lead to interesting possibilities."

"Such as?"

Munro shook his head. "Just thinking out loud. Time to think of moving Steiner anyway. What would you suggest?"

"There's the London Cage in Kensington," Carter said.

"Come off it, Jack. That's only used for processing transients, isn't it? Prisoners of war such as Luftwaffe aircrews."

"There's Cockfosters, sir, but that's just a cage, too, and the school opposite Wandsworth Prison. A number of German agents have been held there." Munro wasn't impressed, and Carter tried again. "Of course there's Mytchett Place in Hampshire. They've turned that into a miniature fortress for Hess."

"Who lives there in splendor so solitary that in June nineteen forty-one he jumped from a balcony and tried to kill himself. No, that's no good." Munro went to the window and looked out. The rain had turned to sleet now. "Time I spoke with friend Steiner, I think. We'll try and make it tomorrow."

"Fine, sir. I'll arrange it."

Munro turned. "Devlin—there is a photo on file?"

"Passport photo, sir. When he was in Norfolk he had to fill in an alien's registration form. That's a must for Irish citizens and it requires a passport photo. Special Branch ran it down. It's not very good."

"They never are, those things." Munro suddenly smiled. "I've got it, Jack. Where to hold Steiner. That place in Wapping. St. Mary's Priory."

"The Little Sisters of Pity, sir? But that's a hospice for terminal cases."

"They also look after chaps who've had breakdowns, don't they? Gallant RAF pilots who've cracked up."

"Yes, sir."

"And you're forgetting that Abwehr agent Baum in February. The one who got shot in the chest when Special Branch and MI-Five tried to pick him up in Bayswater. They nursed him at the priory and interrogated him there. I've seen the reports. MI-Five don't use it regularly, I know that for a fact. It would be perfect. Built in the seventeenth century. They used to be an enclosed order, so the whole place is walled. Built like a fortress."

"I've never been, sir."

"I have. Strange sort of place. Protestant for years when Roman Catholics were proscribed, then some Victorian industrialist who was a religious crank turned it into a hostel for people off the street. It stood empty for years, and then in nineteen ten some benefactor purchased it. The place was reconsecrated Roman Catholic, and the Little Sisters of Pity were in business." He nodded, full of enthusiasm. "Yes, I think the priory will do nicely."

"There is one thing, sir. I would remind you that this is a counter-espionage matter, which means it's strictly an MI-Five and Special Branch affair."

"Not if they don't know about it." Munro smiled. "When Vargas phones, see him at once. Tell him to leave it three or four days, then to notify his cousin that Steiner is being moved to St. Mary's Priory."

"Are you actually inviting them to try and mount this operation, sir?"

"Why not, Jack? We'd bag not only Devlin but any contacts he would have. He couldn't work alone. No, there are all sorts of possibilities to this. Off you go."

"Right, sir."

Carter limped to the door, and Munro said, "Silly me, I'm forgetting the obvious. Walter Schellenberg is going to want a source for this information. It's got to look good."

"May I make a suggestion, sir?"

"By all means."

"José Vargas is a practicing homosexual, sir, and there's a company of Scots Guards on duty at the Tower at the moment. Let's say Vargas has picked one of them up in one of those pubs the soldiers frequent round the Tower.''

"Oh, very good, Jack. Excellent," Munro said. "Get on with it then.''

From a discreet vantage point on the concourse at the airport outside Lisbon, Frear watched Schellenberg and Berger walk across the apron and board the Junkers. He stayed there, watching it taxi away, and only went out to the cab rank when the plane had actually taken off.

Half an hour later he went into the Lights of Lisbon and sat at the bar. He ordered a beer and said to the barman, "Where's our Irish friend today?''

"Oh, him? Gone." The barman shrugged. "Nothing but trouble. The boss sacked him. There was a guest here last night. Nice man. A German, I think. This Devlin had a row with him. Nearly came to blows. Had to be dragged off.''

"Dear me," Frear said. "I wonder what he'll do now.''

"Plenty of bars in Alfama, senhor," the barman said.

"Yes, you're certainly right there." Frear swallowed his beer. "I'll be off then.''

He went out, and Devlin stepped through the bead curtain at the back of the bar. "Good man yourself, Miguel. Now let's have a farewell drink together.''

It was late afternoon and Munro was at his desk in his office at SOE headquarters when Carter came in.

"Another signal from Frear, sir. Schellenberg left for Berlin by plane this morning, but Devlin didn't go with him.''

"If Devlin is as smart as I think he is, Jack, he's been onto Frear from the start. You can't be a military attaché at any embassy in a place like Lisbon without people knowing.''

"You mean he's gone to Berlin by another route, sir?''

"Exactly. Twisting and turning like the fox he is, and all to no avail." Munro smiled. "We have Rivera and Vargas in our pockets, and that means we'll always be one step ahead.''

"So what happens now, sir?''

"We wait, Jack, we just wait and see what their next move is. Did you arrange the meeting with Steiner?''

"Yes, sir.''

Munro went to the window. The sleet had turned to rain, and he snorted. "Looks as if we're going to get some fog now. Bloody weather." He sighed. "What a war, Jack, what a war.''

4

As the car went along Tower Hill, fog rolled in from the Thames. Munro said, "What's the situation here now?"

"The whole place is guarded, Brigadier. Public aren't allowed in like they used to be before the war. I understand they run sightseeing trips for Allied servicemen in uniform some days."

"And the Yeomen?"

"Oh, they still function and still live in the married quarters with their families. The whole place has been bombed more than once. Three times while Rudolf Hess was there, remember?"

They were stopped at a sentry post to have passes checked and moved on through the wool of the fog, traffic sounds muted, an anguished cry from the Thames as a ship sounded its foghorn on the way down to the sea.

They were checked again, then drove on over the drawbridge and through the gate. "Not exactly a day to fill the heart with joy," Munro observed.

There wasn't much to see with the fog, only gray stone walls as they moved on, eventually reaching the Inner Ward, everything cut off around them.

"The hospital's over there, sir," Carter said.

"You've made the arrangements as I ordered?"

"Yes, sir, but with some reluctance."

"You're a nice man, Jack, but this isn't a nice war. Come on, we'll get out here and walk across."

"Right, sir."

Carter struggled to follow him, his leg the usual problem. The fog was yellow and acrid and bit at the back of the throat like acid.

"Shocking, isn't it?" Munro said. "Real pea-souper. What was it Dickens called it? A London Particular?"

"I believe so, sir."

They started to walk. "What a bloody place, Jack. Supposed to be haunted by ghosts. That wretched little girl Lady Jane Grey and Walter Raleigh ceaselessly prowling the walls. I wonder what Steiner makes of it."

"I shouldn't think it exactly helps him to sleep, sir."

336

One of the Tower's famous black ravens emerged from the fog, enormous wings flapping as it cawed at them.

Munro started violently. "Get away, you filthy great creature." He shuddered. "There, what did I tell you, spirits of the dead."

The small hospital room was painted dark green. There was a narrow bed, a cupboard and a wardrobe. There was also a bathroom adjacent to it. Kurt Steiner, in pajamas and terry-cloth robe, sat by the window reading. The window was barred, although it was possible to reach through and open the casement. He preferred to sit there because in better weather he could see out into the Inner Ward and the White Tower. It gave an illusion of space, and space meant freedom.

There was a rattle of bolts at the stout door. It opened and a military policeman stepped in. "Visitors for you, Colonel."

Munro moved in followed by Carter. "You may leave us, Corporal," he told the MP.

"Sir." The man went out, locking the door.

Munro, more for the effect than anything else, was in uniform. He shrugged off his British Warm greatcoat, and Steiner took in the badges of rank and red tabs of a staff officer.

"Oberstleutnant Kurt Steiner?"

Steiner stood up. "Brigadier?"

"Munro, and this is my aide, Captain Jack Carter."

"Gentlemen, I gave my name, my rank and my number some time ago," Steiner said. "I've nothing to add except to say I'm surprised no one's tried to squeeze more out of me since, and I apologize for the fact that there's only one chair here, so I can't ask you to sit down."

His English was perfect, and Munro found himself warming to him. "We'll sit on the bed if we may. Jack, give the colonel a cigarette."

"No, thanks," Steiner said. "A bullet in the chest was a good excuse to give it up."

They sat down. Munro said, "Your English is really excellent."

"Brigadier"—Steiner smiled— "I'm sure you're aware that my mother was American and that I lived in London for many years as a boy when my father was military attaché at the German Embassy. I was educated at St. Paul's."

He was twenty-seven and in good shape except for a slight hollowing in the cheeks, obviously due to his hospitalization. He was quite calm, a slight smile on his lips, a kind of self-sufficiency there that Munro had noticed in many airborne soldiers.

"You haven't been pressured into any further interrogation, not only because of the condition you were in for so long," Munro said, "but because we know everything there is to know about Operation Eagle.''

"Really?" Steiner said dryly.

"Yes. I work for Special Operations Executive, Colonel. Knowing things is our business. I'm sure you'll be surprised to discover that the man you tried to shoot that night at Meltham House wasn't Mr. Churchill.''

Steiner looked incredulous. "What are you trying to tell me now? What nonsense is this?''

"Not nonsense," Jack Carter said. "He was one George Howard Foster, known in the music halls as the Great Foster. An impressionist of some distinction.''

Steiner laughed helplessly. "But that's wonderful. So bloody ironic. Don't you see? If it had all succeeded and we'd taken him back . . . My God, a music-hall artist. I'd love to have seen that bastard Himmler's face.'' Concerned that he was going too far, he took a deep breath and pulled himself together. "So?''

"Your friend Liam Devlin was wounded but survived," Carter said. "Walked out of a Dutch hospital and escaped to Lisbon. As far as we know, your second-in-command, Neumann, still survives and is hospitalized.''

"As is Colonel Max Radl, your organizer," Munro put in. "Had a heart attack.''

"So, not many of us left," Steiner said lightly.

"Something I've never understood, Colonel," Carter said. "You're no Nazi, we know that. You ruined your career trying to help a Jewish girl in Warsaw, and yet that last night in Norfolk you still tried to get Churchill.''

"I'm a soldier, Captain. The game was in play, and it is a game, wouldn't you agree?''

"And in the end the game was playing you," Munro said shrewdly.

"Something like that.''

"Nothing to do with the fact that your father, General Karl Steiner, was being held at Gestapo headquarters at Prinz Albrechtstrasse in Berlin for complicity in a plot against the Führer?'' Carter asked.

Steiner's face shadowed. "Captain Carter, Reichsführer Himmler is noted for many things, but charity and compassion are not among them.''

"And it was Himmler behind the whole business," Munro told him. "He pressured Max Radl into working behind Admiral Canaris's back. Even the Führer had no idea that was going on. Still hasn't.''

"Nothing would surprise me," Steiner said. He stood up and paced to the wall. He turned. "Now, gentlemen, what is this all about?''

"They want you back," Munro told him.

Steiner stared at him, incredulous. "You're joking. Why would they bother?''

"All I know is that Himmler wants you out of here."

Steiner sat down again. "But this is nonsense. With all due respect to my fellow countrymen, German prisoners of war have not been noted for escaping from England, not since the First World War."

"There has been one," Carter told him. "Luftwaffe pilot, but even he had to do it from Canada into the States before they were in the war."

"You miss the point," Munro said. "We're not talking of a prisoner simply making a run for it. We're talking about a plot, if you like. A meticulously mounted operation masterminded by General Walter Schellenberg of the SD. Do you know him?"

"Of him only," Steiner replied automatically.

"Of course it would require the right man to pull it off, which is where Liam Devlin comes in," Carter added.

"Devlin?" Steiner shook his head. "Nonsense. Devlin is one of the most remarkable men I have ever known, but even he couldn't get me out of this place."

"Yes, well it wouldn't be from here. We're moving you to a safe house in Wapping. St. Mary's Priory. You'll be given the details later."

"No, I can't believe it. This is some trick," Steiner said.

"Good God, man, what profit would there be in it for us?" Munro demanded. "There's a man at the Spanish Embassy here in London called José Vargas, a commercial attaché. He works for your side on occasion for money. Operates via his cousin at the Spanish Embassy in Berlin using a diplomatic pouch."

"He works for us, you see, also for money," Carter said. "And they have been in touch, indicated their interest in pulling you out, and requesting more information as to your whereabouts."

"And we've told him what he needs to know," Munro put in. "Even your new home at the priory."

"So, now I understand," Steiner said. "You allow the plan to proceed, Devlin comes to London. He will need help, of course, other agents or what have you, and at the appropriate moment you arrest the lot."

"Yes, that is one way," Munro said. "There is another possibility, of course."

"And what would that be?"

"That I simply allow it all to happen. You escape to Germany—"

"Where I work for you?" Steiner shook his head. "Sorry, Brigadier. Carter was right. I'm no Nazi, but I'm still a soldier—a German soldier. I'd find the word traitor difficult to handle."

"Would you say your father and others were traitors because they tried to remove the Führer?" Munro asked.

"In a sense that's different. Germans trying to handle their own problem."

"A neat point." Munro turned and said, "Jack."

Carter went and knocked on the door. It opened and the MP appeared. Munro got up. "If you'd be kind enough to follow me, Colonel, there's something I'd like you to see."

As far as Adolf Hitler was concerned there was to be no possibility of an honorable death for a traitor. No officer convicted of plotting against him met his end at the hands of a firing squad. The punishment was statutory, death by hanging, usually from a meat hook, and often piano wire was employed. Victims frequently took a long time to die, often very unpleasantly. The Führer had ordered all such executions to be recorded on film. Many were so appalling that even Himmler had been known to walk out of the showings sick to the stomach.

The one which was being shown now in the large stockroom at the end of the corridor was flickering and rather grainy. The young intelligence sergeant, anonymous behind the film projector in the darkness, was using the white-painted wall as a screen. Steiner sat on a chair alone, Munro and Carter behind him.

General Karl Steiner, carried in by two SS men, was already dead from a heart attack, the only good thing about the entire proceedings. They hung him to the hook anyway and moved away. For a little while the camera stayed on that pathetic figure, swaying slightly from side to side, then the screen went blank.

The projectionist switched on the light. Kurt Steiner stood, turned and moved to the door without a word. He opened it, went past the MP and walked down the corridor to his room. Munro and Carter followed. When they went into the room, Steiner was standing at the window gripping the bars and looking out. He turned, his face very pale.

"You know I really think it's about time I took up smoking again, gentlemen."

Jack Carter fumbled a cigarette out of a packet of Players and gave him a light.

"I'm sorry about that," Munro said, "but it was important you knew that Himmler had broken his promise."

"Come off it, Brigadier," Steiner said. "You're not sorry about anything. You wanted to make your point, and you've made it. I never thought my father stood much of a chance of survival whatever I did. As far as Himmler is concerned, keeping promises is a low priority."

"And what do you think now?" Munro asked.

"Ah, so we come to the purpose of the exercise? Will I now, in a white hot rage, offer my services to the Allies? Allow myself to be spirited off to Germany, where I assassinate Hitler at the first opportunity?" He shook his head. "No, Brigadier. I'll have some bad nights over this. I may even ask to see a priest, but the essential point remains the same. My father's involvement in a plot on Hitler's life was as a German. He was doing it for Germany."

It was Carter who said, "Yes, one sees that."

Steiner turned to him. "Then you must also realize that for me to do what the brigadier suggests would be a betrayal of everything my father stood for and gave his life for."

"All right." Munro stood up. "We're wasting our time. You'll be transferred to St. Mary's Priory in the New Year, Colonel. Your friend Devlin hasn't a hope of getting you out, of course, but we'd love him to try." He turned to Carter. "Let's get moving, Jack."

Steiner said, "One thing, Brigadier, if I may."

"Yes?"

"My uniform. I would remind you that under the Geneva Convention I am entitled to wear it."

Munro glanced at Carter, who said, "It has been repaired, Colonel, and cleaned. I'll arrange for you to have it later today together with all your medals, naturally."

"That's all right then," Munro said and went out. Carter took out his packet of cigarettes and a box of matches and laid them on the locker. "You mentioned a priest. I'll arrange for one if you like."

"I'll let you know."

"And a supply of cigarettes?"

"Better not. This one tasted terrible." Steiner managed a smile.

Carter went to the door, hesitated and turned. "If it helps at all. Colonel, it was apparently a heart attack your father died of. I don't know the circumstances."

"Oh, I can imagine them well enough, but my thanks anyway," Steiner answered.

He stood there, hands thrust into the pockets of his robe, quite calm, and Carter, unable to think of anything else to say, stepped into the corridor and went after Munro.

As they drove through the fog along Tower Hill, Munro said, "You don't approve, do you, Jack?"

"Not really, sir. An unnecessary cruelty in my opinion."

"Yes, well, as I told you before, it's not a nice war. At least we know where we stand with friend Steiner now."

"I suppose so, sir."

"As for Devlin, if he's mad enough to try, let him come whenever he wants. With Vargas tipping us off on every move he makes, we can't go wrong.''

He settled back in the seat and closed his eyes.

It was actually New Year's Day when Devlin finally arrived in Berlin. It had taken him two days to get a seat on the Paris Express from Madrid. In Paris itself, his priority, thanks to Schellenberg, had got him on the Berlin Express, but B-17 bombers of the American 8th Air Force operating out of England had inflicted severe damage on the Frankfurt railway marshaling yards. This had necessitated a rerouting of most rail traffic from France and the Netherlands into Germany.

The weather was bad in Berlin, the kind of winter that couldn't make up its mind, a thin snow changing to sleet and driving rain. Devlin, still wearing a suit more apt for Portugal, had managed to procure a raincoat in Paris, but he was freezing and quite miserable as he trudged through the crowds in the railway station in Berlin.

Ilse Huber recognized him at once from his file photo as she stood at the barrier beside the security police. She had already made arrangements with the sergeant in charge, and when Devlin appeared, bag in hand, his papers ready, she intervened at once.

"Herr Devlin? Over here, please." She held out her hand. "I am Ilse Huber, General Schellenberg's secretary. You look awful."

"I feel bloody awful."

"I have transport waiting," she said.

The car was a Mercedes saloon with an SS pennant conspicuously on display. Devlin said, "I suppose that thing makes people get out of the way fast.''

"It certainly helps," she said. "It occurred to General Schellenberg that you might be caught out by the weather."

"You can say that again."

"I've made arrangements to take you to a secondhand shop. We'll get everything you need there. And you'll need someplace to stay. I have an apartment not too far from headquarters. There are two bedrooms. If it suits, you can have one of them while you're here."

"More to the point, does it suit you?" he asked.

She shrugged. "Mr. Devlin, my husband was killed in the Winter War in Russia. I have no children. My mother and father died in an RAF raid on Hamburg. Life could be difficult except for one thing. Working for General Schellenberg usually takes at least sixteen hours out of my day, so I'm hardly ever home."

She smiled and Devlin warmed to her. "It's a deal, then. Ilse, is it? Let's get on with the clothes. I feel as if some of my more particular parts have frozen solid."

When they emerged forty minutes later from the secondhand shop she'd taken him to, he wore a tweed suit, laced boots, a heavy overcoat almost ankle-length, gloves and a trilby hat.

"So, you are equipped to handle Berlin in January," she said.

"Where to now, your apartment?"

"No, we can go there later. General Schellenberg wants to see you as soon as possible. He's at Prinz Albrechtstrasse now."

Devlin could hear the sounds of shooting as they descended the steep stairway. "And what's all this then?"

Ilse said, "The basement firing range. The general likes to keep in practice."

"Is he any good?"

She looked almost shocked. "The best. I've never seen anyone shoot better."

"Really?" Devlin was unconvinced.

But he had cause to revise his opinion a moment later when they opened the door and went in. Schellenberg was firing at a series of cardboard Russian soldiers, watched by an SS sergeant major who was obviously in charge. He worked his way across three targets, placing two rounds neatly in each heart. As he paused to reload, he noticed their presence.

"Ah, Mr. Devlin, so you finally got here."

"A hell of a journey, General."

"And Ilse's taken care of your wardrobe I see."

"And how did you guess?" Devlin said. "It can only have been the smell of the mothballs."

Schellenberg laughed and reloaded his Mauser. "Schwarz," he said to the sergeant major, "something for Mr. Devlin. I believe he's quite a marksman."

Schwarz rammed a magazine into the butt of a Walther PPK and handed it to the Irishman.

"All right?" Schellenberg asked.

"Your shout, General."

Fresh targets sprang up, and Schellenberg fired six times very fast, again two holes in the heart area on three separate targets.

"Now isn't that something?" Devlin's hand swung up, he fired three rounds so close together that they might almost have been one. A hole appeared between the eyes of all three targets.

He laid the Walther down, and Ilse Huber said, "My God!"

Schellenberg handed his pistol to Schwarz. "A remarkable talent, Mr. Devlin."

"Remarkable curse more like. Now what happens, General?"

"The Reichsführer has expressed a desire to see you."

Devlin groaned. "He didn't like me the last time around. A glutton for punishment that man. All right, let's get it over with."

The Mercedes turned out of Wilhelmplatz and into Vosstrasse and drove toward the Reich Chancellery.

"What's all this?" Devlin demanded.

"Times have changed since Göring said that if a single bomb fell on Berlin you could call him Meier."

"You mean he got it wrong?"

"I'm afraid so. The Führer has had a bunker constructed below the Chancellery. Subterranean headquarters. Thirty meters of concrete, so the RAF can drop as many bombs as they like."

"Is this where he intends to make his last stand then?" Devlin inquired. "Wagner playing over the loudspeakers?"

"Yes, well we don't like to think about that," Schellenberg said. "The important people have secondary accommodation down there, which obviously includes the Reichsführer."

"So what goes on now? Are they expecting the RAF to plaster the city tonight or what?"

"Nothing so exciting. The Führer likes to have staff meetings now and then in the map room. He gives them dinner afterwards."

"Down there?" Devlin shuddered. "I'd rather have a corned-beef sandwich."

The Mercedes drew into the car ramp, and an SS sentry approached. In spite of Schellenberg's uniform the sentry checked their identities thoroughly before allowing them through.

Devlin followed Schellenberg down a seemingly endless passage, concrete walls, dim lighting. There was a soft humming from electric fans in the ventilating system, the occasional blast of cold air. There were SS guards here and there, but no great evidence of people, and then a door opened, a young corporal emerged, and behind him Devlin saw a room crammed with radio equipment and a number of operatives.

"Don't make the mistake of thinking there's no one here," Schellenberg said. "Rooms everywhere. A couple of hundred people tucked in all over the place like that radio room."

A door opened farther along the passage, and to Devlin's astonishment, Hitler emerged followed by a broad, rather squat man in a nondescript uniform. As they approached, Schellenberg pulled Devlin to one side and stood at attention. The Führer was talking to the other man in a low voice and totally ignored them as he passed and descended the stairs at the other end of the passage.

"The man with him was Bormann," Schellenberg said. "Reichsleiter Martin Bormann. Head of the Nazi Party Chancellery. A very powerful man."

"So that was the Führer," Devlin said. "And me almost getting to touch the hem of his robe."

Schellenberg smiled. "Sometimes, my friend, I wonder how you've managed to last as long as you have."

"Ah, well it must be my good looks, General."

Schellenberg tapped on a door, opened it and led the way in. A young woman, an SS auxiliary in uniform, sat at a typewriter in the corner. The rest of the room was mainly taken up by filing cabinets and the desk behind which Himmler sat, working through a file. He glanced up and removed his pince-nez.

"So, General, he's arrived."

"God bless all here," Devlin said cheerfully.

Himmler winced and said to the girl, "Leave us. Come back in fifteen minutes." She went out and he carried on. "I expected you in Berlin sooner, Herr Devlin."

"Your railway system seemed to be having trouble with the RAF," Devlin told him and lit a cigarette, mainly because he knew Himmler detested the habit.

Himmler was annoyed but didn't tell him to stop. Instead, he said to Schellenberg, "You seem to have wasted an inordinate amount of time so far, General. Why didn't Herr Devlin return from Lisbon with you?"

"Ah, the general did a fine job," Devlin said. "It was me had plans for Christmas, you see. No, the general was very reasonable. More than I can say for the other fella, Berger. We didn't get on at all."

"So I understand," Himmler said. "But that scarcely matters, as Sturmbannführer Berger has other duties to take care of." He leaned back. "So, you think this thing can be done? You believe you could get Steiner out?"

"Depends on the plan," Devlin said, "but anything's possible."

Himmler nodded. "It would be a remarkable coup for all of us."

"That's as may be," Devlin said. "It's getting back in one piece that worries me. I only just made it last time."

"You were well paid then, and I would remind you that you're being well paid this time."

"And that's a fact," Devlin said. "As my old mother used to say, money will be the death of me."

Himmler looked extremely annoyed. "Can't you take anything seriously, you Irish?"

"When I last had the pleasure of meeting your honor, I gave you the answer to that one. It's the rain."

"Oh, get him out of here," Himmler said. "And get on with it,

General. Needless to say I expect a regular progress report.''

"Reichsführer.'' Schellenberg ushered Devlin out.

The Irishman was grinning hugely. "I enjoyed that.'' He dropped his cigarette on the floor and stamped on it as Berger came around the corner, a rolled-up map under his arm.

He was in uniform and wore Iron Crosses First and Second Class. He stiffened when he saw them, and Devlin said cheerfully, "Very pretty, son, but it looks to me as if someone's been spoiling your good looks.''

Berger's face was very pale, and although the swelling had subsided it was obvious his nose was broken. He ignored Devlin and nodded formally to Schellenberg. "General.'' He passed on and knocked at Himmler's door.

"He must be well in there," Devlin observed.

"Yes.'' Schellenberg nodded. "Interesting.''

"Where to now? Your office?''

"No, tomorrow will be soon enough. I'll take you for a meal and drop you at Ilse's place afterwards. You'll get a good night's sleep and we'll go over things in the morning.''

As they reached the mouth of the tunnel, fresh air drifted in and Devlin took a deep breath. "Thank God for that.'' And then he started to laugh.

"What is it?'' Schellenberg demanded.

Devlin pointed to a poster on the wall that carried a picture of a rather idealized SS soldier that underneath it said, *At the end stands victory*.

Devlin laughed again. "God save us, General, but some people will believe anything.''

Berger clicked his heels in front of Himmler's desk. "I have the plan of the Château de Belle-Île here, Reichsführer.''

"Excellent,'' Himmler said. "Let me see.''

Berger unrolled the plan, and the Reichsführer examined it. "Good. Very good.'' He looked up. "You will be in sole charge, Berger. How many men would you suggest for the honor guard?''

"Twenty-five. Thirty at the most, Reichsführer.''

"Have you visited the place yet?'' Himmler asked.

"I flew down to Cherbourg the day before yesterday and drove out to the château. It's quite splendid. The owners are French aristocrats who fled to England. There is at the moment only a caretaker and his wife. I've informed him that we'll be taking the place over in the near future, but not why, naturally.''

"Excellent. No need to go near the place again for another couple of weeks. In other words, wait as long as possible before you and your men take over. You know what this so-called French Resistance is like. Terrorists, all of them. They bomb—murder.'' He rolled the plan up and returned it to Berger. "After all, the Führer will be our direct responsibility at this conference, Major. A sacred responsibility."

"Of course, Reichsführer."

Berger clicked his heels and went out. Himmler picked up his pen and started to write again.

The Mercedes moved along the Kurfurstendamm as snow started to fall again. There was evidence of bomb damage everywhere, and with the blackout and dusk falling, the prospect was less than pleasing.

"Look at it," Schellenberg said. "Used to be a great city this. Art, music, theater. And the clubs, Mr. Devlin. The Paradise and the Blue Nile. Always filled with the most beautifully dressed transvestites you've ever seen."

"My tastes never ran that way," Devlin told him.

"Nor mine." Schellenberg laughed. "I always think they're missing out on a good thing. Still, let's eat. I know a little restaurant in a back street not far from here where we'll do reasonably well. Black market, but then they do know me, which helps."

The place was homely enough with no more than a dozen tables. It was run by a man and his wife who obviously did know Schellenberg well. The general apologized for the dearth of corned-beef sandwiches, but was able to produce a mutton broth, lamb, potatoes and cabbage and a bottle of hock to go with it.

The booth they sat in was quite private, and as they finished the meal Schellenberg said, "Do you really think it is possible, this thing?"

"Anything's possible. I remember a case during the Irish Revolution. Nineteen twenty, it was. The Black and Tans had captured a fella called Michael Fitzgerald, an important IRA leader. Held him in Limerick Prison. A man called Jack O'Malley who served in the British army in Flanders as a captain got his old uniform out, dressed up half a dozen of his men as soldiers and went to Limerick Prison with a fake order that said they wanted Fitzgerald at Dublin Castle."

"And it worked?"

"Like a charm." Devlin poured the last of the wine into both their glasses. "There is one problem here though, a very important problem."

"And what's that?"

"Vargas."

"But that's taken care of. We've told him we must have firm information as to where they intend to move Steiner."

"You're convinced they will move him?"

"Certain of it. They won't continue to keep him in the Tower. It's too absurd."

"So you think Vargas will come up with the right information?"

Devlin shook his head. "He must be good."

"He always has been in the past, so the Abwehr have found. This is a Spanish diplomat, Mr. Devlin, a man in a privileged position. No ordinary agent. I have had his cousin, this Rivera fellow, thoroughly vetted."

"All right, I accept that. Let's say Rivera's as clean as a whistle, but who checks out Vargas? There is no one. Rivera is just a conduit through which the messages come and go, but what if Vargas is something else?"

"You mean a neat British intelligence plot to entice us in?"

"Well, let's look at the way they would see it. Whoever drops in needs friends in London, some sort of organization. If I was in charge on the Brit side, I'd give a little rope, let things get started, then arrest everybody in sight. From their point of view, quite a coup."

"Are you telling me you're having second thoughts? That you don't want to go?"

"Not at all. What I'm saying is that if I do, I have to go on the supposition that I'm expected. That Vargas has sold us out. Now that's a very different thing."

"Are you serious?" Schellenberg demanded.

"I'd look a right idiot if we organize things on the basis that Vargas is on our side and I get there and he isn't. Tactics, General, that's what's needed here. Just like chess. You've got to think three moves ahead."

"Mr. Devlin, you are a remarkable man," Schellenberg told him.

"A genius on my good days," Devlin replied solemnly.

Schellenberg settled the account and they went outside. It was still snowing lightly as they walked to the Mercedes.

"I'll take you to Ilse's now and we'll meet up in the morning." At that moment the sirens started. Schellenberg called to his driver, "Hans, this way." He turned to Devlin. "On second thought, I think we'll go back to the restaurant and sit in their cellar with the other sensible people. It's quite comfortable. I've been there before."

"Why not," Devlin said and turned with him. "Who knows—they might find us a bottle of something in there."

Behind them, gunfire was already rumbling like thunder on the edge of the city.

5

AS THEY APPROACHED SCHELLENBERG'S OFFICE at Prinz Albrechtstrasse, the morning air was tainted with smoke. "They certainly hit the target last night," he said.

"You can say that again," Devlin replied.

The door opened and Ilse Huber nodded good morning. "There you are, General. I was a little worried."

"Mr. Devlin and I spent the night in the cellar of that restaurant in Marienstrasse."

"Rivera's on his way," she told him.

"Oh, good. Send him in when he arrives."

She went out and ten minutes later ushered Rivera in. The Spaniard stood there clutching his hat, nervously glancing at Devlin.

"You may speak freely," Schellenberg said.

"I've had another message from my cousin, General. He says they are moving Steiner from the Tower of London to a place called St. Mary's Priory."

"Did he give an address for that?"

"He just said it was in Wapping, by the river."

Devlin said, "A remarkable fella, your cousin, to come up with such a prime piece of information so easily."

Rivera smiled eagerly. "José is certain his information is correct, señor. He got it from a friend of his, a soldier in the Scots Guards. They have a company serving the Tower at the moment. They use the public houses nearby, and my cousin . . . " Rivera shrugged. "A matter of some delicacy."

"Yes, we understand, Rivera." Schellenberg nodded. "All right, you can go for now. I'll be in touch when I need you."

Ilse showed him out and came back. "Is there anything you'd like me to do, General?"

"Yes, find me one of those gazetteers from the files. You know the sort of thing. London street-by-street. See if this place is mentioned."

She went out. "I used to know Wapping well at one stage of my career," Devlin said.

"With the IRA?"

349

"The bombing campaign. They were always having a go, the hard men, those who'd blow up the Pope if they thought it would help the cause. Nineteen thirty-six, there was an active service unit who set a bomb or two off in London. You know the sort of thing. Women, kids, passersby. I was used as an enforcer in those days, and the men at the top wanted it stopped. Lousy publicity, you see."

"And this is when you knew Wapping?"

"A friend from my youth in County Down. Friend of my mother's actually."

"Who is this friend?"

"Michael Ryan. Ran a safe house. Not active at all. Very deep cover."

"And you took care of this active service unit?"

"There were only the three of them." Devlin shrugged. "They wouldn't be told. After that, I went to Spain. Joined the Lincoln-Washington Brigade. Did my bit against Franco till the Italians took me prisoner. Eventually the Abwehr pulled me out."

"And this friend of yours in Wapping, this Ryan—I wonder what happened to him."

"Still in deep, old Michael, I should imagine. He wouldn't want to know any more. That kind of man. Had doubts about the use of violence. When the Abwehr sent me to Ireland in forty-one, I met a friend of his in Dublin. From what he told me, I know for a fact the IRA didn't use Mick during their bombing campaign in England at the beginning of the war."

"Could this be of any use?" Schellenberg suggested.

"Jesus, General, you've got the cart running before the horse, haven't you?"

Ilse came in with an orange-colored book. "I've found it, General, St. Mary's Priory, Wapping. See, right on the edge of the Thames."

Schellenberg and Devlin examined the map. "That isn't going to tell us much," Devlin said.

Schellenberg nodded. "I've just had a thought. Operation Sea Lion, nineteen forty."

"You mean the invasion that never was?"

"Yes, but it was thoroughly planned. One task the SD was given was a comprehensive survey of London. Buildings, I'm talking about. Their usefulness if London were occupied."

"You mean which place was suitable for Gestapo headquarters? That sort of thing."

Schellenberg smiled amiably. "Exactly. There was a listing of many hundreds of such places on file and plans, where obtainable." He turned to Ilse Huber. "See what you can do."

"At once, General."

Devlin sat by the window, Schellenberg at his desk. They lit cigarettes.

Schellenberg said, "You said last night you preferred to proceed with the notion of Vargas being a traitor."

"That's right."

"So what would you do? How would you handle it?"

"Easy. A stroke of genius hit me at the height of the bombing, General. We don't tell Vargas I'm going."

"I don't understand."

"We extract what information we need. In fact, we probably have enough already. Then, once a week, Rivera asks for more information on your behalf. Steiner's regime at the priory, the guard system, that sort of thing, only I'll already be in London. Now, Walter, my old son, you've got to admit that's good."

Schellenberg laughed helplessly, then got up. "Very good—bloody marvelous. Let's go down to the canteen and have a coffee on it."

Later, Schellenberg called for his Mercedes, and they drove to the Tiergarten and walked around the lake, feet crunching in the light powdering of snow.

"There's another difficulty," Devlin said. "The Special Branch managed to hunt me down when I was in Norfolk. A little late in the day, as it happened, but they did, and one of the things that helped was the fact that as an Irish citizen I had to be entered on the aliens' register by the local police, and that required a passport photo."

"I see. So what are you saying?"

"A complete change in appearance—a real change."

"You mean hair coloring and so on?"

Devlin nodded. "Add a few years as well."

"I think I can help there," Schellenberg said. "I have friends at the UFA film studios here in Berlin. Some of their makeup artists can achieve remarkable things."

"Another thing. No aliens' register this time. I was born in County Down, which is in Ulster, and that makes me officially a British citizen. We'll stick with that when it comes to false papers and so on."

"And your identity?"

"Last time I was a war hero. A gallant Irishman who'd been wounded at Dunkirk and invalided out." Devlin tapped the bullet scar on the side of his head. "This helped the story, of course."

"Good. Something like that then. What about method of entry?"

"Oh, parachute again."

"Into England?"

Devlin shook his head. "Too chancy, and if I'm seen, it's bound to be reported. No, make it Ireland like last time. If they see me there, no one gives a bugger. A stroll across the border into Ulster, the breakfast train to Belfast and I'm on British soil.''

''And afterwards?''

''The boat. Belfast to Heysham in Lancashire. Last time, I had to take the other route from Larne to Stranraer in Scotland. The boats get full, just like the train.'' Devlin grinned. ''There's a war on, General.''

''So, you are in London. What happens then?''

Devlin lit a cigarette. ''Well, if I keep away from Vargas, that means no help from any of your official sources.''

Schellenberg frowned. ''But you will need the help of others. Also weapons, a radio transmitter, because without the ability to communicate—''

''All right,'' Devlin said. ''So a few things are going to have to be taken on trust. We were talking about my old friend in Wapping earlier, Michael Ryan. Now the odds are good that he's still around, and if he is, he'll help, at least with suitable contacts.''

''Such as?''

''Michael ran a cab and he worked for the bookies on the side. He had a lot of underworld friends in the old days. The kind of crooks who'd do anything for money, deal in guns, that sort of thing. That IRA active service unit I had to knock off in London back in thirty-six—they used underworld contacts a lot, even to buy their explosives.''

''So, this would be excellent. The help of your IRA friend and the assistance, when needed, of some criminal element. But for all you know, your friend could no longer he in London.''

''Or killed in the Blitz, General. Nothing is guaranteed.''

''And you're still willing to take a chance?''

''I reach London, I assess the situation because I have to do that however clever the plan looks that we put together here. If Michael Ryan isn't around, if it simply looks impossible, the whole thing, I'm on the next boat back to Belfast and over the border and safe in Dublin before you know it.'' Devlin grinned. ''I'll give you the bad news from your Embassy there. Now could we go back to your office? It's so damn cold I think my bollocks are going to fall off.''

In the office, after lunch, they started again. Ilse sitting in the corner taking notes.

Schellenberg said, ''say, for arguments sake, that you got Steiner out one dark evening in London.''

''Broke him out of the priory, you mean?''

''Exactly. And that's only the first step. How do you get him back? Do you take him to Ireland? Return the way you came?''

"Not so healthy that," Devlin said. "De Valera, the Irish Prime Minister, has played it very cleverly. Kept Ireland out of the war, but that doesn't mean he's putting himself out for your people. All the Luftwaffe crews who've ended up in Ireland have been put in prison camps. On the other hand, if an RAF plane strays and crash-lands, they usually give them bacon and eggs for breakfast and send them home."

"And he's been imprisoning IRA members, I understand."

Devlin said, "In forty-one, I got back on a neutral boat, a Brazilian cargo ship from Ireland that put in at Lisbon, but that's a tricky one. Nothing guaranteed at all."

Ilse said diffidently, "Surely the moment the colonel is out they'll be looking for him."

"Exactly," Devlin said. "Police, army, Home Guard, the security services. Every port watched, especially the Irish routes." He shook his head. "No, once out we've got to leave England almost immediately. Be on our way before they know what's hit them."

Schellenberg nodded, thinking about it. "It occurs to me that one of the cleverest things about Operation Eagle was the way Colonel Steiner and his men were transported to England."

"The Dakota, you mean?" Devlin said.

"An RAF Dakota which had crash-landed in Holland and was put back into service. To all intents, a British plane flying home if anyone saw it, and all it had to do to make the drop was fly in under eight hundred feet, because many sections of the English coast have no low-level radar."

"Worked like a charm," Devlin said, "except on the way back. Gericke, the pilot, was in the same hospital as me. He was shot down by a Luftwaffe night fighter."

"Unfortunate, but an intriguing thought. A small plane flying in under radar. A British plane. A suitable landing place. It could have you and Steiner out and safely in France in no time at all."

"And pigs might fly, General. Not only would you need a suitable plane. You'd need the landing place. May I also point out you'd need an exceptional pilot."

"Come now, Mr. Devlin, anything is possible. We have what's called the Enemy Aircraft flight where the Luftwaffe tests captured British and American planes of every kind. They even have a B-seventeen. I've seen it." He turned to Ilse. "Get in touch with them at once. Also extend your research on Operation Sea Lion to cover any sites in the general area of London that we intended to use for covert operations, landings by night, that sort of thing."

"And a pilot," Devlin told her. "Like I said, someone special."

"I'll get right on to it."

As she turned, there was a knock at the door and a young woman in

SS auxiliary uniform came in carrying a large file. "St. Mary's Priory, Wapping. Was that what the general wanted?"

llse laughed triumphantly. "Good girl, Sigrid. Wait for me in the office. I've got something else for you." She turned and handed the file to Schellenberg. "I'll get her started on the other thing."

As she reached the door, Schellenberg said, "Another possibility, Ilse. Check the files on those British right-wing organizations that flourished before the war, the ones that sometimes had members of Parliament on their books."

She went out and Devlin asked, "And who in the hell would they be, General?"

"Anti-Semitics, people with Fascist sympathies. Many members of the British aristocracy and upper classes rather admired the Führer, certainly before the war."

"The kind who were disappointed not to see the Panzers driving up to Buckingham Palace?"

"Something like that." Schellenberg opened the bulky file. extracted the first plan and opened it. "So, Mr. Devlin, there you have it in all its glory. St. Mary's Priory."

Asa Vaughan was twenty-seven years of age. He was born in Los Angeles and his father was a film producer. Asa had been fascinated by flying from an early age, had taken his pilot's license even before going to West Point. Afterwards he had completed his training as a fighter pilot, performing so well that he was assigned to take an instructors' course with the navy at San Diego. And then came the night his whole world had collapsed, the night he'd got into a drunken brawl in a harborside bar and punched a major in the mouth.

October 5, 1939. The date was engraved on his heart. No scandal, no court-martial. No one wanted that. Just his resignation. One week at his parents' opulent home in Beverly Hills was all he could bear. He packed a bag and made for Europe.

The war had started in September, and the RAF were accepting a few Americans, but they didn't like his record. And then on November 30 the Russians invaded Finland. The Finns needed pilots badly, and volunteers from many nations flooded in to join the Finnish air force, Asa among them.

It was a hopeless war from the start, in spite of the gallantry of the Finnish army, and most of the fighter planes available were outdated. Not that the Russians were much better, but they did have a few of the new German FW-190s which Hitler had promised to Stalin as a goodwill gesture over the Poland deal.

Asa had flown biplanes like the Italian Fiat Falco and the British Gloucester Gladiator, hopelessly outclassed by the opposition, only his superior skill as a pilot giving him an edge. His personal score stood at seven, which made him an ace, and then came that morning of ferocious winds and driving snow when he'd come in at four hundred feet, flying blind, lost his engine at the last moment and crash-landed.

That was in March 1940, two days before the Finns capitulated. His pelvis fractured and back broken, he'd been hospitalized for eighteen months, was undergoing final therapy and still a lieutenant in the Finnish air force, when on June 25, 1941, Finland joined forces with Nazi Germany and declared war on Russia.

He'd returned to flying duties gradually, working as an instructor, not directly involved in any action. The months had gone by, and suddenly the roof had fallen in. First Pearl Harbor and then the declaration of war between Germany and Italy and the U.S.A.

They held him in a detention camp for three months, the Germans, and then the officers had come to see him from the SS. Himmler was extending the SS foreign legions—Scandinavian, French, the neutral Swedes, Indian prisoners of war from the British army in North Africa. There was even the Britisches Freikorps with their collar patches of three leopards instead of SS runes and the Union Jack on the left sleeve. Not that they'd had many takers, no more than fifty, mostly scum from prison camps attracted by the offer of good food, women and money.

The George Washington Legion was something else again. Supposedly for American sympathizers to the Nazi cause, as far as Asa knew, they never had more than half a dozen members, and he hadn't met the others. He had a choice. To join or be sent to a concentration camp. He argued as best he could. The final agreement was that he would serve only on the Russian Front. As it happened, he seldom flew in straight combat, for his skill as a pilot was so admired he was employed mainly on the courier service, ferrying high-ranking officers.

So here he was, not too far from the Russian border with Poland, at the controls of a Stork, forest and snow five thousand feet below, Hauptsturmführer Asa Vaughan from the U.S. of A. An SS Brigadeführer called Farber was sitting behind him examining maps.

Farber looked up. "How long now?"

"Twenty minutes," Asa told him. He spoke excellent German, although with an American accent.

"Good. I'm frozen to the bone."

How in the hell did I ever get into this? Asa asked himself. *And how do I get out?* A great shadow swooped in. The Stork bucked wildly and Farber cried out in alarm. A fighter plane took station to starboard for a moment, the Red Star plain on its fuselage, then it banked away.

"Russian Yak fighter. We're in trouble," Asa said.

The Yak came in fast from behind, firing both cannon and machine guns, and the Stork staggered, pieces breaking from the wings. Asa banked and went down, the Yak followed, turning in a half-circle, and took up station again. The pilot, conscious of his superiority in every department, waved, enjoying himself.

"Bastard!" Asa said.

The Yak banked again, came in fast, cannon shell punching into the Stork, and Farber cried out as a bullet caught him in the shoulder. As the windscreen shattered, he screamed, "Do something, for God's sake."

Asa, blood on his cheek from a splinter, cried, "You want me to do something, I'll do something. Let's see if this bastard can fly."

He took the Stork straight down to two thousand, waited until the Yak came in, banked and went down again. The forest in the snow plain below seemed to rush toward them.

"What are you doing?" Farber cried.

Asa took her down to a thousand, then five hundred feet, and the Yak, hungry for the kill, stayed on his tail. At the right moment, the American dropped his flaps, the Yak banked to avoid the collision and plowed straight down into the forest at 350 miles an hour. There was a tongue of flame, and Asa pulled back the column and leveled out at two thousand feet.

"You okay, General?"

Farber clutched his arm, blood pumping through. "You're a genius— a genius. I'll see you get the Iron Cross for this."

"Thanks." Asa wiped blood from his cheek. " That's all I need."

At the Luftwaffe base outside Warsaw, Asa walked toward the officers' mess feeling unaccountably depressed. The medical officer had put two stitches in his cheek but had been more concerned with Brigadeführer Farber's condition.

Asa went into the mess and took off his flying jacket. Underneath he wore a beautifully tailored uniform in Held gray, SS runes on his collar patch. On his left sleeve was a Stars and Stripes shield, and the cuff title on his left wrist said, *George Washington Legion.* He had the ribbon of the Iron Cross Second Class on his tunic and the Finnish Gold Cross of Valor.

His very uniqueness made most other pilots avoid him. He ordered a cognac, drank it quickly, and ordered another.

A voice said, "And it's not even lunchtime."

As Asa turned, the Gruppenkommandant, Colonel Erich Adler, sat on the stool next to him. "Champagne," he told the barman.

"And what's the occasion?" Asa demanded.

"First, my miserable Yankee friend, the good Brigadeführer Farber has recommended you for an immediate Iron Cross First Class, which, from what he says, you deserve."

"But Erich, I've got a medal," Asa said plaintively.

Adler ignored him, waiting for the champagne, then passed him a glass. "Second, you're out of it. Grounded immediately."

"I'm what?"

"You fly out to Berlin on the next available transport, priority one. That's usually Goring. You report to General Walter Schellenberg at SD headquarters in Berlin."

"Just a minute," Asa told him. "I only fly on the Russian Front. That was the deal."

"I wouldn't argue if I were you. This order comes by way of Himmler himself." Adler raised his glass. "Good luck, my friend."

"God help me, but I think I'm going to need it," Asa Vaughan told him.

Devlin came awake about three in the morning to the sound of gunfire in the distance. He got up and padded into the living room and peered out through a chink in the blackout curtains. He could see the flashes on the far horizon beyond the city.

Behind him, Ilse switched on the light in the kitchen. "I couldn't sleep either. I'll make some coffee."

She was wearing a robe against the cold, her hair in two pigtails that made her look curiously vulnerable. He went and got his overcoat and put it on over his pajamas and sat at the table smoking a cigarette.

"Two days and no suitable landing site for a plane," he said. "I think the general's getting impatient."

"He likes to do things yesterday," Ilse said. "At least we've found a suitable base on the French coast, and the pilot looks promising."

"You can say that again," Devlin told her. "A Yank in the SS, not that the poor sod had much choice from what the record says. I can't wait to meet him."

"My husband was SS, did you know that? A sergeant major in a Panzer regiment."

"I'm sorry," Devlin said.

"You must think we're all very wicked sometimes, Mr. Devlin, but you must understand how it started. After the First War, Germany was on her knees, ruined."

"And then came the Führer."

"He seemed to offer so much. Pride again—prosperity. And then it started—so many bad things, the Jews most of all." She hesitated. "One of my great-grandmothers was Jewish. My husband had to get special permission to marry me. It's there on my record, and sometimes I wake in the night and think what would happen to me if someone decided to do something about it."

Devlin took her hands. "Hush now, girl, we all get that three-o'clock-in-the-morning feeling when everything looks bad." There were tears in her eyes. "Here, I'll make you smile. My disguise for this little jaunt I'm taking. Guess what?"

She was smiling slightly already. "No, tell me."

"A priest."

Her eyes widened. "You, a priest?" She started to laugh. "Oh, no, Mr. Devlin."

"Wait now while I explain. You'd be surprised at the religious background I have. Oh, yes." He nodded solemnly. "Altar boy, then after the British hanged my father in nineteen twenty-one, my mother and I went to live with my old uncle, who was a priest in Belfast. He sent me to a Jesuit boarding school. They beat religion into you there, all right." He lit another cigarette. "Oh, I can play the priest as well as any priest, if you follow me."

"Well, let's hope you don't have to celebrate Mass or hear Confession." She laughed. "Have another coffee."

"Dear God, woman, you've given me an idea there. Where's your briefcase? The file we were looking at earlier—the general file?"

She went into her bedroom and came back with it. "Here it is."

Devlin leafed through it quickly, then nodded. "I was right. It's here in his record. The Steiners are an old Catholic family."

"What are you getting at?"

"This St. Mary's Priory. It's the sort of place priests visit all the time to hear the Confessions. The Little Sisters of Pity are saints compared to the rest of us, but they need Confession before they partake of Communion, and both functions need a priest. Then there would be those patients who were Catholic."

"Including Steiner, you mean?"

"They couldn't deny him a priest, and him in a place like that." He grinned. "It's an idea."

"Have you thought any more about your appearance?" she asked.

"Ah, we can leave that for another few days, then I'll see one of these film people the general mentioned. Put myself in their hands."

She nodded. "Let's hope we come up with something in those Sea Lion files. The trouble is there's so much to wade through." She got up. "Anyway, I think I'll go back to bed."

Outside, the air-raid siren sounded. Devlin smiled wryly. "No you won't. You'll get dressed like a good girl, and we'll go down and spend another jolly night in the cellars. I'll see you in five minutes."

✤

Schellenberg said, "A priest? Yes, I like that."

"So do I," Devlin said. "It's like a uniform, you see. A soldier, a postman, a railway porter—it's the appearance of things you remember, not the face. As I say, the uniform. Priests are like that. Nice and anonymous."

They were standing at a collapsible map table Schellenberg had erected, the plans of St. Mary's Priory spread before them.

"Having studied these on and off for some days, what is your opinion?" Schellenberg asked.

"The most interesting thing is this plan." Devlin tapped it with a finger. "The architect's plans for the changes made in nineteen hundred and ten when the priory was reconsecrated Roman Catholic and the Little Sisters took over."

"What's your point?"

"Underneath, London is a labyrinth, a subterranean world of sewers. I read once there's over a hundred miles of rivers under the city, like the Fleet, which rises in Hampstead and comes out into the Thames at Blackfriars, all underground."

"So?"

"Seven or eight hundred years of sewers, underground rivers, tunnels, and nobody knows where half of them are until they're excavating or making changes, as they were at the priory. Look at the architect's plan here. Regular flooding of the crypt beneath the chapel. They were able to deal with the problem because they discovered a stream running through an eighteenth-century tunnel next door. See, it's indicated there on the plan running into the Thames."

"Very interesting," Schellenberg said.

"They built a grille in the wall of the crypt to allow water to draw into that tunnel. There's a note here on the plan."

"A way out, you mean?"

"It's a possibility. Would have to be checked." Devlin threw down his pencil. "It's knowing what goes on in that place that's the thing, General. For all we know, it could be dead easy. A handful of guards, slack discipline."

"On the other hand, they could be waiting for you."

"Ah, but not if they think I'm still in Berlin," Devlin reminded him.

At that moment Ilse Huber came in, very excited. "You were right to recommend me to check on British right-wing organizations, General. I found details of a man in there cross-referenced to Sea Lion.''

''What's his name?'' Schellenberg demanded.

''Shaw,'' she said. ''Sir Maxwell Shaw.'' She laid two bulky files on the table.

6

🙰

ROMNEY MARSH, SOME FORTY-FIVE MILES southeast of London on the coast of Kent, is a two-hundred-square-mile area reclaimed from the sea by a system of dikes and channels started as far back as Roman times. Much of it is below sea level, and only innumerable drainage ditches prevent it from reverting to its natural state.

Charbury was not even a village. A hamlet of no more than fifteen houses, a church and a village store. There wasn't even a pub any longer, and half the cottages were empty, only the old folk left. The younger people had departed long ago for war work or service in the armed forces.

It was raining that morning as Sir Maxwell Shaw walked down the village street, a black Labrador at his heels. He was a heavily built man of medium height, face craggy, the evidence of heavy drinking there, and the black mustache didn't help. He looked morose and angry much of the time, ready for trouble, and most people avoided him.

He wore a tweed hat, the brim turned down, a waterproof shooting jacket and Wellingtons. He carried a double-barreled twelve-bore shotgun under one arm. When he reached the store, he bent down and fondled the Labrador's ears, his face softening.

''Good girl, Nell. Stay.''

A bell tinkled as he went in the shop. There was an old man in his seventies leaning against the counter talking to a woman behind who was even older.

''Morning, Tinker,'' Shaw said.

''Morning, Sir Maxwell.''

''You promised me some cigarettes, Mrs. Dawson.''

The old lady produced a package from beneath the counter. ''Managed to get you two hundred Players from my man in Dymchurch, Sir

Maxwell. Black market, I'm afraid, so they come expensive."

"Isn't everything these days? Put it on my bill."

He placed the package in one of his game pockets and went out. As he closed the door, he heard Tinker say, "Poor sod."

He took a deep breath to contain his anger and touched the Labrador. "Let's go, girl," he said and went back along the street.

It was Maxwell Shaw's grandfather who had made the family's fortune, a Sheffield ironmaster who had risen on the high tide of Victorian industrialization. It was he who had purchased the estate, renamed Shaw Place, where he had retired, a millionaire with a baronetcy, in 1885. His son had shown no interest in the family firm, which had passed into other hands. A career soldier, he had died leading his men into battle at Spion Kop during the Boer War.

Maxwell Shaw, born in 1890, had followed in his father's footsteps. Eton, Sandhurst, a commission in the Indian army. He served in Mesopotamia during the First World War, came home in 1916 to transfer to an infantry regiment. His mother was still alive. Lavinia, his younger sister, was married to a pilot in the Royal Flying Corps and was serving as a nurse. In 1917 he returned from France badly wounded and with an MC. During his convalescence he met the girl who was to become his wife at the local hunt ball and married her before returning to France.

It was in 1918, the last year of the war, when everything seemed to happen at once. His mother died, then his wife, out with the local hunt, when she took a bad fall. She'd lasted ten days, long enough for Shaw to rush home on compassionate leave to be with her when she died. It was Lavinia who had supported him every step of the way, kept him upright at the graveside, yet within a month she, too, was alone, her husband shot down over the Western Front.

After the war, it was a different world they inherited like everyone else, and Shaw didn't like it. At least he and Lavinia had each other and Shaw Place, although as the years went by and the money grew less, things became increasingly difficult. He was a Conservative member of Parliament for a while and then humiliatingly lost his seat to a Socialist. Like many of his kind, he was violently anti-Semitic, and this, exacerbated by the crushing political blow, led to his involvement with Sir Oswald Mosley and the British Fascist movement.

In all this, he was backed by Lavinia, although her main interest lay in trying to keep their heads above water and hanging on to the estate. Disenchanted with the way society had changed and their own place in it, again like many of their kind, they looked to Hitler as a role model, admired what he was doing for Germany.

And then at a dinner in London in January 1939 they were introduced to a Major Werner Keitel, a military attaché at the German Embassy. For several months Lavinia enjoyed a passionate affair with him, and he was frequently a visitor at Shaw Place, for he was a Luftwaffe pilot and shared Lavinia's love of flying. She kept a Tiger Moth at the time, housed in an old barn, and used the South Meadow as an airstrip. They frequently flew together in the two-seater biplane, covering large sections of the south coast, and Keitel had been able to indulge in his interest for aerial photography.

Shaw never minded. Lavinia had had relationships before, although he himself had little interest in women. The Keitel thing was different, however, because of what it led to.

"Well, we know where we are with him," Devlin said of Shaw. "He's the kind who used to have children transported to Australia for stealing a loaf of bread."

Schellenberg gave him a cigarette. "Werner Keitel was an Abwehr agent employed at the time to select deep cover agents. Not the usual kind at all. A war was coming, that was obvious, and there was much forward planning for Sea Lion."

"And the old sod's place was perfect," Devlin observed. "The back of beyond and yet only forty-five miles from London, and this South Meadow to land a plane on."

"Yes. Keitel, according to his report, found it amazingly easy to recruit both of them. He supplied them with a radio. The sister already knew Morse code. They were expressly forbidden to engage in any other activities, of course. Keitel, by the way, was killed in the Battle of Britain."

"Did they have a code name?"

Ilse, who had been sitting quietly, produced another sheet from the file. " 'Falcon.' He was to be alerted by the message *Does the Falcon still wait? It is now time to strike.*"

Devlin said, "So there they were. Waiting for the great day, the invasion that never came. And what's the situation now, I wonder?"

"As it happens, there is some further information available," Ilse told him. "We have an article here which appeared in an American magazine." She checked the date. "March nineteen forty-three. 'The British Fascist Movement,' it's called. The journalist got an interview with Shaw and his sister. There's a photo."

Lavinia was sitting on a horse, a scarf around her head, and was far more attractive than Devlin had expected. Shaw stood beside her, a shotgun under his arm.

Schellenberg read the article quickly and passed it to Devlin. "Rather sad. You'll see there that like most of his kind he was detained without trial for a few months under Regulation Eighteen-B in nineteen forty."

"Brixton Prison? That must have been a shock," Devlin said.

"The rest is even more sad. The estate sold off, no servants. Just the two of them hanging on in that decaying old house," Schellenberg said. "It could be perfect, you know. Come and have a look at a map of the Channel." They went to the map table. "Here. Cap de la Hague and Chernay. Used to be a flying club. It's used as a landing strip for emergencies only by the Luftwaffe—refueling, that sort of thing. Only half a dozen men there. It's perfect for our purposes because it's only some thirty miles from the Château de Belle-Île, where the Führer's conference takes place."

"How far to our friends in Romney Marsh?"

"A hundred and fifty miles, most of it over the sea."

"Fine," Devlin said. "Except for one thing. Would the Shaws be willing to be activated?"

"Couldn't Vargas find out?"

"Vargas could drop the lot of us, as I told you. This would be exactly what British intelligence wanted. The chance to pull in everyone they could." Devlin shook his head. "No, the Shaws will have to wait till I get there just like everything else. If they'll do it, then we're in business."

"But how will you communicate?" Ilse demanded.

"They may still have that radio, and I can handle one of those things. When the Abwehr recruited me to go to Ireland in forty-one, I did the usual radio and Morse code course."

"And if they haven't?"

Devlin laughed. "Then I'll beg, borrow or steal one. Jesus, General, you worry too much."

Shaw saw a rabbit, flung his shotgun up to his shoulder, already too late, and missed. He cursed, took a flask from his pocket and drank. Nell whined, gazing up at him, anxiously. The reeds here were as high as a man, water gurgling in the creeks, running toward the sea. It was a scene of complete desolation, the sky black, swollen with rain. As it started to fall, Lavinia appeared on horseback, galloping along a dike toward him.

She reined in. "Hello, my darling. I heard your shot."

"Can't hit a brick wall these days, old girl." He put the flask to his lips, then gestured dramatically. "Look at it—a dead world, Lavinia, everything bloody dead, including me. If only something would happen—anything.'' And he raised the flask to his lips again.

Asa Vaughan closed the file and looked up. Schellenberg leaned across the desk and offered him a cigarette. ''What do you think?''

''Why me?''

''Because they tell me you're a great pilot who can fly anything.''

''Flattery usually gets you everywhere, General, but let's examine this. When I was, shall we say, inducted into the SS, the deal was that I only operated against the Russians. It was made clear to me that I wouldn't have to take part in any act detrimental to my country's cause.''

Devlin, sitting by the window, laughed harshly. ''What a load of bollocks, son. If you believed that, then you'd believe any old thing. They had you by your short and curlies the minute they got you into that uniform.''

''I'm afraid he's right, Captain,'' Schellenberg said. ''You wouldn't get very far with the Reichsführer with that argument.''

''I can imagine,'' Asa said, and an expression of gloom settled on his face.

''What's your problem?'' Devlin demanded. ''Where would you rather be? Back on the Eastern Front or here? And you've no choice. Say no, and that old sod Himmler will have you in a concentration camp.''

''Sounds like no contest, except for one small point,'' Asa told him. ''I end up getting caught in England in this uniform, I'll get the fastest court-martial in American history and a firing squad.''

''No you won't, my old son,'' Devlin said. ''They'll hang you. Now the flight. Do you reckon you could make it in?''

''No reason why not. If I am going to do it, I'd need to know the English Channel approach backwards. From what I can see, I'd stay over the water for almost the whole trip. Turn inland for the last few miles.''

''Exactly,'' Schellenberg said.

''This house, Shaw Place. It would mean a night landing. Even with a moon I'd need some sort of guidance.'' He nodded, thinking about it. ''When I was a kid in California, my flying instructor was a guy who had flown with the Lafayette Escadrille in France. I remember him telling me how in those days, things being more primitive, they often used a few cycle lamps arranged in an inverted L-shape with the crossbar at the upwind end.''

''Simple enough,'' Devlin said.

''And the plane. It would have to be small. Something like a Fieseler Stork.''

"Yes, well I'm hoping that's taken care of," Schellenberg said. "I've spoken to the officer in command of Enemy Aircraft Flight. They are at Hildorf. It's a couple hours' drive from Berlin, and they're expecting us in the morning. He thinks he's found us a suitable plane."

"Guess that's it." Asa got up. "What happens now?"

"We eat, son," Devlin told him. "The best the black market can offer. Then you come back to Frau Huber's apartment with me, where we'll share the spare room. Don't worry, it's got twin beds."

The chapel at St. Mary's Priory of the Little Sisters of Pity was cold and damp and smelled of candle grease and incense. In the Confession box, Father Frank Martin waited until the sister whose Confession he had heard was gone. He switched off the lights and went out.

He was the pastor of St. Patrick's, two streets away, and with St. Patrick's came the job of father confessor to the priory. He was seventy-six, a small, frail man with very white hair. If it hadn't been for the war, they'd have retired him, but it was like everything else these days, all hands to the pumps.

He went into the sacristy, removed his alb and carefully folded his violet stole. He reached for his raincoat, debating the virtues of an early night, but compassion and Christian charity won the day as usual. Eighteen patients at the moment, seven of them terminal. A last round of the rooms wouldn't come amiss. He hadn't visited since early afternoon, and that wasn't good enough.

He went out of the chapel and saw the mother superior, Sister Maria Palmer, mopping the floor, a menial task designed to remind herself of what she saw as her greatest weakness: the sin of pride.

Father Martin paused and shook his head. "You are too hard on yourself."

"Not hard enough," she said. "I'm glad to see you. There's been a development since you were here earlier. They've given us a German prisoner of war again."

"Really?" They walked out of the chapel into the entrance hall.

"Yes, a Luftwaffe officer, recently wounded, but well on the way to recovery. A Colonel Kurt Steiner. They've put him on the top floor like the other ones we've had."

"What about guards?"

"Half a dozen military police. There's a young second lieutenant called Benson in charge."

At that moment Jack Carter and Dougal Munro came down the main staircase. Sister Maria Palmer said, "Is everything satisfactory, Brigadier?"

"Perfectly," Munro said. "We'll try to inconvenience you as little as possible."

"There is no inconvenience," she said. "This, by the way, is Father Martin, our priest."

"Father," Munro said and turned to Carter. "I'll be off now, Jack. Don't forget to get a doctor in to check him over."

Sister Maria Palmer said, "Perhaps it was not made clear to you that I am a doctor, Brigadier. Whatever Colonel Steiner's requirements are, I'm sure we can take care of them. In fact now that you're finished, I'll visit him to make sure he's settled in properly."

Jack Carter said, "Well actually, Sister, I'm not too sure about that."

"Captain Carter, let me remind you that this priory, of which I am in charge, is not only a house of God, it is a place where we attend to the sick and the dying. I have seen Colonel Steiner's medical record and note that it's only been a matter of weeks since he was gravely wounded. He will need my attention, and as I note from his record that he is also a Roman Catholic by religion, he may also need the ministrations of Father Martin here."

"Quite right, Sister," Munro said. "See to it, Jack, will you?"

He went out, and Carter turned and led the way up the stairs. There was a door at the top, heavily studded and banded with steel. An MP sat at a small table beside it.

"Open up," Carter told him. The MP knocked on the door, which was opened after a moment by another MP. They passed inside. Carter said, "We're using the other rooms as billets for the men."

"So I see," Sister Maria Palmer said.

The door to the first room stood open. There was a small desk beside a narrow bed, and the young lieutenant, Benson, sat at it. He jumped to his feet. "What can I do for you, sir?"

"Sister and Father Martin have access whenever they require it. Brigadier Munro's orders. We'll talk to the prisoner now."

There was another MP sitting on a chair outside the room at the far end where the passage ran into a blank wall.

"God help us, you're guarding this man well enough," Father Martin said.

Benson unlocked the door, and Steiner, standing by the window, turned to greet them, an impressive figure in the blue-gray Luftwaffe uniform, the Knight's Cross with Oak Leaves at his throat, his other medals making a brave show.

Carter said, "This is the mother superior, Sister Maria Palmer. You didn't get a chance to speak earlier. And Father Martin."

Sister Maria Palmer said, "Tomorrow I'll have you down to the dispensary for a thorough check, Colonel."

"Is that all right, sir?" Benson asked.

"For goodness sake, bring him down yourself, Lieutenant. Surround him with all your men, but if he's not in the dispensary at ten, we'll have words," she told him.

"No problem," Carter said. "See to it, Benson. Anything else, Sister?"

"No, that will do for tonight."

Father Martin said, "I'd like a word with the colonel, in private, if you wouldn't mind."

Carter nodded and turned to Steiner. " I'll check on you from time to time."

"I'm sure you will."

They all went out except for Father Martin, who closed the door and sat on the bed. "My son, you've had a bad time, I can see it in your face. When were you last at Mass?"

"So long ago I can't remember. The war, Father, tends to get in the way."

"No Confession either? A long time since you were able to ease the burden of your sins."

"I'm afraid so." Steiner smiled, warming to the man. "I know you mean well, Father."

"Good heavens, man, I'm not concerned with you and me. I'm interested only in you and God." Father Martin got up. "I'll pray for you, my son, and I'll visit every day. The moment you feel the need for Confession and Mass, tell me and I'll arrange for you to join us in the chapel."

"I'm afraid Lieutenant Benson would insist on coming too," Steiner said.

"Now wouldn't that do his immortal soul some good too?" The old priest chuckled and went out.

Asa Vaughan sat at the dining table in the living room at Ilse Huber's apartment, Devlin opposite him.

"You really think this thing can work?" the American asked.

"Anything will as long as the engine keeps ticking over, isn't that a fact?"

Asa got up and paced restlessly across the room. "What in the hell am I doing here? Can you understand? Everything kind of overtook me. It just happened. I don't seem to have had a choice. Don't now, when it comes right down to it."

"Of course you do," Devlin said. "You go through with it, fly the plane to England, land and give yourself up."

"And what good would that do? They'd never believe me, Devlin."

There was a kind of horror on his face when he added, "Come to think of it, they never will."

"Then you'd better hope Adolf wins the war," Devlin said.

ᘑᖇ

But the following morning at the air base at Hildorf the American seemed in much better spirits as Major Koenig, the officer commanding the Enemy Aircraft Flight, showed them around. He seemed to have examples of most Allied planes. There was a B-17, a Lancaster bomber, a Hurricane, a Mustang, all bearing Luftwaffe insignia.

"Now this is what I thought might suit your purposes," he said. "Here in the end hangar."

The plane standing there was a high wing-braced monoplane with a single engine and a wing span of more than fifty feet.

"Very nice," Asa said. "What is it?"

"A Westland Lysander. Has a maximum speed of two hundred and thirty at ten thousand feet. Short landing and take-off. Only needs two hundred and forty yards fully loaded."

"That means you could make the flight in just under an hour," Schellenberg said to Asa.

Asa ignored him. "Passengers?"

"How many are you thinking of?" Koenig asked.

"Two."

"Perfect comfort. Can manage three. Even four at a pinch." He turned to Schellenberg. "I thought of it at once when you made your inquiries. We picked this up in France last month. It was RAF. The pilot caught a bullet in the chest when attacked by a Ju night fighter. Managed to land and collapsed before he could destroy it. These planes are used by British intelligence for covert operations. They operate with the French Resistance movement, ferrying agents across from England, taking others out. This is the perfect plane for such work."

"Good—then it's mine," Schellenberg said.

"But, General—" Koenig began.

Schellenberg took the Führer Directive from his pocket. "Read that."

Koenig did and returned it, positively clicking his heels. "At your orders, General."

Schellenberg turned to Asa. "So, what are your requirements?"

"Well, obviously I'll want to try her out. Get used to the thing, though I don't think that should be a problem."

"Anything else?"

"Yes, I'll want the RAF roundels back in place for the flight into England. But I'd like that to be temporary. Some sort of canvas covers that can be stripped so that I'm Luftwaffe again for the trip back."

"Easily taken care of," Koenig said.

"Excellent," Schellenberg told him. "Hauptsturmführer Vaughan will remain and test-fly the plane now and as much as he wants for the rest of the day. After that you will do whatever work is needed and have the aircraft delivered at the weekend to the destination in France that my secretary will notify you of."

"Certainly, General," Koenig said.

Schellenberg turned to Asa. "Enjoy yourself while you can. I've arranged to borrow a Fieseler Stork from the Luftwaffe. We'll fly down to Chernay and inspect the airstrip tomorrow. I'd also like to have a look at this Château de Belle-Île while we're there."

"And you want me to do the flying?" Asa asked.

"Don't worry, son, we have every confidence in you," Devlin told him as he and Schellenberg went out.

In London, Dougal Munro was working at his desk when Jack Carter came in.

"What is it, Jack?"

"I've had a medical report from Sister Maria Palmer, sir, on Steiner."

"What's her opinion?"

"He's still not a hundred percent. Some residual infection. She asked me to help her get hold of some of this new wonder drug penicillin. Apparently it cures just about everything, but it's in short supply."

"Then get it for her, Jack, get it."

"Very well, sir. I'm sure I can."

He hesitated at the door, and Munro said impatiently, "For God's sake, what is it, Jack? I'm up to my ears in work here, not least amongst my worries being a meeting at three of headquarters staff at SHAEF presided over by General Eisenhower himself."

"Well, it's the Steiner thing, sir. I mean, here he is, installed at the priory. What happens now?"

"Liam Devlin, if it is Devlin they choose, is hardly going to parachute into the courtyard at St. Mary's Priory tomorrow night, Jack, and if he did, so what? The only way we could guard Steiner any closer is by having an MP share his bed, and that would never do."

"So we just wait, sir?"

"Of course we do. If they intend to have a go, it'll take weeks to organize, but that doesn't matter. After all, we have Vargas in our pocket. Anything happens, and we'll be the first to know."

"Very well, sir."

As Carter opened the door, Munro added, "We've got all the time in the world, Jack. So has Steiner."

❧

When Steiner went into the chapel that evening, he was escorted by Lieutenant Benson and an MP corporal. The chapel was cold and damp, slightly eerie with the candles down at the altar and the ruby light of the sanctuary lamp. Instinctively he dipped his fingers in the holy water, a kind of regression to childhood, and went and sat on the end of a bench beside two nuns and waited his turn. The mother superior emerged from the confessional box, smiled at him, and passed on. One of the nuns went in. After a while she came out and was replaced by the other.

When it came to Steiner's turn, he went in and kneeled down, finding the darkness surprisingly comforting. He hesitated, and then that ghost from childhood rose again and he said, almost automatically, "Bless me, Father . . . "

Father Martin knew it was him of course, had to. He said, "May the Lord Jesus bless you and help you tell your sins."

"Dammit, Father," Steiner exploded, "I don't even know why I'm here. Maybe I just wanted to get out of that room."

"Oh, I'm sure God will forgive you that, my son." Steiner had an insane desire to laugh. The old man said, "Is there anything you want to say to me? Anything?"

And suddenly Steiner found himself saying, "My father. They butchered my father. Hung him up on a hook like a piece of meat."

"Who did this thing, my son?"

"The Gestapo—the bloody Gestapo." Steiner could hardly breathe, his throat dry, eyes hot. "Hate, that's all I feel and revenge. I want revenge. Now what good is that to a man like you, Father? Am I not guilty of a very great sin?"

Father Martin said quietly, "May our Lord Jesus Christ absolve you, and I, by his authority, absolve you from your sins in the name of the Father, and the Son and the Holy Spirit."

"But, Father, you don't understand," Kurt Steiner said. "I can't pray anymore."

"That's all right, my son," Father Martin told him. "I'll pray for you."

7

THE FLIGHT FROM BERLIN TO Cap de la Hague took just over three hours, Asa charting a course that took them over parts of occupied Holland, Belgium and then France. They came in to Chernay from the sea. It was a desolate-looking little place. Not even a control tower, just a grass runway, with a wind sock at one end, three old prewar hangars and several huts that looked like Luftwaffe additions. There was also a fuel dump.

Asa raised them on the radio. "Stork as expected from Gatow."

A voice said, "Chernay control. Permission to land granted. Wind southeast, strength three to four and freshening."

"Takes himself seriously," Asa said over his shoulder. "Here we go."

He made a perfect landing and taxied toward the hangars, where half a dozen men waited in Luftwaffe coveralls. As Schellenberg and Devlin got out, a sergeant emerged from the hut with the radio mast and hurried toward them.

He took in Schellenberg's uniform and got his heels together. "General."

"And your name is?"

"Leber, General. Flight sergeant."

"And you are in charge here?"

"Yes, General."

"Read this." Schellenberg handed him the Führer Directive. "You and your men are now under my command. A matter of the utmost importance to the Reich."

Leber got his heels together again, handed the letter back. "At your orders, General."

"Hauptsturmführer Vaughan will be making a hazardous and highly secret flight across the English Channel. The aircraft he will use is an unusual one. You'll see that for yourself when it's delivered."

"And our duties, General?"

"I'll inform you later. Is your radio receiving equipment up to scratch?"

"Oh, yes, General, the best the Luftwaffe can offer. Sometimes

371

aircraft returning across the Channel are in a bad way. We have to be able to talk them in when necessary.''

"Good." Schellenberg nodded. "Do you happen to know a place called Château de Belle-Île? According to the map it's about thirty miles from here in the general direction of Carentan.''

"I'm afraid not, General.''

"Never mind. We'll manage. Now find us a *Kübelwagen*."

"Certainly, General. May I ask if you'll be spending the night?''

Schellenberg glanced around at the desolate landscape. "Well, I'd prefer not to, Sergeant, but one never knows. Have the Stork refueled and made ready for the return trip.''

"Jesus," Devlin said as Leber led them toward a jeep parked outside the radio hut. "Would you look at this place? What a lousy posting. I wonder they can put up with it.''

"Better than Russia," Asa Vaughan said.

Asa drove, Devlin beside him, Schellenberg in the rear, a map spread across his knees. "Here it is. The road south from Cherbourg goes to Carentan. It's off there somewhere on the coast.''

"Wouldn't it make more sense to land at the Luftwaffe base at Cherbourg?'' Asa asked.

"As the Führer will when he comes." Schellenberg shook his head. "I prefer to keep our heads down for the moment. We don't need to go through Cherbourg at all. There's a network of country roads south that cut across to the coast. Thirty miles, thirty-five at the most.''

"What's the purpose of this little trip anyway?'' Devlin asked him.

"This Belle-Île place intrigues me. I'd like to see what we've got there as long as we're in the neighborhood.'' He shrugged.

Devlin said, "I was wondering. Does the Reichsführer know we're here?''

"He knows about our flight to Chernay, or he will soon. He likes a regular report.''

"Ah, yes, General, that's one thing, but this Belle-Île place would be another.''

"You could say that, Mr. Devlin, you could.''

"Sweet Mother of God, what a fox you are," Devlin said. "I pity the huntsman when you're around.''

Many of the country lanes were so narrow that it would not have been possible for two vehicles to pass each other, but after half an hour they cut into the main road that ran south from Cherbourg to Carentan. It was here that Schellenberg had trouble with his map, and then they had a stroke of luck, a sign at the side of the road outside the village of St. Aubin that said *12th Parachute Detachment*. There was a spread of farm buildings visible beyond the trees.

"Let's try here," Schellenberg said, and Asa turned off the road.

The men in the farmyard were all *Fallschirmjäger*, hard young men, old before their time, with cropped hair. Most of them wore camouflaged smocks and jump boots. A number sat on benches against the wall cleaning weapons. A couple worked on the engine of a troop carrier. They glanced up curiously as the *Kübelwagen* arrived, rising to their feet when they saw Schellenberg's uniform.

"That's all right, carry on with what you're doing," he said.

A young captain emerged from the farmhouse. He had the Iron Cross First and Second Class, the cuff titles for Crete and the Afrika Korps. He also had a Winter War ribbon, a tough, hard-faced young man.

"You are in charge here?" Schellenberg asked.

"Yes, General. Hauptmann Erich Bramer. In what way may I help you?"

"We're looking for a place called Château de Belle-Île," Schellenberg told him. "Do you know it?"

"Very well. About ten miles east of here on the coast. Let me show you on my area map."

They followed him into the farmhouse. The living room was fitted out as a command post with radio and large scale maps on the wall. The back road to Belle-Île was plain enough.

"Excellent," Schellenberg said. "Tell me something. What's your unit's purpose here?"

"Security duties, General. We patrol the area, try to keep the French Resistance in place."

"Do you get much trouble from them?"

"Not really." Kramer laughed. "I only have thirty-five men left in this unit. We were lucky to get out of Stalingrad. This is a rest cure for us."

They went outside, and as they got back into the *Kübelwagen* Devlin said, "Crete and Afrika Korps, I see, and Stalingrad? Did you know Steiner?"

Even the men cleaning their weapons looked up at the mention of the name. Kramer said, "Oberst Kurt Steiner? Who doesn't in our line of work? A legend in the Parachute Regiment."

"You've met him then?"

"Several times. You know him?"

"You could say that."

Kramer said, "We heard a rumor he was dead."

"Ah, well, you mustn't believe everything you hear," Devlin told him.

"Captain." Schellenberg returned his salute as Asa drove away.

"Dear God," Devlin said, "I sometimes wonder why Steiner doesn't make his own way back across the Channel walking on water."

Belle-Île was quite spectacular, a castle crowning a hill beside the sea, a vast estuary stretching beyond it, sand where the tide had just retreated. Asa took the *Külbelwagen* up the single winding road. There was a narrow bridge across a gap that was more ravine than moat. Two great doors stood open in an arched entrance, and they came out into a cobbled courtyard. Asa braked at the foot of broad steps leading up to the front entrance, walls and towers rising above them.

They got out and Schellenberg led the way. The door was of oak, buckled with age and studded with rusting iron bolts and bands of steel. There was a bell hanging from the wall beside it. Schellenberg pulled the chain, and the jangling echoed around the courtyard, bouncing from the walls.

"Jesus," Devlin said. "All we need is Quasimodo."

A moment later the door creaked open and he appeared, or a fair facsimile, a very old man with gray hair down to his shoulders, a black dress coat of velvet that had seen better days, a pair of very baggy corduroy trousers of the type worn by peasants.

His face was wrinkled and he badly needed a shave. "*Oui, monsieurs*," he said. "What can I do for you?"

"You are the caretaker?" Schellenberg asked.

"Yes, monsieur. Pierre Dissard."

"You live here with your wife?"

"When she is here, monsieur. At present she is with her niece in Cherbourg."

Devlin said to Asa, "Are you getting all this?"

"Not a word. I don't speak French."

"I suppose you spent all your time playing football. The general and I, on the other hand, being men of intellect and learning, can understand everything the old bugger is saying. I'll translate freely when necessary."

Schellenberg said, "I wish to inspect the premises."

He walked past Dissard into a great entrance hall, flagged in granite, a carpet here and there. There was an enormous fireplace to one side and a staircase to the first floor wide enough to take a regiment.

"You are of the SS, monsieur?" Dissard asked.

"I should think that was obvious," Schellenberg told him.

"But the premises have already been inspected, monsieur, the other day. An officer in a similar uniform to your own."

"Do you recall his name?"

"He said he was a major." The old man frowned, trying. "His face was bad on one side."

Schellenberg said calmly, "Berger. Was that his name?"

Dissard nodded eagerly. "That's it, monsieur, Major Berger. His French was very bad."

Asa said, "What's going on?"

"He's telling us someone's been here before us. An SS major named Berger," Devlin said.

"Do you know him?"

"Oh, intimately, particularly his nose, but I'll explain later."

Schellenberg said, "Then you are aware that these premises are required in the near future. I would appreciate a conducted tour."

"The château has been closed since nineteen forty, monsieur. My master, the Comte de Beaumont, went to England to fight the Boche."

"Really?" Schellenberg said dryly. "So, let's get on with it. We'll go upstairs and work down."

The old man led them up the staircase in front of them. There were innumerable bedrooms, some with four-posters, the furniture draped in sheets, two doors leading to separate wings so long disused that the dust lay thick on the floor.

"Mother of God, is this the way the rich live?" Devlin asked as they went down. "Have you seen how far it is to the bathroom?"

Schellenberg noticed a door at one end of the landing above the entrance. "What's through there?"

"I'll show you, monsieur. Another way into the dining hall."

They found themselves in a long dark gallery above a massive room. The ceiling had arched oaken beams, below was a massive fireplace in a medieval pattern. In front of it was an enormous oak table surrounded by high-backed chairs. Battle standards hung above the fireplace.

They went down the stairs and Schellenberg said, "What are the flags?"

"Souvenirs of war, monsieur. The de Beaumonts have always served France well. See, in the center there, the standard in scarlet and gold. An ancestor of the count carried that at Waterloo."

"Is that a fact?" Devlin commented. "I always thought they lost that one."

Schellenberg looked around the hall, then led the way out through high oak doors back into the entrance hall.

"I have seen enough. What did Major Berger say to you?"

"That he would be back, monsieur." The old man shrugged. "One week, maybe two."

Schellenberg put a hand on his shoulder. "No one must know we have been here, my friend, especially Major Berger."

"Monsieur?" Dissard looked puzzled.

Schellenberg said, "This is a matter of the greatest secrecy and of considerable importance."

"I understand, monsieur."

"If the fact that we had been here came out, the source of the information would be obvious." He patted Dissard's shoulder with his gloved hand. "This would be bad for you."

The old man was thoroughly frightened. "Monsieur—please. Not a word. I swear it."

They went out to the *Kübelwagen* and drove away. Devlin said, "Walter, you can be a cold-blooded bastard when you want to be."

"Only when necessary." Schellenberg turned to Asa. "Can we get back to Berlin tonight?"

The light was already fading, dark clouds dropping toward the sea, and rain drifted in across the wet sands.

"Possible," Asa said. "If we're lucky. We might have to overnight at Chernay. Get off first thing in the morning."

Devlin said, "What a prospect." He pulled up the collar of his overcoat and lit a cigarette. "The glamour of war."

On the following afternoon Devlin was delivered to the UFA film studios for his appointment with the chief makeup artist. Karl Schneider was in his late forties, a tall, broad-shouldered man who looked more like a dock worker than anything else.

He examined a passport-type photo which Devlin had had taken. "You say this is what they've got on the other side?"

"Something like that."

"It's not much, not for a policeman looking for a face in the crowd. When would you be going?"

Devlin made the decision then for himself, for Schellenberg, for all of them. "Let's say two or three days from now."

"And how long would you be away?"

"Ten days at the most. Can you do anything?"

"Oh, yes." Schneider nodded. "One can change the shape of the face by wearing cheek pads in the mouth and all that sort of thing, but I don't think it's necessary for you. You don't carry a lot of weight, my friend, not much flesh on your bones."

"All down to bad living," Devlin said.

Schneider ignored the joke. "Your hair—dark and wavy and you wear it long. I think the key is what I do to the hair. What role do you intend to play?"

"A priest. Ex-army chaplain. Invalided out."

"Yes, the hair." Schneider draped a sheet around his shoulders and reached for a pair of scissors.

By the time he was finished, Devlin's hair was cropped close to the skull.

"Jesus, is that me?"

"That's only a start. Let's have you over the basin." Schneider washed the hair then rubbed some chemical in. "I've worked with the best actors. Marlene Dietrich before she cleared out. Now she had marvelous hair. Oh, and there was Conrad Veidt. What a wonderful actor. Chased out by these Nazi bastards, and he ends up, so I'm told, playing Nazi bastards in Hollywood."

"A strange old life," Devlin said. He kept his eyes closed and let him get on with it.

He hardly recognized the face that stared out at him. The close-cropped hair was quite gray now, accentuating the cheekbones, putting ten or twelve years on his age.

"That's bloody marvelous."

"One more touch." Schneider rummaged in his makeup case, took out several pairs of spectacles and examined them. "Yes, these, I think. Clear glass, naturally." He placed a pair of steel-rimmed glasses on Devlin's nose and adjusted them. "Yes, excellent. I'm pleased with myself."

"God help me, but I look like Himmler," Devlin said. "Will it last? The hair, I mean."

"A fortnight, and you said you'd be away ten days at the most." Schneider produced a small plastic bottle. "A rinse with this would keep things going, but not for long."

"No," Devlin told him. "I said ten days and I meant it. It's all one in the end anyway. Any longer and I'll be dead."

***

"Astonishing!" Schellenberg said.

"I'm glad you think so," Devlin told him. "So let's have the right photos taken. I want to get on with it."

"And what does that mean?"

"I want to go as soon as possible. Tomorrow or the day after."

Schellenberg looked at him gravely. "You're sure about this?"

"There's nothing else to hang about for now that your friend at UFA has given me a new lace. We have the setup at Chernay, Asa and the

Lysander. That leaves us with three uncertainties. My IRA friend Michael Ryan, the Shaws and the priory.''

"True," Schellenberg said. "No matter what the situation at the priory, if your friend Ryan is not available you would be presented with real difficulty. The same with the Shaws.''

Devlin said, "Without the Shaws it would be an impossibility, so the sooner I get there the sooner we know.''

"Right," Schellenberg said briskly, and rang for Ilse Huber, who came in. "Papers for Mr. Devlin from the forgery department.''

"They'll need photos of the new me," Devlin told her.

"But, Mr. Devlin, the British identity card is what you need. A ration book for certain items of food, clothing coupons, driving license. None of these require a photo.''

"That's a pity," Devlin told her. "It you're being checked out by someone, the fact that they can compare you with a photo is so satisfying that you're on your way before you know it.''

"Have you decided on your name and circumstances yet?" Schellenberg asked.

"As I've often said, the best kind of lie is the one that sticks closest to the truth," Devlin said. "No sense in trying to sound completely English. Even the great Devlin wouldn't get away with that. So I'm an Ulsterman.''He turned to Ilse. "Are you getting this?''

"Every word.''

"Conlon. Now there's a name I've always liked. My first girlfriend was a Conlon. And my old uncle, the priest in Belfast I lived with as a boy. He was a Henry, though everyone called him Harry.''

"Father Harry Conlon then?" she said.

"Yes, but more than that. Major Harry Conlon, army chaplain, on extended leave after being wounded.''

"Where?" Schellenberg asked.

"In my head." Devlin tapped the bullet scar. "Oh, I see what you mean. Geographically speaking.''

"How about the Allied invasion of Sicily this year?" Schellenberg suggested.

"Excellent. I got clipped in an air strike on the first day. That way I don't need too much information about the place if anyone asks me.''

"I've seen a cross-reference with British army chaplains in the military documentation file," Ilse said. "I remember because it struck me as being unusual. May I go and check on it, General? It would only take a few minutes.''

Schellenberg nodded. She went out and he said, "I'll make the arrangements for your flight to Ireland. I've already done some checking with the Luftwaffe. They suggest you take off from the Laville base outside Brest.''

"Talk about déjà vu," Devlin said. "That's where I left from before.

It wouldn't happen to be a Dornier bomber they suggest, the good old Flying Pencil?''

"Exactly."

"Ah, well, it worked last time, I suppose."

Ilse came in at that moment. "I was right. Look what I found."

The pass was in the name of a Major George Harvey, army chaplain, and there was a photo. It had been issued by the War Office and authorized unrestricted access to both military bases and hospitals.

"Astonishing how powerful the need for spiritual comfort is," Schellenberg said. "Where did this come from?"

"Documents taken from a prisoner of war, General. I'm certain that forging will have no difficulty copying it, and it would give Mr. Devlin the photo he wanted."

"Brilliant," Devlin said. "You're a marvel of a woman."

"You'll need to see the clothing department as well," she said. "Will you want a uniform?"

"It's a thought. I mean, it could come in useful. Otherwise a dark suit, clerical collar, dark hat, raincoat, and they can give me a Military Cross. If I'm a priest, I might as well be a gallant one. Always impressive. And I'll want a travel voucher from Belfast to London. The kind the military use, just in case I do want to play the major."

"I'll get things started."

She went out and Schellenberg said, "What else?"

"Cash. Five thousand quid, I'd say. That's to take care of my having to hand a few bribes out as well as supporting myself. If you find one of those canvas military holdalls officers carry these days, the money could go in a false bottom of some sort."

"I'm sure there'll be no problem."

"Fivers, Walter, and the real thing. None of the false stuff I happen to know the SS has been printing."

"You have my word on it. You'll need a code name."

"We'll stick with Shaw's. Falcon will do fine. Give me the right details for contacting your radio people at this end and I'll be in touch before you know it."

"Excellent. The Führer's conference at Belle-Île is on the twenty-first. We could be cutting it fine."

"We'll manage." Devlin stood up. "I think I'll try the canteen." He turned at the door. "Oh, just one thing."

"What's that?"

"When I was dropped by parachute into Ireland in forty-one for the Abwehr, I had ten thousand pounds in a suitcase, funds for the IRA. When I opened it I found neat bundles of fivers, each one with a Bank of Berlin band around it. Do you think they could do better this time?"

Schellenberg said, "And they wonder why we're losing the war."

Asa was in the canteen drinking a beer and reading a copy of *Signal*, the magazine for German forces, when Devlin came in. The Irishman got a coffee and joined him.

"I can't believe it," Asa said. "I hardly recognized you."

"The new me, Father Harry Conlon, very much at your service. Also Major Harry Conlon, army chaplain, and I'm on my way tomorrow night."

"Isn't that pushing it?"

"Jesus, son, I want to get on with it."

"Where are you flying from?"

"Laville, near Brest."

"And the plane?"

"Dornier two-fifteen."

"Okay, I'll fly you myself."

"No you won't. You're too valuable. Say you got me to Ireland and dropped me off, then got shot down by a British night fighter off the French coast on your way back. A right old balls-up that would be."

"Okay," Asa said reluctantly. "But at least I can fly you down to Laville. Nobody can object to that."

"Always nicer to have a friend see you off," Devlin said.

❦

It was just after nine the following night, rain pounding in from the Atlantic, when Asa stood in the control tower at Laville and watched the Dornier take off. He opened a window, listened to it fade into the night. He closed the window and said to the radio man, "Send this message."

Devlin, sitting at the back of the Dornier in a flying suit, his supply bag beside him, was approached by the wireless operator. "A message for you, sir. A bad joke on someone's part."

"Read it."

"It just says, 'Break a leg.' "

Devlin laughed. "Well, son, you'd have to be an actor to understand that one."

The Dornier made good time, and it was shortly after two in the morning when Devlin jumped at five thousand feet. As on the last occasion, he had chosen County Monaghan, which was an area he knew well and adjacent to the Ulster border.

The necessity of a supply bag to the parachutist is that, dangling twenty feet below him on a cord, it hits the ground first, a useful precaution when landing in the dark. A crescent moon showed occasionally, which helped. Devlin made an excellent landing and within minutes had his suitcase and a trenching shovel out of the supply bag, a dark raincoat and trilby. He found a ditch, scraped a hole, put the supply bag, parachute, and flying suit in it, then tossed the shovel into a nearby pool.

He put on his raincoat and hat, opened the case and found the steel-rimmed spectacles which he carried in there for safety. Underneath the neatly folded uniform was a webbing belt and holster containing a Smith & Wesson .38 revolver, the type frequently issued to British officers. There was a box of fifty cartridges to go with it. Everything seemed in order. He put on the spectacles and stood up.

"Hail Mary full of grace, here am I, a sinner," he said softly. "Do what you can for me." And he crossed himself, picked up his suitcase and moved on.

The Ulster border, to anyone who knew it, was never a problem. He followed a network of country lanes and the occasional field path and by four-fifteen was safe in Ulster and standing on British soil.

And then he had an incredible piece of luck. A farm truck passed him, stopped, and the driver, a man in his sixties, looked out. "Jesus, Father, and where would you be walking to at this time of the morning?"

"Armagh," Devlin said. "To catch the milk train to Belfast."

"Now isn't that the strange thing and me going all the way to Belfast market."

"God bless you, my son," Devlin said and climbed in beside him.

"Nothing to it, Father," the farmer told him as he drove away. "After all, if a priest can't get a helping hand in Ireland where would he get one?"

*

It was later that morning at ten o'clock when Schellenberg knocked on the Reichsführer's door and went in.

"Yes?" Himmler said. "What is it?"

"I've had confirmation from Laville, Reichsführer, that Devlin jumped into Southern Ireland at approximately two A.M."

"Really?" Himmler said. "You've moved fast, Brigadeführer. My congratulations."

"Of course none of this guarantees success, Reichsführer. We have to take even Devlin's safe landing on faith, and the whole business when he gets to London is very open-ended."

"There's been a change in our plans," Himmler said. "The Führer's conference at Belle-Île will now take place on the fifteenth."

"But, Reichsführer, that only gives us a week."

"Yes, well we're in the Führer's hands. It is not for us to query his decisions. Still, I know you'll do your best. Carry on, General.''

Schellenberg went out, closing the door, feeling totally bewildered. ''For God's sake, what's the bastard playing at?'' he said softly and went back to his office.

8

In Belfast, Devlin found it impossible to get a ticket for the crossing to Heysham in Lancashire. There was a waiting list, and the situation was no better on the Glasgow route. Which left Larne, north of Belfast to Stranraer, the way he had got across the water for Operation Eagle. It was a short run, with a special boat train all the way to London, but this time he wasn't going to take any chances. He caught the local train from Belfast to Larne, went into a public toilet on the docks and locked himself in. When he came out fifteen minutes later, he was in uniform.

It paid off immediately. The boat was full, but not to military personnel. He produced the travel voucher they had given him in Berlin. The booking clerk hardly looked at it, took in the major's uniform, the ribbon for the Military Cross and the clergyman's dog collar and booked him on board immediately.

It was the same at Stranraer, where in spite of the incredible number of people being carried by the train, he was allocated a seat in a first-class carriage. Stranraer to Glasgow, Glasgow down to Birmingham and then to London, arriving at King's Cross at three o'clock the following morning. When he walked from the train, one face among the crowd, the first thing he heard was an air-raid siren.

The beginning of 1944 became known to Londoners as the Little Blitz as the Luftwaffe, the performance of its planes greatly improved, turned attention to night raids on London again. The siren Devlin heard heralded the approach of Ju-88 pathfinders from Chartres in France. The heavy bombers came later, but by then he was, like thousands of others, far below ground, sitting out a hard night in the comparative safety of a London tube station.

Mary Ryan was a girl that people remarked on, not because she was particularly beautiful but because there was a strange, almost ethereal look to her. The truth was her health had never been good, and the pressures of wartime didn't help. Her face was always pale, with dark smudges beneath her eyes, and she had a heavy limp which had been a fact of life for her since birth. She was only nineteen and looked old beyond her years.

Her father, an IRA activist, had died of a heart attack in Mountjoy Prison in Dublin just before the war, her mother of cancer in 1940, leaving her with only one relative, her Uncle Michael, her father's younger brother who had lived in London for years, on his own since the death of his wife in 1938. She had moved from Dublin to London and now kept house for him and worked as an assistant in a large grocery store in Wapping High Street.

No more though, for when she reported for work at eight o'clock that morning, the shop and sizable section of the street was reduced to a pile of smoking rubble. She stayed, watching the ambulances, the firemen dousing things down, the men of the heavy rescue unit sifting through the foundations for those who might still be alive.

After doing what she could to help, she turned and walked away, a strange figure in her black beret and old raincoat, limping rapidly along the pavement. She stopped at a back street shop, purchased milk and a loaf of bread, some cigarettes for her uncle, then went out again. It started to rain as she turned into Cable Wharfe.

There had originally been twenty houses backing onto the river. Fifteen had been demolished by a bomb during the Blitz. Four more were boarded up. She and her uncle lived in the end one. The kitchen door was at the side, opening onto an iron terrace, the waters of the Thames below. She paused at the rail, looking down toward Tower Bridge and the Tower of London in the near distance. She loved the river, never tired of it. The large ships from the London docks passing to and fro, the constant barge traffic. There was a wooden stairway at the end of the terrace dropping down to a small private jetty. Her uncle kept two boats moored there. A rowing skiff and a larger craft, a small motorboat with a cabin. As she looked over, she saw a man smoking a cigarette and sheltering from the rain. He wore a black hat and raincoat, and a suitcase was on the jetty beside him.

"Who are you?" she called sharply. "It's private property down there."

"Good day to you *a colleen*," he called cheerfully and lifted the case and came up the stairs.

"What do you want?" she said.

Devlin smiled. "It's Michael Ryan I'm after. Would you be knowing him? I tried the door, but there was no answer."

"I'm his niece, Mary," she said. "Uncle Michael's not due home just yet. He was on a night shift."

"A night shift?" Devlin asked.

"Yes, on the cabs. Ten till ten. Twelve hours."

"I see." He glanced at his watch. "Another hour and a half then."

She was slightly uncertain, unwilling to ask him in, he sensed that. Instead she said, "I don't think I've seen you before."

"Not surprising and me only just over from Ireland."

"You know Uncle Michael then?"

"Oh, yes, old friends from way back. Conlon's my name. Father Harry Conlon," he added, opening the top of his dark raincoat so that she could see the dog collar.

She relaxed at once. "Would you like to come in and wait, Father?"

"I don't think so. I'll take a little walk and come back later. Could I leave my suitcase?"

"Of course."

She unlocked the kitchen door, he followed her in and put the case down. "Would you know St. Mary's Priory, by any chance?"

"Oh, yes," she said. "You go along Wapping High Street to Wapping Wall. It's near St. James's Stairs on the river. About a mile."

He stepped back outside. "The grand view you have here. There's a book by Dickens that starts with a girl and her father in a boat on the Thames searching for the bodies of the drowned and what was in their pockets."

"*Our Mutual Friend*," she told him. "The girl's name was Lizzie."

"By God, girl, and aren't you the well-read one."

She warmed to him for that. "Books are everything."

"And isn't that the fact?" He touched his hat. "I'll be back."

He walked away along the terrace, his footsteps echoing on the boards, and she closed the door.

From Wapping High Street the damage done to the London docks in the Blitz was plain to see, and yet the amazing thing was how busy they were, ships everywhere.

"I wonder what old Adolf would make of this," Devlin said softly. "Give him a nasty surprise, I shouldn't wonder."

He found St. Mary's Priory with no trouble. It stood on the other side of the main road from the river, high walls in gray stone, darkened even more by the filth of the city over the years. The roof of the chapel was clear to see on the other side, a bell tower rising above it. Interestingly enough, the great oak door that was the entrance stood open.

The notice board beside it said, *St Mary's Priory, Little Sisters of Pity, Mother Superior: Sister Maria Palmer.* Devlin leaned against the wall and lit a cigarette and watched. After a while a porter in a blue uniform appeared. He stood on the top step looking up and down the road, then went back in.

Below, there was a narrow band of shingle and mud between the river and the retaining wall. Some little distance away were steps down from the wall. Devlin descended casually and strolled along the strip of shingle, remembering the architect's drawings and the old drainage tunnel. The shingle ran out, water lapped in against the wall, and then he saw it, an arched entrance almost completely flooded, a couple of feet of headroom only.

He went back up to the road and on the next corner from the priory found a public house called The Bargee. He went into the saloon bar. There was a young woman in headscarf and slacks mopping the floor. She looked up, surprise on her face.

"Yes, what do you want? We don't open till eleven."

Devlin had unbuttoned his raincoat and she saw the dog collar. "I'm sorry to bother you. Conlon—Father Conlon."

There was a chain around her neck, and he saw the crucifix. Her attitude changed at once. "What can I do for you, Father?"

"I knew I was going to be in the neighborhood, and a colleague asked me to look up a friend of his. Father Confessor at St. Mary's Priory. Stupid of me, but I've forgotten his name."

"That would be Father Frank." She smiled. "Well, that's what we call him. Father Frank Martin. He's priest in charge at St. Patrick's down the road, and he handles the priory as well. God alone knows how he manages at his age. Has no help at all, but then there's a war on I suppose."

"St. Patrick's you say? God bless you," Devlin told her and went out.

There was nothing very remarkable about the church. It was late Victorian in architecture like most Catholic churches in England, built after changes in English law had legitimized that branch of the Christian religion.

It had the usual smells, candles, incense, religious images, the Stations of the Cross, things which, in spite of his Jesuit education, had never meant very much to Devlin. He sat down in a pew, and after a while

Father Martin came out of the sacristy and genuflected at the altar. The old man stayed on his knees praying, and Devlin got up and left quietly.

Michael Ryan was a little over six feet and carried himself well for his sixty years. Sitting at the kitchen table, he wore a black leather jacket and white scarf, a tweed cap beside him. He was drinking tea from a large mug Mary had given him.

"Conlon, you say?" He shook his head. "I never had a friend called Conlon. Come to think of it, I never had a friend who was a priest."

There was a knock at the kitchen door. Mary went and opened it. Devlin stood there in the rain. "God bless all here," he said and stepped inside.

Ryan stared at him, frowning, and then an expression of bewilderment appeared on his face. "Dear God in heaven. It can't be—Liam Devlin. It is you?"

He stood up, and Devlin put his hands on his shoulders. "The years have been kind to you, Michael."

"But you, Liam, what have they done to you?"

"Oh, don't believe everything you see. I needed a change in appearance. A few years added on." He took his hat off and ran his fingers through the gray stubble. "The hair owes more to the chemical industry at the moment than it does to nature."

"Come in, man, come in." Ryan shut the door. "Are you on the run or what?"

"Something like that. It needs explaining."

Ryan said, "This is my niece, Mary. Remember my elder brother, Seamus? He that died in Mountjoy Prison."

"A good man on the worst of days," Devlin said.

"Mary, this is my old friend Liam Devlin."

The effect on the girl was quite extraordinary. It was as if a light had been turned on inside. There was a look on her face that was almost holy. "You are Liam Devlin? Sweet Mother of Jesus, I've heard of you ever since I was a little girl."

"Nothing bad, I hope," Devlin said.

"Sit down, please. Will you have some tea? Have you had your breakfast?"

"Come to think of it, I haven't."

"I've got some eggs and there's a little of Uncle Michael's black market bacon left. You can share it."

While she busied herself at the stove, Devlin took off his coat and sat opposite Ryan. "Have you a telephone here?"

"Yes. In the hall."

"Good. I need to make a call later."

"What is it, Liam? Has the IRA decided to start up again in London?"

"I'm not from the IRA this time," Devlin told him. "Not directly. To be frank, I'm from Berlin."

Ryan said, "I'd heard the organization had had dealings with the Germans, but to what purpose, Liam? Are you telling me you actually approve of that lot?"

"Nazi bastards most of them," Devlin said. "Not all, mind you. Their aim is to win the war, mine is a united Ireland. I've had the odd dealing with them, always for money, money paid into a Swiss account on behalf of the organization."

"And you're here for them now? Why?"

"British intelligence have a man under guard not far from here at St. Mary's Priory. A Colonel Steiner. As it happens, he's a good man and no Nazi. You'll have to take my word for that. It also happens that the Germans want him back. That's why I'm here."

"To break him out?" Ryan shook his head. "There was never anyone else like you. A raving bloody lunatic."

"I'll try not to involve you too much, but I do need a little help. Nothing too strenuous, I promise. I could ask you to do it for old times' sake, but I won't." Devlin picked up the case, put it on the table and opened it. He pushed the clothes out of the way, ran a finger around the bottom and pulled out the lining, revealing the money he had carried in there. He took out a bundle of five-pound notes and laid them on the table. "A thousand pounds, Michael."

Ryan ran his fingers through his hair. "My God, Liam, what can I say?"

The girl put plates of egg and bacon in front of each of them. "You should be ashamed to take a penny piece after the stories you've told me about Mr. Devlin. You should be happy to do it for nothing."

"Oh, what it is to be young." Devlin put an arm around her waist. "If only life were like that, but hang on to your dreams, girl." He turned to Ryan. "Well, Michael?"

"Christ, Liam, you only live once, but to show I'm a weak man, I'll take the thousand quid."

"First things first. Do you happen to have a gun about the place?"

"A Luger pistol from before the war under the floorboards in my bedroom. Must have been there five years, and the ammunition to go with it."

"I'll check it over. Is it convenient for me to stay here? It won't be for long."

"Fine. We've plenty of room."

"Transport. I saw your black cab outside. Is that it?"

"No, I have a Ford van in the shed. I only use it now and then. It's the petrol situation, you see."

"That's fine. I'll use your phone now if I may."

"Help yourself."

Devlin closed the door and stood alone at the telephone. He rang directory inquiries and asked for the telephone number for Shaw Place. There was a delay of two or three minutes only and then the girl gave him the number and he wrote it down. He sat on a chair beside the phone, thinking about it for a while, then picked it up, dialed the operator and gave her the number.

After a while the phone was picked up at the other end and a woman's voice said. "Charbury three-one-four."

"Would Sir Maxwell Shaw be at home?"

"No, he isn't. Who is this?"

Devlin decided to take a chance. Remembering from the file that she had reverted to using her maiden name years ago, he said, "Would that be Miss Lavinia Shaw?"

"Yes it is. Who are you?"

Devlin said, "Does the Falcon still wait? It is now time to strike."

The effect was immediate and dramatic. "Oh, my God!" Lavinia Shaw said, and then there was silence.

Devlin waited for a moment, then said, "Are you there, Miss Shaw?"

"Yes, I'm here."

"I must see you and your brother as soon as possible. It's urgent."

She said, "My brother's in London. He had to see his solicitor. He's staying at the Army and Navy Club. He told me he'd have lunch there and catch the train back this afternoon."

"Excellent. Get in touch with him and tell him to expect me. Let's say two o'clock. Conlon—Major Harry Conlon."

There was a pause. She said, "Is it coming?"

"Is what coming, Miss Shaw?"

"You know—the invasion."

He stifled a strong desire to laugh. "We'll speak again I'm sure after I've seen your brother."

He went back to the kitchen, where Ryan still sat at the table. The girl, washing dishes at the sink, said, "Is everything all right?"

"Fine," he said. "Every journey needs a first step." He picked up his case. "If you could show me my room. I need to change."

She took him upstairs, led him into a back bedroom overlooking the river. Devlin unpacked his case, laid the uniform out on the bed. The Smith & Wesson he slipped under the mattress with the webbing belt and holster together with an ankle holster in leather which he also took from the case. He found the bathroom at the end of the corridor, had a quick shave and brushed his hair, then returned to the bedroom and changed.

He went downstairs fifteen minutes later resplendent in his uniform. "Jesus, Liam, I never thought I'd see the day," Ryan said.

"You know the old saying, Michael," Devlin told him. "When you're a fox with a pack on your tail you stand a better chance if you look like a hound." He turned to Mary and smiled. "And now, girl dear, another cup of tea would go down just fine."

It was at that moment that the poor girl fell totally in love with him, what the French call a *coup de foudre*, a thunderclap. She felt herself blush and turned to the cooker. "Of course, Mr. Devlin. I'll make some fresh."

To its members, the Army and Navy Club was simply known as the Rag. A great gloomy palazzo of a place in Venetian style and situated on Pall Mall. Its governing committee had been renowned since Victorian times for its leniency toward members disgraced or in trouble, and Sir Maxwell Shaw was a case in point. No one had seen the slightest necessity to blackball him over the business of his detention under Regulation 18B. He was, after all, an officer and a gentleman who had been both wounded and decorated for gallantry in the service of his country.

He sat in a corner of the morning room drinking the Scotch the waiter had brought in and thinking about Lavinia's astonishing telephone call. Quite unbelievable that now, after so long, the summons should come. My God, but he was excited. Hadn't felt such a charge in years.

He called for another Scotch, and at the same moment a porter approached him. "Your guest is here, Sir Maxwell."

"My guest?"

"Major Conlon. Shall I show him in?"

"Yes. Of course. At once, man."

Shaw got to his feet, straightening his tie as the porter returned with Devlin, who held out his hand and said cheerfully, "Harry Conlon. Nice to meet you, Sir Maxwell."

Shaw was dumbfounded, not so much by the uniform, but by the dog collar. He shook hands as the waiter brought his glass of Scotch. "Would you like one of these, Major?"

"No, thanks." The waiter departed and Devlin sat down and lit a cigarette. "You look a little shaken, Sir Maxwell."

"Well goodness, man, of course I am. I mean, what is all this about? Who are you?"

"Does the Falcon still wait?" Devlin asked. "Because it is now time to strike."

"Yes, but—"

"No buts, Sir Maxwell. You made a pledge a long time ago when Werner Reitel recruited you and your sister to, shall we say, the cause? Are you in or are you out? Where do you stand?"

"You mean you've got work for me?"

"There's a job to be done."

"The invasion is finally coming?"

"Not yet," Devlin said smoothly, "but soon. Are you with us?"

He'd been prepared to bring pressure to bear, but in the event, it was unnecessary. Shaw gulped down the whisky. "Of course I am. What do you require of me?"

"Let's take a little walk," Devlin said. "The park across the road will do fine."

It had started to rain, bouncing from the windows. For a moment, there wasn't a porter in the cloakroom. Shaw found his bowler hat, raincoat and umbrella. Among the jumble of coats there was a military trench coat. Devlin picked it up, followed him outside and put it on.

They went across to St. James's Park and walked along the side of the lake toward Buckingham Palace, Shaw with his umbrella up. After a while they moved into the shelter of some trees and Devlin lit a cigarette.

"You want one of these things?"

"Not at the moment. What is it you want me to do?"

"Before the war your sister used to fly a Tiger Moth. Does she still have it?"

"The RAF took it for training purposes in the winter of thirty-nine."

"She used a barn as a hangar. Is that still there?"

"Yes."

"And the place she used to land and take off. The South Meadow, I think you called it. It's not been plowed up for the war effort or anything?"

"No, all the land around Shaw Place, the land that used to be ours, is used for sheep grazing."

"And South Meadow is still yours?"

"Of course. Is that important?"

"You could say so. A plane from France will be dropping in, and in the not too distant future."

Shaw's face became extremely animated. "Really? What for?"

"To pick up me and another man. The less you know the better, but he's important. Does any of this give you a problem?"

"Good heavens, no. Glad to help, old man." Shaw frowned slightly. "You're not German, I take it?"

"Irish," Devlin told him. "But we're on the same side. You were given a radio by Werner Keitel. Do you still have it?"

"Ah, well there you have me, old man. I'm afraid we don't. You see back in forty-one the government brought in this stupid regulation. I was in prison for a few months."

"I know about that."

"My sister, Lavinia, you know what women are like. She panicked. Thought the police might arrive and turn the house upside down. There's a lot of marsh around our place, some of it bottomless. She threw the radio in, you see." He looked anxious. "Is this a problem, old man?"

"Of a temporary nature only. You're going back home today?"

"That's right."

"Good I'll be in touch. Tomorrow or the next day." Devlin ground out his cigarette. "Jesus, the rain. That's London for you. Never changes." And he walked away.

When he turned along the terrace at the side of the house at Cable Wharfe, the rain was drifting across the river. There was an awning stretching from the cable of the motorboat over the cockpit. Mary Ryan sat under it, safe from the rain, reading a book.

"Are you enjoying yourself down there?" Devlin called.

"I am. Uncle Michael's in the kitchen. Can I get you anything?"

"No, I'm fine at the moment."

When Devlin went in, Ryan was sitting at the table. He'd covered it with newspaper and was stripping a Luger pistol, oil on his fingers. "God help me, Liam, I've forgotten how to do this."

"Give me a minute to change and I'll handle it," Devlin told him.

He was back in five minutes wearing dark slacks and a black polo-neck sweater. He reached for the Luger parts and got to work oiling them, then put the whole weapon together expertly.

"Did it go well?" Ryan asked.

"If meeting a raving lunatic could ever go well, then yes," Devlin told him. "Michael, I'm dealing with an English aristocrat so totally out of his skull that he's still eagerly awaiting a German invasion, and that's when he's sober."

He told Ryan about Shaw Place, Shaw and his sister. When he was finished, Ryan said, "They sound mad, the both of them."

"Yes, but the trouble is I need a radio and they haven't got one."

"So what are you going to do?"

"I was thinking about the old days when I came over to handle that active service unit. They got weapons and even explosives from underworld sources. Am I right?"

Ryan nodded. "That's true."

"And you, Michael, as I recall, were the man with the contacts."

"That was a long time ago."

"Come off it, Michael. There's a war on, black market in everything from petrol to cigarettes. Just the same in Berlin. Don't tell me you aren't in it up to your neck, and you a London cabbie."

"All right." Ryan put up a hand defensively. "You want a radio, but the kind you want would have to be army equipment."

"That's right."

"It's no good going to some back-street trader."

There was a silence between them. Devlin broke the Luger down and wiped each piece carefully with a rag. "Then who would I go to?"

Ryan said, "There's a fella called Carver—Jack Carver. Has a brother called Eric."

"What are they, black marketeers?"

"Much more than that. Jack Carver's probably the most powerful gangster in London these days. Anything, but anything, that goes down, Carver gets a piece. Not just black market. Girls, gambling, protection. You name it."

"I used to know a fella in Dublin in the same line of work," Devlin said. "He wasn't so bad."

"Jack Carver's the original bastard, and young Eric's a toad. Every girl on the pavement is terrified of him."

"Do you tell me?" Devlin said. "I'm surprised nobody's stepped in here before now."

"It wasn't New York gangsters who invented cementing dead bodies into new roadways," Ryan said. "Jack Carver patented that idea. He's the one who supplied that active service unit with their guns and explosives back in thirty-six. If he had a grandmother he'd sell her to the Germans if he thought there was money in it."

"I'm frightened to death," Devlin said. "Well, Carver is the kind of man who can lay his hands on anything, so if I want a radio . . . "

"Exactly."

"Fine. Where do I find him?"

"There's a dance hall a couple of miles from here in Limehouse. It's called the Astoria Ballroom. Carver owns it. Has a big apartment upstairs. He likes that. Convenient for his brother to pick up the girls."

"And himself, I suppose?"

"You'd suppose wrong, Liam. Girls don't interest him in the slightest."

Devlin nodded. "I take your drift."

His hands moved suddenly with incredible dexterity, putting the Luger together again. He was finished in seconds and rammed a magazine up the butt.

"Jesus, you look like death himself when you do that," Ryan said.

"It's just a knack, Michael." Devlin wrapped up the oily newspapers and put them in the bin under the sink. "And now I think we'll take a little walk down by the river. I'd like your opinion on something."

He went down the stairway to the boat and found Mary still reading. The rain dripped from the edge of the awning, and there was a slight mist on the river. Devlin was wearing the military trench coat he'd stolen from the Army and Navy Club. He leaned against the rail, hands in his pockets.

"What are you reading?"

She held the book up. "*Our Mutual Friend.*"

"I've started something."

She stood up. "We're going to have fog in the next few days. A real pea-souper."

"How can you tell that?"

"I'm not sure, but I'm always right. It's the smell I recognize first."

"And do you like that?"

"Oh, yes. You're alone, enclosed in your own private world."

"And isn't that what we're all looking for?" He took her arm. "Your Uncle Michael and I are taking a little walk in the rain by the river. Why don't you come with us? That's if you've got nothing better to do."

They drove to St. Mary's Priory in Ryan's cab. He parked at the side of the road, and they sat looking at the entrance. There was a Morris saloon car parked outside painted olive green. It said *Military Police* on the side. As they watched, Lieutenant Benson and a corporal came out of the entrance, got in the car and drove off.

"You're not going to get far through the front door," Ryan said.

"More ways of skinning a cat than one," Devlin said. "Let's take that little walk."

The strip of shingle he'd walked along earlier seemed wider, and when he stopped to indicate the archway there was more headroom. "It was almost under the surface this morning," he said.

"The Thames is a tidal river, Liam, and the tide's going out. There'll be times when that thing's under the water entirely. Is it important?"

"Runs close to the foundations of the priory. According to the plans, there's a grille into the crypt under the priory chapel. It could be a way in."

"You'd need to take a look then."

"Naturally, but not now. Later when it's nice and dark."

The rain increased to monsoonlike proportions, and Ryan said, "For Christ's sake, let's get in out of this," and he started back to the steps.

Devlin took Mary's arm. "Would you happen to have yourself a pretty frock tucked away somewhere, because if you do, I'll take you dancing this evening."

She paused, staring at him, and when she started walking again the limp seemed more pronounced. "I don't dance, Mr. Devlin. I can't."

"Oh, yes you can, my love. You can do anything in the whole wide world if you put your mind to it."

9

THE ASTORIA WAS A TYPICAL London dance hall of the period and very crowded. There was a band on each side of the room, one in blue tuxedos, the other in red. Devlin wore his dark clerical suit, but with a soft white shirt and black tie he'd borrowed from Ryan. He waited outside the cloakroom for Mary, who'd gone in to leave her coat. When she came out, he saw that she had on a neat cotton dress and brown stockings. She wore white plastic earrings, fashionable at the moment, and just a hint of lipstick.

"My compliments on the dress," he said. "A vast improvement."

"I don't get a chance to dress up very often," she told him.

"Well let's make the most of it."

He took her hand and pulled her onto the floor before she could protest. One of the bands was playing a slow foxtrot. He started to hum the tune. "You do that well," she said.

"Ah, well, I have a small gift for music. I play the piano badly. You, on the other hand, dance rather well."

"It's better out here in the middle of all these people. Nobody notices."

She was obviously referring to her limp. Devlin said, "Girl dear, nobody notices anyway."

She tightened her grip, putting her cheek against his shoulder, and they moved into the crowd, the glitter-ball revolving on the ceiling, its rays bathing everything with blue light. The number came to an end and the other band broke into a fast, upbeat quickstep.

"Oh, no," she protested. "I can't manage this."

"All right," Devlin said. "Coffee it is then."

They went up the stairs to the balcony. "I'm just going to the cloakroom," she said.

"I'll get the coffee and see you back here."

She went around to the other side of the balcony, limping noticeably, passing two young men leaning on the rail. One of them wore a pin-striped double-breasted suit and hand-painted tie. The other was a few years older, in a leather jacket with the flattened nose of a prize fighter and scar tissue around the eyes.

"You fancy that, Mr. Carver?" he asked as they watched Mary go into the cloakroom.

"I certainly do, George," Eric Carver said. "I haven't had a cripple before."

Eric Carver was twenty-two years of age with thin wolfish features and long blond hair swept back from the forehead. A tendency to asthma attacks had kept him out of the army. At least that's what it said on the medical certificate his brother's doctor had provided. His father had been a drunken bully who'd died under the wheels of a cart in the Mile End Road. Jack, already a criminal of some renown and fifteen years his senior, had looked after Eric and their mother until cancer had carried her off just before the war. Her death had brought them even closer. There was nothing Eric couldn't do, no girl he couldn't have, because he was Jack Carver's brother and he never let anyone forget it.

Mary emerged from the cloakroom and limped past them, and Eric said, "I'll see you later, George."

George smiled, turned and walked away and Eric moved around the balcony to where Mary leaned over the rail watching the dancers. He slipped his arm around her waist and then ran one hand up to cup her left breast. "Now then darling and what's your name?"

"Please don't," she said and started to struggle.

"Oh, I like it," he said, his grip tightening.

Devlin arrived, a cup of coffee in each hand. He put them down on a nearby table. "Excuse me." he said.

As Eric turned, slackening his grip, Devlin stood on his right foot, bearing down with all his weight. The young man snarled, trying to pull away, and Devlin picked up one of the cups of coffee and poured it down Eric's shirtfront.

"Jesus, son, I'm sorry," he said.

Eric looked down at his shirt, total amazement on his face. "Why you little creep," he said and swung a punch.

Devlin blocked it easily and kicked him on the shin. "Now why don't you go and play nasty little boys elsewhere?"

There was rage on Eric's face. "You bastard. I'll get you for this. You see if I don't."

He hobbled away, and Devlin sat Mary down and gave her the other cup of coffee. She took a sip and looked up at him. "That was awful."

"A worm, girl dear, nothing to worry about. Will you be all right while I go and see this Carver fella? I shouldn't be long."

She smiled. "I'll be fine, Mr. Devlin." He turned and walked away.

The door at the other end of the balcony said *Manager's Office*, but when he opened it he found himself in a corridor. He went to the far end and opened another door into a carpeted landing. Stairs went down to what was obviously a back entrance, but the sound of music drifted from above, so up he went to the next landing where a door stood open. It was only a small room with a desk and a chair on which the man George sat reading a newspaper while music sounded over the radio.

"Nice that." Devlin leaned on the doorway. "Carroll Gibbons from the Savoy. He plays the grand piano, that man."

George looked him over coldly. "And what do you want?"

"A moment of Jack Carver's valuable time."

"What's it about? Mr. Carver don't see just anybody."

Devlin took out a five-pound note and laid it on the table. "That's what it's about, my old son, that and another one hundred and ninety-nine like it."

George put the newspaper down and picked up the banknote. "All right. Wait here."

He brushed past Devlin and knocked on the other door, then went in. After a while he opened it and looked out. "All right, he'll see you."

Jack Carver sat behind a walnut Regency desk that looked genuine. He was a hard, dangerous-looking man, his face fleshy, the signs of decay setting in early. He wore an excellent suit in navy worsted tailored in Savile Row, a discreet tie. To judge by outward appearances, he could have been a prosperous businessman, but the jagged scar that ran from the corner of the left eye into the dark hairline and the look in the cold eyes belied that.

George stayed by the door, and Devlin glanced around the room, which was furnished in surprisingly good taste. "This is nice."

"All right, so what's it about?" Carver said, holding up the fiver.

"Aren't they beautiful, those things?" Devlin said. "A work of genuine art, the Bank of England five-pound note."

Carver said, "According to George, you said something about another hundred and ninety-nine. That came to a thousand quid when I went to school."

"Ah, you remembered, George," Devlin said.

At that moment, a door opened and Eric entered wearing a clean shirt and fastening his tie. He stopped dead, astonishment on his face that was quickly replaced by anger. "Here, that's him, Jack, the little squirt who spilled coffee down me."

"Oh, an accident surely," Devlin told him.

Eric started toward him, and Jack Carver snapped, "Leave it out, Eric, this is business." Eric stayed by the desk, rage in his eyes, and Carver said, "Now what would I have to do for a thousand quid? Kill somebody?"

"Come off it, Mr. Carver, we both know you'd do that for fun," Devlin said. "No, what I need is an item of military equipment. I hear you're a man who can get anything. At least that's what the IRA seem to think. I wonder what Special Branch at Scotland Yard might make of that tidbit."

Carver smoothed the fiver between his fingers and looked up, his face blank. "You're beginning to sound right out of order."

"Me and my big mouth. I'll never learn," Devlin said. "And all I wanted was to buy a radio."

"A radio?" For the first time Carver looked puzzled.

"Of the transmitting and receiving kind. There's a rather nice one the army uses these days. It's called a twenty-eight set, Mark Four. God knows why. Fits in a wooden box with a carrying handle. Just like a suit case. Very handy." Devlin took a piece of paper from his pocket and put it on the desk. "I've written the details down."

Carver looked at it. "Sounds a fancy piece of work to me. What would a man want a thing like that for?"

"Now that, Mr. Carver, is between me and my God. Can you handle it?"

"Jack Carver can handle anything. A thousand, you said?"

"But I must have it tomorrow."

Carver nodded. "All right, but I'll take half in advance."

"Fair enough."

Devlin had expected as much, had the money waiting in his pocket. He took it out and dropped it on the table. "There you go."

Carver scooped it up. "And it'll cost you another thousand. Tomorrow night, ten o'clock. Just down the road from here. Black Lion Dock. There's a warehouse with my name over the door. Be on time."

"Sure and you're a hard man to do business with," Devlin said. "But then we have to pay for what we want in this life."

"You can say that again," Carver said. "Now get out of here."

Devlin left, George closing the door behind him. Eric said, "He's mine, Jack. I want him."

"Leave it out. Eric. I've got this." Carver held up the five hundred pounds. "And I want the rest of it. Then he gets squeezed. I didn't like that IRA crack he made at all. Very naughty. Now get out of it. I want to make a phone call."

Mary was sitting quietly watching the dancers when Devlin joined her. "Did it go all right with Carver?" she asked.

"I'd rather shake hands with the devil. That little rat I chastised turned out to be his brother, Eric. Would you like to go now?"

"All right. I'll get my coat and see you in the foyer."

When they went out, it was raining. She took his arm and they walked down the wet pavements toward the main road. There was an alley to the right, and as they approached it, Eric Carver and George stepped out, blocking the way.

"Saw you leaving. Thought we'd say goodnight," Eric said.

"Mother of God!" Devlin put the girl to one side.

"Go on, George, do him up," Eric cried.

"A pleasure." George came in, enjoying himself.

Devlin simply stepped to the left and kicked sideways at his kneecap. George screamed in agony, doubled over, and Devlin raised a knee into his face. "Didn't they teach you that one, George?"

Eric backed away in terror. Devlin took Mary's arm and walked past him. "Now where were we?"

Jack Carver said, "I told you to leave it out, Eric. You never learn."

"The bastard's half crippled George. Dislodged his kneecap. I had to take him to Dr. Aziz round the corner."

"Never mind George. I phoned Morrie Green. He knows more about surplus military equipment than any man in London."

"Does he have this radio the little bastard wanted?"

"No, but he can get one. No trouble. He'll drop it in tomorrow. The interesting thing is what he said about it. It's no ordinary radio. Sort of thing the army would use operating behind enemy lines."

Eric looked bewildered. "But what's it mean, Jack?"

"That there's a lot more to that little sod than meets the eye. I'm going to have some fun with him tomorrow night." Carver laughed harshly. "Now pour me a Scotch."

Devlin and Mary took the turning down to Harrow Street. "Shall I try and get a cab?" he asked.

"Oh, no, it's not much more than a mile and a half, and I like walking in the rain." She kept her hand lightly on his arm. "You're very quick, Mr. Devlin, you don't hesitate. Back there, I mean."

"Yes, well I never could see the point."

They walked in companionable silence for a while alongside the river toward Wapping. There was a heavy mist on the Thames, and a large cargo boat slipped past them, green and red navigation lights plain in spite of the blackout.

"I'd love to be like that boat," she said. "Going to sea, to faraway distant places, something different every day."

"Jesus, girl, you're only nineteen. It's all waiting for you out there, and this bloody war can't last forever."

They paused in the shelter of a wall while he lit a cigarette. She said, "I wish we had time to walk all the way down to the Embankment."

"Too far surely."

"I saw this film once. I think it was Fred Astaire. He walked along the Embankment with a girl and his chauffeur followed along behind in a Rolls-Royce."

"And you liked that?"

"It was very romantic."

"Ah, there's a woman for you."

They turned along Cable Wharfe and paused on the little terrace before going into the house.

"I've had a lovely time."

He laughed out loud. "You must be joking, girl."

"No, really. I like being with you."

She still held his arm and leaned against him. He put his other arm around her and they stayed there for a moment, rain glistening as it fell through the shaded light above the door. He felt a sudden dreadful sadness for everything there had never been in his life, remembering a girl in Norfolk just like Mary Ryan, a girl he had hurt very badly indeed.

He sighed and Mary looked up. "What is it?"

"Oh, nothing, I was just wondering where it had all gone. It's a touch of that three o'clock in the morning feeling when you feel past everything there ever was."

"Not you, surely. You've got years ahead of you."

"Mary, my love. You are nineteen and I am an old thirty-five who's seen it all and doesn't believe in much anymore. In a few days I'll be on my way, and a good thing." He gave her one small hug. "So let's get inside before I lose what few wits I have entirely."

Ryan, sitting on the other side of the table, said, "Jack Carver's bad news, Liam, always was. How can you be certain he'll play straight?"

"He couldn't if he wanted to," Devlin said, "but there's more to this. Much more. The radio I need, the twenty-eight set. It's an unusual piece of equipment, and the more Carver realizes that, the more he's going to want to know what's going on."

"So what are you going to do?"

"I'll think of something, but that can wait. What can't is an inspection of that drainage tunnel under the priory."

"I'll come with you," Ryan said. "We'll go in the motorboat. Only take fifteen minutes to get there."

"Would that be likely to cause attention?"

"No problem." Ryan shook his head. "The Thames is the busiest highway in London these days. Lots of craft work the river at night. Barges. Freighters."

Mary turned from the sink. "Can I come?"

Before Devlin could protest, Ryan said, "A good idea. You can mind the boat."

"But you stay on board," Devlin told her. "No funny business."

"Right, I'll go and change." She rushed out.

"Oh, to be young," Devlin said.

Ryan nodded. "She likes you, Liam."

"And I like her, Michael old friend, and that's where it will end. Now, what do we need?"

"The tide is low, but it's still going to be wet. I'll dig out some overalls and boots," Ryan told him and went out.

The small motorboat moved in toward the strand, its engine a muted throbbing. The prow carved its way into mud and sand, and Ryan cut the engine. "Right, Mary. Keep an eye on things. We shouldn't be long."

He and Devlin in their dark overalls and boots went over the side and faded into the darkness. Ryan carried a bag of tools and Devlin a large torch of the type used by workmen. There was three feet of water in the tunnel.

Ryan said, "So we'll have to wade."

As they moved into the water, the smell was pungent. Devlin said, "Christ, you can tell it's a sewer."

"So try not to fall down, and if you do, keep your mouth closed," Ryan said. "The terrible place for diseases, sewers."

Devlin led the way, the tunnel stretching ahead of them in the rays of the lamp. The brickwork was obviously very old, corroded and rotting. There was a sudden splash and two rats leapt from a ledge and swam away.

"Filthy creatures," Ryan said in disgust.

"It can't be far," Devlin said. "A hundred yards. Not much more surely."

Suddenly there it was, an iron grille perhaps four feet by three, just above the surface of the water. They looked through into the crypt, and Devlin played the light across the interior. There were a couple of tombs almost completely covered with water and stone steps in the far corner going up to a door.

"One thing's for sure," Ryan said. "The grille's done nothing to help their drainage system."

"It was put in nearly forty years ago," Devlin said. "Maybe it worked then."

Ryan got a crowbar from his bag of tools. Devlin held the bag for him while the other man pushed into the mortar in the brickwork beside the grille. He jumped back in alarm as the wall buckled and five or six bricks tumbled into the water. "The whole place is ready to come down. We can have this grille out in a fast ten minutes, Liam."

"No, not now. I need to know what the situation is upstairs. We've found out all we need for the moment, which is that the grille can be pulled out anytime we want. Now let's get out of here."

At the same moment in Romney Marsh, the wind from the sea rattled the French windows of the drawing room as Shaw closed the curtains. The furniture was no longer what it had been, the carpets were faded, but there was a log fire burning in the hearth, Nell lying in front of it. The door opened and Lavinia came in. She was wearing slacks and carried a tray. "I've made coffee, darling."

"Coffee!" he roared. "To hell with the coffee. I found a bottle of champagne in the cellar. Bollinger. That's what we need tonight."

He took it from a bucket on the table, opened it with a flourish and poured some into two glasses.

"This man Conlon," she said. "What did you say he was like?"

"I've told you about five times, old girl."

"Oh, Max, isn't it exciting? To you, my darling."

"And to you, old girl," he said and toasted her back.

In Berlin, it was very quiet in Schellenberg's office as he sat working through some papers in the light of a desk lamp. The door opened and Ilse looked in. "Coffee, General?"

"Are you still here? I thought you'd gone home."

"I'm going to spend the night in the emergency accommodation. Asa's stayed on too. He's in the canteen."

"We might as well join him." Schellenberg stood up and buttoned his tunic.

"Are you worried, General, about Devlin?"

"My dear Ilse. Liam Devlin is a man of infinite resource and guile. Given those attributes, you could say I've nothing to worry about." He opened the door and smiled. "Which is why I'm frightened to death instead."

From Steiner's window he could see across to the river. He peered through a chink in his blackout curtain and closed it again. "A large ship going downriver. Amazing how active things are out there even at night."

Father Martin, sitting by the small table, nodded. "As the song says, Old Father Thames, just goes rolling along."

"During the day I sometimes sit at the window and watch for a couple of hours at a time."

"I understand, my son. It must be difficult for you." The priest sighed and got to his feet. "I must go. I have a Midnight Mass."

"Good heavens, Father, do you ever stop?"

"There's a war on, my son." Father Martin knocked on the door.

The MP on duty unlocked it and the old priest went along the corridor to the outer door. Lieutenant Benson was sitting at the desk in his room and glanced up. "Everything all right, Father?"

"As right as it will ever be," Martin said and passed through.

As he went down the stairway to the foyer, Sister Maria Palmer came out of her of office. "Still here, Father? Don't you ever go home?"

"So much to do, Sister."

"You look tired."

"It's been a long war." He smiled. "Goodnight and God bless you."

The night porter came out of his cubbyhole, helped him on with his raincoat and gave him his umbrella, then unbolted the door. The old man paused, looking out at the rain, then put up his umbrella and walked away wearily.

Munro was still in his office, standing at a map table, charts of the English Channel and the Normandy approaches spread before him, when Carter limped in.

"The invasion, sir?"

"Yes, Jack. Normandy. They've made their decision. Let's hope the Führer still believes it will be the Pas de Calais."

"I understand his personal astrologer's convinced him of it," Carter said.

Munro laughed. "The ancient Egyptians would only appoint generals who'd been born under the sign of Leo."

"I never knew that, sir."

"Yes, well you learn something new every day. No going home tonight, Jack. Eisenhower wants a blanket report on the strength of the French Resistance units in this general area and he wants it in the morning. We'll have to snatch a few hours here."

"Very well, sir."

"Was there anything else?"

"Vargas gave me a call."

"What did he want?"

"Another message from his cousin in Berlin. Could he send as much information as possible about St. Mary's Priory."

"All right, Jack, cook something up in the next couple of days, staying as close to the truth as possible, and pass it on to Vargas. We've got more important things to take care of at the moment."

"Fine, sir. I'll organize some tea and sandwiches."

"Do that, Jack. It's going to be a long night."

Carter went out and Munro returned to his maps.

10

〜

THE FOLLOWING MORNING FATHER MARTIN knelt at the altar rail and prayed, eyes closed. He was tired, that was the trouble, had felt so tired for such a long time, and he prayed for strength to the God he had loved unfalteringly all his life and the ability to stand upright.

"I will bless the Lord who gives me Counsel, who even at night directs my heart. I keep the Lord ever in my sight."

He had spoken the words aloud and faltered, unable to think of the rest. A strong voice said, *"Since He is at my right hand I shall stand firm."* Father Martin half turned and found Devlin standing there in uniform, the trench coat over one arm. "Major?" The old man tried to get off his knees, and Devlin put a hand under his elbow.

"Or Father. The uniform is only for the duration. Conlon—Harry Conlon."

"And I'm Frank Martin, pastor. Is there something I can do for you?"

"Nothing special. I'm on extended leave. I was wounded in Sicily," Devlin told him. "Spending a few days with friends not too far from here. I saw St. Pat's and thought I'd look in."

"Well then, let me offer you a cup of tea," the old man said.

Devlin sat in the small crowded sacristy while Martin boiled water in an electric kettle and made the tea.

"So you've been in it from the beginning?"

Devlin nodded. "Yes, November thirty-nine I got my call."

"I see they gave you an MC."

"The Sicilian landings, that was," Devlin told him.

"Was it bad?" Father Martin poured the tea and offered an open tin of condensed milk.

"Bad enough." The old man sipped his tea and Devlin lit a cigarette. "Just as bad for you, though. The Blitz, I mean. You're rather close to the London docks."

"Yes, it was hard." Martin nodded. "And it doesn't get any easier. I'm on my own here these days."

He suddenly looked very frail, and Devlin felt a pang of conscience, and yet he had to take this as far as it would go, he knew that. "I called in at the local pub, The Bargee I think it was called, for some cigarettes. I was talking to a girl there who mentioned you warmly."

"Ah, that would be Maggie Brown."

"Told me you were father confessor at the hospice near here. St. Mary's Priory?"

"That's right."

"Must give you a lot of extra work, Father."

"It does indeed, but it must be done. We all have to do our bit." The old man looked at his watch. "In fact, I'll have to be off there in a few minutes. Rounds to do."

"Do you have many patients there?"

"It varies. Fifteen, sometimes twenty. Many are terminal. Some are special problems. Servicemen who've had breakdowns. Pilots occasionally. You know how it is."

"I do indeed," Devlin said. "I was interested when I walked by earlier to see a couple of military policemen going in. It struck me as odd. I mean, military police in a hospice."

"Ah, well there's a reason for that. Occasionally they keep the odd German prisoner of war on the top floor. I don't know the background, but they're usually special cases."

"Oh, I see the reason for the MPs then. There's someone there now?"

"Yes, a Luftwaffe colonel. A nice man. I've even managed to persuade him to come to Mass for the first time in years."

"Interesting."

"Well, I must make a move." The old man reached for his raincoat, and Devlin helped him on with it. As they went out into the church, he said, "I've been thinking, Father. Here's me with time on my hands and you carrying all this burden alone. Maybe I could give you a hand? Hear a few Confessions for you at least."

"Why, that's extraordinarily kind of you," Father Martin said.

Liam Devlin had seldom felt lower in his life, but he went on. "And I'd love to see something of your work at the priory."

"Then so you shall," the old man said and led the way down the steps.

The priory chapel was as cold as could be. They moved down to the altar and Devlin said, "It seems very damp. Is there a problem?"

"Yes, the crypt has been flooded for years. Sometimes quite badly. No money available to put it right."

Devlin could see the stout oak door banded with iron in the shadows in the far corner. "Is that the way in then?"

"Yes, but no one goes down there anymore."

"I once saw a church in France with the same trouble. Could I take a look?"

"If you like."

The door was bolted. He eased it back and ventured halfway down the steps. When he flicked on his lighter, he saw the dark water around the tombs and lapping at the grille. He retraced his steps and closed the door.

"Dear, yes, there's not much to be done for it," he called.

"Yes. Well, make sure you bolt it again," the old man called back. "We don't want anyone going down there. They could do themselves an injury."

Devlin rammed the bolt home, the solid sound echoing through the chapel, then quietly eased it back. Shrouded in shadows, the door was in the corner; it would be remarkable if anyone noticed. He rejoined Father Martin, and they moved up the aisle to the outer door. As they opened it, Sister Maria Palmer came out of her office.

"Ah, there you are," Father Martin said. "I looked in when we arrived, but you weren't there. I've been showing Father Conlon—" He laughed, correcting himself. "I'll start again. I've been showing Major Conlon the chapel. He's going to accompany me on my rounds."

"Father suits me just fine." Devlin shook her hand. "A pleasure, Sister."

"Major Conlon was wounded in Sicily."

"I see. Have they given you a London posting?" she asked.

"No, I'm still on sick leave. In the neighborhood for a few days. Just passing through. I met Father Martin at his church."

"He's been kind enough to offer to help me out at the church. Hear a few Confessions and so on," Father Martin said.

"Good, you need a rest. We'll do the rounds together." As they started up the stairs, she said, "By the way, Lieutenant Benson's gone on a three-day pass. That young sergeant's in charge. What's his name? Morgan, isn't it?"

"The Welsh boy?" Father Martin said. "I called in on Steiner last night. Did you?"

"No, we had an emergency admission after you'd gone, Father. I didn't have time. I'll see him now though. I'm hoping the penicillin's finally cleared the last traces of his chest infection."

She went up the stairs in front of them briskly, skirts swirling, and Devlin and Father Martin followed.

They worked their way from room to room, staying to talk here and there to various patients, and it was half an hour before they reached the top floor. The MP on duty at the table outside the outer door jumped up and saluted automatically when he saw Devlin. The door was opened by another MP and they passed through.

The young sergeant sitting in Benson's room stood up and came out. "Sister—Father Martin."

"Good morning, Sergeant Morgan," Sister Maria Palmer said. "We'd like to see Colonel Steiner."

Morgan took in Devlin's uniform and the dog collar. "I see," he said uncertainly.

"Major Conlon's having a look round with us," she informed him.

Devlin took out his wallet and produced the fake War Office pass Schellenberg's people had provided, the one that guaranteed unlimited access. He passed it across.

"I think you'll find that takes care of it, Sergeant."

Morgan examined it. "I'll just get the details for the admittance sheet, sir." He did so and handed it back. "If you'd follow me."

He led the way along to the end of the corridor, nodded, and the MP on duty unlocked the door. Sister Maria Palmer led the way in followed by Father Martin, Devlin bringing up the rear. The door closed behind them.

Steiner, sitting by the window, stood up, and Sister Maria Palmer said, "And how are you today, Colonel?"

"Fine, Sister."

"I'm sorry I couldn't see you last night. I had an emergency, but Father Martin tells me he called in."

"As usual." Steiner nodded.

The old priest said, "This is Major Conlon, by the way. As you can see, an army chaplain. He's on sick leave. Like yourself, recently wounded.''

Devlin smiled amiably and put out his hand. ''A great pleasure, Colonel.''

Kurt Steiner, making one of the most supreme efforts of his life, managed to keep his face straight. ''Major Conlon.'' Devlin gripped the German's hand hard, and Steiner said, ''Anywhere interesting? Where you picked up your wound, I mean.''

''Sicily,'' Devlin said.

''A hard campaign.''

''Ah, well, I wouldn't really know. I got mine the first day there.'' He walked to the window and looked out down to the road beside the Thames. ''A fine view you've got here. You can see right down to those steps and that little beach, the boats passing. Something to look at.''

''It helps pass the time.''

''So, we must go now,'' Sister Maria Palmer said and knocked at the door.

Father Martin put a hand on Steiner's shoulder. ''Don't forget I'll be in the chapel tonight at eight to hear Confessions. All sinners welcome.''

Devlin said, ''Now then, Father, didn't you say I'd take some of the load off your shoulders? It's me who'll be sitting in the box tonight.'' He turned to Steiner. ''But you're still welcome, Colonel.''

''Are you sure you don't mind?'' Father Martin said.

As the door opened, Sister Maria Palmer cut in. ''An excellent idea.''

They moved along the corridor and Morgan opened the outer door for them. Father Martin said, ''Just one thing. I usually start at seven. The MPs bring Steiner down at eight because everyone's gone by then. They prefer it that way.''

''So you see him last?''

''That's right.''

''No problem,'' Devlin said.

They reached the foyer and the porter handed them their raincoats. Sister Maria Palmer said, ''We'll see you tonight then, Major.''

''I'll look forward to it,'' Devlin said and went down the steps with the old priest.

''God save us, talk about Daniel in the lion's den,'' Ryan said. ''You've the cheek of Old Nick himself.''

''Yes, well it worked,'' Devlin said. ''But I wouldn't like to hang about there too much. Asking for trouble that.''

''But you will go back this evening?''

''I have to. My one chance of speaking properly to Steiner.''

Mary, sitting at one end of the table hugging herself, said, "But Mr. Devlin, to sit there in the box and hear people's Confessions, and some of them nuns. That's a mortal sin."

"I've no choice, Mary. It must be done. It doesn't sit well with me to make a fool of that fine old man, but there it is."

"Well, I still think it's a terrible thing to be doing." She left the room, came back a moment later in her raincoat and went outside.

"The temper on her sometimes," Ryan said.

"Never mind that now, we've things to discuss. My meeting tonight with Carver. Black Lion Dock. Could we get there in your boat?"

"I know it well. Take about thirty minutes. Ten o'clock you said."

"I'd like to be there earlier. To review the situation, if you follow me."

"Leave at nine then. You'll be back from the priory before, surely."

"I would think so." Devlin lit a cigarette. "I can't go down to Shaw Place in your taxi, Michael. A London cab would definitely look out of place in Romney Marsh. This Ford van of yours. Is it in running order?"

"Yes. As I said, I use it now and then."

"One very important point," Devlin said. "When I get Steiner out, we move and move fast. Two hours to Shaw Place, the plane waiting and out of it before the authorities know what's hit them. I'll need the van that night and it would be a one-way trip. It wouldn't be a good idea for you to try and get it back."

Ryan smiled. "I took it as payment for a bad debt from a dealer in Brixton two years ago. The logbook's so crooked it's a joke and so is the numberplate. No way could it be traced back to me, and it's in good order. You know me and engines. They're my hobby."

"Ah, well, a bob or two extra for you for that," Devlin said and got up. "I'll go and make my peace with your niece now."

She was sitting under the awning in the boat reading again as he went down the steps.

"What is it this time?" he said.

"*The Midnight Court,*" she told him reluctantly.

"In English or Irish?"

"I don't have the Irish."

"The great pity. I used to be able to recite the whole of it in Irish. My uncle gave me a Bible for doing that. He was a priest."

"I wonder what he'd say about what you're doing this evening," she said.

"Oh, I know very well," Devlin told her. "He'd forgive me." And he went back up the steps.

◆

Devlin sat in the box in uniform, just a violet stole about his neck, and listened patiently to four nuns and two male patients as they confessed their sins. It was nothing very dreadful that he heard. Sins of omission in the main, or matters so petty they were hardly worth a thought, and yet they were to those anonymous people talking to him on the other side of the grille. He honestly did the best he could, tried to say the right thing, but it was an effort. His last client departed. He sat there in the silence, and then the chapel door opened and he heard the ring of army boots on the stone floor.

The confessional box door opened and closed. From the darkness Steiner said, "Bless me, Father, for I have sinned."

"Not as much as I have, Colonel." Devlin switched on his light and smiled through the grille at him.

"Mr. Devlin," Steiner said. "What have they done to you?"

"A few changes just to put the hounds off." Devlin ran his hands through his gray hair. "How have you been?"

"Never mind that. The British were hoping you would turn up. I was interviewed by a Brigadier Munro of Special Operations Executive. He told me they'd made sure my presence in London was known in Berlin by passing the information through a man at the Spanish Embassy called Vargas. He works for them."

"I knew it," Devlin said. "The bastard."

"They told me two things. That General Walter Schellenberg was in charge of organizing my escape and that they expected him to use you. They're waiting for you, hoping you'll show up."

"Yes, but I allowed for British intelligence handling it the way they have. Vargas is still getting messages asking for more information. They will be thinking I'm still in Berlin."

"Good God!" Steiner said.

"How many MPs escort you down here?"

"Two. Usually Benson the lieutenant, but he's on leave."

"Right. I'm going to have you out of here in the next two or three days. We'll exit through the crypt. It's pretty well organized. There'll be a boat waiting on the river. After that a two-hour drive to a place where we'll be picked up by plane from France."

"I see. Everything organized down to the last detail, just like Operation Eagle, and remember how that turned out."

"Ah, yes, but I'm in charge this time." Devlin smiled. "The evening we go you'll come down to Confession just like tonight. Usual time."

"How will I know?"

"A fine view from your window and the steps down to the little beach by the Thames. Remember?"

"Ah, yes."

"The day we decide to go, there'll be a young girl standing by the wall at the top of those steps. She'll be wearing a black beret and an old raincoat. She'll be there at noon exactly, so watch at noon each day, and she has a strong limp, Colonel, very pronounced. You can't miss her.''

"So, I see her, then we go that evening?" Steiner hesitated. "The MPs?"

"A detail only." Devlin smiled. "Trust me. Now three Hail Marys and two Our Fathers and be off with you.''

He switched off the light. The door banged, there was a murmur of voices, the sound of boots again and the outer door opening and closing.

Devlin came out and moved toward the altar. "God forgive me," he murmured.

He checked that the bolt of the crypt door was still pulled back, then went into the sacristy, got his trench coat and left.

Ryan stood at the door as Devlin changed quickly from the uniform into dark slacks and sweater. He pulled up his right trouser leg and strapped the ankle holster to it, tucking his sock up around the end. He slipped the Smith & Wesson .38 into it and pulled down his trouser.

"Just in case." He picked up the old leather jacket Ryan had loaned him and put it on. Then he opened his suitcase, took out a wad of fivers and put them in his inside pocket.

They went downstairs and found Mary sitting at the table reading again. "Is there any tea in the pot?" Devlin asked.

"A mouthful, I think. Are we going now?" She poured the tea into a cup.

He opened the kitchen table drawer, took out the Luger, checked it and slipped it inside his jacket. "You're not going anywhere, girl dear, not this time," he told her and swallowed his tea.

She started to protest, but her uncle shook his head. "He's right, girl, it could get nasty. Best stay out of it.''

She watched, disconsolate, as they went down the steps to the boat and cast off. As Ryan started the engine, Devlin moved into the little wheelhouse beside him and lit a cigarette in cupped hands.

"And the same applies to you, Michael," he said. "Stay out of it. My affair, not yours.''

Jack and Eric Carver arrived at the Black Lion Dock at nine forty-five in a Humber limousine, George driving. The dock was almost completely dark except for the light over the main warehouse doors, shaded as required by the blackout regulations. The sign on the warehouse said,

Carver Brothers—Export and Import, and Jack Carver looked up at it with satisfaction as he got out of the car.

"Very nice that. The sign writer did a good job."

It was very quiet, the only sounds those of shipping on the river. Eric followed him, and George limped around to the back of the car, opened the boot and took out the radio set in its wooden case painted olive green.

"I'll carry that, it's worth money." Carver turned to his brother. "All right, Eric, let's get on with it."

Eric unlocked the Judas gate in the main door, stepped inside and found the light switch. His brother and George followed him. The warehouse was stacked with packing cases of every kind. There was a table in the center and a couple of chairs, obviously used by a shipping clerk.

"Right, put it on the table." George did as he was told, and Carver added, "You've got the shooter?"

George took a Walther PPK from one pocket, a silencer from the other and screwed it into place.

Carver lit a cigar. "Look at that, Eric, bloody marvelous. Just sounds like a cork popping."

"I can't wait for that little bastard to get here," Eric said.

But Devlin had actually been there for some time, hidden in the shadows at the rear of the building, having gained access through an upstairs window. He watched George position himself behind a stack of packing cases, the Carver brothers sitting down at the table, then he turned and slipped out the way he had come.

A couple of minutes later he approached the main door, whistling cheerfully, opened the Judas gate and went in. "God save all here," he called and approached the table. "You got it then, Mr. Carver?"

"I told you. I can get anything. You didn't mention your name last night, by the way."

"Churchill," Devlin said. "Winston."

"Very funny."

Devlin opened the case. The radio fitted inside, headphones, Morse tapper, aerials, everything. It looked brand-new. He closed the lid again.

"Satisfied?" Carver asked.

"Oh, yes."

"Then cash on the table."

Devlin took the thousand pounds from his pocket and passed it over. "The hard man, eh, Mr. Carver?"

"Hard enough." Carver dropped the money back on the table. "Of course, we now come to the other matter."

"And what matter would that be?"

"Your insulting treatment of my brother and your threats to me. IRA and Special Branch. I can't have that. I've got a reputation to think of. You need chastising, my son." He blew cigar smoke in Devlin's face. "George."

George moved fast, considering his damaged knee, had the Walther at the back of Devlin's neck in a second. Eric reached inside the Irishman's jacket and relieved him of the Luger. "Look at that, Jack. Cunning bastard."

Devlin spread his arms. "All right, Mr. Carver, so you've got me. What happens now?"

He walked across to a packing case, sat down and took out a cigarette. Carver said, "You're a cool bastard, I'll give you that."

"I'll tell you what happens now," Eric said, taking a cut-throat razor from his pocket and opening it. "I'm going to slice your ears off, that's what I'm going to do."

"While George holds the gun on me?" Devlin asked.

"That's the general idea," Eric told him.

"Only one problem with that," Devlin said. "That gun is a Walther PPK and you have to pull the slider back to put yourself in business and I don't think George has done that."

George pulled at the slider desperately, Devlin hitched up his trouser, yanked the Smith & Wesson from the ankle holster and fired, all in one smooth motion, drilling him through the upper arm so that he cried out and dropped the Walther.

Devlin picked it up. "Nice," he said. "Thanks very much." He pushed it into his waistband.

Carver sat there, a look of total disbelief on his face. Eric looked frightened to death as Devlin put first the money and then the Luger inside his leather jacket. He picked up the case containing the radio and walked away.

As he reached the door, he turned. "Jesus, Eric, I was forgetting. You said something about slicing my ears off."

His arm swung up, he fired, and Eric screamed as the lower half of his right ear disintegrated. He grabbed at it, blood spurting.

Devlin said, "A good job you don't wear earrings."

He stepped out and the Judas gate banged behind him.

Schellenberg was in his office when the door burst open and Ilse appeared. Asa Vaughan was at her shoulder, excitement on his face.

"What on earth is it?" Schellenberg demanded.

"You must come to the radio room now. It's Devlin." She could hardly get the words out. "It's Devlin, General, calling from London."

～

The radio was open on the kitchen table, the aerials looped all the way around the walls. Ryan and Mary sat watching in fascination as Devlin tapped away in Morse code.

"Jesus," he said, frowning. There was a little more action and then he stopped. "That's it. Get the aerials down."

Mary moved around the kitchen coiling up the wires. Ryan said, "Is everything all right, Liam?"

"All wrong, old son. We were supposed to try and be back in France for the twenty-first. Now they say the great occasion is on the fifteenth, and as tonight is the twelfth, that doesn't give us much time."

"Is it possible, Liam?"

Devlin said, "First thing in the morning we'll take a run down to Romney Marsh. See what the situation is at Shaw Place." He turned to Mary. "Would you like a day out in the country?"

"It sounds just fine to me."

"Good, then I'll give the Shaws a call and warn them to expect me."

～

Back in his office, Schellenberg sat at his desk studying the message in front of him, Asa Vaughan and Ilse watching.

"So, what do we know?" Schellenberg said. "He's there at his IRA friend's house, he's made contact with Shaw and now with Steiner."

"Everything fits," Asa said.

"Perhaps, but he can't make the fifteenth, it would be impossible, even for Devlin."

"I'm beginning to wonder if anything is impossible to that guy," Asa said.

" 'Stand by tomorrow,' " Schellenberg commented. "That was his final instruction. Well, we shall see." He stood up. "I doubt whether the canteen can run to champagne, but whatever they can manage is on me."

11

SOUTH OF THE THAMES, THEY took the road to Maidstone, Ryan driving, Devlin squeezed in beside him. He wasn't in uniform, but wore his trench coat over the clerical suit and dog collar, the black trilby slanted over one ear. Ryan had told him the truth. The Ford's engine was in apple pie order in spite of the vehicle's rattletrap appearance.

"You were right, Michael," Devlin said. "She's a runner, this old van of yours."

"Sure and I could race her at Brooklands if they were still racing at Brooklands." Ryan grinned.

Mary was sitting in the back of the van reading a book as usual. "Are you all right back there?" Devlin asked her.

"I'm fine."

"We'll stop for a cup of tea in a while."

In Maidstone, Ryan drove around the center of the town until he found a cycle shop. Devlin went in and bought half a dozen standard bicycle lamps with fresh batteries.

"I've cleaned him out," he said when he returned. "Told him I wanted them for my church scout troop. There's no doubt about it this collar comes in useful on occasion."

"And why would you want those?" Mary asked.

"An airplane coming in through the darkness at night is like a lost bird, girl dear. It needs a welcome. A little light on the situation, you might say."

On the other side of Ashford they pulled in at the side of the road and Mary opened a Thermos flask and they had tea. There was a track leading to a little copse. It had stopped raining but was still very damp. The sky was dark and threatening all the way to Romney Marsh and the sea in the distance. Mary and Devlin strolled along the track and stood under a tree, taking it all in.

He nodded at her book. "What this time?"

"Poetry," she said. "Robert Browning. Do you like poetry?"

"I had some published once. What's called in the trade a slim volume." He laughed. "I could make the stuff up at the drop of a hat, and then I realized one day just how bad it was."

"I don't believe you. Make something up about me."

He stuck a cigarette in his mouth. "All right." He thought for a moment then said, "Mystery girl, who are you? Hurrying nowhere in your tight skirt and frizzled hair, legs heavy with promise."

There was a look of mischief on his face, and she struck him lightly with her clenched fist. "That's terrible."

"I warned you." He lit his cigarette. "Good poetry says it all for you in a few lines."

"All right, what would sum me up?"

"Easy. 'Now, Voyager, sail thou forth to seek and find.' "

"That's marvelous," she said. "Did you write that?"

"Not exactly. A Yankee fella called Walt Whitman thought of it first." It started to rain, and he put a hand on her elbow. "But I wish I'd written it for you. Let's get moving." And they hurried back to the van.

At the apartment over the Astoria, Jack Carver was sitting at the table by the window having a late breakfast when Eric came in. His ear was heavily bandaged, tape running diagonally up across his forehead holding the dressing in place. He looked terrible.

"How do you feel?" Carver asked.

"Shocking, Jack, the pain's bloody awful. Aziz gave me some pills, but they don't seem to have much effect."

"He tells me George is in a bad way. That bullet splintered the bone. He could be left with a permanently stiff arm, as well as the leg."

Eric poured coffee, his hand shaking. "That little sod, Jack. We've got to get our hands on him. We've got to."

"We will, son," Jack said. "And then it'll be our turn. I've put his description out all over London. He'll turn up. Now drink your coffee and have something to eat."

Using the road map, Ryan found Charbury easily enough and an inquiry at the little village store led them to Shaw Place. The great rusting iron gates at the end of the drive stood open; the drive, stretching toward the old house, had grass growing through the gravel.

"This place has seen better days," Ryan commented.

Devlin stepped out, opened the van doors and got the radio and the bag of cycle lamps out. "You can leave me here," he said. "I'll walk up to the house."

"What time shall we call back?" Ryan asked.

"Give me four hours, and if I'm not here, just wait. Go and have a look at Rye or one of those places."

"Fine," Ryan said. "Take care, Liam." And he drove away.

Devlin picked up the case and started up the long drive. The house showed every evidence of lack of money. The long shutters at the windows badly needed a coat of paint, as did the front door. There was a bell pull. He gave it a heave and waited, but there was no response. After a while he picked up the case and went around to the rear of the house, where there was a cobbled courtyard. One of the stable doors stood open and there were sounds of activity. He put the case down and looked in.

Lavinia Shaw wore riding breeches and boots, her hair bound in a scarf as she curried a large black stallion. Devlin put a cigarette in his mouth and snapped open his lighter. The sound startled her and she looked around.

"Miss Lavinia Shaw?" he inquired.

"Yes."

"Harry Conlon. I phoned your brother last night. He's expecting me."

"Major Conlon." There was a sudden eagerness about her. She put down the brush and comb she was using and ran her hands over her breeches. "Of course. How wonderful to have you here."

The well-bred upper-class voice, her whole attitude, was quite incredible to Devlin, but he took the hand she offered and smiled. "A pleasure, Miss Shaw."

"Maxwell is out on the marsh somewhere with his gun. Goes every day. You know how it is. Food shortages. Anything's good for the pot." She didn't seem to be able to stop talking. "We'll go into the kitchen, shall we?"

It was very large, the floor flagged with red tiles, an enormous pine table in the center with chairs around it. There were unwashed dishes in the sink, and the whole place was cluttered and untidy, the lack of servants very evident.

"Tea?" she said. "Or would you like something stronger?"

"No, tea would be fine."

He put the case carefully on the table with the bag of cycle lamps, and she boiled water and made the tea quickly, so excited and nervous that she poured it before it had brewed properly.

"Oh, dear, I've ruined it."

"Not at all. It's wet isn't it and hot?" Devlin said.

He poured a little milk in, and she sat on the other side of the table, arms folded under her full breasts, eyes glittering now, never leaving him. "I can't tell you how absolutely thrilling all this is. I haven't been so excited for years."

She was like a character in a bad play, the duke's daughter coming in through the French windows in her riding breeches and gushing at everyone in sight.

"You've been in Germany recently?" she asked.

"Oh, yes," he told her. "I was in Berlin only the other day."

"How marvelous to be part of all that. People here are so complacent. They don't understand what the Führer's done for Germany."

"For all of Europe you might say," Devlin told her.

"Exactly. Strength, a sense of purpose, discipline. Whereas here—" She laughed contemptuously. "That drunken fool Churchill has no idea what he's doing. Just lurches from one mistake to another."

"Ah, yes, but he would, wouldn't he?" Devlin said dryly. "Do you think we could have a look round? The old barn you used for your Tiger Moth and the South Meadow."

"Of course." She jumped up so eagerly that she knocked over the chair. As she picked it up, she said, "I'll just get a coat."

The meadow was larger than he had expected and stretched to a line of trees in the distance. "How long?" Devlin asked. "Two-fifty or three hundred yards?"

"Oh, no," she said. "Getting on for three-fifty. The grass is so short because we leased it to a local farmer to graze sheep, but they've gone to market now."

"You used to take off and land here a lot in the old days?"

"All the time. That's when I had my little Puss Moth. Great fun."

"And you used the barn over there as a hangar?"

"That's right. I'll show you."

The place was quite huge, but like everything else the massive doors had seen better days, dry rot very evident, planks missing. Devlin helped her open one of the doors slightly so they could go inside. There was a rusting tractor in one corner, some moldering hay at the back. Otherwise it was empty, rain dripping through holes in the roof.

"You'd want to put a plane in here?" she asked.

"Only for a short while, to be out of sight. A Lysander. Not too large. It would fit in here and no trouble."

"When exactly?"

"Tomorrow night."

"My goodness, you are pushing things along."

"Yes, well time's important."

They went out and he closed the door. Somewhere in the far distance a shotgun was fired. "My brother," she said. "Let's go and find him, shall we?"

As they walked across the meadow, she said, "We had a German friend who used to come here in the old days, Werner Keitel. We used to fly all over the place together. Do you happen to know him?"

"He was killed in the Battle of Britain."

She paused for a moment only, then carried on. "Yes, I thought it would be something like that."

"I'm sorry," Devlin told her.

She shrugged. "A long time ago, Major." And she started to walk faster.

They followed a dike through the small reeds, and it was Nell who appeared first, splashing through water, gamboling around them before running away again. There was another shot, and then Shaw emerged from the reeds in the distance and came toward them.

"Look at this, old girl." He held up a couple of rabbits.

"See who's here," she called.

He paused and came forward again. "Conlon, my dear chap. Nice to see you. Won't shake hands. Blood on them." He might have been welcoming Devlin to a weekend in the country. "Better get home and find you a drink."

They started back along the dike. Devlin looked out across the expanse of reeds intersected by creeks. "Desolate country this."

"Dead, old man. Everything about the damn place is dead. Rain, mist and the ghosts of things past. Of course it was different in my grandfather's day. Twenty-five servants in the house alone. God knows how many on the estate." He didn't stop talking for a moment as they walked along. "People don't want to work these days, that's the trouble. Damn Bolshies all over the place. That's what I admire about the Führer. Gives people some order in their lives."

"Makes them do as they're told, you mean," Devlin said.

Shaw nodded enthusiastically. "Exactly, old man, exactly."

Devlin set up the radio in a small study behind the old library. Shaw had gone to have a bath, and it was Lavinia who helped festoon the aerials around the room and watched intently as the Irishman explained the set to her.

"Is it much different from the one you had before?" he asked.

"A bit more sophisticated, that's all."

"And your Morse code. Can you still remember it?"

"Good heavens, Major Conlon, you never forget something like that. I was a Girl Guide when I first learned it."

"Right," Devlin said. "Let's see what you can do then."

In the radio room at Prinz Albrechtstrasse, Schellenberg studied Devlin's first message, then turned to Ilse and Asa Vaughan. "Incredible. He intends to pull Steiner out tomorrow evening. He wants you at Shaw Place in time to leave no later than midnight.''

''Then we'll have to get moving,'' Asa told him.

''Yes, well the Lysander was delivered to Chernay yesterday,'' Schellenberg said. ''It's only a matter of getting ourselves down there.'' He said to the radio operator, ''Take this message to Falcon. *Will meet your requirements. Departure time will be confirmed to you tomorrow night.*''

He started to walk out, and the operator called, ''I have a reply, General.''

Schellenberg turned. ''What is it?''

''A pleasure to do business with you.''

Schellenberg smiled and kept going, Asa and Ilse Huber following him.

In the study, Lavinia turned from the radio set. ''Did I do all right?''

Her brother was sitting by the empty fireplace, a tumbler of whisky in his hand. ''Seemed fine to me.''

''You were excellent,'' Devlin said. ''Now this set is different from the one you threw away in one respect. It has a direct voice capacity for short ranges only. Say twenty-five miles. That was why I gave them the frequency reading. I've adjusted it, and all you do is switch on and you're in business. That means you can talk to the pilot when he's close.''

''Marvelous. Anything else?''

''Sometime after seven they'll contact you from the French base to confirm departure time, so stand by. Afterwards, you place the cycle lamps in the meadow as I described to you.''

''I will. You may depend on it.'' She turned to Shaw. ''Isn't it marvelous, darling?''

''Terrific, old girl,'' he said, eyes already glazed, and poured another drink.

But by then Devlin had had enough and he got up. ''I'll be on my way. See you tomorrow night.''

Shaw mumbled something, and Lavinia took Devlin back to the kitchen where he got his coat and hat.

''Will he be all right?'' Devlin asked as she took him to the front door.

''Who, Max? Oh, yes. No need to worry there, Major.''

''I'll see you then.''

It started to rain as he went down the drive, and there was no sign of the van. He stood there, hands in pockets, and it was thirty minutes before it turned up.

''Did it go well?'' Ryan asked

Mary cut in. "We've had a lovely time. Rye was a fine place."

"Well, I'm happy for you," Devlin said sourly. "Those two didn't even offer me a bite to eat."

Asa was just finishing a late lunch in the canteen when Schellenberg hurried in. "A slight change in plan. I've had a message saying the Reichsführer wants to see me. The interesting thing is I'm to bring you."

"What in the hell for?"

"It seems you've been awarded the Iron Cross First Class, and the Reichsführer likes to pin them on SS officers himself."

Asa said, "I wonder what my old man would say. I went to West Point, for Christ's sakes."

"The other complication is that he's at Wewelsburg. You've heard of the place, of course?"

"Every good SS man's idea of heaven. What does this do to our schedule?"

"No problem. Wewelsburg has a Luftwaffe feeder base only ten miles away. We'll fly there in the Stork and carry on to Chernay afterwards." Schellenberg glanced at his watch. "The appointment's for seven, and he takes punctuality for granted."

At six-thirty it was totally dark on the Thames as Ryan nudged the motorboat in toward the shingle strand. He said to Mary, "Just sit tight. It shouldn't take long."

Devlin picked up the bag of tools and the torch. "Right, let's get moving." And he went over the side.

The water in the tunnel was deeper than it had been before, at one point chest high, but they pressed on and reached the grille in a few minutes.

"Are you sure about this?" Ryan asked.

"Michael, you said you thought it would come away easy. Now wouldn't I look the original fool if I turned up to grab Steiner tomorrow night and found the damn grille wouldn't budge?"

"All right, let's get on with it," Ryan said.

"And no banging. I don't want someone on their knees up there in the chapel wondering what's happening down here."

Which is what made the whole thing rather more difficult than it had at first appeared. The slow, careful probing between the brickwork took time. On occasion, several bricks fell out of place at once, but others proved more difficult. It took half an hour to clear one side.

Fifteen minutes into working on the other, Ryan said, "You were right, dammit, the thing's a sod."

He pulled at the grille angrily and it fell forward. Devlin grabbed at his arm, pulling him out of the way and got a hand to the side of the grille at the same time, easing it down.

He took the lamp and peered inside, then handed it to Ryan. "You hold the light while I go and take a look."

"Watch your step now."

Devlin went through the hole and waded inside. In there, the water was now up to his armpits, covering the tops of the tombs. He made it to the steps and started up. A rat scurried past him and dived into the water. He paused on the top step, then very gently tried the handle.

There was the faintest of creaks and the door eased open. He could see the altar, the Virgin on the other side floating in candlelight. He peered around the door cautiously. The chapel was quite deserted, and then the outer door opened and a nun came in. Very quietly Devlin closed the door and retreated down the steps.

"Perfect," he said to Ryan as he clambered through the hole. "Now let's get out of here."

At the Luftwaffe base, Schellenberg gave orders for the Stork to be refueled, commandeered the station commander's Mercedes and driver and set out for Wewelsburg with Asa. It started to snow, and as they approached, Wewelsburg was plain to see, light at the windows and over the main gate in total disregard of any blackout regulations.

Asa looked up at the castle and its towers in the falling snow. "My God!" he said in awe. "It's incredible."

"I know." Schellenberg reached forward and closed the glass partition so that the Luftwaffe driver couldn't hear what they were saying. "Looks like a film set. Actually it's a personal retreat for the Reichsführer, a center for racial research and a home-from-home to the elite of the SS."

"But what do they do there?"

"The Reichsführer is obsessed with King Arthur and the Knights of the Round Table. So he has his twelve most trusted lieutenants sit at a round table. His knights, you see."

"And you're not one of them, I take it."

"Very definitely not. No, you have to be a lunatic to indulge in those games. They have a memorial hall with a swastika in the ceiling, a pit in which the remains of these special ones will be burnt on death. There are twelve pedestals and urns waiting for the ashes."

"You've got to be kidding!" Asa said.

"No, quite true. I'll show you if we get a chance." Schellenberg laughed and shook his head. "And people like these are handling the destinies of millions."

They booked in at the entrance hall and left their greatcoats and caps with the sergeant of the guard, who checked his register.

"Yes, General Schellenberg, the Reichsführer is expecting you for seven o'clock in his private sitting room in the south wing. I'll take you up, sir."

"No need. I know the way."

As Asa followed Schellenberg across the hall and they turned along a corridor, he said, "You're right. This place puts Louis B. Mayer to shame."

Schellenberg checked his watch. "We've got fifteen minutes. Come on, I'll show you that memorial hall I told you about. It's just along here. There's a little gallery, as I remember. Yes, here we are."

There were perhaps a dozen steps up to an oak door. It opened easily, and he could immediately hear voices. He paused, frowning, then turned to Asa and put a finger to his lips. Then he opened the door cautiously and they went in.

The circular room was a place of shadows, only dimly lit. Asa was aware of the pedestals and urns Schellenberg had described, the pit beneath the ceiling swastika, but it was the people present who were most interesting. Rossman, Himmler's aide, stood to one side waiting. The Reichsführer stood in the pit itself, face to face with Sturmbannführer Horst Berger. They all wore black dress uniforms.

"I have brought you here, Berger, to this holy place before you depart on what I can only describe as your sacred mission."

"An honor, Reichsführer."

"Now let's go over the details. You will meet the Führer's plane, which will land at the Luftwaffe base at Cherbourg at six tomorrow night. I shall be with him. You will escort us to this Château de Belle-Île, where we will spend the night. At seven o'clock the following morning the Führer will have breakfast with Rommel and Admiral Canaris. They will arrive by road."

"And when do I take action, Reichsführer?"

Himmler shrugged. "It doesn't really matter. I suppose the end of the meal might be appropriate. How many men will you have in the guard?"

"Thirty."

"Good. That should be enough."

"Hand-picked, Reichsführer."

"Good—the fewer the better. We are a special brotherhood, those of us involved in this, for there are some who would not agree with what we intend."

"As you say, Reichsführer."

"General Schellenberg, for instance, but he's cleverer than the proverbial fox. That's why I wanted him elsewhere these past three weeks. So I gave him this ridiculous mission to occupy him. To bring Steiner out of England. An impossibility. I happen to know from our intelligence people that the agent working for us in London, Vargas, also works for the British. We didn't tell Schellenberg that, did we Rossman?''

"No, Reichsführer."

"So we may deduce that the Irishman Devlin will not last too long over there."

"I couldn't be more pleased, Reichsführer," Berger said.

"We could have won this war at Dunkirk, Berger, if the Führer had allowed the Panzers to roll onto the beaches. Instead he ordered them to halt. Russia, one disaster after another. Stalingrad, the most catastrophic defeat the German army has ever suffered." Himmler shuffled away and turned. "Blunder after blunder and he still won't listen."

"I see, Reichsführer," Berger said. "All men of sense would."

"And so inexorably Germany, our beloved country, sinks deeper into the pit of defeat, and that is why the Führer must die, Berger, and to accomplish that is your sacred task. Rommel, Canaris, the Führer. A dastardly attack on their part leading to the Führer's unfortunate death, followed by their own deaths at the hands of loyal SS men."

"And afterwards?" Berger said.

"We of the SS will naturally assume all governmental powers. The war may then be continued as it should be. No weakness, no shirking by anyone." He put a hand on Berger's shoulder. "We belong to the same sacred brotherhood, Major. I envy you this opportunity."

Schellenberg nodded to Asa, edged him out and closed the door.

"Jesus!" Asa said. "Now what happens?"

"We keep the appointment. If he finds out we overheard that lot, we'll never get out of here alive." As they hurried along the corridor, Schellenberg said, "Whatever he wants, follow my lead and not a mention that Devlin's got things to the stage they are."

He led the way up a back stair, along a corridor, and reached the door to Himmler's sitting room in the south wing very quickly.

Schellenberg sat in the chair behind Rossman's desk. "Now we wait. They'll probably come up by the back entrance to his room."

A moment later the door opened and Rossman looked out. "Ah, there you are."

"Right on time." Schellenberg led the way in.

Himmler, behind his desk, looked up. "So, General, and this is Hauptsturmführer Vaughan, the pilot you recruited for the Steiner affair?"

"Yes, Reichsführer."

"Any news of your Mr. Devlin?"

Schellenberg said, "I'm afraid not, Reichsführer."

"Ah, well, it was always a problematical mission to say the least. The Führer flies to Cherbourg, arrives at Belle-Île tomorrow night. Canaris and Rommel are to have breakfast the following morning at seven. I'll be there, of course. The idiots are junketing around Normandy at the moment. They have a crazy idea the invasion will come there and hope to persuade the Führer to agree with them."

"I see, Reichsführer."

"However, to the reason for your visit and why I asked you to bring the officer with you." He turned. "Rossman."

As he stood up, Rossman opened a medal case. Himmler took the Iron Cross it contained, came around the table and pinned it to Asa Vaughan's tunic.

"To you, Hauptsturmführer Asa Vaughan of the George Washington Legion, in acknowledgment of supreme valor in aerial combat over Poland."

"Reichsführer," said Asa, keeping his face straight with a supreme effort.

"And now you may go. I have work to do."

Schellenberg and Asa hurried down the stairs, retrieved their greatcoats and caps and went out to the waiting Mercedes.

"Back to the base," Schellenberg said to the driver, and he and Asa got in.

As they drove away, Asa closed the glass partition and said, "What do you make of it?"

"I know one thing," Schellenberg said. "Killing Hitler is the worst thing that could happen. At least with the Führer making one foul-up after another, there's a prospect of a reasonably early end to the war, but Himmler would be another story. Can you imagine that animal in total control, the SS in charge of government, the army? The war could go on for years."

"So what are you going to do? Warn Rommel and Canaris?"

"First of all, I don't know exactly where they are, and second, it's a question of belief, Asa. Why should anyone believe me? My word against that of the Reichsführer of the SS."

"Come off it, General. According to Liam Devlin, you're a very smart guy. Surely you can come up with something."

"I'll put my heart and soul into it," Schellenberg promised him. "But for the moment, let's concentrate on getting back to the airfield and the Stork. We fly out at once. The sooner we're at Chernay, the happier I'll be."

12

THE DUTY MP USUALLY BROUGHT Steiner a cup of tea at eleven each morning. He was five minutes late and found the German by the window reading.

"There you go, General."

"Thank you, Corporal."

"I suppose you'd prefer coffee, sir," the corporal said, lingering, for he rather liked Steiner.

"But I was raised on tea, Corporal." Steiner told him "I went to school right here in London. St. Paul's."

"Is that a fact, sir?"

He turned to the door and Steiner said, "Is Lieutenant Benson back yet?"

"His leave is up at midnight, sir, but if I know him, he'll look in this evening. You know what these young officers are like. Dead keen. Looking for that second pip on his shoulders."

He left, the bolt rammed home and Steiner went back to his seat by the window, waiting for noon as he had on the previous day, drinking his tea and trying to compose himself to patience.

It was raining again and there was fog in the city, so heavy already that he could barely see the other side of the river. A very large cargo boat eased down from the London docks followed by a line of barges. He watched for a while, wondering where it was going, and then he saw the girl, just as Devlin had described—black beret and shabby raincoat.

Mary limped along the pavement, collar up, hands thrust deep into her pockets. She stopped at the entrance leading down to the strand and leaned on the wall, watching the boats on the river. She didn't look up at the priory at all. Devlin had been most explicit about that. She just stayed there watching for ten minutes, then turned and walked away.

Steiner was aware of intense excitement and gripped the bars at his window to steady himself. The door opened behind him and the corporal reappeared.

"If you're finished, Colonel, I'll take your tray."

"Yes, I am, thank you." The MP picked up the tray and turned to the door. "Oh, I don't know who's on duty this evening, but I'll be going down to Confession," Steiner said.

"Right, sir. I'll make a note of it. Eight o'clock as usual."

He went out and locked the door. Steiner listened to the sound of his boots receding along the corridor, then turned, gripping the bars again.

"Now we pray, Mr. Devlin," he said softly. "Now we pray."

When Devlin went into St. Patrick's, he was in his military trench coat and uniform. He wasn't really sure why he had come. Conscience again, he supposed, or perhaps just tying up loose ends. He only knew he couldn't leave without a word with the old priest. He'd used him, he knew that, and it didn't sit well. What was worse was the fact that they would meet again and for the last time in the chapel at St. Mary's that evening. No avoiding that or the distress it would cause.

The church was quiet, only Frank Martin down at the alter arranging a few flowers. He turned at the sound of Devlin's approach, and there was genuine pleasure on his face. "Hello, Father."

Devlin managed a smile. "I just dropped in to tell you I'm on my way. I got my orders this morning."

"That's unexpected, isn't it?"

"Yes, well, they're easing me back in." Devlin lied in his teeth. "I'm to report to a military hospital in Portsmouth."

"Ah, well, as they say, there's a war on."

Devlin nodded. "The war, the war, the bloody war, Father. It's gone on too long, and we all of us have to do things we normally would never do. Every soldier, whichever side he's on. Things to shame us."

The old man said gently, "You're troubled, my son. Can I help in any way?"

"No, Father, not this time. Some things we have to live with ourselves." Devlin put out his hand and the old priest took it. "It's been a genuine pleasure, Father."

"And for me," Frank Martin said.

Devlin turned and walked away, the door banged. The old priest stood there for a moment, puzzlement on his face, and then he turned and went back to his flowers.

There was the merest hint of fog at Chernay too at four o'clock when Schellenberg went in search of Asa. He found him in the hangar with the Lysander and Flight Sergeant Leber.

"How is it?" Schellenberg asked.

"Perfection, General," Leber told him. "Couldn't be better," He smiled. "Naturally, the Hauptsturmführer has just been checking everything out for the fifth time, but that's understandable."

The Lysander had RAF roundels in place on canvas strips as Asa had requested, and the swastika on the tailplane had been blocked out with black canvas.

"Of course there's no absolute guarantee that they won't come off in flight," Asa said. "We'll just have to keep our fingers crossed."

"And the weather?" Schellenberg asked.

Leber said, "It's uncertain. Visibility could be restricted. There are a couple of conflicting fronts moving in. I've checked with our base at Cherbourg, and the truth is it's one of those times when they don't really know."

"But the plane is ready?"

"Oh, yes," Asa told him. "One good thing about this beauty is that she's fitted with an emergency fuel tank. I suppose the RAF had that done because of the kind of operation it was employed on. I'm allowing an hour and a half for the flight, and thanks to Luftwaffe intelligence at Cherbourg, I can tune my radio to the RAF frequency as I approach the English coast."

"Good. Let's go for a walk. I feel like the air."

It was raining only slightly as they walked along the airfield and Schellenberg smoked a cigarette, not speaking for a while. They reached the end and leaned on a fence, looking out to sea.

Schellenberg said, "You feel all right about this?"

"The trip?" Asa shrugged. "The flight itself doesn't worry me. It's the situation at the other end that's problematical."

"Yes, we are all in Mr. Devlin's hands there."

Asa said, "Assuming everything goes well and I put down here with our friends sometime early tomorrow morning, what happens then? What about the Belle-Île situation? Have you any ideas?"

"Only one and it would be a desperate venture. On the other hand simple, and I like simplicity. It pleases me."

"I'm all ears."

"Well, the Führer will be having breakfast with Rommel, the admiral and the Reichsführer. Berger will strike at the end of the meal."

"Yes, I know that. I was there, remember?"

"What if you and I and Mr. Devlin arrived to join them for breakfast and exposed the plot."

"But we'd go down the hole too, that's obvious," Asa said. "Even if you said your piece to the Führer, Berger and his chums would just get on with it."

"Oh, yes, and it would suit the Reichsführer to have me out of the war." Schellenberg smiled. "There is a wild card I haven't mentioned.

Remember when we were driving to Belle-Île? The Twelfth Parachute Detachment outside St.-Aubin? Hauptmann Erich Kramer and thirty-five paratroopers?''

"Sure I do.''

"What do you think would happen if Colonel Kurt Steiner, the living legend of the Parachute Regiment, appeared and told them he needed their services because there was an SS plot ten miles up the road to kill the Führer?''

"Jesus!" Asa said. "Those guys would follow Steiner anywhere.''

"Exactly. And the *Fallschirmjäger* have always been notorious for their dislike of the SS.''

"It could work,'' Asa said.

"If everything else did.''

"Let me get this straight. We'd go in first? Steiner would follow on?''

"Yes, let's say fifteen minutes later.''

Asa said, "That could be one hell of a breakfast.''

"Yes, well, I prefer not to think of it right now,'' Schellenberg said. "I've got other things on my mind. Let's go and have a cup of coffee.''

ᜃ

In Ryan's kitchen, Devlin had various items laid out on the table. "Let's see what I've got here,'' he said. "Those MPs carry handcuffs, but I'll take a little extra twine for emergencies, just in case.''

"I've made up three gags,'' Ryan said. "Bandages and sticking plaster. You've the priest too, remember.''

"I'd prefer to forget him, but there you are,'' Devlin said.

"And a weapon?''

"I'll take the Smith and Wesson in the ankle holster for emergencies and that Walther with the silencer I got from Carver.''

"Would you anticipate any killing?'' Ryan asked and looked troubled.

"The last thing I want. Have you got that sap of yours?''

"God, I was forgetting.''

Ryan opened the kitchen table drawer and produced the leather sap. It was loaded with lead and there was a loop for the wrist. It was a thing carried by many London taxi drivers for self-protection. Devlin weighed it in his hand and put it down beside the Walther.

"That's everything then,'' Ryan said.

Devlin smiled lightly. "All we need is Steiner now.''

The door opened and Mary came in. Her uncle said, "God, I'm starving, girl. Bacon and eggs all round if you can manage it.''

"No problem,'' she said, "but we're out of bread and tea. I'll just run along to the High Street before the shop closes. I shan't be long.''

And she took her beret and raincoat down from behind the door and went out.

The old lady at the shop managed her a tin of black market salmon and some cigarettes as well as the bread and tea, and Mary was carrying them in a carrier bag when she left. The fog was rolling in, the traffic slow, and she stopped cautiously on the next corner before crossing the road.

Eric Carver, at the wheel of his brother's Humber limousine, had stopped at the lights. She was only a yard or two away as she passed, but he saw her clearly. She crossed the road and turned into a side street. As the lights changed, he went after her, pulled the Humber in at the curb, got out and followed cautiously.

Mary turned into Cable Wharfe, walking as quickly as she could, and crossed to the house. As she went around the corner, Eric hurried across and peered around cautiously. She had just reached the kitchen door.

It opened, and he heard Devlin say, "Ah, there you are, girl. Will you come in out of that?"

The door closed. Eric said softly, "Right, you bastard. I've got you." And he turned and hurried away.

Jack Carver was in his bedroom when Eric burst in. Carver said, "How often have I told you, Eric? I don't like anyone coming in here when I'm dressing, and that includes you."

"But I've found him, Jack. I've found where that rotten little bastard's shacked up. I saw the girl. I followed her home and he was there."

"You're sure?"

"Of course I bloody am."

"Where was this?"

"A place called Cable Wharfe. It's in Wapping."

"Right." Carver nodded in satisfaction, put on his jacket and went through to the sitting room, Eric following.

"So, what are we going to do?" Eric demanded as his brother sat behind his desk.

"Do? We're going to sort him," Carver said.

"When?"

Carver checked his watch. "I've got a big game on tonight, you know that. Probably finish around ten. We'll pay him a call after that, when he thinks he's nicely tucked up for the night." Carver smiled, opened a drawer and took out a Browning. "Just you and me and our friend here."

There was an unholy look on Eric's face. "Christ, Jack, I can't wait," he said.

Lieutenant Benson arrived at the priory just before seven. He said hello to the porter who admitted him and went straight upstairs. Strictly speaking, as the MP had told Steiner that morning, Benson's leave wasn't up until midnight, but the only available train to London from his parents' home in Norwich had been an early one. When he was admitted to the corridor in the upper floor, he found a corporal sitting in his office who jumped to his feet at once.

"You're back, sir."

"I should have thought that was obvious, Smith. Where's Sergeant Morgan?"

"Went off about an hour ago, sir."

"Everything calm while I've been away?"

"I think so, sir."

"Let's have a look at the log." Smith handed it over and Benson leafed through it. "What's this entry here on the admittance sheet? Major Conlon?"

"Oh, yes, sir, the padre. He did a tour of the place with the sister and Father Martin."

"Who gave him permission?"

"He had a War Office pass, sir. You know, those unrestricted access things. I think you'll find Sergeant Morgan put the details down."

"I can see that. The point is, what was Conlon doing here?"

"Search me, sir. Nice-looking man. Gray hair, glasses. Looked like he'd had a hard time. Oh, and he had an MC, sir."

"Yes, well, that could mean anything," Benson said sourly. "I'm going down to see Sister."

She was in her office when he knocked and went in; she glanced up and smiled. "You're back. Did you have a good leave?"

"Yes, not bad. Is Father Martin around?"

"Just went into the chapel to hear Confessions. Anything I can do?"

"There was a Major Conlon here when I was away."

"Ah, yes, the army chaplain. A nice man. On sick leave. I understand he was wounded in Sicily last year."

"Yes, but what was he doing here?"

"Nothing. We just showed him round and he took over for Father Martin one evening. He's not been well, you know."

"Has he been back?"

"No. I understand from Father Martin that he's been posted. A military hospital in Portsmouth, I believe." She looked slightly bewildered. "Is anything wrong?"

"Oh, no, it's just that when unexpected guests turn up with War Office passes one likes to know who they are.''

"You worry too much," she said.

"Probably. Goodnight, Sister."

But it wouldn't go away, the nagging doubt, and when he got back upstairs to his office he phoned Dougal Munro.

Jack Carter had gone to York for the day. His train wasn't due into London until ten, so Munro was working alone in his office when he took the call. He listened patiently to what Benson had to say.

"You were right to call me," he said. "I don't much like the idea of officers with War Office passes sticking their noses into our business, but there it is. One of the problems with using a place like the priory, Benson. These religious types don't behave like other people."

"I've got Conlon's details here on the admission sheet, sir. Do you want them?"

"Tell you what. I'm packing up here quite soon and going home," Munro said. "I'll call in and see you. About an hour and a half."

"I'll expect you, sir."

Benson put down the phone, and Corporal Smith, standing at the door, said, "You'll see Colonel Steiner's booked for chapel, sir."

"What in the hell has he got to confess cooped up in here?" Benson demanded.

"Eight o'clock as usual, sir. Shall I do it with Corporal Ross?"

"No," Benson said. "Well do it together. I'm expecting Brigadier Munro, but he won't be here until half past eight. Now get me a cup of tea."

At Chernay, the elements were very definitely against them, fog rolling in from the sea and rain with it. Schellenberg and Asa Vaughan stood in the radio room waiting while Flight Sergeant Leber checked the situation with Cherbourg.

After a while he turned to them. "The Führer's plane got in all right, General. Landed at six just before this lot started."

"So, what's the verdict?" Asa demanded.

"Parts of the Channel you'll find winds gusting up to force eight."

"Hell, I can handle wind," Asa said. "What else do they say?"

"Fog over southern England, from London down to the Channel coast. Another thing. They say it will get worse here during the night." He looked worried. "To be frank, sir, it stinks."

"Don't worry, Sergeant, I'll find a way."

Asa and Schellenberg went out into the wind and rain and hurried across to the hut they were using. Schellenberg sat on one of the beds and poured schnapps into an enamel cup. "Do you want some?"

"Better not." Asa lit a cigarette instead.

There was silence, then Schellenberg said, "Look, if you think it's not on, if you don't want to go . . . "

"Don't be silly," Asa told him. "Of course I'm going. Devlin's depending on me. I can't leave him in the lurch. Wind doesn't bother me. I flew for the Finns in their Winter War, remember, when we had blizzards every day. Let me tell you about fog. Taking off in it's nothing, but landing is something else and it worries me that I might not be able to land when I get there."

"Then you'll have to come back."

"Fine, except for the fact that, as Leber has just informed us, it's not going to get any better here."

"So what do you want to do?"

"Leave it as late as possible. Devlin wanted me there for a midnight departure. Let's cut it really close. I won't leave until ten o'clock. That will give the weather a chance to clear."

"And if it doesn't?"

"I go anyway."

"Fine." Schellenberg got up. "I'll send a signal to that effect to Shaw Place now."

Lavinia Shaw, seated at the radio in the study in her headphones, took the message. She tapped out a quick reply: *Message received and understood.* She took off her headphones and turned. Her brother sat by the fire cleaning his shotgun, Nell at his feet, a tumbler of Scotch beside him.

"They won't be leaving until ten o'clock, darling. It's this damn weather."

She went to the French windows, pulled back the curtains and opened the windows, looking out at the fog.

Shaw moved to her side. "I should have thought this bloody stuff was all to the good for this kind of secret landing."

Lavinia said, "Don't be silly, Max, the worst thing in the world for any pilot. Don't you remember when I couldn't land at Helmsley back in thirty-six? Stooged around until I ran out of fuel and crashed into that field wall. I was nearly killed."

"Sorry, old girl, I was forgetting." Rain started to spot the terrace in front of them in the light from the window. "There you are," Shaw said. "That should help clear it. Now close the window and let's have another drink."

"You've got everything?" Michael Ryan asked as the motorboat coasted in to the little strand.

Devlin wore loose blue overalls and boots. He tapped at his pockets, checklisting each item. "Everything in perfect working order."

Ryan said, "I wish you'd let me come with you."

"My affair, this one, Michael, and if there's the slightest hint of trouble you and Mary get the hell out of it. This bloody fog is a blessing in a way." He turned and smiled at Mary through the darkness. "You were right about that."

She reached up and kissed him on the cheek. "God bless you, Mr. Devlin. I've prayed for you."

"Then everything will be all right." And he went over the side.

The water was not quite as deep, which was something, and he moved on, the light from his lamp splaying against the tunnel until he reached the hole in the wall. He checked his watch. It was a couple of minutes past eight. He climbed in and waded through the water then started up the steps.

Dougal Munro had finished a little earlier than he had intended, so he called a staff car and told the driver to take him to St. Mary's Priory. It was a difficult journey, crawling along at fifteen miles an hour in the fog, and it was just after eight o'clock when they arrived.

"I shan't be long," the brigadier said as he got out.

"I'll get off the road, sir, while I'm waiting," his driver replied. "Otherwise someone will be shunting me up the rear. I'll just turn up the side, sir. There's a yard there."

"I'll find you." Munro went up the steps and rang the bell at the door.

The night porter opened it to him. "Good evening, Brigadier," he said.

"Sister Maria about?" Munro asked.

"No, she was called to the Cromwell Road Hospital."

"All right. I'll go on upstairs. I want to see Lieutenant Benson."

"I saw him go into the chapel a few minutes ago, sir, with one of the corporals and that German officer."

"Really?" Munro hesitated, then crossed to the chapel door.

Devlin eased open the door at the top of the steps and got the shock of his life. Corporal Smith was standing with his back to him no more than six feet away. He was examining a religious figure. Benson was up by the door. Devlin didn't hesitate. He pulled out the sap and lashed Smith across the back of the neck and moved back into the shelter of the door as the corporal went down with a clatter.

Benson called, "Smith, what's going on?"

He ran along the aisle and paused, staring down at the body. It was then, sensing too late that something was very wrong indeed, that he reached for the Webley revolver in his holster.

Devlin stepped out, the silenced Walther in his left hand, the sap in his right. "I wouldn't do that, son. This thing makes no more noise than you or me coughing. Now turn round."

Benson did as he was told, and Devlin gave him the same as Smith. The young lieutenant groaned, sank to his knees and fell across the corporal. Quickly Devlin searched them for handcuffs, but only Smith appeared to be carrying them.

"Are you there, Colonel?" he called.

Steiner stepped out of the confessional box, and Father Martin, joined him. The old priest looked shocked and bewildered. "Major Conlon? What's happening here."

"I'm truly sorry, Father." Devlin turned him around and handcuffed his wrists behind him.

He sat the old man down in a pew and took out one of his makeshift gags. Martin said, "You're not a priest, I take it."

"My uncle was, Father."

"I forgive you, my son," Frank Martin said and submitted himself to the gag.

At that moment, the door opened and Dougal Munro walked in. Before he could say a word, Kurt Steiner had him around, an arm like steel across his throat.

"And who might this be?" Devlin demanded.

"Brigadier Dougal Munro," Steiner told him. "Of SOE."

"Is that a fact?" Devlin held the Walther in his right hand now. "This thing is silenced, as I'm sure you will know, Brigadier. So be sensible."

Steiner released him and Munro said bitterly, "My God, Devlin— Liam Devlin."

"As ever was, Brigadier."

"What happens now?" Steiner asked.

Devlin was excited, a little cocky. "A short trip down river, a gentle drive through the country and you'll be away while this lot are still running round in circles looking for us."

"Which must mean you intend to fly," Munro said. "Very interesting."

"Me and my big mouth," groaned Devlin. He tapped Munro under the chin with the gun. "If I leave you, you'll have the RAF on the job before we know where we are. I could kill you, but I'm in a very generous mood.''

''Which leaves what alternative?''

''We'll have to take you with us.'' He nodded to Steiner. ''Watch him.'' And he eased open the door.

At that moment the night porter emerged from his cubbyhole with a tray containing a pot of tea, two cups and a milk jug. He went up the stairs whistling.

Devlin said, ''Wonderful. No need for you lads to get your feet wet. We're going straight out of the front door and across the road. It's thick fog, so no one will notice a thing.'' He opened the door and urged Munro across the hall, the Walther at his back. ''Don't forget, Brigadier, a wrong word and I blow your spine out.''

It was Steiner who opened the door and led the way down to the pavement. The fog was thick and brown as only a London pea-souper could be and tasted sour at the back of the throat. Devlin pushed Munro across the road, Steiner followed. They didn't see a soul, and alone in their private world they went down the steps to the strand. At the bottom, Devlin paused and passed the gun to Steiner.

''I've got friends I don't want this old bugger to see or he'll be hanging them at Wadsworth Prison for treason.''

''Only if they deserve it,'' Munro told him.

''A matter of opinion.''

Devlin quickly tied the brigadier's hands with some of the twine he'd brought. Munro was wearing a silk scarf against the cold. The Irishman took that and bound it around his eyes.

''Right, let's go.''

He started along the strand, a hand at Munro's elbow, and the motorboat loomed out of the darkness.

''Is that you, Liam?'' Ryan called softly.

''As ever was. Now let's get the hell out of here,'' Devlin replied.

In the bedroom, Devlin changed quickly into the clerical suit and a dark polo-neck sweater. He collected what few belongings he needed, put them in a holdall together with the Luger and the Walther. He checked the Smith & Wesson in the ankle holster, picked up the bag and went out. When he went into the kitchen, Steiner was sitting at the table drinking tea with Ryan, Mary watching him in awe.

''Are you fit, Colonel?'' Devlin demanded.

''Never better, Mr. Devlin.''

Devlin tossed him the military trench coat he'd stolen from the Army and Navy Club the day he'd met Shaw. ''That should do to cover the uniform. I'm sure Mary can find you a scarf.''

''I can indeed.'' She ran out and returned with a white silk scarf which she gave to Steiner.

''That's kind of you,'' he said.

''Right, let's move it.'' Devlin opened the cupboard under the stairs to reveal Munro sitting in the corner with his hands tied and still wearing the scarf around his eyes. ''Let's be having you, Brigadier.''

He pulled Munro up and out and walked him to the front door. Ryan had already got the van from the garage, and it stood at the curb. They put Munro in the back, and Devlin checked his watch.

''Nine o'clock. A long hour, Michael, me old son. We'll be off now.''

They shook hands. When he turned to Mary, she was in tears. Devlin put his bag in the van and opened his arms. She rushed into them and he embraced her.

''The wonderful life you'll have ahead of you and the wonderful girl you are.''

''I'll never forget you.'' She was really crying now. ''I'll pray for you every night.''

He was too full to speak himself, got in beside Steiner and drove away. The German said, ''A nice girl.''

''Yes,'' Devlin said. ''I shouldn't have involved them or that old priest, but there was nothing else I could do.''

''The nature of the game we're in, Mr. Devlin,'' Munro said from the rear. ''Tell me something, just to assuage my idle curiosity. Vargas.''

''Oh, I smelt a rat there from the beginning,'' Devlin said. ''It always seemed likely you were inviting us in, so to speak. I knew the only way to fool you was to fool Vargas as well. That's why he's still getting messages from Berlin.''

''And your own contacts? Nobody recently active, am I right?''

''That's about it.''

''You're a clever bastard, I'll say that for you. Mind you, as that fine old English saying has it: *There's many a slip between the cup and the lip.*''

''And what's that supposed to mean?''

''Fog, Mr. Devlin, fog,'' Dougal Munro said.

13

Jack Carver's big game in the back room at the Astoria Ballroom had not gone his way at all, and if there was one thing guaranteed to put him in a bad mood it was losing money. He broke off the game angrily at eight-thirty, lit a cigar and went down to the ballroom. He leaned on the balcony rail watching the crowd; and Eric, dancing down there with a young girl, saw him at once.

"Sorry, sweetness, another time," he said and went up the stairs to join his brother. "You've finished early, Jack."

"Yes, well I got bored, didn't I?"

Eric, who knew the signs, didn't pursue the matter. Instead he said, "I was thinking, Jack. You're sure you don't want to take some of the boys along when we pay that call?"

Carver was furiously angry. "What are you trying to say? That I can't take care of that little squirt on my own? That I need to go in team-handed?"

"I didn't mean anything, Jack, I was just thinking—"

"You think too bloody much, my son," his brother told him. "Come on, I'll show you. We'll go and see that little Irish bastard now."

The Humber, Eric at the wheel turned into Cable Wharfe no more than ten minutes after the van had left.

"That's the house at the far end," Eric said.

"Right, we'll leave the motor here and walk. Don't want to alert them." Carver took the Browning from his pocket and pulled the slider. "Got yours?"

"Sure I have, Jack." Eric produced a Webley .38 revolver.

"Good boy. Let's go and give him some stick."

Mary was sitting at the table reading and Ryan was poking the fire when the kitchen door burst open and the Carvers entered. Mary screamed and Ryan turned, poker in hand.

"No you don't." Carver extended his arm, the Browning rigid in his hand. "You make one wrong move and I'll blow your head off. See to the bird, Eric."

"A pleasure, Jack." Eric slipped his revolver into his pocket, went and stood behind Mary and put his hands on her shoulders. "Now you be a good girl."

He kissed her neck and she squirmed in disgust. "Stop it!"

Ryan took a step forward. "Leave her alone."

Carver tapped him with the barrel of the Browning. "I give the orders here, so shut your face. Where is he?"

"Where's who?" Ryan demanded.

"The other Mick. The one who came dancing at the Astoria with the kid here. The clever little bastard who shot half my brother's ear off."

It was Mary who answered defiantly, "You're too late, they've gone."

"Is that a fact?" Carver said to Eric, "Leave her. Check upstairs and make sure you have your shooter in your hand."

Eric went out and Carver gestured at the other chair. "Sit," he ordered Ryan. The Irishman did as he was told, and Carver lit a cigarette. "She didn't say we'd missed him, she said we'd missed them."

"So what?" Ryan said.

"So who was that pal of yours and who's he mixed up with? I want to know and you're going to tell me."

"Don't say a word, Uncle Michael," Mary cried.

"Not me, girl."

Carver hit him across the side of the face with the Browning, and Ryan went over backwards in the chair. As Mary screamed again, Carver said "You should have stayed back home in the bogs where you belong, you and your mate."

Eric came back at that moment. "Here, what have I missed?"

"Just teaching him his manners. Anything?"

"Not a sausage. There was a major's uniform in one of the bedrooms."

"Is that a fact?" Carver turned back to Ryan, who was wiping blood from his face. "All right, I haven't got all night."

"Go stuff yourself."

"A hard man, eh? Watch the girl, Eric."

Eric moved behind her, pulled her up from the chair, his arms about her waist. "You like that, don't you? They all do."

She moaned, trying to get away, and Carver picked up the poker from the hearth and put it into the fire. "All right, hard man, we'll see how you like this. Either you tell me what I want to know or I put this, once it's nice and hot, to your niece's face. Not that she's much in the looks department, but this would really finish her off."

Mary tried to move, but Eric held her, laughing. Ryan said, "You bastard."

"It's been said before," Carver told him. "But it ain't true. Slur on my old lady, that."

He took the poker out. It was white hot. He put it to the tabletop and the dry wood burst into flame. Then he moved toward Mary, and the girl screamed in terror.

It was the scream which did it and Ryan cried out, "All right, I'll tell you."

"Okay," Carver said. "His name."

"Devlin—Liam Devlin."

"IRA? Am I right?"

"In a way."

"Who was with him?" Ryan hesitated and Carver turned and touched the girl's woolen cardigan so that it smoldered. "I ain't kidding, friend."

"He was doing a job for the Germans. Breaking out a prisoner they had here in London."

"And where is he now?"

"Driven off to a place near Romney. He's going to be picked up by a plane."

"In this fog? He'll be bleeding lucky. What's this place they're going to?" Ryan hesitated, and Carver touched the poker to the girl's hair. The stench of burning was terrible and she screamed again.

Ryan broke completely. He was a good man, but it was impossible to accept what was happening. "Like I said, a place near Romney."

"Don't, Uncle Michael," Mary cried.

"A village called Charbury. Shaw Place is the house."

"Marvelous." Carver put the poker down on the hearth. "That wasn't too bad, was it?" He turned to Eric. "Fancy a little drive down to the country?"

"I don't mind, Jack." Eric kissed Mary on the neck again. "As long as I can have ten minutes upstairs with this little madam before we go."

She cried out in terror and revulsion, reached back and clawed his face. Eric released her with a howl of pain, then, as he turned, slapped her. She backed away as he advanced on her slowly, reached behind her and managed to get the kitchen door open. He grabbed at her, she kicked out at him, then staggered back across the terrace against the wall. There was an ugly snapping sound as it gave way and she disappeared into darkness.

Ryan gave a cry and started forward, and Carver had him by the collar, the barrel of the Browning at his ear. "Go and check on her," he called to Eric.

Ryan stopped struggling and waited in silence. After a while Eric appeared, his face pale. "She's croaked, Jack. Fell on a jetty down there. Must have broken her neck or something."

Ryan kicked back against Carver's shin, shoving him away. He picked up the poker from the hearth, turned with it raised above his head, and Carver shot him in the heart.

There was silence. Eric wiped blood from his face. "What now, Jack?"

"We get out of here, that's what."

He led the way and Eric followed, closing the kitchen door. They turned along the wharf and got in the Humber. Carver lit a cigarette. "Where's that RAC map book?" Eric found it in the glove compartment, and Carver flipped through it. "Here we are, Romney Marsh and there's Charbury. Don't you remember? Before the war I used to take you and Mum down there to Rye for a day out by the sea."

Eric nodded. "Mum liked Rye."

"Let's get going then."

"To Charbury?" Eric said.

"Why not? We don't have anything better to do, and there's one aspect to all this that doesn't seem to have occurred to you, my old son. We catch up with Devlin and this German and take care of them, we'll be bleeding heroes." He tossed his cigarette out and replaced it with a cigar. "Move it, Eric," he said and leaned back in his seat.

At Chernay, visibility was no more than a hundred yards. Schellenberg and Asa stood in the radio room and waited while Leber checked the weather. The American wore a leather helmet, fur-lined flying jacket and boots. He smoked a cigarette nervously.

"Well?" he demanded.

"They've listened to RAF weather reports for the south of England. It's one of those situations, Captain—thick fog, but every so often the wind blows a hole in it."

"Okay," Asa said. "Let's stop monkeying around."

He went out, Schellenberg following, and walked to the plane. Schellenberg said, "Asa, what can I say?"

Asa laughed and pulled on his gloves. "General, I've been on borrowed time ever since I crash-landed in that blizzard in Finland. Take care of yourself."

He clambered into the cockpit and pulled down the cupola. Schellenberg stepped back out of the way. The Lysander started to move. It turned at the end of the field and came back into the wind. Asa boosted power and gave it everything, rushing headlong into that wall of fog, darkness and rain. He pulled back the column and started to climb, turning out to sea.

Schellenberg watched him go in awe. "Dear God," he murmured, "where do we find such men?"

He turned and walked back to the radio room.

In the study at Shaw Place Lavinia turned from the radio and removed her headphones. She hurried out and found Shaw in the kitchen cooking bacon and eggs.

"Felt a bit peckish, old girl." There was the usual tumbler of whisky close to hand, and for once she felt impatient.

"Good God, Max, the plane's on its way, and all you can think of is your wretched stomach. I'm going down to South Meadow."

She got her shooting jacket, one of her brother's old tweed hats, found the bag of cycle lamps and set off, Nell following her. There was electricity in the barn, so she switched on the lights when she got there. It was obvious that, considering the weather, breaking the blackout regulations wouldn't matter, and there wasn't another house for two miles. She put the cycle lamps by the door and stood outside checking the wind direction. The fog was as thick as ever, showed no sign of lifting at all. Suddenly it was like a curtain parting and she could see a chink of light from her house three hundred yards away.

"How marvelous, Nell." She leaned down to fondle the dog's ears, and the fog dropped back into place as the wind died.

Getting out of London itself was the worst part, as Devlin discovered, crawling along in a line of traffic at fifteen to twenty miles an hour.

"A sod this," he said to Steiner.

"It will make us late for the rendezvous, I presume," Steiner said.

"A midnight departure was the aim. We're not done yet."

Munro said from the back, "Put a bit of a spoke in your wheel this lot, Mr. Devlin."

Devlin ignored him and kept on going. Once they were through Greenwich, there was much less traffic and he was able to make better time. He lit a cigarette with one hand. "We're on our way now."

Munro said, "I wouldn't count your chickens."

Devlin said, "You're a great man for the sayings, Brigadier. What about one from the Bible? 'The laughter of fools is as the crackling of thorns under a pot.' " And he increased speed.

The Carver brothers in the Humber had exactly the same problem getting out of London, and Eric managed to take the wrong turning in Greenwich town center, going three miles in the other direction. It was Jack who sorted him, getting out the RAC handbook and checking their route.

"It's bleeding simple. Greenwich to Maidstone, Maidstone to Ashford. From there you take the road to Rye and we turn off halfway for Charbury."

"But there's hardly any road signs these days, you know that, Jack," Eric said.

"Yes, well there's a war on, isn't there, so just get on with it."

Jack Carver leaned back, closed his eyes and had a nap.

There was a school of thought in both the Luftwaffe and RAF that recommended approaching an enemy coastline below the radar screen all the way on important missions. Asa remembered trying that with his old squadron during the Russo-Finnish war, coming in low off the sea to catch the Reds by surprise, all nice copy-book stuff, only nobody had counted on the presence of the Russian navy. Five planes that one had cost.

So he charted a course for Dungeness that took him along the Channel in a dead straight line. There were strong crosswinds, and that slowed him down, but it was good monotonous flying, and all he had to do was check for drift every so often. He stayed at eight thousand for most of the way, well above the fog, keeping a weather eye cocked for other planes.

When it came, it took even an old hand like him by surprise, the Spitfire that lifted out of the fog, banked and took up station to starboard. Up there, visibility was good with a half-moon, and Asa could see the pilot of the Spitfire clearly in the cockpit in helmet and goggles. The American raised a hand and waved.

A cheerful voice crackled over his radio. "Hello, Lysander, what are you up to?"

"Sorry," Asa replied. "Special Duties Squadron, operating out of Tempsford."

"A Yank, are you?"

"In the RAF," Asa told him.

"Saw the movie, old man. Terrible. Take care." The Spitfire banked away to the east very fast and disappeared into the distance.

Asa said softly, "That's what comes of living right, old buddy."

He went down into the fog until his altimeter showed a thousand feet, then turned in toward Dungeness and Romney Marsh.

Shaw had his meal and a considerable amount of whisky after it. He was slumped in his chair beside the sitting-room fire, his shotgun on the floor, when Lavinia came in.

"Oh, Max," she said. "What am I going to do with you?"

He stirred when she put a hand on his shoulder and looked up. "Hello, old girl. Everything all right?"

She went to the French windows and opened the curtains. The fog was as thick as ever. She closed the curtains and went back to him. "I'm going to go down to the barn, Max. It must be close now, the plane, I mean."

"All right, old girl."

He folded his arms and turned his head, closing his eyes again, and she gave up. She went into the study and hurriedly took down the radio's aerial, and then she packed everything into the carrying case. When she opened the front door, Nell slipped out beside her and they went down to the South Meadow together.

She stood outside the barn listening. There was no sound, the fog embracing everything. She went in and switched on the light. There was a workbench by the door. She set the radio up there, running the aerial wires along the wall, looping them over rusting old nails. She put on the headphones and switched to the voice frequency as Devlin had shown her and heard Asa Vaughan's voice instantly.

"Falcon, are you receiving me? I say again, are you receiving me?"

It was eleven forty-five, and the Lysander was only five miles away. Lavinia stood in the entrance to the barn looking up, holding the headphones in one hand against her left ear. Of the plane, there was no sound.

"Am receiving you, Lysander. Am receiving you."

"What are conditions in your nest?" Asa's voice crackled.

"Thick fog. Visibility down to fifty yards. Wind gusting occasionally. I estimate strength four to five. It only clears things intermittently."

"Have you placed your markers?" he asked.

She'd totally forgotten. "Oh, God, no, give me a few minutes."

She put down the headphones, got the bag of cycle lamps and ran out into the meadow. She arranged three of them in an inverted L shape, the cross bar at the upwind end, and switched them on so that their beams shone straight up into the sky. Then she ran to a point two hundred yards along the meadow, Nell chasing after her, and spaced out three more lamps.

She was panting for breath when she returned to the barn and reached for the headphones and mike. "Falcon here. Markers in place."

She stood in the doorway of the barn looking up. She could hear the

Lysander clearly. It seemed to pass at a few hundred feet and moved away.

"Falcon here," she called. "I heard you. You were directly overhead."

"Can't see a thing," Asa replied. "It's bad."

At that moment Sir Maxwell Shaw appeared from the darkness. He was not wearing a raincoat or hat and was very drunk, his speech slurred and halting. "Ah, there you are, old girl, everything all right?"

"No it isn't," she told him.

Asa said, "I'll keep circling, just in case things change."

"Right, I'll stand by."

There was a crash of some sort just outside Ashford, a large produce truck and a private car, potatoes all over the road. Devlin, gripping the wheel impatiently, sat there in a queue of traffic for fifteen minutes before pulling out and turning the van.

"Already midnight," he said to Steiner. "We can't afford to hang about here. We'll find another way."

"Oh, dear," Munro said. "Having trouble are we, Mr. Devlin?"

"No, you old sod, but you will be if you don't shut up," Devlin told him and took the next road on the left.

It was at about the same time that Asa Vaughan took the Lysander down for the fourth attempt. The under carriage was of the nonretractable type, and there were landing spotlights fitted in the wheel spats. He had them on, but all they showed him was the fog.

"Falcon, it's impossible. I'm not getting anywhere."

Strangely enough it was Maxwell Shaw who came up with the solution. "Needs more light," he said. "Lots more light. I mean, he'd see the bloody house if it was on fire, wouldn't he?"

"My God!" Lavinia said and reached for the mike. "Falcon here. Now listen carefully. I'm a pilot so I know what I'm talking about."

"Let's hear it," Asa said.

"My house is three hundred yards south of the meadow and down wind. I'm going to go up there now and put on every light in the place."

"Isn't that what they call advertising?" Asa said.

"Not in this fog, and there isn't another house for two miles. I'm going now. Good luck." She put down her headphones and mike. "You stay here, Max, I shan't be long."

"All right, old girl."

She ran all the way to the house, got the front door open, gasping for breath, and started. She climbed the stairs first, going into every room, even the bathrooms, switched on the lights and yanked back the blackout curtains. Then she went down to the ground floor and did the same thing. She left quickly, and when she stopped after some fifty yards to look back, the house was ablaze with lights.

Maxwell Shaw was drinking from a hip flask when she returned. "Bloody place looks like a Christmas tree," he told her.

She ignored him and reached for the mike. "Right, I've done it. Is that any better?"

"We'll take a look," Asa said.

He took the Lysander down to five hundred feet, suddenly filled with a strange fatalism. "What the hell, Asa," he said softly. "If you survive this damn war, they'll only give you fifty years in Leavenworth, so what have you got to lose?"

He went in hard, and now the fog was suffused with a kind of glow, and a second later Shaw Place, every window alight, came into view. He had always been a fine pilot, but for a moment greatness took over as he pulled back the column and lifted over the house with feet to spare. And there on the other side were the lights of the meadow, the open barn door.

The Lysander landed perfectly, turned and taxied toward the barn. Lavinia got the doors fully open, her brother watching, and gestured Asa inside. He switched off the engine, took off his flying helmet and got out.

"I say, that was a bit hairy," she said and stuck out her hand. "I'm Lavinia Shaw and this is my brother Maxwell."

"Asa Vaughan. I really owe you one."

"Not at all. I'm a pilot myself. Used to fly a Tiger Moth from here."

"Good heavens, the fellow sounds like a damn Yank," Maxwell Shaw said.

"Well you could say I grew up there." Asa turned to Lavinia. "Where are the others?"

"No sign of Major Conlon, I'm afraid. Fog all the way from London to the coast. I expect they've got held up."

Asa nodded. "Okay, let's get a message out to Chernay right now telling them I'm down in one piece."

At Chernay in the radio room Schellenberg was in despair, for the RAF weather report Cherbourg had been monitoring indicated just how impossible the situation was. And then Leber, sitting by the radio in headphones, was convulsed into action.

"It's Falcon, General." He listened, writing furiously on his pad at the same time, tore off the sheet and passed it to Schellenberg. "He's made it, General, he managed to set that lovely bitch down."

"Yes," Schellenberg said. "He certainly did, but his passengers weren't waiting for him."

"He said delayed by the fog, General."

"Yes, well let's hope so. Tell him we'll be standing by."

Leber tapped out the message quickly and pulled the headphones down to his neck. "Why don't you go and put your feet up for an hour, General? I'm all right here."

"What I will do is go and have a shower and freshen myself up," Schellenberg told him. "When we'll have some coffee together, Flight Sergeant."

He walked to the door, and Leber said, "After all, there's no rush. He'd never be able to get the Lysander in here until this weather improves."

"Yes, well let's not think about that for now," Schellenberg said and went out.

At Shaw Place, Asa helped Lavinia put out all the lights, going from room to room. Shaw was slumped in his chair by the fire, eyes glazed, very far gone indeed.

"Is he often like that?" Asa asked.

She left the French windows open but drew the curtains. "My brother isn't a happy man. Sorry, I didn't ask you your rank."

"Captain," he said.

"Well, Captain, let's say the drink helps. Come into the kitchen. I'll make some tea or coffee if you'd like it."

"Coffee would be great."

He sat on the edge of the table smoking a cigarette while she made the coffee, very handsome in the SS uniform, and she was acutely aware of him. He took off his flying jacket, and she saw the cuff title on his sleeve.

"Good heavens, the George Washington Legion. I didn't know there was such a thing. My brother was right. You are an American."

"I hope you won't hold it against me," he said.

"We won't, you beautiful Yankee bastard." As Asa turned, Liam Devlin came through the door and threw his arms around him. "How in the hell did you manage to land in that stuff, son? It took us all our time to make it from London by road."

"Genius, I suppose," Asa said modestly.

Munro appeared behind Devlin, still with his wrists bound and the scarf around his eyes. Steiner was at his shoulder. "Colonel Kurt Steiner, the object of the exercise, plus a little excess baggage we acquired along the way," Devlin said.

"Colonel, a pleasure." Asa shook Steiner's hand.

Lavinia said, "Why don't we all go into the living room and have a cup of coffee? It's just made."

"What a charming idea," Munro said.

"What you like and what you get are two different things, Brigadier," Devlin told him. "Still, if it's made, there's no harm. Five minutes and we're away."

"I wouldn't count on that. I'll have to check the situation at Chernay," Asa said to him as they moved through. "The weather was just as bad there when I left."

Devlin said, "That's all we need." In the living room he pushed Munro down into the other chair by the fire and looked at Maxwell Shaw in disgust. "Christ, if you struck a match he'd catch fire."

"He's really tied one on," Asa said.

Shaw woke up and opened his eyes. "What's that, eh?" He focused on Devlin. "Conlon, that you?"

"As ever was," Devlin answered.

Shaw sat up and looked across at Munro. "Who in the hell is that? What's he got that stupid thing round his eyes for?" He reached across and pulled off the scarf before anyone could stop him. Munro shook his head, blinking in the light. Shaw said, "I know you, don't I?"

"You should, Sir Maxwell," Dougal Munro told him. "We've been fellow members of the Army and Navy Club for years."

"Of course." Shaw nodded foolishly. "Thought I knew you."

"That's torn it, Brigadier," Devlin told him. "I'd intended to dump you somewhere in the marsh before we left to find your own way home, but now you know who these people are."

"Which means you have two choices. Shoot me or take me with you."

It was Steiner who said, "Is there room, Captain?"

"Oh, sure. we could manage," Asa said.

Steiner turned to the Irishman. "It's up to you, Mr. Devlin."

Munro said, "Never mind, my friend. I'm sure your Nazi masters will pay well for me."

Asa said, "I haven't had the chance to fill you in on what the score is over there yet. You'd better know now, because you'll be up to your necks in it if we get back over there in one piece."

"You'd better tell us then," Steiner said.

So Asa did.

The fog was as bad as ever as they all stood around the radio in the barn, Lavinia scribbling on the pad in front of her. She handed the message to Asa, who read it and passed it to Devlin. "They suggest we delay take-off for another hour. There's a slight chance conditions at Chernay might have improved by then."

Devlin glanced at Steiner. "We don't seem to have much choice."

"Well, I can't say I'm sorry for you." Munro turned to Lavinia with a smile of devastating charm. "I was wondering, my dear. Do you think when we get back to the house I might have tea this time."

Shaw was sprawled in his chair by the fire fast asleep. Munro sat opposite, wrists still bound. Asa was in the kitchen helping Lavinia.

Devlin said to Steiner, "I was thinking, Colonel, you might need a sidearm." He picked up his holdall, put it on the table and opened it. The silenced Walther was lying inside on top of a couple of shirts.

"A thought," Steiner said.

There was a gust of wind, a creaking at the French windows, and then the curtains were pulled back and Jack and Eric Carver stepped into the room, guns in their hands.

14

DEVLIN SAID, "LOOK WHAT THE wind's blown in."

Steiner said calmly, "Who are these men?"

"Well, the big ugly one is Jack Carver. He runs most of London's East End. Makes an honest bob out of protection, gambling, prostitution."

"Very funny," Carver said.

"The other one, the one who looks as if he's just crawled out of his hole, is his brother, Eric."

"I'll teach you." Eric advanced on him, his face pinched and angry. "We'll give you what we gave that pal of yours and his niece."

Devlin went cold inside, his face on the instant turned deathly pale. "What are you telling me?"

"No funny stuff this time," Carver said. "Check to see if he has that bleeding gun up his trouser leg."

Eric dropped to one knee and relieved Devlin of the Smith & Wesson. "It won't work twice, you cunning sod."

"My friends?" Devlin said calmly. "What happened to them?"

Carver was enjoying himself. He took a cigar from his pocket, bit off the end and stuck it in his mouth. "I put the word out on you, my son. Didn't get anywhere, and then we had a stroke of luck. Eric saw the bird in Wapping High Street last evening. Followed her home."

"And?"

"We paid them a visit not long after you left. A little persuasion was all it took and here we are."

"And he talked, my friend, as easily as that?" Devlin asked. "I find that hard to believe." He turned to Steiner. "Don't you, Colonel?"

"I do indeed," Steiner said.

"Oh, I wouldn't think too badly of him." Carver flicked his lighter and put the flame to his cigar. "I mean, it was his niece he was concerned about. He had to do the decent thing there."

"Not that it did either of them much good." Eric smiled sadistically. "Want to know what happened to her? She made a run for it, went over the rail down to that jetty by the house. Broke her neck."

"And Michael?" Devlin asked Carver, barely managing to keep from choking.

"I shot him, didn't I? Isn't that what you do with dogs?"

Devlin took a step toward him, and the look on his face was terrible to see. "You're dead, the both of you."

Carver stopped smiling. "Not us, you little sod—you. What's more, I'm going to give you it in the belly so it takes time."

It was at that moment that Shaw came back to life. He opened his eyes, stretched and looked around him. "Now then, what's all this?"

At the same moment, the double doors were flung open and Lavinia appeared holding a tray, Asa beside her. "Tea everyone," she said, then froze.

"Just hold it right there, the both of you," Carver told them.

She looked absolutely terrified but didn't say a word.

It was Dougal Munro who tried to help her. "Steady, my dear. Just keep calm."

Shaw, on his feet, swayed drunkenly, eyes bloodshot, speech slurred. "You bloody swine. Who do you think you are coming into my house waving guns about?"

"Another step, you old fool, and I'll blow you away," Carver told him.

Lavinia shouted, "Do as he says, Max." She dropped the tray with a crash and took a step forward.

Carver turned and shot her, more as a reflex action than anything else. Maxwell Shaw, with a cry of rage, jumped at him, and Carver fired again, shooting him twice at close quarters.

Asa was on his knees beside Lavinia. He looked up. "She's dead."

"I warned you, didn't I?" Carver said, his face contorted.

"You certainly did, Mr. Carver," Kurt Steiner told him.

His hand went into Devlin's open holdall on the table, found the butt of the silenced Walther, brought it out in one smooth motion and fired once. The bullet caught Carver in the center of the forehead and he went back over the chair.

"Jack!" Eric screamed. And as he took a step forward, Devlin grabbed for his wrist, twisting it until Eric dropped the revolver.

Eric backed away and Devlin said. "You killed that girl, is that what you're telling me?"

He leaned down and picked up Maxwell Shaw's shotgun from the floor beside the chair.

Eric was terrified. "It was an accident. She was running away. Went over the rail." The curtains billowed in the wind from the open French windows, and he backed out onto the terrace.

"But what made her run? That's the thing," Devlin said, thumbing back the hammers.

"No!" Eric cried, and Devlin gave him both barrels, lifting him over the balustrade.

At Chernay it was almost two o'clock. Schellenberg was dozing in the chair in the corner of the radio room when Leber called to him.

"Falcon coming in, General."

Schellenberg hurried to his side. "What is it?"

"Another check on the weather. I've told him how bad things are here."

"And?"

"Just a moment, General, he's coming in again." He listened intently and looked up. "He says he's not prepared to wait any longer. He's leaving now."

Schellenberg nodded. "Just say good luck."

He went to the door, opened it and went out. The fog rolled in from the sea remorselessly, and he turned up the collar of his greatcoat to walk aimlessly along the side of the airstrip.

At roughly the same time, Horst Berger was sitting by the window in the room they had allocated to him at Belle-Île. He had found himself unable to sleep, the prospect of the morning was too momentous, so he sat there in the darkness, the window open, listening to the rain falling through the fog. There was a knock at the door, it opened, light falling into the room.

One of the SS duty sentries stood there. "Sturmbannführer," he called softly.

"I'm here. What is it?"

"The Reichsführer wants you. He's waiting now at his apartment."

"Five minutes," Berger told him, and the man went out.

In the sitting room of his apartment, Himmler was standing by the fire in full uniform when Berger knocked and entered. The Reichsführer turned. "Ah, there you are."

"Reichsführer."

"The Führer obviously can't sleep. He's sent for me. Asked particularly that I bring you."

"Does the Reichsführer think this is of any significance?"

"Not at all," Himmler said. "The Führer's health has been something of a problem for quite some time. His inability to sleep is only one of many symptoms. He has come to rely on the ministrations of his personal physician, Professor Morell, to an inordinate degree. Unfortunately, from the Führer's point of view at the moment, Morell is in Berlin and the Führer is here."

"Morell is of such vital importance then?" Berger asked.

"There are those who would consider him a quack," Himmler said. "On the other hand, the Führer can't be considered an easy patient."

"I see, Reichsführer. But why am I commanded?"

"Who knows? Some whim or other." Himmler consulted his watch. "We are due at his suite in fifteen minutes. With the Führer, Berger, time is everything. Not one minute more, not one minute less. There's fresh coffee on the table there. Time for you to have a cup before we go."

In the barn at Shaw Place, everyone waited while Devlin tapped out his message on the radio. He put down the headphones, switched off and turned to Steiner and Asa, who stood there, Dougal Munro, his hands still bound, between them.

"That's it," Devlin said. "I've told Schellenberg we're leaving."

"Then let's get the plane out," Asa said.

Munro stood against the wall while the three of them manhandled the Lysander out into the fog. They rolled it some distance away from the barn. Asa got the cupola up and reached for his helmet.

"What about our friend in the barn?" Steiner asked.

"He stays," Devlin said.

Steiner turned to him. "You're sure?"

"Colonel," Devlin said, "you're a nice man, and due to the vagaries of war, I happen to be on your side at the moment, but this is a personal thing. I haven't the slightest intention of handing over the head of Section D at SOE to German intelligence. Now you two get in and start up. I'll be with you in a minute."

When he went in the barn, Munro was half sitting on the table by the radio, struggling with the twine around his wrists. He paused as Devlin entered. The Irishman took a small pocketknife from his pocket and opened the blade.

"Here, let me, Brigadier."

He sliced through the twine, freeing him, and Munro rubbed at his wrists. "What's this?"

"Sure and you didn't really think I was going to hand you over to those Nazi bastards, now did you? There was a small problem for a while, Shaw exposing you to things, as it were, but there's no one left. My good friend Michael Ryan and Mary, his niece, at Cable Wharfe, the Shaws here. All gone. No one you could hurt."

"God help me, Devlin, I'll never understand you."

"And why should you, Brigadier, when I don't understand myself most of the time?" The engine of the Lysander started up, and Devlin stuck a cigarette in his mouth. "We'll be going now. You could alert the RAF, but they'd need the luck of the devil to find us in this fog."

"True," Munro agreed.

Devlin flicked his lighter. "On the other hand, it's just possible you might think Walter Schellenberg has the right idea."

"Strange," Munro said. "There have been moments in this war when I'd have jumped for joy at the idea of someone killing Hitler."

"A great man once said that as the times change, sensible men change with them." Devlin moved to the door. "Goodbye, Brigadier, I don't expect we'll be seeing each other again."

"I wish I could count on that," Munro said.

The Irishman hurried across to the Lysander, where Steiner was stripping the canvas with the RAF roundels from the wings, revealing the Luftwaffe insignia. Devlin ran to the tailplane, did the same there, then scrambled inside after Steiner. The Lysander taxied to the end of the meadow and turned into the wind. A moment later, it roared down the runway and took off. Munro stood there listening to the sound of it disappear into the night. There was a sudden whimper, and Nell slipped out of the darkness and sat there looking up at him. When he turned and started back to the house, she followed him.

Jack Carter, in the outer office at SOE headquarters, heard the red phone's distinctive sound and rushed in at once to answer it.

"Jack?" Munro said.

"Thank God, sir, I've been worried as hell. I got in from York and walked straight into a minefield. All hell broken loose at St. Mary's Priory, and the porter said you were there, sir. I mean, what the hell happened?"

"It's quite simple, Jack. A rather clever gentleman called Liam Devlin made fools of the lot of us and is at this very moment flying back to France with Colonel Kurt Steiner."

"Shall I alert the RAF?" Carter asked.

"I'll take care of it. More important things to do. Number one, there's a house on Cable Wharfe in Wapping owned by a man called Ryan. You'll find him and his niece there dead. I want a disposal team as soon as possible. Use that crematorium in North London."

"Right, sir."

"I also want a disposal team here, Jack. That's Shaw Place outside the village of Charbury in Romney Marsh. Come yourself. I'll wait for you."

He put the phone down. No question of phoning the RAF of course. Schellenberg was right and that was that. He left the study and went to the front door. When he opened it, the fog was as thick as ever. Nell whined and sat on her haunches, staring up at him.

Munro bent down and fondled her ears. "Poor old girl," he said. "And poor old Devlin. I wish him luck."

When Himmler and Berger were admitted to the Führer's apartment, Adolf Hitler was sitting beside an enormous stone fireplace in which a log fire burned brightly. He had a file open on his knees which he continued to read as they stood there waiting. After a while he looked up, a slightly vacant look in his eyes.

"Reichsführer?"

"You wished to see me and Sturmbannführer Berger."

"Ah, yes." Hitler closed the file and put it on a small table. "The young man who has so brilliantly organized my security here. I'm impressed, Reichsführer." He stood and put a hand on Berger's shoulder. "You've done well."

Berger held himself stiff as a ramrod. "My honor to serve, my Führer."

Hitler touched Berger's Iron Cross First Class with one finger. "A brave soldier too, I see." He turned to Himmler. "Obersturmbannführer would be more appropriate here, I think."

"I'll take care of it, my Führer," Himmler told him.

"Good." Hitler turned back to Berger and smiled indulgently. "Now off you go. The Reichsführer and I have things to discuss."

Berger clicked his heels and raised his right arm. "Heil Hitler," he said, turned on his heel and went out.

Hitler returned to his chair and indicated the one opposite. "Join me, Reichsführer."

"A privilege."

Himmler sat down and Hitler said, "Insomnia can be a blessing in disguise. It gives one extra time to ponder the really important things. This file, for example." He picked it up. "A joint report from Rommel and Canaris in which they try to persuade me that the Allies will attempt an invasion by way of Normandy. Nonsense, of course. Even Eisenhower couldn't be so foolish."

"I agree, my Führer."

"No, it's obvious that the Pas de Calais will be the target, any idiot can see that."

Himmler said carefully, "And yet you still intend to confirm Rommel as Commander of Army Group B with full responsibility for the Atlantic Wall defenses?"

"Why not?" Hitler said. "A brilliant soldier, we all know that. He'll have to accept my decision in this matter with good grace and follow orders, as will Canaris."

"But will they, my Führer?"

"Do you doubt their loyalty?" Hitler asked. "Is that what you are implying?"

"What can I say, my Führer. The admiral has not always been as enthusiastic toward the cause of National Socialism as I would like. As for Rommel"—Himmler shrugged— "the people's hero. Such popularity easily leads to arrogance."

"Rommel will do as he is told," Hitler said serenely. "I am well aware, as are you, of the existence of those extremists in the army who would destroy me if they could. I am also aware that it is a distinct possibility that Rommel is in sympathy with such aims. At the right moment there will be a noose waiting for all such traitors."

"And richly deserved, my Führer."

Hitler got up and stood with his back to the fire. "One must learn how to handle these people, Reichsführer. That's why I insisted they join me for breakfast at seven. As you know, they're staying in Rennes overnight. This means they must rise at a rather early hour to get here in time. I like to keep people like this slightly unbalanced. I find it pays."

"Brilliant, my Führer."

"And before you go, remember one thing." Hitler's face was very calm, and Himmler stood up. "Since I took power, how many attempts on my life? How many plots?"

Himmler for once was caught. "I'm not sure."

"At least sixteen," Hitler said. "And this argues divine intervention. The only logical explanation."

Himmler swallowed hard. "Of course, my Führer."

Hitler smiled benignly. "Now be off with you. Try and get a little sleep and I'll see you at breakfast." He turned to look down at the fire, and Himmler left quickly.

The English Channel was fogged in for most of the way to Cap de la Hague, and Asa took advantage of it, using the cover, making good time, finally turning in toward the French coast just after three.

He called Chernay over the radio. "Chernay, Falcon here. What's the situation?"

In the radio room, Schellenberg sprang from his chair and crossed to Leber. The flight sergeant said, "We've had some clearance with wind but not enough. Ceiling zero one minute, then it clears to maybe a hundred feet, then back again."

"Is there anywhere else to go?" Asa demanded.

"Not round here. Cherbourg's totally closed in."

Schellenberg took the mike. "Asa, it's me. Are you all there?"

"We sure as hell are. Your Colonel Steiner, Devlin and me, only we don't seem to have any place to go."

"What's your fuel position?"

"I figure I'm good for about forty-five minutes. What I'll do is stooge around for a while. Keep on the line and let me know the second there's any kind of improvement."

Leber said, "I'll have the men light runway flares, General, it might help."

"I'll take care of that," Schellenberg told him. "You stay on the radio." And he hurried out.

After twenty minutes, Asa said, "This is no good. Sit tight and I'll give it a shot."

He took the Lysander down, his wheel spots on, and the fog enveloped him, just as it had done at Shaw Place. At six hundred feet he pulled the column back into his stomach and went up, coming out of the mist and fog at around a thousand.

The stars still glistened palely, and what was left of the moon was low, dawn streaking the horizon. Asa called, "It's hopeless. Suicide to try and land. I'd rather put her down in the sea."

"The tide's out, Captain," Leber answered.

"Is that a fact? How much beach do you get down there?"

"It runs for miles."

"Then that's it. It's some sort of a chance anyway."

Schellenberg's voice sounded. "Are you sure, Asa?"

"The only thing I'm sure of, General, is that we don't have any choice. We'll see you or we won't. Over and out."

Schellenberg dropped the mike and turned to Leber. "Can we get down there?"

"Oh, yes, General, there's a road leading to an old slipway."

"Good. Then let's get moving."

"If I have to land in the sea, this thing's not going to float for very long," Asa said over his shoulder to Steiner and Devlin. "There's a dinghy pack there behind you. The yellow thing. Get it out fast, pull the red tag and it inflates itself."

Steiner smiled. "You swim, of course, Mr. Devlin."

Devlin smiled back. "Some of the time."

Asa started down, easing the column forward, sweat on his face, all the way to five hundred and his altimeter kept on going. The Lysander bucked in a heavy gust of wind, and they passed three hundred.

Devlin cried, "I saw something."

The fog seemed to open before them, as if a curtain was being pulled to each side and there were great waves surging in from the Atlantic, half a mile of wet sand stretching toward the cliffs of Cap de la Hague. Asa heaved the column back, the Lysander leveled out no more than fifty feet above the whitecaps that pounded into surf on the shore.

Asa slammed the instrument panel with one hand. "You beautiful, beautiful bitch. I love you," he cried and turned into the wind to land.

The truck containing Schellenberg, Leber and several Luftwaffe mechanics had reached the slipway at the very moment the Lysander burst into view.

"He made it, General," Leber cried. "What a pilot!" He ran forward waving, followed by his men.

Schellenberg felt totally drained. He lit a cigarette and waited as the Lysander taxied toward the end of the slipway. It came to a halt, and Leber and his men cheered as Asa switched off the engine. Devlin and

Steiner got out first and Asa followed, taking off his flying helmet and tossing it into the cockpit:

Leber said, "Quite a job, Captain."

Asa said, "Treat her with care, Flight Sergeant. Only the best. She's earned it. Will she be safe here?"

"Oh, yes, the tide is on the turn, but it doesn't come up this far."

"Fine. Do an engine check, and you'll have to refuel by hand."

"As you say, Captain."

Schellenberg stood waiting as Steiner and Devlin came toward him. He held out his hand to Steiner. "Colonel, a pleasure to see you here."

"General," Steiner said.

Schellenberg turned to Devlin. "As for you, my mad Irish friend, I still can't believe you're here."

"Well, you know what I always say, Walter, me old son, all you have to do is live right." Devlin grinned. "Would you think there might be a bit of breakfast somewhere? I'm starved."

They sat around the table in the little canteen drinking coffee. Schellenberg said, "So, the Führer arrived safely last night."

"And Rommel and the admiral?" Devlin asked.

"I've no idea where they've been staying, but they will be joining him very soon now. Must be on their way."

Steiner said, "This plan of yours makes a wild kind of sense, but there is a considerable uncertainty."

"You don't think the men of this parachute detachment will follow you?"

"Oh, no, I mean what happens to the three of you in the château before we arrive."

"Yes, well, we've no choice," Schellenberg said. "There's no other way."

"Yes, I see that."

There was a moment's silence, and Schellenberg said, "Are you with me in this, Colonel, or not? There isn't much time."

Steiner got up and moved to the window. It had started to rain heavily, and he stared out for a moment and turned. "I have little reason to like the Führer and not just because of what happened to my father. I could say he's bad for everybody, a disaster for the human race, but for me, the most important thing is that he's bad for Germany. Having said that, Himmler as head of state would be infinitely worse. At least with the Führer in charge, one has the prospect of an end to this bloody war."

"So you will join with me in this?"

"I don't think any of us have a choice."

Asa shrugged. "What the hell, you can count me in."

Devlin stood up and stretched. "Right, well, let's get on with it." And he opened the door and went out.

ᦆᦊ᦮

When Schellenberg went into the hut he and Asa had been using, Devlin had a foot on the bed, his trouser leg rolled up as he adjusted the Smith & Wesson in the ankle holster.

"Your ace in the hole, my friend?"

"And this." Devlin took the silenced Walther from his holdall and put it into his waistband at the rear. Then he took out the Luger. "This is the one for the pocket. I doubt those SS guards will let us through the door armed, so best to have something to give them."

"Do you think it will work?" Schellenberg asked.

"Uncertainty—and from you at this stage, General?"

"Not really. You see the Allies have made one thing very clear. No negotiated peace. Total surrender. The last thing Himmler could afford."

"Yes, there's a rope waiting for him all right one of these days."

"And me also, perhaps. I am, after all, a general of the SS," Schellenberg said.

"Don't worry, Walter." Devlin smiled. "If you end up in a prison cell, I'll break you out and for free. Now let's get moving."

ᦆᦊ᦮

Field Marshal Erwin Rommel and Admiral Canaris had left Rennes at five o'clock in a Mercedes limousine driven, for reasons of security, by Rommel's aide, a Major Carl Ritter. Two military police motorcyclists were their only escort and led the way as they twisted and turned through the narrow French lanes in the early morning gloom.

"Of course, the only reason we've had to turn out at such a ridiculous time is because he wants us at a disadvantage," Canaris said.

"The Führer likes all of us at a disadvantage, Admiral," Rommel said. "I'd have thought you'd have learned that long ago."

"I wonder what he's up to," Canaris said. "We know he's going to confirm your appointment as Commander of Army Group B, but he could have made you fly to Berlin for that."

"Exactly," Rommel said. "And there are such things as telephones. No, I think it's the Normandy business."

"But surely we can make him see sense there," Canaris said. "The report we've put together is really quite conclusive."

"Yes, but unfortunately the Führer favors the Pas de Calais, and so does his astrologer."

"And Uncle Heini?" Canaris suggested.

"Himmler always agrees with the Führer, you know that as well as I do."

Beyond, through a break in the rain, they saw Belle-Île. "Impressive," Rommel said.

"Yes, very Wagnerian," Canaris said dryly. "The castle at the end of the world. The Führer must like that. He and Himmler must be enjoying themselves."

"Have you ever wondered how it came to happen, Admiral? How we came to allow such monsters to control the destinies of millions of people?" Erwin Rommel asked.

"Every day of my life," Canaris replied.

The Mercedes turned off the road and started up to the château, the motorcyclists leading the way.

15

IT WAS JUST AFTER SIX, and Hauptmann Erich Kramer, commanding the 12th Parachute Detachment at St. Aubin, was having coffee in his office when he heard a vehicle drive into the farmyard. He went to the window and saw a *Kübelwagen*, its canvas hood up against the rain. Asa got out first, followed by Schellenberg and Devlin.

Kramer recognized them instantly from the last visit and frowned. "Now what in the hell do they want?" he said softly.

And then Kurt Steiner emerged. Having no cap, he had borrowed a Luftwaffe sidecap from Flight Sergeant Leber, what was commonly referred to as a *Schiff*. It was, as it happened, an affectation of many old-timers in the Parachute Regiment. He stood there in the rain in his blue-gray flying blouse with the yellow collar patches, jump trousers and boots. Kramer took in the Knight's Cross with Oak Leaves, the silver and gold eagle of the paratrooper's badge, the Kreta and Afrika Korps cuff titles. He recognized him, of course, a legend to everyone in the Parachute Regiment.

"Oh, my God," he murmured as he reached for his cap and opened the door, buttoning his blouse. "Colonel Steiner—sir." He got his heels together and saluted, ignoring the others. "I can't tell you what an honor this is."

"A pleasure. Captain Kramer, isn't it?" Steiner took in Kramer's cuff titles, the ribbon for the Winter War. "So, we are old comrades, it would seem."

"Yes, Colonel."

Several paratroopers had emerged from their canteen, curious about the arrivals. At the sight of Steiner they all jumped to attention. "At ease, lads," he called and said to Kramer, "What strength have you here?"

"Thirty-five only, Colonel."

"Good," Steiner told him. "I'm going to need everyone, including you, of course, so let's get in out of this rain and I'll explain."

The thirty-five men of the 12th Parachute Detachment stood in four ranks in the rain in the farmyard. They wore the steel helmets peculiar to the Parachute Regiment, baggy jump smocks, and most of them had Schmeisser machine pistols slung across their chests. They stood there, rigid at attention, as Steiner addressed them, Schellenberg, Devlin and Asa Vaughan behind him, Kramer at one side.

Steiner hadn't bothered with niceties, only the facts. "So there it is. The Führer is to meet his death very shortly at the hands of traitorous elements of the SS. Our job is to stop them. Any questions?"

There wasn't a word, only the heavy rain drumming down, and Steiner turned to Kramer. "Get them ready, Captain."

"*Zu befehl, Herr Oberst.*" Kramer saluted.

Steiner turned to the others. "Will fifteen minutes be enough for you?"

"Then you arrive like a Panzer column," Schellenberg told him. "Very fast indeed."

He and Asa got in the *Kübelwagen*. Devlin, the black hat slanted over one ear, his trench coat already soaked, said to Steiner, "In a way, we've been here before."

"I know, and the same old question. Are we playing the game or is the game playing us?"

"Let's hope we have better luck than we did last time, Colonel." Devlin smiled and got in the back of the *Kübelwagen*, and Asa drove away.

At the Château de Belle-Île, Rommel, Canaris and Major Ritter went up the steps to the main entrance. One of the two SS guards opened the door and they went inside. There seemed to be guards everywhere.

Rommel said to Canaris as he unbuttoned his coat, "It looks rather like some weekend SS convention, the kind they used to have in Bavaria in the old days."

Berger came down the stairs and advanced to meet them. "Herr Admiral, Herr Field Marshal, a great pleasure. Sturmbannführer Berger in charge of security."

"Major." Rommel nodded.

"The Führer is waiting in the dining hall. He has requested that no one bears arms in his presence."

Rommel and Ritter took their pistols from their holsters. "I trust we're not late," the field marshal said.

"Actually, you are early by two minutes." Berger gave him the good-humored smile of one soldier to another. "May I show you the way?"

He opened the great oak door and they followed him in. The long dining table was laid for four people only. The Führer was standing by the stone fireplace looking down into the burning logs. He turned and faced them. "Ah, there you are."

Rommel said, "I trust you are well, my Führer."

Hitler nodded to Canaris. "Herr Admiral." His eyes flickered to Ritter, who stood rigidly at attention clutching a briefcase. "And who have we here?"

"My personal aide, Major Carl Ritter, my Führer. He has further details on the Normandy situation that we have already discussed," Rommel said.

"More reports?" Hitler shrugged. "If you must, I suppose." He turned to Berger. "Have another place laid at the table and see what's keeping the Reichsführer."

As Berger moved to the door, it opened and Himmler entered. He wore the black dress uniform and his face was pale, a faint edge of excitement to him that he found difficult to conceal. "I apologize, my Führer, a phone call from Berlin as I was about to leave my room." He nodded. "Herr Admiral, Field Marshal."

"And the field marshal's aide, Major Ritter." Hitler rubbed his hands together. "I really feel extraordinarily hungry. You know, gentlemen, perhaps one should do this more often. The early breakfast, I mean. It leaves so much of the day for matters of importance. But come. Sit."

He himself took the head of the table. Rommel and Canaris on his right, Himmler and Ritter on the left. "So," he said. "Let's begin. Food before business."

He picked up the small silver bell at his right hand and rang it.

~

It was no more than ten minutes later that the *Kübelwagen* arrived at the main gate. Schellenberg leaned out. The sergeant who came forward took in his uniform and saluted.

"The Führer is expecting us," Schellenberg told him.

The sergeant looked uncertain. "I've orders to admit no one, General."

"Don't be stupid, man," Schellenberg said. "That hardly applies to me." He nodded to Asa. "Drive on, Hauptsturmführer."

They drove into the inner courtyard and stopped. Devlin said, "You know what the Spaniards call the instant when the bullfighter goes in for the kill and doesn't know whether he'll live or die? The moment of truth."

"Not now, Mr. Devlin," Schellenberg said. "Let's just keep going." And he marched up the wide steps and reached for the handle of the front door.

Hitler was enjoying himself, working his way through a plate of toast and fruit. "One thing about the French, they really do make rather excellent bread," he said and reached for another slice.

The door opened and an SS sergeant major entered. It was Himmler who spoke to him. "I thought I made it clear we were not to be disturbed for any reason."

"Yes, Reichsführer, but General Schellenberg is here with a Hauptsturmführer and some civilian. Says it is imperative he sees the Führer."

Himmler said, "Nonsense, you have your orders!"

Hitler cut in at once. "Schellenberg? Now I wonder what that can be about. Bring them in, Sergeant Major."

~

Schellenberg, Devlin and Asa waited in the hall by the door. The sergeant major returned. "The Führer will see you, General, but all weapons must be left here. I have my orders. It applies to everyone."

"Of course." Schellenberg took his pistol from its holster, slapping it down on the table.

Asa did the same, and Devlin took the Luger from his coat pocket. "All contributions graciously given."

The sergeant major said, "If you would follow me, gentlemen." He turned and led the way across the hall.

When they went in, Hitler was still eating. Rommel and Canaris looked up curiously. Himmler was deathly pale.

Hitler said, "Now then, Schellenberg, what brings you here?"

"I regret the intrusion, my Führer, but a matter of the gravest urgency has come to my attention."

"And how urgent would that be?" Hitler demanded.

"A question of your very life, my Führer, or should I say an attempt on your life."

"Impossible," Himmler said.

Hitler waved him to silence and glanced at Devlin and Asa Vaughan. "And who have we here?"

"If I may explain. The Reichsführer recently gave me the task of planning the safe return to the Reich of a certain Colonel Kurt Steiner, who was held prisoner in the Tower of London for a while. Herr Devlin here and Hauptsturmführer Vaughan succeeded triumphantly in this matter, delivered Steiner to me at the small Luftwaffe base nearby a short time ago."

Hitler said to Himmler, "I knew nothing of this."

Himmler looked quite wretched. "It was to be a surprise, my Führer."

Hitler turned again to Schellenberg. "This Colonel Steiner, where is he?"

"He'll be here soon. The thing is, I received an anonymous telephone call only a couple of hours ago. I regret to have to say this in the presence of the Reichsführer, but whoever it was spoke of treachery, even within the ranks of the SS."

Himmler was almost choking. "Impossible."

"An officer named Berger was referred to."

Hitler said, "But Sturmbannführer Berger is in charge of my security here. I've just had him promoted."

"Nevertheless, my Führer, that is what I was told."

"Which just goes to show you can't trust anyone," Horst Berger called, and moved out of the shadows at the end of the dining hall, an SS man on either side of him holding a machine pistol.

Steiner and Captain Kramer led the way up the hill to the château in a *Kübelwagen*, the top down in spite of the rain. The paratroopers followed packed into two troop carriers. Steiner had a stick grenade tucked into the top of one of his jump boots and a Schmeisser ready in his lap.

"When we go, we go hard, no stopping, remember that," he said.

"We're with you all the way, Colonel," Kramer told him.

He slowed at the outer gate, and the SS sergeant came forward. "What's all this?"

Steiner raised the Schmeisser, lifted him back with a quick burst, was on his feet and swinging to cut down the other guard as Kramer took the *Kübelwagen* forward with a surge of power.

As they reached the bottom of the steps leading to the front door, more SS appeared from the guardhouse on the right. Steiner pulled the stick grenade from his boot and tossed it into the center of them, then he leapt from the *Kübelwagen* and started up the steps. Behind him the paratroopers jumped from the troop carriers and stormed after him, firing across the courtyard at the SS.

"You dare to approach me like this, a gun in your hand?" Hitler said to Berger, his eyes blazing.

"I regret to have to say it, my Führer, but your moment has come—you, Field Marshal Rommel here, the admiral." Berger shook his head. "We can no longer afford any of you."

Hitler said, "You can't kill me, you young fool, it's an impossibility."

"Really?" Berger said. "And why would that be?"

"Because it is not my destiny to die here," Hitler told him calmly. "Because God is on my side."

Somewhere in the distance was the sound of shooting. Berger half turned to glance at the door, and Major Ritter leapt to his feet, threw his briefcase at him and ran for the door. "Guards!" he shouted.

One of the SS men fired his Schmeisser, shooting him in the back several times.

Schellenberg said, "Mr. Devlin."

Devlin's hand found the butt of the silenced Walther in his waistband against the small of his back. His first bullet caught the man who had just machine gunned Ritter in the temple, the second took the other SS man in the heart. Berger swung to face him, his mouth open in a terrible cry of rage, and Devlin's third bullet hit him between the eyes.

Devlin walked across and looked down at him, the Walther slack in his hand. "You wouldn't be told, son, would you? I said you needed a different class of work."

Behind him the doors burst open and Kurt Steiner rushed in at the head of his men.

When Schellenberg knocked and entered Himmler's room, he found the Reichsführer standing at the window. It was instantly evident that he intended to brazen it out.

"Ah, there you are, General. A most unfortunate business. It reflects so terribly on all of us of the SS. Thank goodness the Führer sees Berger's abominable treachery as an individual lapse."

"Fortunate for all of us, Reichsführer."

Himmler sat down. "The anonymous phone call you mentioned. You've absolutely no idea who it was?"

"I'm afraid not."

"A pity. Still . . . " Himmler looked at his watch. "The Führer intends to leave at noon, and I shall fly back to Berlin with him. Canaris goes with us. Rommel has already left."

"I see," Schellenberg said.

"Before he leaves, the Führer wants to see you and the other three. I believe he thinks decorations are in order."

"Decorations?" Schellenberg said.

"The Führer is never without them, General, carries a supply in his personal case wherever he goes. He believes in rewarding loyal service, and so do I."

"Reichsführer."

Schellenberg turned to the door, and Himmler said, "Better for all of us if this shocking affair never happened. You follow me, General? Rommel and Canaris will keep their mouths shut, and easy enough to handle those paratroopers. A posting back to the Russian Front will take care of them."

"I see, Reichsführer," Schellenberg said carefully.

"Which, of course, leaves us with Steiner, Hauptsturmführer Vaughan and the man Devlin. I feel they could all prove a serious embarrassment, as I'm sure you will agree."

"Is the Reichsführer suggesting . . . " Schellenberg began.

"Nothing," Himmler told him. "I'm suggesting nothing. I simply leave it to your own good sense."

It was just before noon in the library, as Schellenberg, Steiner, Asa and Devlin waited, that the door opened and the Führer entered followed by Canaris and Himmler, who carried a small leather briefcase.

"Gentlemen," Hitler said.

The three officers jumped to attention, and Devlin, sitting on the window seat, got up awkwardly. Hitler nodded to Himmler, who opened the case which was full of decorations.

"To you, General Schellenberg, the German Cross in Gold, and also to you, Hauptsturmführer Vaughan." He pinned on the decorations, then turned to Steiner. "You, Colonel Steiner, already have the Knight's Cross with Oak Leaves. I now award you the Swords."

"Thank you, my Führer," Kurt Steiner replied with considerable irony.

"And to you, Mr. Devlin," the Führer said, turning to the Irishman, "the Iron Cross First Class."

Devlin couldn't think of a thing to say, stifled an insane desire to laugh as the cross was pinned to his jacket.

"You have my gratitude, gentlemen, and the gratitude of all the German people," Hitler told them. He turned and went out, Himmler trailing behind.

Canaris lingered for a moment at the door. "A most instructive morning, but I'd take care if I were you from now on, Walter."

The door closed. Devlin said, "What happens now?"

"The Führer returns to Berlin at once," Schellenberg said. "Canaris and Himmler go with him."

"What about us?" Asa Vaughan asked.

"There's a slight problem there. The Reichsführer has made it plain he doesn't want you three back in Berlin. In fact, he doesn't want you around at all."

"I see," Steiner said. "And you're supposed to take care of us?"

"Something like that."

"The old sod," Devlin said.

"Of course there is the Lysander waiting on the beach at Chernay," Schellenberg said. "Leber will have had it checked out by now and refueled."

"But where in the hell do we go?" Asa Vaughan demanded "We just got out of England by the skin of our teeth, and Germany's certainly too hot for us."

Schellenberg glanced inquiringly at Devlin, and the Irishman started to laugh. "Have you ever been to Ireland?" he asked Vaughan.

It was cold on the beach, the tide much higher than it had been that morning, but there was still ample space to take off.

"I've checked everything," flight Sergeant Leber said to Asa. "You shouldn't have any problems, Hauptsturmführer."

Schellenberg said, "You go back to the airfield now, Flight Sergeant. I'll join you later."

Leber saluted and walked away. Schellenberg shook hands with Steiner and Asa. "Gentlemen, good luck." They got into the Lysander, and he turned to Devlin. "You are a truly remarkable man."

Devlin said, "Come with us, Walter, nothing for you back there."

"Too late, my friend. As I've said before, far too late to get off the merry-go-round now."

"And what will Himmler say when he hears that you let us go?"

"Oh, I've thought of that. An excellent marksman like you should have no difficulty in shooting me in the shoulder. Let's make it the left one. A flesh wound, naturally."

"Jesus, it's the cunning old fox you are."

Schellenberg walked away, then turned. Devlin's hand came out of his pocket holding the Walther. It coughed once and Schellenberg staggered, clutching at his shoulder. There was blood between his fingers, and he smiled. "Goodbye, Mr. Devlin."

The Irishman scrambled in and pulled down the cupola. Asa turned into the wind, the Lysander roared along the beach and lifted off. Schellenberg watched as it sped out to sea. After a while he turned and, still clutching his shoulder, walked back toward the slipway.

Lough Conn, in the County of Mayo and not too far from Killala Bay on the west coast of Ireland, is better than ten miles long. On that evening in the failing light as darkness swept down from the mountains, its surface was like black glass.

Michael Murphy farmed close to the southern end of the lough, but that day he had been fishing and drinking poteen until, in the words of his old grannie, he didn't know whether he was here or there. It started to rain with a sudden rush, and he reached for his oars, singing softly to himself.

There was a roaring in his ears, a rush of air and what he could only describe afterwards as a great black bird that passed over his head and vanished into the shadows at the other end of the lough.

Asa made a masterly landing on the calm surface several hundred yards from the shore, dropping his tail at the last moment. They skidded to a halt and rested there and then water started to come in. He got the cupola up and heaved the dinghy package out. It inflated at once.

"How deep is it here?" he asked Devlin.

"Two hundred feet."

"That should take care of her then. Poor lovely bitch. Let's get moving."

He was into the dinghy in a moment, followed by Steiner and Devlin. They paddled away and then paused to look back. The Lysander's nose went under. For a moment there was only the tailplane showing with the Luftwaffe swastika, and then that too disappeared below the surface.

"That's it, I guess," Asa said.

They started to paddle toward the darkening shore. Steiner said, "What now, Mr. Devlin?"

"A long walk before us, but the whole night to do it in. My great aunt Eileen O'Brien has an old farmhouse above Killala Bay. Nothing but friends there."

"And then what?" Asa demanded.

"God knows, my old son. We'll have to see," Liam Devlin told him.

The dinghy drifted in to a small beach. Devlin went first, knee deep, and pulled them in to shore.

"*Cead mile failte,*" he said, putting out a hand to Kurt Steiner.

"And what's that?" the German demanded.

"Irish." Liam Devlin smiled. "The language of kings. It means a hundred thousand welcomes."

BELFAST
1975

16

IT WAS ALMOST FOUR IN the morning. Devlin stood up and opened the sacristy door. The city was quiet now, but there was the acrid smell of smoke. It started to rain, and he shivered and lit a cigarette.

"Nothing quite like a bad night in Belfast."

I said, "Tell me something. Did you ever have dealings with Dougal Munro again?"

"Oh, yes." He nodded. "Several times over the years. He liked his fishing did old Dougal."

As usual I found it difficult to take him seriously and tried again. "All right, what happened afterwards? How did Dougal Munro manage to keep it all under wraps?"

"Well, you must remember that only Munro and Carter knew who Steiner really was. To poor old Lieutenant Benson, Sister Maria Palmer and Father Martin he was just a prisoner of war. A Luftwaffe officer."

"But Michael Ryan and his niece? The Shaws?"

"The Luftwaffe had started on London again at the beginning of that year. The Little Blitz it was called, and that was very convenient for British intelligence."

"Why?"

"Because people died in the bombing raids, people like Sir Maxwell Shaw and his sister, Lavinia, killed in London during a Luftwaffe raid in January nineteen forty-four. Look up *The Times* for that month. You'll find an obituary."

"And Michael Ryan and Mary? Jack and Eric Carver?"

"They didn't rate *The Times*, but they ended up in the same place, a crematorium in North London. Five pounds of gray ash and no need for an autopsy. All listed as victims of the bombing."

"Nothing changes," I said. "And the others?"

"Canaris didn't last much longer. Fell out of favor later that year, then the attempt to kill Hitler in July failed. Canaris was arrested amongst others. They killed him in the last week of the war. Whether Rommel was involved or not has always been a matter of speculation, but the Führer thought he was. Couldn't bear to have the people's hero revealed as a traitor to the Nazi cause, so Rommel was allowed to commit suicide with the promise that his family would be spared."

"What bastards they all were," I said.

"We all know what happened to the Führer holed up in his bunker at the end. Himmler tried to make a run for it. Shaved off his mustache, even wore an eye patch. Didn't do him any good. Took cyanide when they caught him."

"And Schellenberg?"

"Now there was a man, old Walter. He fooled Himmler when he got back. Said we'd overpowered him. The wound helped, of course. He became head of the Combined Secret Services before the end of the war. Outlasted the lot of them. When it came to the war crimes trials, the only thing they could get him for was being a member of an illegal organization, the SS. All sorts of witnesses came forward to speak for him at the trial, Jews amongst them. He only served a couple of years in jail, and they let him out. He died in Italy in fifty-one—cancer."

"So that's it," I said.

He nodded. "We saved Hitler's life. Did we do right?" He shrugged. "It seemed like a good idea at the time, but I can imagine why they put a hundred-year hold on that file."

He opened the door again and looked out. I said, "What happened afterwards? To you and Steiner and Asa Vaughan! I know you were a professor at some American college in the years after the war, but what happened in between?"

"Ah, Jesus, son, and haven't I talked enough? I've given you enough for another book. The rest will have to wait until next time. You should be getting back to your hotel. I'll go a step of the way with you."

"Is that safe?"

"Well, you're clean enough if we meet an army patrol, and who's going to worry about a poor old priest like me?"

He wore a hat and a raincoat over his cassock and sheltered us with his umbrella as we walked through the mean streets, passing here and there the devastation of a bombing.

"Would you look at this place?" he demanded. "Rat's alley where the dead men left their bones."

"Why do you keep on?" I asked him. "The bombings, the killings?"

"When it started, back in August sixty-nine, it seemed like a good idea. Orange mobs trying to burn Catholics out, the B Special Police giving them a hand."

"And now?"

"To be honest with you, son, I'm getting tired, and I never did like soft target hits, the indiscriminate bomb that kills passersby, women, children. That farmhouse above Killala Bay. My old aunt Eileen left it to me, and there's a job waiting as professor of English at Trinity College in Dublin whenever I want." He stopped on the corner and sniffed the smoky air. "Time to get the hell out of this and let those who want to get on with it."

"You mean you've finally got tired of the game playing you instead of you playing the game?"

He nodded. "That's what Steiner always says."

"Interesting," I commented. "You said, 'Steiner *says.*' "

He smiled. "Is that a fact?" The rain increased suddenly. We were on the corner of the Falls Road. In the distance was a foot patrol of the Parachute Regiment and a Saracen armored car. "I think I'll leave you here, son."

"A wise decision." I took his hand.

"You can look me up in Killala any time." He turned away and paused. "One thing."

"What's that?" I asked.

"The Cohen girl, the hit-and-run accident. You were right. Convenient for someone, that. I'd watch my back if I were you."

I lit a cigarette in cupped hands and watched him go, the cassock like skirts around his ankles, the umbrella against the rain. I glanced down the Falls Road. The patrol was nearer now, but when I turned to take a last look at Liam Devlin, he'd gone, disappeared into the shadows as if he had never been.

NIGHT OF THE FOX

For Vivienne Mylne

1

THE ROMANS USED TO THINK that the souls of the departed stayed near their tombs. It was easy to believe that on a cold March morning, with a sky so black that it was as if night was about to fall.

I stood in the granite archway and looked in at the graveyard. The notice board said *Parish Church of St. Brelade* and the place was crammed with headstones and tombs, and here and there a granite cross reared up. There was a winged angel on the far side, I noticed that, and then thunder rumbled on the horizon and rain swept in across the bay.

The porter at the hotel had given me an umbrella and I put it up and ventured in. On Sunday in Boston I'd never heard of the British Channel Islands off the coast of France or the Island of Jersey. Now it was Thursday and here I was having traveled halfway round the world to seek the final answer to something that had taken three years out of my life.

The church was very old and built of granite. I moved toward it through the tombstones, pausing to look out over the bay. The tide was out and there was a fine sweep of golden sands extending to a concrete seawall and I could see my hotel.

I heard voices and, turning, saw two men in cloth caps, sacks over their shoulders, crouching under a cypress tree by the far wall of the graveyard. They stood up and moved away, laughing together as if at some joke, and I noticed they were carrying spades. They disappeared around the back of the church and I crossed to the wall.

There was a freshly dug grave, covered with a tarpaulin although the tree gave it some protection from the rain. I don't think I've ever felt so excited. It was as if it had been waiting for me and I turned and moved through the headstones to the entrance of the church, opened the door and went inside.

I'd expected a place of darkness and gloom, but the lights were on and it was really very beautiful, the vaulted ceiling unusual in that it was constructed of granite, no evidence of wooden beams there at all. I walked toward the altar and stood for a moment, looking around me, aware of the quiet. There was the click of a door opening and closing. A man approached.

He had white hair and eyes of the palest blue. He wore a black cassock and carried a raincoat over one arm. His voice was dry and very old and there was a hint of Irish to it when he spoke. "Can I help you?"

"Are you the rector?"

"Oh, no." He smiled good-humoredly. "They put me out to grass a long time ago. My name is Cullen. Canon Donald Cullen. You're an American?"

"That's right." I shook hands. He had a surprisingly firm grip. "Alan Stacey."

"Your first visit to Jersey?"

"Yes," I said. "Until a few days ago I never knew the place existed. Like most Americans, I'd only heard of *New* Jersey."

He smiled. We moved toward the door and he carried on, "You've chosen a bad time of the year for your first visit. Jersey can be one of the most desirable places on earth, but not usually during March."

"I didn't have much choice," I said. "You're burying someone here today. Harry Martineau."

He had started to pull on his raincoat and paused in surprise. "That's right. I'm performing the ceremony myself, as a matter of fact. Two o'clock this afternoon. Are you a relative?"

"Not exactly, although I sometimes feel as if I am. I'm an assistant professor of philosophy at Harvard. I've been working on a biography of Martineau for the past three years."

"I see." He opened the door and we went out into the porch.

"Do you know much about him?" I asked.

"Very little, besides the extraordinary way he met his end."

"And the even more extraordinary circumstance of his last rites," I said. "After all, Canon, it isn't often you get to bury a man forty years after his death."

The bungalow was at the other end of St. Brelade's Bay, close to L'Horizon Hotel where I was staying. It was small and unpretentious, but the living room was surprisingly large, comfortable and cluttered, two walls lined with books. Sliding windows opened to a terrace and a small garden, the bay beyond. The tide was rushing in, the wind lifting the sea into whitecaps, and rain rattled against the window.

My host came in from the kitchen and put a tray on a small table by the fire. "I hope you don't mind tea."

"Tea will be fine."

"My wife was the coffee drinker in the family, but she died three years ago. I could never abide the stuff myself."

He filled my cup and pushed it toward me as I sat down on the other side of the table from him. The silence hung between us. He raised his cup and drank very precisely, waiting.

"You're very comfortable here," I said.

"Yes," he said. "I do very well. Lonely, of course. The great weakness of all human beings, Professor Stacey, is that we all need somebody." He refilled his cup. "I spent three years in Jersey as a boy and grew to love the place very much."

"That would be easy enough." I looked out at the bay. "It's very beautiful."

"I returned on holiday on many occasions. When I retired, I was a canon of Winchester Cathedral. Our only son moved to Australia many years ago, so . . . " He shrugged. "Jersey seemed an obvious choice as my wife had owned this bungalow for many years. A legacy from an uncle."

"That must have been convenient."

"Yes, especially with the housing laws the way they are here." He put down his cup, took out a pipe and started to fill it from a worn leather pouch. "So," he said briskly. "Now you know all about me. What about you and friend Martineau?"

"Do you know much about him?"

"I'd never heard of the man until a few days ago when my good friend, Dr. Drayton, came to see me, explained the circumstances in which the body had been recovered and told me it was being shipped from London for burial here."

"You're aware of the manner of his death?"

"In a plane crash in 1945."

"January 1945, to be precise. The RAF had a unit called the Enemy Aircraft Flight during the Second World War. They operated captured German planes to evaluate performance and so on."

"I see."

"Harry Martineau worked for the Ministry of Economic Warfare. In January 1945, he went missing when traveling as an observer in an Arado 96, a German two-seater training plane being operated by the Enemy Aircraft Flight. It was always believed to have gone down in the sea."

"And?"

"Two weeks ago it was found during excavations in an Essex marsh. Work on the building site was halted while an RAF unit recovered what was left."

"And Martineau and the pilot were still inside?"

"What was left of them. For some reason the authorities kept a low profile on the affair. News didn't filter through to me until last weekend. I caught the first plane out. Arrived in London on Monday morning."

He nodded. "You say you've been working on a biography of him. What makes him so special? As I told you, I'd never even heard his name before."

"Nor had the general public," I said. "But in the thirties, in academic circles . . . '' I shrugged. ''Bertrand Russell considered him one of the most brilliant and innovative minds in his field.''

''Which was?''

''Moral philosophy.''

''An interesting study,'' the canon said.

''For a fascinating man. He was born in Boston. His father was in shipping. Wealthy, but not outrageously so. His mother, although born in New York, was of German parentage. Her father taught for some years at Columbia then returned to Germany in 1925 as professor of surgery at Dresden University.'' I got up and walked to the window, thinking about it as I peered out. ''Martineau went to Harvard, did a doctorate at Heidelberg, was a Rhodes scholar at Oxford, a Fellow of Trinity College and Croxley Professor of Moral Philosophy by the age of thirty-eight.''

''A remarkable achievement,'' Cullen said.

I turned. ''But you don't understand. Here was a man who was questioning everything. Turning his whole field upside down. And then the Second World War broke out and the rest is silence. Until now, that is.''

''Silence?''

''Oh, he left Oxford, we know that. Worked for the Ministry of Defence and then the Ministry of Economic Warfare, as I told you. Many academics did that. But the tragedy was that he seems to have stopped working altogether in his chosen field. No more papers and the book he'd been writing for years was left unfinished. We've got the manuscript at Harvard. Not a line written after September nineteen thirty-nine.''

''How very strange.''

I went back and sat down. ''We have all his papers in the Harvard Library. What really intrigued me on going through them was a personal thing.''

''And what was that?''

''When I finished high school at eighteen, instead of going straight to Harvard I joined the Marines. Did a year in Vietnam until a bullet in the left kneecap sent me home for good. Martineau did the same sort of thing. Joined the American Expeditionary Force in the last few months of the First World War, underage, I might say, and served as an infantry private in the trenches in Flanders. I was fascinated by the fact that in turning from what we'd gone through, we'd both sought another answer in the same way.''

''From the hell of war to the cool recesses of the mind.'' Canon Cullen knocked out his pipe in the hearth. ''I can't remember who said that. Some war poet or other.''

''God save me from those,'' I said. ''Nam cost me a permanently stiff left leg, three years in the hands of psychiatrists and a failed marriage.''

The clock on the mantelpiece struck twelve. Cullen got up, moved to the sideboard and poured whisky from a cut glass decanter into two glasses. He brought them back and handed me one. "I was in Burma during the war myself, which was bad enough." He sipped a little whisky and put down his glass on the hearth. "And so, Professor, what about the rest?"

"The rest?"

"Priests are supposed to be ingenuous souls who know nothing of the reality of life," he said in that dry, precise voice. "Rubbish, of course. Our business is confession, human pain, misery. I know people, Professor, after fifty-two years as an ordained priest, and one learns to know when they are not telling you everything." He put a match to his pipe and puffed away. "Which applies to you, my friend, unless I'm very much mistaken."

I took a deep breath. "He was in uniform when they found him."

He frowned. "But you said he was working for the Ministry of Economic Warfare."

"German Luftwaffe uniform," I said. "Both he and the pilot."

"Are you certain?"

"I have a friend from the Vietnam days in the Marines called Tony Bianco. He's with the CIA at our embassy in London. They get to know things, these people. I had problems with the Ministry of Defence the other day. They were giving very little away about Martineau and that plane."

"Your friend checked up for you?"

"And found out something else. The newspaper report about that Arado being from the Enemy Aircraft Flight. That's suspect, too."

"Why?"

"Because they always carried RAF rondels. And according to Bianco's informant, this one still had Luftwaffe markings."

"And you say you couldn't get any more information from official sources?"

"None at all. Ridiculous though it may seem, Martineau and that flight are still covered by some wartime security classification."

The old man frowned. "After forty years?"

"There's more," I said. "I had this kind of problem last year when I was researching. Ran into roadblocks, if you know what I mean. I discovered that Martineau was awarded the Distinguished Service Order in January 1944. One of those awards that appears in the list without explanation. No information about what he'd done to earn it."

"But that's a military award and a very high one at that. Martineau was a civilian."

"Apparently civilians have qualified on rare occasions, but it all begins to fit with a story I heard when researching at Oxford three years ago. Max Kubel, the nuclear physicist, was a professor at Oxford for many years and a friend of Martineau's."

"Now I *have* heard about him," Cullen said. "He was a German Jew, was he not, who managed to get out before the Nazis could send him to a concentration camp?"

"He died in nineteen seventy-three," I said. "But I managed to interview the old man who'd been his manservant at his Oxford college for more than thirty years. He told me that during the big German offensive in nineteen forty that led to Dunkirk, Kubel was held by the Gestapo under house arrest at Freiburg, just across the German border from France. An SS officer arrived with an escort to take him to Berlin."

"So?"

"The old boy, Howard his name was, said that Kubel told him years ago that the SS officer was Martineau."

"Did you believe him?"

"Not at the time. He was ninety-one and senile, but one has to remember Martineau's background. Quite obviously he could have passed for a German any time he wanted. He not only had the language but had the family background."

Cullen nodded. "So, in view of more recent developments you're prepared to give more credence to that story?"

"I don't know what to think anymore." I shrugged. "Nothing makes any sense. Martineau and Jersey, for example. To the best of my knowledge he never visited the place and he died five months before it was freed from Nazi occupation." I swallowed the rest of my whisky. "Martineau has no living relatives, I know that because he never married, so who the hell is this Dr. Drayton of yours? I know one thing. He must have one hell of a pull with the Ministry of Defence to get them to release the body to him."

"You're absolutely right." Canon Cullen poured me another Scotch whisky. "In all respects, but one."

"And what would that be?"

"Dr. Drayton," he said, "is not a he, but a she. Dr. Sarah Drayton, to be precise." He raised his glass to toast me.

I am the resurrection and the life, saith the Lord: he that believeth in me, though he were dead, yet shall he live.

Cullen sounded even more Irish as he lifted his voice bravely against the heavy rain. He wore a dark cloak over his vestments and one of the funeral men stood beside him holding an umbrella. There was only one mourner, Sarah Drayton, standing on the other side of the open grave, an undertaker behind her with another umbrella.

She looked perhaps forty-eight or fifty although, as I discovered later, she was sixty, small and with a figure still trim in the black two-piece suit and hat. Her hair was short, expertly cut and iron gray. She was not in any way conventionally beautiful, with a mouth that was rather too large and hazel eyes above wide cheekbones. It was a face of considerable character with an impression of someone who had seen the best and worst that life had to offer, and there was an extraordinary stillness to her. If I had seen her only in passing, I'd have turned for a second look. She was that sort of woman.

She ignored me completely and I stayed back under what shelter the trees provided, getting thoroughly damp in spite of my umbrella. Cullen concluded the service, then moved toward her and spoke briefly. She kissed him on the cheek and he turned and moved away toward the church, followed by the funeral men.

She stayed there for a while at the graveside and the two gravediggers waited respectfully a few yards away. She still ignored me as I moved forward, picked up a little damp soil and threw it down on the coffin.

"Dr. Drayton?" I said. "I'm sorry to intrude. My name is Alan Stacey. I wonder if I might have a few words? I'm not a reporter, by the way."

Her voice was deeper than I had expected, calm and beautifully modulated. She said, without looking at me, "I know very well who you are, Professor Stacey. I've been expecting you at any time these past three years." She turned and smiled and suddenly looked absolutely enchanting and about twenty years of age. "We really should get out of this rain before it does us both a mischief. That's sound medical advice and for free. My car is in the road outside. I think you'd better come back for a drink."

The house was no more than five minutes away, reached by a narrow country lane along which she drove expertly at considerable speed. It stood in about an acre of well-tended garden surrounded by beech trees through which one could see the bay far below. It was Victorian from the look of it, with long narrow windows and green shutters at the front and a portico at the entrance. The door was opened instantly as we went up the steps by a tall, somber-looking man in a black alpaca jacket. He had silver hair and wore steel-rimmed glasses.

"Ah, Vito," she said as he took her coat. "This is Professor Stacey."

"Professore." He bowed slightly.

"We'll have coffee in the library later," she said. "I'll see to the drinks."

"Of course, Contessa."

He turned away and paused and spoke to her in Italian. She shook her head and answered fluently in the same language. He went through a door at the rear of the hall.

"Contessa?" I asked.

"Oh, don't listen to Vito." She dismissed my query politely, but firmly. "He's a terrible snob. This way."

The hall was cool and pleasant. Black and white tiled floor, a curving staircase and two or three oil paintings on the wall. Eighteenth-century seascapes. She opened a double mahogany door and led the way into a large library. The walls were lined with books, and French windows looked out to the garden. There was an Adam fireplace with a fire burning brightly in the basket grate and a grand piano, the top crammed with photos, mostly in silver frames.

"Scotch all right for you?" she asked.

"Fine."

She crossed to a sideboard and busied herself at the drinks tray. "How did you know who I was?" I asked. "Canon Cullen?"

"I've known about you since you started work on Harry." She handed me a glass.

"Who told you?"

"Oh, friends," she said. "From the old days. The kind who get to know things."

It made me think of Tony Bianco, my CIA contact at the embassy, and I was immediately excited. "Nobody seems to want to answer any of my questions at the Ministry of Defence."

"I don't suppose they would."

"And yet they release the body to you. You must have influence?"

"You could say that." She took a cigarette from a silver box, lit it and sat in a wing chair by the fire, crossing slim legs. "Have you ever heard of SOE, Professor?"

"Of course," I said. "Special Operations Executive. Set up by British Intelligence in 1940 on Churchill's instructions to coordinate resistance and the underground movement in Europe."

" 'Set Europe ablaze,' that's what the old man ordered." Sarah Drayton flicked ash in the fire. "I worked for them."

I was astonished. "But you can't have been more than a child."

"Nineteen," she said. "In 1944."

"And Martineau?"

"Look on the piano," she said. "The end photo in the silver frame."

I crossed to the piano and picked the photo up and her face jumped out at me, strangely unchanged except in one respect. Her hair was startlingly blond and marcelled—that's the term I think they used to use. She wore a little black hat and one of those coats from the wartime period with big shoulders and tight at the waist. She also wore silk stockings and high-heeled shoes and clutched a black patent-leather bag.

The man standing next to her was of medium height and wore a leather military trenchcoat over a tweed suit, hands thrust deep into the pockets. His face was shadowed by a dark slouch hat and a cigarette dangled from the corner of his mouth. The eyes were dark, no expression to them at all, and his smile had a kind of ruthless charm. He looked a thoroughly dangerous man.

Sarah Drayton got up and joined me. "Not much like the Croxley Professor of Moral Philosophy at Oxford there, is he?"

"Where was it taken?" I asked.

"In Jersey. Not too far from here. May nineteen forty-four. The tenth, I think."

"But I've been in Jersey long enough to know that it was occupied by the Germans at that time," I said.

"Very much so."

"And Martineau was here? With you?"

She crossed to a Georgian desk, opened a drawer and took out a small folder. When she opened it I saw at once that it contained several old photographs. She passed one to me. "This one I don't keep on top of the piano for obvious reasons."

She was dressed pretty much as she had been in the other photo and Martineau wore the same leather trenchcoat. The only difference was the SS uniform underneath, the silver death's-head badge in his cap. "Standartenführer Max Vogel," she said. "Colonel, to you. He looks rather dashing, doesn't he?" She smiled as she took it from me. "He had a weakness for uniforms, Harry."

"Dear God," I said. "What is all this?"

She didn't answer, but simply passed me another photo. It was faded slightly, but still perfectly clear. A group of German officers. In front of them stood two men on their own. One was Martineau in the SS uniform, but it was the other who took my breath away. One of the best-known faces of the Second World War. Field Marshal Erwin Rommel. The Desert Fox himself.

I said, "Was that taken here too?"

"Oh yes." She put the photos back in the desk and picked up my glass. "I think you could do with another drink."

"Yes, I believe I could."

She got me one, handed the glass to me, and we moved to the fire. She took a cigarette from the box. "I should stop, I suppose. Too late now. Another bad habit Harry taught me."

"Do I get an explanation?"

"Why not?" she said, and turned as rain drummed against the French windows. "I can't think of anything better to do on an afternoon like this, can you?"

LONDON
1944

2

IT STARTED, IF ONE CAN ever be certain where anything starts, with a telephone call received by Brigadier Dougal Munro at his flat in Haston Place, ten minutes' walk from the London headquarters of SOE in Baker Street. As head of Section D at SOE he had two phones by his bed, one routed straight through to his office. It was this that brought him awake at four o'clock on the morning of April 28, 1944.

He listened, face grave, then swore softly. "I'll be right over. One thing, check if Eisenhower is in town."

Within five minutes he was letting himself out of the front door, shivering in the damp cold, lighting the first cigarette of the day as he hurried along the deserted street. He was at that time sixty-five, a squat, powerful-looking man with white hair, his round, ugly face set off by steel-rimmed spectacles. He wore an old Burberry raincoat and carried an umbrella.

There was very little of the military in either his bearing or his appearance, which was hardly surprising. His rank of brigadier was simply to give him the necessary authority in certain quarters. Until 1939, Dougal Munro had been an archaeologist by profession. An Egyptologist, to be more precise, and fellow of All Souls at Oxford. For three years now, head of Section D at SOE. What was commonly referred to in the trade as the dirty tricks department.

He turned in at the entrance of Baker Street, nodded to the night guard and went straight upstairs. When he went into his office, Captain Jack Carter, his night duty officer, was seated behind his desk. Carter had a false leg, a legacy of Dunkirk. He reached for his stick and started to get up.

"No, stay where you are, Jack," Munro told him. "Is there any tea?"

"Thermos flask on the map table, sir."

Munro unscrewed the flask, poured a cup and drank. "God, that's foul, but at least it's hot. Right, get on with it."

Carter now got up and limped across. There was a map of the southwest of England on the table, concentrating mainly on Devon, Cornwall and the general area of the English Channel.

"Exercise Tiger, sir," he said. "You remember the details?"

"Simulated landings for Overlord."

491

"That's right. Here in Lyme Bay in Devon there's a place called Slapton Sands. It bears enough similarities to the beach we've designated Utah in the Normandy landings to make it invaluable for training purposes. Most of the young Americans going in have no combat experience."

"I know that, Jack," Munro said. "Go on."

"Last night's convoy consisted of eight landing craft. Five from Plymouth and three from Brixham. Under naval escort, of course. They were to do a practice beach landing at Slapton."

There was a pause. Munro said, "Tell me the worst."

"They were attacked at sea by German E-boats, we think the Fifth and Ninth Schnellboote Flotillas from Cherbourg."

"And the damage?"

"Two landing craft sunk for certain. Others torpedoed and damaged."

"And the butcher's bill?"

"Difficult to be accurate at the moment. Around two hundred sailors and four hundred and fifty soldiers."

Munro said, "Are you trying to tell me we lost six hundred and fifty American servicemen last night? Six hundred and fifty and we haven't even started the invasion of Europe?"

"I'm afraid so."

Munro walked restlessly across the room and stood at the window. "Has Eisenhower been told?"

"He's in town, sir, at Hayes Lodge. He wants to see you at breakfast. Eight o'clock."

"And he'll want the facts." Munro turned and went to his desk. "Were there any Bigots among those officers lost?"

"Three, sir."

"Dear God, I warned them. I warned them about this," Munro said. "No Bigot to in any way undertake hazardous duty."

Some months previously it had become regrettably clear that there were serious breaches of security, in some cases by high-ranking American officers, in connection with the projected invasion of Europe. The Bigot procedure had been brought in as an answer to the situation. It was an intelligence classification above Most Secret. Bigots knew what others did not—the details of the Allied invasion of Europe.

"The three are missing so far," Carter said. "I've got their files."

He laid them on the desk and Munro examined them quickly. "Stupid," he said. "Unbelievably stupid. Take this man, Colonel Hugh Kelso."

"The engineering officer?" Carter said. "He's already visited two of the Normandy beaches by night, courtesy of Four Commando, to check on the suitability of the terrain for vehicles."

"Sword Beach and Utah Beach." Munro groaned. "For God's sake,

Jack, what if he was picked up by one of those E-boats? He could be in enemy hands right now. And they'll make him talk if they want to, you know that.''

''I don't think it's likely that any of those missing were picked up by the Germans, sir. The captain of the destroyer *Saladin*, which was one of the escorts, said the E-boats attacked at a range of fifteen hundred meters, then got the hell out of it fast. Typical hit and run. A lot of darkness and confusion on both sides. And the weather isn't too good. Wind force five to six and freshening, but I'm informed that the way the currents are in Lyme Bay, most of the bodies will come ashore. Already started.''

''Most, Jack, most.'' Munro tapped the map on the table. ''The Germans know we're coming. They're expecting the invasion. They're ready for it. Hitler's put Rommel himself in charge of all coastal fortifications. But they don't know where and they don't know when.'' He shook his head, staring down at the map. ''Wouldn't it be ironic if the greatest invasion in history had to be called off because one man with all the right information fell into the wrong hands.''

''Not likely, sir, believe me,'' Carter said gently. ''This Colonel Kelso will come in on the tide with the rest of them.''

''God help me, but I pray that he does, Jack. I pray that he does,'' Dougal Munro said fervently.

But at that precise moment, Colonel Hugh Kelso was very much alive, more afraid than he had ever been in his life, cold and wet and in terrible pain. He lay huddled in the bottom of a life raft in several inches of water about a mile offshore from the Devon coast, a contrary current carrying him fast toward Start Point on the southernmost tip of Lyme Bay, and beyond Start Point were the open waters of the English Channel.

Kelso was forty-two, married with two daughters. A civil engineer, he had been managing director of the family firm of construction engineers in New York for several years and had a high reputation in the field. Which was why he'd been drafted into the Engineering Corps in 1942 with the immediate rank of major. His experience with the engineering problems involved in beach landings on various islands in the South Pacific had earned him a promotion and a transfer to SHAEF Headquarters in England to work on the preparation for the invasion of Europe.

He'd taken part in Exercise Tiger on the request of the commanding officer for one reason only. The American 1st Engineer Special Brigade was one of the units assigned to take the beach designated as Utah during the coming Normandy landings, and Hugh Kelso had actually visited Utah Beach six weeks previously, under cover of darkness, guarded by British commandos. Slapton Sands was as close to the terrain as they could get. It had seemed sensible to seek his opinion, which was why he'd sailed on LST 31 from Plymouth.

Like everyone on board, Kelso had been taken totally by surprise by the attack. A considerable number of flares had been noticed in the distance which had been assumed to be from British MTBs. And then the first torpedo had struck and the night had become a living hell of burning oil and screaming men. Although Kelso didn't know it then, 413 men were killed from LST 31 alone. In his own case, he was blown off his feet by the force of the explosion and slammed against a rail, toppling into the water. His life jacket kept him afloat, of course, but he lost consciousness, coming to his senses to find himself being towed through the icy water.

The flames were a hundred yards away and in the reflected light he was aware only of an oil-soaked face.

"You're okay, sir. Just hang on. There's a life raft here."

The life raft loomed out of the darkness. It was the new model of inflatable developed from Pacific experience. A round, fat orange sphere riding high in the water and intended to carry as many as ten men. There was a canopy on top to protect the occupants from wind and weather, the entrance flap standing open.

"I'll get you in, sir, then I'll go back for some more. Come on, up you go."

Kelso felt weak, but his unknown friend was strong and muscular. He pushed hard, shoving Kelso in headfirst through the flap. And then Kelso was aware of the pain in his right leg, like a living thing and worse than anything he had ever known. He screamed and fainted.

When he came to, he was numb with cold and it took him a few moments to work out where he was. There was no sign of his unknown friend. He felt around in the darkness, then peered out through the open flap. Spray dashed in his face. There was no light anywhere, only the dark and the wind and the sound of the sea running. He checked the luminous dial of his waterproof watch. It was almost five o'clock and then he remembered that these life rafts carried an emergency kit. As he turned to feel for it, the pain started in his leg again. He gritted his teeth as his hands found the emergency kit box and got the lid open.

There was a waterproof flashlight in a clip on the inside of the lid and he switched it on. He was alone, as he had thought, in the orange cave, about a foot of water slopping around him. His uniform trousers were badly torn below the right knee, and when he put his hand inside gingerly he could feel the raised edges of bone in several places.

There was a Verey pistol in the box and he fingered it for a moment.

It seemed the obvious thing to send up one of its parachute distress flares, but then he paused, trying to make his tired brain think straight. What if the German naval units that had attacked them were still in the area? What if it was the enemy that picked him up? He couldn't take that chance. He was, after all, a Bigot. In a matter of weeks an armada of six thousand ships would sail across the narrow waters of the English Channel and Kelso knew time and place. No, better to wait until dawn.

The leg was really hurting now and he rummaged in the box and found the medical kit with its morphine ampules. He jabbed one in his leg and, after a moment's hesitation, used another. Then he found the bailer and wearily started to throw water out through the open flap. God, but he was tired. Too much morphine perhaps, but at least the pain had dulled and he dropped the bailer and pulled the plastic zip at the entrance and leaned back and was suddenly asleep.

On his right, a few hundred yards away, was Start Point. For a while he seemed to be drifting toward the rocks and then a contrary current pulled him away. Ten minutes later, the life raft passed that final point of land and a freshening wind drove it out into the cold waters of the English Channel.

Eisenhower was seated in the Regency bow window of the library at Hayes Lodge having breakfast of poached eggs, toast and coffee when the young aide showed Dougal Munro in.

"Leave us, Captain," the general said and the aide withdrew. "Difficult to smile this morning, Brigadier."

"I'm afraid so."

"Have you eaten?"

"I haven't eaten breakfast for years, General."

For a moment, Eisenhower's face was illuminated by that famous and inimitable smile. "Which shows you aren't an old military hand. You prefer tea, don't you?"

"Yes, General."

"You'll find it on the sideboard behind you—special order. Help yourself, then tell me what you know of this wretched business. My own people have already given me their version, but I've always had considerable respect for your people at SOE, you know that."

Munro helped himself to the tea and sat in the window seat and gave Eisenhower a brief résumé of the night's events.

"But surely the naval escorts should have been able to prevent such a thing happening," the general said. "On the other hand, I hear the weather wasn't too good. It's past belief. I visited Slapton myself only three days ago to see how the exercises were going. Went down by special train with Tedder and Omar Bradley.''

"Most of the crews of your LSTs are new to those waters, and the English Channel at the best of times can be difficult.'' Munro shrugged. "We've had torpedo boats from the Royal Navy hanging around off Cherbourg regularly during these exercises because Cherbourg, as the General knows, is the most important E-boat base on the French coast. There was a sea mist and the Germans obviously slipped out with their silencers on and probably with their radar sets switched off. They do more than forty knots, those things. Nothing afloat that's faster and they boxed rather cleverly on their approach. Fired off parachute flares so the people in the convoy assumed they were ours.''

"Goddammit, you never assume anything in this game. I'm tired of telling people that.'' Eisenhower poured another coffee, stood up and went to the fire. "Bodies coming ashore by the hundred, so they tell me.''

"I'm afraid so.''

"Needless to say, this whole thing stays under wraps. We're going to arrange for some kind of mass grave down there in Devon for the time being. At least it's a defense area under military rule, which should help. If this got out, so close to the invasion, it could have a terrible effect on morale.''

"I agree.'' Munro hesitated and said carefully, "There is the question of the Bigots, General.''

"Who should never have been there in the first place. No one knows the regulations on Bigots better than you.''

"It could be worse, sir. There were three in all. Two of the bodies have already been recovered. The third, this man.'' Munro took a file from his briefcase and pushed it across. "Is still missing.''

Eisenhower read the file quickly. "Colonel Hugh Kelso.'' His face darkened. "But I know Kelso personally. He checked out two beaches in Normandy only weeks ago.''

"Utah and Sword. On those occasions he had commandos nursing him and he also had an L pill with him, just in case he was caught. As the General knows, the cyanide in those things kills instantaneously.''

Eisenhower pushed the file across. "He knows, Brigadier, both when we're going and where. The implications are past belief.''

"We've men on the beaches around Slapton looking for him now, General. I've little reason to doubt that his body will turn up with the rest of them.''

"Don't try to make me feel good,'' Eisenhower told him sharply. "Some of those bodies will never come in on the tide. I know that and so do you, and if Kelso is one of them, we can never be certain that he wasn't picked up by the enemy.''

"That's true, General,'' Munro admitted because there wasn't really anything else he could say.

Eisenhower walked to the window. Rain dashed against the pane. "What a day," he said morosely. "One thing's for sure. I can only think of one man who'll have a smile on his face this morning."

At that very moment Adolf Hitler was reading a report on the Slapton Sands affair in the map room of his underground headquarters known as Wolf's Lair, near Rastenburg, deep in the forests of East Prussia.

Most of those important in the Nazi hierarchy were present. Heinrich Himmler, Reichsführer of the SS and Chief of both State and Secret Police, Josef Goebbels, Reichsminister for Propaganda, Reichsleiter Martin Bormann, Secretary to the Führer among other things, and Oberführer Rattenhuber, Himmler's Chief of Security and Commander of the SS guard at Rastenburg.

Hitler almost danced with delight and crumpled the thin paper of the message in one hand. "So, our Navy can still strike, and hard, right in the enemy's own backyard! Three ships sunk, and hundreds of casualties." His eyes sparked. "A bad morning for General Eisenhower, gentlemen."

There was general enthusiasm. "Good news indeed, my Führer," Goebbels said and delivered his usual high laugh.

Bormann, who had been the first to see the message, said quietly, "If we can do this to them off the coast of Devon, my Führer, all things are possible off the coast of France."

"They won't even get ashore," Himmler put in.

"Probably not," Hitler said, in high good humor. "But now, gentlemen, to the purpose of our meeting." They grouped around the circular table and he tapped the large-scale map of France. "The Westwall proceeds, I think." He turned to Bormann. "The report on Army Group B which I asked for? Has it arrived?"

Bormann turned inquiringly to Rattenhuber who said, "I've just had a report from the airfield. The courier, a Captain Koenig, landed five minutes ago. He's on his way."

"Good." Hitler seemed abstracted now, as if somehow alone as he stared down at the map. "So, gentlemen, where do we start?"

On December 26, 1943, a remarkable and gifted young German officer, Colonel Klaus von Stauffenberg, reported for a meeting at Rastenburg with a time bomb in his briefcase. Unfortunately, the meeting did not take place, as the Führer had already departed for Bavaria for the Christmas holiday. In spite of having lost his left eye and right hand in action, von Stauffenberg was Chief of Staff to General Olbricht of the General Army Office and the center of a conspiracy of army generals whose aim was to assassinate the Führer and save Germany from disaster.

His own abortive attempt at Christmas 1943 was only one of many that had failed. Yet there was no shortage of volunteers to the cause, as witness Captain Karl Koenig traveling in the rear of the military car from the airfield to Wolf's Lair on that gray April morning with the papers from Berlin that Hitler had requested. He was in a highly nervous state, which was hardly surprising when one considered the time bomb carefully placed in the false bottom of the briefcase. He had told the pilot at Rastenburg airfield to be ready for a quick turnaround and his fingers trembled as he lit a cigarette.

The SS driver and guard in front stared woodenly ahead, and as time passed, Koenig's nervousness increased. There were minefields on either side in the gloomy woods, electric fences, guards patrolling everywhere with savage dogs and three gates to pass through to reach the inner compound. Still, time to arm the bomb. Once done, it would give him exactly thirty minutes, they had told him.

He reached for the lock on the left-hand strap of the briefcase and depressed it. There was an immediate and very powerful explosion which killed Koenig and the two guards instantly and blew the car apart.

Hitler was beside himself with rage, pacing up and down in the map room. "Again and yet again they try." He turned on Rattenhuber. "And you, Oberführer? What about you? Sworn to protect my personal safety."

"My Führer," Rattenhuber stammered. "What can I say?"

"Nothing!" Hitler stormed and turned on the rest of them. "You say nothing of use to me—not any of you."

In the shocked silence, it was Himmler who spoke, his voice dry and precise. "That there has been negligence here is true, my Führer, but surely we see further proof, in the failure of this dastardly attempt, of the certainty of your own destiny. Further proof of Germany's inevitable victory under your inspired guidance."

Hitler's eyes blazed, his head went back. "As always, Reichsführer, you see. The only one who does." He turned on the others. "Get out, all of you. I wish to talk to the Reichsführer alone."

They went without a murmur, Goebbels the last one to leave. Hitler stood staring down at the map desk, hands clasped behind him. "In what way may I serve my Führer?" Himmler asked.

"There is a plot, am I not right?" Hitler said. "A general conspiracy to destroy me, and this Captain Koenig was simply an agent?"

"Not so much a general conspiracy as a conspiracy of generals, my Führer."

Hitler turned sharply. "Are you certain?"

"Oh, yes, but proof—that is something else."

Hitler nodded. "Koenig was an aide of General Olbricht. Is Olbricht one of those you suspect?" Himmler nodded. "And the others?"

"Generals Stieff, Wagner, von Hase, Lindemann. Several more, all being closely watched."

Hitler stayed remarkably cool. "Traitors each and every one. No firing squad. A noose each when the time comes. No one higher, though? It would seem our field marshals are loyal at least."

"I wish I could confirm that, my Führer, but there is one who is heavily suspect. I would be failing in my duty not to tell you."

"Then tell me."

"Rommel."

Hitler smiled a ghastly smile that was almost one of triumph, turned and walked away and turned again, still smiling. "I think I expected it. Yes, I'm sure I did. So, the Desert Fox wishes to play games."

"I'm almost certain of it."

"The people's hero," Hitler said. "We must handle him carefully, wouldn't you say?"

"Or outfox him, my Führer," Himmler said softly.

"Outfox him. Outfox the Desert Fox." Hitler smiled delightedly. "Yes, I like that, Reichsführer. I like that very much indeed."

Hugh Kelso slept until noon and when he awakened, he was sick. He turned over in the violently pitching life raft and pulled down the zip of the entrance flap. His heart sank. There was nothing but sea, the life raft twisting and turning on the angry waves. The sky was black, heavy with rain and the wind was gusting 5 or 6, he could tell that. Worst of all, there wasn't a hint of land anywhere. He was well out in the English Channel, so much was obvious. If he drifted straight across, wasn't picked up at all, he'd hit the coast of France, possibly the Cherbourg Peninsula. Below that, in the Gulf of St. Malo, were the Channel Islands. Alderney, Guernsey and Jersey. He didn't know much about them except that they were British and occupied by the enemy. He was not likely to be carried as far south as that, though.

He got the Verey light out, and fired an orange distress flare. There was seldom any German naval traffic in the Channel during daylight. They tended to keep to the inshore run behind their minefields. He fired another flare and then water cascaded in through the flap and he hurriedly zipped it up. There were some field rations in the emergency kit. He tried to eat one of the dried fruit blocks and was violently sick and his leg was on fire again. Hurriedly, he got another morphine ampule and injected himself. After a while, he pillowed his head on his hands and slept again.

Outside, the sea lifted as the afternoon wore on. It started to get dark soon after five o'clock. By that time the wind was blowing sou'westerly, turning him away from the French coast and the Cherbourg Peninsula so that by six o'clock he was ten miles to the west of the Casquets Light off the island of Alderney. And then the wind veered again, pushing him down along the outer edge of the Gulf of St. Malo toward Guernsey.

Kelso was aware of none of these things. He awakened around seven o'clock with a high temperature, washed his face with a little water to cool it, was sick again and dropped into something approaching a coma.

In London, Dougal Munro was working at his desk, the slight scratching of his pen the only sound in the quiet of the room. There was a knock at the door and Jack Carter limped in with a folder in one hand. He put it down in front of Munro.

"Latest list from Slapton, sir."

"Anything on Kelso?"

"Not a thing, sir, but they've got every available ship out there in the bay looking for the missing bodies."

Dougal Munro got up and moved to the window. The wind moaned outside, hurling rain against the pane. He shook his head and said softly, "God help sailors at sea on a night like this."

3

AS COMMANDER OF ARMY GROUP B, Field Marshal Erwin Rommel was responsible for the Atlantic Wall defenses, his sole task to defeat any Allied attempt to land in northern France. Since taking command in January of 1944 he had strengthened the coastal defenses to an incredible degree, tramping the beaches, visiting every strongpoint, impressing his own energetic presence on everyone from divisional commanders to the lowliest private.

His headquarters seemed permanently on the move so that no one could be sure where he was from one day to the next. He had an uncomfortable habit of turning up in his familiar black Mercedes accompanied only by his driver and his most trusted aide from Afrika Korps days, Major Konrad Hofer.

On the evening of that fateful day at about the time Hugh Kelso was somewhere in the general area of the Casquets Light, west of Alderney, the field marshal was sitting down to an early dinner with the officers of the 21st Parachute Regiment in a chateau at Campeaux some ten miles from St. Lo in Normandy.

His primary reason for being there was sound enough. The High Command, and the Führer himself, believed that the invasion, when it came, would take place in the area of the Pas de Calais. Rommel disagreed and had made it clear that if he were Eisenhower, he would strike for Normandy. None of this had done anything for his popularity among the people who counted at OKW, High Command of the Armed Forces, in Berlin. Rommel didn't give a damn about that anymore. The war was lost. The only thing that was uncertain was how long it would take.

Which brought him to the second reason for being in Normandy. He was involved in a dangerous game and it paid to keep on the move, for since taking command of Army Group B he had renewed old friendships with General von Stulpnagel, military governor of France, and General Alexander von Falkenhausen. Both were involved, with von Stauffenberg, in the conspiracy against Hitler. It had not taken them long to bring Rommel around to their point of view.

They had all been aware of the projected assassination attempt at Rastenburg that morning. Rommel had sent Konrad Hofer by air to Berlin the previous day to await events at General Olbricht's headquarters, but there had been no news at all. Not a hint of anything untoward on the radio.

Now, in the mess, Colonel Halder, commanding the regiment, stood to offer the loyal toast. "Gentlemen—to our Führer and total victory."

"So many young men," Rommel thought to himself, "and what for?" But he raised his glass and drank with them.

"And now, Field Marshal Erwin Rommel, the Desert Fox himself, who does our mess so much honor tonight."

They drained their glasses, then applauded him, cheering wildly, and Rommel was immensely touched. Colonel Halder said, "The men have arranged a little entertainment in your honor, Field Marshal. We were hoping you might be willing to attend."

"But of course." Rommel held out his glass for more champagne. "Delighted."

The door opened at the back of the mess and Konrad Hofer entered. He looked tired and badly needed a shave, his field gray greatcoat buttoned up to his neck.

"Ah, Konrad, there you are," Rommel called. "Come and have a glass of champagne. You look as if you could do with it."

"I've just flown in from Berlin, Field Marshal. Landed at St. Lo."

"Good flight?"

"Terrible, actually." Hofer swallowed the champagne gratefully.

"My dear boy, come and have a shower and we'll see if they can manage you a sandwich." Rommel turned to Colonel Halder. "See if you can delay this little show the men are putting on for half an hour."

"No problem, Field Marshal."

"Good—we'll see you later then." Rommel picked up a fresh bottle of champagne and two glasses and walked out followed by Hofer.

As soon as the bedroom door was closed, Hofer turned in agitation. "It was the worst kind of mess. All that fool Koenig managed to do was blow himself up outside the main gate."

"That seems rather careless of him," Rommel said dryly. " Now calm yourself, Konrad. Have another glass of champagne and get under the shower and just take it slowly."

Hofer went into the bathroom and Rommel straightened his uniform, examining himself in the mirror. He was fifty-three at that time, of medium height, stocky and thick-set with strong features, and there was a power to the man, a force, that was almost electric. His uniform was simple enough, his only decorations the Pour le Mérite, the famous Blue Max, won as a young infantry officer in the First World War, and the Knight's Cross with Oak Leaves, Swords and Diamonds, both of which hung around his neck. On the other hand, one hardly needed anything else if one had those.

Hofer emerged in a bathrobe toweling his hair. "Olbricht and a few more up there are in a blue funk and I don't blame them. I mean the Gestapo or the SD could be on to this at any time."

"Yes," Rommel conceded. "Himmler may have started life as a chicken farmer, but whatever else you may say about him he's no fool. How was von Stauffenberg?"

"As determined as ever. He suggests you meet with Generals von Stulpnagel and Falkenhausen within the next few days."

"I'll see what I can do."

Hofer was back in the bathroom pulling on his uniform again. "I'm not so sure it's a good idea. If Himmler does have his suspicions about you, you could be under close surveillance already."

"Oh, I'll think of something," Rommel said. "Now hurry up. The men are laying on a little show for me and I don't want to disappoint them."

ᡃᢦᠵᡃ

The show was presented in the main hall of the chateau. A small stage had been rigged at one end with some makeshift curtains. Rommel, Hofer and the regimental officers sat down in chairs provided at the front; the men stood in the hall behind them or sat on the grand staircase.

A young corporal came on, bowed and sat down at the grand piano and played a selection of light music. There was polite applause. Then he moved into the song of the Fallschirmjäger, the paratroopers' own song, sung everywhere from Stalingrad to North Africa. The curtains parted to reveal the regimental choir singing lustily. There was a cheer from the back of the hall and everyone started to join in, including the officers. Without pause, the choir moved straight into several choruses of *We March Against England*, an unfortunate choice, Rommel told himself. It was interesting to note that no one tried singing the *Horst Wessel*. The curtain came down to a storm of cheering and several instrumentalists came on, grouped themselves around the pianist and played two or three jazz numbers. When they were finished, the lights went down and there was a pause.

"What's happening?" Rommel demanded.

"Wait and see, Herr Field Marshal. Something special, I assure you."

The pianist started to play the song that was most popular of all with the German forces, *Lili Marlene*. The curtains parted to reveal only a pool of light on a stool in the center of the stage from a crude spotlight. Suddenly, Marlene Dietrich stepped into the light straight out of *Blue Angel*, or so it seemed. Top hat, black stockings and suspenders. She sat on the stool to a chorus of wolf whistles from the men and then she started to sing *Lili Marlene*, and that haunting, bittersweet melody reduced the audience to total silence.

A man, of course, Rommel could see that, but a brilliant impersonation and he joined in the applause enthusiastically. "Who on earth is that?" he asked Colonel Halder.

"Our orderly room corporal, Berger. Apparently he used to be some sort of cabaret performer."

"Brilliant," Rommel said. "Is there more?"

"Oh, yes, Herr Field Marshal. Something very special."

The instrumentalists returned and the choir joined them in a few more numbers. There was another pause when they departed and then a steady, muted drum roll. The curtain rose to reveal subdued lighting. As the choir started to sing the song of the Afrika Korps from the side of the stage, Rommel walked on. And it was quite unmistakably he. The cap with the desert goggles, the white scarf carelessly knotted at the neck, the old leather greatcoat, the field marshal's baton in one gloved hand, the other arrogantly on the hip. The voice, when he spoke, was perfect as he delivered a few lines of his famous battlefield speech before El Alamein.

"I know I haven't offered you much. Sand, heat and scorpions, but we've shared them together. One more push and it's Cairo, and if we fail . . . well, we tried—together."

There was total silence from the body of the hall as Colonel Halder glanced anxiously at Rommel. "Field Marshal, I hope you're not offended."

"Offended? I think he's marvelous," Rommel said and jumped to his feet. "Bravo!" he called and started to clap and behind him, the entire audience joined in with the chorus of the Afrika Korps song, cheering wildly.

In the makeshift dressing room next to the kitchen, Erich Berger slumped into a chair and stared at himself in the mirror. His heart was beating and he was sweating. A hell of a thing for any actor to perform in front of the man he was taking off, and such a man. A name to conjure with. The most popular soldier in Germany.

"Not bad, Heini," he said softly. "Mazel tov." He took a bottle of schnapps from the drawer, drew the cork and swallowed some.

A Yiddish phrase on the lips of a corporal in a German Fallschirmjäger regiment might have seemed strange to anyone who had overhead. His secret was that he wasn't Erich Berger at all, but Heini Baum, Jewish actor and cabaret performer from Berlin and proud of it.

His story was surprisingly simple. He had performed with success in cabarets all over Europe. He had never married. To be frank, his inclinations ran more toward men than women. He had persisted in living in Berlin, even as the Nazis came to power, because his aging parents had always lived there and would not believe that anything terrible could ever happen. Which it did, of course, though not for a long time. As an entertainer, Baum was of use to the Reich. He still had to wear his Star of David on his coat, but a series of special permits kept him afloat and his parents with him, while all around them their friends were taken away.

And then there was the fateful night in 1940 when he had arrived at the end of his street, coming home from cabaret, in time to see the Gestapo taking his mother and father from their house. He had turned and run, like the coward he was, pausing only in a side street to tear the Star of David from his coat. He was forty-four years of age and looked ten years younger on a good day. Nowhere to go, for his papers told the world he was a Jew.

So, he'd caught a train to Kiel with the wild idea that he might be able to get a ship from there to somewhere—anywhere. He'd arrived just after one of the first of the devastating RAF raids on that city, had stumbled through the chaos and flames of the city center, searching for shelter as the RAF came back for a second go. Lurching down into a cellar, he'd found a man and a woman and a twelve-year-old girl dead, all from the same family he learned when he examined their identity cards. Erich Berger, his wife and daughter. And one thing more. In Berger's pocket were his call-up papers, ordering him to report the following week.

What better hiding place could a Jew who was afraid to be a Jew find? Sure, he was ten years older than Berger, but it wouldn't show. To change the photos on the two identity cards was simple enough so that the body he dragged out to leave in the rubble of the street to be found later was that of Heini Baum, Jew of Berlin. It had been necessary to obliterate most of the dead man's face with a brick, just to help things along, but after what he'd been through that part was easy.

How ironic that it was the paratroops he'd been inducted into. He'd been everywhere. Crete, Stalingrad, North Africa, a nice flashy hero in his Luftwaffe blouse and baggy paratroopers' pants and jump boots, with the Iron Cross Second and First Class to prove it. He took another pull at the schnapps bottle, and behind him the door opened and Rommel, Colonel Halder and Hofer entered.

It was midnight and Hugh Kelso had never been happier, up at Cape Cod at the summer bungalow, sitting on the veranda in the swing seat, reading a book, a cool glass to his hand and Jane, his wife, was calling, on her way up from the beach, her face shaded by a sun hat, the good legs tanned under the old cotton dress, and the girls in swimming suits and carrying buckets and spades, voices faint on the warm afternoon air. Everyone so happy. So very happy. he didn't feel cold anymore, didn't really feel anything. He reached out to take Jane's hand as she came up the steps to the veranda and the voices faded and he came awake, shaking all over.

It was pitch dark and the sea wasn't as rough, and yet he seemed to be moving very fast. He pulled down the zip on the flap with stiff fingers and peered out. Only a slight phosphorescence as the water turned over and a vast darkness. His eyes were weary, sore from the salt water. For a wild moment he thought he saw a light out there. He shook his head, closed then opened his eyes again. A mistake, of course. Only the never-ending night. He zipped up the flap, lay back and closed his eyes, trying to think of Jane and his two daughters. Perhaps they would come back again?

Although he didn't know it, he had already drifted something like seventy miles since leaving Lyme Bay on the Devon coast and his eyes had not deceived him. What he had just seen through the darkness was a momentary flash of light as a sentry at the German guard post on Pleinmont Point on the southwest corner of the island of Guernsey had opened a door to go out on duty. To the southeast, perhaps thirty miles away, was Jersey, the largest of the Channel Islands. It was in this general direction that the freshening wind bore him as he slept on.

Rommel leaned on the mantelpiece and stirred the fire with his boot. "So, the others would like me to talk with von Stulpnagel and Falkenhausen?"

"Yes, Herr Field Marshal," Hofer said. "But as you point out, one must take things very carefully at the moment. For such a meeting, secrecy would be essential."

"And opportunity," Rommel said. "Secrecy and opportunity." The clock on the mantelpiece chimed twice and he laughed. "Two o'clock in the morning. The best time for crazy ideas."

"What are you suggesting, Herr Field Marshal?"

"Quite simple, really. What is it now, Saturday? What if we arranged a meeting next week at some agreed rendezvous with von Stulpnagel and Falkenhausen while I was actually supposed to be somewhere else? Jersey, for example?"

"The Channel Islands?" Hofer looked bewildered.

"The Führer himself suggested not two months ago that I inspect the fortifications there. You know my feelings about the military importance of the islands. The Allies will never attempt a landing. It would cause too many civilian casualties. British civilian casualties, I might add."

"And yet they tie up the 319 Infantry Division," Hofer said. "Six thousand troops in Jersey alone. Ten thousand service personnel in all, if you include Luftwaffe and Navy people."

"And yet we've poured so much into them, Konrad, because the Führer wants to hang onto the only piece of British territory we've ever occupied. The strongest fortifications in the world. The same number of strongpoints and batteries as we have to defend the entire European coast from Dieppe to St. Nazaire." He turned and smiled. "The Führer is right. As commander of the Atlantic Wall, I should certainly inspect such an important part of it."

Hofer nodded. "I see that, Herr Field Marshal, but what I don't see is how you can be in two places at once. Meeting with Falkenhausen and Stulpnagel in France and inspecting fortifications in Jersey."

"But you saw me in two places earlier this evening," Rommel said calmly, "both in the audience and on stage at the same time."

The room was so quiet that Hofer could hear the clock ticking. "My God," he whispered. "Are you serious?"

"Why not? Friend Berger even fooled me when he came on stage. The voice, the appearance."

"But would he be intelligent enough to carry it off? There are so many things he wouldn't know how to handle. I mean, being a Field Marshal is rather different from being an orderly room clerk," Hofer said.

"He seems intelligent enough to me," Rommel told him. "He's obviously talented and a brave soldier to boot. Iron Cross First and Second Class. And you mustn't forget one important thing."

"What's that, Herr Field Marshal?"

"He'd have you at his shoulder every step of the way to keep him straight." Suddenly Rommel sounded impatient. "Where's your enthusiasm, Konrad? If you're that worried, I'll give you a few days to prepare him. Let's see, it's Saturday now. How about descending on Jersey next Friday. I'm only thinking of thirty-six hours or so. Back in France on Saturday night or Sunday at the latest. If Berger can't carry it off for that length of time, I'll eat my hat."

"Very well, Herr Field Marshal. I'll notify the Channel Islands that you'll be arriving next Friday."

"No, you won't," Rommel said. "We box more cleverly than that. Who's the commander-in-chief?"

"Major General Count von Schmettow. His headquarters are in Guernsey."

"I've met him," Rommel said. "Good officer."

"With a reputation for being pro-English, which didn't do him any good in some quarters," Hofer said.

"On the other hand, the fact that he's Field Marshall von Rundstedt's nephew certainly helped there. Who's military commander in Jersey?"

"I'll check." Hofer took a file from his briefcase and worked his way down a unit situation list. "Yes, here we are. Colonel Heine is military commander."

"And civil administration?"

"The important people there are Colonel Baron von Aufsess and Captain Heider."

"And the inhabitants themselves? Who are their representatives?"

"There's an organization called the Superior Council of the States of Jersey. The president is the bailiff of the island. A man called Alexander Coutanche."

"Good," said Rommel. "This is what we do. Send General von Schmettow a signal ordering him to hold a coordinating meeting in Guernsey to consider the implications for the islands of the invasion of France threatened this summer."

"And you want them all there?"

"Oh, yes. Military commander Jersey, the civil affairs people, the bailiff and his lot, and whoever's in charge of the Navy and Luftwaffe contingents in the islands."

"Which will leave only junior officers in command."

"Exactly."

"There's not too much flying in and out of the Channel Islands these days. The RAF are far too active in that area. It's usual to travel between the islands by sea and at night."

"I know," Rommel said. "I've taken advice on that point from Naval Headquarters in Cherbourg. Tell von Schmettow to call his meeting for next Saturday. In the circumstances they must travel either Thursday night or in the early hours of Friday to make sure they get there. I'll fly in on Friday morning in the Storch."

"A risky flight, Herr Field Marshal."

"For you, Konrad, and Berger, of course, not for me." Rommel smiled with a kind of ruthless charm. "The first thing they'll know about my arrival is when you ask the tower for permission to land at the airfield."

"And what will von Schmettow think?"

"That the whole thing has been a deliberate ploy so that I can make a snap inspection of the military situation in the island and its defenses."

"That's really rather clever," Hofer said.

"Yes, I think it is." Rommel started to unbutton his tunic. "In the meantime, I'll meet with Falkenhausen and Stulpnagel at some quiet spot and get on with it." He yawned. "I think I'll go to bed. See that signal goes to von Schmettow in Guernsey tomorrow. Oh, and speak to Colonel Halder first thing in the morning. Tell him I'm much taken with Corporal Berger and want to borrow him for a while. I don't think he'll make any difficulties."

"I doubt it, Herr Field Marshal," Hofer said. "Sleep well," and he went out.

Dougal Munro slept on a small military bed in the corner of his office at Baker Street that night. It was about three o'clock in the morning when Jack Carter shook him gently awake. Munro opened his eyes instantly and sat up. "What is it?"

"Latest lists from Slapton, sir. You asked to see them. Still over a hundred bodies missing."

"And no sign of Kelso?"

"I'm afraid not. General Montgomery isn't too happy, but he has had an assurance from the Navy that the E-boats couldn't have picked survivors up. They were too far away.''

''The trouble with life, Jack, is that the moment someone tells you something is impossible, someone else promptly proves that it isn't. What time is first light?''

''Just before six. That should make a big difference to the final search.''

''Order a car for eight o'clock. We'll take a run down to Slapton and see for ourselves.''

''Very well, sir. Are you going back to sleep?''

''No, I don't think so.'' Munro stood up and stretched. ''Think I'll catch up on some paperwork. No peace for the wicked in this life, Jack.''

At six o'clock on that same morning, Kelso came awake from a strange dream in which some primeval creature was calling to him from a great distance. He was very, very cold, feet and hands numb, and yet his face burned and there was sweat on his forehead.

He unzipped the flap and peered out into the gray light of dawn, not that there was anything much to see for he was shrouded in a sea fog of considerable density. Somewhere in the distance, the beast called again, only now he recognized it for what it was—a foghorn. Although he didn't know it, it was the Corbiere Light on the tip of the southernmost coast of Jersey, already behind him as the current swept him along. He sensed land, could almost smell it and, for a little while, came back to life again.

He could hear waves breaking on an unseen shore, and then the wind tore a hole in the curtain and he glimpsed cliffs, concrete gun emplacements on top. The place, although it meant nothing to Kelso, was Noirmont Point, and as the sea fog dropped back into place, the current carried him into St. Aubin's Bay, close inshore.

There were waves taking him in, strange, twisting currents carrying him round. At one side, a wave broke sending spray high in the air, and all around him was white foam, rocks showing through. And then there was a voice, high and clear, and the fog rolled away to reveal a small beach, rocks climbing steeply to a pine wood above. There was someone there, a man running along the shore, in woolen cap, heavy reefer coat and rubber boots.

The life raft slewed broadside in the surf, lifted high and smashed against rocks, pitching Kelso headfirst through the flap into the water. he tried to stand up, his scream as his right leg collapsed under him drowned by the roaring of the surf, and then the man was knee-deep in water, holding him. It was only then that he realized it was a woman.

''All right, I've got you. Just hang on.''

"Leg," he mumbled. "Leg broken."

He wasn't sure what happened after that, and he came to in the shelter of some rocks. The woman was dragging the landing craft out of the water. When he tried to sit up, she turned and came toward him. Kelso said as she knelt down, "Where am I, France?"

"No," she said. "Jersey."

He closed his eyes for a moment and shivered. "You're British, then?"

"I should hope so. The last I heard of my husband, he was a major in the Tanks Corps serving in the Western Desert. My name's Helen de Ville."

"Colonel Hugh Kelso."

"American Air Force, I suppose? Where did your plane come down?"

"It didn't. I'm an army officer."

"An army officer? But that doesn't make sense. Where on earth have you come from?"

"England. I'm a survivor of a ship that was torpedoed in Lyme Bay." He groaned suddenly as pain knifed through his leg and almost lost his senses.

She opened his torn trouser leg and frowned. "That's terrible. You'll have to go to hospital."

"Will that mean Germans?"

"I'm afraid so."

He clutched at the front of her reefer coat. "No—no Germans."

She eased him back down. "Just lie still. I'm going to leave you for a little while. I'm going to need a cart."

"Okay," he said. "But no Germans. They mustn't get their hands on me. You must promise. If you can't do that, then you must kill me. See, there's a Browning pistol here."

He plucked at it and she leaned over him, face set, and took the pistol from its holster on his left thigh. "You're not going to die and the Jerries aren't going to have you either—that's the only promise I'm prepared to give. Now wait for me."

She slipped the pistol into her pocket, turned and hurried away. He lay there on that fog-shrouded shore, trying to get his bearings, and then the leg started to hurt again and he remembered the morphine in the emergency kit. He began to crawl toward the life raft. That, of course, was very definitely the final straw, and he plunged into darkness.

4

HELEN DE VILLE LEFT THE cart track which was the usual way down to the beach and took a shortcut, scrambling up the steep hillside through the pine trees. She was strong and wiry, not surprising after four years of enemy occupation and the food restrictions that had caused her to lose nearly thirty pounds in weight. She often joked that it had given her back the figure she'd enjoyed at eighteen, an unlooked-for bonus at forty-two. And like most people, the lack of a car and a public transport system meant she was used to walking many miles each week.

She stood at the edge of the trees and looked across at the house. De Ville Place was not one of the largest manors on the island. It had been once in days of family glory, but a disastrous fire at the end of the nineteenth century had destroyed one entire wing. It was very old, constructed of Jersey granite weathered by the years. There were rows of French windows at the front on either side of the entrance, a granite wall dividing the house from a courtyard at one side.

She paused, taking her time, for there was an old Morris sedan parked in the courtyard, one of those requisitioned by the enemy. For two years now she'd had German naval officers billeted on her. They came and went, of course, sometimes staying only a night or two when E-boats of the 5th Schnellboote Flotilla came over from Guernsey.

Mostly they were regulars, young officers serving with various naval units based in Jersey. The war took its toll. There were often engagements with British MTBs in the area of the Channel Islands, and the RAF frequently attacked convoys to Granville, St. Malo and Cherbourg, even when they made a night run. Men died, but some survived. As she started across the lawn, the door opened and one of them came out.

He wore a white sweater, old reefer coat and seaboots and carried a duffel bag in one hand. The face beneath the salt-stained naval cap was good-humored and recklessly handsome. A bravo, this one, straight out of the sixteenth century, who wore a white top to his cap, usually an affectation of German U-boat commanders, but then Lieutenant Guido Orsini was a law unto himself, an Italian on secondment to the German Navy, trapped in the wrong place at entirely the wrong time when the Italian government had capitulated. Helen de Ville had long since given up pretending that she felt anything but considerable affection for him.

"Morning, Guido."

"Helen, cara mia." He blew her a kiss. "I'm the last, as usual."

"Where to today?"

"Granville. Should be fun in this fog. On the other hand, it keeps the Tommies at home. Back tomorrow. Do you want to go into St. Helier? Can I give you a lift?"

"No thanks. I'm looking for Sean."

"I saw the good General not ten minutes ago coming out of the south barn with a felling axe and walking down toward his cottage. See you tomorrow. I must fly. Ciao, cara."

He went through the small gate to the courtyard. A moment later, she heard the Morris start up and drive away. She crossed the courtyard herself, went through a field gate and ran along the track through trees. Sean Gallagher's cottage stood by a stream in a hollow. She could see him now in old corduroy pants and riding boots, the sleeves of the checked shirt rolled up above muscular arms as he split logs.

"Sean!" she called and stumbled almost falling.

He lowered the axe and turned, pushing a lock of reddish brown hair from his eyes as he looked toward her. He dropped the axe and reached out to catch her as she almost fell again.

Sean Martin Gallagher was fifty-two and, as an Irish citizen, officially neutral in this war. He had been born in Dublin in 1892, his father a professor of surgery at Trinity College, a man who had taken no interest in women until, in his fiftieth year during a professional visit to Jersey, he had met a young nurse called Ruth le Brocq. He'd married her within a month and taken her back to Dublin.

She'd died in childbirth the following year and the boy Sean grew up spending the long summers each year in Jersey with his grandparents, the rest of the time in Dublin with his father. Sean's ambition was to be a writer, and he'd taken a degree in literature at his father's university, Trinity College. The exigencies of life made him a soldier, for as he finished college the First World War started.

He'd joined the Irish Fusiliers, a regiment that many Jerseymen served in, and by 1918 was a very old twenty-six. A major, twice wounded, and with an MC for gallantry on the Somme. As he used to say, any real experience of war came after that, fighting with the IRA in Ireland under Michael Collins' leadership, as commander of a flying column in County Mayo.

The treaty with the British government which had ended the conflict in 1922 had only proved a prelude to a bloody and vicious civil war between those elements of the IRA who refused to accept the treaty and those who chose to fight for the Irish Free State government under Collins. Sean Gallagher had chosen the Free State and found himself a general at the age of thirty, sweeping through the west of Ireland, ruthlessly hunting down old comrades.

Afterward, sick of killing, he'd traveled the world, living on money left to him by his father, writing the odd novel when he had a mind, finally settling in Jersey in 1930. Ralph de Ville had been a boyhood friend, and Helen he had loved desperately and hopelessly from the first moment they had met. His home in St. Lawrence, deep in the country, had been requisitioned by the Germans in 1940. Helen, with Ralph away serving with the British Army, needed a strong right arm, which explained his presence at the dower cottage on the estate. And he still loved her, of course, and still quite hopelessly.

The old cart had seen better days and the horse was considerably leaner than it should have been as they negotiated the track down to the beach, Sean Gallagher leading the horse, Helen at his side.

"If this goes wrong," he said gravely. "If they find out you're helping this man, it won't just be a prison sentence. It could mean a firing squad or one of those concentration camps they're talking about."

"And what about you?"

"Jesus, woman, I'm a neutral, don't I keep telling you that?" He smiled mischievously, the gray eyes full of humor. "If they want to keep that old bastard, de Valera, sweet back in Dublin, they've got to handle me with dress gloves. Mind you, after the way I chased the arse off him all over Ireland in the Civil War, he might welcome the news that they want to shoot me."

She burst out laughing. "I love you, Sean Gallagher. You always make me feel good at the worst times." She put an arm around the small, lean man's shoulders and kissed him on the cheek.

"As a brother," he said. "You love me as a brother, as you often remind me, so keep your mad passion in your pocket, woman, and concentrate. Colonel Hugh Kelso, he said, an American army officer torpedoed off Devon?"

"That's right."

"And what was all that about how the Germans mustn't get their hands on him?"

"I don't know. He was half out of his mind and his leg's in a terrible state, but at the suggestion he might have to go to hospital he went crazy.

Said it would be better if I shot him.''

"A fine old mess from the sound of it,'' Gallagher said, and led the horse down onto the fog-shrouded beach.

It was very quiet, the sea calm, so quiet that they could hear the whistle of the German military train from across the bay as it ran along the front from St. Helier to Millbrook.

Hugh Kelso lay face-down on the sand unconscious. Sean Gallagher turned him over gently and examined the leg. He gave a low whistle. "He needs a surgeon, this lad. I'll get him in the cart while he's still out. You gather as much driftwood as you can and hurry.''

She ran along the beach and he lifted Kelso up, taking his weight easily, for he was surprisingly strong for a small man. Kelso groaned but stayed out, and the Irishman eased him onto the sacks in the cart and draped a few across him.

He turned as Helen came back with an armful of wood.

"Cover him with that while I see to the life raft.''

It was still bumping around in the shallows, and he waded into the water and pulled it up on the sand. He looked inside, removed the emergency kit, then took out a spring-blade gutting knife and slashed at the skin of the life raft fiercely. As air rushed out, it crumpled and he rolled it up and carried it to the cart, shoving it onto the rack underneath.

Helen arrived with another armful of wood which she put in the back with the rest. "Will that do?''

"I think so. I'll stop by the paddock and we'll put the life raft down the old well shaft. But let's get moving.''

They started up the track, Helen sitting on the shaft of the cart, Sean leading the horse. Suddenly there was laughter up ahead and a dog barked. The Irishman paused and took his time over lighting one of the vile French cigarettes that he smoked. "Nothing to worry about, I'll handle it,'' he told her.

The Alsatian arrived first, a splendid animal which barked once, then recognized Gallagher as an old friend, and licked his hand. Two German soldiers in field gray and helmets, rifles over their shoulders, came next. "Guten morgen, Herr General,'' they both called eagerly.

"And good morning to you two daft buggers.'' Gallagher's smile was his friendliest as he led the horse on.

"Sean, you're quite mad,'' she hissed.

"Not at all. Neither of those two lads speak a word of English. It might have been fun if they'd looked under the cart though.''

"Where are we going?'' she demanded. "There's no one at the Place at the moment.''

It was always referred to in that way, never as a house.

"Isn't Mrs. Vibert in?''

"I gave her the day off. Remember that niece of hers had a new baby last week."

"Naughty girl," Gallagher said. "And her man away serving in the British Army. I wonder what he'll think when he comes home and finds a bouncing boy with blue eyes and blond hair called Fritz."

"Don't be cruel, Sean. She's not a bad girl. A little weak perhaps. People get lonely."

"Do you tell me?" Gallagher laughed. "I haven't exactly noticed you chasing me around the barn this week."

"Be sensible," she said. "Now where do we take him? There's the Chamber."

During the English Civil War, Charles de Ville, the Seigneur of the manor at that time, had espoused the Royalist cause. He'd had a room constructed in the roof with a secret staircase from the master bedroom known to the family over the years as the Chamber. It had saved his life during the time of Cromwell's rule when he was sought as a traitor.

"No, too awkward at the moment. He needs help and quickly. We'll take him to my cottage first."

"And what about a doctor?"

"George Hamilton. Who else could you trust? Now hang on while I get this life raft down the well."

He tugged it out and moved into the trees. She sat there, aware of her uneven breathing in the silence of the wood. Behind her, under the sacking and the driftwood, Hugh Kelso groaned and stirred.

At Slapton Sands just before noon, the tide turned and a few more bodies came in. Dougal Munro and Carter sat in the lee of a sand dune and had an early lunch of sandwiches and shared a bottle of beer. Soldiers tramped along the shoreline, occasionally venturing into the water at some officer's command to pull in another body. There were already about thirty laid out on the beach.

Munro said, "Someone once said the first casualty when war comes is truth."

"I know exactly what you mean, sir," Carter said.

A young American officer approached and saluted. "The beach is cleared of new arrivals at the moment, sir. Thirty-three since dawn. No sign of Colonel Kelso." He hesitated. "Does the Brigadier wish to view the burial arrangements? It's not too far."

"No thank you," Munro told him. "I think I can manage without that."

The officer saluted and walked away. Munro got up and helped Carter to his feet. "Come on, Jack. Nothing we can do here."

"All right, sir."

Carter balanced on his walking stick and Munro stood, hands in pockets, and looked out to sea. He shivered suddenly. "Anything wrong, sir?" Carter asked.

"Someone just walked over my grave, Jack. To be honest, I've got a bad feeling about this. A very bad feeling. Come on, let's get back to London," and he turned and walked away along the beach.

"So, Berger, you understand what I am saying to you?" Konrad Hofer demanded.

Heini Baum stood rigidly at attention in front of the desk in the office which the CO had been happy to lend to the field marshal at Campeaux. He tried to ignore the fact that Rommel stood at the window looking out into the garden.

"I'm not sure, Herr Major. I think so."

Rommel turned. "Don't be stupid, Berger. You're an intelligent man, I can see that, and a brave one." He tapped the Iron Cross First Class with the tip of his crop and the band around the left sleeve with the Gothic lettering. "The Afrika Korps cuff-title, I see. So, we are old comrades. Were you at Alamein?"

"No, Field Marshal. Wounded at Tobruk."

"Good. I'm a plain man so listen carefully. You did a wonderful impersonation of me last night, in both appearance and voice. Very professional."

"Thank you."

"Now I require a second performance. On Friday, you will fly to Jersey for the weekend accompanied by Major Hofer. You think you could fool them in Jersey for that long, Berger? King for a day? Would you like that?"

Baum smiled. "Actually, I think I would, sir."

Rommel said to Hofer, "There you are. Sensible and intelligent, just as I told you. Now make the arrangements, Konrad, and let's get out of here."

The cottage was built in the same kind of granite as the house. There was one large living room with a beamed ceiling and a dining table and half-a-dozen chairs in a window alcove. The kitchen was on the other side of the hall. Upstairs, there was one large bedroom, a storeroom and a bathroom.

Rather than negotiate the stairs, Gallagher had laid Kelso out on a

long comfortable sofa in the living room. The American was still unconscious, and Gallagher found his wallet and opened it. There was his
security card with photo, some snaps of a woman and two young girls,
obviously his family, and a couple of letters which were so immediately
personal that Gallagher folded them up again. He could hear Helen's
voice from the kitchen as she spoke on the telephone. Kelso opened his
eyes, stared blankly at him and then noticed the wallet in Gallagher's
hand.

"Who are you?" He grabbed at it weakly. "Give it back to me."

Helen came in and sat on the sofa and put a hand on his forehead.
"It's all right. Just be still. You're burning up with fever. Remember
me, Helen de Ville?"

He nodded slowly. "The woman on the beach."

"This is a friend, General Sean Gallagher."

"I was just checking his papers," Gallagher told her. "The identity
card is a little damp. I'll leave it out to dry."

She said to Kelso, "Do you remember where you are?"

"Jersey." He managed a ghastly smile. "Don't worry. I'm not quite
out of my mind yet. I can think straight if I concentrate."

"All right, then, listen to me," Sean Gallagher said. "Your leg is very
bad indeed. You need hospital and a good surgeon."

Kelso shook his head. "Not possible. As I told this lady earlier, no
Germans. It would be better to shoot me than let them get their hands
on me."

"Why?" Sean Gallagher demanded bluntly.

"She called you General. Is that true?"

"I was once in the Irish Army and I served with the Brits in the last
war. Does that make a difference?"

"Perhaps."

"All right, what's your unit?"

"Engineers—assault engineers, to be precise. We lead the way in
beach landings."

Sean Gallagher saw it all. "Is this something to do with the invasion?"

Kelso nodded. "It's coming soon."

"Sure and we all know that," Gallagher said.

"Yes, but I know where and I know when. If the Germans could
squeeze that out of me, can you imagine what it would mean? All their
troops concentrated in the right place. We'd never get off the beach."

He was extremely agitated, sweat on his forehead. Helen soothed him,
easing him down. "It's all right, I promise you."

"Is George Hamilton coming?" Gallagher asked.

"He was out. I left a message with his housekeeper that you wanted
to see him urgently. I said you'd cut your leg and thought it needed a
stitch or two."

"Who's Hamilton?" Kelso demanded.

"A doctor," Helen said. "And a good friend. He'll be here soon to see to that leg of yours."

Kelso was shaking again as the fever took hold. "More important things to think of at the moment. You must speak to your resistance people here. Tell them to get on the radio as soon as possible and notify Intelligence in London that I'm here. They'll have to try to get me out."

"But there is no resistance movement in Jersey," Helen said. "I mean, there's a hell of a lot of people who don't care to be occupied and make life as awkward for the enemy as they can, but we don't have anything like the French Resistance, if that's what you mean."

Kelso stared at her in astonishment and Gallagher said, "This island is approximately ten miles by five. There are something like forty-five thousand civilians. A good-size market town, that's all. How long do you think a resistance movement would last here? No mountains to run to, nowhere to take refuge. Nowhere to go, in fact."

Kelso seemed to have difficulty in taking it in. "So, there's no resistance movement. No radio?"

"No links with London at all," Gallagher told him.

"Then what about France?" Kelso asked desperately. "Granville, St. Malo. They're only a few hours away across the water, aren't they? There must be a local unit of the French Resistance in those places."

There was a significant pause, then Helen turned to Gallagher. "Savary could speak to the right people in Granville. He knows who they are and so do you."

"True."

"Guido was leaving as I came up from the beach," she said. "He told me they were trying for Granville this afternoon. Taking advantage of the fog." She glanced at her watch. "They won't have the tide until noon. You could take the van. There are those sacks of potatoes to go into St. Helier for the troops' supply depot and the market."

"All right, you've convinced me," Gallagher said. "But if I know Savary, he won't want any of this, not in his head. That means writing it down, which is taking one hell of a chance."

"We don't have any choice, Sean," she said simply.

"No, I suppose you're right." Gallagher laughed. "The things I do for England. Look after our friend here. I'll be back as soon as I can."

As he reached the door she called, "And Sean?"

He turned. "Yes?"

"Don't forget to drive on the right-hand side of the road."

❦

It was an old joke, but not without a certain amount of truth. One of the first things the German forces had done on occupying Jersey was to change the traffic flow from the left- to the right-hand side of the road. After four years, Gallagher still couldn't get used to it, not that he drove very often. They only had the old Ford van as a special dispensation because the de Ville farmlands supplied various crops for the use of the German forces. The size of the petrol ration meant the van could be used only two or three times a week anyway. Gallagher stretched it by coasting down the hills with the engine off, and there was always a little black-market petrol available if you knew the right people.

He drove down through the tiny picturesque town of St. Aubin and followed the curve of the bay to Bel Royal, St. Helier in the distance. He passed a number of gun emplacements with a few troops in evidence, but Victoria Avenue was deserted on the run into town. One of the French trains the Germans had brought over passed him on its way to Millbrook, the only sign of activity until he reached the Grand Hotel. He checked his watch. It was just before eleven. Plenty of time to catch Savary before the Victor Hugo left for Granville, so he turned left into Gloucester Street and made his way to the market.

There weren't too many people about, mainly because of the weather. The scarlet and black Nazi flag with its swastika on the pole above the Town Hall entrance hung limply in the damp air. The German for Town Hall is Rathaus. It was, therefore, understandable that the place was now known as the Rat House by the local inhabitants.

He parked outside the market in Beresford Street. It was almost deserted, just a handful of shoppers and a sprinkling of German soldiers. The market itself was officially closed, open for only two hours on a Saturday afternoon. There would be enough people in evidence then, desperately hoping for fresh produce.

Gallagher got two sacks of potatoes from the van, kicked open the gate and went inside. Most of the stalls in the old Victorian Market were empty, but there were one or two people about. He made straight for a stall on the far side where a large genial man in heavy sweater and cloth cap was arranging turnips in neat rows under a sign *D. Chevalier*.

"So, it's swedes today?" Gallagher said as he arrived.

"Good for you, General," Chevalier said.

"Do you tell me? Mrs. Vibert gave me swede jam for breakfast the other day." Gallagher shuddered. "I can still taste it. Two sacks of spuds for you here."

Chevalier's eyes lit up. "I knew you wouldn't let me down, General. Let's have them in the back."

Gallagher dragged them into the room at the rear, and Chevalier opened a cupboard and took out an old canvas duffel bag. "Four loaves of white bread."

"Jesus," Gallagher said. "Who did you kill to get those?"

"A quarter pound of China tea and a leg of pork. Okay?"

"Nice to do business with you," Gallagher told him. "See you next week."

His next stop was at the troop supply depot in Wesley Street. It had originally been a garage and there were half-a-dozen trucks parked in there. There wasn't much happening, but a burly Feldwebel called Klinger was sitting in the glass office eating a sandwich. He waved, opened the door and came down the steps.

"Herr General," he said genially.

"God, Hans, but you do well for yourself," Gallagher said in excellent German and prodded the ample stomach.

Klinger smiled. "A man must live. We are both old soldiers, Herr General. We understand each other. You have something for me?"

"Two sacks of potatoes for the official list."

"And?"

"Another sack for you, if you're interested."

"And in exchange?"

"Petrol."

The German nodded. "One five-gallon can."

"Two five-gallon cans," Gallagher said.

"General." Klinger turned to a row of British Army issue petrol cans, picked two up and brought them to the van. "What if I turned you in? You're so unreasonable."

"Prison for me and a holiday for you," Gallagher said. "They say the Russian Front's lovely at this time of the year."

"As always, a practical man." Klinger pulled the three sacks of potatoes out of the van. "One of these days a patrol is going to stop you for a fuel check, and they'll discover your petrol is the wrong color."

"Ah, but I'm a magician, my friend, didn't I tell you that?" and Gallagher drove away.

Military petrol was dyed red, the ration for agricultural use was green, and doctors enjoyed a pink variety. What Klinger hadn't discovered was that it was a simple matter to remove the dye by straining the petrol through the filter of the gas mask issued to the general public at the beginning of the war. A little green dye added afterward turned military petrol to the agricultural variety very quickly indeed.

Survival was what it was all about. This was an old island, and the Le Brocq half of him was fiercely proud of that. Over the centuries, the island had endured many things. As he passed the Pomme d'Or Hotel, German Naval Headquarters, he looked up at the Nazi flag hanging above the entrance and said softly, "And we'll still be here when you bastards are long gone."

5

GALLAGHER PARKED THE VAN AT the weighbridge and walked along the
Albert Pier, going up the steps to the top section. He paused to light one
of his French cigarettes and looked out across the bay. The fog had
thinned just a little and Elizabeth Castle, on its island, looked strange
and mysterious, like something out of a fairy story. Walter Raleigh had
once ruled there as governor. Now Germans with concrete fortifications
and gun emplacements up on top.

He looked down into the harbor. As always it was a hive of activity. The Germans used Rhine barges, among other vessels, to carry
supplies to the Channel Islands. There were several moored on the far
side at the New North Quay. There were a number of craft of various
kinds from the 2 Vorpostenbootsflotille and two M40 Klasse mine-
sweepers from the 24th Minesweeper Flotilla. Several cargo vessels,
mostly coasters, among them the SS *Victor Hugo*, were moored
against the Albert Pier.

Built in 1920 by Ferguson Brothers in Glasgow for a French firm
engaged in the coastal trade, she had definitely seen better days. Her
single smokestack was punctured in several places by cannon shell from
RAF Beaufighters in an attack on one of the night convoys from Granville two weeks previously. Savary was the master with a crew of ten
Frenchmen. The antiaircraft defenses consisted of two machine guns and
a Bofors gun, manned by seven German naval ratings commanded by
Guido Orsini.

Gallagher could see him now on the bridge, leaning on the rail, and
called in English, "Heh, Guido? Is Savary about?"

Guido cupped his hands. "In the café."

The hut farther along the pier which served as a café was not busy,
four French seamen playing cards at one table, three German sailors
at another. Robert Savary, a large, bearded man in a reefer coat and
cloth cap, a greasy scarf knotted at his neck, sat on his own at a table
next to the window, smoking a cigarette, a bowl of coffee in front of
him.

"Robert, how goes it?" Gallagher demanded in French and sat
down.

"Unusual to see you down here, Mon General, which means you want something."

"Ah, you cunning old peasant." Gallagher passed an envelope under the table. "There, have you got that?"

"What is it?"

"Just put it in your pocket and don't ask questions. When you get to Granville, there's a café in the walled city called Sophie's. You know it?"

Savary was already beginning to turn pale. "Yes, of course I do."

"You know the good Sophie Cresson well and her husband Gerard?"

"I've met them." Savary tried to give him the envelope back under the table.

"Then you'll know that their business is terrorism carried to as extreme a degree as possible. They not only shoot the Boche, they also like to make an example of collaborators, isn't that the colorful phrase? So if I were you, I'd be sensible. Take the letter. Needless to say, don't read it. If you do, you'll probably never sleep again. Just give it to Sophie with my love. I'm sure she'll have a message for me, which you'll let me have as soon as you're back."

"Damn you, General," Savary muttered and put the envelope in his pocket.

"The Devil took care of that long ago. Don't worry. You've nothing to worry about. Guido Orsini's a good lad."

"The Count?" Savary shrugged. "Flashy Italian pimp. I hate aristocrats."

"No Fascist, that one, and he's probably got less time for Hitler than you have. Have you any decent cigarettes in your bag? I'm going crazy smoking that filthy tobacco they've been importing for the official ration lately."

Savary looked cunning. "Not really. Only a few Gitanes."

"Only, the man says." Gallagher groaned aloud. "All right, I'll take two hundred."

"And what do I get?"

Gallagher opened the bag Chevalier had given him. "Leg of pork?"

Savary's jaw dropped. "My God, my tongue's hanging out already. Give me."

Gallagher passed it under the table and took the carton of cigarettes in return. "You know my telephone number at the cottage. Ring me as soon as you get back."

"All right."

Savary got up and they went outside. Gallagher, unwilling to wait, got a packet of Gitanes out, opened it and lit one. "Jesus, that's wonderful."

"I'll be off then." Savary made a move to walk toward the gangway of the *Victor Hugo*.

Gallagher said softly, "Let me down on this one and I'll kill you, my friend. Understand?"

Savary turned, mouth open in astonishment as Gallagher smiled cheerfully and walked away along the pier.

George Hamilton was a tall, angular man whose old Harris tweed suit looked a size too large. A distinguished physician in his day, at one time professor of pharmacology at the University of London and a consultant of Guy's Hospital, he had retired to a cottage in Jersey just before the outbreak of war. In 1940, with the Germans expected at any day, many people had left the island, a number of doctors among them, which explained why Hamilton, an M.D. and Fellow of the Royal College of Physicians, was working as a general practitioner at the age of seventy.

He pushed a shock of white hair back from his forehead and stood up, looking down at Kelso on the couch. "No good. He should be in hospital. I really need an x-ray to be sure, but I'd say at least two fractures of the tibia. Possibly three."

"No hospital," Kelso said faintly.

Hamilton made a sign to Helen and Gallagher, and they followed him into the kitchen. "If the fractures were compound—in other words, if there was any kind of open wound, bone sticking through, then we wouldn't any choice. The possibility of infection, especially after all he's been through, would be very great. The only way of saving the leg would be a hospital bed and traction."

"What exactly are you saying, George?" Gallagher asked.

"Well, as you can see, the skin isn't broken. The fractures are what we term comminuted. it might be possible to set the leg and plaster it."

"Can you handle that?" Helen demanded.

"I could try, but I need the right conditions. I certainly wouldn't dream of proceeding without an x-ray." He hesitated. "There is one possibility."

"What's that?" Gallagher asked.

"Pine Trees. It's a little nursing home in St. Lawrence run by Catholic Sisters of Mercy. Irish and French mostly. They have x-ray facilities there and a decent operating theater. Sister Maria Teresa, who's in charge, is a good friend. I could give her a ring."

"Do the Germans use it?" Helen asked.

"Now and then. Usually young women with prenatal problems, which is a polite way of saying they're in for an abortion. The nuns, as you may imagine, don't like that one little bit, but there isn't anything they can do about it."

"Would he be able to stay there?"

"I doubt it. They've very few beds and surely it would be too dangerous. The most we could do is patch him up and bring him back here."

Gallagher said, "You're taking a hell of a risk helping us like this, George."

"I'd say we all are," Hamilton told him dryly.

"It's vitally important that Colonel Kelso stay out of the hands of the enemy," Helen began.

Hamilton shook his head. "I don't want to know, Helen, so don't try to tell me, and I don't want the nuns to be involved either. As far as Sister Maria Teresa is concerned, our friend must be a local man who's had a suitable accident. It would help if we had an identity card for him, just in case."

Helen turned on Gallagher. "Can you do anything? You managed a card for that Spanish Communist last year when he escaped from the working party at those tunnels they've been constructing in St. Peter."

Gallagher went to the old eighteenth-century pine desk in the corner of the kitchen, pulled out the front drawer, then reached inside and produced a small box drawer of the kind people had once used to hide valuables. There were several blank identity cards in there, signed and stamped with the Nazi eagle.

"Where on earth did you get those?" Hamilton asked in astonishment.

"An Irishman I know, barman in one of the town hotels, has a German boyfriend, if you follow me. A clerk at the Feldkommandatur. I did him a big favor last year. He gave me these in exchange. I'll fill in Kelso's details and we'll give him a good Jersey name. How about Le Marquand?" He took out pen and ink and sat at the kitchen table. "Henry Ralph Le Marquand. Residence?"

He looked up at Helen. "Home Farm, de Ville Place," she said.

"Fair enough. I'll go and get the color of his eyes, hair and so on while you phone Pine Trees." He paused at the door. "I'll enter his occupation as fisherman. That way we can say it was a boating accident. And one more thing, George."

"What's that?" Hamilton asked as he lifted the phone.

"I'm going with you. We'll take him up in the van. No arguments. We must all hang together, or all hang separately." He smiled wryly and went out.

Pine Trees was an ugly house, obviously late Victorian in origin. At some time, the walls had been faced in cement which had cracked in many places, here and there, large pieces having flaked away altogether. Gallagher drove the van into the front courtyard, Hamilton sitting beside him. As they got out, the front door opened and Sister Maria Teresa came down the sloping concrete ramp to meet them. She wore a simple black habit, a small woman with calm eyes and not a wrinkle to be seen on her face though she was in her sixties.

"Dr. Hamilton." Her English was good, but with a pronounced French accent.

"This is General Gallagher. He manages de Ville Place where the patient is employed."

"We'll need a trolley," Gallagher said.

"There's one just inside the door."

He got it and brought it to the back of the van. He opened the doors, revealing Kelso lying on an old mattress, and they eased him out onto the trolley.

Sister Maria Teresa led the way inside, and as he pushed the trolley up the ramp, Gallagher whispered to Kelso, "Don't forget, keep your trap shut, and if you have to moan in pain, try not to sound American."

Hamilton stood in the operating theater examining the x-ray plates which young Sister Bernadette had brought in. "Three fractures," Sister Maria Teresa said. "Not good. He should be in hospital, Doctor, but I don't need to tell you that."

"All right, Sister. I'll tell you the truth," Hamilton said. "If he goes down to St. Helier they'll want to know how it happened. Our German friends insist on it. You know what sticklers for detail they are. Le Marquand was fishing illegally when the accident took place."

Gallagher cut in smoothly, "Which could earn him three months in jail."

"I see." She shook her head. "I wish I had a bed to offer, but we're quite full."

"Any Germans about?"

"Two of their girlfriends," she said calmly. "The usual thing. One of the army doctors handled that yesterday. Major Speer. Do you know him?"

"I've worked with him on occasion at the hospital," Hamilton said. "I've known worse. Anyway, Sister, if you'd care to assist me, you and Sister Bernadette, we'll get started."

She eased him into a robe and he went to scrub up at the sink in the corner. As Sister Bernadette helped him on with rubber gloves, he said to Maria Teresa, "A short-term anesthetic only. Chloroform on the pad will do." He moved to the operating table and looked down at Kelso. "All right?"

Kelso, gritting his teeth, nodded and Hamilton said to Gallagher. "You'd better wait outside."

Gallagher turned to leave, and at that moment, the door opened and a German officer walked in.

"Ah, there you are, Sister," he said in French, then smiled and changed to English. "Professor Hamilton, you here?"

"Major Speer," Hamilton said, gloved hands raised.

"I've just looked in on my patients, Sister. Both are doing well."

Speer was a tall, handsome man with a good-humored, rather fleshy face. His greatcoat hung open, and Gallagher noticed an Iron Cross First Class on the left breast and the ribbon for the Russian Winter War. A man who had seen action.

"Anything interesting, Doctor?"

"Fractures of the tibia. An employee of General Gallagher here. Have you met?"

"No, but I've heard of you many times, General." Speer clicked his heels and saluted. "A pleasure." He moved to the x-rays and examined them. "Not good. Not good at all. Comminuted fracture of the tibia in three places."

"I know hospitalization and traction should be the norm," Hamilton said. "But a bed isn't available."

"Oh, I should think it perfectly acceptable to set the bones and then plaster." Speer smiled with great charm and took off his greatcoat. "But, Herr Professor, this is hardly your field. It would be a pleasure to take care of this small matter for you."

He was already taking a gown down from a peg on the wall and moved to the sink to scrub up. "If you insist," Hamilton said calmly. "There's little doubt this is more your sort of thing than mine."

A few minutes later, Speer was ready, leaning down to examine the leg. He looked up at Sister Maria Teresa. "Right, Sister, chloroform now, I think. Not too much and we'll work very quickly."

From the corner, Gallagher watched, fascinated.

❧

Savary wasn't feeling too pleased with life as he walked along the cobbled streets of the walled city in Granville. For one thing, the trip from Jersey in the fog had been lousy, and he was distinctly unhappy at the situation Gallagher had placed him in. He turned into a quiet square. Sophie's Bar was on the far side, a chink of light showing here and there through the shutters. He walked across, slowly and reluctantly, and went in.

Gerard Cresson sat in his wheelchair playing the piano, a small man with the white intense face of the invalid, black hair hanging almost to his shoulders. He'd broken his back in an accident on the docks two years before the war. Would never walk again, not even with crutches.

There were a dozen or so customers scattered around the bar, some of them seamen whom Savary knew. Sophie sat on a high stool behind the marble counter, bottles ranged behind her against an ornate mirror, and read the local newspaper. She was in her late thirties, dark hair piled high on her head, black eyes, the face sallow like a gypsy's, the mouth wide and painted bright red. She had good breasts, the best Savary had ever seen. Not that it would have done any good. With a knife or a bottle she was dynamite, and there were men in Granville with scars to prove it.

"Ah, Robert, it's been a long time. How goes it?"

"It could be worse, it could be better."

As she poured him a cognac, he slipped the letter across. "What's this?" she demanded.

"Your friend Gallagher in Jersey uses me as a postman now. I don't know what's in it and I don't want to, but he expects an answer when I return. We sail tomorrow at noon. I'll be back." He swallowed his cognac and left.

She came round the counter and called to one of the customers, "Heh, Marcel, look after the bar for me."

She approached her husband who had stopped playing and was lighting a cigarette. "What was that all about?"

"Let's go in the back and find out."

She pulled his wheelchair from the piano, turned and pushed him along the bar to the sitting room at the rear. Gerard Cresson sat at the table and read Gallagher's letter, then pushed it across to her, face grave.

She read it quickly, then got a bottle of red wine and filled two glasses. "He's in a real mess this time, our friend the General."

"And then some."

Between them they had controlled the Resistance movement from Granville to Avranches and St. Malo for three years now. Gerard provided the organizing ability and Sophie was his good right arm. They were a very successful team. Had to be to have survived so long.

"You'll radio London?"

"Of course."

"What do you think?" she said. "Maybe they'll ask us to try to get this Yank out of Jersey."

"Difficult at the best of times," he said. "Not possible with the state he's in." He held out his glass for more wine. "Of course, there is a rather obvious solution. Much better for everyone in the circumstances, I should have thought."

"And what's that?"

"Send someone across to cut his throat."

There was silence between them. She said, "It's been a long war."

"Too long," he said. "Now take me to the storeroom and I'll radio London."

Major Speer turned from the sink, toweling his hands. Sister Bernadette was already mixing the plaster of Paris, and he crossed to the operating table and looked down at Kelso who was still unconscious.

"An excellent piece of work," George Hamilton said.

"Yes, I must say I'm rather pleased with it myself." Speer reached for his greatcoat. "I'm sure you can handle the rest. I'm already late for dinner at the officers' club. Don't forget to let me know how he progresses, Herr Professor. General." He saluted and went out.

Hamilton stood, looked down at Kelso, suddenly drained as he stripped off his gloves and gown. Kelso moaned a little as he started to come round and said softly, "Janet, I love you."

The American accent was unmistakable. Sister Bernadette appeared not to have noticed, but the older woman glanced sharply at Hamilton and then at Gallagher.

"He seems to be coming around," Hamilton said lamely.

"So it would appear," she said. "Why don't you and General Gallagher go to my office. One of the nuns will get you some coffee. We have some of the real stuff thanks to Major Speer. Sister Bernadette and I will put the cast on for you."

"That's very kind of you, Sister."

The two men went out and along the corridor, past the kitchen where two nuns worked, to the office at the end. Hamilton sat behind the desk and Gallagher gave him one of his Gitanes and sat in the window seat.

"The moment he came through that door will stay with me forever," the Irishman said.

"As I told you, he's not a bad sort," Hamilton commented. "And a damn fine doctor."

"You think Kelso will be all right?"

"I don't see why not. We should be able to move him in an hour or so. We'll have to watch him closely for the next few days. The possibility of infection mustn't be discounted, but there were some ampules of this new wonder drug, penicillin, in that emergency kit from his life raft. I'll start him on that if he gets the wrong sort of reaction."

"Sister Maria Teresa—she knows things aren't what they seem."

"Yes, I feel rather bad about that," George Hamilton said. "As if I've used her. She won't tell, of course. It would be contrary to every belief she holds dear."

"She reminds me of my old aunt in Dublin when I was a lad," Gallagher said. "Incense, candles and the Holy Water."

"Do you still believe, Sean?" Hamilton asked.

"Not since the first of July, nineteen sixteen, on the Somme," Gallagher said. "I was attached to a Yorkshire Regiment, the Leeds Pals. The idiots at headquarters sent those lads over the top, packs on their backs, into heavy machine-gun fire. By noon, there were around forty or so survivors out of eight hundred. I decided then that if God existed, he was having a bad joke at my expense."

"I take your point," Hamilton said gravely.

Gallagher stood up. "I think I'll sample the night air for a while," and he opened the door and went out.

George Hamilton rested his head on his arms on the desk and yawned. It had been a long day. He closed his eyes and was asleep within a couple of minutes.

It was just after ten and Dougal Munro was still working away at his desk in his office at Baker Street when the door opened and Jack Carter limped in, his face grim. He placed a signal flimsy on the brigadier's desk. "Brace yourself, sir."

"What is this?" Munro demanded.

"Message just in from our Resistance contact in Granville. That's in Normandy."

"I know where it is, for God's sake." Munro started to read and suddenly sat up straight. "I don't believe it."

Munro read the signal through again. "It couldn't be worse. There isn't a resistance movement in Jersey. No one to call on. I mean, this de Ville woman and the Gallagher man, how long can they manage, especially if he's ill? And how long can he get by on a small island like that? It doesn't bear thinking of, Jack."

For the first time since Carter had known him he sounded close to despair, uncertain which way to go. "You'll think of something, sir, you always do," Carter said gently.

"Thanks for the vote of confidence." Munro stood up and reached for his coat. "Now you'd better phone through to Hayes Lodge and get me an immediate appointment with General Eisenhower. Tell them I'm on my way."

Helen de Ville had been waiting anxiously for the sound of the van returning, and when it drove into the courtyard, at the side of de Ville

Place, she ran out. As Gallagher and Hamilton got out of the van, she cried, "Is he all right?"

"Still doped up, but the leg's doing fine," Gallagher told her.

"There's no one in at the moment. They're either in Granville or at sea or at the officers' club, so let's get him upstairs."

Gallagher and Hamilton got Kelso out of the van, joined hands and lifted him between them. They followed Helen through the front door, across the wide paneled hall and up the great staircase. She opened the door of the master bedroom and led the way in. The furniture was seventeenth-century Breton, including the four-poster bed. There was a bathroom through a door on the right side of the bed, on the left, carved library shelving from wall to ceiling crammed with books. Her fingers found a hidden spring and a section swung back to disclose a stairway. She led the way up and Gallagher and Hamilton followed with some difficulty, but finally made it to a room under the roof. The walls were paneled in oak, and there was a single window in the gable end. It was comfortable enough with carpet on the floor and a single bed.

They got Kelso onto the bed and Helen said, "There's everything you need, and the only entrance is from my room, so you should be quite safe. An ancestor of mine hid here from Cromwell's people for years. I'm afraid the convenience hasn't improved since his day. It's that oak commode over there."

"Thanks, but all I want to do is sleep," Kelso said, his face tired and strained.

She nodded to Gallagher and the old doctor and they went out and downstairs. Hamilton said, "I'll get off myself. Tell Helen I'll look in tomorrow."

Sean Gallagher took his hand for a moment. "George, you're quite a man."

"All in a doctor's day, Sean." Hamilton smiled. "See you tomorrow." And he went out.

Gallagher went through the hall and along the rear passage to the kitchen. He put the kettle on the stove, and was pushing a few pieces of wood in among the dying embers when Helen came in.

"Is he all right?" he asked.

"Fast asleep already." She sat on the edge of the table. "Now what do we do?"

"Nothing we can do until Savary gets back from Granville with some sort of message."

"And what if there isn't any message?"

"Oh, I'll think of something. Now sit down and have a nice cup of tea."

She shook her head. "We've got a choice of either bramble or beet tea and, tonight, I just can't face either."

"Oh, ye of little faith." Gallagher produced the packet of China tea which Chevalier had given him that morning at the market.

She started to laugh helplessly and put her arms around his neck. "Sean Gallagher, what would I do without you?"

Eisenhower was in full uniform for he'd been attending a dinner party with the prime minister when he'd received Munro's message. He paced up and down the library at Hayes Lodge, extremely agitated. "Is there no way we can put someone in?"

"If you mean a commando unit, I don't think so, sir. The most heavily defended coast in Europe."

Eisenhower nodded. "What you're really saying is that it's impossible to get him out."

"No, sir, but very, very difficult. It's a small island, General. It's not like hiding someone on the back of a truck and driving three hundred miles overnight to the Pyrenees or arranging for one of our Lysanders to fly in to pick him up."

"Right, then get him across to France where you can fix those things."

"Our information is that he's not capable of traveling."

"For God's sake, Munro, everything could hang on this. The whole invasion. Months of planning."

Munro cleared his throat and nervously for him. "If worse came to worst, General, would you be willing to consider Colonel Kelso as expendable?"

Eisenhower stopped pacing. "You mean have him executed?"

"Something like that."

"God help me, but if there's nothing else for it, then so be it." Eisenhower walked up to the huge wall map of western Europe. "Six thousand ships, thousands of planes, two million men and the war in balance. If they find out our exact points of landing, they'll mass everything they've got." He turned. "Intelligence reported a Rommel speech of a few weeks ago in which he said just that. That the war would be won or lost on those beaches."

"I know, General."

"And you ask is Kelso expendable?" Eisenhower sighed heavily. "If you can save him, do. If you can't . . . " He shrugged. "In any case, considering what you've already said about the Jersey situation, how would you go about getting an agent in? I should think a new face would stick out like a sore thumb."

"That's true, General. We'll have to think about it."

Jack Carter, standing respectfully quiet by the fire, coughed. "There is one way, General."

"What's that, Captain?" Eisenhower inquired.

"The best place to hide a tree is in a wood. It seems to me the people who are most free to come and go are the Germans themselves. I mean, new personnel must be posted there all the time."

Eisenhower turned sharply to Munro. "He's got a point. Have you got any people capable of that kind of work?"

Munro nodded. "Here and there, sir. It's a rare skill. Not just a question of speaking fluent German, but thinking like a German and that isn't easy."

Eisenhower said, "I'll give you a week, Brigadier. One week and I expect you to have this matter resolved."

"My word on it, sir."

Munro walked out briskly, Carter limping along behind. "Radio Cresson in Granville to relay a message to Gallagher in Jersey saying someone will be with him by Thursday."

"Are you sure, sir?"

"Of course I am," Munro said cheerfully. "That was a masterly suggestion of yours in there, Jack. Best place to hide a tree is in a wood. I like that."

"Thank you very much, sir."

"German personnel moving in and out all the time. What would one new arrival be among many, especially if provided with the right kind of credentials?"

"It would take a very special man, sir."

"Come off it, Jack," Munro said as they reached the street and the car. "There's only one man for this job. You know it and I know it. Only one man capable of playing a Nazi to the hilt and ruthless enough to put a bullet between Kelso's eyes if necessary. Harry Martineau."

"I must remind you, sir, that Colonel Martineau was given a definite promise after that business in Lyons that his services wouldn't be required again. His health alone should make it impossible."

"Nonsense, Jack. Harry could never resist a challenge. Find him. And another thing, Jack. Check SOE files. See if we've got anyone with a Jersey background."

"Men only, sir?"

"Good God, Jack, of course not. Since when have we been interested in men only in our business."

He tapped on the partition and the driver took them away from the curb.

6

THE COTTAGE IN DORSET, NOT far from Lulworth Cove, had been loaned to Martineau by an old friend from Oxford days. It stood in a tiny valley above the cliffs, and the way to the beach was blocked by rusting barbed wire. There had once been a notice warning of mines, not that there were any. That had been the first thing the landlord at the village pub had told Martineau when he'd moved into the area, which explained why he was walking along the shoreline, occasionally throwing stones into the incoming waves, the morning after Dougal Munro's meeting with Eisenhower at Hayes Lodge.

Harry Martineau was forty-four, of medium height, with good shoulders under the old paratrooper's camouflaged jump jacket which he wore against the cold. His face was very pale, with the kind of skin that never seemed to tan, and wedge-shaped, the eyes so dark that it was impossible to say what their true color was. The mouth was mobile, with a slight ironic smile permanently in place. The look of a man who had found life more disappointing than he had hoped.

He'd been out of hospital for three months now and things were better than they'd been for a while. He didn't get the chest pain anymore, except when he overdid things, but the insomnia pattern was terrible. He could seldom sleep at night. The moment he went to bed, his brain seemed to become hyperactive. Still, that was only to be expected. Too many years on the run, of living by night, danger constantly at hand.

He was no use to Munro anymore, the doctors had made that clear. He could have returned to Oxford, but that was no answer. Neither was trying to pick up the threads of the book he'd been working on in 1939. The war had taught him that if nothing else. So, he'd dropped out as thoroughly as a man could. The cottage in Dorset by the sea, books to read, space to find himself in.

"And where the hell have you gone, Harry?" he asked morosely as he started up the cliff path. "Because I'm damned if I can find you."

533

The living room of the old cottage was comfortable enough. A Persian carpet on the flagged floor, a dining table and several rush-backed chairs and books everywhere, not only on the shelves but piled in the corner. None of them were his. Nothing in this place was his except for a few clothes.

There was a sofa on each side of the stone fireplace. He put a couple of logs on the embers, poured himself a scotch, drank it quickly and poured another. Then he sat down and picked up the notepad he'd left on the coffee table. There were several lines of poetry written on it and he read them aloud.

The station is ominous at midnight. Hope is a dead letter. He dropped the notepad back on the table with a wry smile. "Admit it, Harry," he said softly. "You're a lousy poet."

Suddenly, he was tired, the feeling coming in a kind of rush, the lack of sleep catching up with him. His chest began to ache a little, the left lung, and that took him back to Lyons, of course, on that final and fatal day. If he'd been a little bit more on the ball it wouldn't have happened. A case of taking the pitcher to the well too often or perhaps, quite simply, his luck had run out. As he drifted into sleep, it all came back so clearly.

Standartenführer Jurgen Kaufmann, the head of the Gestapo in Lyons, was in civilian clothes that day as he came down the steps of the Town Hall and got into the back of the black Citroën. His driver was also in civilian clothes, for on Thursday afternoons Kaufmann visited his mistress and liked to be discreet about it.

"Take your time, Karl," he said to his driver, an SS sergeant who'd served with him for two years now. "We're a little early. I said I wouldn't be there till three and you know how she hates surprises."

"As you say, Standartenführer." Karl smiled as he drove away.

Kaufmann opened a copy of a Berlin newspaper which he had received in the post that morning and settled back to enjoy it. They moved through the outskirts of town into the country. It was really quite beautiful, orchards of apples on either side of the road, and the air was heavy with the smell of them. For some time Karl had noticed a motorcycle behind them, and when they turned into the side road leading to the village of Chaumont, it followed.

He said, "There's a motorcyclist been on our tail for quite some time, Standartenführer." He took a Luger from his pocket and laid it on the seat beside him.

Kaufmann turned to look through the rear window and laughed. "You're losing your touch, Karl. He's one of ours."

The motorcyclist drew alongside and waved. He was SS Feldgendarmerie in helmet, heavy uniform raincoat, a Schmeisser machine pistol slung across his chest just below the SS Field Police metal gorget that was only worn when officially on duty. The face was anonymous behind the goggles. He waved a gloved hand again.

"He must have a message for me," Kaufmann said. "Pull up."

Karl turned in at the side of the road and braked to a halt and the motorcyclist pulled up in front. He shoved his machine up on the stand and Karl got out. "What can we do for you?"

A hand came out of the raincoat pocket holding a Mauser semiautomatic pistol. He shot Karl once in the heart, hurling him back against the Citroën. He slid down into the road. The SS man turned him over with his boot and shot him again very deliberately between the eyes. Then he opened the rear door.

Kaufmann always went armed, but he'd taken off his overcoat and folded it neatly in the corner. As he got his hand to the Luger in the right pocket and turned, the SS man shot him in the arm. Kaufmann clutched at his sleeve, blood oozing between his fingers.

"Who are you?" he cried wildly. The other man pushed up his goggles and Kaufmann stared into the darkest, coldest eyes he had ever seen in his life.

"My name is Martineau. I'm a major in the British Army serving with SOE."

"So, you are Martineau." Kaufmann grimaced with pain. "Your German is excellent. Quite perfect."

"So it should be. My mother was German," Martineau told him.

Kaufmann said, "I'd hoped to meet you before long, but under different circumstances."

"I'm sure you did. I've wanted to meet you for quite some time. Since nineteen thirty-eight, in fact. You were a captain at Gestapo Headquarters in Berlin in May of that year. You arrested a young woman called Rosa Bernstein. You probably don't even remember the name."

"But I recall her very well," Kaufmann told him. "She was Jewish and worked for the Socialist Underground."

"I was told that by the time you'd finished with her she couldn't even walk to the firing squad."

"That's not true. The firing squad never came into it. She was hanged in cellar number three. Standard procedure. What was she to you?"

"I loved her." Martineau raised his pistol.

Kaufmann cried, "Don't be a fool. We can do a deal. I can save your life, Martineau, believe me."

"Is that so?" Harry Martineau said, and shot him between the eyes, killing him instantly.

He pushed the heavy motorcycle off its stand and rode away. He was perfectly in control in spite of what he had just done. No emotion— nothing. The trouble was, it hadn't brought Rosa Bernstein back, but then, nothing ever could.

He rode through a maze of country lanes for over an hour, working his way steadily westward. Finally, he turned along a narrow country lane, grass growing so tall on either side that it almost touched. The farmhouse in the courtyard at the end of the lane had seen better days, a window broken here and there, a few slates missing. Martineau got off the bike, pushed it up on the stand and crossed to the front door.

"Heh, Pierre, open up!" He tried the latch and hammered with his fist and then the door opened so suddenly that he fell on his knees.

The muzzle of a Walther touched him between the eyes. The man holding it was about forty and dressed like a French farm laborer in beret, corduroy jacket and denim trousers, but his German was impeccable. "Please stand, Major Martineau, and walk inside very slowly."

He followed Martineau along the corridor into the kitchen. Pierre Duval sat at the table, tied to a chair, a handkerchief in his mouth, eyes wild, blood on his face.

"Hands on the wall and spread," the German said, and ran his hands expertly over Martineau, relieving him of the Schmeisser and the Mauser.

He moved to the old-fashioned telephone on the wall and gave the operator a number. After a while he said, "Schmidt? He turned up. Yes, Martineau." He nodded. "All right, fifteen minutes."

"Friend of yours?" Martineau inquired.

"Not really. I'm Abwehr. Kramer's the name. That was the Gestapo. I don't like those swine any more than you do, but we all have a job to do. Take your helmet and raincoat off. Make yourself comfortable."

Martineau did as he was told. Evening was falling fast outside, the room was getting quite dark. He put the helmet and coat down and stood there in the SS uniform, aware of Pierre on the other side of the table, eyes glaring wildly, leaning back in his chair, his feet coming up.

"What about a drink?" Martineau asked.

"My God, they told me you were a cool one," Kramer said admiringly.

Pierre lunged with his feet at the edge of the table ramming it into the German's back. Martineau's left hand deflected the pistol and he closed, raising his knee. But Kramer turned a thigh, raising stiffened fingers under Martineau's chin, jerking back his head. Martineau hooked Kramer's left leg, sending the German crashing to the ground, going down with him, reaching for the wrist of the hand that held the pistol, smashing his fist into the side of Kramer's neck, aware of the pistol exploding between them.

There was the distinct sound of bone cracking and the German lay still, alive, but moaning softly. Martineau got to his feet feeling suddenly weak and faint, opened the table drawer, spilling its contents on the floor and picked up a breadknife. He moved behind Pierre and sliced the ropes that bound him to the chair. The old Frenchman jumped up, pulling the gag from his mouth.

"My God, Harry, I've never seen so much blood."

Martineau glanced down. The front of the SS blouse was soaked in blood. His own blood and there were three bullet holes that he could see, one of them smoldering slightly from powder burns.

He slumped into the chair. "Never mind that."

"Did you get him, Harry? Did you get Kaufmann?"

"I got him, Pierre," Martineau said wearily. "When's the pickup?"

"The old aero club at Fleurie at seven, just before dark."

Martineau looked at his watch. "That only gives me half an hour. You'll have to come too. Nowhere else for you to go now."

He got to his feet and started for the door, swaying a little, and the Frenchman put an arm around him. "You'll never make it, Harry."

"I'd better because about five minutes from now the Gestapo are going to be coming up that road," Martineau told him and went outside.

He got the bike off the stand and threw a leg across the saddle, then he kicked it into life, feeling curiously as if everything was happening in slow motion. Pierre climbed up behind and put his arms around him and they rode away, out of the yard and along the lane.

As they turned into the road at the end, Martineau was aware of two dark sedans coming up fast on his left. One of them skidded to a halt, almost driving him into the ditch. He swung the motorcycle to the right, wheels spinning as he gunned the motor, was aware of shots, a sudden cry from Pierre, hands loosening their hold as the old Frenchman went backward over the rear wheel.

Martineau roared down the road toward the canal at the far end, swerved onto the towpath, one of the Gestapo cars following close. Two hundred yards away there was a lock, a narrow footbridge for pedestrians crossing to the other side. He rode across with no difficulty. Behind him, the car braked to a halt. The two Gestapo operatives inside jumped out and began to fire wildly, but by then he was long gone.

He could never remember clearly afterward any details of that cross-country ride to Fleurie. In the end, it was all something of an anticlimax anyway. The field had been headquarters of an aero club before the war. Now it lay derelict and forlorn and long disused.

He was aware of the roaring of the Lysander's engine in the distance as he rode up to the airfield himself. He paused, waiting, and the Lysander came in out of the darkness for a perfect touchdown, turned and taxied toward him. He got off the bike, allowing it to fall to one side. He promptly fell down himself, got up again and lurched forward. The

*door swung open and the pilot leaned across and shouted, "I wasn't
too sure when I saw the uniform."*

*Martineau hauled himself inside. The pilot reached over and closed
and locked the door. Martineau coughed suddenly, his mouth and chin
red.*

The pilot said, "My God, you're choking on your own blood."

"I've been doing that for at least four years now," Martineau said.

*The pilot had other things on his mind, several vehicles converging
on the other end of the runway by the old buildings. Whoever they were,
they were too late. The Bristol Perseus engine responded magnificently
when fully boosted. The Westland Lysander was capable of taking off
from rough ground, fully loaded, in two hundred and forty yards. At
Fleurie, that night, they managed it in two hundred, clearing the cars
at the end of the runway and climbing up into the gathering darkness.*

"Very nice," Martineau said. "I liked that." And then he fainted.

"So, he's in Dorset, is he?" Munro said. "Doing what?"

"Not very much from what I can make out." Carter hesitated. "He
did take two bullets in the left lung, sir, and . . . "

"No sad songs, Jack, I've other things on my mind. You've had a
look at my ideas on a way of getting him into Jersey? What do you
think?"

"Excellent, sir. I would have thought it all pretty foolproof, at least
for a few days."

"And that's all we need. Now, what else have you got for me?"

"As I understand it from your preliminary plan, sir, what you're seeking is someone to go in with him to establish his credentials. Someone
who knows the island and the people and so on?"

"That's right."

"There's an obvious flaw, of course. How on earth would you explain
their presence? You can't just pop up in the island after four years of
occupation without some sort of an explanation."

"Very true." Munro nodded. "However, I can tell by the throb in
your voice that you've already come up with a solution, so let's get on
with it, Jack. What have you got?"

"Sarah Anne Drayton, sir, age nineteen. Born in Jersey. Left the island
just before the war to go out to Malaya where her father was a rubber
planter. He was a widower apparently. Sent her home a month before
the fall of Singapore."

"Which means she hasn't been back in Jersey since when?" Munro
looked at the file. "Nineteen thirty-eight. Six years. That's a long time
at that age. Jack. Girls change out of all recognition."

"Yes, sir."

"Mind you, she's young."

"We've used them as young as this before, sir."

"Yes, but rarely and only in extremes. Where did you find her?"

"She was put forward for SOE consideration two years ago, mainly because she speaks fluent French with a Breton accent. Her maternal grandmother was Breton. Naturally, she was turned down because of her youth."

"Where is she now?"

"Probationer nurse here in London at Cromwell Hospital."

"Excellent, Jack." Munro stood up and reached for his jacket. "We'll go and see her. I'm sure she'll prove to be intensely patriotic."

That the Luftwaffe had been chased from British skies, the Blitz had long gone, was a tale for the front pages of newspapers only. In the spring of 1944 night attacks were renewed on London, using the JU88S with devastating results. That Sunday was no exception. By eight o'clock the casualty department at Cromwell Hospital was working flat out.

Sarah Drayton had been supposed to come off shift at six. She had now been on duty for fourteen hours without a break, but there were simply not enough nurses or doctors available. She worked on, helping with casualties laid out in the corridors, trying to ignore the crump of bombs falling in the middle distance, the sound of fire engines.

She was a small, intense girl, dark hair pushed up under her cap, her face very determined, the hazel eyes serious. Her gown was filthy, stained with blood, her stockings torn. She knelt to help the matron sedate a panic-stricken young girl who was bleeding badly from shrapnel wounds. They stood up to allow porters to carry the girl away on a stretcher.

Sarah said, "I thought night raids were supposed to be a thing of the past."

"Tell that to the casualties," the matron said. "Almost a thousand of them in March. Right, you clear off, Drayton. You'll be falling down soon from sheer fatigue. No arguments."

She walked wearily along the corridor, aware that the sound of the bombing now seemed to have moved south of the river. Someone was sweeping up broken glass, and she stepped around them and moved to the reception desk to book out.

The night clerk was talking to two men. She said, "Actually, this is Nurse Drayton coming now."

Jack Carter said, "Miss Drayton, this is Brigadier Munro and I'm Captain Carter."

"What can I do for you?" Her voice was rather low and very pleasant.

Munro was much taken with her at once, and Carter said, "Do you recall an interview you had two years ago? An Intelligence matter?"

"With SOE?" She looked surprised. "I was turned down."

"Yes, well, if you could spare us some time we'd like a word with you." Carter drew her over to a bench beside the wall, and he and Munro sat on either side of her. "You were born in Jersey, Miss Drayton?"

"That's right."

He took out his notebook and opened it. "Your mother's name was Margaret de Ville. That has a particular interest for us. Do you by any chance know a Mrs. Helen de Ville?"

"I do. My mother's cousin, although she was always Aunty Helen to me. She was so much older than I was."

"And Sean Gallagher?"

"The General? Since I was a child." She looked puzzled. "What's going on here?"

"In good time, Miss Drayton," Munro told her. "When did you last see your aunt or General Gallagher?"

"Nineteen thirty-eight. My mother died that year and my father took a job in Malaya. I went out to join him."

"Yes, we know that," Carter said.

She frowned at him for a moment, then turned on Munro. "All right, what's this about?"

"It's quite simple really," Dougal Munro said. "I'd like to offer you a job with SOE. I'd like you to go to Jersey for me."

She stared at him in astonishment, but only for a moment, and then she started to laugh helplessly and the sound of it was close to hysteria. It had, after all, been a long day.

"But, Brigadier," she said. "I hardly know you."

"Strange chap, Harry Martineau," Munro said. "I've never known anybody quite like him."

"From what you tell me, neither have I," Sarah said.

The car taking them down to Lulworth Cove was a huge Austin, a glass partition separating them from the driver. Munro and Jack Carter were in the rear, side by side, and Sarah Drayton sat on the jump seat opposite. She wore a tweed suit with pleated skirt, tan stockings and black brogues with half-heels, blouse in cream satin with a black string tie at her neck. She looked very attractive, cheeks flushed, eyes flickering everywhere. She also looked extremely young.

"It was his birthday the week before last," Carter told her.

She was immediately interested. "How old was he?"

"Forty-four."

"What they call a child of the century, my dear," Munro told her. "Born on the seventh of April, nineteen hundred. That must seem terribly old to you."

"Aries," she said.

Munro smiled. "That's right. Before the advent of our so-called enlightened times astrology was a science. Did you know that?"

"Not really."

"The ancient Egyptians always chose their generals from Leos, for example."

"I'm a Leo," she said. "July twenty-seventh."

"Then you *are* in for a complicated life. Something of a hobby of mine. Take Harry, for instance. Very gifted, brilliant analytical mind. A professor in the greatest university in the world at thirty-eight. Then look at what he became in middle life."

"How do you explain that?" she demanded.

"Astrology explains it for us. Aries is a warrior sign, but very commonly those born around the same time as Harry are one thing on the surface, something else underneath. Mars decanate in Gemini, you see, and Gemini is the sign of the twins."

"So?"

"People like that can be very schizophrenic. On one level, you're Harry Martineau, scholar, philosopher, poet, full of sweet reason, but on the dark side . . . " He shrugged. "A cold and ruthless killer. Yes, there's a curious lack of emotion to him, wouldn't you agree, Jack? Of course, all this has been extremely useful in the job he's been doing for the past four years. Suppose that's what's kept him alive when most of the others have died."

Carter said, "Just in case you're getting a rather bad impression of Harry Martineau, two things, Sarah. Although his mother was born in the States, she was of German parentage, and Harry spent a lot of time with them in Dresden and Heidelberg as he grew up. His grandfather, a professor of surgery, was an active Socialist. He died in a fall from the balcony of his apartment. A nasty accident."

"Aided by two Gestapo thugs taking an arm and a leg each to help him on his way," Munro put in.

"And then there was a Jewish girl named Rosa Bernstein."

"Yes," Sarah put in. "I was beginning to wonder whether females had ever entered into his life. No mention of marriage."

"He met Rosa Bernstein when she did a year at an Oxford College, St. Hugh's, in nineteen thirty-two. He was spending increasing time in Europe by then. Both his parents were dead. His father had left him reasonably well off, and as an only child, he had no close relatives."

"But he and Rosa never married?"

"No," Munro said, and added bluntly: "You'll often find prejudice on both sides of the fence, my dear. Rosa's parents were Orthodox Jews, and they didn't like the idea of their daughter marrying a Gentile. She and Harry pursued what you might term a vigorous affair for some years. I knew them both well. I was at Oxford myself in those days."

"What happened?"

It was Carter who answered her. "She was active in the Socialist underground. Went backward and forward from England to Germany as a courier. In May, nineteen thirty-eight, she was apprehended, taken to Gestapo Headquarters at Prince Albrechtstrasse in Berlin. A good address for a very bad place. There, she was interrogated with extreme brutality and, according to our information, executed."

There was a long silence. She seemed abstracted, staring out of the window into the distance. Munro said, "You don't seem shocked? I find that strange in one so young."

She shook her head. "I've been nursing for two years now. I deal with death every day of my life. So Harry Martineau doesn't particularly care for Germans?"

"No," Carter said. "He doesn't like Nazis. There's a difference."

"Yes, I can see that."

She stared out of the window again, feeling restless, on edge, and it was all to do with Martineau, this man she had never met. He filled her mind. Would not go away.

Carter said, "One thing we didn't ask. I hope you don't mind my being personal, but is there anyone in your life at the moment? Anyone who would miss you?"

"A man?" She laughed harshly. "Good heavens, no! I never work less than a twelve-hour daily shift at the Cromwell. That leaves one just about enough time to have a bath and a meal before falling into bed." She shook her head. "No time for men. My father's in a Japanese prison camp. I've an old aunt in Sussex, his elder sister, and that's about it. No one to miss me at all. I'm all yours, gentlemen."

She delivered the speech with an air of bravado and an illusion of calm sophistication that in one so young was strangely moving.

Munro, unusually for him, felt uncomfortable. "This is important, believe me." He leaned forward, put a hand on her arm. "We wouldn't ask you if it wasn't."

She nodded. "I know, Brigadier, I know." She turned and stared out of the window again at the passing scenery, thinking about Martineau.

He awoke with a dull ache just behind the right eye and his mouth tasted foul. Only one answer to that. He pulled on an old tracksuit and grabbed a towel, left by the front door and ran down to the sea.

He stripped and ran out through the shallows, plunging through the waves. It wasn't even a nice morning, the sky the color of slate gray, and there was rain on the wind. Yet quite suddenly, he experienced one of those special moments. Sea and sky seemed to become one. For a little while all sounds faded as he battled his way through the waves. Nothing mattered. Not the past or the future. Only this present moment. As he turned on his back, a herring gull fled overhead and it started to rain.

A voice called out, "Enjoying yourself, Harry?"

Martineau turned toward the shore and found Munro standing there in old tweed coat and battered hat, holding an umbrella over his head. "My God," he said. "Not you, Dougal?"

"As ever was, Harry. Come on up to the cottage. There's someone I'd like you to meet."

He turned and walked back across the beach without another word. Martineau floated there for a while, thinking about it. Dougal Munro wasn't just paying a social call, that was for sure, not all the way from London. Excitement surged through him and he waded out of the water, toweled himself briskly, pulled on the old tracksuit and ran across the beach and up the cliff path. Jack Carter was standing on the porch, watching the rain and smoking a cigarette.

"What, you too, Jack?" Martineau smiled with real pleasure and took the other man's hand. "Does the old sod want me to go back to work?"

"Something like that." Carter hesitated, then said, "Harry, I think you've done enough."

"No such word in the vocabulary, Jack, not until they nail down the lid and put you six feet under." Martineau brushed past Carter and went inside.

Munro was sitting by the fire, reading the notepad he'd found on the table. "Still writing bad poetry?"

"Always did." Martineau took the pad from him, tore off the top sheet, crumpled it up and tossed it into the fireplace. It was then that he became aware of Sarah Drayton standing in the kitchen doorway.

"I'm making tea for everyone. I hope that's all right, Colonel Martineau. I'm Sarah Drayton."

She didn't bother holding out her hand, for it would have trembled too much. She was aware that she was close to tears and her stomach was hollow with excitement, throat dry. *Coup de foudre*, the French called it. The thunderclap. The best kind of love of all. Instant and quite irrevocable.

And at first, he responded, brushing a lock of black hair back from the white forehead, his face illuminated by a smile of great natural charm, and then the smile faded and he turned on Munro, anger in his voice, as if seeing everything.

"My God, what a bastard you are, Dougal. So now we're using schoolgirls?"

Hugh Kelso's adventures did not take long in the telling, but when he was finished, Munro carried on.

"The other month we knocked off a man called Braun in Paris. Jack has the details. I think you'll find it interesting."

"What was he, Gestapo?" Martineau asked.

"No, SD." Carter turned to Sarah Drayton sitting on the other side of the fire. "That's the Secret Intelligence Department of the SS, responsible only to Himmler himself. More powerful than any other organization in Germany today."

"Go on about Braun," Martineau said.

"Well, according to his papers, he was RFSS." Carter turned again to Sarah. "That means Reichsführer SS. It's a cuff title that members of Himmler's personal staff wear on their uniform sleeve." He took a paper from the file he was holding and offered it to Martineau. "It seems Braun was a kind of roving ambassador, empowered to make his own investigations wherever he pleased."

"With supreme authority over everyone he came into contact with," Munro said. "Read that letter."

Martineau took it from its envelope and unfolded it.

It was on excellent paper, the heading embossed in black.

DER REICHSFÜHRER—SS   Berlin,
                                                 9 November 1943

SS—STURMBANNFÜHRER
BRAUN ERWIN, SS-NR 107863

This officer acts under my personal orders on business of the utmost importance to the Reich. All personnel, military and civil, without distinction of rank, must assist him in any way he sees fit.

                                                      H. HIMMLER

A remarkable document in itself. Even more astonishing was that it was countersigned across the bottom: *Adolf Hitler, Führer und Reichskanzler.*

"He obviously had a certain amount of influence," Martineau said dryly, handing it back to Carter.

Munro said, "Well the bastard's dead now, but our Paris people got some useful information out of him before he left."

"I bet they did," Martineau said, and lit a cigarette.

"He has a dozen or so of these special envoys floating around Europe, putting the fear of God into everyone wherever they turn up. All highly secret. Nobody knows who they are. I've got our forgery department preparing a complete set of papers for you. SD identity card and a copy of that letter and whatever else you need. Name of Max Vogel. We thought we'd give you a little rank, just to help the ship along, so it's Standartenführer." He turned to Sarah, "Colonel to you."

"I get the picture," Martineau said. "I arrive on Jersey's fair shore and frighten the hell out of everyone."

"You know as well as I, dear boy, that there's nothing more frightening than a schoolmaster in a leather overcoat turned revolutionary. Lenin for a start. And you must admit, you do a very good Nazi, Harry."

"And the child?" Martineau inquired. "Where does she fit in?"

"You need someone with you to establish your credentials with Mrs. de Ville and this chap Gallagher. Sarah is related to one and knows the other. Another thing, she was last in Jersey six years ago, aged thirteen—all plaits and ankle socks, I shouldn't wonder. Still herself enough for Helen de Ville and Gallagher to recognize, but different enough to pass as a stranger with other people, especially when we've finished with her."

"And what's that supposed to mean?"

"Well, there's a fair trade in ladies of the night between France and Jersey."

"You mean whores? You're not suggesting she play one of those?"

"Most senior German officers in France have French girlfriends. Why should you be any different? To start off, Sarah speaks excellent French with a Breton accent because that's what her grandmother was. By the time our people at Berkley Hall have finished with her, changed her hair color, got her into the right clothes—"

"You mean, turned her into a little French tart?" Martineau interrupted.

"Something like that. Perfect cover for her."

"And when are we supposed to go in?"

"Day after tomorrow. A Lysander drop near Granville. Two-hour flight, Harry. Piece of cake. Sophie Cresson will meet you. Afterward, you use your authority to cross to Jersey on one of the night boats from Granville. Once over there, you make it up as you go along. You've got till Sunday at the outside."

"And what if it's impossible to get him out? What then?"

"Up to you."

"I see. I play executioner for you again?" He turned on Sarah. "What do you think about all this?"

He was angry, the face whiter than ever, the eyes very dark. "Oh, I don't know," she said. "It sounds as if it could be rather interesting."

In a sense, the flippancy of her remarks was an attempt to control her feelings, and when she turned and moved to the table to pour more tea into her cup, her hand shook slightly. The death of her mother had sent her to live with her father on a plantation deep in the Malayan jungle. A life of discomfort and considerable danger, an extraordinary upbringing for a girl of thirteen, and yet she'd loved every minute of it. In moments of the greatest danger, she seemed to come alive. The hospital by night, the bombing, the casualties who needed her. Once again, she'd loved every minute of it.

And now this. It was not just sexual desire, although she was enough of a woman to know that she wanted Martineau. But that was only part of it. It was what this strange, intense, tortured man offered. The promise of danger, excitement of a kind she had never even dreamed of before.

"Rather interesting? Dear God!" Martineau poured himself a scotch. "Have you read any of the works of Heidegger, Jack?"

"I'm familiar with them."

"An interesting man. He believed that for authentic living what was necessary was the resolute confrontation of death."

"That sounds fine by me," Munro said.

"Really?" Martineau laughed harshly. "As far as I'm concerned, it's idiots like that who made me give up on philosophy." He raised his glass and toasted them all. "Here we go then. Berkley Hall next stop."

7

THE FIRING RANGE AT BERKLEY Hall was in the basement. The armorer was an Irish Guards staff sergeant named Kelly, long past retirement and back in harness only because of the war. The place was brightly lit at the target end where cutout replicas of charging Germans stood against sandbags. Kelly and Sarah Drayton were the only people on the firing line. They'd given her battle dress to wear, slacks and blouse of blue serge, the kind issued to girls in the Women's Auxiliary Air Force. She'd tied her hair up and tucked it inside the peaked cap, leaving her neck bare. It somehow made her look very vulnerable.

Kelly had various weapons laid out on the table. "Have you ever fired a handgun before, miss?"

"Yes," she said, "in Malaya. My father was a rubber planter. He used to be away a great deal so he made sure I knew how to use a revolver. And I've fired a shotgun a few times."

"Anything here that looks familiar?"

"That revolver." She pointed. "It looks like the Smith and Wesson my father owned."

"That's exactly what it is, miss," Kelly said. "Obviously in more normal circumstances you'd be given a thorough grounding in weaponry as part of your course, but in your case, there just isn't time. What I'll do is show you a few things, just to familiarize you with some basic weapons you're likely to come across. Then you can fire a few rounds and that will have to do."

"Fair enough," she said.

"Rifles are simple," he said. "I won't waste your time with those. Here we've got two basic submachine guns. The British Sten in standard use with our own forces. This is a Mark 11S. Silenced version, developed for use with the French Resistance groups. Thirty-two rounds in that magazine. Automatic fire burns out the silencer, so use it semiautomatic or single burst. Like to have a go?"

It was surprisingly light and gave her no problems at all when she fired it from the shoulder, the only sound being the bolt reciprocating. She tore a sandbag apart to one side of the target she aimed at.

"Not much good," she said.

"Few people are with these things. They're good at close quarters when you're up against several people and that's all," Kelly told her. "The other submachine gun's German. An MP40. Popularly known as the Schmeisser. The Resistance use those a lot too."

He went through the handguns with her then, both the revolvers and the automatics. When she tried with the Smith & Wesson, arm extended, she only managed to nick the shoulder of the target once out of six shots.

"I'm afraid you'd be dead, miss."

As he reloaded, she said, "What about Colonel Martineau? Is he any good?"

"You could say that, miss. I don't think I've ever known anyone better with a handgun. Now, try this way." He crouched, feet apart, holding the gun two-handed. "See what I mean?"

"I think so." She copied him, the gun out in front of her in both hands.

"Now squeeze with a half breath of a pause between each shot."

This time, she did better, hitting the target once in the shoulder and once in the left hand.

"Terrific," Kelly said.

"Not if you consider she was probably aiming for the heart."

Martineau had come in quietly behind them. He wore a dark polo neck sweater and black corduroy pants and he came to the table and examined the guns. "As I'm going to have to look after this infant and as time is limited, do you mind if I take a hand?"

"Be my guest, sir."

Martineau picked up a pistol from the table. "Walther PPK, semiautomatic. Seven-round magazine goes in the butt, like so. Pull the slider back and you're in business. It's not too large. You wouldn't notice it in your handbag, but it will do the job and that's what matters. Now come down the range."

"All right."

They moved so close that the targets were no more than ten or twelve yards away. "If he's close enough for you to hold it against him when you pull the trigger, do it that way, but you should never be farther away than you are now. Simply throw up your arm and point the gun at him. Keep both eyes open and fire very fast."

She hit the target six times in the general area of the chest and belly. "Oh, my word," she said, very excited. "That wasn't bad, was it?"

As they walked back to the firing line he said, "Yes, but could you do it for real?"

"I'll only know when the time comes, won't I?" she said. "Anyway, what about you? I hear a lot of talk, but not much to justify it."

There was another Walther on the table with a round cylinder of polished black steel screwed on to the end of the barrel. "This is what's called a Carswell silencer," Martineau told her. "Specially developed for use by SOE agents."

His arm swung up. He didn't appear to take aim, firing twice, shooting out the heart of the target. The only sound had been two dull thuds, and the effect was quite terrifying.

He laid the gun down and turned, eyes blank in the white face. "I've got things to do. Dougal wants us in the library in half an hour. I'll see you then."

He walked out. There was an awkward silence. Sarah said, "He seemed angry."

"The colonel gets like that, miss. I don't think he likes what he sees in himself sometimes. Last November he killed the head of the Gestapo at Lyons. Man called Kaufmann. A real butcher. They brought him back from over there in a puddle of blood in a Lysander. Two bullets in his left lung for starters. He's been different since then."

"In what way?"

"I don't know, miss." Kelly frowned. "Here, don't you go getting silly ideas about him. I know what you young girls can be like. I've got a daughter your age on an antiaircraft battery in London. Just remember he's got twenty-five years on you."

"You mean he's too old?" Sarah said. "Isn't that like saying you can't love someone because they're Catholic or Jewish or American or something? What's the difference?"

"Too clever for me, that kind of talk." Kelly opened a drawer and took out a cloth bundle which he unwrapped. "A little present for you, miss, in spite of what the colonel says." It was a small black automatic pistol, very light, almost swallowed up by her hand. "Belgian. Only .25, but it'll do the trick when you need it and, at that size, very easy to hide." He looked awkward. "I've known ladies to tuck them in the top of their stocking, not intending to be disrespectful, miss."

She reached up and kissed him on the cheek. "I think you're wonderful."

"You can't do that, miss, you being an officer. Against regulations."

"But I'm not an officer, Sergeant."

"I think you'll find you are, miss. Probably one of the things the brigadier wants to tell you. I'd cut off and go to the library now if I were you."

"All right and thank you."

She went out and Kelly sighed and started to clear away the weapons.

Munro, Carter and Martineau were already in the library when she went in, sitting by the fire having afternoon tea. "Ah, there you are," Munro said. "Do join us. The crumpets are delicious."

Carter poured her a cup of tea. She said, "Sergeant Kelly said something about my being an officer now. What was he talking about?"

"Yes, well, we do prefer our women operatives to hold some sort of commissioned rank. In theory it's supposed to help you if you fall into enemy hands," Munro told her.

"In practice, it doesn't do you any good at all," Martineau interrupted.

"However, for good or ill, you are now a flight officer in the WAAF," Munro said. "I trust that is satisfactory. Now, let's look at the map."

They all got up and went to the table where there were several large-scale maps, together making a patchwork that included the south of England, the Channel, and the general area of the Channel Islands and Normandy and Brittany.

"All those jolly films they make at Elstree showing you our gallant secret agents at work usually have them parachuting into France. In fact, we prefer to take people in by plane wherever possible."

"I see," she said.

"Our popular choice is the Lysander. These days the pilot usually manages on his own. That way we can take up to three passengers. They're operated by a Special Duties Squadron at Hornley Field. It's not too far from here."

"How long will the flight take?"

"No more than an hour and a half, perhaps less depending on wind conditions. You'll land not far from Granville. The local Resistance people will be on hand to take care of you. We find the early hours of the morning best. Say four or five."

"Then what?"

"The evening of the same day you'll leave Granville by ship for Jersey. Most convoys go by night now. We have air superiority during daylight hours." He turned to Martineau. "Naturally, the question of passage is a matter for Standartenführer Max Vogel, but I doubt whether anyone is likely to do anything other than run round in circles when they see your credentials."

Martineau nodded. "We'll be in trouble if they don't."

"As regards your dealings with Mrs. de Ville and General Gallagher. Well, you have Sarah to vouch for you."

"And Kelso?"

"Entirely in your hands, dear boy. You're the officer in the field. I'll back whatever you decide to do. You know how critical the situation is."

"Fair enough."

Munro picked up the phone at his side. "Send Mrs. Moon in now." He put the phone down and said to Sarah, "We're very lucky to have Mrs. Moon. We borrow her from Denham Studios by courtesy of Alexander Korda. There's nothing she doesn't know about makeup, dress and so on."

Hilda Moon was a large fat woman with a cockney accent. Her own appearance inspired little confidence, for her hair was dyed red and it showed, and she wore too much lipstick. A cigarette dangled from the corner of her mouth, ash spilling down on her ample bosom.

"Yes." She nodded, walking round Sarah. "Very nice. Of course I'll have to do something with the hair."

"Do you think so?" Sarah asked in alarm.

"Girls who get by the way you're supposed to in this part, dear, always carry it up front. They make a living from pleasing men, which means they have to make the best of what they've got. You trust me, I know what's best for you."

She took Sarah by the arm and led her out. As the door closed, Martineau said, "We probably won't even recognize her when we see her again."

"Of course," Munro said. "But then, I should have thought that was the general idea."

🙦

It was early evening when the phone rang at Gallagher's cottage. He was in the kitchen, working through farm accounts at the table, and answered it instantly.

"Savary here, General. The matter of the package we discussed."

"Yes."

"My contact in Granville was in touch with their head office. It seems someone will be with you by Thursday at the latest to give you the advice you need."

"You're certain of that."

"Absolutely."

The phone went dead. Gallagher sat there thinking about it, then he put on his old corduroy jacket and went up to de Ville Place. He found Helen in the kitchen with Mrs. Vibert, preparing the evening meal. The old lady didn't live on the premises, but just down the road in another farm cottage with her niece and young daughter. She was a widow herself, a good-hearted woman of sixty-five, devoted to Helen.

She dried her hands and took a coat down from behind the door. "If that's all, I'll be off now, Mrs. de Ville."

"See you in the morning," Helen told her.

As the door closed behind her, Gallagher said, "She doesn't suspect anything, does she?"

"No, and I want it to stay that way, for her own good, as much as anyone else's."

"I've just had Savary on the phone. They got through to London. Someone will be with us by Thursday."

She turned quickly. "Are you certain?"

"As much as I can be. How is the good colonel?"

"Still feverish. George saw him this afternoon. He seems satisfied. He's trying him on this penicillin stuff."

"I'm surprised Savary was in so early. They must have made the run this afternoon."

"They did," she said. "Taking advantage of the fog again. Most of the officers have turned up here within the past hour."

"Most?"

"Two dead. Bohlen and Wendel. Two of the ships were attacked by Hurricanes."

At that moment, the green baize door leading to the dining room opened and Guido Orsini came in. He was wearing his best uniform, his hair still damp from the shower, and looked rather dashing. He wore the Italian Medal for Military Valor in gold, a medal equivalent to the British Victoria Cross and very rarely awarded. On his left breast he also wore an Iron Cross First Class.

Gallagher said in English, "Still in one piece are you? Hear you had a bad time."

"It could have been worse," Guido told him. "They're all sitting in there doing their conspicuous mourning bit." He put a bag he was carrying on the table. "Dozen bottles of Sancerre there from Granville."

"You're a good boy," she said.

"So I believe. Don't you think I also look rather beautiful tonight?"

"Very possibly." He was mocking her as usual, she knew that. "Now move to one side while I dish up the food."

Guido inched open the serving hatch to the dining room and whispered to Gallagher. "Sean, come and look at this."

The hall was paneled in oak, darkly magnificent, and the long oaken table down the center could accommodate twenty-five. There were only eight in there now, all naval officers, seated at various places. In each gap, where someone was missing, a lighted candle stood at the plate. There were six such candles, each representing a member of the mess who had died in action. The atmosphere was funereal to say the least.

"They have to make everything into a Shakespearean tragedy," Orsini said. "It's really very boring. If it wasn't for Helen's cooking I'd go elsewhere. I discovered a remarkably good black-market restaurant in St. Aubin's Bay the other night. Amazing what one got and without coupons."

"Now that is interesting," Gallagher said. "Tell me more."

As Mrs. Moon and her two assistants worked on Sarah, the fat woman talked incessantly. "I've been everywhere. Denham, Elstree, Pinewood. I do all Miss Margaret Lockwood's makeup and Mr. James Mason. Oh, and I've worked with Mr. Coward. Now he *was* a gentleman."

When Sarah came out from under the dryer, she couldn't believe what she saw. Her dark hair was now a golden blond, and they'd marcelled it tight against her face. Now, Mrs. Moon started with the makeup, plucking hairs from the eyebrows painfully then lining them into two thin streaks.

"Plenty of rouge, dear. A little too much, if you know what I mean, and lots of lipstick. Everything just a little overdone, that's what we want. Now, what do you think?"

Sarah sat looking into the mirror. It was the face of a stranger. Who am I? she thought. Did Sarah Drayton ever exist at all?

"We'll try one of the dresses. Of course, the underwear and every individual item will be of French origin, but you only need the dress at the moment, just for the effect."

It was black satin, very tight and rather short. She helped Sarah into it and zipped it at the back. "It certainly helps your breasts along, dear. They look very good."

"I don't know about that, I can't breathe." Sarah pulled on a pair of high-heeled shoes and looked at herself in the mirror. She giggled. "I look the most awful tart."

"Well, that *is* the idea, love. Now go and see what the brigadier thinks."

Munro and Carter were still sitting by the fire when she went in, talking in low tones. Sarah said, "No one told me my name."

"Anne-Marie Latour," Carter said automatically and then looked up. "Good God!" he said.

Munro was far more positive. "I like it. Like it very much indeed." Sarah pirouetted. "Yes, they'll go for you in the German officers' club in St. Helier."

"Or in the Army and Navy in London, I should have thought," Carter said dryly.

The door opened and Martineau entered. She turned to face him, hands on hips in a deliberate challenge. "Well?" she demanded.

"Well, what?"

"Oh, damn you." She was cross enough to stamp a foot. "You're the most infuriating man I've ever met. Is there a village near here with a pub?"

"Yes."

"Will you take me for a drink?"

"Like that?"

"You mean I don't look nice enough?"

"Actually, you transcend all Mrs. Moon's efforts. You couldn't be a tart if you tried, brat. I'll see you in the hall in fifteen minutes," and he turned and went out.

There was a spring fete on in the village in aid of war charities. Stalls and sideshows on the village green and a couple of old-fashioned roundabouts. Sarah wore a coat over the dress and hung onto his arm. She was obviously enjoying herself as they moved through the noisy and good-humored crowd.

There was a tent marked *Fortunes—Gypsy Sara*. "Sara without the H," she said. "Let's give it a try."

"All right," he said, humoring her.

Surprisingly, the woman inside had dispensed with the usual gypsy trappings, the headscarf and the earrings. She was about forty with a sallow face, neat black hair and wore a smart gabardine suit. She took the girl's hand. "Just you, lady, or your gentleman as well?"

"But he isn't my gentleman," she protested.

"He'll never belong to anyone else, never know another woman."

She took a deep breath as if trying to clear her head, and Martineau said, "Now let's hear the good news."

She handed a tarot pack to Sarah, folded her own hands over Sarah's, then shuffled the pack several times and extracted three cards.

The first was Fortitude, a young woman grasping the jaws of a lion. "There is an opportunity to put an important plan into action if one will take risks," Gypsy Sara said.

The next card was the Star, a naked girl kneeling by a pool. "I see fire and water, mingling at the same time. A contradiction and yet you come through both unscathed."

Sarah turned to Martineau. "I had that last month at the Cromwell. Incendiary bombs on the nurses' quarters and water everywhere from the fire hoses."

The third card was the Hanged Man. The woman said, "He will not change however long he hangs in the tree. He cannot alter the mirror image, however much he fears it. You must journey on alone. Adversity will always be your strength. You will find love only by not seeking it, that is the lesson you must learn."

Sarah said to Martineau, "Now you."

Gypsy Sara gathered up the cards. "There is nothing I can tell the gentleman that he does not know already."

"Best thing I've heard since the Brothers Grimm." Martineau pushed a pound across the table and stood up. "Let's go."

"Are you angry?" Sarah demanded as they pushed through the crowd to the village pub.

"Why should I be?"

"It was only a bit of fun. Nothing to be taken seriously."

"Oh, but I take everything seriously," he assured her.

The bar was crowded but they managed to find a couple of seats in the corner by the fire, and he ordered her a shandy and had a scotch for himself. "Well, what do you think of it so far?" he asked.

"Rather more interesting than the wards at the Cromwell."

"In other circumstances you'd be trained for about six weeks," he said. "The Scottish Highlands to toughen you up. Courses in unarmed combat and so on. Twelve ways of killing someone with your bare hands."

"That sounds very gruesome."

"But effective. I remember one of our agents, a journalist in civilian life, who stopped going into pubs when he was home. He was afraid to get into an argument because of what he might do."

"Can you do that sort of thing?" she asked him.

"Anybody can be taught to do it. It's brains that's important in this game."

There were three soldiers in khaki battle dress at the bar, an older man who was a sergeant and a couple of privates. Hard young men who kept laughing, heads together, as they looked across at Martineau. When he went to replenish the drinks, one of them deliberately jogged his arm as he turned from the bar, spilling a little scotch.

"You want to be more careful, mate," the youth told him.

"If you say so." Martineau smiled cheerfully, and the sergeant put a hand on the youth's sleeve and muttered something.

When he sat down Sarah said, "Jack Carter tells me you knew Freud."

"Yes, I last saw him in London in nineteen thirty-nine just before he died."

"Do you agree with psychoanalysis?"

"Everything coming down to sex? God knows, old Sigmund had enough problems in that direction himself. He was once doing a lecture tour in the States with Jung and told him one day that he kept dreaming of prostitutes. Jung simply asked him why he didn't do something about it. Freud was terribly shocked. 'But I'm a married man,' he said."

She laughed helplessly. "That's marvelous."

"Talking of great minds, I used to have dealings with Bertrand Russell, who liked the ladies more than somewhat, which he justified by his strongly held personal belief that you couldn't get to know a woman properly until you'd slept with her."

"That doesn't sound very philosophical to me," she said.

"On the contrary."

She got up and excused herself. "I'll be back in a minute."

As she went out to the cloakroom the three soldiers watched her go, then glanced at Martineau, and there was a burst of laughter. As she returned, the young soldier who had bumped Martineau at the bar grabbed her arm. She struggled to pull away and Martineau was on his feet and pushing through the crowd to her side.

"That's enough."

"Who the hell are you, her father?" the boy demanded.

Martineau took him by the wrist, applying leverage in the way the instructor had shown him on the silent killing course at Arisaig in Scotland in the early days. The boy grimaced in pain. The sergeant said, "Leave off. He didn't mean any harm. Just a bit of fun."

"Yes, I can see that."

As he took her back to the table she said, "That was quick."

"When I feel, I act. I'm a very existentialist person."

"Existentialist?" She frowned. "I don't understand."

"Oh, a new perspective to things a friend of mine's come up with. A French writer called Jean-Paul Sartre. When I was on the run in Paris three years ago I holed up at his apartment for a couple of weeks. He's involved with the Resistance."

"But what does it mean?"

"Oh, lots of things. The bit I like is the suggestion that you should create values for yourself through action and by living each moment to the full."

"Is that how you've got yourself through the last four years?"

"Something like that. Sartre just put it into words for me." He helped her into her coat. "Let's go."

It was dark outside, music and merriment drifting from the direction of the fair, although most of the stands were already closed because of the blackout regulations. They started across the deserted car park to where Martineau had left the car, and there was a sound of running footsteps. He turned as the two young soldiers ran up. The sergeant emerged on the porch at the rear of the pub and stood watching.

"Now then," the young soldier who'd caused the scene at the bar said. "You and me aren't finished yet. You need to be taught a lesson."

"Is that a fact?" Martineau demanded, and as the youth moved in, swinging a punch, he caught the wrist, twisted it up and around, locking the shoulder. The soldier cried out as the muscle tore. The other soldier gave a cry of alarm and recoiled as Martineau dropped his friend on the ground and the sergeant ran forward angrily.

"You bastard!" he said.

"Not me, you for letting it happen." Martineau had his identity card out. "I think you'd better look at that."

The sergeant's face dropped. "Colonel, sir!" He sprang to attention.

"That's better. You're going to need a doctor. Tell chummy here when he's capable of listening that I hope he's learned something. Next time it could be the death of him."

As they drove away, Sarah said, "You don't hesitate at all, do you?"

"What's the point?"

"I think I understand what Jack Carter meant. You have an aptitude for killing, I think."

"Words," he said. "Games in the head. That's all I had for years. Nothing but talk, nothing but ideas. Let's have some facts. Let's stop playing games in black satin dresses with our hair blonded. You know what the first technique is that the Gestapo employ in breaking down any woman agent who falls into their hands?"

"You're obviously going to tell me."

"Multiple rape. If that doesn't do the trick, the electric shock treatment comes next. I used to have a girlfriend in Berlin. She was Jewish."

"I know. Carter told me about her as well."

"How they tortured, then murdered her in the Gestapo cellars at Prince Albrechtstrasse?" Martineau shook his head. "He doesn't know everything. He doesn't know that Kaufmann, the head of the Gestapo in Lyons who I killed last November, was the man responsible for Rosa's death in Berlin in nineteen thirty-eight."

"I see now," she said softly. "Sergeant Kelly said you were different and he was right. You hated Kaufmann for years and when you finally took your revenge, you found it meant nothing."

"All this wisdom." He laughed coldly. "Going over there and taking on the Gestapo isn't like one of those movies they make at Elstree Studios. There are fifty million people in France. You know how many we estimate are active members of the Resistance?"

"No."

"Two thousand, Sarah. Two lousy thousand." He was disgusted. "I don't know why we bother."

"Then why do you? Not just for Rosa or your grandfather." He turned briefly and she said, "Oh, yes, I know about that too."

There was a silence. He opened his cigarette case one-handed. "Do you want one of these things? A bad habit, but a great comfort in the clinches."

"All right," she said and took one.

He gave her a light. "Something I've never talked about. I was due to go to Harvard in nineteen seventeen. Then America joined in the war. I was seventeen, officially under age. Joined up on sheer impulse and ended up in the trenches in Flanders." He shook his head. "Whatever you mean by hell on earth, that was the trenches. So many dead you lost count."

"It must have been terrible," she said.

"And I loved every minute of it. Can you understand that? I lived more in one day, felt more, than in a year of ordinary living. Life became real, bloody, exciting. I couldn't get enough."

"Like a drug?"

"Exactly. I was like the man in the poem, constantly seeking Death on the battlefield. That was what I ran away from, back to Harvard and Oxford cloisters and the safe world of classrooms and books, everything in the head."

"And then the war came round again."

"And Dougal Munro yanked me out into the real world. . . . And the rest, as they say, you know."

Later, lying in bed smoking a cigarette, listening to the rain tapping at the window, he heard the door open. She said softly through the darkness, "It's only me."

"Really?" Martineau said.

She took off her robe and got into bed beside him. She was wearing a cotton nightdress and he put an arm around her automatically. "Harry," she whispered. "Can I make a confession?"

"You obviously intend to."

"I know you probably imagine, along with everyone else, that I'm a delicate little middle-class virgin, but I'm afraid I'm not."

"Is that a fact?"

"Yes, I met a Spitfire pilot at the hospital last year. He used to come in for treatment for a broken ankle."

"And true love blossomed?"

"Not really. More like mutual lust, but he was a nice chap and I don't regret it. He was shot down over the Channel three months ago."

She started to cry, for no reason that made any kind of sense, and Martineau held her tight, wordless in the dark.

8

THE FOLLOWING DAY JUST AFTER noon at Fermanville on the Cherbourg Peninsula, Karl Hagan, the duty sergeant at the central strongpoint of the 15th Coastal Artillery Battery, was leaning on a concrete parapet idly enjoying a cigarette in the pale afternoon sunshine when he observed a black Mercedes coming up the track. No escort so it couldn't be anyone important—and then he noticed the pennant fluttering on the bonnet. Too far away to see what it was, but to an old soldier it was enough. He was inside the operations room in a flash, where Captain Reimann, the battery commander, sprawled at his desk, tunic buttons undone, reading a book.

"Someone coming, sir. Looks like top brass to me. Shock inspection perhaps."

"Right. Klaxon alarm. Get the men to fall in, just in case."

Reimann buttoned his tunic, buckled his belt and adjusted his cap to a satisfactory angle. As he went out on the redoubt, the Mercedes pulled in below. The driver got out. The first person out was an army major with staff stripes on his pants. The second was Field Marshal Erwin Rommel in leather trenchcoat, white scarf knotted carelessly at his neck, desert goggles pulled up above the peak of his cap.

Reimann had never been so shocked in his life and he grabbed at the parapet. At the same moment he heard Sergeant Hagan's voice and the battery personnel doubled out in the courtyard below. As Reimann hurried down the steps the two battery lieutenants, Scheel and Planck, took up their positions.

Reimann moved forward and remembering what he'd heard of Rommel's preferences chose the military rather than the Nazi salute. "Herr Field Marshal. You do us a great honor."

Rommel tapped the end of his field marshal's baton against the peak of his cap. "Your name?"

"Reimann, Herr Field Marshal."

"Major Hofer, my aide."

Hofer said, "The Field Marshal will see everything, including the subsidiary strongpoints. Please lead the way."

"First, Major, I'll inspect the troops," Rommel told him. "An army is only as strong as its weakest point, always remember that."

"Of course, Herr Field Marshal," Hofer said.

Rommel moved down the line, stopping here and there to talk to an individual who took his fancy. Finally he turned. "Good turnout. Highly satisfactory. Now we go."

For the next hour he tramped the clifftop from one strongpoint to another as Reimann led the way. Radio rooms, men's quarters, ammunition stores, even the urinals. Nothing escaped his attention.

"Excellent, Reimann," he told the young artillery officer. "First-rate performance. I'll endorse your field unit report personally."

Reimann almost fainted with pleasure. "Herr Field Marshal—what can I say?"

He called the honor guard to attention. Rommel tapped the baton against his cap again and got into the Mercedes. Hofer joined him on the other side, and as the driver drove away, the major checked that the glass partition was closed tight.

"Excellent," Hofer said. "Have a cigarette. I think you carried that off very well, Berger."

"Really, Herr Major?" Heini Baum said. "I get the booking then?"

"One more test, I think. Something a little bit more ambitious. Dinner at some officers' mess, perhaps. Yes, that would be good. Then you'll be ready for Jersey."

"Anything you say." Baum leaned back, inhaling deeply on the cigarette.

"So, back to the field marshal to report," Konrad Hofer said.

When Sarah and Harry Martineau went into the library at Berkley Hall, Jack Carter was sitting at the table, the maps spread before him.

"Ah, there you are," he said. "Brigadier Munro has gone up to London to report to General Eisenhower, but he'll be back tonight. We'll both see you off from Hornley Field. Any problems?''

"None that I can think of." Martineau turned to Sarah. "What about you?"

"I don't think so."

"Your clothes have all been double-checked for Frenchness," Carter said. "So that's taken care of. Here are your papers, Sarah. French identity card with photo. German Ausweis, with different photo. Now you know why they asked you to change clothes at the photography session. Ration cards. Oh, and a tobacco ration card."

"You're supposed to have one of those even if you don't smoke," Martineau told her.

"These documents are one hundred percent," Carter said. "Right paper, same watermarks. Typewriters, ink—everything perfect. I can assure you that there is no way that even the most skilled Abwehr or Gestapo operative could find them anything but genuine." He handed her a slip of paper. "There are your personal details. Anne-Marie Latour. We've kept to your own age and birthdate. Born in Brittany naturally, to explain your accent. We've made your place of birth Paimpol on the coast. I believe you know it well?"

"Yes, my grandmother lived there. I spent many holidays with her."

"Normally you'd have some considerable length of time to get used to your new identity. In this case that just isn't possible. However, you will have Harry with you and it should be for no more than three days. Four at the most."

"I understand."

"One more thing. Your relationship with Standartenführer Vogel must at all times seem convincing. You do appreciate what that could entail?"

"Sharing a room?" The smile when she turned to Martineau was mischievous. "Is that all right with you, Colonel?"

For once, Martineau was put out and he frowned. "You little bitch!"

It was as if they were alone for a moment and she touched his face gently with her fingertips. "Oh, Harry Martineau, you are lovely when you're angry." She turned to Carter. "I think you can take it there'll be no problem, Captain."

Carter, hugely embarrassed, said hurriedly, "All right. Then read this, both of you. Regulations, Sarah."

It was a typical SOE operations order, cold, flat, precise, no-nonsense language. It laid out the task ahead of them, procedure, communication channel via the Cressons in Granville. Everything was covered, even down to a code name for the operation, JERSEYMAN. At the end of the flimsy it said: NOW DESTROY NOW DESTROY.

"All right?" Martineau asked her.

She nodded and he struck a match and touched it to the paper, dropping it into the ashtray. "That's it then," he said. "I'll go and do my packing. See you two later."

On the bed in his room, the wardrobe people had laid out a three-piece suit in light-gray tweed, shoes, some white shirts, two black ties. There was also a military overcoat in soft black leather of a kind worn by many SS officers.

The gray-green SS uniform hung behind the door. He checked it carefully. On the left sleeve was the RFSS cuff title of Himmler's personal staff, an SD patch above it. The Waffenfarben, the colored piping on the uniform and cap, was toxic green, indicating that he belonged to the SS Security Service. The oak leaves of his collar patches indicating his rank were in silver thread. There was an Iron Cross First Class on the left side of the tunic. His only other decoration was the Order of Blood, a medal struck specially for old comrades of the Führer who had served prison sentences for political crimes during the twenties.

He decided to try the uniform on and undressed quickly. Everything fit to perfection. He buttoned the tunic and fastened the belt, a rare specimen that had an eagle on the buckle with a swastika in one claw and SS runes in the other. He picked up the cap and examined the silver death's-head badge, running his sleeve across it, then reached inside, scratched a slight tear in the silk lining and withdrew the rigid spring so that the cap crumpled. It was an affectation of many oldtimers, although against regulations.

He put it on his head at a slight angle. From behind, Sarah said quietly, "You look as if you're enjoying yourself. I get the feeling you like uniforms."

"I like getting it right," he said. "I often think I missed my vocation. I should have been an actor. Getting it right is important, Sarah. You don't get second chances."

There was a kind of distress on her face and she moved close and gripped his arm. "I'm not sure if it's you anymore, Harry."

"It isn't, not in this uniform. Standartenführer Max Vogel, of the SD. Feared by his own side as much as the French. You'll see. This isn't a game anymore."

She shivered and put her arms around him. "I know, Harry, I know."

"Are you frightened?"

"Good God, no." She smiled up at him. "Not with Gypsy Sara in my corner."

Eisenhower sat at his desk in the study at Hayes Lodge, reading glasses perched on his nose as he worked his way through the file. He sat back, removed the glasses and looked across at Dougal Munro.

"Quite a man, Martineau. Extraordinary record, and an American."

"Yes, sir. He told me once that his great-grandmother had immigrated to Virginia in the eighteen-fifties from England. Small town in Lancashire, I believe."

"It sounds a kind of exotic name for Lancashire."

"Not unknown, General. I believe it goes back to Norman times."

He realized that Eisenhower was simply stalling for time while he thought about things. He got up and peered out the window, then turned. "Flight Officer Drayton. She's very young."

"I'm aware of that, General. However, she is in a unique position to help us."

"Of course. You really think this could work?"

"I believe we can put Colonel Martineau and Flight Officer Drayton into France with no trouble. I can't see any problem with their continuing onward to Jersey by boat. Martineau has unique authority. No one would dare question it. If you want to query the Reichsführer's personal representative, the only way you can do it is to ring the Reichsführer himself in Berlin."

"Yes, I see that," Eisenhower said.

"However, once they're in Jersey, the game is really wide open. There is no way I can give you any assurance about what happens. We'll be entirely in Martineau's hands." There was silence for a while, and then Munro added, "They should be in Jersey by Thursday. Martineau has until Sunday. That's his deadline. It's only a few days."

"And a hell of a lot of lives depending on it." Eisenhower sat down behind the desk. "Okay, Brigadier. Carry on and keep me informed at all times."

Hornley Field had been an aero club before the war. It had also been used as a temporary fighter station during the Battle of Britain. It was now used for clandestine flights to the continent only, mainly Lysanders and the occasional Liberator. The runway was grass, but long enough. There was a tower, several huts and two hangars.

The commanding officer was a Squadron Leader Barnes, an ex-fighter pilot who'd lost his left arm in the summer of 1940. The pilot of the Lysander was a flight lieutenant named Peter Green. Sarah, standing at the window, saw him now, bulky in his flying jacket and helmet, standing by the plane.

It was two-thirty in the morning, but warm enough, the stove roaring away. "Can I offer you some more coffee, Flight Officer?" Barnes asked Sarah.

She turned and smiled. "No thanks. I shouldn't imagine Westland included a toilet facility in their Lysander.''

He smiled. ''No, I'm afraid there wasn't the room.''

Martineau stood by the stove, hands in the pockets of his leather trenchcoat. He wore the tweed suit and a dark slouch hat and smoked a cigarette. Carter sat by the stove, tapping his stick restlessly on the floor.

''We're really going to have to get moving, I'm afraid,'' Barnes said. ''Just the right conditions at the other end if you go now. Too light if we wait.''

''I can't imagine what's happened to the brigadier,'' Carter said.

''It doesn't matter.'' Martineau turned to Sarah. ''Ready to go?''

She nodded and very carefully pulled on her fashionable leather gloves. She was wearing a black coat over her dress, nipped in at the waist with large shoulders, all very fashionable.

Barnes put a very large fur-lined flying jacket over her shoulders. ''It might be cold up there.''

''Thank you.''

Martineau picked up their two suitcases and they went out and crossed to the Lysander where Green waited. ''Any problems?'' Martineau asked.

''Coastal fog, but only in patches. Slight headwind.'' He glanced at his watch. ''We'll be there by four-thirty at the outside.''

Sarah went first and strapped herself in. Martineau passed up the suitcases then turned and shook hands with Carter. ''See you soon, Jack.''

''You've got the call sign,'' Carter said. ''All Cresson has to do is send that. No message needed. We'll have a Lysander out to the same field at ten o'clock at night of the same day to pick you up.''

Martineau climbed in next to Sarah and fastened his seat belt. He didn't look at her or say anything, but he took her hand as Green climbed into the pilot's seat. The sound of the engines shattered the night. They started to taxi to the far end of the runway and turned. As they started to roll between the two lines of lights, gradually increasing speed, the Austin Princess turned in through the main gate, hesitated for the sentry's inspection then bumped across the grass to the huts. As Dougal Munro got out, the Lysander lifted over the trees at the far end of the field and was swallowed by darkness.

''Damnation!'' he said. ''Held up at Baker Street, Jack. Something came up. Thought I'd just make it.''

''They couldn't wait, sir,'' Barnes told him. ''Might have made things difficult at the other end.''

''Of course,'' Munro said.

Barnes walked away and Carter said, ''What did General Eisenhower have to say, sir?''

''What could he say, Jack? What can any of us say?'' Munro shrugged. ''The ball's in Harry Martineau's court now. All up to him.''

"And Sarah Drayton, sir."

"Yes, I liked that young woman." Aware suddenly that he had spoken in the past tense, Munro shivered as if at an omen. "Come on, Jack, let's go home," he said, and he turned and got back into the Austin.

Sophia Cresson waited on the edge of a wood beside the field seven miles northwest of Granville which was the designated landing strip. She was on her own and stood beside an old Renault van smoking a cigarette in her cupped hands. The door of the van was open, and a Sten gun lay ready to hand on the passenger seat. There was also the homing beacon. She'd waited at the bar until Gerard had received the message that they had actually left Hornley. Timing was critical in these things.

She wore a woolen cap pulled down over her ears against the cold, an old fur-lined hunting coat of Gerard's, belted at the waist, and slacks. She wasn't worried about problems with any security patrol she might run across. She knew all the soldiers in the Granville area and they knew her. As for the police, they did as they were told. There wasn't one she didn't know too much about. In the back of the van were several dead chickens and a few pheasants. Out on another black-market trip, that was her cover.

She checked her watch and switched on the homing beacon. Then she took three torches from the van and ran forward into the broad meadow and arranged them in an inverted L-shape with the crossbar at the upwind end. Then she moved back to the van and waited.

The flight had been completely uneventful, mainly because Green was an old hand, with more than forty such sorties under his belt. He had never belonged to the school of thought that recommended approaching the French coast below the radar screen. The one time he had tried this tactic the Royal Navy had fired at him. So, it was at 8,000 feet that the Lysander crossed over the Cherbourg Peninsula and turned slightly south.

He spoke over the intercom. "Fifteen minutes, so be ready."

"Any chance of running into a night fighter?" Martineau asked.

"Unlikely. Maximum effort strike by Bomber Command on various towns in the Ruhr. Jerry will have scrambled every night fighter in France to go and protect the Fatherland."

"Look!" Sarah cut in. "I can see lights."

The L-shape was clearly visible below as they descended rapidly. "That's it," Green told them. "I've landed here twice before so I know my stuff. In and out very fast. You know the drill, Colonel.''

And then they were drifting down over the trees into the meadow, rolling forward across the lights. Sophie Cresson ran forward, waving, the Sten gun in one hand. Martineau got the door open, threw out the suitcases and followed them. He turned to help Sarah. Behind her, Green reached for the door and slammed it shut, locking the handle. The engine note deepened to a full-throated roar as the Lysander raced across the meadow and took off.

Sophie Cresson said, ''Come on, let's get out of here. Bring your suitcases while I get my lamps.'' They followed her to the van and she opened the rear door. ''There's just enough room for both of you to sit behind the two barrels. Don't worry, I know every flic in the district. If they stop me, all they'll do is take a chicken and go home.''

''Some things never change,'' Sarah said.

''Heh, a Breton girl?'' Sophie flashed her torch on Sarah's face and grunted. ''My God, now they send little girls.'' She shrugged. ''In you get and let's be out of here.''

Sarah crouched behind the barrels, her knees touching Martineau as Sophie drove away. So, this was it, she thought, the real thing. No more games now. She opened her handbag and felt for the butt of the Walther PPK inside. The little Belgian automatic Kelly had given her was in her case. Would she be able to use them if necessary? Only time would tell. Martineau lit a cigarette and passed it to her. When she inhaled, nothing had ever felt better, and she leaned back against the side of the van feeling wonderfully, marvelously alive.

It was noon before she awoke, yawning and stretching her arms. The small bedroom under the roof was plainly furnished but comfortable. She threw back the sheets and crossed to the window. The view across the walls down to the harbor was really quite special. Behind her the door opened and Sophie came in with a bowl of coffee on a tray.

''So, you're up.''

''It's good to be back.'' Sarah took the bowl from her and sat on the window seat.

Sophie lit a cigarette. ''You've been here before?''

''Many times. My mother was a de Ville. Half-Jersey, half-Breton. My grandmother was born at Paimpol. I used to come over to Granville from the island when I was a little girl. There was a fishermen's café on the quay that had the finest hot rolls in the world. The best coffee.''

''Not anymore,'' Sophie said. ''The war has changed everything. Look down there.''

The harbor was crammed with shipping. Rhine barges, three coasters and a number of German naval craft. It was a scene of considerable activity as dockers unloaded the contents of a line of trucks on the quay into the barges.

"They're definitely sailing for the islands tonight?" Sarah asked.

"Oh yes. Some for Jersey, the rest on to Guernsey."

"How do you find them?"

"The Boche?" Sophie shrugged. "I'm a reasonable woman. I don't want to hate anybody. I just want them out of France."

"It's just that we hear such bad things about them in England."

"True," Sophie said. "SS and Gestapo are devils, but they frighten the hell out of the ordinary German soldier as much as they do anyone else. In any case, we've got those among our own people who are as bad as the Gestapo. Darnan's *milice*. Frenchmen who work with the Nazis to betray Frenchmen."

"That's terrible," Sarah said.

"It's life, child, and what it means is you can never really trust anyone. Now get dressed and come downstairs and we'll have some lunch."

At Gavray in what had once been the country home of the count of that name, Heini Baum sat at one end of the table in the officers' mess of the 41st Panzer Grenadiers and smilingly acknowledged the cheers as the officers toasted him then applauded. When they were finished, he nodded his thanks.

The young colonel of the regiment, a veteran of the Russian Front, his black panzer uniform scattered with decorations, said, "If you could manage a few words, Herr Field Marshal. It would mean so much to my officers."

There was a worried look in Hofer's eye when Baum glanced at him, but he disregarded it and stood up, straightening his tunic. "Gentlemen, the Führer has given us a simple task. To keep the enemy off our beaches. Yes, I say our beaches. Europe, one and indivisible, is our goal. The battle will be won on those beaches. There is no possibility of our losing. The destiny of the Führer is God-given. So much is obvious to anyone with a grain of sense." His irony was lost on them as they gazed up, enraptured, drinking in every word. He raised his glass. "So, gentlemen, join me. To our beloved Führer, Adolf Hitler."

"Adolf Hitler!" they chorused.

Baum tossed his glass into the fire, and with a stirring of excitement, they all followed him. Then they applauded again, forming two lines as he walked out, followed by Hofer.

"Rather heavy on the glasses, I should have thought," Hofer said as they drove back to Cressy where Rommel had established temporary headquarters at the old castle there.

"You didn't approve?" Baum said.

"I didn't say that. Actually, the speech was rather good."

"If the Herr Major will excuse my saying so, it was heavily over the top, to use theatrical vernacular," Baum told him.

"I take your point," Hofer said. "On the other hand, it's exactly what they wanted to hear."

Crazy, Baum thought. *Am I the only sane man left alive?* But by then, they were drawing into the courtyard of the castle. He went up the steps fast, acknowledging the salutes, Hofer trailing him, all the way up to the suite on the second floor.

Rommel had locked himself in the study and only came out on Hofer's knock. "How did it go?"

"Perfect," Hofer said. "Passed with flying colors. You should have heard the speech you made."

"Excellent." Rommel nodded. "Everything progresses in the Channel Islands? You spoke to von Schmettow in Guernsey?"

"Personally, Herr Field Marshal. He's also had his orders in writing. As you were told by Naval HQ at Cherbourg, they do most of their traveling between the islands by night these days because of the enemy air superiority in the area. So they will travel from Jersey to Guernsey on Thursday night for the conference, returning on Sunday night."

"Good," Rommel said. "Which still leaves you and Berger flying in out of the dawn in a Fiesler Storch with all that RAF superiority in the area that you speak of." He turned to Baum. "What do you think about that, Berger?"

"I think it could be interesting if the Herr Major and I went down in flames into the sea. The Desert Fox is dead." He shrugged. "That could lead to some strange possibilities, you must admit, Herr Field Marshal."

Gerard Cresson sat in his wheelchair at the table in the sitting room and refilled the glasses with red wine. "No, I hate to dispel your illusions," he said to Sarah, "But out in Jersey, just as in France and every other occupied country in Europe, the real enemy is the informer. Without them the Gestapo couldn't operate."

"But I was told there weren't any Gestapo in Jersey," Sarah said.

"Officially they have a Geheime Feldpolizei setup there. That's Secret Field Police, and they're supposed to be controlled by the Abwehr. Military Intelligence. The whole thing is part of the ruling-by-kindness policy, a cosmetic exercise aimed at fooling the people. The implication is that because you're British we won't sick the Gestapo onto you."

"Which is shit," Sophie said as she came in from the kitchen with fresh coffee, "because several of the men working for the GFP in Jersey are Gestapo operatives on loan."

"Do you know where they are?" Sarah asked.

"A hotel at Havre des Pas called Silvertide. You know it?"

She nodded. "Oh yes. I used to go swimming at Havre des Pas when I was a child."

"Gestapo, Secret Field Police, SD, Abwehr. Wherever you go, whoever the man is who knocks on the door, it's the Gestapo to the poor devil being arrested."

"Exactly the same in Jersey," Gerard told him. "To the locals, they're Gestapo and that's it. Mind you, it's a Mickey Mouse operation compared to what goes on in Lyons or Paris, but watch out for a Captain Muller. He's temporarily in command, and his chief aide, an inspector called Kleist."

"Are they SS?"

"I don't know. Probably not. They've never been seen in uniform. Probably seconded from the police in some big city. Full of themselves, like all flics. Out to prove something." He shrugged. "You don't have to be in the SS to be in the Gestapo. You don't even have to be a member of the Nazi Party."

"True," Martineau said. "Anyway, how do you rate our chances of bringing Kelso over from Jersey?"

"Very difficult indeed. That's one item they are very tight on, civilian traffic. It would be impossible in a small boat at the moment."

"And if he isn't able to walk . . . " Sophie shrugged expressively.

"They'll be standing by at SOE for a call from you at any time this weekend," Martineau said. "The Lysander can pick up on Sunday night."

Gerard laughed suddenly. "I've just had a brilliant thought. You could always arrest Kelso. Find him and arrest him, if you follow me. Bring him over here officially, then cut out."

"That's all very well," Sarah put in, "but where would that leave Aunt Helen and the General? Wouldn't they have to be arrested too?"

Martineau nodded. "It's one of those ideas that sounds good until you think about it. Never mind. We'll think of something when we get there."

"Like a bullet in the head maybe?" Cresson suggested. "I mean, if this man is as important as they say . . . "

"He's entitled to a chance," Martineau said. "If there's any way I can pull him out I will, if not . . . " He shrugged. "Now, what's the procedure for booking passage to the island tonight?"

"There's a movement officer in the office in the green hut on the quay. He issues the passes. No difficulty in your case."

"Good," Martineau said. "That seems to be about it then."

Sophie filled four glasses with red wine. "I'm not going to wish you luck, I'm just going to tell you something."

"What's that?" Martineau inquired.

She put an arm around Sarah's shoulders. "I like the kid here very much. Whatever happens over there, you bring her back in one piece, because if you don't, and you show your face here again, I'll put a bullet in you myself."

She smiled genially and toasted him.

9

THE 5TH SCHNELLBOOTE FLOTILLA, AS was common with all German navy E-boat units, was used to living on the move. On returning to their Cherbourg base after the Slapton Sands affair, three boats had been ordered to Guernsey for temporary duty as convoy escorts. One of them, S92, was tied up at the quay at Granville now.

Darkness was already falling and the harbor was a scene of frenzied activity as the convoy got ready to leave. Chief Petty Officer Hans Richter, checking the 40-mm Bofors gun in the stern, paused to watch dockers working on the *Victor Hugo* which was moored next to them. Now that her holds were crammed full, they were dumping sacks of coal and bales of hay on her decks so that there was hardly room to move.

The *Hugo*'s antiaircraft defenses were 7.92-mm machine guns and a Bofors gun—not too much use when the Tommies swept in from the darkness in those damned Beaufighters with their searchlights on, but that's the way things were these days, and the Luftwaffe didn't seem to be able to do much about it. Richter could see the master of the *Hugo*, Savary, on the bridge talking to the officer in command of the gun crew, the Italian lieutenant, Orsini. Flamboyant as usual with the white top to his cap and the scarf at his neck. A good seaman for all that. They said he'd sunk a British destroyer off Taranto before being seconded to the 5th Schnellboote as an E-boat commander. They were only using him on secondary duties these days because nobody trusted the Italians anymore. After all, most of them were fighting for the Allies now.

As Richter watched, Guido Orsini went down the ladder and then the gangway to the quay and walked toward the port officer's hut. Richter turned back to the gun and a voice called "Petty Officer!"

Richter looked over the rail. Standing a few feet away was an SS officer, a black leather trenchcoat over his uniform, the silver death's-head on the cap gleaming dully in the evening light. When Richter saw the oak leaf collar patches of a full colonel his heart sank.

He got his heels together quickly. "Standartenführer. What can I do for you?"

The young woman standing at the colonel's shoulder was pretty in her little black beret and belted raincoat, the hair very fair, just like his daughter's back home in Hamburg. Too young for an SS bastard like this, Richter thought.

"Your commanding officer, Kapitanleutnant Dietrich, commands the convoy, I understand?" Martineau said. "Is he on board?"

"Not at the moment."

"Where is he?"

"Port officer's hut. The green one over there, Standartenführer."

"Good. I'll have a word with him." Martineau gestured to the two suitcases. "See these go on board. We'll be traveling with you as far as Jersey."

Which was a turnup for the book. Richter watched them walk away, then nodded to a young seaman who'd been listening with interest. "You heard the man. Get those cases."

"He was SD," the sailor said. "Did you notice?"

"Yes," Richter said. "As it happens I did. Now get on with it."

Erich Dietrich was thirty years of age, a young architect in Hamburg before the war who had discovered his true vocation. He had never been happier than when he was at sea and in command, especially in E-boats. He did not want the war to end. It had taken its toll, of course, on him as much as anyone. Just now, leaning over the chart table with the port officer, Lieutenant Schroeder, and Guido Orsini, he was in the best of humors.

"Winds three to four at the most with rain squalls. Could be worse."

Schroeder said, "Intelligence is expecting big raids on the Ruhr again tonight, so things should be reasonably clear for us down here as regards the RAF."

"If you believe that, you'll believe anything," Orsini said.

"You're a pessimist, Guido," Erich Dietrich told him. "Expect good things and they'll always fall into your lap. That's what my old mother used to say."

The door opened behind him, Schroeder's face dropped and Guido stopped smiling. Dietrich turned and found Martineau standing there, Sarah at his shoulder.

"Kapitanleutnant Dietrich? My name is Vogel." Martineau produced his SD identity card and passed it across, then he took Himmler's letter from its envelope. "If you would be kind enough to read this also."

Sarah couldn't understand a word. He sounded like someone else, held himself like another person, the voice cold and dry. Dietrich read the letter, and Guido and Schroeder peered over his shoulder. The Italian made a face and Dietrich handed the document back.

"You noticed, of course, that the Führer himself was kind enough to countersign my orders?"

"Your credentials are without doubt the most remarkable I've ever seen, Standartenführer," Dietrich said. "In what way can we serve you?"

"I need passage for myself and Mademoiselle Latour to Jersey. As you are convoy commander I shall naturally travel with you. I've already told your petty officer to take our cases on board."

Which would have been enough to reduce Erich Dietrich to speechless rage at the best of times, but there was another factor here. The Kriegsmarine had always been notoriously the least Nazi of all the German armed forces. Dietrich personally had never cared for the Party one little bit, which hardly disposed him in Standartenführer Max Vogel's favor. There were limits, of course, to what he could do, but he still had one possible objection on his side.

"Happy to oblige, Standartenführer," he said smoothly. "There is one problem, however. Naval regulations forbid the carrying of civilians on a fighting ship at sea. I can accommodate you, but not, alas, this charming young lady."

It was difficult to argue with him because he was right. Martineau tried to handle it as a man like Vogel would have done, arrogant, demanding, determined not to be put down. "What would you suggest?"

"One of the convoy ships, perhaps. Lieutenant Orsini here is in command of the gun crew on the SS *Victor Hugo*, whose cargo is destined for the port of St. Helier on Jersey. You could go with him."

But Vogel would not have allowed himself to lose face completely. "No," he said calmly. "It is good that I should see something of your work, Kapitanleutnant. I shall travel with you. Mademoiselle Latour, on the other hand, can proceed on the *Victor Hugo* if Lieutenant Orsini has no objections."

"Certainly not," said Guido who had hardly been able to take his eyes off her. "A distinct pleasure."

"Unfortunately Mademoiselle Latour speaks no German." Martineau turned to her and carried on in French. "We must separate for the journey across, my dear. A matter of regulations. I'll keep your luggage with me, so don't worry about that. This young officer will take care of you."

"Guido Orsini, at your service, signorina," he said gallantly and saluted. "If you come with me I'll see you safely on board. We sail in thirty minutes."

She turned to Martineau. "I'll see you later then Max."

"In Jersey." He nodded calmly.

She went out, Orsini holding the door open for her. Dietrich said, "A charming girl."

"I think so." Martineau leaned over the chart table. "Are we to enjoy an uneventful run tonight? I understand your convoys are often attacked by RAF night fighters."

"Frequently, Standartenführer," Schroeder told him. "But the RAF will be busy elsewhere tonight."

"Terror bombing the civilian population of our major cities as usual," Martineau said because it was the kind of thing they would expect a Party fanatic like him to say. "And the British Royal Navy?"

"Yes, their MTBs are often active in the area," Dietrich admitted and tapped the map. "From bases at Falmouth and Devonport."

"And this doesn't worry you?"

"Standartenführer, there are more of them these days, but our E-boats are still the fastest thing of their kind afloat, as I will certainly have the chance to show you tonight." He gathered up his charts. "Now, if you will follow me, we'll go on board."

The convoy left just after ten o'clock, eleven ships in all, including the barges. S92 led the way out of harbor, then swung hard to port. There was a light rain falling, and Dietrich stood on the bridge, probing into the darkness with his Zeiss night glasses. Martineau was at his right shoulder. Below them the wheelhouse was even more cramped with the helmsman and engine room telegraphist in there and the navigating officer at his small table behind. The wireless room was down a passage farther on.

"Not much room on these things," Martineau commented.

"All engines, that's what we say," Dietrich told him.

"And armaments?"

"The torpedoes. Bofors gun aft, twenty-millimeter cannon in the forward well deck. Eight machine guns. We manage."

"And radar, of course?"

"Yes, but that's a difficult one in these waters. Lots of reefs, rocks, small islands. It makes for a lot of clutter on the screen. When the Tommies come down here they do exactly what I do when I'm operating out of Cherbourg and hitting their convoys."

"What's that?"

"Turn off our radar so they can't find us with their location equipment and maintain radio silence."

Martineau nodded and looked astern at the other ships bulking in the dark. "What speed will the convoy maintain?"

"Six knots."

"You must feel like a racing horse pulling a cart sometimes."

Dietrich laughed. "Yes, but I've got two thousand horses under me." He slapped the rail. "Nice to know just how fast they can get up and go when I ask them to."

On the bridge of the *Victor Hugo* it was like being in a safe and enclosed world, rain and spray drifting against the glass. Savary stood beside the helmsman, and Sarah and Guido Orsini leaned over the chart table.

"This is the convoy route, what the Navy call Weg Ida, from Granville, east of the Chausey isles."

She liked him a lot, had from the moment he'd turned to look at her in the hut on the quay. He was certainly good-looking. Too handsome, really, in a way that Latins could be sometimes, but there was strength there too, and when he smiled . . .

His shoulder was touching hers. He said, "Come to the saloon. I'll get you a coffee and you can use my cabin if you'd like to lie down."

Savary turned. "Not just now, Count. I want to check the engine room. You'll have to take the bridge."

He went out. Sarah said, "Count?"

"Lots of counts in Italy. Don't let it worry you."

He offered her a cigarette and they smoked in companionable silence, looking out into the night, the noise of the engines a muted throbbing. "I thought Italy capitulated last year?" she said.

"Oh, it did, except for those Fascist fanatics who decided to fight on under the Germans, especially when Otto Skorzeny hoisted Mussolini off that mountaintop and flew him to Berlin to continue the holy struggle."

"Are you a Fascist?"

He looked down into that appealing young face, aware of a tenderness that he had never experienced with any woman in his life before. It was perhaps because of that fact that he found himself speaking so frankly.

"To be honest, I'm not anything. I loathe politics. It reminds me of the senator in Rome who's supposed to have said: 'Don't tell my mother I'm in politics. She thinks I play the piano in a brothel.' "

She laughed. "I like that."

"Most of my former comrades are now working with the British and American Navies. I, on the other hand, was seconded on special duties to serve with the Fifth Schnellboote Flotilla in Cherbourg. When Italy decided to sue for peace, there wasn't a great deal I could do about it, and I didn't fancy a prison camp. Of course, they don't trust me enough to allow me to command an E-boat anymore. I suppose they think I might roar across to England.''

"Would you?''

Savary returned to the bridge at that moment, and the Italian said, "Right, let's go below now and get that coffee.''

She moved ahead of him. As he watched her descend the companionway he was conscious of a curious excitement. He'd known many women, and many who were more beautiful than Anne-Marie Latour with her ridiculous dyed hair. Certainly more sophisticated. And there was something about her that was not quite right. The image was one thing, but the girl herself, when he spoke to her, was something else again.

"Mother of God, Guido, what's happening to you?'' he asked softly as he went down the companionway after her.

Captain Karl Muller, the officer in command of the Secret Field Police in Jersey, sat at his desk in the Silvertide Hotel at Havre des Pas and worked his way through a bulky file. It was wholly devoted to anonymous letters, the tip-offs that led to whatever success his unit enjoyed. The crimes were varied. Anything from possession of an illegal radio to helping a Russian slave worker on the run or involvement in the black market. Muller always insisted on his men tracking down the writers of anonymous letters. Once uncovered, they could be used in many ways because of his threat to expose them to friends and neighbors.

It was all very small beer, of course. Nothing like it had been at Gestapo Headquarters at Rue des Saussaies in Paris. Muller was not SS, but he was a Party member, a onetime Chief Inspector of Police in the Hamburg Criminal Investigation Department. Unfortunately, a young Frenchwoman in his hands for interrogation had died without disclosing the names of her associates. As she had been involved with the principal Resistance circuit in Paris, it had been a matter of some importance. To his superiors he'd botched things badly by being too eager. The posting to this island backwater had followed. So now, he was a man in a hurry, seeking any way he could to get back into the mainstream of things.

He stood up, a shade under six feet, with hair that was still dark brown in spite of the fact that he was in his fiftieth year. He stretched, started to the window to look out at the weather, and the phone rang.

He picked it up. "Yes.''

It wasn't a local call, he could tell by the crackling. "Captain Muller? This is Schroeder, port officer at Granville.''

Ten minutes later he was standing at the window, staring out into the dark, when there was a knock at the door. He turned and went to his desk and sat down.

The two men who entered were, like Muller, in civilian clothes. The GFP never wore uniform if they could help it. The one who led the way was broad and squat with a Slavic face and hard gray eyes. This was Inspector Willi Kleist, Muller's second-in-command, also seconded from the Gestapo and, like Muller, a former detective with the Hamburg police. They had known each other for years. The man with him was much younger with fair hair, blue eyes and a weak mouth. A suggestion of perverse cruelty there, but when confronted with Muller, so eager to please that it showed. This was Sergeant Ernst Greiser, who had been transferred from the Army's Field Police to the GFP six months earlier.

"An interesting development," Muller told them. "I've had Schroeder on the phone from Granville. Apparently an SD Standartenführer Vogel presented himself on the quay with a young French woman and demanded passage to Jersey. The put the woman on the *Victor Hugo*. He comes on the S92 with Dietrich."

"But why, Herr Captain?" Kleist asked. "We've had no notification. Why would he be coming? "

"The bad news," Muller said, "is that he's traveling under a special warrant from Reichsführer Himmler. According to Schroeder it's countersigned by the Führer."

"My God!" Greiser said.

"So, my friends, we must be ready for him. You were going to take care of the passenger checks when the convoy ships get into St. Helier, isn't that so, Ernst?" he inquired of Greiser.

"Yes, Herr Captain."

"Inspector Kleist and I will join you. Whatever his reason for being here, I want to be in on the action. I'll see you later."

They went out. He lit a cigarette and went to the window, more excited than he had been in months.

It was just after eleven when Helen de Ville took the tray to her room, using the back stairs that led straight up from the kitchen. None of the officers ever used it, keeping strictly to their own end of the house. In any case, she was careful. Only one cup on the tray. Everything for one. If she chose to have late supper in her room, that was her affair.

She went into the bedroom, locking the door behind her, crossed to the bookshelves, opened the secret entrance and moved inside, closing it before going up the narrow stairway. Kelso was sitting up in bed, propped against pillows, reading by the light of an oil lamp. The wooden shutters in the gable window were closed, a heavy curtain drawn across.

He looked up and smiled. "What have we got here?"

"Not much. Tea, but at least it's the real stuff, and a cheese sandwich. I make my own cheese these days, so you'd better like it. What are you reading?"

"One of the books you brought up. Eliot. *The Four Quartets.*"

"Poetry and you an engineer?" She sat on the end of the bed and lit one of the Gitanes Gallagher had given her.

"I certainly wasn't interested in that kind of thing in the old days, but this war." He shrugged. "Like a lot of people I want answers, I suppose. In my end is my beginning, that's what the man says. But what comes in between? What's it all mean?"

"Well, if you find out, don't forget to let me know." She noticed the snap of his wife and daughters on the bedside locker and picked it up. "Do you think of them often?"

"All the time. They mean everything. My marriage really worked. It was as simple as that. I never wanted anything else, and then the war came along and messed things up."

"Yes, it has a bad habit of doing that."

"Still, I can't complain. Comfortable bed, decent cooking, and the oil lamp gives things a nicely old-fashioned atmosphere."

"They cut off the electricity to this part of the island at nine o'clock sharp," she said. "I know people who would be glad of that oil lamp."

"Are things really as bad as that?"

"Of course they are." There was a trace of anger in her voice. "What on earth would you expect? You're lucky to have that cup of tea. Elsewhere in the island it could be a rather inferior substitute made from parsnips or blackberry leaves. Or you could try acorn coffee. Not one of life's great experiences."

"And food?"

"You just have to get used to getting by with a lot less of it, that's all. The same with tobacco." She held up her cigarette. "This is real and very black market, but you can get anything if you have the right connections or plenty of cash. The rich here still do very well. The banks just operate in reichsmarks instead of pounds." She smiled. "Do you want to know what it's really like being occupied in Jersey?"

"It would be interesting."

"Boring." She plumped up his pillows. "I'm going to bed now."

"The big day tomorrow," he said.

"If we're to believe the message Savary brought." She picked up the tray. "Try and get some sleep."

⚶

Orsini had given Sarah his cabin. It was very small indeed, with a cupboard and washstand and a single bunk. It was hot and stuffy, the porthole blacked over, and the noise of the engine churning below gave her a headache. She lay on the bunk and closed her eyes and tried to relax. The ship seemed to stagger. An illusion, of course. She sat up and there was an explosion.

Things seemed to happen in slow motion after that. The ship fell perfectly still, as if everything waited, and then there was another violent shock. The explosion this time caused the walls to tremble. She cried out and tried to stand up, and then the floor tilted and she fell against the door. Her handbag, thrown from the locker top, was on the floor beside her. She picked it up automatically and tried the door handle, but the door stuck fast. She shook the handle desperately and then the door opened so unexpectedly that she was hurled back against the opposite wall.

Orsini stood in the entrance, his face wild. "Move!" he ordered. "Now! No time to lose."

"What is it?" she demanded as he grabbed her hand and pulled her after him.

"Torpedo attack. We've been hit twice. We've only got minutes. This old tub will go down like a stone."

They went up the companionway to the saloon which was deserted. He took off his reefer coat and held it out to her. "Get this on." She hesitated, aware suddenly that she was still clutching her handbag, then did as she was told, stuffing the bag into one of the reefer coat's ample pockets. He pulled her arms roughly through a life jacket and laced it up. Then he put one on himself as he led the way out onto the boat deck.

There was a scene of indescribable confusion as the crew tried to launch the boats and, above them, the machine-gun crews fired into the night. Fire arced toward them in return, raking the bridge above, where Savary shouted orders. He cried out in fear and jumped over the rail, bouncing off some bales of hay below. Cannon shell ripped into one of the lifeboats a few yards away, tearing great holes in it.

Orsini pushed Sarah down behind some sacks of coal. At the same moment there was another explosion, inside the ship this time, and a portion of the deck in the stern disintegrated, flames billowing into the night. The entire ship tilted sharply to port, and the deck cargo started to break free, sacks of coal, bales of hay, sliding down against the rail.

It had not been possible to launch a single boat, so rapidly had disaster struck, and men were already going over the rail, Savary leading the way. Orsini lost his balance and Sarah fell on her back, felt herself slide down the slippery deck, and then the rail dipped under and she was in the water.

～～

The E-boat surged forward at speed within seconds of the first explosion, Dietrich scanning the darkness with his night glasses. Martineau almost lost his balance at the sudden burst of speed and hung on grimly.

"What is it?"

"I'm not sure," Dietrich said, and then flames blossomed in the night five hundred yards away and he focused on the *Victor Hugo*. A dark shape flashed across that patch of light like a shadow and then another. "British MTBs. They've hit the *Hugo*."

He pressed the button on the battle stations alarm, and the ugly sound of the klaxon rose above the roaring of the Mercedes Benz engines winding up to top speed. Already the crew were moving to their stations. The Bofors gun and the well-deck cannon started to fire, lines of tracer curving into the night.

The only thing Martineau could think of was Sarah, and he grabbed Dietrich by the sleeve. "But the people on that ship. We must help them."

"Later!" Dietrich shrugged him aside. "This is business. Now keep out of the way."

Sarah kicked desperately to get as far from the ship as possible as the *Victor Hugo* continued to tilt. There was burning oil on the water toward the stern, men swimming hard to get away from it as it advanced relentlessly. One man was overtaken. She heard his screams as he disappeared.

She moved awkwardly because of the life jacket and the reefer coat was bulky, already saturated with water. She realized now why Orsini had given it to her as the cold started to eat at her legs. Where was he? She turned trying to make sense of the oil-stained faces. An MTB spun around the stern of the *Victor Hugo*, the violence of its wash hurling some of those in the sea up out of the water. There was a burst of machine-gun fire.

A hand grabbed at her life jacket from behind, and she turned and Orsini was there. "Over here, cara. Just do as I say."

There was wreckage floating everywhere, the bales of hay from the deck cargo buoyant in the water. He towed her toward one of these and they hung onto its binding ropes.

"Who were they?" she gasped.

"MTBs."

"British?"

"Or French or Dutch. They all operate out of Falmouth."

There was another mighty rushing sound in the night and machine-gun bullets churned the water as an MTB again carved its way through men and wreckage. A tracer flashed through the darkness in a great arc and a starshell burst. A moment later, a parachute flare illuminated the scene.

Some distance away two MTBs ran for cover, and the E-boat roared after them. "Go get the bastards, Erich!" Orsini shouted.

She almost joined in. My God, she thought, what a way to go. My own people trying to kill me. She hung onto the rope and said, gasping, "Did they have to do that? Machine-gun men in the water?"

"War, cara, is a nasty business. It makes everyone crazy. Are you managing?"

"My arms are tired."

A hatch drifted by and he swam to it and towed it toward her. "Let's get you onto this."

It was a struggle, but she finally managed it. "What about you?"

"I'll be fine hanging on." He laughed. "Don't worry, I've been in the water before. My luck is good, so stick with me."

And then she remembered the spring fete and Gypsy Sara and her fire and water and she started to laugh shakily. "Are you all right?" he demanded.

"Lovely. Nothing like the Channel Islands for a holiday at this time of the year. Perfect for sea bathing," and then she realized, to her horror, that she'd spoken in English.

He floated there, staring up at her, and then said in excellent English, "Did I tell you I went to Winchester? My father felt that only an English public school could give me the backbone I needed." He laughed. "Oh, I do so like to be right, and I knew there was something different about you from the first moment, cara." He laughed again, excitedly this time. "Which means there's something unusual about the good Standarten-führer Vogel."

"Please," she said desperately.

"Don't worry, cara, I fell in love with you the moment you came through the door of that hut on the quay. I like you, I don't like them— whoever they are. We Italians are a very simple people."

He coughed, rubbing oil from his face, and she reached for his hand. "You saved my life, Guido."

There was the sound of a throttled-down engine approaching. He glanced over his shoulder and saw an armed trawler, one of the escorts, approaching. "Yes," he said. "I'm pleased to say I probably did."

A moment later, the trawler was looming above them, a net over the side. Two or three German sailors clambered down, reaching for Sarah, and pulled her up. Guido followed and collapsed on the deck beside her.

A young lieutenant came down the ladder from the bridge and hurried forward. "Guido, is that you?" he said in German.

"As ever, Bruno," Guido answered in the same language.

"And you, fraulein, are you all right? We must get you to my cabin."

"Mademoiselle Latour, Bruno, and she speaks no German," Guido told him in French. He smiled at Sarah and helped her to her feet. "Now let's take you below."

10

ᴡᴏ

As SARAH PULLED THE HEAVY white sweater over her head there was a knock on the door of Bruno's cabin. She opened it and a young rating said in poor French, "Lieutenant Feldt's compliments. We're entering St. Helier Harbor."

He closed the door and she went to the basin and tried to do something with her hair, which was impossible. The effects of salt water had proved disastrous, and it was now a tangled straw-colored mess. She gave up and rolled the Kriegsmarine dungarees up at her ankles.

The contents of her handbag, which she had stuffed into a pocket of Orsini's reefer before leaving the *Victor Hugo*, had survived surprisingly well. Her identity card and other papers were soaked, of course. She had laid them out now on the hot-water pipes to dry with her handbag. She replaced them all and retrieved the Walther PPK from under the pillow. The Belgian pistol Sergeant Kelly had given her was in her suitcase on board the E-boat. She sat on the edge of the bunk and pulled on a pair of old tennis shoes one of the young ratings had given her.

There was a knock and Guido came in. "How are you?" he asked in French.

"Fine," she said, "except for the hair. I look like a scarecrow."

He was carrying a Kriegsmarine reefer coat. "Put this on. A damp morning out there."

As she stood her handbag fell to the floor, spilling some of the contents, including the Walther. Guido picked it up and said softly, "What a lot of gun for a little girl. Mystery piles on mystery with you."

She took it from him and returned it to her handbag. "All part of my fatal attraction."

"Very fatal if an item like that is involved."

His eyes were serious now, but she smiled lightly and, on impulse, kissed him on the cheek. Then she went out and he followed her.

〜〜

A scene so familiar from her childhood. The harbor, Elizabeth Castle on her left in the bay, the Albert Pier, the sprawl of St. Helier, Fort Regent on the hill above. The same and yet not the same. Military strongpoints everywhere and the harbor more crammed with vessels than she had ever known it. The Rhine barges from the convoy were already safely in, but there was no sign of S92.

"Where's the E-boat?" Sarah asked Guido as she leaned on the bridge rail beside him and Lieutenant Feldt.

"Probably having a last look for survivors," he said as they nosed in toward the Albert Pier.

Dockers were already starting to unload the barges, and there seemed to be soldiers everywhere. Below, half-a-dozen French seamen, survivors of the crew of the *Victor Hugo* picked up by the trawler after Guido and Sarah, waited at the rail in borrowed clothes. Two had sustained facial burns and were heavily bandaged. Another man who had swallowed oil lay on a stretcher.

"No sign of Savary," Orsini said.

"Someone else may have picked him up," Bruno Feldt said. "I see the GFP are ready and waiting. Why is it that policemen always look like policemen?"

"GFP?" Sarah asked in a deliberate display of ignorance. "What's that?"

"Geheime Feldpolizei," Guido told her. "As a matter of interest, the tall one, Captain Muller, is on loan from the Gestapo. So is the thug next to him, the one built like a brick wall. That's Inspector Willi Kleist. The young one with the fair hair is Sergeant Ernst Greiser. Now he *isn't* ex-Gestapo."

"But wishes he were," Bruno Feldt put in.

The three were the first up the gangway when it went over. Greiser paused among the French seamen, and Muller came on up the ladder to the ridge followed by Kleist. Sarah was aware of Guido's hand going into the pocket of her reefer coat and fumbling inside her handbag. She turned to glance briefly at him. As she realized it was the Walther he was seeking, it was already too late, as Muller reached the bridge.

"Herr Leutnant." He nodded to Feldt and said to Orsini, "You had quite a night of it, I hear?" He wore an old Burberry raincoat and felt hat and there was something curiously gentle about him as he turned to Sarah and said in French, "You were a passenger on the *Hugo*, mademoiselle . . . ?"

"Latour," Orsini put in. "We were in the water together."

"A remarkable escape," Muller nodded. "You lost your papers?"

"No," she said. "I have them here." She took the handbag from her pocket and started to open it. Muller held out his hand. "The bag, if you please, mademoiselle."

There was a moment only as if everyone waited, then Sarah handed it to him. "Of course."

He turned to Bruno Feldt. "We'll use your cabin for a few minutes, if we may."

He seemed so reasonable, Sarah thought, so polite, when very obviously most of those standing around were frightened to death of him. Not Guido, of course, who smiled and squeezed her arm. "I'll wait for you, cara, and if the colonel doesn't arrive you can come up to my billet at de Ville Place. I have a very superior landlady. She'll look after you, I promise. All very high class. Only naval officers."

She went down the companionway and back into Lieutenant Feldt's cabin. Muller followed her in and Kleist leaned against the open door.

"So, mademoiselle." Muller sat on the bed, turned the handbag upside down and emptied it. Her papers fell out, her makeup case, powder compact and comb, and also the Walther. He made no comment. He opened her French identity card, examined it, the German Ausweis and the ration cards. He replaced them carefully in the bag and lit a cigarette. Only then did he pick up the Walther, a finger through the trigger guard. "You are, I'm sure, aware that there is only one penalty for a civilian caught in possession of any kind of firearm?"

"Yes," Sarah said.

"This is yours, I take it?"

"Certainly. It was a gift from a friend. He was concerned for my safety. These are troubled times, Captain."

"And what kind of friend would encourage you to break the law so flagrantly? Would it not make him as guilty as you?"

From behind, a cold voice said in German, "Then perhaps you should address that question to me?"

Harry Martineau stood in the doorway. Guido just behind him in the corridor. He presented a supremely menacing figure in the SS uniform and black leather trenchcoat, the silver death's-head in the crumpled cap.

Karl Muller knew the devil when he met him face-to-face and got to his feet very fast indeed. "Standartenführer."

"You are?"

"Captain Karl Muller, in charge of Geheime Feldpolizei here in Jersey. This is my second in command, Inspector Kleist."

"My name is Vogel." Martineau took out his SD pass and handed it over. Muller examined it and passed it back. Martineau produced the Himmler warrant. "Read that—both of you."

Muller did as he was told. Kleist, peering over his shoulder, was awe-struck and gazed at Martineau in astonishment. Muller took it much more calmly, folded the letter and handed it back. "In what way can I serve you, Standartenführer?"

"Mademoiselle Latour travels under my protection." Martineau picked up the Walther and put it back in her handbag. "She has done me the honor of choosing my friendship. There are those among her countrymen who do not approve. I prefer that she should be in a position to defend herself should any unfortunate situation arise."

"Of course, Standartenführer."

"Good, then kindly wait for me on deck."

Muller didn't even hesitate. "Certainly, Standartenführer." He nodded to Kleist and they went out.

Martineau closed the door and turned. He smiled suddenly, turning Vogel into Harry. "You look awful. Are you all right?"

"Yes," she said. "Thanks to Guido."

"Guido is it?"

"He saved my life, Harry. It wasn't good when we went down. Burn-ing oil, men dying." She shuddered. "And the MTBs machine-gunned us in the water. I thought it was only the Germans who were supposed to do that?"

"Only at the cinema, sweetheart." He gave her a cigarette. "In real life everybody does it."

"We've got a problem," she said. "At one point when we were in the water I spoke to Guido in English."

"Good God!"

She put up a hand defensively. "It was pretty confusing out there to put it mildly. Anyway, he speaks good English himself. It seems he went to Winchester."

"Stop!" Martineau said. "It gets worse."

"Not really. After we were saved he told the officer commanding the ship that I only spoke French. And he knows about the Walther and kept quiet about that."

"You *have* been careless."

"He's no Fascist, Harry. He's an Italian aristocrat who doesn't give a damn about politics, stuck here because he happened to be in the wrong place when the Italian government capitulated."

"I see. So why should he go to all this trouble to lay himself on the line for you?"

"He likes me?"

"Likes you? He only met you last night."

"You know what these Latins are like."

She smiled mischievously and Martineau shook his head. "Nineteen they told me. More like a hundred and nineteen."

"Another thing, Harry, Guido's billeted on Aunt Helen at de Ville Place. Apparently a number of naval officers are. He was going to take me up there if you hadn't arrived."

"Perfect," Martineau said. "As for the other business, we'll tell him your mother was English. You've kept quiet about this during the Occupation years in case it caused you problems."

"Will he believe it?"

"I don't see why not. Are you going to be all right for clothes?"

"Yes. I've got a coat, shoes, hat, everything I need in the large case. A good job it traveled with you on the E-boat."

They went up the companionway. Muller was standing on the bridge talking to Feldt and Orsini. Below, Kleist and Greiser were shepherding the French seamen ashore.

Martineau said to Orsini in French, "Anne-Marie tells me you are billeted in most congenial circumstances. Some country house called de Ville Place?"

"That's right, Colonel."

Martineau turned to Muller. "It sounds as if it would suit my needs exactly. Would there be any objection?"

Muller, eager to please, said, "None at all, Standartenführer. It has, by tradition, been allocated to officers of the Kriegsmarine, but Mrs. de Ville, the owner, is seven or eight below her complement."

"That's settled then."

Orsini said, "I'll take you up there now, if you like. I have a car parked at the end of the pier."

"Good," Martineau said. "I suggest we get moving then."

They went down the gangway to the pier, and a Kriegsmarine rating, standing by the E-boat waiting, picked up the two suitcases and followed. Orsini and Sarah walked in front, Martineau followed with Muller at his side.

"Naturally once I'm settled in, I'll return to town to pay my respects to the military commandant. Colonel Heine, isn't it?"

"That's correct, Standartenführer. I understand he's leaving for Guernsey first thing in the morning for a weekend meeting with General von Schmettow."

"I need to see him only to present my compliments," Martineau told him. "One thing I will need is a vehicle. A Kubelwagen would serve my purposes best in case I wish to use it over rough country."

The Kubelwagen was the German Army's equivalent of the jeep, a general purpose vehicle that would go virtually anywhere.

"No problem, Standartenführer. I will also be happy to provide one of my men as a driver."

"Not necessary," Martineau said. "I prefer to do things for myself, Muller. I'll find my way about this little island of yours, believe me."

Muller said, "If I could have some idea of the purpose of your visit."

"I am here on special instruction from Reichsführer Himmler himself, countersigned by the Führer. You have seen my orders," Martineau told him. "Are you querying them?"

"Certainly not."

"Good." They had reached Orsini's Morris sedan, and the sailor was stowing the suitcases. "When the time comes, you will be informed, if and when necessary. I'll possibly call in on you later today. Where are your headquarters?"

"Silvertide Hotel. Havre des Pas."

"I'll find it. In the meantime have the Kubelwagen delivered to me."

Sarah was already in the back, Orsini behind the wheel. Martineau got into the front passenger seat beside him and the Italian moved away.

As they drove along Victoria Avenue, the military railway tracks between them and the bay, Martineau wound down the window and lit one of the Gitanes he'd got from the Cressons. "You like it here?" he asked Orsini.

"There are worse places to wait out the end of a war. In the summer it's particularly beautiful."

Martineau said, "I believe there's a misunderstanding to be cleared up. Anne-Marie has a Breton father, but an English mother. She felt it sensible to keep quiet about this in case it caused problems with the occupying powers. In fact it was one of my own people who first made the discovery, a happy one for me as it brought us together. Isn't that so, my love?"

"An intriguing story, Colonel," Orsini said. "You may rely on my discretion in the matter. The last thing I would wish to do is embarrass Mademoiselle Latour in any way."

"Good," Martineau said. "I felt sure you'd understand."

Back in his office at the Silvertide, Muller sat behind his desk thinking about things. After a while, he flipped the intercom. "Have Inspector Kleist and Sergeant Greiser come in."

He went to the window and looked out. The sky was clear now, suddenly blue, and the tide, still advancing, blanketed the rocks on the shore with white foam. The door opened and the two policemen entered.

"You wanted us, Herr Captain?" Kleist asked.

"Yes, Willi." Muller sat down, leaned back in his chair, lit a cigarette and blew smoke to the ceiling.

"What is it?" the Inspector asked.

"Remember old Dieckhoff, Chief of Detectives in Hamburg?"

"How could I forget him?"

"I always recall his number-one rule when I was a young detective. Dieckhoff's Law, he called it."

"That it doesn't matter how good an egg looks. If it smells, there's something wrong," Kleist said.

"Exactly." Muller nodded. "And this smells, Willi." He got up and paced around the room. "Nothing to do with evidence or appearance. Just every instinct I have as a detective tells me things aren't as they seem. I'd like to know more about Standartenführer Vogel."

Kleist was obviously worried. "But, Herr Captain, his background is impeccable. You can't very well ring up Reichsführer Himmler and ask him to fill you in on his personal envoy."

"No, of course not." Muller turned. "But there is another possibility. Your brother used to work at Gestapo headquarters at Prince Albrecht-strasse in Berlin, Ernst?"

"Peter? Yes, Herr Captain, but now he's at Stuttgart Headquarters. Criminal records," Greiser said.

"He must still have connections in Berlin. Book a call through to him. Ask about Vogel. I want to know how important he is."

"Shall I telex? It would be quicker."

"I want a judicious inquiry, you fool," Muller told him wearily. "Not a public one."

"But I would remind you, sir, that calls for Germany are routed, as you know, via Cherbourg and Paris. They've been taking fifteen or sixteen hours recently, even at priority level."

"Then book one now, Ernst." The young man went out, and Muller said to Kleist, "See about a Kubelwagen. Have it delivered to de Ville Place. Let's keep him happy for the time being."

❧

In the kitchen, Helen was rolling out the pastry made from potato flour when Gallagher came in. "Good, you can clean the fish for me," she said.

There were some plaice on the marble slab beside the sink. Gallagher took a knife from his pocket. The handle was of yellowing ivory. When he pressed one end, a razor-sharp double-edged blade sprang into view.

"You know I loathe that thing," she said.

"When my old grandfather, Harvey Le Brocq, was twelve he made his first trip in a schooner, all the way from Jersey to the Grand Banks off Newfoundland for cod. This knife was his father's gift to him. He left it to me in his will. Knives, guns—it's how they're used that's important, Helen."

"What do you want me to do, applaud?" she asked as he started to clean the fish. At that moment there was the sound of a car drawing up outside. "Probably Guido. I wonder what kind of a run they had?"

There were steps in the passageway, a knock on the door, and Guido came in carrying two suitcases. He put them down and straightened. "A good passage?" Helen asked.

"No, the *Hugo* was torpedoed. Savary missing, three crew members dead and four of my gun crew." Sarah stepped in through the door followed by Martineau, and Orsini carried on, "This is Anne-Marie Latour. She was a passenger on the *Hugo*. We were in the water together." He nodded to Martineau. "Standartenführer Vogel."

Helen looked bewildered. "What can I do for you?"

"Put us up, Mrs. de Ville," Martineau spoke in English. "I'm in the island for a few days. We need quarters."

"Impossible," Helen told him. "This is a billet for officers of the Kriegsmarine only."

"And you are well short of your complement," Martineau told her. "However inconvenient, the matter is an accomplished fact. If you would be kind enough therefore to show us to a suitable room."

Helen was angrier than she had been in years. The ice-cold assurance of the man, the SS uniform and the silly little tart traveling with him, with the tousled hair almost swallowed up by the huge reefer coat.

Guido said hurriedly, "Right, I'm going to have a bath and catch up on a little sleep. I'll see you all later."

The door closed behind him. Gallagher still stood by the sink, the knife in hand. Helen turned, pushing him out of the way angrily, washing the potato flour from her hands under the tap. She was aware of the SS officer still at the door with the girl.

Very softly, a voice said, "Aunt Helen, don't you know me?" Helen went quite still. Gallagher was looking over her shoulder in astonishment. "Uncle Sean?" And then, as Helen turned, "It's me, Aunt Helen. It's Sarah."

Helen dropped the cloth, moved forward and grabbed her by the shoulders, gazing at her searchingly. With recognition, there were sudden tears in her eyes. She laughed unsteadily and ran her fingers through the girl's hair.

"Oh, my God, Sarah, what have they done to you?" And then they were in each other's arms.

Hugh Kelso said, "So what happens now? You two have obviously had one hell of a trip just getting to Jersey, so where do we go from here?"

"I know where Sarah goes. Straight into a hot bath," Helen de Ville said. "You three can carry on talking as long as you like."

As she moved to the door Gallagher said, "I've been thinking. Mrs. Vibert's due this afternoon. It might be an idea to give her a few days off."

"All right," Helen told him. "You can take care of it."

They went out and Kelso said, "What *does* happen now?" There was impatience in his voice.

Martineau said, "I just got here, my friend, so give me time to catch my breath. When it's time to go, you'll be the first to know."

"Does that include a bullet in the head, Colonel?" Kelso demanded, "If that's the decision, do we get to talk about it or just do it?"

Martineau didn't bother to answer. He simply went downstairs and waited in the master bedroom for Gallagher. The Irishman closed the secret door and shrugged. "He's had a hard time and that leg gives him a lot of pain."

"We're all in pain one way or another," Martineau said.

As he was about to open the door, Gallagher put a hand on his shoulder. "Could he be right? About the bullet in the head, I mean?"

"Maybe," Martineau said. "We'll have to see, won't we? Now I think I'll have a bath as well."

〜

In London, Dougal Munro was just finishing breakfast at his flat when Jack Carter came in. "Some mixed news, sir, about Jerseyman."

"Tell me the worst, Jack."

"We've heard from Cresson. Everything went according to plan, and Martineau and Sarah left Granville for Jersey last night."

"And?"

"We've had another message from Cresson to say the word is the convoy ran into trouble. Attacked by MTBs. They don't have any hard facts."

"Have you?"

"I've checked with Naval Intelligence. Apparently MTBs of the Royal Dutch Navy operating out of Falmouth last night did hit that convoy, and they claim one merchantman sunk. They were driven off by the escorts."

"Good God, Jack, you're not seriously suggesting that Harry and the Drayton girl were on that boat?"

"We just don't know, sir, and what's more, there's no possible way we can find out."

"Exactly, so sit down, stop worrying about it and have a cup of tea, Jack. You know what your trouble is." Munro reached for the toast. "You don't have enough faith."

ᴡᴡ

Sarah had washed her hair, using some homemade soft soap Helen had provided. She still looked a mess, and when Helen came into the bathroom she said, "It's no good. You need a hairdresser."

"Are there still such things?"

"Oh, yes, if you go into St. Helier. The general run of shops still function. The opening hours are shorter. Two hours in the mornings and two in the afternoon for most places."

She tried combing the girl's hair into some semblance of a style and Sarah said, "What's it been like?"

"Not good, but not too bad if you behave yourself. Plenty of people think the Germans are all right and a lot of the time they are, but step out of line and see what happens. You have to do as you're told, you see. They even made the Jersey States pass anti-Semitic laws. A lot of people try to excuse it by saying all the Jews had left, but I know two living in St. Brelade now."

"What happens if the German authorities discover them?"

"God knows. We've had people sent off to those concentration camps we hear about for keeping Russian slave workers who were on the run. I have a friend, a teacher at Jersey College for Girls, whose father kept an illegal radio. She used to spread the BBC news around to her friends until an anonymous letter brought the Gestapo to the house. They sent her to prison in France for a year."

"An anonymous letter? You mean from a local person? But that's terrible."

"You get bad apples in every barrel, Sarah. Jersey is no different from anywhere else in that respect. And we've got the other kind as well. The postmen at the sorting office who try to lose as many of the letters addressed to Gestapo Headquarters as possible." She finished combing. "There, that's the best I can do."

Sarah sat down, pulled on silk stockings and fastened them. "My God!" Helen said. "I haven't seen anything like that for four years. And that dress." She helped Sarah pull it over her head and zipped it up. "You and Martineau. What's the situation there? He's old enough to be your father."

"My father he very definitely is not." Sarah smiled as she pulled on her shoes. "He's probably the most infuriating man I've ever met and the most fascinating."

"And you sleep with him?"

"I *am* supposed to be Vogel's tart, Aunt Helen."

"And to think that the last time I saw you, you had pigtails," Helen said.

In the kitchen, she put two spoonfuls of her precious China tea into the pot, but Gallagher made his excuses. "I'll go and put Mrs. Vibert off," he said. "It'll only complicate things having her around. Always the chance she might recognize you, Sarah. She knew you well enough, God knows."

He went out and Helen, Sarah and Martineau sat around the table drinking tea and smoking. There was a knock at the door. When Helen opened it, Willi Kleist stood there.

Martineau got up. "You want me?"

"We've brought your Kubelwagen, Standartenführer," Kleist told him.

Martineau went out to have a look at it. The canvas top was up and the body was camouflaged. He looked inside and said, "That seems satisfactory."

Ernst Greiser was sitting behind the wheel of a black Citroën. Kleist said, "If there's anything else we can do . . . "

"I don't think so."

"By the way, Captain Muller wanted me to tell you he's spoken to Colonel Heine, the military commandant. Apparently he'll be at the Town Hall this afternoon if you'd care to call in and see him."

"Thank you, I will."

They drove away and Martineau went back inside. "Transport problems taken care of. I'll go into town this afternoon, call on the military commandant, then Muller and his friends at this Silvertide place."

"You'd better go in with him and get your hair done," Helen told Sarah. "There's a good hairdresser at Charing Cross. You can tell her I sent you." She turned to Martineau. "Very convenient. It's close to the Town Hall."

"Fine," he said, "except for one thing. She mustn't say you sent her. In the circumstances that would be quite wrong." He got up. "I feel like a breath of air. How about showing me round the estate, Sarah?"

"A good idea," Helen said. "I've got things to do. I already had eight to cook for tonight so I've got my work cut out. I'll see you later."

After leaving de Ville Place, Kleist and Greiser started down the road, but after about a quarter of a mile, the inspector touched the young man on the arm. "Let's pull in here, Ernst. Stick the car in that track over there. We'll take a walk back through the woods."

"Any particular reason?"

"I'd just like to have a look around, that's all."

The cart track was heavily overgrown. Greiser drove along it until they were out of sight of the road, and they got out and left the Citroën there, taking a field path across the woods of the de Ville estate. It was very quiet and really rather pleasant, only the sound of the birds, and then a young woman carrying a basket appeared unexpectedly from beyond the high granite wall at the end of the field. It was impossible to see her face. For one thing, she was wearing a headscarf, but the old cotton frock was tight enough to reveal, even at a distance, a body that was full and ripe. She didn't notice them and followed the path into the wood.

Kleist said, "Now that's interesting." He turned to Greiser and smiled. "Would you say we should investigate, Sergeant?"

"Very definitely, Herr Inspector," the younger man said eagerly and they quickened their pace.

The young woman was in fact Mrs. Vibert's daughter, Mary. After Sean Gallagher's visit to tell her to take the weekend off, the old woman had remembered the eggs she had promised Helen de Ville for the evening meal. It was these that the girl was taking to the house now.

She was only sixteen and already blossoming into womanhood, but not very bright, with a simple, kindly face. She loved the countryside, the flowers, the birds, was never happier than when walking alone in the woods. Some little way in, there was an old granite barn long disused, the roof gaping, the doors hanging crazily. It always made her feel uneasy, and yet drawn to it by a strange fascination, she paused, then walked across the grass between crumbled walls to peer inside.

A harsh voice called, "Now then. What do you think you're doing?"

She turned quickly and saw Kleist and Greiser advancing toward her.

After leaving Mrs. Vibert's, Sean Gallagher walked down to the south meadow where he had three cows grazing, tethered to long chains in the Jersey manner. They were a precious commodity in these hard times and he stayed with them there in the sunshine for a while then started back to his cottage.

When he was still two fields away he saw the Germans walking toward the wood, saw and recognized Mary. He paused, shading his eyes against the sun, saw the girl disappear into the trees, the Germans following. Suddenly uneasy, he started to hurry. It was when he was halfway across the field that he heard the first scream. He cursed softly and broke into a run.

The weather was the best of spring, delightfully warm as Sarah and Martineau followed the track from the house through the pine trees. There were daffodils everywhere, crocuses and snowdrops in profusion, camellias blooming. Beyond, through the trees, the waters of the bay were blue merging into green in places. Birds sang everywhere.

Sarah held his arm as they strolled along. "God, that wonderful marvelous smell. Straight back to childhood and those long hot summers. Did they ever exist, I wonder, or was it all an impossible dream?"

"No," he said. "They were the only true reality. It's the past four years that have been the nightmare."

"I love this place," she said. "It's an old race, the Norman stock here, and the de Villes are as old as any of them. We go back a long way. Robert de Ville fought at the Battle of Hastings with Duke William of Normandy."

"Good old William the Conqueror?"

"That's right. He ruled Jersey before he became king of England, so it's we who colonized the English, if you like, not the other way about."

"There's arrogance for you."

"These are my roots," she said. "Here I belong. This is home. Where do you belong, Harry?"

"Stateless person, that's me," he said lightly. "For years an American living and working in Europe. No family left worth speaking of."

"Citizen of the world?"

"Not really." He was upset and it showed in a sudden angry unease. "I just don't belong. Don't belong anywhere. Could be I should have died in those trenches back in nineteen eighteen. Maybe the man upstairs made a mistake. Perhaps I shouldn't be here at all."

She pulled him around, angry. "That's a terrible thing to say. I'm beginning to get rather tired of the cynical and sardonic bit, Harry Martineau. Can't you drop your guard just occasionally? Even with me?"

Before he could reply there was a sudden scream. They turned and looked down to the barn in the clearing through trees and saw Mary struggling in Kleist's arms, Greiser standing to one side laughing.

"For God's sake, Harry, do something," Sarah said.

"I will, only you stay out of it."

He started down the slope as Sean Gallagher ran out of the trees.

Kleist was excited, the supple young body squirming against him. "Shut up!" he told her. "Just be a good girl and I won't hurt you."

Greiser's eyes were shining, the mouth loose. "Don't forget, Inspector, fair shares for all, that's my motto."

Gallagher arrived on the run, shouldering the sergeant out of the way like a rugby forward. As he reached Kleist, he stamped hard behind the German's left knee, causing the leg to buckle and punched him hard in the kidneys. Kleist grunted and went down, releasing the terrified girl.

Gallagher picked up Mary's basket and gave it to her and patted her face. "It's all right now, love," he said. "You run on up to the house to Mrs. de Ville. Nobody's going to harm you this day."

She ran like a frightened rabbit. As Gallagher turned, Greiser took a Mauser from his pocket, his eyes wild. Kleist called, "No, Ernst, and that's an order. He's mine." He got up, easing his back, and took off his raincoat. "Like all the Irish you're cracked in the head. Now I shall teach you a lesson. I shall break both your arms."

"Half-Irish, so only half-cracked, let's get it right." Sean Gallagher took off his jacket and tossed it to one side. "Didn't I ever tell you about my grandfather, old Harvey le Brocq? He was sailing in cod schooners at the age of twelve, bosun on windjammers on the grain run from Australia. Twelve times round the Horn by the age of twenty-three."

"Talk away," Kleist said circling him. "It won't do you any good."

He rushed in and swung a tremendous punch which Gallagher avoided with ease. "In those days a bosun was only as good as his fists, and he was good. Very good." He ducked in and landed a punch under the German's left eye. "When I used to come over from Ireland as a kid to stay with him, the village lads would work me over because I talked funny. When I went home crying, he took me out in the orchard and gave me the first of many lessons. Science, timing, punching, that's what counts, not size. God, as he often reminded me, and he was a lay preacher, had never intended the brutes to rule on earth."

Every punch the German threw was sidestepped, and in return, Gallagher seemed to be able to hit him wherever he wanted. On the hillside a few yards away, Sarah, Martineau and the Vibert girl watched as the Irishman drove the inspector back across the grass.

And then there was a sudden moment of disaster, for as Gallagher moved in, his right foot slipped on the grass and he went down. Kleist seized his chance, lifting a knee into his forehead and kicking him in the side as he went down. Gallagher rolled away with surprising speed and came up on one knee.

"God save us, you can't even kick straight."

As he came up, Kleist rushed at him, arms reaching to destroy. Gallagher slipped to one side, tripping the German so that he went headfirst into the wall of the barn. The Irishman gave him a left and a right in the kidneys. Kleist cried out sharply and Gallagher swung him around. He grabbed him by the lapels and smashed his forehead against the bridge of the German's nose, breaking it. Then he stepped back. Kleist swayed and fell.

"Bastard!" Greiser called.

Gallagher swung around to find the sergeant confronting him with the Mauser, but in the same moment a shot rang out, kicking up dirt at Greiser's feet. They turned as Martineau walked down the slope, Walther in hand.

"Put it away!" he ordered.

Greiser stood there, staring at him, and it was Kleist, getting to his feet, who said hoarsely, "Do as he says, Ernst."

Greiser obeyed and Martineau said, "Good. You are, of course, a disgrace to everything the Reich stands for. This I shall discuss with your commanding officer later. Now leave."

Greiser tried to give Kleist his arm. The big man shoved him away and walked off through the trees. Gallagher turned and shouted to Mary Vibert, "Go on girl, go up to the house."

She turned and ran. Sarah took out a handkerchief and wiped blood from Gallagher's mouth. "I never realized what a deadly combination Jersey was with the Irish."

"A fine day for it, thanks be to God." Gallagher squinted up at the sun through the trees. "Better times coming." He grinned and turned to Martineau. "You wouldn't happen to have a cigarette on you? I seem to have left mine at home."

11

MARTINEAU AND SARAH DROVE DOWN through St. Aubin and along toward Bel Royal, passing a number of fortifications and gun positions on the way. The sky was very blue, the sun bright, and yet on the horizon, beyond Fort Elizabeth, there was a dark curtain.

"Rain," she said. "Typical Jersey spring weather. Wonderful sunshine and then the squalls sweep in across the bay, sometimes only for a few minutes."

"It's warmer than I'd expected," he said. "Quite Mediterranean." he nodded at the gardens as they passed. "Especially with all those palm trees. I didn't expect those."

She leaned back and closed her eyes. "This island has a special smell to it in the spring. Nothing quite like it anywhere else in the world." She opened her eyes again and smiled. "That's the de Ville side of me speaking. Hopelessly prejudiced. Tell me something. Why have you taken off your uniform?"

He was wearing the leather military trenchcoat, but underneath was a gray tweed suit with a waistcoat and white shirt with a black tie. The slouch hat was also in black, the brim down at the front and back.

"Tactics," he said. "Everybody who is anybody will know I'm here, will know who I am, thanks to Muller. I don't need to appear in uniform if I don't want to. SD officers wear civilian clothes most of the time. It emphasizes our power. It's more frightening."

"You said *our* power."

"Did I?"

"Yes. You frighten me sometimes, Harry."

He pulled the Kubelwagen in at the side of the road and switched off. "Let's take a walk."

He helped her out and they paused as one of the military trains approached and moved past, then they crossed the track to the seawall. There was a café there, all closed up, probably from before the war, a huge bunker not too far away.

A new unlooked-for delight was music, two young soldiers on the seawall, a portable radio between them. Below, on the sands, children played, their mothers sitting against the wall, faces turned to the sun. A number of German soldiers swam in the sea, two or three young women among them.

Martineau and Sarah leaned on the wall. "Unexpectedly domestic, isn't it?" He gave her a cigarette.

The soldiers glanced at them, attracted by the girl, but turned from his dark stare. "Yes," she said. "Not what I expected."

"If you look closely you'll see that most of the soldiers on the beach are boys. Twenty at the most. Difficult to hate. When someone's a Nazi, then it's explicit. You know where you stand. But the average twenty-year-old German in uniform"—he shrugged—"is just a twenty-year-old in uniform."

"What do you believe in, Harry? Where are you going?" Her face was strained, intense.

"As I once told you, I'm a very existentialist person. 'Action this day'—Churchill's favorite phrase. And that means defeating the Nazis because they must be destroyed totally. Hitler's personal philosophy is unacceptable in terms of any kind of common humanity."

"And afterward, when it's all over? What happens to you?"

He stared out to sea, eyes very dark, leaning on the wall. "When I was young I used to love railway stations, especially at night. The smell of the steam, the dying fall of a train whistle in the distance, the platforms in those great deserted Victorian palaces at night, waiting to go somewhere, anywhere. I loved it and yet I also used to get a feeling of tremendous unease. Something to do with getting on the wrong train." He turned to her. "And once the train's on its way, you see, you can't get off."

"The station is ominous at midnight," she said softly. "Hope is a dead letter."

He stared at her. "Where did you hear that?"

"One of your bad poems," she said. "That first day I met you at the cottage the brigadier was reading it. You took it from him, crumpled it up and threw it into the fireplace."

"And you retrieved it?"

"Yes."

For a moment she thought he would be angry. Instead he smiled. "Wait here." He left her and crossed the line to the Kubelwagen and opened the door. When he returned he was carrying a small Kodak camera. "Helen gave me this. As the film is four years old she can't guarantee the results."

He walked up to the soldiers. There was a brief exchange in which they put their heads together for a moment, standing stiffly to attention. Martineau gave one of them the camera and returned to her.

"Don't forget to smile." He lit a cigarette and turned, hands in the pockets of the trenchcoat.

Sarah took his arm. "What's this for?"

"Something to remember me by."

It made her feel uneasy and she held his arm even more tightly. The young soldier took the photo. "Another," Martineau called in German, "just to make sure."

The boy returned the camera, smiling shyly, then saluted and walked away. "Did you tell him who you were?" she asked.

"Of course I did." He took her arm. "Let's get going. I've got things to do." They crossed the railway track and returned to the Kubelwagen.

Karl Muller prided himself on his control, his remarkable lack of emotion in all situations. He thought of it as his greatest asset, and yet, standing by the window in his office at the Silvertide Hotel, it almost deserted him for the first time.

"You what?" he demanded.

Kleist's face was in a dreadful state, flesh around the eyes purple and dark, the broken nose swollen. "A misunderstanding, Herr Captain."

Muller turned to Greiser. "And that's your version also? A misunderstanding?"

"We were only questioning the girl, Herr Captain. She panicked, then Gallagher arrived. He placed entirely the wrong construction on the affair."

"As your face proves, Willi," Muller said. "And Vogel was involved."

"He arrived on the scene at an unfortunate moment," Greiser told him.

"And *he* also placed entirely the wrong construction on things." Muller was furious. "Leaving me to get you off the hook when he turns up here this afternoon. Go on, get out of my sight!"

He turned to the window and slammed his palm against the wall.

Following Sarah's instructions, Martineau drove along Gloucester Street past the prison. "One thing," he said. "When we're together in the town speak French. You never know who's listening, understand?"

"Of course."

They could hear music now and turned into the Parade to find a German military band playing on the grass between the statue of General Don, a previous governor of the island, and the Cenotaph. There was quite a crowd standing listening, mainly civilians with a few soldiers.

"Just like *Workers' Playtime* on the BBC back in the UK," Martineau said. "Supposed to make people feel better about being occupied."

"Pull in here," she said. "The Town Hall is just at the end."

He parked at the curb and they got out, people turning to stare curiously, attracted by the sight of the military vehicle. Many seemed indifferent, but there were those unable to hide their anger when they looked at Sarah, especially the older women.

Someone muttered "Gerrybag!" as they walked past. It was an ugly word meant to express the contempt most people felt for a girl who consorted with the enemy. Martineau swung around, Vogel to the life, and confronted the gray-haired woman who had spoken.

"You said something, madam?" he asked in English.

She was immediately terrified. "No—not me. You're mistaken." She turned and hurried away in a panic.

Sarah took his arm and said softly, "There are times when I hate you myself, Harry Martineau."

They passed the entrance of the Town Hall with the Nazi flag flying above and a Luftwaffe sentry on the steps with a rifle. They crossed to the other side of York Street and came to Charing Cross. Some of the shop windows were still taped to avoid flying glass, probably from the first year of the war. The Luftwaffe had bombed St. Helier once in 1940. It was obviously the last thing the RAF intended to do, which probably explained why a lot of shopkeepers had cleaned the tape off.

They paused at a doorway between two shops. The sign indicated that the hairdresser was upstairs. Sarah said, ''I remember this place.''

''Would you be recognized?''

''I shouldn't think so. The last time I was in here was to have my hair cut when I was ten years old.''

She led the way up the stairs, pushed open a door with a frosted glass pane and Martineau followed her in. It was only a small salon with two washbasins and a couple of hairdriers. The woman who sat in the corner reading a magazine was about forty with a round, pleasant face. She glanced up smiling, and then the smile was wiped clear away.

''Yes?'' she said.

''I need my hair fixed rather badly,'' Sarah said in French.

''I don't speak French,'' the woman replied.

Martineau said in English, ''The young lady was a passenger on the Victor Hugo from Granville last night. As I am sure you are aware of the fate of that unhappy vessel, you will appreciate that she was in the water for some time. As she has no English I must speak for her. Her hair, as you can see, requires attention.''

''I can't help. I'm booked up.''

Martineau looked around the empty salon. ''So I see. You're identity card, if you please.''

''Why should I? I've done nothing.''

''Would you rather continue this conversation at Silvertide?''

There was fear in her eyes. Sarah had never felt so wretched in her life and waited as the unfortunate woman found her handbag and produced the identity card. It was in the name of Mrs. Emily Johnson. Martineau examined it and handed it back.

''My name is Vogel—Standartenführer Max Vogel. I have an appointment at the Town Hall with Colonel Heine, the commandant. I'll be gone for an hour, perhaps a little longer. While I am away you will do whatever is necessary to the young lady's hair. When I return, I am sure it will look quite delightful.'' He opened the door. ''If it doesn't, I'll close this establishment so fast you won't know what's hit you.''

They listened to him descend the stairs. Mrs Johnson took a robe down from behind the door and turned to Sarah with a delightful smile. ''All right, you dirty little French tart. Let's make you look pretty for that butcher,'' she said in English. Her smile became even more charming. ''And I can only hope you get what you deserve.''

Sarah felt like cheering her out loud. Instead she stayed in control and replied in French, "Ah, the coat."

She took it off, handed it to her, put on the robe and went to the nearest chair.

—❧—

As Martineau crossed to the Town Hall he saw a policeman in traditional British bobby's uniform and helmet standing on the steps talking to the sentry. They stopped talking, watching him warily as he approached.

"Standartenführer Vogel for the commandant."

The sentry jumped to attention and the police constable faded away discreetly. "The commandant arrived twenty minutes ago, Standartenführer."

Martineau moved into the hall and found a table at the bottom of the stairs, an army sergeant sitting there. He glanced up and Martineau said, "My name is Vogel. I believe Colonel Heine is expecting me."

The sergeant leaped to his feet and picked up the phone. "Standartenführer Vogel is here, Herr Major." He replaced the receiver. "Major Necker will be down directly, sir."

"Thank you." Martineau walked away and looked out through the open door. Within moments there was the sound of boots on the stairs. He turned to find a young man hurrying down, an infantry major, no more than thirty from the look of him.

He was all cordiality, but then he would be, pausing briefly to click his heels before putting out a hand. "Felix Necker, Standartenführer."

He'd seen action, that was plain enough from the shrapnel scar running into the right eye. As well as the Iron Cross First Class he wore the Wounded Badge in silver, which meant he'd been a casualty at least three times, the Infantry Assault Badge and a Close Combat Clasp in gilt. It was recognition and familiarity with such items that kept Martineau alive. What they told him about people was important. What they said about this man was that he was a war hero.

"A pleasure to meet you, Herr Major," he said. "You've been in Jersey long?"

"Only a couple of months," Necker told him. "I'm not with the 319th Division normally. Only on loan."

They went upstairs, he knocked and opened a door, stood to one side and Martineau went in first. It was a pleasant enough room, obviously originally the office of some official. The officer who stood up and came around the desk to meet him was a type he recognized instantly. A little stiff in manner, rather old-fashioned regular army and very definitely no Nazi. An officer and a gentleman.

"Standartenführer. A pleasure to see you." The handshake was firm, friendly enough, but the eyes said something else. Only surface courtesy here.

"Colonel Heine." Martineau opened his coat and produced his SD card.

Heine examined it and handed it back. "Please sit down. In what way can we serve you? You've met Felix Necker, of course. He's only on loan from Paris. Temporarily my second in command. A holiday for him. Just out of hospital. He was on the Russian Front."

"Indeed?" Martineau said. He took out the Himmler letter and passed it across.

Heine read it slowly, his face grave, then passed it to Necker. "If I could know the purpose of your visit?"

"Not at this stage." Martineau took the letter as Necker handed it back to him. "All I need is assurance of total cooperation as and when required."

"That goes without saying." Heine hesitated. "As for billeting arrangements, I understand you are staying at de Ville Place."

"Yes, I spoke to Captain Muller of the GFP on the pier when we arrived. He was most cooperative. He has already supplied me with a suitable vehicle, so for the moment, there is really nothing else I require. It would be useful if you informed all unit commanders of my presence."

"Of course. There is one thing," Heine added. "I have to go to Guernsey and so does the civil affairs commander. A weekend conference with General von Schmettow."

Martineau turned to Necker. "Presumably you will be in command?"

"That is correct."

"Then I can see no problem." He got to his feet and picked up his hat.

Heine said, "I'll see you when I get back then?"

"Possibly." Martineau shook hands. "A pleasure, Herr Colonel. I'll let you get on with it now. Don't bother to see me out, Major."

The door closed behind him. Heine's whole demeanor changed. "My flesh crawls when these SS security people appear. What in the hell does he want, Felix?"

"God alone knows, Herr Colonel, but his credentials . . . " Necker shrugged. "Not only signed by Himmler, but by the Führer himself."

"I know." Heine put up a hand defensively. "Just watch him, that's all. I'll see what von Schmettow thinks when I get to Guernsey. But at all costs keep him sweet. Trouble with Himmler is the last thing we need."

"Of course, Herr Colonel."

"Good. Now show in these good citizens from the Food Control Committee and let's get on with it."

Martineau had time in hand so he walked through the town. There were plenty of people about, more civilians than soldiers. Most people looked underweight, but that was to be expected, and clothes looked old and well-worn. There were few children about, they'd be at school. The ones he did see were in better shape than he had expected, but then, people always did put their children first.

So, people managed. He knew, because Helen de Ville had told them, of the communal kitchens and bakeries to conserve fuel. It occurred to him that people in the town obviously had a more difficult time of it than those in the country. At that moment, as he moved into Queen Street, he saw a crowd overflowing the pavement ahead, all staring into a shop window.

It contained an amazing display of food of every description. Canned goods, sacks of potatoes and flour, hams, bottles of red wine and champagne. People said nothing, just looked. A notice in the window said: *Black market goods. The enemy may be your own neighbor. Help defeat him.* It was signed by Muller. The pain in the faces of ordinary people deprived too long was unbearable. Martineau turned and went back to Charing Cross.

When he went upstairs to the salon, Sarah was just adjusting her hat in the mirror. Her hair looked excellent. He helped her on with her coat.

Emily Johnson said, "Satisfied?"

"Very much so." He opened his wallet and took out a ten-mark note.

"No!" Her anger overflowed. "I don't want your money. You told me to do her hair and I've done it." There were tears of frustration in her eyes. "Just go."

Martineau pushed Sarah out of the door. When he turned, his voice, to Emily Johnson's astonishment, was quite gentle. It was as if, for a moment, he had stepped out of the role of brutal SS officer that he had played so well. "I salute you, Mrs. Johnson. You are a brave woman."

The door closed behind him. She sat down, head in hands, and started to cry.

Martineau parked the Kubelwagen outside the Silvertide Hotel at Havre des Pas beside several other cars. "I shan't be long."

She smiled. "Don't worry about me. I'll just take a walk along the seawall. I used to come to swim in the pool here when I was a kid."

"As you please. Just try not to talk to any strange men."

Muller had seen him arrive from the window of his office. When Martineau went inside, a young military policeman in plain clothes was waiting to greet him. "Standartenführer Vogel? This way please."

He ushered Martineau into Muller's office and closed the door. The captain stood up behind the desk. "A great pleasure."

"I wish I could say the same," Martineau said. "You've spoken to Kleist and Greiser?"

"About this misunderstanding at de Ville Place? Yes, they did explain . . . "

"Misunderstanding?" Martineau said coldly. "You will have them in here now, Herr Captain, if you please, and quickly. My time is limited."

He turned away and stood at the window, hands behind his back, as Muller asked for Kleist and Greiser over the intercom. They came in only a few moments. Martineau didn't bother to turn around, but looked out across the road to the seawall where Sarah was standing.

He said softly, "Inspector Kleist, I understand you have put this morning's events at de Ville Place down to a misunderstanding?"

"Well, yes, Standartenführer."

"Liar!" Martineau's voice was low and dangerous. "Both of you liars." He turned to face them. "As I walked through the wood with Mademoiselle Latour we heard a girl scream. A child, Captain, barely sixteen, being dragged toward a barn by this animal here while the other stood and laughed. I was about to interfere when General Gallagher came on the scene and gave a bully the thrashing he deserved."

"I see," Muller said.

"Just to make things worse, I was obliged to draw my own pistol and fire a warning shot to prevent this idiot shooting Gallagher in the back. God in heaven, what kind of an imbecile are you Greiser?" He spoke slowly as if to a child. "The man is Irish, which means he is a neutral, and the Führer's declared policy is good relations with Ireland. On top of that he is a famous man back there in the old country. A hero of their revolution. A general. We don't shoot people like that in the back. Understand?"

"Yes, Standartenführer."

Now he turned his attention to Kleist. "And as the Führer's declared policy toward the inhabitants of Jersey has been one of reconciliation, we do not attempt to rape sixteen-year-old girls." He turned to Muller. "The actions of these men are an affront to every ideal the Reich holds dear and to German honor."

He was thoroughly enjoying himself, especially when Kleist's anger overflowed. "I'm not a child to be lectured like this."

"Kleist!" Martineau said. "As a member of the Gestapo you took an oath to our Führer. A holy oath. As I recall it runs: I vow to you and the superiors you appoint, obedience unto death. Is it not so?"

"Yes," Kleist answered.

"Then remember from now on that you are here to obey orders. If I ask a question you answer, '*Jawohl, Standartenführer.*' If I give you an order it's '*Zu befehl, Standartenführer.*' Do you follow?"

There was a pause before Kleist said in a low voice, "*Jawohl, Standartenführer.*"

Martineau turned on Muller. "And you wonder why Reichsführer Himmler thought it worthwhile sending me here?"

He walked out without another word, went through the foyer and crossed the road to the Kubelwagen. Sarah was sitting on the bonnet. "How did it go?" she asked.

"Oh, I think you could say I put the fear of God in them all rather satisfactorily." He opened the door for her. "Now you can take me on a Cook's tour of this island of yours."

Muller started to laugh. "I wish you could see yourself standing there in front of the desk, Willi. All you need is short pants."

"I swear to God I'll . . . "

"You'll do nothing, Willi, just like the rest of us. You'll do just as you're told." He went to a cupboard, opened it and found a glass and a bottle of cognac. "I must say he sounded just like the Reichsführer on a bad day. All that German purity nonsense. All those platitudes."

"Do you still want me to speak to my brother, Herr Captain?" Greiser asked. "I've got a call booked through to Stuttgart for ten o'clock tonight."

"Why not?" Muller poured some cognac into his glass and said impatiently, "For God's sake, go down to the hospital and get that nose seen to, Willi. Go on, get out of my sight, both of you."

Rommel was staying at a villa near Bayeux, in a place deep in the countryside and quite remote. It had been used as a weekend retreat by the commanding general of the area who had been happy to offer it to the field marshal when he'd expressed a desire for a quiet weekend. The Bernards, who ran the house, were extremely discreet. The wife was an excellent cook, the husband acted as butler.

Baum drove to the house ahead of the field marshal that afternoon in a Kubelwagen wearing his own Fallschirmjäger uniform. He also affected a heavy black patch over the right eye on Rommel's insistence. To Baum, he did not resemble the field marshal until he put on the clothes, changed his appearance with a few artful touches of makeup, the rubber cheekpads that made the face squarer. But the real change was in himself—the change that started inside. He thought Rommel, so he became Rommel. That was his unique talent as a performer.

Rommel and Hofer arrived later in the afternoon in the Mercedes driven by an engineer sergeant named Dreschler, an Afrika Korps veteran whom Hofer had specially selected. Madame Bernard provided the field marshal with a late luncheon in the drawing room. Afterward, Hofer brought Baum in to join them.

"Right, let's go over things," Rommel said.

"According to my information the people from Jersey will leave for Guernsey at around two in the morning. Berger and I will leave here in the Kubelwagen at nine. There is an empty cottage on the estate a kilometer from here where we stop for him to change."

"And afterward?"

"To a Luftwaffe reserve airstrip only ten kilometers from here. There is a pilot, an Oberleutnant Sorsa, waiting there under your personal order with a Fiesler Storch."

"Sorsa? Isn't that a Finnish name?" Rommel asked.

"That's right."

"Then what's he doing with the Luftwaffe? Why isn't he on the Eastern Front shooting down Russians with his own people?"

"Sorsa is hot stuff, a real ace. One of the greatest night fighter pilots in the business. These days he's of more use flying over the Reich knocking down Lancaster bombers. He's an excellent choice for this venture. He doesn't fit into the usual Luftwaffe command structure. An outsider."

"They don't like us very much, the Finns," Rommel said. "I've never trusted them." He lit a cigarette. "Still, carry on."

"Sorsa won't know his destination until we join the plane. I estimate we will land in Jersey around eleven o'clock. I've given orders for Headquarters of Army Group B to notify Berlin at noon that you've flown to Jersey. The reason for not letting them know earlier being the need to consider your safety when in flight."

"And what happens here?"

"Generals Stulpnagel and Falkenhausen arrive later in the day. Stay overnight and leave on Saturday morning."

"And you return in the evening?"

"Of course. This couple here at the house, the Bernards, will know you are here, but then they won't know you're also in Jersey. Neither will Sergeant Dreschler. He worships you anyway. An old desert hand. If there is any problem with him later, I can handle it."

Rommel turned to Baum. "And you, my friend, can you handle it?"

"Yes, Herr Field Marshal. I really think I can," Baum told him.

"Good." Rommel took the bottle of Dom Perignon from the ice bucket that Monsieur Bernard had brought in earlier and uncorked it. He filled three glasses and gave them one each. "So, my friends, to the Jersey enterprise."

Sarah and Martineau had spent an enlightening afternoon, driving to Gorey where she had intended to show him Mont Orgeuil, one of the most magnificent castles in Europe, only to find that it was now a heavily defended enemy strongpoint.

At Fliquet Bay, they had come across a party of slave workers cutting a new road through to a coastal artillery battery. They were the most ragged, filthy, undernourished creatures even Martineau had seen. He had made himself known to the sergeant in charge of the detail who told him they were Russians. It was particularly ironic, therefore, to discover a battalion of the Russian Liberation Army staffed mainly by Ukrainians, guarding the north coast around Bonne Nuit Bay.

They carried on to Grosnez with the few stones remaining of its medieval castle and spectacular views of Sark, Herm and Jethou, all reaching toward Guernsey. The interesting thing was that not once were they stopped or challenged, even when they drove along the Five Mile Road following the curve of St. Ouens Bay, which looked to Martineau like the most heavily defended stretch they'd seen.

It was evening when they stopped at the church at the end of St. Brelade's Bay. Sarah got out and he followed her. They stood in the archway and peered inside. There was an entire section devoted to the military, rows of crosses, each one at the end of a neat grave.

"I don't know what Christ would have made of those crosses," Martineau said. "There's a swastika in the center of each one."

She shivered. "I used to attend this church. I had my first communion here."

Martineau walked idly between the rows of German crosses. "There's a couple of Italians here and a Russian." He carried on, moving into the older section of the cemetery, passing between granite headstones and tombs. "Strange," he said. "I feel quite at home."

"That's a morbid thought." Sarah told him.

"Not really. I just find it extraordinarily peaceful and the view of the bay is sensational. Still I suppose we should be getting back now."

They got in the Kubelwagen and drove past the bay along Mont Sohier. Sarah said, "So, now you've had the guided tour. What do you think?"

"A tight little island."

"And how do we get Hugh Kelso off it?"

"To tell you the truth, I haven't the slightest idea, so if you think of anything, let me know."

He carried on driving, whistling tunelessly between his teeth.

Dinner was a strange affair. Martineau and Sarah joined the officers in the main dining room. Guido Orsini, Bruno Feldt, Kapitanleutnant Erich Dietrich and several others. There was a fresh lighted candle at each empty place which Sarah found rather macabre, but the young officers were polite and considerate, would obviously have put themselves out even more if it had not been for Martineau's presence. He was wearing his uniform in deference to the formality of the meal, and its effect on the others had been definitely depressing.

Helen de Ville passed in and out with the plates, and Sarah, bored with the stilted conversation, insisted on helping her to clear the table and joined her in the kitchen, where Sean Gallagher sat at the table eating the leftovers.

"Terrible in there. Harry's like a specter at the feast," she said.

Helen had just prepared a tray for Kelso. "I'll just take this up while they're all still in the dining room."

She went up the back stairs and opened the door to the master bedroom at the same moment that Guido Orsini passed the end of the corridor. He saw her, noted the tray in astonishment and moved cautiously along the corridor. He hesitated, then tried the door of her bedroom. Helen, for once, had omitted to turn the key. He peered inside, saw the secret door ajar and tiptoed across. There was a murmur of voices from upstairs. He listened for a moment, then turned and went out again, closing the door.

Sarah and Gallagher were talking in low voices when Guido went into the kitchen. "Ah, there you are," he said. "They're into politics now. Can I take you for a walk on the terrace?"

"Is he to be trusted?" she asked Gallagher.

"No more than most men I know, especially around a darling like you."

"I'll have to take a chance then. If Colonel Vogel comes looking for me, tell him I'll be back soon." she added formally.

There was a half-moon, the sky bright with stars, a luminosity to everything, palm trees etched against the sky. Everywhere there was the smell of flowers, drenched from the rain earlier.

"Azaleas." She breathed deeply. "One of my favorites."

"You are a remarkable girl," he said in English. "You don't mind if we use English, do you? There's no one about and it helps me keep my hand in.''

"All right,'' she said reluctantly, "but not for long.''

"You've never been to Jersey before?''

"No. I was raised by my grandmother in Paimpol after my mother died.''

"I see. And it was your mother who was English?''

"That's right.''

She was wary at this questioning and sat on a low granite wall, the moon behind her. He gave her a cigarette. "You smoke Gitanes, don't you?''

She was used to cigarettes by now and nodded. "On the other hand, one has to be content with whatever is available these days.''

He gave her a light. "Yes, it's really quite remarkable. You speak French with a very Breton accent.''

"What's strange about that? My grandmother was Breton.''

"I know. It's your English that's so interesting. Very upper class. I went to Winchester, remember, so I can tell.''

"Really? I'm a lucky girl, then.'' She stood up. "I'd better get back now, Guido. Max can get rather restless if I'm out of his sight too long with another man.''

"Of course.'' She took his arm and they strolled back through the azaleas. "I like you, Anne-Marie Latour. I like you a lot. I want you to remember that.''

"Only like?'' she said. "I thought you said you loved me.'' A dangerous game she was playing here. She knew that and yet could not resist taking it as far as it would go.

"All right,'' he said. "I love you,'' and he pulled her into his arms and kissed her passionately. "Now do you understand?''

"Yes, Guido,'' she said softly. "I think I do.''

Martineau appeared on the terrace in the moonlight. "Anne-Marie, are you there?'' he shouted in French.

"Coming!'' she called back and reached to touch the Italian's face. "I'll see you tomorrow, Guido,'' and she ran up the steps to the terrace.

They were all in the private sitting room at the back of the house overlooking the terrace, Gallagher, Martineau, Helen and Sarah. Gallagher poured Burgundy into four glasses while Helen opened the French window a little. It was very close. She breathed in the perfumed air for a few moments, then drew the heavy curtains across.

"So, what happens now?'' Sean Gallagher asked.

"He certainly can't walk at the moment,'' Helen de Ville said.

"George Hamilton saw him this afternoon. A real chance he could lose the leg if he disturbs things."

"At least he's safe for the time being upstairs," Sarah said.

"He can't sit out the war there," Martineau pointed out. "We need to get him to Granville. Once there, Cresson can radio London and have a Lysander over any night we want."

"But how to get him there, that's the thing," Gallagher said. "They've really got the small boat traffic closed up tight here. Observation posts all along the coast as you saw for yourself today. You wouldn't get far without being spotted. Any fishing boat that leaves harbor, even the lifeboat, has to have German guards on board when they put to sea."

"So what *is* the solution?" Sarah demanded. "We must do something."

There was a movement at the window; the curtains parted. Martineau turned, drawing his Walther, and Guido Orsini stepped into the room. "Perhaps I can help," he said in English.

12

‿‿

THE FOLLOWING MORNING MARTINEAU WAS on the upper level of the Albert Pier as Colonel Heine, the civil administration commander, and the bailiff and his party left for Guernsey on the E-boat with Dietrich. He watched them go as he leaned on the seawall, waiting for Orsini, who had gone to Kriegsmarine Headquarters at the Pomme d'Or Hotel.

The Italian's entry through the curtains the night before had certainly been as dramatic as it was unexpected. But his offer to throw in his lot with them made sense. Even if Orsini had been a thoroughgoing Fascist, it was reasonably certain who was going to win this war, and in Italy many of Mussolini's most fervent followers had transferred their allegiance to the winning side without a moment's hesitation. In any case, Orsini was not one of those. So Helen and Gallagher had assured him and so had Sarah, most fervently of all.

The young Italian came up the steps, saluted a couple of Kriegsmarine ratings and joined Martineau. "Let's walk to the end of the pier."

"What did you find out?" Martineau asked as they strolled along.

"A possible break. There's a small convoy due in from Guernsey early Sunday morning. The master of one of the ships, a Dutch coaster called the *Jan Kruger*, was taken ill yesterday. The bosun is handling her as far as Jersey."

"And then?"

"Our old friend Robert Savary takes command for the run to Granville."

"That certainly is interesting," Martineau said. "When can you speak to him?"

"There's the snag. He was picked up after the *Victor Hugo* went down by one of the search and rescue craft from St. Malo. He's due over from Granville early evening tomorrow on a fast patrol craft. What we call the dispatch boat."

"And you think he might be willing to smuggle Kelso over?"

Orsini shrugged. "From what you have told me of his part in this business already, I should imagine him an eminently suitable candidate for applied pressure. After what he's already done, I fail to see how he can say no."

"True," Martineau said. "And he knows that if he puts a foot wrong the Cressons and their friends will arrange his funeral, priest included, free of charge." He smiled. "You know something, Count? I think you may well prove to be an asset to the corporation."

"Fine," said Guido. "Only let us understand each other."

"Go on."

"I've had my bellyful of death and destruction. I'm tired of killing and sick of politics. The Allies are going to win this war, that is inevitable, so Jersey was the perfect billet for a sensible man to sit out the last few months in comfort. And don't let's pretend that anything that happens here will make the slightest difference. If the Germans got their hands on Kelso, Eisenhower's invasion plans would, at the most, be seriously inconvenienced. He'd still win in the end. We're engaged in a rather interesting game here. It's true that it's also a dangerous one, but still only a game."

"Then why throw your hat in the ring?" Martineau asked.

"I think you know why," Guido told him as they went down the steps to where his car was parked. He smiled amiably. "Be warned, my friend. There is nothing more dangerous than the libertine who suddenly finds he has fallen in love with a good woman."

When the phone rang in his office at command headquarters Felix Necker was just about to leave to go riding on the beach at St. Aubin. He picked up the receiver and listened and a look of horror appeared on his face. "My God! What's his estimated time of arrival? All right. Arrange a guard of honor. I'll be there as soon as I can."

He slammed down the receiver and sat there for a moment thinking about things, then he picked it up again and dialed GFP Headquarters at the Silvertide.

"Herr Major," Muller said when he was put through. "What can I do for you?"

"Rommel is due in at the airport in forty-five minutes."

"Who did you say?" Muller demanded.

"Field Marshal Erwin Rommel, you idiot. He's arriving with his aide, a Major Hofer, from Normandy in a Fiesler Storch."

"But why?" Muller demanded. "I don't understand."

"Well I do," Necker told him. "It all makes perfect sense. First of all his orders for Heine and the others to join General von Schmettow in Guernsey for the weekend, getting them all nicely out of the way so that he can fly in out of the blue and take the place apart. I know how Rommel operates, Muller. He'll go everywhere. Check every machine-gun post."

"At least one mystery is solved," Muller said.

"What's that?"

"The reason for Vogel being here. The whole thing ties in now."

"Yes, I suppose you're right," Necker said. "Anyway, never mind that now. I'll see you at the airport."

He put down the receiver, hesitated, then picked it up again and told the operator to connect him with de Ville Place. Martineau and Orsini had just returned, and it was Helen who answered the phone in the kitchen.

"It's for you," she said to Martineau. "Major Necker."

He took the receiver from her. "Vogel here."

"Good morning," Necker greeted him. "I'm sure it will come as no surprise to you to know that Field Marshal Rommel arrives at the airport in just over half-an-hour."

Martineau, concealing his astonishment, said, "I see."

"Naturally, you'll wish to greet him. I'll see you at the airport."

Martineau put the phone down slowly as Sarah and Gallagher came in from the garden. "What is it, Harry?" Sarah demanded. "You look awful."

"I should," he said. "I think the roof just fell in on me."

❧

At the Silvertide, Muller was hurriedly changing into uniform in the bathroom next to his office. He heard the outside door open and Kleist called, "Are you there, Herr Captain? You wanted us."

"Yes, come in," Muller called.

He went into the office buttoning his tunic, picked up his belt with the holstered Mauser and fastened it quickly.

"Something up?" Kleist asked. He looked terrible. The bruising around the eyes had deepened, and the plaster they had taped across his nose at the hospital didn't improve things.

"You could say that. I've just heard Rommel's flying in on what looks like a snap inspection. I'll have to get up to the airport now. You can drive me, Ernst," he told Greiser.

"What about me?" Kleist asked.

"With a face like that? I don't want you within a mile of Rommel. Better take a couple of days off, Willi. Just keep out of the way." He turned to Greiser. "Let's get moving."

After they had gone, Kleist went to the cupboard where the captain kept his drink, took out a bottle of cognac and poured a large one into a glass. He swallowed it in one quick gulp and went into the bathroom and examined himself in the mirror. He looked awful and his face hurt. It was all that damned Irishman's fault.

He poured himself another cognac and said softly, "My turn will come, you swine, and when it does . . . " He toasted himself in the mirror and emptied his glass.

As the Citroën moved past the harbor and turned along the esplanade, Greiser said, "By the way, that call I had booked to my brother in Stuttgart last night."

"What did he have to say?"

"He didn't. He was on leave. Due back today on the night shift. I'll speak to him then."

"Not that it matters all that much now," Muller said. "Nothing very mysterious about friend Vogel any longer. He obviously came here in advance of the field marshal, that's all."

"But what does Rommel want?" Greiser asked.

"If you consider the beach fortifications, strongpoints and batteries for the entire French coast south from Dieppe, exactly half are in these islands alone," Muller told him. "Perhaps, with the invasion coming, he thought it was time to see what he was getting for his money." He glanced at his watch. "But never mind that now. Just put your foot down hard. We've only got about ten minutes."

At the airport, Martineau paused briefly to have his pass checked by the sentry. As he was in uniform, it was the merest formality. Several cars were parked outside the main entrance, drivers standing by them, obviously the official party. The big black Austin limousine in front carried the military commander's pennant.

Martineau parked the Kubelwagen behind Muller's Citroën. Greiser was at the wheel, the only driver in civilian clothes. Martineau ignored him and went inside the airport building. There were uniforms everywhere, mainly Luftwaffe. He felt a sense of detachment as he walked on through, no fear at all. He would have to do the best he could with the cards fate had dealt him.

Necker and a party of officers, Muller among them, were waiting on the apron outside, a Luftwaffe guard drawn up. The major came across, a slightly nervous smile on his face, followed by Muller. "They'll be here in a few minutes." He offered a cigarette from a silver case. "A tremendous shock for us all, the field marshal coming in out of the blue like this, but not to you, I think."

Martineau saw it all then. They thought there was some connection between his own unexplained presence in the island and Rommel's unexpected visit. "Really? I can't imagine what you mean, my dear Necker."

Necker glanced at Muller in exasperation. It was obvious that neither of them believed him, which was fine and suited his situation perfectly. He walked a few yards away and stood, hands behind his back, examining the airport. There were seven blister hangars, obviously constructed by the Luftwaffe. The doors to one of them stood open revealing the three engines and distinctive corrugated metal fuselage of a JU52, the Junkers transport plane that was the workhorse of the German Army. There was no sign of any other aircraft.

"He still persists in playing the man of mystery," Necker said to Muller out of the side of his mouth.

Martineau rejoined them. "The Luftwaffe doesn't seem to have much to offer."

"Unfortunately not. The enemy has an overwhelming superiority in the air in this region."

Martineau nodded toward the far blister hangar. "What's the JU52 doing there?"

"That's the mail plane. He makes the run once a week, just the pilot and a crewman. Always under cover of darkness. They came in last night."

"And fly out again?"

"Tomorrow night."

There was the sound of an airplane engine in the distance. As they turned, the Storch came in across St. Ouen's Bay and made a perfect landing. Konrad Hofer put a hand on Baum's for a moment in reassur-

ance as the pilot, Oberleutnant Sorsa, taxied toward the waiting officers.
Baum turned to nod briefly at Hofer, then adjusted the brim of his cap
and tightened his gloves. Showtime, Heini, he told himself, so let's give
a performance.

Sorsa lifted the door and Hofer got out, then turned to help Baum,
who unbuttoned his old leather coat revealing the Blue Max and the
Knight's Cross at his throat. Felix Necker advanced to meet him and
gave him a punctilious military salute, one soldier to another. "Field
Marshal. A great honor."

Baum negligently touched the peak of his cap with his field marshal's
baton. "You are?"

"Felix Necker, sir. I'm temporarily in command. Colonel Heine has
gone to Guernsey for the weekend. A conference with General von
Schmettow."

"Yes, I know about that."

"If only we'd been aware that you were coming," Necker went on.

"Well, you weren't. Konrad Hofer, my aide. Now then, who have we
here?"

Necker introduced the officers, starting with Martineau. "Standartenführer Vogel, who I think you may know."

"No," Martineau said. "I have never had the pleasure of meeting the
field marshal before."

Rommel's dislike was plain for everyone to see. He passed on, greeting Muller and the other officers and then inspecting the guard of honor.
Afterward, he simply took off, walking toward the nearest flak gun,
everyone trailing after him. He spoke to the gun crew, then cut across
the grass to a hangar where Luftwaffe ground crew waited rigidly at
attention.

Finally he turned and walked back toward the airport buildings, looking up at the sky. "Fine weather. Will it stay like this?"

"The forecast is good, Herr Field Marshal," Necker told him.

"Excellent. I want to see everything. You understand? I'll be returning
tomorrow, probably in the evening, so we'll need a suitable billet for
tonight. However, that can wait until later."

"The officers of the Luftwaffe mess have had a light luncheon prepared, Herr Field Marshal. It would be a great honor if you would con-
sent to join them."

"Certainly, Major, but afterward, work. I've a lot to see. So, where
do we go?"

The officers' mess was upstairs in what had been the restaurant before
the war. There was a buffet of salad, roast chicken and tinned ham,
served rather self-consciously by young Luftwaffe boys in white coats

acting as waiters. The officers hung eagerly on the field marshal's every word, conscious of their proximity to greatness. Baum, a glass of champagne in his hand, was more than enjoying himself. It was as if he were somewhere else looking in, observing. One thing was certain. He was good.

"We were surprised that you chose to fly in during daylight hours, Herr Field Marshal," Necker said.

"And with no fighter escort," Muller added.

"I've always believed in doing the unexpected thing," Baum told them. "And you must remember we had Oberleutnant Sorsa as pilot, one of our gallant Finnish comrades. He normally flies a JU88S night fighter and has thirty-eight Lancasters to his credit, which explains his Knight's Cross." Sorsa, a small, vital man of twenty-five with very fair hair, looked suitably modest, and Baum carried on, "I must also tell you that we flew across the sea so low that we were in more danger from the waves than anything the RAF might have come up with."

There was a general laugh and he excused himself and went off to the toilet followed by Hofer.

Martineau had been standing against the wall, observing everything and drinking very little. Muller approached. "A remarkable man."

"Oh, yes." Martineau nodded. "One of the few real heroes of the war. And how is your Inspector Kleist?"

"A stupid man," Muller observed. "But then, I think you know that. More champagne?"

In the toilet, Baum checked himself in the mirror and said to Hofer, "How am I doing?"

"Superbly." Hofer was exhilarated. "There are times when I really think it's the old man himself talking."

"Good." Baum combed his hair and adjusted the cheek pads. "What about the SS colonel? I didn't expect that."

"Vogel?" Hofer was serious for a moment. "I was talking to Necker about him. He just turned up in the island yesterday, backed by a special pass signed by Himmler and the Führer himself. So far he's given no information as to why he's here."

"I don't know," Baum said. "Those bastards always make me feel funny. You're certain his presence here has nothing to do with us?"

"How could it be? Army Group B Headquarters only released the news that you were in Jersey an hour ago. So, no need to panic, and back to the fray."

Necker said, "If you wouldn't mind coming into the CO's office, Field Marshal. General von Schmettow is on the line from Guernsey."

Baum sat carelessly on the edge of the desk and took the receiver offered to him. "My dear von Schmettow, it's been a long time."

General von Schmettow said, "An unexpected honor for my entire command. Heine is quite shocked and wishes to return at once."

"Tell him if he does, it's the firing squad for him," Baum said good-humoredly. "Young Necker can show me around just as well. A fine officer. No, this suits me perfectly."

"Do you intend to visit Guernsey?"

"Not this time. I return to France tomorrow."

"May we expect you at some future date?" The line was crackling now.

"Of course, and before long, I promise you. Best wishes."

Baum put down the receiver and turned to Necker. "To work. Coastal defenses, that's what I wish to see, so let's get started."

∽

In the garden at de Ville Place Sarah sat on the wall looking out over the bay and Guido leaned beside her, smoking a cigarette. "Sarah," he said in English. "It's as if I have to get to know you all over again." He shook his head. "Whoever told you that you could pass yourself off as a French tart was gravely mistaken. I knew there was something wrong with you from the start."

"And Harry? Did you think there was something wrong about him?"

"No. He worries me, that one. He plays Vogel too well."

"I know." She shivered. "I wonder how he's getting on?"

"He'll be fine. The last person I'd ever worry about. You like him, don't you?"

"Yes," she said. "You could put it that way." Before they could take the conversation any further, Helen and Gallagher crossed the grass to join them.

"What are you two up to?" Helen demanded.

"Nothing much," Sarah told her. "We were wondering how Harry was getting on."

"The devil looks after his own," Gallagher said. "He can take care of himself, that one. More important at the moment is a decision on what to do with Kelso. I think we should move him from the chamber to my cottage."

Guido nodded. "That makes sense. Much easier to take him from there down to the harbor once I get Savary sorted out."

"Do you really think it has a chance of working?" Sarah demanded.

"Fake papers as a French seaman. The General and I can fix that up between us," Guido told her.

"We'll bandage his face. Say he was in the water after the attack on the convoy and sustained burns," Gallagher said. "We'll move Kelso late tonight." He smiled reassuringly and put an arm around Sarah. "It's going to work. Believe me."

Martineau joined on the end of the cavalcade of cars as it left the airport and took the road through St. Peter's. Rommel fascinated him, so did the idea of being so close to one of the greatest soldiers the war had produced, the commander of the Westwall himself. The man dedicated to smashing the Allies on the beaches where they landed.

He was certainly energetic. They visited Meadowbank in the Parish of St. Lawrence where for two years military engineers and slave workers had labored on tunnels designed to be an artillery depot. Now it was in process of being converted into a military hospital.

Afterward they saw the Russians in Defense Sector North and the strongpoints at Greve de Lecq, Plemont and Les Landes. It all took time. The field marshal seemed to want to look in every foxhole personally, visit every gun post.

He asked to see the war cemetery at St. Brelade and inspected the church while he was there. The Soldatenheim, the Soldiers' Home, was just along the road in a requisitioned hotel overlooking the bay. He insisted on calling in there, much to the delight of the matron in charge, and discovered a proxy wedding taking place. It was a system devised by the Nazi government to take care of the fact that it was increasingly difficult for soldiers on active duty to get married in the normal way any longer, as they seldom got furloughs back home in Germany. The groom was a burly sergeant and a Red Cross nursing sister stood in for his bride, who was in Berlin.

It was very much a Nazi marriage, totally without any religious significance at all. The insistence on the lack of Jewish blood in either the bride of bridegroom was something Baum found especially ironic, but he toasted the sergeant's good health with a glass of schnapps and moved on.

By the time they reached St. Aubin it was evening, and most of the party were beginning to flag. Baum, examining the map Necker had provided, noticed the artillery positions on Mont de la Rocque and asked to be taken up there.

Martineau followed, still on the tail of the line of cars climbing the steep hill of the Mont until they came to a narrow turning that led out on top where there were a number of flat-roofed houses.

"A gun platoon only now, Field Marshal," Necker assured Baum as he got out.

The house at the very end with a courtyard behind a wall was called

Septembertide. The one next to it had a French name, Hinguette. In its garden, a narrow entrance gave access to a series of underground bunkers and machine-gun posts which ran along the crest of the hill under the gardens. There were no civilians living in any of the houses, only troops, who were overwhelmed to have the Desert Fox in proximity to them, none more so than the commanding officer, a Captain Heider.

It transpired that his personal billet was Septembertide. When the field marshal expressed an interest in it, he eagerly led the way. They all trooped down into the garden. The views across the bay, St. Aubin on the right and St. Helier on the left, were breathtaking. The garden was edged with a low concrete wall, and the ground fell almost vertically down through trees and heavy undergrowth to the road far below.

Baum said, "You'd need the Alpine Corps to get up here, gentlemen." He looked up at the house. There was a large terrace in front of the sitting room and another above running the full length at bedroom level. "Nice." He turned to Heider. "I need somewhere to lay my head tonight. Will you lend it to me?"

Heider was beside himself with joy. "An honor, Herr Field Marshal. I can move into Hinguette for the night with my second in command."

"I'm sure you can find us a decent cook among your men."

"No problem, Field Marshal."

Baum turned to Necker. "You see, my dear Necker, all taken care of. This will suit me very well indeed. Impregnable on this side and Captain Heider and his boys guarding the front. What more could one ask for?"

"It was hoped you might join us for dinner at the officers' club at Bagatelle," Necker said diffidently.

"Another time. It's been a long day and frankly, I'd welcome an early night. Call for me in the morning. Not too early. Let's say at ten, and we can do the other side of the island."

"At your orders, Herr Field Marshal."

They all went around to the front of the house where there was a general leavetaking. Heider took Baum and Hofer inside and showed them around. The living room was large and reasonably well furnished.

"It was like this when we moved in," Heider said. "If you'll excuse me, I'll get my things out of the bedroom, Field Marshal, then I'll arrange a cook."

He went upstairs. Baum turned to Hofer. "Did I do well?"

"Superb," Hofer said. "And this place is perfect. Just the right amount of isolation. You're a genius, Berger."

The evening meal had already started at de Ville Place when Martineau got back. He peered in at the window and saw Sarah sitting with Guido and half-a-dozen other naval officers at the table. He decided not to go in and, instead, went round to the back door and let himself into the kitchen. Helen was washing dishes at the sink and Gallagher was drying for her.

"How did things go?" the Irishman demanded.

"Well enough. Absolutely no problems, if that's what you mean."

"Did you see the great man?"

"As close as I am to you, but he made it clear the SS is not exactly his favorite organization."

Helen poured him a cup of tea, and Gallagher said, "We've been making decisions while you've been away."

He told him how they'd decided to move Kelso. When he was finished, Martineau nodded. "That makes sense to me. We'll make it later though. Say around eleven."

"Should be safe enough then," Gallagher said.

Martineau went upstairs and lay on the bed of the room he shared with Sarah. Although they slept in the same bed he had not made love to her again since that first night. There was no particular reason. There just didn't seem to be the need. But no. He wasn't being honest. It wasn't Sarah, it was him, something inside, some old wound of the spirit that made him afraid to give himself fully. A morose fear that it would all prove to be just another disappointment or perhaps simply the fear that this strange, enchanting, tough young woman was forcing him back into the real world again. Bringing him back to life.

He lay on the bed smoking a cigarette, staring at the ceiling, strangely restless, thinking of Rommel and the energy of the man—and what a target he was. He got up and put on his belt with the holstered PPK, then he opened his suitcase, found the Carswell silencer and put it in his pocket.

When he went downstairs, they were still eating in the great hall. He went back to the kitchen. Helen looked up in surprise. "You're going out again?"

"Things to do." He turned to Gallagher. "Tell Sarah I'll be back soon."

The Irishman frowned. "Are you all right? Is something wrong?"

"Not in the whole wide world," Martineau assured him. "I'll see you later," and he went out.

There was a half moon again and in its light, he saw the line of white houses high overhead on the ridge above the trees. He turned the Kubelwagen into La Haule Hill and parked in a track where it joined with Mont de la Rocque. For a while, he sat there thinking about it, and then he got out and started up through the trees.

It was nonsense, of course. Shoot Rommel and they'd have the island sewn up tight within an hour. Nowhere to go. On top of that they'd probably take hostages until the assassin gave himself up. They'd done that in other countries. No reason to think Jersey would be any different. But in spite of all reason and logic, the thought titillated, would not go away. He kept on climbing.

13
⟜

MULLER WAS WORKING IN HIS office at the Silvertide, trying to catch up on his paperwork when there was a knock on the door and Greiser looked in. "Working late tonight, Herr Captain."

"The field marshal accounted for most of my time today, and he's likely to take up more tomorrow," Muller said. "I've at least twelve case reports to work through for court appearances next week. I thought I'd try to get rid of them tonight." He stretched and yawned. "Anyway, what are you doing here?"

"The phone call I booked to my brother in Stuttgart. I've just been talking to him."

Muller was immediately interested. "What did he have to say about Vogel?"

"Well, he certainly never came across him at Gestapo Headquarters in Berlin. But he does point out that the SD are housed in a building at the other end of Prince Albrechtstrasse. He simply wasn't familiar with who was who, except for the big noises like Heydrich before they murdered him and Walter Schellenberg. However, it was an open secret during his time in Berlin, that the Reichsführer uses mystery men like Vogel with special powers and so on. He says nobody was all that sure who they were."

"Which is exactly the point of the whole exercise," Muller observed.

"Anyway, he says people like that operate out of the SD unit attached to the Reichsführer's office at the Reich Chancellery. As it happens, he knows someone on the staff there rather well."

"Who?"

"An SS auxiliary named Lotte Neumann. She was his mistress during his Berlin period. She's secretary to one of the Reichsführer's aides.''

"And he's going to speak to her?''

"He has a call booked through to Berlin in the morning. He'll get back to me as soon as he can. At least it will tell us just how important Vogel is. She's bound to know something about him.''

"Excellent." Muller nodded. "Have you seen Willi tonight?''

"Yes," Greiser admitted reluctantly. "At the club. Then he insisted on going to a bar in some back street in St. Helier.''

"He's drinking?" Greiser hesitated and Muller said, "Come on, man, tell me the worst.''

"Yes, Herr Captain, heavily. I couldn't keep up. As you know I drink very little. I stayed with him for a while, but then he grew morose and angry as he does. He told me to clear off. Became rather violent.''

"Damnation!" Muller sighed. "Nothing to be done now. He's probably ended up with some woman. You'd better get off to bed. I'll need you again in the morning. Ten o'clock at Septembertide.''

"Very well, Herr Captain.''

He went out, and Muller opened another file and picked up his pen.

Kleist was at that moment parking his car on a track on the edge of the de Ville estate very close to Gallagher's cottage. He was dangerously drunk, way beyond any consideration of common sense. He had half a bottle of schnapps with him. He took a pull at it, put it in his pocket, got out of the car and walked unsteadily along the track toward the cottage.

There was a chink of light at the drawn curtains covering one of the sitting room windows. He kicked on the front door vigorously. There was no response. He kicked again, then tried the handle and the door opened. He peered into the sitting room. There was an oil lamp on the table, the embers of a fire on the hearth, but no other sign of life. The kitchen was also empty.

He stood at the bottom of the stairs. "Gallagher, where are you?''

There was no reply. He got the oil lamp and went upstairs to see for himself, but both bedrooms were empty. He descended the stairs again, slowly and with some difficulty, went into the sitting room and put the lamp on the table.

He turned it down, leaving the room in darkness except for a dull glow from the embers of the fire. He pulled back the curtain at the window and sat there in a wing chair, looking at the yard outside, clear in the moonlight. "Right, you bastard. You've got to come home sometime.''

He took a Mauser from his right-hand pocket and sat there nursing it in his lap as he waited.

⤳

At Septembertide, Baum and Hofer had enjoyed a surprisingly excellent meal. Cold roast chicken, Jersey new potatoes and a salad, washed down with a bottle of excellent Sancerre provided by Captain Heider. The half moon gave a wonderful view of St. Aubin's Bay, and they went out onto the terrace to finish their wine.

After a while, the corporal who had cooked the meal appeared. "All is in order, Herr Major," he told Hofer, "the kitchen is clear again. I've left coffee and milk on the side. Will there be anything else?"

"Not tonight," Hofer told him. "We'll have breakfast at nine sharp in the morning. Eggs, ham, anything you can lay your hands on. You can return to your billet now."

The corporal clicked his heels and withdrew. Baum said, "What a night."

"My dear Berger, what a day," Hofer told him. "The most remarkable of my life."

"And the second act still to come." Baum yawned. "Speaking of tomorrow, I could do with some sleep," and he went back inside.

Hofer said, "You, of course, in deference to your superior rank, will take the large bedroom above this, which has its own bathroom. I'll take the small room at the end of the corridor. It overlooks the front of the house so I'll be more aware of what's going on there."

They went upstairs, Baum still carrying his glass of wine. "What time?" he said.

"If you're not already up I'll wake you at seven-thirty," Hofer told him.

"Rommel would be up at five, but one can take playacting too far." Baum smiled. He closed the outer door to the bedroom suite, walked through the dressing area into the bedroom itself. It was plainly furnished with two wardrobes, a dressing table and a double bed, presumably left by the owners from whom the house had been requisitioned. The corporal had drawn the curtains at the windows. They were large and heavy, made of red velvet and touched the floor. When he parted them, he found a steel and glass door, which he opened and stepped out onto the upper terrace.

The view was even better at this height, and he could see down into St. Aubin's Harbor in the distance on his right. It was very still, the only sound a dog barking a couple of fields away. The blackout in St. Helier was anything but complete, lights dotted here and there. The sea was calm, a white line of surf down there on the beach, the sky luminous with stars in the moonlight. A night to thank God for.

He raised his glass. "L'chayim," he said softly and he turned, parted the curtains and went back inside, leaving the door open.

It took Martineau twenty minutes to make his way up through the trees. The undergrowth was thick in places and the going was rough, but he'd expected that and there was no barbed wire on the final approach to the garden, he'd noticed that earlier. He still had no idea what he intended and pulled himself up over the concrete block wall cautiously, aware of voices. He stood in the shadow of a palm tree, and looked up to see Hofer and Rommel on the terrace in the moonlight.

"What a night," the field marshal said.

"My dear Berger, what a day," Hofer told him.

"And the second act still to come."

Martineau stayed in the shadow of the palm tree, astonished at this amazing exchange. It didn't make sense. After they had gone inside, he advanced cautiously across the lawn and paused by the covered way. A moment later, the field marshal appeared on the upper terrace and stood at the rail looking out over the bay.

He raised his glass. "L'chayim," he said softly, turned and went back inside.

L'chayim, which meant "to life," the most ancient of Hebrew toasts. It was enough. Martineau stood on the low wall, reached for the railings on the first terrace and pulled himself over.

Heini Baum took the Blue Max and the Knight's Cross with Oak Leaves, Swords and Diamonds from around his neck and laid them on the dressing table. He removed his cheek pads and examined his face in the mirror, running his fingers through his hair.

"Not bad, Heini. Not bad. I wonder what the great man would say if he knew he was being taken off by a Jew boy?"

He started to unbutton his tunic and Martineau, who had been standing on the other side of the curtain screwing the Carswell silencer on the barrel of the Walther, stepped inside. Baum saw him instantly in the mirror, and old soldier that he was, reached at once for the Mauser pistol in its holster on his belt which lay on the dressing table.

"I wouldn't," Martineau told him. "They've really done wonders with this new model silencer. If I fired it behind your back you wouldn't even know about it. Now, hands on head and sit on the stool."

"Is this some plot of the SS to get rid of me?" Baum asked, playing his role to the hilt. "I'm aware that Reichsführer Himmler never liked me, but I didn't realize how much."

Martineau sat on the edge of the bed, took out a packet of Gitanes one-handed and shook one up. As he lit it he said, "I heard you and Hofer talking on the terrace. He called you Berger."

"You've been busy."

"And I was outside a couple of minutes ago when you were talking to yourself, so let's get down to facts. Number one, you aren't Rommel."

"If you say so."

"All right," Martineau said, "let's try again. If I am part of an SS plot to kill you on Himmler's orders, there wouldn't be much point if you aren't really Rommel. Of course, if you are . . . "

He raised the PPK and Baum took a deep breath. "Very clever."

"So you aren't Rommel?"

"I should have thought that was sufficiently obvious by now."

"What are you, an actor?"

"Turned soldier, turned actor again."

"Marvelous," Martineau said. "I saw him in Paris last year and you fooled me. Does he know you're Jewish?"

"No." Baum frowned. "Listen, what kind of an SS man are you anyway?"

"I'm not." Martineau laid the PPK down on the bed beside him. "I'm a colonel in the British Army."

"I don't believe you," Baum said in astonishment.

"A pity you don't speak English and I could prove it," Martineau said.

"But I do." Baum broke into very good English indeed. "I played the Moss Empire circuit in London, Leeds and Manchester in nineteen thirty-five and six."

"And you went back to Germany?" Martineau said. "You must have been crazy."

"My parents." Baum shrugged. "Like most of the old folk, they didn't believe it would happen. I hid in the army using the identity of a man killed in an air raid in Kiel. My real name is Heini Baum. To Rommel, I'm Corporal Erich Berger, 21st Parachute Regiment."

"Harry Martineau."

Baum hesitated then shook hands. "Your German is excellent."

"My mother was German," Martineau explained. "Tell me, where is Rommel?"

"In Normandy."

"And what's the purpose of the masquerade or don't you know?"

"I'm not supposed to, but I can listen at doors as well as anybody." Baum took a cigarette from the field marshal's silver case, fitted it into the ivory holder Rommel had given him and lit it. "He's having a quiet get-together with Generals von Stulpnagel and Falkenhausen. A highly illegal business as far as I can make out. Apparently they and a number of other generals, realizing they've lost the war, want to get rid of Hitler and salvage something from the mess while there's still a chance.''

"Possible,'' Martineau said. ''There have been attempts on Hitler's life before.''

"Fools, all of them,'' Baum told him.

"You don't approve? That surprises me.''

"They've lost the war anyway. It's only a question of time so there's no point in their scheming. By the time that mad bastard Himmler's finished with them, they'll be hanging on hooks, not that it would worry me. Most of them helped Hitler to power in the first place.''

"That's true.''

"On the other hand, I'm a German as well as a Jew. I've got to know Rommel pretty well in the past few days. He's a good man. He's on the wrong side, that's all. Now you know all about me. What about you? What are you doing here?''

Martineau told him briefly about Kelso, although omitting, for the moment, any mention of the Operation Overlord connection. When he was finished, Baum said, ''I wish you luck. From the sound of it, it's going to be tricky trying to get him out by boat. At least I fly out tomorrow night. A nice fast exit.''

Martineau saw it then, the perfect answer to the whole situation. Sheer genius. ''Tell me,'' he said. ''Once back, you'll be returned to your regiment?''

"I should imagine so.''

"Which means you'll have every chance of having your head blown off during the next few months because the invasion's coming and your paratroopers will be in the thick of it.''

"I expect so.''

"How would you like to go to England instead?''

"You've got to be joking,'' Baum said in astonishment. ''How could such a thing be?''

"Just think about it.'' Martineau got up and paced around the room. ''What's the most useful thing about being Field Marshal Erwin Rommel?''

"You tell me.''

"The fact that everyone does what you tell them to do. For example, tomorrow evening you go to the airport to return to France in the little Storch you came in.''

"So what.''

"There's a JU52 transport up there, the mail plane, due to leave for France around the same time. What do you think would happen if Field Marshal Rommel turned up just before takeoff with an SS Standartenführer, a wounded man on a stretcher, a young Frenchwoman, and commandeered the plane? What do you think they'd say?''

Baum smiled. ''Not very much, I imagine.''

"Once in the air,'' Martineau said, ''and the nearest point on the

English coast would be no more than half an hour's flying time in that mail plane.''

"My God!" Baum said in awe. "You really mean it."

"Do you want to go to England or don't you?" Martineau asked. "Make up your mind. Of course, if you hadn't met me you'd have gone back to France to rejoin the field marshal, and who knows what would happen. Another mad plot to kill the Führer fails, which would mean an unpleasant end for Erwin Rommel. I suspect that might also apply to anyone connected with him and, let's face it—the Gestapo and Himmler would find you very suspect indeed."

"You really do have a way with the words," Baum told him.

Martineau lit a cigarette. "Even if you survive, my friend, Berlin will resemble a brickyard before long. The Russians want blood, and I think you'll find that the Allies will stand back and let them get on with it." He peered out through the curtains. "No, I really do think my alternative is the only option that would make sense to an intelligent man."

"You could make an excellent living selling insurance," Baum told him. "As it happens, I used to have a cousin in Leeds which is in the north of England. Yorkshire, to be precise. My only relative, if he's still alive. I need someone to say kaddish for me. That's prayers for the dead, by the way."

"I know what it is," Martineau said patiently. "Do we have a deal?"

"Berlin a brickyard." Baum shook his head and smiled. "I like that."

"That's settled then." Martineau unscrewed the silencer and put the PPK back in its holster.

"So what about Hofer?"

"What about him?"

"He's not so bad. No different from the rest of us. I wouldn't like to have to hurt him."

"I'll think of something. I'll discuss it with my friends. I'll join your tour of the east of the island tomorrow morning. Be more friendly toward me. At a suitable point when Necker is there, ask me where I'm staying. I'll tell you de Ville Place—all about it. It's magical location, wonderful grounds, and so on. You tell Necker you like the sound of it. That you'd like to have lunch there. Insist on it. I'll finalize things with you then."

"The third act, rewritten at so late a date we don't get any chance to rehearse," Baum said wryly.

"You know what they say," Martineau told him. "That's show business," and he slipped out through the curtain.

It was just after midnight when Sean Gallagher and Guido took Hugh Kelso down the narrow stairway to Helen's bedroom. Sarah waited by the partially open door for Helen's signal from the other end of the corridor. It came and she opened the door quickly.

"Now," she said.

Gallagher and Guido linked arms again and hurried out, Hugh Kelso between them. The back stairs were wider and easier to negotiate, and they were in the kitchen within a couple of minutes. They sat Kelso down and Helen closed the door to the stairs, turning the key.

"So far so good," Gallagher said. "Are you all right, Colonel?"

The American looked strained, but nodded eagerly. "I'm feeling great just to be moving again."

"Fine. We'll take the path through the woods to my place. Ten minutes, that's all."

Helen motioned him to silence. "I think I hear a car."

They waited and Sarah hurriedly turned down the lamp, went to the window and drew the curtains as a vehicle entered the yard outside. "It's Harry," she said.

Helen turned up the lamp again and Sarah unbolted the back door for him. He slipped in and closed the door behind him. After events at Mont de la Rocque he was on a high, full of energy, and the excitement was plain to see on the pale face shadowed by the SS cap.

"What is it, Harry?" Sarah demanded. "Has something happened?"

"I think you could definitely say that, but it can wait until later. Ready to go, are we?"

"As ever was," Kelso said.

"Let's get it done then."

"Sarah and I will go on ahead to make sure everything's ready for you," Helen said as she took a couple of old macs down from a peg, gave one to the girl and put the other one on herself.

She turned the lamp down again, opened the door and she and Sarah hurried across the yard. Gallagher and Guido linked hands and Kelso put his arms around their necks.

"Right," Martineau said. "Here we go. I'll lead the way. If anyone wants a rest, just say so."

He stood to one side to let them go out, closed the door behind him and they started across the courtyard.

The pale moonlight filtered through the trees, and the track was clear before them, the night perfumed with the scent of flowers again. Sarah took Helen's arm. For a moment, there was an intimacy between them, and she was very aware of that warm, safe feeling she had known in the time following her mother's death when Helen had been not only a strong right arm but the breath of life to her.

"What happens afterward?" Helen said. "When you get back?"

"Assuming that we do."

"Don't be silly. It's going to work. If ever I met a man who knows what he's doing it's Harry Martineau. So, what happens on your return? Back to nursing?"

"God knows," Sarah told her. "Nursing was always only a stopgap. It was medicine I was interested in."

"I remember."

"But after this, who knows?" Sarah said. "The whole thing's been like a mad dream. I've never known a man like Harry, never known such excitement."

"Temporary madness, Sarah, just like the war. Not real life. Neither is Harry Martineau. He's not for you, Sarah. God help him, he's not even for himself."

They paused on the edge of the clearing, the cottage a few yards away, bathed in the moonlight. "It's nothing to do with me," Sarah said. "It never was. I had no control over what happened. It's beyond reason."

In the cottage, sitting at the window, Kleist had seen them the moment they had emerged from the wood, and it was the intimacy that struck him at once. There was something wrong here, and he got up, moved to the door and opened it a little. It was then, of course, as they approached, that he realized they were speaking together in English.

Helen said, "Loving someone is different from being in love, darling. Being in love is a state of heat and that passes, believe me. Still, let's get inside. The others will be here in a moment." She put a hand to the door and it moved. "It seems to be open."

And then the door swung, a hand had her by the front of her coat, and Kleist tapped the muzzle of the Mauser against her cheek. "Inside, Frau de Ville," he said roughly. "And let us discuss the curious fact that this little French bitch not only speaks the most excellent English, but would appear to be a friend of yours."

For a moment, Helen was frozen, aware only of a terrible fear as the Mauser tapped again against her face. Kleist reached and got Sarah by the hair.

"And you are expecting others, I gather. I wonder who?" He walked backward, pulling Sarah by the hair, the gun still probing into Helen's flesh. "No stupidities or I pull the trigger." He released Sarah suddenly. "Go and draw the curtains." She did as she was told. "Good, now turn up the lamp. Let's have everything as it should be." She could see the sweat on his face, now, the terror and pain on Helen's. "Now come back here."

His fingers tightened in her hair again. The pain was dreadful. She wanted to cry a warning, but was aware of Helen's head back, the Mauser under her chin. Kleist stank of drink, was shaking with excitement as they waited, listening to the voices approaching across the yard. Only at the very last moment, as the door swung open and Gallagher and Guido backed in, Kelso between them, did he push the women away.

"Harry, look out!" Sarah cried as Martineau slipped in after them, but by then, her anguished cry was too late to help anyone.

Kelso lay on the floor and Helen, Sarah and the three men leaned against the wall in a row, arms outstretched. Kleist relieved Martineau of his PPK and slipped it into his pocket. "The SS must be doing its recruiting in some strange places these days."

Martineau said nothing, waiting, coldly, for his chance and Kleist moved on to Guido Orsini, running his hands over him expertly. "I never liked you, pretty boy," he said contemptuously. "All you sodding Italians have ever done is give us trouble. The Führer should have sorted you lot out first."

"Amazing." Guido turned his head and said amiably to Gallagher, "It can actually talk."

Kleist kicked his feet from under him and put a boot in his side, then he turned to Gallagher, running a hand over him quickly, feeling for a gun. He found nothing and stood back. "Now then, you bastard, I've been waiting for this."

He smashed his right fist into the base of the Irishman's spine. Gallagher cried out and went down. Kleist booted him in the side and Helen screamed. "Stop it!"

Kleist smiled at her. "I haven't even started." He stirred Gallagher with his boot. "Get up and put your hands on your head." Gallagher stayed on his hands and knees for a moment and Kleist prodded him with a toe. "Come on, move it, you thick piece of Irish dung."

Gallagher got to his feet and stood there, a half-smile on his face, arms at his sides. "Half-Irish," he said, "and half-Jersey. As I told you before, a bad combination."

Kleist struck him backhanded across the face. "I told you to get your hands on your head."

"Anything you say."

The gutting knife was ready in Gallagher's left hand, had been for several minutes, skillfully palmed. His arm swung, there was a click as he pressed the button, the blade flickered in the lamplight, catching Kleist in the soft flesh under the chin. Kleist discharged the Mauser once into the wall, then dropped it and fell back against the table, wrenching the knife from Gallagher's grasp. He tried to get up, one hand tearing at the handle protruding from beneath his chin, then fell sideways to the floor, kicked convulsively and was still.

"Oh, my God!" Helen said and turned and stumbled into the kitchen, where she was immediately violently sick.

Martineau said to Sarah, "Go and help her."

The girl went out and he crouched down and took his Walther from the dead man's pocket. He looked up at Gallagher. "They teach that trick in the SOE silent killing course. Where did you learn it?"

"Another legacy from my old grandfather," Gallagher said.

"He must have been a remarkable man."

He and Guido got Kelso onto the couch while Gallagher retrieved his knife. It took all his strength to pull it free. He wiped it on the dead man's coat. "Do you think this was an official visit?"

"I shouldn't imagine so." Martineau picked up the empty bottle of schnapps. "He'd been drinking and he had blood in his eye. He wanted revenge, came up here looking for you, and when you weren't here, he waited." He shook his head. "Poor sod, he almost got lucky for once. It would have been the coup of his career."

"But what happens now?" Kelso demanded. "This could ruin everything. I mean, a Gestapo man doesn't turn up for work, they start looking."

"No need to panic." Martineau picked up a rug and covered Kleist. "There's always a way out. First, we find his car. It's bound to be parked nearby." He nodded to Guido and Gallagher and led the way out.

It was Guido who found the Renault within ten minutes and whistled up the others. Martineau and Gallagher joined him. "Now what?" Guido asked.

"Kelso's right. If Kleist doesn't turn up for work in the morning, Muller will turn this island inside out," Gallagher said. "So what do we do?"

"Give him to them," Martineau said crisply. "He was drunk and ran off the road in his car, it's as simple as that."

"Preferably over a cliff," Guido put in.

"Exactly." Martineau turned to Gallagher. "Have you anywhere suitable to suggest? Not too far, but far enough for there to be no obvious connection with here."

"Yes," Gallagher said. "I think I've got just the place."

"Good. You lead the way in the Renault, and I'll follow in the Kubelwagen."

"Shall I come?" Guido asked.

"No," Martineau said. "You hold the fort here. I'll go up to the house and get the Kubelwagen. You two take the Renault back to the cottage and put Kleist in the boot."

He turned and hurried away through the wood.

⌇⌇

When Martineau arrived back at the cottage they already had Kleist's body in the boot of the car, and Gallagher was ready to go. Martineau asked, "How long will it take us to get to this place?"

"The far side of La Moye Point." Gallagher unfolded an old pocket touring map of the island. "About fifteen or twenty minutes at this time in the morning."

"Are we likely to run into anybody?"

"We have an honorary police system out here in the parishes, and they don't turn out to work for the enemy unless they have to."

"And the Germans?"

"The odd military police patrol, no more than that. We've every chance of driving to La Moye without seeing a soul."

"Right, then let's get moving." Martineau turned to Guido and the two women standing in the doorway. "Wait for us here. There are things to discuss," and he drove away.

Gallagher was right. Their run from Noirmont to Woodbine Corner and along the main road to Red Houses passed without incident, no sign of another vehicle all the way along La Route Orange and moving toward Corbiere Point. Finally, Gallagher turned into a narrow lane. He stopped the Renault and got out.

"There's a strongpoint down there on our right at Corbiere, an artillery battery on the left toward La Moye Point. The area up ahead is clear, and the road turns along the edge of the cliffs about two hundred yards from here. It's always been a hazard. No protecting wall."

"All right," Martineau said. "We'll leave the Kubelwagen here."

He got a can of petrol and stood on the running board of the Renault as Gallagher drove along the bumpy road between high hedges. They came out on the edge of the cliffs, going down into a small valley, a defile on the left running down to rocks and surf below.

"This will do." Martineau hammered on the roof.

Gallagher braked to a halt, got out and went around to the boot. He and Martineau got Kleist out between them, carried him to the front and put him behind the wheel. Gallagher had left the engine running. As he shut the door the dead man slumped forward.

"All right?" Gallagher demanded in a low voice.

"In a minute." Martineau opened the can and poured petrol over the front seat and the dead man's clothes. "Okay, let him go."

Gallagher released the handbrake, leaving the engine in neutral and turned the wheel. He started to push and the Renault left the track, moving across the grass.

"Watch yourself!" Martineau called and struck a match and dropped it through the open passenger window.

For a moment, he thought it had gone out and then, as the Renault bumped over the edge, orange and yellow flame blossomed. They turned and ran back along the lane, and behind them, there was a grinding crash and then a brief explosion.

When they reached the Kubelwagen, Martineau said, "You get down in the back, just in case."

It was too good to last, of course, and five minutes later, as he turned from the Corbiere Road into Route du Sud, he found two military police motorcycles parked at the side of the road. One of them stepped out, hand raised in the moonlight. Martineau slowed at once.

"Military police," he whispered to Gallagher. "Stay low."

He opened the door and got out. "Is there a problem?" At the sight of the uniform, the two policemen jumped to attention. One of them still had a lighted cigarette between the fingers of his left hand. "Ah, now I see, what we might term a smoke break," Martineau said.

"Standartenführer, what can I say?" the man replied.

"Personally, I always find it better to say nothing." There was something supremely menacing in the way he delivered the words. "Now, what did you want?"

"Nothing, Standartenführer. It's just that we don't often see a vehicle at this time in the morning in this sector."

"And you were quite properly doing your duty." Martineau produced his papers. "My SD card. Come on, man, hurry up!" He raised his voice and it was harsh and ugly.

The policeman barely glanced at it, hands shaking as he handed it back. "All is in order."

"Good, you can return to your duties then." Martineau got back in the car. "As for smoking, be a little more discreet, that's my advice."

He drove away. Gallagher said, voice slightly muffled, "How in the hell do you manage to sound such a convincing Nazi?"

"Practice, Sean, that's what it takes. Lots of practice," Martineau told him, and he turned into La Route Orange and moved toward Red Houses.

When they got back to the cottage, Sarah opened the door instantly to them. "Everything all right?"

"Perfect," Gallagher told her as he followed Martineau inside. "We put the car over a cliff near La Moye and made sure it burned."

"Was that necessary?" Helen shivered, clasping her arms around herself.

"We want him to be found," Martineau said. "And if the sentries at the coastal strongpoints in the area are even half-awake they'll have noticed the flames. On the other hand, we don't want him in too good a condition, because if he was, there would be that knife wound to explain.''

Kelso said, ''So, you had no trouble at all?''

''A military police patrol stopped us on the way back,'' Gallagher said. ''I was well out of sight and Harry did his Nazi bit. No problem.''

''So, all that remains now is for Guido to contact Savary in the morning,'' Sarah said.

''No,'' Martineau said. ''Actually, there's been a rather significant change of plan.''

There was general astonishment. Gallagher said, ''Sweet Jesus, what have you been up to now?''

Martineau lit a cigarette, stood with his back to the fire and said calmly, ''If you'll all sit down, I'll tell you.''

14

🙰

AT NINE THE FOLLOWING MORNING Gallagher drove down to St. Helier, two more sacks of potatoes in the van. He didn't call at the central market, but went straight to the troop supply depot in the old garage in Wesley Street. The first trucks went out with military supplies to various units around the island at eight-thirty, which was why he had chosen his time carefully. Feldwebel Klinger was up in his glass office eating his breakfast. Sausage, eggs, bacon, all very English. The coffee was real, Gallagher could smell that as he went up the stairs.

''Good morning, Herr General, what have you got for me today?''

''A couple of sacks of potatoes if you're interested. I'll take canned food in exchange, whatever you've got, and coffee.'' He helped himself to a piece of bacon from Klinger's plate. ''Whenever I see you, you're eating.''

''And why not? The only pleasure left to me in this lousy life. Here, join me in a coffee.'' Klinger poured it out. ''Why are human beings so stupid? I had a nice restaurant in Hamburg before the war. All the best people came. My wife does her best, but more bomb damage last week and no compensation.''

''And worse to come, Hans,'' Gallagher told him. ''They'll be on the beaches soon, all those Tommies and Yanks, and heading for the Fatherland and the Russians coming the other way. You'll be lucky to have a business at all. Those Reichsmarks you keep hoarding won't be worth the paper they're printed on.''

Klinger wiped a hand across his mouth. ''Don't, you'll give me indigestion with talk like that so early in the morning.''

''Of course, this kind of money never loses its value.'' Gallagher took a coin from his pocket, flicked it in the air, caught it and put it down on the table.

Klinger picked it up and there was awe on his face. ''An English sovereign.''

''Exactly,'' Gallagher said. ''A gold sovereign.''

Klinger tried it with his teeth. ''The real thing.''

''Would I offer you anything less?'' Gallagher took a small linen bag from his pocket and held it up tantalizingly. ''Another forty-nine in there.''

He placed the bag on the table and Klinger spilled the coins out and touched them with his fingers. ''All right, what do you want?''

''A sailor's uniform. Kriegsmarine,'' Gallagher told him. ''No big deal, as our American friends say. You've got stacks of them in store here.''

''Impossible,'' Klinger said. ''Absolutely.''

''I'd also expect boots, reefer coat and cap. We're doing a play at the Parish Hall at St. Brelade. Very good part for a German sailor in it. He falls in love with this Jersey girl and her parents . . . ''

''Stop this nonsense,'' Klinger said. ''Play? What play is this?''

''All right.'' Gallagher shrugged. ''If you're not interested.''

He started to pick up the coins and Klinger put a hand on his arm. ''You know the GFP at Silvertide would be very interested to know what you wanted with a German uniform, Herr General.''

''Of course they would, only we're not going to tell them, are we? I mean, you don't want them nosing around in here, Hans. All that booze and cigarettes in the cellar and the canned goods. And then there's the coffee and the champagne.''

''Stop it!''

''I know it's spring now,'' Gallagher carried on relentlessly. ''But it still can't be too healthy on the Russian Front serving with a penal battalion.''

The threat was plain in his voice and the prospect too horrible to contemplate. Klinger was trapped, angry that he'd ever got involved with the Irishman. Too late to cry about that now. Better to give him what he wanted and hope for the best.

"All right, I hear you." Klinger scooped up the sovereigns, put them in one of his tunic pockets. "I've always loved the theater. It would be a privilege to assist."

"I knew I could rely on you," Gallagher told him. "Here are the sizes," and he pushed a piece of paper across the desk.

At ten o'clock the cavalcade left Septembertide and drove to Beaumont and Bel Royal and then along Victoria Avenue to St. Helier. The first stop was Elizabeth Castle. The tide was out and they parked the cars opposite the Grand Hotel and clambered on board an armored personnel carrier which followed the line of the causeway across the beach, its half-tracks churning sand.

"When the tide is in, the causeway is under water, Herr Field Marshal," Necker told him.

Baum was in his element, filled with excitement at the turn events had taken. He could see Martineau seated at the other end of the truck talking to a couple of young officers and Muller and for a wild moment wondered whether he might have dreamed the events of the previous night. Martineau certainly played a most convincing Nazi. On the other hand, he didn't do too bad a job on field marshals himself.

The carrier drove up from the causeway through the old castle gate and stopped. They all got out and Necker said, "The English fortified this place to keep out the French in Napoleon's time. Some of the original guns are still here."

"Now we fortify it further to keep out the English," Baum said. "There's irony for you."

As he led the way along the road to the moat and the entrance to the inner court, Martineau moved to his shoulder. "As a matter of interest, Herr Field Marshal, Sir Walter Raleigh was governor here in the time of Queen Elizabeth Tudor."

"Really?" Baum said. "An extraordinary man. Soldier, sailor, musician, poet, historian."

"Who also found time to introduce tobacco to the Western world," Martineau reminded him.

"For that alone he should have a statue in every major city," Baum said. "I remember the Italian campaign in nineteen seventeen. A terrible time. I think the only thing that got us through the trench warfare was the cigarettes."

He strode on ahead, Martineau at his shoulder, talking animatedly, and Hofer trailed anxiously behind with Necker. An hour later, after a thorough inspection of every gun and strongpoint Baum could find, they returned to the personnel carrier and were taken back across the beach to the cars.

On the cliffs near La Moye Point a group of field engineers hauled on a line, helping the corporal on the other end walk up the steep slope. He came over the edge and unhooked himself. The sergeant in charge of the detail gave him a cigarette. "You don't look too good."

"Neither would you. He's like a piece of badly cooked meat, the driver down there."

"Any papers?"

"Burned along with most of his clothes. The car is a Renault and I've got the number."

The sergeant wrote it down. "The police can handle it now." He turned to the other men. "All right, back to the post, you lot."

Mont Orgeuil at Gorey on the east coast of Jersey is probably one of the most spectacular castles in Europe. The Germans had garrisoned it with coastal artillery batteries. In fact there were two regimental headquarters situated in the castle. Baum visited both of them, as well as conducting his usual energetic survey. In the observation post which had been constructed on the highest point of the castle, he stood with a pair of field-glasses and looked across at the French coast, which was clearly visible. He was for the moment slightly apart from the others and Hofer moved to his shoulder.

"Is everything all right?" Baum asked, the glasses still to his eyes.

"Vogel seems to be pressing his attentions," Hofer said softly.

"He wanted to talk, so I let him," Baum replied. "I'm keeping him happy, Major. I'm trying to keep them all happy. Isn't that what you want?"

"Of course," Hofer told him. "Don't take it the wrong way. You're doing fine. Just be careful, that's all."

Necker moved up to join them, and Baum said, "Fantastic, this place. Now I would like to see something in the country. The sort of strongpoint one might find in a village area."

"Of course, Herr Field Marshal."

"And then some lunch."

"Arrangements have been made. The officers' mess at Battle HQ were hoping to entertain you."

"No, Necker, something different, I think. I'd like to see the other side of island life. Vogel tells me he's billeted at some manor house called de Ville Place. You know it?''

"Yes, Herr Field Marshal. The owner, Mrs. Helen de Ville, is married to the Seigneur who is an officer in the British Army. A most charming woman.''

"And a delightful house according to Vogel. I think we'll have lunch there. I'm sure Mrs. de Ville won't object, especially if you provide the food and wine.'' He looked up at the cloudless blue sky. "A beautiful day for a picnic.''

"As you say, Herr Field Marshal. If you'll excuse me I'll go and give the orders.''

Ten minutes later, as the cavalcade of officers moved out through the main entrance to where the cars waited, a military police motorcyclist drove up. He pulled in beside Greiser, who sat behind the wheel of Muller's Citroën. Greiser read the message the man handed him, then got out of the car and hurried across to Muller, who was talking to a couple of officers. Martineau, standing nearby, heard everything.

"The bloody fool,'' Muller said softly and crumpled the message up in his hand. "All right, we'd better get moving.''

He went to Necker, spoke briefly to him and then got into the Citroën. It moved away quickly, and Martineau walked over to Necker. "Muller seemed agitated.''

"Yes,'' Necker said. "It would seem one of his men has been killed in a car accident.''

"How unfortunate.'' Martineau offered him a cigarette. "Allow me to compliment you on the way you've handled things at such short notice.''

"We do what we can. It's not every day a Rommel comes visiting.''

"On the other hand, I expect you'll heave a sigh of relief when that Storch of his takes off tonight. Is he leaving before or after the mail plane?''

"In my opinion he should make the flight under cover of darkness. The mail plane usually leaves at eight for the same reason.''

"Don't worry, Major.'' Martineau smiled. "I'm sure he'll see sense. I'll speak to him personally about it.''

On a wooded slope in the parish of St. Peter with distant views of St. Ouen's Bay, the field marshal visited a complex of machine-gun nests, talking to gun crews, accepting a cigarette here and there. With the men, he was a sensational success, Necker had to admit that, although God alone knew where all the energy came from.

They had visited every part of the defense complex, were circling back through the wood, when an extraordinary incident took place. They came out of the trees, Baum in the lead. Below them, a gang of slave laborers worked on the track. They were the most wretched creatures Baum had ever seen in his life, dressed, for the most part, in rags.

"What have we here?" he demanded.

"Russians, Herr Field Marshal, plus a few Poles and Spanish Reds."

No one below was aware of their presence, especially the guard who sat on a tree trunk and smoked a cigarette, his rifle across his knees. A cart emerged from the lower wood pulled by a rather thin horse, a young woman in a headscarf and overalls leading it. There was a little girl of five or six in the back of the cart. As they passed the road gang, she tossed them several turnips.

The German guard shouted angrily and ran along the track after the cart. He grabbed the horse by the bridle and brought it to a halt. He said something to the woman and then walked to the back of the cart, reached up and pulled the child down roughly. He slapped her face and, when the young woman ran to help her, knocked the woman to the ground.

Baum did not say a word, but went down the hillside like a strong wind. As he reached the track, the guard's hand rose to strike the child again. Baum caught him by the wrist, twisting it up and around. The guard turned, the anger on his face quickly replaced by astonishment, and Baum punched him in the mouth. The guard bounced off the side of the cart and fell on his hands and knees.

"Major Necker," the field marshal said. "You will oblige me by arresting this animal." He ignored them all, turning to the young woman and the child clutching her. "Your name, Fraulein?" he asked in English.

"Jean le Couteur."

"And this is?" Baum picked the child up.

"My sister Agnes."

"So?" He nodded. "You are a very brave girl, Agnes le Couteur." He put her up in the cart again, turned and saluted the young woman courteously. "My deepest regrets."

She gazed at him, bewildered, then grabbed the bridle and led the horse away along the track. Just before they disappeared from view into the trees, the child raised an arm and waved.

There was general laughter from all the officers present. Baum turned and said to Necker, "Honor being satisfied, I suggest we adjourn to the de Ville Place for lunch."

Muller stood on the edge of the cliff with Greiser and looked down at the wreck of the Renault. "There was a fire," Greiser told him. "From what the engineer sergeant I spoke to says, he's pretty unrecognizable.''

''I can imagine.'' Muller nodded. ''All right, make arrangements with them to get the body up sometime this afternoon. We'll need a post-mortem, but discreetly handled. We must keep the drunkenness factor out of it.''

He turned away and Greiser said, ''But what was he doing out here? That's what I can't understand.''

''So far the only thing we do know is that he was drinking heavily last night. Check with military police for this area, just in case someone saw his car,'' Muller told him. ''I'll have to get back to the official party now so I'll take the Citroën. You'll have to commandeer something from the military police. The moment you have any information at all, let me know.''

The mess sergeant and his men who had descended on de Ville Place from the officers' club at Bagatelle brought ample supplies of food and wine. They simply took over, carrying tables and chairs from the house, covering them with the white linen tablecloths they had brought with them, working very fast. The mess sergeant was polite but made it clear to Helen that as the field marshal was due at any time, he would appreciate it if she did not get in the way.

She went up to her bedroom, searched through the wardrobe and found a summer dress in pale green organdy from happier days. As she was pulling it over her head, there was a tap on the door and Sarah came in.

''Getting ready to play hostess?''

''I don't have much choice, do I?'' Helen told her. ''Even if he was the real thing.''

She brushed back her hair and fitted ivory side combs. Sarah said, ''You look very nice.''

''And so do you.'' Sarah was wearing a dark coat and tiny black hat, the hair swept up.

''We do our best. I'll be glad when it's all over.''

''Not long now, love.'' Helen put her arms around her and held her for a moment, then turned and smoothed her dress.

''You haven't changed your mind, you and Sean? You won't come with us?''

''Good heavens no. Can you imagine what would happen to de Ville Place if I wasn't here? Nothing for Ralph to come home to, and remember that Sean, as he keeps telling us, is a neutral.'' She applied a little lipstick. ''I certainly have nothing to worry about. You and Standarten-führer Vogel were uninvited guests here. Anyway, there's always Guido in the background to back me up.''

"You're really quite a remarkable woman," Sarah said.

"All women are remarkable, my darling. They have to be to get by. It's a man's world." She moved to the window. "Yes, I thought so. They're here." She turned, smiled. "Don't forget that down there among all those officers you and I are formally polite. French only."

"I'll remember."

"Good. Into battle then. I'll go first. Give me a few minutes," and she went out.

When Sarah went into the Great Hall she found Guido, Bruno Feldt and three other young naval officers, all hovering uncertainly around the front door, peering outside. "Ah, Mademoiselle Latour," Guido said in French. "You look ravishing as usual. The field marshal has just arrived."

They moved out onto the steps. Baum was being introduced to Helen by Necker, and Sarah saw Harry standing at the back of the group of officers. Someone took the field marshal's leather coat, baton and gloves. He turned back to Helen, smoothing his tunic, and spoke in English.

"This is most kind of you, Frau de Ville. A gross imposition, but I felt I wanted to see for myself one of your famous Jersey manor houses. De Ville Place comes highly recommended."

"Quite modest compared to some, Herr Field Marshal. St. Ouen's Manor, for example, is much more spectacular."

"But this is delightful. Truly delightful. The gardens, the flowers and palm trees and the sea down there. What a fantastic color." He offered her his arm gallantly. "And now, if you would do me the honor. A little lobster? Some champagne? Perhaps we can forget the war for a while?"

"Difficult, Herr Field Marshal, but I'll try." She took his arm and they walked across the grass to the tables.

The afternoon started off well. Guido Orsini asked permission to take photos which the Field Marshal graciously agreed to, posing with the assembled officers, Martineau standing next to him. The whole affair was obviously a huge success.

Necker, on his fourth glass of champagne, was standing by the drinks table with Hofer and Martineau. "I think he's enjoying himself."

Hofer nodded. "Most definitely. A marvelous place and a most charming hostess."

"However reluctant," Martineau commented acidly. "But too well bred to show it. The English upper classes are always the same."

"Perhaps," Necker said coldly. "And understandably so. Her husband, after all, is a major in the British Army."

"And therefore an enemy of the Reich, but then I hardly need remind you of that."

Martineau picked up another glass of champagne and walked away. Sarah was surrounded by the naval officers and Guido was taking a photo. She waved and Martineau joined them.

"Please, Max," she said. "We must have a photo together."

He laughed lightly and handed his glass to Bruno. "Why not?"

The others moved to one side and he and Sarah stood there together in the sunshine. She felt strange, remembering what Helen had said, her hand tightening on his arm as if trying desperately to hold on.

Guido smiled. "That's fine."

"Good." Martineau retrieved his champagne from Bruno. "And now I must speak to the field marshal. You'll look after Anne-Marie for me, Lieutenant?" he said to Guido and walked away.

He'd noticed Muller arrive, rather later than everyone else. He was standing talking to Necker, and behind him, a military police motorcycle drove up with Greiser in the saddle. Martineau paused, watching. Greiser got off, pushed the motorcycle up on its stand and approached Muller, who made his excuses to Necker and moved away, listening to what the sergeant had to say. After a while, he looked around as if searching for someone. When he found Martineau, he crossed the grass toward him.

"I wonder if I might have a few words in private, Standartenführer?"

"Of course," Martineau said, and they moved away from the others, walking toward the trees. "What can I do for you?"

"My man Kleist was killed last night. A messy business. His car went over a cliff at La Moye."

"Not good," Martineau said. "Had he been drinking?"

"Perhaps," Muller replied cautiously. "The thing is we can't think of any convincing reason for him having been there. It's a remote sort of place."

"A woman perhaps?" Martineau suggested.

"No sign of another body."

"A mystery then, but what has it to do with me?" Martineau knew, of course, what was to come.

"We ran a routine check with the military police patrols in that sector in case they'd noticed his car."

"And had they?"

"No, but we have got a report that you were stopped in your Kubelwagen on Route du Sud at approximately two o'clock this morning."

"Correct," Martineau told him calmly. "But what has that to do with the matter in hand?"

"To get to the area of La Moye where Kleist met with his unfortunate accident it would be necessary to drive along Route du Sud, then take the Corbiere road."

"Do get to the point, Muller, the field marshal is expecting me."

"Very well, Standartenführer. I was wondering what you were doing there at two o'clock in the morning."

"It's quite simple," Martineau said. "I was about my business, under direct orders of the Reichsführer, as you well know. When I return to Berlin he will expect a report on what I found here in Jersey. I'm sorry to say it will not be favorable."

Muller frowned. "Perhaps you could explain, Standartenführer."

"Security for one thing," Martineau told him. "Or the lack of it. Yes, Muller, I was stopped by a military police patrol on Route du Sud this morning. I left de Ville Place at midnight, drove through St. Peter's Valley, up to the village and along to Greve de Lecq. Just after one o'clock I reached L'Etacq at the north end of St. Ouen's Bay, having taken a back lane around Les Landes. A defense area, am I right?"

"Yes, Standartenführer."

"And the places all have important military installations?"

"True."

"I'm glad you agree. I then drove along the bay to Corbiere lighthouse and was eventually stopped in Route du Sud by two military policemen who appeared to be having a smoke at the side of the road. You do get the point, don't you, Muller?" His face was hard and dangerous. "I drove around this island in the early hours of the morning close to some of our most sensitive installations and only got stopped once." He allowed his voice to rise so that officers nearby turned curiously. "Would you say that was satisfactory?"

"No, Standartenführer."

"Then I suggest you do something about it." Martineau put his glass down on a nearby table. "And now I think I've kept the field marshal waiting long enough."

As he walked away, Greiser joined Muller. "What happened?"

"Nothing very much. He says he was on a tour of inspection. Says that in two hours of touring the west of the island, he was only stopped once—on Route du Sud."

"Do you believe him, Herr Captain?"

"Oh, it fits well enough," Muller said. "Unfortunately we're back with that policeman's nose of mine. He was in the area, that's a fact, and I hate coincidences."

"So what shall I do?"

"When they get poor old Willi's body up, get it straight in for a postmortem. If he was awash with schnapps when he died, at least it will show and we'll know where we are."

"All right, Herr Captain, I'll see to it." Greiser went back to his motorcycle, mounted and rode away quickly.

Baum, talking to Helen and a couple of officers, turned as Martineau approached. "Ah, there you are, Vogel. I'm in your debt for suggesting my visit to such a delightful spot."

"A pleasure, Herr Field Marshal."

"Come, we'll walk awhile and you can tell me how things are in Berlin these days." He took Helen's hand and kissed it. "You'll excuse us, Frau de Ville?"

"Of course, Herr Field Marshal."

Martineau and Baum turned away and strolled across the grass toward the trees, taking the path that led to the rampart walk with its view of the bay. "This whole thing becomes more like a bad play by the minute," Baum said.

"Yes, well we don't have time right now to discuss what Brecht might have made of it. This is what happens. The mail plane leaves at eight. They expect you to fly out in the Storch at about the same time."

"So?"

"I'll turn up at Septembertide at seven. I'll have Sarah with me, also Kelso in Kriegsmarine uniform and heavily bandaged."

"And how does Hofer react?"

"He does exactly as he's told. I've got a syringe and a strong sedative, courtesy of the doctor who's been treating Kelso. An armful of that and he'll be out for hours. We'll lock him in his bedroom."

"When does this happen?"

"I'd say the best time would be at the end of your tour when you return to Septembertide. Probably around five o'clock. Get rid of Necker and the others, but ask me to stay for a drink."

"But how do I explain his absence at the airport?"

"Simple. Necker will be there with his staff to bid you a fond farewell. It's at that point you announce you intend to fly out in the mail plane. You can't arrange it earlier because Hofer would want to know what you were up to. You tell Necker that the chief medical officer at the hospital has made representations on behalf of this sailor, badly wounded in the convoy attack the other night and in urgent need of specialist treatment on the mainland. As you're using the bigger plane, you're giving me and Sarah a lift."

"And Hofer?"

"Tell Necker that Hofer is following behind. That he's going to fly out in the Storch on his own."

"And you think all this will work?"

"Yes," Martineau said, "because it's actually rather simple. I could have tried something like it without you, using my letter from the Reichsführer, but perhaps the Luftwaffe commanding officer here would have insisted on getting permission from Luftwaffe HQ in Normandy." He smiled. "But to Erwin Rommel, nobody says no."

Baum sighed, took the cigarette Martineau offered and fitted it into the holder. "I'll never get a role as good as this again. Never."

15

ᴗᴗ

ON THE SLAB IN THE postmortem room at the general hospital, Willi Kleist's corpse looked even more appalling. Major Speer stood waiting while the two medical corporals who were assisting him carefully cut away the burned clothing. Greiser, standing by the door, watched in fascinated horror.

Speer turned to look at him. "If you feel like being sick, the bucket is over there. Nothing to be ashamed of."

"Thank you, Herr Major. Captain Muller asked me to tell you how much he appreciates your attending to him personally."

"I understand, Sergeant. Discretion, in a case like this, is of the utmost importance. So, we are ready?"

The last vestiges of clothing were stripped away, and one of the corporals washed the body down with a fine spray, while the other wheeled across a trolley on which a selection of surgical instruments had been laid out.

"I'd normally start with taking out the brain," Speer said cheerfully. "But in this case, speed being of the essence, or so you inform me, we'll have the organs out first so the lab technicians can get on with their side of things."

The scalpel in his right hand didn't seem particularly large, but when he ran it down from just below the throat to the belly, the flesh parted instantly. The smell was terrible, but Greiser hung on, a handkerchief to his mouth. Speer worked at speed, removing the heart, the liver, the kidneys, all being taken away in enamel basins to the laboratory next door.

Speer seemed to have forgotten about Greiser. One of the corporals passed him a small electric saw which plugged into a floor socket. When he started on the skull, Greiser could take no more and removed himself hurriedly to the lavatory where he was violently sick.

Afterward, he sat outside in the corridor and smoked. A young nurse with an Irish accent came up and put a hand on his shoulder. "You look awful."

"I've just been watching them do a postmortem," Greiser told her.

"Yes, well it gets you like that the first time. I'll bring you a coffee."

She meant well, but it was not the real thing: acorn coffee, a taste Greiser found particularly loathsome. He lit another cigarette and walked down to the main entrance and phoned through to Muller at the Silvertide from the porter's desk.

"It's Greiser, Herr Captain."

"How are things going?" Muller asked.

"Well, it's hardly one of life's great experiences, but Major Speer obviously knows his stuff. I'm waiting for his conclusions now. They're doing lab tests."

"You might as well hang on until they're ready. An interesting development. I've had your brother on the phone from Stuttgart. He's heard from this Neumann woman in Berlin. The one who works in the Reichsführer's office at the Chancellery."

"And?"

"She's never heard of Vogel. She's kept her inquiries discreet for the moment. Of course, as your brother points out, these special envoys of Himmler are mystery men to everyone else."

"Yes, but you'd think someone like Lotte Neumann would have at least heard of him," Greiser said. "What are you going to do?"

"Think about it. As soon as Speer's ready with those results, give me a ring and I'll come around myself to see what he has to say."

It was just before five when the cavalcade of cars returned to Septembertide. Baum and Hofer got out and Necker joined them with one or two officers. Martineau stood at the back of the group and waited. "A memorable day, Major," Baum said. "I'm truly grateful."

"I'm pleased everything has gone so well, Herr Field Marshal."

"How long does it take to the airport from here?"

"No more than ten minutes."

"Good. We'll see you up there sometime between seven-thirty and eight."

Necker saluted, turned and got back into his car. As the officers dispersed, Baum and Hofer turned to the front door and Martineau stepped forward. "Might I have a word, Herr Field Marshal?"

Hofer was immediately wary, but Baum said cheerfully, "Of course, Standartenführer. Come in."

At that moment Heider, the platoon commander, appeared in the gateway and saluted. "Is there anything I can do for you, Herr Field Marshal?"

"What about the cook we had last night?"

"I'll send him over."

"Not for half an hour, Heider."

He went inside followed by Hofer and Martineau. They went into the living room. Baum took off his leather coat and his cap and opened the glass door to the terrace. "A drink, Standartenführer?"

"That would be very acceptable."

"Konrad." Baum nodded to Hofer. "Cognac, I think. You'll join us?"

He fitted a cigarette to his holder, and Martineau gave him a light as Hofer poured the drinks. "What an extraordinary view," Baum said, looking down at St. Aubin's Bay. "In peacetime, with the lights on at night down there, it must resemble Monte Carlo. Wouldn't you think so, Konrad?"

"Perhaps, Herr Field Marshal." Hofer was nervous and trying not to show it, wondering what Vogel wanted.

"To us, gentlemen." Baum raised his glass. "To soldiers everywhere who always bear the burden of man's stupidity." He emptied his glass, smiled and said in English, "All right, Harry, let's get on with it."

Hofer looked totally bewildered and Martineau produced the Walther with the Carswell silencer from his trenchcoat pocket. "It would be stupid to make me shoot you. Nobody would hear a thing." He removed the Mauser from Hofer's holster. "Sit down."

"Who are you?" Hofer demanded.

"Well I'm certainly not Standartenführer Max Vogel any more than Heini here is the Desert Fox."

"Heini?" Hofer looked even more bewildered.

"That's me," Baum said. "Heini Baum. Erich Berger was killed in an air raid on Kiel. I took his papers and joined the paratroops."

"But why?"

"Well, you see, Herr Captain, I happen to be Jewish, and what better place for a Jew to hide?"

"My God!" Hofer said hoarsely.

"Yes, I thought you'd like that. A Jew impersonating Germany's greatest war hero. A nice touch of irony there."

Hofer turned to Martineau. "And you?"

"My name is Martineau. Lieutenant Colonel Harry Martineau. I work for SOE. I'm sure you've heard of us."

"Yes." Hofer reached for his glass and finished the rest of his brandy. "I think you can say that."

"Your boss is a lucky man. I was close to putting a bullet in him last night after you'd gone to bed. Happily for our friend here, he likes to talk to himself and I discovered all was not as it seemed."

"So what do you intend to do?" Hofer asked.

"Simple. Field Marshal Rommel flies out in the mail plane tonight, not the Storch, which means I can leave with him, along with a couple of friends. Destination England."

"The young lady?" Hofer managed a smile. "I liked her. I presume she also is not what she seems."

"One more thing," Martineau said, "but it's important. You might wonder why I don't shoot you. Well, Heini having a bad habit of listening at doors, I know where Rommel has been this weekend and what he's been up to. The assassination of Hitler at this stage of the war would suit the Allied cause very well. In the circumstances, when we get back to England and I tell my people about this business, I think you'll find they keep very quiet. We wouldn't want to make things too difficult for Field Marshal Rommel, if you follow me. More power to his arm. I want you to live so you can tell him that."

"And how does he explain to the Führer what happened here?"

"I should have thought that rather simple. There's been more than one plot against Rommel's life already by French Resistance and Allied agents. The British nearly got him in North Africa, remember. To use Berger to impersonate him on occasion made good sense, and what happened here in Jersey proved it. If he'd come himself, he'd have died here. The fact that Berger has decided to change sides is regrettable, but hardly your fault."

"Now you say Berger again."

"I think he means you might overcomplicate things if you introduce the Jewish bit," Heini told him.

"Something like that." Martineau stood up. "All right, let's have you upstairs."

Hofer did as he was told, because he didn't have any choice in the matter, and they followed him up and along the corridor to the small bedroom he had been using.

Through the half-drawn curtains he could see into the courtyard and over the wall to where Heider stood beside one of the armored personnel carriers.

"Obviously you don't intend to kill me," he said.

"Of course not. I need you to tell all to Rommel, don't I?" Martineau replied. "Just keep still and don't make a fuss and you'll be fine."

There was a burning pain in Hofer's right arm and almost instantaneous darkness. Baum emptied the contents of the syringe before pulling it out, and Martineau eased the major down onto the bed, arranged his limbs in a comfortable position and covered him with a blanket.

They went down to the hall. Martineau said, "Seven o'clock."

As he opened the front door, the cook corporal from the night before walked across the courtyard. Baum said, "I'll see you later then, Standartenführer."

He turned and walked back inside to the living room and the corporal followed. "At your orders, Herr Field Marshal."

"Something simple," Baum said. "Scrambled eggs, toast and coffee, I think. Just for me. Major Hofer isn't feeling too well. He's having a rest before we leave."

In Gallagher's cottage, he and Martineau eased Kelso into the Kriegsmarine uniform while Sarah stayed discreetly out of the way in the kitchen. Gallagher cut the right trouser leg so that it would fit over the cast.

"How's that?" he asked.

"Not bad." Kelso hesitated then said awkwardly, "There's a lot of people putting themselves on the line because of me."

"Oh, I see," Martineau said. "You mean you deliberately got yourself blown over the rail of that LST in Lyme Bay?"

"No, of course not."

"Then stop agonizing," Martineau told him and called to Sarah: "You can come in now."

She entered from the kitchen with two large bandage rolls and surgical tape. She went to work on Kelso's face and head, leaving only one eye and the mouth visible.

"That's really very professional," Gallagher said.

"I am a professional, you fool," she told him.

He grinned amiably. "Jesus, girl, I bet you look great in that nurse's uniform."

Martineau glanced at his watch. It was almost six o'clock. "We'll go up to the house now, General. You keep an eye on him. I'll be back with the Kubelwagen in an hour."

He and Sarah left, and Gallagher went into the hall and came back with a pair of crutches. "Present for you." He propped them against the table. "See how you get on."

Kelso pushed himself up on one leg, got first one crutch under an arm and then the other. He took one hesitant step forward, paused, then moved on with increasing confidence, until he reached the other side of the room.

"Brilliant!" Gallagher told him. "Long John Silver to the life. Now try again."

"Are you certain?" Muller asked.

"Oh, it's quite definite," Speer said. "I'll show you." The brain slopped about in the enamel basin and he turned it over in gloved hands. "See the pink discoloration at the base? That's blood, and that's what gave me the clue. Something sharp sheared right up through the roof of the mouth into the brain."

"Is it likely such an injury would be explained by the kind of accident he was in?"

"Oh, no," Speer said. "Whatever did this was as razor sharp as a scalpel. The external flesh of the face and neck is badly burned and I can't be certain, but if you want my opinion, he was stabbed under the chin. Does that make any kind of sense?"

"Yes," Muller said. "I think it does. Thanks very much." He nodded to Greiser. "Let's go."

As he reached the door and opened it, Speer said, "Oh, one more thing."

"What's that?"

"You were quite right. He had been drinking heavily. I'd say, from the tests, about a bottle and a half of spirits."

On the steps outside the main entrance of the hospital, Muller paused to light a cigarette. "What do you think, Herr Captain?" Greiser asked.

"That another word with Standartenführer Vogel is indicated, Ernst, so let's get moving."

He got into the passenger seat of the Citroën. Greiser slid behind the wheel and drove away.

In the kitchen at de Ville Place, Sarah, Helen and Martineau sat round the table. The door opened and Guido came in with a bottle. "Warm champagne," he said. "The best I can do."

"Are you certain the place is empty?" Sarah asked.

"Oh, yes. Bruno was the last to leave. They're all on tonight's convoy to Granville. Kriegsmarine Headquarters haven't come up with a new assignment for me yet."

He pulled the cork and poured champagne into the four kitchen glasses Helen provided. She raised hers. "What shall we drink to?"

"Better days," Sarah said.

"And life, liberty and the pursuit of happiness," Guido added, "not forgetting love."

"You wouldn't." Sarah kissed his cheek and turned to Martineau. "And you, Harry, what do you wish?"

"One day at a time is all I can manage." He finished the champagne. "My God, that tastes awful." He put down the glass. "I'll go and get Kelso now. Be ready to leave when I get back, Sarah."

He went out, got into the Kubelwagen and drove away, taking the track down through the wood. At the same time, two hundred yards to the right, the Citroën carrying Muller and Greiser moved along the road to de Ville Place and turned into the courtyard.

In the bedroom, Sarah put on her hat and coat, turning to check in the mirror that her stocking seams were straight. She freshened her mouth with lipstick and made a face at herself in the mirror. "Goodbye, little French tart, it's been nice knowing you."

At that moment she heard a car outside and glanced out of the window and saw Muller get out of the Citroën. It was trouble, she knew that instantly. She opened her handbag. The PPK was in there but also the little Belgian automatic Kelly had given her. She lifted her skirt and slipped the smaller gun into the top of her right stocking. It fit surprisingly snugly. She smoothed down her coat and left the room.

Muller was in the hall talking to Helen, Greiser over by the entrance. Guido was standing by the green baize door leading to the kitchen. As Sarah came down the stairs, Muller looked up and saw her.

"Ah, there you are, mademoiselle," Helen said in French. "Captain Muller was looking for the Standartenführer. Do you know where he is?"

"I've no idea," Sarah said continuing on down. "Is there a problem?"

"Perhaps." Muller took her handbag from her quite gently, opened it and removed the PPK which he put in his pocket. He handed the bag back to her. "You've no idea when he'll be back?"

"None at all," Sarah said.

"But you are dressed to go out?"

"Mademoiselle Latour was going to take a walk in the grounds with me," Guido put in.

Muller nodded. "Very well, if the Standartenführer isn't available, I'll have to make do with you." He said to Greiser. "Take her out to the car."

"But I protest," Sarah started to say.

Greiser smiled, his fingers hooking painfully into her arm. "You protest all you like, sweetheart. I like it," and he hustled her through the door.

Muller turned to Helen who managed to stay calm with difficulty. "Perhaps you would be good enough to tell Standartenführer Vogel on his return that if he wishes to see Mademoiselle Latour, he must come to the Silvertide,'' and he turned and walked out.

Kelso was doing quite well with the crutches. He made it to the Kubelwagen under his own steam, and Gallagher helped him into the rear seat. ''Nice going, me old son.''

Martineau got behind the wheel and Guido emerged from the trees on the run. He leaned against the car, gasping.

''What is it, man?'' Gallagher demanded.

''Muller and Greiser turned up. They were looking for you, Harry.''

''And?'' Martineau's face was very pale.

''They've taken Sarah. Muller says if you want to see her, you'll have to go to the Silvertide. What are we going to do?''

''Get in!'' Martineau said and drove away as the Italian and Gallagher scrambled aboard.

He braked to a halt in the courtyard where Helen waited anxiously on the steps. She hurried down and leaned in the Kubelwagen. ''What are we going to do, Harry?''

''I'll take Kelso up to Septembertide to connect with Baum. If worse comes to worst, they can fly off into the blue together. Baum knows what to do.''

''But we can't leave Sarah,'' Kelso protested.

''I can't,'' Martineau said, ''but you can, so don't give me a lot of false sentimentality. You're what brought us here in the first place. The reason for everything.''

Helen clutched his arm. ''Harry!''

''Don't worry. I'll think of something.''

''Such as?'' Gallagher demanded.

''I don't know,'' Martineau said. ''But you keep out of it, that's essential. We'll have to go.''

The Kubelwagen moved away across the yard, and the noise of the engine faded. Gallagher turned to Guido. ''Get the Morris out and you and I'll take a run down to the Silvertide.''

''What do you have in mind?'' Guido asked.

''God knows. I never could stand just sitting around and waiting, that's all.''

Martineau drove into the courtyard at Septembertide and braked to a halt. He helped Kelso out and the American followed him, swinging between his crutches. The door was opened by the corporal. As they went in, Baum appeared from the sitting room.

"Ah, there you are, Vogel! And this is the young man you told me about?" He turned to the corporal. "Dismissed. I'll call you when I want you."

Baum stood back and Kelso moved past him into the sitting room. Martineau said, "There's been a change of plan. Muller came looking for me at de Ville Place. As it happens, I wasn't around at the right moment, but Sarah was. They've taken her to the Silvertide."

"Don't tell me, let me guess," Baum said. "You're going to go to the rescue."

"Something like that."

"And what about us?"

Martineau glanced at his watch. It was just after seven. "You and Kelso keep to your schedule. Getting him out of here is what's important."

"Now look here," Kelso began, but Martineau had already walked out.

The Kubelwagen roared out of the courtyard. Kelso turned and found Baum pouring cognac into a glass. He drank it slowly. "That's really very good."

"What goes on here?" the American demanded.

"I was thinking of Martineau," Baum said. "I might have known that under all that surface cynicism he was the kind of man who'd go back for the girl. I was at Stalingrad, did you know that? I've had enough of heroes to last me for a lifetime."

He pulled on his leather trenchcoat and gloves, twisted the white scarf around his neck, adjusted the angle of the cap and picked up his baton.

"What are you going to do?" Kelso demanded.

"Martineau told me that the important thing about being Field Marshal Erwin Rommel was that everyone would do what I told them to do. Now we'll see if he's right. You stay here."

He strode through the courtyard into the road and the men leaning beside the personnel carrier sprang to attention. "One of you get Captain Heider."

Baum took out a cigarette and fitted it in his holder. A sergeant sprang forward with a light. A second later Heider hurried out. "Herr Field Marshal?"

"Get through to the airport. A message for Major Necker. I shall be a little later than I thought. Tell him also that I shall leave for France, not in my Storch, but in the mail plane. I expect it waiting and ready to go when I arrive, and I'd like my personal pilot to fly it."

"Very well, Herr Field Marshal."

"Excellent. I need them all, fully armed and ready to go in five minutes. You'll find a wounded sailor in Septembertide. Have a couple of men help him out and put him in the personnel carrier. And they can bring the corporal you loaned me with them, too. No sense in leaving him hanging around the kitchen.''

"But Herr Field Marshal, I don't understand," the captain said.

"You will, Heider," the field marshal told him. "You will. Now send that message to the airport."

Muller had drawn the curtains in his office and Sarah sat on a chair in front of his desk, hands folded in her lap, knees together. They'd made her take off her coat and Greiser was searching the lining while Muller went through the handbag.

He said, "So you are from Paimpol?"

"That's right."

"Sophisticated clothes for a Breton girl from a fishing village."

"Oh, but she's been around this one, haven't you?" Greiser ran his fingers up and down her neck, making her flesh crawl.

Muller said, "Where did you and Standartenführer Vogel meet?"

"Paris," she said.

"But there is no visa for Paris among your papers."

"I had one. It ran out."

"Have you ever heard of the Cherche Midi or the women's prison at Troyes? Bad places for a young woman like you to be."

"I don't know what you're talking about. I've done nothing," she said.

Her stomach contracted with fear, her throat was dry. Oh, God, Harry, she thought, fly away. Just fly away. And then the door opened and Martineau walked into the office.

There were tears in her eyes and she had never known such emotion as Greiser stood back and Harry put an arm around her gently.

The emotion she felt was so overwhelming that she committed the greatest blunder of all then. "Oh, you bloody fool," she said in English. "Why didn't you go?"

Muller smiled gently and picked up the Mauser that lay on his desk. "So, you speak English also, mademoiselle. This whole business becomes even more intriguing. I think you'd better relieve the Standartenführer of his Walther, Ernst."

Greiser did as he was told, and Martineau said in German, "Do you know what you're doing, Muller? There's a perfectly good reason for Mademoiselle Latour to speak English. Her mother was English. The facts are on file at SD headquarters in Paris. You can check."

"You have an answer for everything," Muller said. "What if I told you that a postmortem has indicated that Willi Kleist was murdered last night? The medical examiner indicates the time of death as being between midnight and two o'clock. I need hardly remind you that it was two o'clock when you were stopped on Route du Sud, no more than a mile from where the body was discovered. What do you have to say to that?''

''I can only imagine you've been grossly over-working. Your career's on the line here, Muller, you realize that. When the Reichsführer hears the full facts he'll . . . ''

For the first time Muller almost lost his temper. ''Enough of this. I've been a policeman all my life—a good policeman and I detest violence. However, there are those with a different attitude. Greiser here, for instance. A strange thing about Greiser. He doesn't like women. He would actually find it pleasurable to discuss this whole affair in private with Mademoiselle Latour, but I doubt that she would.''

''Oh, I don't know.'' Greiser put an arm around Sarah and slipped a hand inside her dress, fondling a breast. ''I think she might get to like it after I've taught her her manners.''

Sarah's left hand clawed down his face, drawing blood, only feeling rage now, more powerful than she had ever known. As Greiser staggered back, her hand went up her skirt, pulling the tiny automatic from her stocking. Her arm swung up and she fired at point-blank range, shooting Muller between the eyes. The Mauser dropped from his nerveless hand to the desk; he staggered back against the wall and fell to the floor. Greiser tried to get his own gun from his pocket, too late as Martineau picked up the Mauser from the desk.

Gallagher and Guido were sitting in the Morris on the other side of the road from the Silvertide when they heard the sound of approaching vehicles. They turned to see a military column approaching. The lead vehicle was a Kubelwagen with the top down and Field Marshal Erwin Rommel standing in the passenger seat for the whole world to see. The Kubelwagen braked to a halt, he got out as the soldiers, carried by the other vehicles in the column, jumped down and ran forward in obedience to Heider's shouted orders.

''Right, follow me!'' Baum called and marched straight in through the entrance of the Silvertide. A moment after Sarah fired the shot that killed Muller, the door crashed open and Baum appeared. He advanced into the room, Heider and a dozen armed men behind him. He peered over the desk at Muller's body.

Greiser said, ''Herr Field Marshal, this woman has murdered Captain Muller.''

Baum ignored him and said to Heider, ''Put this man in a cell.''

"Yes, Herr Field Marshal." Heider nodded and three of his men grabbed the protesting Greiser. Heider followed them out.

"Back in your vehicles," Baum shouted to the others and held Sarah's coat for her. "Can we go now?"

Gallagher and Guido saw them come out of the entrance to the hotel and get into the Kubelwagen, Martineau and Sarah in the back, Baum standing up in front. He waved his arm, the Kubelwagen led off, the whole column following.

"Now what do we do?" Guido asked.

"Jesus, is there no poetry in you at all?" Gallagher demanded. "We follow them, of course. I wouldn't miss the last act for anything."

At Septembertide, on the bed in the small room, Konrad Hofer groaned and moved restlessly. The sedative the doctor had given Martineau was, like most of his drugs, of prewar vintage, and Hofer was no longer completely unconscious. He opened his eyes, mouth dry, and stared at the ceiling, trying to work out where he was. It was like awaking from a bad dream, something you knew had been terrible and yet already forgotten. And then he remembered, tried to sit up and rolled off the bed to the floor.

He pulled himself up, head swimming, and reached for the door handle. It refused to budge and he turned and lurched across to the window. He fumbled with the catch and then gave up the struggle and slammed his elbow through the pane.

The sound of breaking glass brought the two soldiers Captain Heider had left on sentry duty at Hinguette next door running into the courtyard. They stared up, machine pistols at the ready, a young private and an older man, a corporal.

"Up here!" Hofer called. "Get me out. I'm locked in."

He sat on the bed, his head in his hands, and tried to breathe deeply, aware of the sound of their boots clattering up the stairs and along the corridor. He could hear voices, saw the handle turn.

"There's no key, Herr Hofer," one of them called.

"Then break it down, you fool!" he replied.

A moment later, the door burst open, crashing against the wall, and they stood staring at him.

"Get Captain Heider," Hofer said.

"He's gone, Herr Major."

"Gone?" Hofer still had difficulty thinking clearly.

"With the field marshal, Herr Major. The whole unit went with them. We're the only two here."

The effects of the drug made Hofer feel as if he were underwater and he shook his head vigorously. "Did they leave any vehicles?"

"There's a Kubelwagen, Herr Major," the corporal told him.

"Can you drive?"

"Of course, sir. Where does the Herr Major wish to go?"

"The airport," Hofer said. "And there's no time to lose, so help me downstairs and let's get moving."

16

~

AT THE AIRPORT, THE LUFTWAFFE honor guard waited patiently as darkness fell. The same group of officers who had greeted the field marshal on his arrival now presented themselves to say goodbye. The Storch was parked on the far side of the JU52, which awaited its illustrious passenger some fifty yards from the terminal building. Necker paced up and down anxiously, wondering what on earth was going on. First of all that extraordinary message from Heider at Mont de la Rocque about the mail plane and now this. Twenty minutes past eight and still no sign.

There was the sudden roar of engines, the rattle of a half-track on concrete. He turned in time to witness the extraordinary sight of the armored column coming around the corner of the main airport building, the field marshal standing up in the Kubelwagen at the front, hands braced on the edge of the windshield.

The column made straight for the Junkers. Necker saw the field marshal wave to Sorsa in the cockpit, who was looking out of the side window. The center engine of the plane coughed into life, and Rommel was turning and waving, barking orders. Soldiers leaped from the trucks, rifles ready. Necker recognized Heider and then saw a bandaged sailor being taken from the personnel carrier by two soldiers who led him to the Junkers and helped him inside.

The whole thing had happened in seconds. As Necker started forward, the field marshal came to meet him. It was noisy now as the Junkers' wing engines also started to turn. To Necker's further astonishment he saw, beyond the field marshal, Standartenführer Vogel and the French girl dismount from the personnel carrier and go up the short ladder into the plane.

Baum was enjoying himself. The ride up from the Silvertide had been truly exhilarating, and he smiled and put a hand on Necker's shoulder. "My deepest apologies, Necker, but I had things to do. Young Heider was good enough to assist me with his men. A promising officer."

Necker was truly bewildered. "But, Herr Field Marshal . . . " he began.

Baum carried on. "The chief medical officer at the hospital told me of this young sailor wounded in some convoy attack the other night and badly in need of treatment at the burns unit in Rennes. He asked me if I'd take him with me. Of course, in the state he's in we'd never have got him into the Storch. That's why I need the mail plane."

"And Standartenführer Vogel?"

"He was going back tomorrow anyway, so I might as well give him and the young woman a lift." He clapped Necker on the shoulder again. "But we must be off now. Again, my thanks for all you've done. I shall, of course, be in touch with General von Schmettow to express my entire satisfaction with the way things are in Jersey."

He saluted and turned to go up the ladder into the plane. Necker called, "But, Herr Field Marshal, what about Major Hofer?"

"He should be arriving any minute," Baum told him. "He'll leave in the Storch as arranged. The mail plane pilot can fly him across."

He scrambled inside the plane; the crewman pulled up the ladder and closed the door. The Junkers taxied away to the east end of the runway and turned. There was a deepening roar from the three engines as it moved faster and faster, a silhouette only in the gathering gloom, and then it lifted, drifting out over St. Ouen's Bay, still climbing.

Guido had parked the Morris a couple of hundred yards along the airport road. Standing there beside it, they saw the Junkers lift into the evening sky and fly west to where the horizon was tipped with fire.

The noise of the engines faded into the distance and Guido said softly, "My God, they actually pulled it off."

Gallagher nodded. "So now we can go home and get our stories straight for when all the questioning starts."

"No problem," Guido said. "Not if we stick together. I am, after all, an authentic war hero, which always helps."

"That's what I love about you, Guido. Your engaging modesty," Gallagher told him. "Now let's move. Helen will be getting worried."

They got into the Morris and Guido drove away quickly, a

Kubelwagen passing them a moment later coming the other way, driving so fast that they failed to see Hofer sitting in the rear seat.

At the airport, most of the officers had dispersed, but Necker was standing by his car talking to Captain Adler, the Luftwaffe duty control officer, when the Kubelwagen came around the corner of the main airport building and braked to a halt. They turned to see Hofer being helped out of the rear seat by the two soldiers.

Necker knew trouble when he saw it. "Hofer? What is it?"

Hofer slumped against the Kubelwagen. "Have they gone?"

"Less than five minutes ago. The field marshal took the mail plane. He said you'd follow in the Storch. He took his own pilot."

"No!" Hofer said. "Not the field marshal."

Necker's stomach contracted. So many things that had worried him and yet . . . He took a deep breath. "What are you saying?"

"That the man you thought was Field Marshal Rommel is his double, a damn traitor called Berger who's thrown in his lot with the enemy. You'll also be happy to know that Standartenführer Max Vogel is an agent of the British Special Operations Executive. So is the girl, by the way. The wounded sailor is an American colonel."

But Necker, by now, was totally bewildered. "I don't understand any of this."

"It's really quite simple," Hofer told him. "They're flying to England in the mail plane." His head was suddenly clearer and he stood up. "Naturally, they must be stopped." He turned to Adler. "Get on the radio to Cherbourg. Scramble a night fighter squadron. Now let's get moving. There's no time to lose." He turned and led the way to the operations building.

The Junkers was a workhorse and not built for comfort. Most of the interior was crammed with mail sacks and Kelso sat on the floor propped against them, legs outstretched. Sarah was on a bench on one side of the plane, Baum and Martineau on the other.

The crewman came out of the cockpit and joined them. "My name is Braun, Herr Field Marshal. Sergeant observer. If there is anything I can get you. We have a thermos flask of coffee and . . ."

"Nothing, thank you." Baum took out his cigarette case and offered Martineau one.

"And Oberleutnant Sorsa would take it as an honor if you would care to come up front."

"You don't have a full crew? Just the two of you?" Martineau inquired.

"All that's necessary on these mail runs, Standartenführer."

"Tell Oberleutnant Sorsa I'll be happy to take him up on his offer a little later. I'll just finish my cigarette," Baum said.

"Certainly, Herr Field Marshal."

Braun opened the door and went back into the cockpit. Baum turned to Martineau and smiled. "Five minutes?"

"That should be about right." Martineau moved across to sit beside Sarah. He gave her his lighted cigarette. "Are you all right?"

"Absolutely."

"You're sure?"

"You mean am I going through hell because I just killed a man?" Her face was very calm. "Not at all. My one regret is that it was Muller instead of Greiser. He was from under a stone. Muller was just a policeman on the wrong side."

"From our point of view."

"No, Harry," she said. "Most wars are a stupidity. This one isn't. We're right and the Nazis are wrong. They're wrong for Germany and they're wrong for everyone else. It's as simple as that."

"Good for you," Kelso said. "A lady who stands up to be counted. I like that."

"I know," Martineau said. "It's wonderful to be young." He tapped Baum on the knee. "Ready?"

"I think so."

Martineau took his Walther from its holster and gave it to Sarah. "Action stations. You'll need that to take care of the observer. Here we go."

He opened the cabin door and he and Baum squeezed into the cockpit behind the pilot and the observer. Oberleutnant Sorsa turned. "Everything to your satisfaction, Field Marshal?"

"I think you could say that," Baum told him.

"If there is anything we can do for you?"

"There is actually. You can haul this thing round and fly forty miles due west until we are completely clear of all Channel Islands traffic."

"But I don't understand."

Baum took the Mauser from his holster and touched it against the back of Sorsa's neck. "Perhaps this will help you."

"Later on when I call you, you'll turn north," Martineau said, "and make for England."

"England?" young Braun said in horror.

"Yes," Martineau told him. "As they say, for you, the war is over. Frankly, the way it's shaping up, you're well out of it."

"This is crazy," Sorsa said.

"If it helps you to believe that the field marshal is proceeding to England as a special envoy of the Führer, why not?" Martineau said. "Now change course like a good boy."

Sorsa did as he was told and the Junkers plowed on through the darkness. Martineau leaned over Braun. "Right, now for the radio. Show me the frequency selection procedure." Braun did as he was told. "Good. Now go and sit down in the cabin and don't do anything stupid. The lady has a gun."

The boy squeezed past him, and Martineau got into the copilot's seat and started to transmit on the frequency reserved by SOE for emergency procedure.

In the control room in the tower at Jersey Airport, Hofer and Necker waited anxiously while Adler spoke on the radio. A Luftwaffe corporal came up and spoke to him briefly.

Adler turned to the two officers. "We've still got them on radar, but they appear to be moving due west out to sea."

"My God!" Necker said.

Adler talked into the microphone for a moment, then turned to Hofer. "All night fighters in the Brittany area were scrambled an hour ago for operations over the Reich. Heavy bombing raids expected over the Ruhr."

"There must be something, for God's sake," Hofer said.

Adler waved him to silence, listening, then put down the mike and turned, smiling. "There is. One JU88S night fighter. Its port engine needed a check and it wasn't finished in time to leave with the rest of the squadron."

"But is it now?" Necker demanded eagerly.

"Oh, yes." Adler was enjoying himself. "He's just taken off from Cherbourg."

"But can he catch them?" Necker asked.

"Herr Major, that old crate they're flying in can do a hundred and eighty flat out. The JU88S with the new engine boosting system does better than four hundred. He'll be with them before they know it."

Necker turned in triumph to Hofer. "They'll have to turn back, otherwise he'll blow them out of the sky."

But Hofer had been thinking about that, among other things. If the mail plane returned, it would mean only one thing. Martineau and the others would be flown to Berlin, and few people survived interrogation in the cellars of Gestapo Headquarters at Prince Albrechtstrasse. That couldn't be allowed to happen. Berger knew about Rommel's connection with the generals' plot against the Führer, and so did Martineau. Perhaps he'd even told the girl.

Hofer took a deep breath. "No, we can't take a chance on their getting away."

"Herr Major?" Adler turned inquiringly.

"Send an order to the pilot of that night fighter to shoot on sight. They mustn't reach England."

"As you say, Herr Major." Adler picked up the microphone.

Necker put a hand on Hofer's shoulder. "You look terrible. let's go down to the mess and get you a brandy. Adler will call us when things start to warm up."

Hofer managed a weak smile. "The best offer I've had tonight." And they went out together.

Dougal Munro was at his Baker Street desk working late when Carter came in with the signal and passed it across. The brigadier read it quickly and smiled. "Good God, this is extraordinary, even for Harry."

"I know, sir. I've alerted Fighter Command about receiving them. Where do you want them to put down? I suppose Cornwall would be closest."

"No, let's bring them all the way in. They can land where they started, Jack. Hornley Field. Let Fighter Command know. I want them down in one piece."

"And General Eisenhower, sir?"

"We'll leave him until Kelso's actually on the ground." Munro stood up and reached for his jacket. "And we'll have the car round, Jack. We can get there in just over an hour. With any luck, we'll be able to greet them."

In the mail plane the atmosphere was positively euphoric as Martineau left Heini Baum in the cockpit to keep an eye on Sorsa and joined the others.

"Everything okay?" Kelso asked.

"Couldn't be better. I've made contact with our people in England. They're going to provide an escort to take us in, courtesy of the RAF." He turned and smiled at Sarah, taking her hand. She'd never seen him so excited. Suddenly he looked ten years younger. "You all right?" he asked her.

"Fine, Harry. Just fine."

"Dinner at the Ritz tomorrow night," he said.

"By candlelight?"

"Even if I have to take my own." He turned to Braun, the observer. "You said something about coffee, didn't you?"

Braun started to get up and the plane bucked wildly as a great roaring filled the night, then dropped like a stone. Braun lost his balance and Kelso rolled on the floor with a cry of pain.

"Harry!" Sarah screamed. "What is it?"

The plane regained some sort of stability and Martineau peered out one of the side windows. A hundred yards away on the port side flying parallel with them he saw a Junkers 88S, one of those deadly black twin-engined planes that had caused such catastrophic losses to RAF Bomber Command in the night skies of Europe.

"We've got trouble," he said. "Luftwaffe night fighter." He turned and wrenched open the cabin door and leaned into the cockpit.

Sorsa glanced over his shoulder, face grim and pale in the cockpit lights. "We've had it. He's come to take us back."

"Has he said so?"

"No. No radio contact at all."

"Why not? It doesn't make sense."

The JU88S suddenly climbed steeply and disappeared, and it was Heini who gave the only possible answer to the question. "Every kind of sense if they don't want us back, my friend."

Martineau saw it all then. Something had gone wrong and it had to involve Hofer, and if that were so, the last thing he'd want was to have them back in Gestapo hands to bring down Erwin Rommel.

"What do I do?" Sorsa demanded. "That thing can blow us out of the skies. I know. I've been flying one for two years now."

At that moment, the roaring filled the night again, and the mail plane shuddered as cannon shell slammed into the fuselage. One came up through the floor of the cockpit, narrowly missing Sorsa, splinters shattering the windscreen. He pushed the column forward, going down in a steep dive into the cloud layer below, and the Junkers 88S roared overhead, passing like a dark shadow.

Martineau fell to one knee, but got the door open and scrambled out. Several gaping holes had been punched into the fuselage of the plane and two windows were shattered. Kelso was on the floor, hanging onto a seat and Sarah was crouched over Braun, who lay on his back, his uniform soaked with blood, eyes rolling. He jerked convulsively and lay still.

Sarah looked up, her face surprisingly calm. "He's dead, Harry."

There was nothing to say, couldn't be, and Martineau turned back to the cockpit, hanging on as the mail plane continued its steep dive down through the clouds. They rocked again in the turbulence as the Junkers 88S passed over them.

"Bastard!" Sorsa said, in a rage now. "I'll show you."

Baum, crouched on the floor, looked up at Harry with a ghastly smile. "He's a Finn, remember? They don't really like us Germans very much."

The mail plane burst out of the clouds at three thousand feet and kept on going down.

"What are you doing?" Martineau cried.

"Can't play hide and seek with him in that cloud. He'd get us for sure. Just one trick up my sleeve. He's very fast and I'm very slow and that makes it difficult for him." Sorsa glanced over his shoulder again and smiled savagely. "Let's see if he's any good."

He kept on going down, was at seven or eight hundred feet when the Junkers 88S came in again on their tail, far too fast, banking to port to avoid a collision.

Sorsa took the mail plane down to five hundred and leveled off. "Right, you swine, let's have you," he said, hands steady as a rock.

In that moment Martineau saw genius at work, understood all those medals the Finn wore, the Knight's Cross, and a strange feeling of calm enveloped him. It was all so unreal, the lights from the instrument panel, the wind roaring in through the shattered windscreen.

And when it happened, it was over in seconds. The Junkers 88S swooped in on their tail again, and Sorsa hauled back the column and started to climb. The pilot of the Junkers 88S banked steeply to avoid what seemed like an inevitable collision, but at that height and speed had nowhere else to go but straight down into the waves below.

Sorsa's face was calm again. "You lost, my friend," he said softly and eased back the column. "All right, let's get back upstairs."

Martineau pushed back the door and glanced out. The inside of the plane was a shambles, wind blowing in through innumerable holes, Braun's blood-soaked body on the floor, Sarah crouched beside Kelso.

"You two all right?" he called.

"Fine. Don't worry about us. Is it over?" Sarah asked.

"You could say that."

He turned back to the cockpit as Sorsa leveled out at six thousand feet. "So, the old girl's leaking like a sieve, but everything appears to be functioning," the Finn said.

"Let's try the radio." Martineau squeezed into the co-pilot's seat. He twisted the dial experimentally but everything seemed to be in working order. "I'll let them know what's happened," he said and started to transmit on the SOE emergency frequency.

Heini Baum tried to light a cigarette but his hands shook so much he had to give up. "My God!" he moaned. "What a last act."

Sorsa said cheerfully, "Tell me, is the food good in British prisoner-of-war camps?"

Martineau smiled. "Oh, I think you'll find we make very special arrangements for you, my friend." And then, he made contact with SOE Headquarters.

At the control room at Jersey, Adler stood by the radio, an expression of disbelief on his face. He removed the earphones and turned slowly.

"What is it, for God's sake?" Necker demanded.

"That was Cherbourg Control. They've lost the JU88S."

"What do you mean, lost it?"

"They had the pilot on radio. He'd attacked several times. They suddenly lost contact and he disappeared from the radar screen. They think he's gone into the drink."

"I might have known," Hofer said softly. "A great pilot, Sorsa. An exceptional man. I should know. I chose him myself. And the mail plane?"

"Still on radar, moving up-Channel toward the English coast. No way on earth of stopping her."

There was silence. A flurry of rain drifted against the window. Necker said, "What happens now?"

"I'll leave in the Storch at dawn," Hofer told him. "The pilot of the mail plane can fly me. It's essential I get to Field Marshal Rommel as soon as possible."

"And what then?" Necker asked. "What happens when Berlin hears about this?"

"God knows, my friend." Hofer smiled wearily. " A bleak prospect—for all of us."

About fifteen minutes after Sorsa had changed course for the second time, Martineau received a response to his message.

"Come in, Martineau,"

"Martineau here," he answered.

"Your destination Hornley Field. Fly at five thousand feet and await further instructions. Escorts will assist. Should be with you in minutes."

Martineau turned to Sorsa who had his headphones on. "Did you get that?"

The Finn shook his head. "I don't understand English."

Martineau translated, then crouched down beside Baum. "So far, so good."

Baum sat up and pointed. "Look out there."

Martineau turned and saw, in the moonlight, a Spitfire take station to port. As he turned to check the starboard side, another appeared. He reached for the copilot's headphones.

A crisp voice said, "Martineau, do you read me?"

"Martineau here."

"You are now twenty miles east of the Isle of Wight. We're going to turn inland and descend to three thousand. I'll lead and my friend will bring up the rear. We'll shepherd you right in."

"Our pleasure." He translated quickly for Sorsa and sat back.

"Everything okay?" Baum asked.

"Fine. They're leading us in. Another fifteen minutes or so, that's all."

Baum was excited. This time when he took a cigarette from his case his hand was steady. "I really feel as if I'm breaking out of something."

"I know," Martineau said.

"Do you really? I wonder. I was at Stalingrad, did I tell you that? The greatest disaster in the history of the German Army. Three hundred thousand down the drain. The day before the airstrip closed I was wounded in the foot. I flew out in a good old JU52, just like this. Ninety-one thousand taken prisoner, twenty-four generals. Why them and not me?"

"I spent years trying to find answers to questions like that," Martineau told him.

"And did you?"

"Not really. In the end, I decided there weren't any answers. Also no sense and precious little reason."

He pulled down the earphones as the voice came over the air again, giving him new instructions and a fresh course. He passed them on to Sorsa. They descended steadily. A few minutes later, the voice sounded again. "Hornley Field, right in front. In you go."

The runway lights were plain to see, and this time Sorsa didn't need any translation. He reduced power and dropped his flaps to float in for a perfect landing. The escorting Spitfires peeled away to port and starboard and climbed into the night.

The Junkers started to slow, and Sorsa turned and taxied toward the control tower. He rolled to a halt, switched off the engines. Baum got up and laughed excitedly. "We made it!"

Sarah was smiling. She reached for Martineau's hand and held on tight and Kelso, on the floor, was laughing out loud. The feeling of release was fantastic. Baum got the door open and he and Martineau peered outside.

A voice called over a bullhorn, "Stay where you are."

A line of airmen in RAF blue, each carrying a rifle, moved toward them. There were other people in the shadows behind them, but Martineau couldn't make out who.

Baum jumped down onto the runway. The voice called again, "Stay where you are!"

Baum knotted the white scarf around his throat and grinned up at Harry, saluting him, touching the field marshal's baton to the rim of his cap. "Will you join me, Standartenführer?" And then he turned and strode toward the line of men, the baton raised in his right hand. "Put the rifles away, you idiots," he called in English. "All friends here."

There was a single shot. He spun around, took a couple of steps back toward the Junkers, then sank on his knees and rolled over.

Harry ran forward, waving his arms. "No more, you fools!" he shouted. "It's me, Martineau."

He was aware of the advancing line slowing and Squadron Leader Barnes was there, telling them to stay back. Martineau dropped to his knees. Baum reached up with his left hand and grabbed him by the front of the uniform.

"You were right, Harry," he said hoarsely. "No sense, no reason to anything."

"Quiet, Heini. Don't talk. We'll get a doctor."

Sarah was crouched beside him and Baum's grip lightened. "Last act, Harry. Say kaddish for me. Promise."

"I promise," Martineau said.

Baum choked, there was blood on his mouth. His body seemed to shake and then the hand lost its grip on Martineau's tunic and he lay still. Martineau got up slowly and saw Dougal Munro and Jack Carter standing in front of the line of RAF men beside Barnes.

"An accident, Harry," Munro said. "One of the lads panicked."

"An accident?" Martineau said. "Is that what you call it? Sometimes I really wonder who the enemy is. If you're still interested, by the way, you'll find your American colonel in the plane."

He went past them and through the line of airmen, walking aimlessly toward the old aero club buildings. Strange, but he had that pain in the chest again, and it hadn't bothered him once in Jersey. He sat down on the steps of the old clubhouse and lit a cigarette, suddenly cold. After a while, he became aware of Sarah sitting a few feet away.

"What did he mean, say kaddish for him?"

"It's a sort of mourning prayer. A Jewish thing. Usually relatives take care of it, but he didn't have any. All gone to the bloody ovens." He took the half-smoked cigarette from his mouth and passed it to her. "Anyway, now you know. Now your education's complete. No honor, no glory, only Heini Baum out there, lying on his back."

He got to his feet and she stood up also. Someone had brought a stretcher and they were carrying Baum away, and Kelso was crossing the runway on his crutches, Munro and Carter on either side of him.

"Did I remember to tell you how well you did?" he asked.

"No."

"You were good. So good that Dougal will probably try to use you again. Don't let him. Go back to that hospital of yours."

"I don't think one should ever go back to anything." They started to walk toward the waiting cars. "And you?" she asked. "What's going to happen to you?"

"I haven't the slightest idea."

She took his arm and held on tight and as the runway lights were switched off, they moved on through the darkness together.

JERSEY
1985

17

IT WAS VERY QUIET THERE in the library, Sarah Drayton standing at the window peering out. "Dark soon. Sometimes I wonder whether the rain will ever stop. A bad winter this year."

The door opened and the manservant, Vito, came in with a tray which he placed on a low table by the fire. "Coffee, Contessa."

"Thank you, Vito, I'll see to it."

He went out and she sat down and reached for the coffeepot. "And afterward?" I asked her.

"You mean what happened to everybody? Well, Konrad Hofer flew out in the Storch the following morning, got to Rommel and filled him in on what had happened."

"And how did Rommel cover himself?"

"Very much as Harry had suggested. He flew to Rastenburg."

"The Wolf's Lair?"

"That's right. He saw Hitler personally. Told him Intelligence sources had warned him of the possibility of plots against his life, which was why he'd used Berger to impersonate him. He stayed pretty much with the facts. If he'd gone to Jersey himself, Harry would have assassinated him. Berger was dismissed as a rat who'd deserted the sinking ship."

"I'm sure he didn't put it to the Führer in quite those terms," I said.

"Probably not. There was an official investigation. I read the Gestapo file on the case a few months after the war ended. They didn't come up with anything very much. They knew nothing about Hugh Kelso, remember, and what made the story so believable from Rommel's point of view was Harry himself."

"I don't understand," I said.

"Remember that Harry had gone to some pains to tell Hofer who he was, and that meant something concrete to the Gestapo. They had him on file, had been after him for a long time. Remember, they only just failed to get their hands on him after that business at Lyons when he shot Kaufmann."

"So Rommel was believed?"

"Oh, I don't think Himmler was too happy, but the Führer seemed satisfied enough. They drew a veil over the whole thing. Hardly wanted it on the front page of national newspapers at that stage in the war. The

669

same thing applied with our people, but for different reasons."

"No publicity?"

"That's right."

"In the circumstances," I said, "the accidental shot that killed Heini Baum was really rather convenient. He could have been a problem."

"Too convenient," Sarah said flatly. "As Harry once said to me, Dougal Munro hated loose ends. Not that it gave anyone any problems. With D Day coming, Eisenhower was only too delighted to have got Kelso back in one piece, and our own Intelligence people didn't want to make things difficult for Rommel and the other generals who were plotting against Hitler."

"And they almost succeeded," I said.

"Yes, the bomb plot in July, later that year. Hitler was injured but survived."

"And the conspirators?"

"Count von Stauffenberg and many others were executed, some of them in the most horrible of circumstances."

"And Rommel?"

"Three days before the attempt on Hitler's life, Rommel's car was machine-gunned by low-flying Allied planes. He was terribly wounded. Although he was involved with the plot it kept him out of things in any practical sense."

"But they caught up with him?"

"In time. Someone broke under Gestapo torture and implicated him. However, Hitler didn't want the scandal of having Germany's greatest war hero in the dock. He was given the chance of taking his own life on the promise that his family wouldn't be molested."

I nodded. "And what happened to Hofer?"

"He was killed in heavy fighting near Caen not long after D Day."

"And Hugh Kelso?"

"He wasn't supposed to return to active duty. That leg never fully recovered, but they needed his engineering expertise for the Rhine crossings in March forty-five. He was killed in an explosion while supervising work on the damaged bridge at Remagen. A booby trap."

I got up and walked to the window and stared out at the rain, thinking about it all. "Amazing," I said. "And the most extraordinary thing is that it never came out, the whole story."

"There was a special reason for that," she said. "The Jersey connection. This island was liberated on the ninth of May, nineteen forty-five. The fortieth anniversary in a couple of months' time. It's always been an important occasion here, Liberation Day."

"I can imagine."

"But after the war, it was a difficult time. Accusations and counter-accusations about those who were supposed to have consorted with the enemy. The Gestapo had actually hunted down some of the people who had sent them anonymous letters denouncing friends and neighbors. Those names were on file. Anyway, there was a government committee appointed to investigate.''

''And what did it find?''

''I don't know. It was put on hold with a special one-hundred-year security classification. You can't read that report until the year twenty forty-five.''

I went back and sat down again. ''What happened to Helen de Ville, Gallagher and Guido?''

''Nothing. They didn't come under any kind of suspicion. Guido was taken prisoner at the end of the war, but Dougal Munro secured his release almost at once. Helen's husband, Ralph, returned in bad shape. He'd been wounded in the desert campaign. He never really recovered and died three years after the war.''

''Did she and Gallagher marry?''

''No. It sounds silly, but I think they'd known each other too long. She died of lung cancer ten years ago. He followed her within a matter of months. He was eighty-three and still one hell of a man. I was with him at the end.''

''I was wondering,'' I said, ''about de Ville Place and Septembertide. Would it be possible to take a look?''

''I'm not sure,'' she said. ''Jersey has changed considerably since those war years. We're now one of the most important banking centers in the world. There's a great deal of money here and a considerable number of millionaires. One of them owns de Ville Place now, perhaps I could arrange something. I'm not certain.''

I'd been putting off the most important question, she knew that, of course. Would be expecting it. ''And you and Martineau? What happened there?''

''I was awarded the MBE, Military Division, the reason for the award unspecified, naturally. For some reason the Free French tossed in the Croix de Guerre.''

''And the Americans? Didn't they come up with anything?''

''Good God, no!'' She laughed. ''From their point of view the whole episode had been far too uncomfortable. They preferred to forget it as quickly as possible. Dougal Munro gave me a job on the inside at Baker Street. I couldn't have said no even if I'd wanted to. He'd made me a serving officer in the WAAF, remember.''

''And Martineau?''

''His health deteriorated. That chest wound from the Lyons affair was always trouble, but he worked on the inside at Baker Street also. There was a lot on after D Day. We lived together. We had a flat within walking distance of the office at Jacobs Well Mansions.''

"Were you happy?"

"Oh, yes." She nodded. "The best few months of my life. I knew it couldn't last, mind you. He needed more, you see."

"Action?"

"That's right. He needed it in the way some people need a drink, and in the end, it did for him. In January nineteen forty-five, certain German generals made contact with British Intelligence with a view to bringing the war to a speedier end. Dougal Munro concocted a scheme in which an Arado operated by the Enemy Aircraft Flight was flown to Germany by a volunteer pilot with Harry as passenger. As you know, the aircraft had German markings and they both wore Luftwaffe uniforms."

"And they never got there?"

"Oh, but they did. Landed on the other side of the Rhine where he met the people concerned and flew back."

"And disappeared?"

"There was a directive to Fighter Command to expect them. Apparently the message hadn't been forwarded to the pilots of one particular squadron. A blunder on the part of some clerk or other."

"Dear God," I said. "How trivial the reasons for disaster can sometimes be."

"Exactly." She nodded. "Records showed that an Arado was attacked by a Spitfire near Margate. Visibility was very bad that day, and the pilot lost contact with it in low clouds. It was assumed to have gone down in the sea. Now we know better."

There was silence. She picked a couple of logs from the basket and put them on the fire. "And you?" I said. "How did you manage?"

"Well enough. I got a government grant to go to medical school. They were reasonably generous to ex-service personnel after the war. Once I was qualified I went to the old Cromwell for a year as a house physician. It seemed fitting somehow. For me, that's where it had all started."

"And you never married." It was a statement, not a question and her answer surprised me, although I should have known, by then, if I'd had my wits about me.

"Good heavens, whatever gave you that idea? Guido visited London regularly. One thing he'd omitted to tell me was just how wealthy the Orsini family was. Each year I was at medical school he asked me to marry him. I always said no."

"And he'd still come back and try again?"

"In between his other marriages. Three in all. I gave in at last on the strict understanding that I would still work as a doctor. The family estate was outside Florence. I was partner in a country practice there for years."

"So you really are a Contessa?"

"I'm afraid so. Contessa Sarah Orsini. Guido died in a car crash three years ago. Can you imagine a man who still raced Ferraris at sixty-four years of age?"

"From what you've told me of him, I'd say it fits."

"This house was my parents'. I'd always hung onto it so I decided to come back. As a doctor on an island like this it's easier to use my maiden name. The locals would find the other rather intimidating."

"And you and Guido? Were you happy?"

"Why do you ask?"·

"The fact that you came back here, I suppose, after so many years."

"But this island is a strange place. It has that kind of effect. It pulls people back, sometimes after many years. I wasn't trying to find some-·thing I'd lost if that's what you mean. At least I don't think so." She shook her head. "I loved Guido dearly. I gave him a daughter and then a son, the present count, who rings me twice a week from Italy, begging me to return to Florence to live with him again."

"I see."

She stood up. "Guido understood what he called the ghost in my machine. The fact of Harry that would not go away. Aunt Helen told me there was a difference between being in love and loving someone."

"She also told you that Martineau wasn't for you."

"She was right enough there. Whatever had gone wrong in Harry's psyche was more than I could cure." She opened the desk drawer again, took out a yellowing piece of paper and unfolded it. "This is the poem he threw away that first day at the cottage at Lulworth. The one I re-covered."

"May I see it?"

She passed it across and I read it quickly. *The station is ominous at midnight. Hope is a dead letter. Time to change trains for something better. No local train now, long since departed. No way of getting back to where you started.*

I felt inexpressibly saddened as I handed it back to her. "He called it a rotten poem," she said. "But it says it all. *No way of getting back to where you started.* Maybe he was right after all. Perhaps he should have died at seventeen in that trench in Flanders."

There didn't seem a great deal to say to that. I said, "I've taken enough of your time. I think I'd better be getting back to my hotel."

"You're staying at L'Horizon?"

"That's right."

"They do you very well there," she said. "I'll run you down."

"There's no need for that," I protested. "It isn't far."

"That's all right. I want to take some flowers down to the grave anyway."

It was raining heavily, darkness moving in from the horizon across the bay as we drove down the hill and parked outside the entrance to St.

Brelade's Church. Sarah Drayton got out and put up her umbrella and I handed the flowers to her.

"I want to show you something," she said. "Over here." She led the way to the older section of the cemetery and finally stopped before a moss-covered granite headstone. "What do you think of that?"

It read: *Here lie the mortal remains of Captain Henry Martineau, late of the 5th Bengal Infantry, died July 7, 1859.*

"I only discovered it last year quite by chance. When I did, I got one of those ancestor-tracing agencies to check up for me. Captain Martineau retired here from the army in India. Apparently he died at the age of forty from the effects of some old wound or other. His wife and children moved to Lancashire and then emigrated to America."

"How extraordinary."

"When we visited this place he told me he had this strange feeling of being at home."

As we walked back through the headstones I said, "What happened to all those Germans who were buried here?"

"They were all moved after the war," she said. "Back to Germany, as far as I know."

We reached the spot where he had been laid to rest earlier that afternoon. We stood there together, looking down at that fresh mound of earth. She laid the flowers on it and straightened and what she said then astonished me.

"Damn you, Harry Martineau," she said softly. "You did for yourself, but you did for me as well."

There was no answer to that, could never be, and suddenly, I felt like an intruder. I turned and walked away and left her there in the rain in that ancient churchyard, alone with the past.

ABOUT THE AUTHOR

JACK HIGGINS is among the world's most popular authors. Since the publication of *The Eagle Has Landed*—one of the biggest selling thrillers of all time—every novel he has written has become an international bestseller, including *A Season in Hell, Storm Warning,* and *Day of Judgement.* He has had simultaneous #1 bestsellers in hardcover and paperback. Many of his books have been made into successful motion pictures, such as *The Eagle Has Landed, To Catch a King,* and *The Valhalla Exchange.* Higgins lives on Jersey in the Channel Islands, and is an expert scuba diver. He and his wife also enjoy exploring the reefs and wrecks in the waters of the Virgin Islands.